INCARNATION

Daniel Easterman was born in Belfast in 1949. Dubbed by *The Purloined Letter* as 'easily the best thriller writer working today', he is the author of eleven critically acclaimed novels including *The Judas Testament*, *Day of Wrath*, *The Final Judgement* and *K*. He lives in the north of England with his wife, Beth, the author of several books on alternative medicine.

INCARNATION

DANIEL EASTERMAN

HarperCollins*Publishers*

HarperCollins*Publishers*,
77–85 Fulham Palace Road,
Hammersmith, London W6 8JB

www.fireandwater.com

This paperback edition 2000
1 3 5 7 9 8 6 4 2

First published in Great Britain by
HarperCollins*Publishers* 1998

Copyright © Daniel Easterman 1998

Daniel Easterman asserts the moral right to
be identified as the author of this work

Unfortunately the publisher has been unable to trace the
copyright holders of the following: *Poems of the Late T'ang*
translated by A C Graham, lines quoted on Dedication page
and in Chapters 15, 36 and 38; *The Wisdom of China* edited
by Lin Yutang, lines quoted in Chapter 58. We would like to
thank the authors for use of the extracts, and if anyone can
be of assistance, please let us know.

ISBN 0 00 651006 X

Typeset in Meridien by
Palimpsest Book Production Limited,
Polmont, Stirlingshire

Printed and bound in Great Britain by
Caledonian International Book Manufacturing Ltd, Glasgow

For Beth.

'The lifetime he shared with the goddess was always a dream . . .'
Li Shang-Yin

ACKNOWLEDGEMENTS

The usual suspects, with even more vigour and vim than before. My editor, Patricia Parkin, took an unwieldy first draft and helped transform it into the bright and polished narrative it is today. She was aided and abetted in that process by Anne O'Brien, who brought very well-honed copy-editorial skills to bear on it all. Outside the editorial hothouse, my tireless agent, Giles Gordon, helped make it all worthwhile, and my equally tireless wife Beth continued with her lifelong effort to transform me from a frog to a handsome prince. I don't mind, if I can keep the princess.

'Iraq signed . . . nuclear arrangements with India and China, US government sources say, although the details have never been revealed.'

Kenneth Timmerman, *The Death Lobby*, p. 93

'American officials say Iraq turned to China for help with the first [nuclear] centrifuges.'

Ibid, p. 358

There are eight stages of dissolution through which the soul passes in its journey to be reborn:

1. Clear Light
2. Radiant Black Sky
3. Radiant Red Sky
4. Radiant White Sky
5. Flame of a Butter-Lamp
6. Fireflies
7. Smoke
8. Mirage

PROLOGUE

Srinagar, Kashmir, Northern India
June

The sun lay across the city like a copper chafing dish, baking everything in sight with its dull, oppressive warmth. It was the hottest summer in living memory, perhaps the hottest since time began. The sky was empty of clouds and birds. Today, not even the orioles were in flight. On Dal Lake, abandoned houseboats lay strewn like broken flowers, and the floating gardens wilted and died. To the east, the blue foothills of the Himalayas rose up behind a ragged haze. In the city, people looked up at them from time to time, thinking how cool it must be up there.

A woman's voice rose in song from the lake's southern shore, light and easy, a hymn to Shiva. First from the Jami Masjid, then from the mosques of Hazratbal and Rosahbal and Shah Hamdan and Pathar and Dastgir, the voices of the city's muezzins rose in the call to the noon prayer. A very different god, and a very different love.

As the worshippers made their way on foot to their places of prayer, clutches of soldiers watched suspiciously from their bunkers. No one walked easily in Srinagar, no one went anywhere unobserved.

Two men stepped down from a four-wheel-drive vehicle that had just drawn up in front of the General Post Office on Guptar Road. They'd scarcely set foot on the parched earth before a chirruping bevy of would-be porters and guides swallowed them whole. V. S. Mukerji's 'Top Number One Taxi Service' was always the choice of rich foreigners coming in on the morning flight from Delhi. Except that nowadays foreigners in Kashmir were as rare as teeth in an old man's gums.

The guides and porters vanished back into the lanes near the Post Office as quickly as they had come. A small Indian wearing cream-coloured *kurta*-pyjamas and impenetrable dark glasses had emerged from the Post Office and was greeting the newcomers, hands folded in the *namaste*, bobbing, smirking, and apologizing for the undignified confusion that had welcomed them to the jewel of the north.

His greetings over, the Indian hurried them past a heap of sandbags topped by a light machine-gun, down narrow steps to the river. The Jhelum was low, its normally muddy brown water stinking and putrid now, as it moved sluggishly between the tall houses that crowded in upon it from either bank.

A *shikara* was waiting, tied up to a wooden pole whose lower half was seeing daylight for the first time in over two hundred years. The boatman, an old man with grizzled hair, helped them into the narrow vessel, as he had helped thousands of tourists in his day, and pushed off towards midstream. But today's passengers were not tourists. They did not carry cameras, and they did not stare at the sights of Old Srinagar as the little boat weaved its way between a clutter of barges and floating shops. Their only luggage was a large, heavy-looking briefcase.

The two foreigners made a curious sight, if anyone

had been willing to pay more than passing attention. The Indian sat up front, whispering directions to the boatman as he steered. Behind him sat the visitors, one old, one young. Bewildered by the heat that pervaded its smallest crevices, the city seemed to sigh as they passed, recognizing in them descendants of a vanished Raj. No one would have turned a hair if a band had appeared out of nowhere and struck up 'God Save the Queen'.

The old man's name was Dennison. No first name, no title, no tactless entry in *Who's Who*. He had the air of tired menace that walks with men and women of a certain age and class. Not even the city's heat could penetrate the invisible wall that stood between him and his surroundings. He sat upright in the pirogue, as aloof as any Rajput prince on a palanquin. His eyes fell on the dun walls and shuttered windows of the jumble of houses clinging frantically to the narrow banks, but he gazed at them with the practised indifference of a demigod.

A drop of sweat beaded the tip of his nose and fell at last to his knee. Another formed, but he did not lift a finger or furrow his brow. He'd been sent here on a wild-goose chase, and he knew it. The business had a smell about it, a smell not much unlike the stench that rose from the muddy river through which he was being rowed. The boy would turn out to be a fake and an illusion, the whole thing a clever trick to wheedle money out of Dennison's bosses in London.

The boatman flexed his arms, twisting the heart-shaped oar through water and sunlight, propelling them deeper into the ancient city. The scent of fear was everywhere. Buildings carried the marks of bullet-holes, the traces of fires, the scars of bombings. It might have been Beirut a decade earlier. Eyes peered through broken lattices, watching, surmising. Two Europeans passing in an open boat: sitting targets for a band of kidnappers. And the Indian, calm and collected as a petty god moving among his worshippers. He looked up the narrow course of the river, humming a bhajan to himself.

A faint sound of hammering came to them from beyond a bend.

'Habba Kadal,' said the Indian, without turning his head. 'Here is where they make copper goods. Advised to stop up ears.'

They passed beneath the old bridge with its weathered beams of deodar. The din of the copper workshops took possession of them for a while. The young man let his hand fall into the water, letting it trail for a moment before pulling it out again as though stung. He shook water from it like a dog. The water was unpleasantly warm to the touch.

'You aren't going to like it,' he said to the older man. 'It isn't what you think.'

'I don't think. I watch and wait. They didn't send me here to like or not to like.'

'You won't understand. He isn't what you want him to be.'

'And what, pray, is that?'

'An impostor.'

He'd found the boy during his last tour of duty up here. It had taken him until now to make them send someone out. He hated to think how much time had been wasted.

'We'll see.'

The young man's name was Ross, Douglas Ross. Born in Edinburgh, into the service. His father had died in a cold room somewhere in East Berlin. The Wall was gone now, but the room remained. In memory. In his mother's heart. She'd told him once her heart was nothing but a single memory.

4

He let his hand fall limply to the water again.

'He'll frighten you,' he said. Something made him want to goad Dennison.

Dennison shook his head. He was beyond fear.

'He told me things he couldn't have known,' said Ross. 'Not if he was a fake.'

The *shikara* glided under another bridge and continued to the next.

'Zaina Kadal,' said the Indian. 'We are getting out here, please.'

The boatman brought the craft up against the bank. No one was waiting for them. People glanced at them with curiosity. Tourists seldom came this way. It was too dangerous. There had been too many kidnappings, and a killing only last week.

The Indian told the boatman to wait, then led them into the tangle of alleyways that made up the quarter in which the boy lived. Stalls festooned with skeins of silk and wool lined the street, narrowing it until there was almost no room in which to pass. Always the Indian went ahead, making space for them. Twice they were stopped by military patrols, but each time the Indian showed a pass and brought them through without further questioning.

They passed into a lane that became a cul-de-sac. It was hotter here than in all the rest of the city, Ross thought. He fingered the pistol in his pocket. If they got caught here, they'd never make it out again. He'd have brought the boy to Delhi, but he'd refused to go, and there'd been no making him.

A wooden door barely wide enough to pass through stood at the end of the alley. The Indian stopped and turned. He took off his sunglasses and looked directly at them for the first time.

'You must understand, Mr Dennison,' he said, 'you are

not in your own world any longer. Whatever happens here, it will not happen according to your rules. Do you understand that?'

Dennison nodded. He only had to sniff the scented air to understand the truth of the man's words.

'Let's go in,' he said. 'I haven't come all this way to stand gaping at a bloody door.'

CLEAR LIGHT

CHAPTER ONE

Secure E-mail Communication via Cadenza Central.
  Not for retransmission.
Time: 17:14:09 hours IST
Date: 20/6/99
To: Controller, East Asia Desk [ConEA@6.gov.uk]
From: Dennison, P. J., London Operations Chief, India
  Section, Srinigar [dennison@embassy.delhi.gov.uk]
Subject: Reincarnation

Maurice,

I recommend we get the boy to London a.s.a.p. I've
made arrangements for him and his family to be taken
to Delhi tonight. There's a flight out just before the
curfew starts. Dubey is being co-operative, but I don't
know how long it will last. Depends what he tells his
own people. They may decide this is more their line
of country than ours. Ordinarily, I'd say bloody right,
but in this case . . .

I think it's vital for UK security to have the boy and
his parents on a plane out of Delhi by tomorrow noon
at the latest. I leave that to you, it's what you're good
at. Put Ross and myself on the same flight. I need
authorization to deal with Dubey.

Is he what he claims to be? Buggered if I know. I'm
not a Buddhist or a Hindu, I'm not up to these tricks.

C of E and the Apostles' Creed suit me down to the ground. But . . . To tell you the truth, I've never been more scared in my life than I was this afternoon.

Dennison

CHAPTER TWO

From transcription of a tape-recording made at
** 10 Pampore Alley, Zaina Kadal, Srinagar,**
** 14.30 hours IST, 20 June 1999**
Operator: D. Ross, Field Agent MI6 Delhi
Recording Time: 2:17:35
Tape logged: 20.15 hours GMT, 23/6/99, Vauxhall
Access: Nil access below Chief MI6/Chairman Joint
* Intelligence Committee*
Transcript logged: 14.07 hours GMT, 24/6/99, Vauxhall annexe
Access: Nil below Chief MI6/CJIC/Controller East Asia

ROSS: Testing, testing. [*Puff, puff, puff.*] Hello, one, two, three, testing . . . I think it's working. Right, this is Douglas Ross. I'm about to interview the boy called Yongden whom I last met here on the eighth of June. Also present are Captain Sunil Dubey of the Indian Intelligence Service, and the man you sent out to act as an observer, Dennison.

I'd like to set the scene for you, if I may. Dennison is sitting on my left, Dubey to my right. We're in a small room, maybe twelve by ten, with a low ceiling. It's hot in here, very hot. We're all uncomfortable, except for the boy. I can feel sweat coiling down my neck, my back is soaking, my socks are wringing wet. Yet the boy is as cool as a cucumber, he looks

11

as if he's sitting on ice. He isn't even bothered by the flies.

He's about twelve years old, I think, good-looking, with jet-black hair and a winning smile. He's simply dressed in white, in the Indian fashion. It's impossible not to like him. And just as impossible not to be frightened of him.

The humming sound you can hear is the big fan up above that goes churning round and round. All it does is cut the hot air into slices and then send dollops of it down on top of us, making us hotter than ever. I find it distracting. I think we all do. Dennison looks up at it from time to time. The kid doesn't seem to notice it. Nothing distracts him. He could be on another planet. Maybe he is.

DUBEY, INDIAN INTELLIGENCE: My name is Captain Dubey. I am here to see all is correct. These gentlemen have come from England to speak with you. Mr Ross you have met already.

BOY: Hello, Mr Ross. How are you keeping?

ROSS: Very well. How about you?

BOY: I thought you'd forgotten me.

ROSS: Now, how would I do a thing like that?

DUBEY: Mr Dennison you have not met. He is an old friend of mine. You can trust him.

BOY: I'm not so sure of that. Peter the Ponce was always a sly fox. Weren't you Pete?

DENNISON: How the hell do you know that nickname?

BOY: I gave it to you, old boy. Back in seventy-five. We'd been to the Gay Hussar for lunch, we were on our way back to Century House, the cabbie passed a remark about the flower in your buttonhole. You were Peter the Ponce from then on.

12

DENNISON: Turn off that bloody machine. I want to know what's going on here. I want to know what bloody fool trick you're trying to play.

ROSS: I'm sorry, Mr Dennison, I have instructions. Everything has to be recorded.

DENNISON: Even that nonsense?

ROSS: Especially that.

CHAPTER THREE

It was just a room. Douglas Ross had been there twice before. The room never changed, the boy never changed. The room and the boy were timeless, unchanged, perhaps even unchangeable.

He was sitting just like he'd sat before, on a wooden chair in the middle of the room. Nothing seemed to affect him, least of all the heat. His parents stood to one side, watching, understanding nothing. They never spoke, not a syllable. The boy did everything for them. He was their messenger, their angel, their interpreter. He said they'd come down from Ladakh, from Leh, along the long road that reaches Kashmir through the pass of Zoji La. That was in the spring. Ross had met them first in the first week of May.

A window had been left open in the vain hope of bringing a little fresh air into the room. Flies went in and out, heavy black flies that came up from the river in droves. They settled on everything. On a little trestle table, the reels turned slowly on the recorder Ross had brought from Delhi.

Dennison's bluster had gone. The boy's use of his nickname had taken the breath from him, left him gasping. Ross took over, questioning the boy gently. Dubey sat on a chair facing them, mentally recording all that passed. Ross knew that Dubey was going to become a problem, that they should never have got Delhi involved.

14

'Tell me, Yongden, you say your real name is Matthew Hyde, that you are his reincarnation?'

'Yes.'

'Mr Dennison finds this hard to believe. He does not believe in reincarnations. His superiors in London will find it even harder to believe.'

'They have not seen me.'

Ross looked at the boy, as though seeing him again for the first time. He no longer wore the tattered Ladakhi *goncha* he'd worn in May. The Indian clothes made him look like a miniature guru. His face and stature suggested a child of ten. He said he was twelve. His eyes were the most penetrating eyes Ross had ever seen. Blue, as blue as the water in Dal Lake. Yongden might have come from almost anywhere east or north of Kashmir. His English was near perfect.

'You have to persuade Mr Dennison of the truth of your claims. Otherwise his bosses will not want to see you.'

'They will want to see me.'

'Tell us about Matthew Hyde. How does Matthew Hyde come to be in the body of a twelve-year-old boy from Ladakh?'

'Why shouldn't I? After all, what do you really know about these things. I found a suitable vessel in a boy called Yongden, and I pushed him aside. After that, it was a doddle. I am no longer Yongden. I am Matthew Hyde.'

'When was this?'

'Two years ago. When Yongden was ten.'

'We have no evidence that Matthew Hyde is dead.'

'I died in the prison-camp at Huancheng. I was shot there.'

'We have had no news of that.'

'Now you know where to ask, you will find what you're looking for.'

A fly circled the boy's head, but it would not land. Yongden's mother went to the next room to prepare tea.

'Where were you born?'

'Durham, of course. Nearby, anyway. My mother went over to Hardwick Hall in Sedgefield. It's a hotel now.'

'When was that?'

'Fifteenth of September nineteen fifty-seven.'

Ross looked across at Dennison.

'Does that check out, sir?'

Dennison nodded.

'Go on,' he said. A voice drifted through the open window, a rough man's voice complaining about something.

'School?'

'Ushaw College.'

'And after that?'

'The usual. Cambridge. My father's college, King's. I read Chinese.'

'The Keynes' building was there then, was it?'

'Naturally.'

'It's next to the chapel, isn't it?'

'Of course not. It's on the other side of college, facing on to King's Parade.'

Dennison grunted. He was a John's man, but he knew the Keynes' building.

'After college?'

'My tutor, Harry Forbes, gave me an address in London. Baker Street. I had a chat with a man there, and the next day I was up for an interview in Carlton Gardens. You know the drill, you've been through it yourself.'

Dennison cleared his throat.

'Who interviewed you?' he asked.

'Peter Doddswell. Michael Patch. De Coverley – it must

have been a couple of months before his retirement. Hugh Creasey looked in.'

Dennison looked away. Ross reached down for a plastic file he'd left on the floor. Opening it, he extracted a handful of photographs. He took one and passed it to Yongden.

'Can you tell me who this is?' he asked.

Yongden glanced at the photograph and handed it back.

'My sister, Juliet.'

'And this?'

He passed across a second photograph.

'My uncle Ralph.'

'This?'

Yongden studied the third photograph briefly and shrugged.

'Never seen him before.'

'Well, well,' said Dennison, smirking for the first time. 'And who is it, Ross?'

Ross put the photograph back in the file.

'My uncle James. He lives in Montreal. He's been there for the past twenty years.'

The smirk vanished from Dennison's face.

'Perhaps you can enlighten us all,' he said, 'as to what this is all about exactly. Why has Matthew Hyde incarnated himself – if that's the correct phrase – in the body of a twelve-year-old coolie from – where the hell is it?'

Ross answered.

'Leh, sir. And he's not a coolie, he's –'

'I'll call him what I damn well please.' He looked back at Yongden.

'Well?'

'I'm in Yongden's body because we need to talk.'

'Talk?'

'About information I have and you need.'

'What sort of information?'

'About Matthew Hyde's last operation. Operation Hong Cha.'

Yongden stopped speaking and looked directly at Dennison. There was total silence in the room. A kind of electricity seemed to have taken hold of it. Dennison looked at the boy, as if suddenly taken unwell. He made to say something to Yongden, then thought better of it. Instead, he turned to Ross.

'Turn off the bloody tape.'

'Sir, I've already –'

'I said turn the tape off. That's a direct order.'

He took a gun from his pocket and pointed it at Ross.

'Or would you like me to blow your bloody brains out?'

Ross's hand reached out and the tape stopped turning.

CHAPTER FOUR

London
23 June

The telephone entered his dreams like a hand reaching into water to bring a drowning man to safety. He'd been dreaming about his mother, something well calculated to cause him the maximum distress. It hadn't really been his mother, of course, it had been Elizabeth; not that it made a great deal of difference. They'd both betrayed him, they'd both erected statues of themselves on heavy stone plinths in the centre of his psyche. It had been Elizabeth in the dream, but it had been his mother's eyes glaring at him that he remembered as he swam up to the surface.

Getting there didn't make anything much better. Dreams gave way to memories, memories to the bitterness of reality. The phone went on ringing as he tried to readjust himself to where and what he was. He glanced at the alarm clock. It was only half past seven. He groaned aloud. Only some bastard at Vauxhall would be ringing at this time, and if they were ringing early, it meant something was up.

He lifted the receiver with numb fingers.

'David Laing.'

'Dad? It's Maddie.'

His daughter's voice brought him fully awake.

'Maddie! Thank God. Where the hell are you? I've been trying to get hold of you for days. I've been worried sick. Barbara said you'd gone off without leaving an address. Are you all right?' He rattled the words out, barely pausing for breath.

'Calm down, Dad. I'm fine.'

Ice trickled through his heart. She sounded drugged.

'Where are you?'

There was a pause. The pause worried him. It was in pauses like that, he'd found, that the darkest revelations lurked to make themselves known.

'I'm with Dr Rose. At his clinic. He'd like to speak to you.'

David felt his heart fall like a coffin sinking into a grave.

'Put him on,' he said.

There followed a series of bumping sounds, then a man's voice came on the line.

'Mr Laing? I'm glad I caught you at home. I tried all yesterday, but there was no reply and no answering machine.'

David closed his eyes. He'd been at GCHQ for two days, all day Monday and Tuesday, working with one of the Chinese-speaking cryptographers, trying to crack a new military code they were using during tank manoeuvres in Kansu. He had to go back again at the weekend.

'I'm sorry. I was away on business. When I got back I found I'd forgotten to switch on the answering machine.'

No, he thought, not forgotten. He just hadn't wanted to come back to any more abuse from Elizabeth. She'd taken to using up the machine's entire memory with long tirades about why she'd left him, how he'd driven her to it, why she wouldn't pay him a penny. It was like having her living with him again.

20

'Well, it's all right. We've got you now. How are you keeping?' The all too familiar voice came down the line like a memory leaping out of some inner darkness. How many years had it been? Six, seven? David had thought all that behind them. Rose had saved Maddie's life and sanity before. He sounded just the same. As though nothing had changed.

'I'm fine,' said David. He sat on the edge of the bed now, fully alert. 'How is Maddie? Why is she at the clinic?'

The brief pause told him everything.

'I'm afraid Maddie's not too good.'

'She sounded . . .'

'I have her under sedation at the moment. I thought it was important for her to speak to you. Later, I'd like you to come over.'

'What's happened?'

'Another breakdown. She was brought here about one o'clock on Monday morning.'

'Jesus.'

'I'd say her mother was the more likely culprit. I need to talk to you about that.'

'Yes, I rather thought that's what you were going to say. How'd she end up at the clinic?'

'The police found her in a street off King's Cross. She was in a distressed state. They were planning to have her admitted to St Pancras, but when she got there she mentioned my name. They're under too much pressure there as it is, so they were only too glad to be able to off-load her.'

'You don't off-load people.'

Rose's shrug could almost be heard down the line.

'A lot of people get off-loaded nowadays. Usually they don't end up somewhere as comfortable as this. I take it her mother will be paying.'

'Elizabeth? You can bank on it. In every possible way.'

'Well, that's for you to sort out. I'll be happy with a few cheques.'

'Has she been sectioned?'

'No, we're treating this as voluntary. But if she tries to leave, it'll have to be done. This is worse than the last time.'

'And you think it's because Elizabeth has left me?'

'Maddie has referred to that, yes. It seems to be what's preying on her mind most at the moment.'

'Has she told you the circumstances?'

'Some of them, yes. I'd much rather get those from you and Mrs Laing.'

'I understand. When can I see her?'

'Not at the moment. I want her to adjust to being back in the clinic. Possibly tomorrow. Will that be all right?'

David looked round the bedroom. The emptiness was palpable. How long was it now since Elizabeth walked out on him? A month? No, more like six weeks. She was living with Farrar now. Openly, without remorse. David had scarcely gone in to the office since then, and only when he thought Farrar was somewhere else. He was frightened the two of them might come to blows.

'That's fine. I have a lot of spare time at the moment.'

'You civil servants get a lot of that. You should try working in the real world for a change. I'll call you tomorrow morning, let you know how she is.'

David put down the phone and took another look at the real world.

Any opportunity he might have hoped to find for calm reflection was rudely swept aside by a nine-year-old voice bellowing outside the door.

'Dad! You've got to come at once! Gromit has poohed all over the kitchen floor, and there's shit on everything.'

Next moment, the door flew open to reveal the human being behind the voice. Sam was still in his pyjamas, his hair tousled, his old, much-loved slippers with their Wallace and Gromit heads squeezed on to feet at least one size too small. He ran through the door and into the room with only a little less than the force of a mature tornado.

'Come on,' he shouted. 'You've got to clean up before she does any more.'

Gromit was three months old and Sam's most jealously guarded possession. He'd picked her out from a litter of six at the pet shop on Cambridge Road. Ordinarily, David would have been wary of buying a pet for a nine-year-old boy of rapidly fluctuating enthusiasms. But with Elizabeth's departure, he could deny Sam nothing.

She hadn't wanted him. That wasn't what she'd said, of course: Elizabeth would never be that direct. She'd just felt that it was more appropriate for the boy to be with his father. 'He's not far from adolescence, he'll soon need a role model, someone masculine to look up to.' David had asked what was wrong with her paramour, the sexual stud Anthony Farrar. 'Oh, Anthony's far too remote for someone like Sam. Sam needs someone more "hands-on". And you are his natural father. He looks like you.'

David waved Sam over to the bed and scrutinized him. The boy did look like him, so much so that it was hard to believe Elizabeth had had anything to do with his gestation. Perhaps her genes were as aloof as she was.

It was as if Sam shared David's own mixed parentage, half English, half Uighur. David's father was Max Laing, emeritus professor of Turkic languages at London University. His mother, Soheila, had been a teacher of English at Sinkiang University, where Max had met her while doing research in the region a few years before the Chinese revolution.

'Gromit is your responsibility,' explained David for what must have been the hundredth time. 'You have to feed her, give her water, and clean up after her.'

Sam wrinkled his nose.

'But it smells horrible! Really yuk. It's all over the kitchen. I can't do it on my own.'

'I'm sure you can. Let's go down and take a look.'

True enough, Gromit had decorated the kitchen floor and most of the working surfaces with copious quantities of a substance that should have been encased beneath several inches of cat litter. The unfortunate creature had retreated to her bed, from which vantage point she let out piercing cries of malaise and anger. They started with Gromit, who was anything but a one-man job, and worked their way round the kitchen (followed by the now curious cat) with paper towel and massive quantities of disinfectant.

In the middle of wiping down the breakfast bar, Sam, who'd been his usual chirpy self until then, inexplicably burst into tears. David dropped the wad of towel he was holding and dashed across.

'Sam? Sam, whatever's wrong?'

It took a while for the child to recover himself enough to respond, and when he did it was only what David had expected.

'I miss Mum. I don't like her not being here. I want her back. Why did she have to go?'

The question David had been dreading all these weeks. At first, it had been quite an adventure, just the two of them in the house alone. Elizabeth had left during school term, and David had made a point of seeing that Sam got to school every day. Now that the summer holidays were here, it was impossible to keep the boy sufficiently occupied. He went out with friends, but most of the time he came home to an empty house. David couldn't just give up work, and he couldn't always arrange to be home at the right times.

They talked for a long time, and David did what he could to explain the inexplicable. No, that wasn't true. Elizabeth's departure hadn't been inexplicable to him. She'd got bored with being a wife and a mother, she'd decided that, being wealthy in her own right, she'd be far better off with a rich man than a mere cog in the wheel of national intelligence. The problem wasn't understanding her motives. The problem was making them comprehensible to a nine-year-old.

Sam's tears subsided. But David knew they were still there, waiting to burst out again every time the sense of abandonment grew at all strong. He had his own tears to fight back, but for now it was more important to get Sam through his struggle. Otherwise Sam would join Maddie in a few years' time, emotionally crippled and dependent on drugs to get her through the ruins of her life.

'Fancy a visit to the Dungeon?' he asked.

'Great. Aren't you going to work?'

'I'm supposed to be in the office later. But let's see if I can't wangle something.'

He shaved in the shower, cutting himself twice. The water slashed his head and shoulders with tiny needles, washing his blood away. He closed his eyes tightly and thought about the mess his life was in. Maybe he should be the one in the clinic, he thought.

Maddie, his daughter, was twenty-five years old, beautiful, intelligent, and totally screwed up. Elizabeth, his wife, his former lover, was forty-six, beautiful, intelligent, and in possession of all her faculties. Except for love. Except for loyalty. Except for devotion. Were those things faculties, he wondered, or blessings?

He stepped out of the shower and towelled himself dry. Going to the mirror, he saw he was bleeding again. He took the styptic pencil from the cupboard and went through the ritual of staunching the little wounds. Time he stopped using cheap razors, he thought.

The face that stared back at him seemed almost that of a stranger. He was forty-seven, in excellent health, possessed of all his teeth and a full head of hair. But when he looked in the mirror, he sought a much younger man. The greying hair and the lines beneath his eyes were a cruel trick dreamed up to convince him he was someone else. He put the styptic pencil away and went to the bedroom to dress.

The phone rang again. He tensed himself, sure it would be Elizabeth this time, knowing there was no point in delaying their inevitable and certain-to-be-painful conversation about Maddie.

'Laing.'

'David, it's Bill Dryden here. Farrar wants you down at Carstairs. This morning.'

'For God's sake, I only got back from Cheltenham last night. I'm due back on Friday.'

'Cheltenham's off. For you, anyway. We're sending Dick Redgrave down.'

'Dick? For God's sake, Dick knows bugger all about military codes. This one's a bastard. He'll balls it up.'

'There's no way round this one, David. If you don't show up at Carstairs by ten o'clock, you're in deep shit.'

'What the hell's going on?'

'Can't tell you over the phone. Except that it's very big. Very serious. And it has to do with an old friend.'

'Are you allowed to say who?'

There was a slight pause. Dryden was a rule-book on two legs. He'd weigh up everything he said seven times before saying it.

'Matthew Hyde,' he said.

'Sam, this isn't easy to explain.'

'You can't take me to the Dungeon.'

'Not today, no. Oh, Sam, I'm really sorry.'

'That's all right.'

But he knew it wasn't all right. At nine, promises mean a lot. In Sam's condition, they meant more than usual.

'Look, I'll make it up to you. It's just . . .'

Sam didn't really know what his father did for a living. As with their friends, David's job description was necessarily vague. He was 'something in the civil service', 'a Whitehall dogsbody', 'a glorified typist'. Now, he thought, Sam had to know a little more.

'Sam, will it help if I tell you something very secret? Something nobody, absolutely nobody else is to know.'

'Stuart Badger's dad had a secret like that. Stuart said he was a sex pervert. Are you one as well?'

'Do you know what a sex pervert is?'

'Stuart said he wore women's clothes. Is that what you do?'

'I'm sorry to disappoint you, Sam, but women's clothes don't look good on me. Let's leave sex out of this for the moment. But I want you to remember that this is very seriously secret. I mean that. You're to tell absolutely nobody, however much you may want to. People's lives could depend on it.'

'Not even Maddie?'

'Maddie knows already. But it's best you don't talk about it with her. She worries about what I do.'

'What *do* you do?'

'I work in something called the Secret Service. Do you know what that is?'

Sam shook his head, but it was obvious his curiosity had been aroused.

'It's an organization that puts together information about other countries. And sometimes we send people in to find out more, or to take defensive action against things like terrorist attacks. My job is to get information about China.'

'Like James Bond?'

'Not quite.'

'Do you have a gun?'

'Most of the time, no. Even when you're in the field, it isn't always safe to carry a weapon.'

'Do you . . . ?'

He held his finger out and put it over his son's lips. They were warm to the touch. He wanted to take the boy and hug him hard, but something held him back.

'Look, Sam, I don't have time to go into all this now. But I will, I promise. All I want to say is that the reason I can't take you out today is that I just had news about a man I knew, an old friend. He was . . . I sent him on a mission and he didn't come back. I thought he was dead, and maybe he is. But it's just possible he's alive, and that he needs my help. I've got to go into the country to find out. Do you understand?'

Sam looked at him gravely.

'You're not making all this up?' he asked. His eyes were wide, like a startled fawn's. David shook his head.

'Scout's honour?'

'Scout's honour.'

'I'll spend the day with Billy Hancock. His mum's taking him to Hyde Park. They're taking a boat out.'

'Terrific. I'll give you money for lunch.'

Sam scampered off to get ready, then scampered back again.

'Dad? Did you ever kill anyone? Like in the films?'

'Enough speculation, Samuel Laing. I need to be on my way.'

Sam turned and hurried upstairs to his bedroom. Watching him leave, David felt his heart could so easily break.

Carstairs was Arwel Hughes's safe house down in the Cotswolds, in a five-acre wood near Temple Guiting. They'd kept everyone there at one time or another: Blake, Blunt, Gordievsky, and dozens more the public had never heard of and never would. Carstairs was stone-roofed, mullioned, and fair, but it was no holiday cottage.

He joined the M4 at Hammersmith, and headed west. There was a tailback on the other carriageway, a mile and more of lonely faces staring through sun-bedazzled windscreens. Some beat with their fingers to the rhythm of Radio One or a cassette, some combed their sleep-tangled hair, some yawned. It was the middle of another week, the end of another month. Life did not change.

David put his foot down, moving past slower traffic with practised ease. The Volvo took the strain gently, and he set the cruise control at 90, settling back to watch the city slip away from him. He held the wheel lightly and did what little steering was needed without thinking.

His thoughts were in turmoil. One moment Sam was there, his face bright and eager, then Maddie rushed to the front, clamouring for attention, then Elizabeth sauntered up, smiling her amused smile, then Matthew Hyde appeared out of dark shadows, tired and hesitant.

Dryden had pleaded ignorance. 'It's something to do

with Matthew Hyde,' he'd said. 'That's why they want you there.'

'Is Matthew alive? Has he made contact?'

'I've told you all I know. Farrar said I was to tell you that. But that's all.'

'Will Farrar be there?'

There'd been a sigh at the other end. Dryden wasn't a close friend, but he knew. David realized that a lot of people had known about Elizabeth's affair a long time before she'd spilled the beans to him.

'David, you've got to face him some time. Either that or resign the service.'

'Will he be there?'

'I don't think so. It's being handled by another desk. You have to be there because of Hyde.'

David had sent Hyde on his last mission three years earlier, to investigate a report that Iraqi scientists had been sighted in Sinkiang, not far from the nuclear testing sites at Lop Nor. Hyde had gone in, made two telephone calls to a Uighur agent in Urumchi, and then gone completely silent. He had not been heard from since. He and David had been old friends, and David hoped what he had not dared hope in years, that Matthew had somehow managed to escape.

He bypassed Windsor and Eton, through countryside fringed by Maidenhead and Slough. The constancy of the road appealed to him. If life was like a motorway, he thought, you'd know what to do, and when: come off here, go back on there, switch lanes, speed up, slow down.

Maddie had never understood the rules of the road. Her life was guided by instinct and impulse, she would quicken or slacken her pace according to the dictates of hormones and mysterious brain chemicals whose promptings were outside her conscious control. She'd had one breakdown after coming home from China six years earlier. His bright-faced little girl had become someone unrecognizable and unapproachable. She'd spent a long time in Dr Rose's clinic in Esher, and when she'd come out they'd thought her cured.

What would Matthew be like? he wondered. Changed? Or the same old blight on the species? Hyde had been a wonder, a pain in everyone's arse, cleverer than a dozen monkeys in a bag of treacle. He had read the 'Analects' more than one hundred times – or so he claimed – and he spoke Chinese like a *hsiao* flute, his pitch perfect, his accent flawless. What would he be now? David asked himself. A broken man? A reed? Or something quite different from anything he could imagine?

The car followed the road like a leaf racing downstream. Sunshine flowed across the countryside. Birds circled in an empty sky. He'd sent Matthew Hyde to the most dangerous place in the world, without back-up. He'd been sent to a desert without a heart or soul, and now he'd come home. Or something had come home.

CHAPTER FIVE

Srinagar
23 June

'Mr Dubey, sir, would you step this way, please?'

The voice came from a little alley on his left. Someone speaking Hindi, with a light Kashmiri accent. He turned to see who it was. Fierce sunlight struck his eyes, making him squint. He'd left his dark glasses behind in his office. The other man was visible only as a shadow.

Sunil Dubey had been the Indian Intelligence Service's eyes and ears in Srinagar since as far back as made no difference. Most of the Service's work was done up here, where every inch of ground was a matter of dispute between India and Pakistan, and Dubey had made a name for himself spotting and betraying agents who worked for the other side. His reports to Delhi were a matter of pride, commented on by Mr Ranjit Bhose, no less, the director of Jammu and Kashmir Regional Unit. He had never met Mr Bhose, but he dreamed of the day when his contribution to national security and public safety would be rewarded with a letter of commendation and a medal. Genuine silver, hallmarked, made in Britain.

He'd spent all day writing his latest, a super-confidential account of proceedings at 10 Pampore Alley, attesting to all that had been heard and witnessed by himself during the interview with the boy from Ladakh. It was with him now, in the canvas bag he carried, nestling next to the *nan* he'd just bought at Jamshid Khosraupur's shop. He'd have liked to have access to the tape the man Ross had made. That would have made it perfect, and impressed Mr Bhose no end; but he knew there'd be no chance of that, not unless someone in Delhi put some pressure where it hurt, some even bigger cheese than Mr Ranjit Bhose. He sang under his breath, *Nahi buleghi voh barsat ki rat*, a song he'd heard Mohammad Rafi sing in an old film they'd shown on television last night.

It worried him a little that they'd spirited the boy away like that – parents, clothes, bags and baggage. The little rooms in Gujwara Alley had been stripped of their possessions: it was as if no one had ever lived there, or ever would again. Someone in Delhi – Mr Ranjit Bhose or maybe someone even more pukka – would be sure to ask him why he'd done nothing to prevent them, and he didn't know what to answer. They should have been there, seen the man called Dennison, tried to face up to him themselves. Well, he'd telephoned Delhi, and it wasn't his fault that the person on the other end was no one of any importance, that his message had been 'logged and noted', and almost certainly not passed on with any alacrity. All the same, they were sure to fix the blame on him if they could. Hence the importance of the report, hence the care he'd taken over it.

The boy worried him a lot. He'd met more than one incarnation in his time, pretty boys and pouting girls who said, 'I've been here before' or 'My mother and father were so-and-so, and I've come back to be with them a second time.' It reduced people to tears, tore families apart, created legal problems that went on for years, like that trial in Mr Dickens's great novel. Most

33

of them were fakes. Ninety-nine per cent *kutcha*, even if you closed your eyes and thought of all the gods in all the heavens. This one was different. This one had scared the Englishmen.

He took a step out of the sunlight, grateful for the shadow play of the alley. The man who had called to him was standing casually near an open doorway. The alley was full of food stalls. A smell of cooked mutton rose from the pots of a *rista* merchant, rich and warm.

With a sense of relief, Dubey recognized the man. His name was Mohammad Faiz, a Muslim saffron-seller who worked off and on for the British. Faiz had even passed occasional snippets of information to Dubey himself from time to time – nothing remarkable, but always worth paying a few rupees for. If his tips were shown up as false – which they often were – he'd simply shrug and say, '*Mongra* is *mongra*, *lochha* is *lochha*,' in reference to the two kinds of saffron he sold: the first prohibitively expensive but genuine, the second cheap and just as yellow, but perfectly worthless.

Faiz also liked to put it about that he had close links to the Hizbul Mujahidin, the main Muslim separatist movement, and that he was even in the confidence of its leaders. To which Dubey would shrug and say, '*Mongra* is *mongra*, *lochha* is *lochha*.' Still, round here, it never paid to be too careful. Never trust anyone, never distrust anyone.

'*Al-salam alaykum*, Mohammad. *Kya hal hai?* It's good to see you. Have you got something for me?'

Mohammad Faiz smiled. He was a thin man with loose, saffron-powdered skin that clung to what there was of his flesh like seaweed clinging to a rock. Yellow teeth gleamed in a soft red mouth.

'Mr Dennison sahib says I must speak with you.'

'Dennison? The Englishman? Where is he?'

'Not here. Dennison has gone. He says I must find you and speak with you directly.'

Dubey looked up the narrow alley ahead of him. Shadow and sunlight, sunlight and shadow. A dog ran gamely between the legs of passers-by. A group of soldiers walked past, their weapons held in nervous hands, fearful of a sudden ambush or a bullet in the back. Hostile eyes followed them to the corner and out of sight.

'Well, what is it he wants you to talk with me about?'

'Not here, Mr Dubey, sir. He is very insistent. He says I must speak with you, sir, in private. Please, we can talk in here.'

He gestured to the open doorway: an odd gesture, one that a pimp or a strip-show tout might employ, luring the unwary into vice or self-degradation. A strange, vapid light came from inside. Dubey caught sight of a large fan turning somnolently in the thick air.

'What is this place?' he asked amiably.

'It is my brother's *karkhana*. His boys weave carpets. The very best Mughal designs. Perhaps you would like to buy one? A present for your dear wife.'

'I can't afford carpets. Your brother should have sold one to Mr Dennison.'

Mohammad moved his head in an apologetic manner.

'Nabil will make a very special price for you when I tell him what an important man you are. You have most significant connections. Nabil always needs contacts to the right people. And he is very generous to those who help him. Come inside, let me introduce you.'

Dubey hesitated for several moments. He did not feel altogether safe in this part of town. But Mohammad had spoken with Dennison.

'You are sure Dennison *sahib* asked you to speak with me?'

35

Mohammad looked at him impatiently and slipped one hand into his shirt pocket. He drew it out holding a slightly crumpled sheet of paper and handed it to Dubey. Dubey unfolded it. It bore a letterhead consisting only of Dennison's name, beneath which someone had scribbled in English the words 'Thanks for your help' and the initials PJD, barely legible. Wordlessly, Dubey handed the paper back to Mohammad and followed him into the workshop.

There was a public area at the front, where carpets had been laid out for sale, some on a long bench, others hanging from the wall. Dubey could tell right away that they were not the very best work, but adequate. He admired one with dark red and gold tones, styled after a Persian model. He fingered it as he passed and admired its delicacy, wondering if he could afford it, even with a discount.

From behind a curtain came the voices of the weavers, chanting the *talim*, the coded instructions that laid down the patterns for each design.

'Let's go through,' said Mohammad. 'My brother's inside.'

They passed through the curtain into a much larger room. Four upright looms took up almost all the available space. The weavers squatted in front of them on wooden boards, their hands moving rapidly as they knotted the pattern through the cords. Tuft of wool was laid upon tuft in strict and ordered sequence, generating birds and flowers and Arabic letters as if from nothing.

'Nabil!' Mohammad spoke the name softly, as though calling upon a spirit of the air to leave its realm and join him on the dusty floor. One of the weavers, a tall man dressed in black, got to his feet and came towards them. He reached out a hand and took Dubey's firmly.

'Mr Dubey. My brother has told me much about you. He says he has business with you. And then, perhaps, I can speak with you as well.'

Dubey nodded and smiled. He turned to Mohammad.

'What did Mr Dennison ask you to speak with me about, Mohammad?'

'Oh, very little really. A trifling thing. He said I was to ask about your report. He said you will have written it by now, and that you will be carrying it with you.'

'What report is that?'

'How should I know? I am only to ask about it. If it is finished. And if it is with you.'

'I don't think it's Mr Dennison's business to know about my report.'

'That's not for me to enquire. He paid me to ask. Is it in your bag?'

'I only have some *nan* in here. My wife expects me home with it for dinner.'

'Who do you buy your *nan* from?'

'Jamshid Khosraupur. He bakes the best.'

'I'm sure he would not mind if I took a look at his *nan*. I've heard it's very good, as you say.'

Mohammad's hand reached out for the bag. Dubey made to push him aside, but he felt his arm taken by Nabil.

'My brother would like to look in your bag, Mr Dubey.' Nabil looked hard at him. There was no warmth in the look. 'I think it's only polite to let him.'

The bag was pulled unceremoniously from Dubey's hands, and opened. Mohammad lifted out the thin file containing the report.

'This is very strange *nan*,' he said. 'Not very edible. Perhaps this Jamshid is not as clever a baker as I'd heard.'

Next to them, one of the weavers paused in his work

and snickered at Mohammad's lame joke. Nabil snapped at him, telling him to keep on weaving. Dubey took his handkerchief from his pocket and wiped his forehead. It felt uncomfortably hot in the *karkhana*.

'Maybe this is your report,' said Mohammad. 'The one Mr Dennison would like to see.'

'My report is confidential. Not even Mr Dennison is authorized to see it. If he wants to see, he must ask through proper channels.'

Mohammad shook his head languidly. Nabil had not let go of Dubey's arm.

'I am Mr Dennison's proper channel. He has paid me to bring him this report. Paid me very well. Much more than you can pay me to leave it alone.'

Suddenly, Nabil twisted his arm behind his back, grabbed his other arm, and held them both pinned hard in that position.

'Don't be such fools,' Dubey shouted. 'You know who I am. There will be a full inquiry if I'm harmed.'

Mohammad took a long knife from an inside pocket. It looked very sharp, as if it had been honed and honed to a perfect edge. When it entered his stomach, Sunil Dubey hardly felt it. He watched it go in with a sense of wonder, and he watched Mohammad draw it upwards, then down again with renewed astonishment, as if it was all happening to another person. Then the pain began, and with it the most terrible nausea. He saw Mohammad's face spin, slowly at first, then at sickening speed. There were words in the air, but he could not catch them. And snatches of an old song, shuddering through his head and out again towards the open sky. He tried to follow where they had gone, but something exploded in his head, and he was blind and deaf and spinning down a dark tunnel that had no end.

CHAPTER SIX

Carstairs

'They're waiting for you in room number seven, Mr Laing.'

Arwel Hughes was the larger-than-life uncle David had never had. A huge man, tall by Welsh standards, he'd played rugby for Neath in his youth, and had continued coaching a local team until a year or two ago. He and the loquacious Mrs Hughes had run the safe house out here in the Cotswolds for as long as anyone in the service could remember, trundling down to South Wales once a month in their battered Volkswagen estate, and coming back laden with laver bread from Bridgend and tubs of Joe's ice-cream packed in ice.

Generations of spies and double agents had breakfasted on Glynis Hughes's fry-ups of laver bread, sausage, and mushrooms, and gone to bed wondering how they'd ever get by back in Moscow or Peking without regular helpings of Joe's strawberry sundae. It had tempted more than one KGB stalwart to consider doing a deal.

'Who's here? Anthony Farrar isn't among them, is he?'

Arwel shook his balding head. He and David had always got on particularly well. They'd played more than one hard game of rugby together over the years, always on the same side, always on the winning side. And afterwards they'd gone to the pub together and talked. Over the years, Arwel had been one of the few people David could talk to about his troubles at home. He was a good listener.

'I'm sorry about what's happened, Mr Laing. I couldn't help hearing.'

'Don't worry. If there's one place you can't keep a secret . . .'

'It's the Secret Service. I know. But, it's not right, all the same, sir. He's your desk head, after all. It's unforgivable to steal someone else's wife at the best of times, sir, but . . .'

'He didn't steal her, Arwel, you know that. She went of her own free will; in fact she was extremely willing. I'd better not say anything more, or you'll be reporting me to our ever-vigilant masters.'

David never liked to be reminded about Anthony Farrar, his boss and successful rival for his wife's affections. He had always had a fundamental dislike of the man even from the early days of their acquaintance; that had been less because of his cuckolding ways, which were notorious, or his looks, which Bronzino might have painted, or his connections, which Madame de Staël might have envied, than by reason of Farrar's inherent unfitness for the job. His appointment had ruffled the usual feathers on the usual birds, but in his case the feathers had stayed ruffled. Of course, the man would have been perfectly suited to the task if all anyone had demanded of him had been polish, an ability to command anything that moved, and an innate knowledge of how to behave in the best clubs. It had been a political appointment at a time when the Desk needed more than ever a man with different abilities.

'What's in room seven?' he asked.

'They have a boy in there, sir. Chinese or something. Around the age of our Megan's Richard. Mr Barker brought him down from London.'

'Who else?'

'Miss Potter; that new man from Section Six, Donaldson . . .'

'The one with the squint?'

'That's him. And a Mr Ross, a Scotsman.'

'Don't know him.'

'He knows you, sir. Or your name.'

David thanked him and set off along the corridor that led to rooms five to nine. The room numbers were an innovation of the Patterson years, part of the cold restructuring that had modernized and dehumanized the service. They'd done well enough in the old days with 'second on the left' or 'the one at the end'. The house was small enough, after all, and homely enough. You could have fooled yourself into thinking you were spending the weekend with old friends. Now it was like a second-rate country house hotel, keeping up the pretensions but providing little of substance. Next thing the fry-ups would give way to pre-packed breakfasts from an outside contractor, and there'd be synthetic ice-cream on Formica tables in the evening.

Like all the rooms on this floor, number seven had a glass pane set in the door. David stopped before entering and looked inside. His colleagues were seated round a small table at whose head sat a boy of perhaps ten. He was not Han Chinese, that much was certain. Possibly Tajik, but more likely Uighur. Sinkiang Province, then. That would provide a link with Matthew.

He opened the door. Heads turned, but no one spoke. Softly, David closed the door behind him. Still no one spoke.

'Something wrong?' he asked. 'Wasn't I expected?'

It was the boy who spoke. He smiled at David, as though greeting an old friend.

'Hello, David. You look surprised. I see you don't recognize me.'

David looked at him blankly.

'I see no reason why I should,' he said. He turned to Pauline Potter. Pauline, like himself, was China Desk staff, an old trooper from the Peking embassy.

'Suppose somebody explains to me what's going on.'

'I'm sorry, David. We wanted to see if he recognized you. It seems he has.'

'Clearly you all have the advantage of me. Who is the boy?'

'All in due course,' said Pauline. 'First let me introduce you. You know Richard Barker. And I think you've met Chris Donaldson from Section Six. The man beside him is Douglas Ross. Douglas is a field agent in northern India. The boy is his discovery. He's been interviewed before this by P. J. Dennison.'

'Why isn't Dennison here?'

Ross answered the question for her.

'He's in London pow-wowing with your boss, Anthony Farrar. He may come down later today.'

'Is this a border problem?'

David Laing was Britain's leading intelligence expert on Chinese military activity in the western province of Sinkiang. Sinkiang, which was inhabited mainly by Uighur Muslims, was separated from India by the Karakoram Mountains, and the border region had long been a bone of contention between the two countries. A frontier problem would explain why Ross and Dennison from the India Desk would be here. But it didn't make sense of Donaldson, whose section dealt with Iraqi nuclear capacity. And it didn't explain the boy or his strange greeting. What had that meant, 'recognized you'?

'Not in the sense you mean,' said Ross. 'Nevertheless, I think there may be a problem with another border entirely.'

'Meaning what exactly?'

'Meaning the border between this life and the next.'

The man said the words flatly, without affectation of any sort. As though he meant them. It was as if they had stepped out of the ordinary world of intelligence-gathering into one of mediumship and astrology.

'Like the *X-Files*?'

Barker chuckled, looked at David, and resumed the expressionless face he had worn until then. He'd be the boy's minder, thought David, there to make sure his charge was treated well.

'Why don't you sit down, David?' Pauline gestured to a chair next to her. She was a small woman, whose neat, nimble movements always surprised David by their delicacy. Her formidable intellect frightened him, and when in her presence he could not help feeling like a small schoolboy brought to explain himself to his headmistress. He sat down and waited.

'Mr Barker, would you please leave us now?' she asked. 'You're welcome to monitor proceedings on the screen in the next room, but the rest of this discussion is above top secret.'

Barker made no protest. That wasn't part of his job. He made his departure in silence.

'Exactly who's in charge here?' David asked when Barker had gone.

'At the moment, I am,' said Pauline. 'By the time we've finished, you will be. Or so I hope.'

'What about Farrar?'

'He has overall responsibility. But this is your baby.'

'Why wasn't I notified before this? If it's to be my baby, as you put it?'

'The boy's story had to be checked,' said Pauline. 'There was no point in pulling you off vital work on the off chance something might come of this.'

'But now?'

'Something will come of it. We're fairly certain of that.'

'And this nonsense about the afterlife?'

'It may not be nonsense. Mr Ross will explain.'

Ross was fresh-faced and nervous, almost juvenile. His imperfectly tanned skin implied a tour of duty that had some years to go.

'It started back in May,' he said. 'I received a message from an Indian intelligence officer in Srinagar, a man called Dubey. He didn't tell me much, just that there was someone he thought I should meet. I went up and was introduced to Yongden here and his parents. Yongden said they had recently arrived in Kashmir from Ladakh. He claimed – this is not easy to explain – that he was the reincarnation of a British intelligence agent named Matthew Hyde. The name meant nothing to me, of course. I'm new in the service, and I believe Mr Hyde worked in quite a different area.'

'And you swallowed this story?'

'Of course not. I swallow nothing I might have to throw up again. Believe me, I took care. I questioned him closely. The interview did not go as I expected. For one thing, the boy speaks almost perfect English. I don't think many children from Ladakh can do that.'

'He's not from Ladakh,' David said.

'How can you know?'

'I only have to look at him.' He turned from Ross to the boy.

'*Khush, yakhshimusiz?*'

The boy smiled, like someone who has been caught out in a minor deceit.

'*Yakhshi,*' he replied, as though he'd known David for years. There was no trace of embarrassment or guilt in his face or voice. '*Özinizchu? Qandaq ahwaliniz?*' Fine. How are you? How are things going?

'He's from Sinkiang,' said David. 'He's a Uighur. Now, perhaps we can drop this silliness about reincarnations.'

'Actually, I don't think we can, David,' Pauline said. 'Where he comes from isn't terribly important. It's what he knows.'

'He lied about where he came from. Presumably the rest is a lie as well.'

Donaldson treated the comment as a cue to speak for the first time.

'I'm sorry, Mr Laing, but I think you're jumping the gun here. The boy's already been through exhaustive questioning. We've determined that, whatever the source of it, his story is basically true. He knows things it would be impossible for any child from Ladakh or, for that matter, Sinkiang to know. He knows about Operation Hong Cha.'

David said nothing. There was nothing he could say in answer to that. Operation Hong Cha was something only he, Matthew Hyde, and Anthony Farrar had known about in the first months. Something only ten people knew about even now. One of British intelligence's most secret operations since the Second World War. Donaldson was right. If the boy knew about Hong Cha, he was more than he seemed.

'He knows the details?'

Pauline nodded.

'Everything,' she said. 'At least, everything Matthew Hyde knew.'

'Go on with your story, Mr Ross. I'm sorry I interrupted.'

'I came away from that first interview feeling as though I'd just been scooped out. Yongden told me enough to convince me he knew about the Secret Service, about London, about places I'd only heard of. Like this house. When I got back to Delhi I made enquiries about Matthew Hyde. It was then I got in touch with Dennison. The boy was brought back here after he spoke with him.'

'Surely this is just some sort of circus trick.'

'I assure you it's not, David.' Pauline's voice was dark and troubled. She didn't like this any more than he did. 'He says Hong Cha was not aborted. That Hyde got into the Taklamakan and out again. That he knows the full co-ordinates and all other details. But he'll only reveal them to you.'

'I see.'

That explained why Donaldson was here then. Operation Hong Cha had been set up three years earlier on the back of rumours that Iraqi nuclear scientists had been spotted near military research centres in western China. Matthew Hyde had been sent on a mission to explore a number of possible sites where, it was rumoured, a super-weapon was being developed for Saddam Hussein. Hyde had made contact twice with a local contact in Charkhliq, then vanished. Every attempt to locate him after that had failed, and in the end Farrar had shut down the operation. And, despite David's protests, given up the hunt for Matthew Hyde.

He looked at the boy.

'What's your real name?' he asked in English.

'Tursun.'

'Why did you lie about coming from Ladakh?'

'It was a necessary lie. If I'd said we were from Sinkiang,

the Indian authorities would have sent us back. Now I'm here, there's no point in it. It makes no difference.'

'Is there a weapon?'

'There was none while I was alive.'

'And now?'

'I can't speak for now. Three years ago they had made considerable progress, but the project was still continuing. They must be very close by now.'

'What is the name of the Iraqi general who handles things at their end?'

'Abd al-Latif Nuri.'

David felt like someone who has started to drown, but who still has enough sense to know when to start swimming.

'Tell me about the project,' he said. 'Tell me everything you know.'

CHAPTER SEVEN

Farrar did not turn up that afternoon. David tried more than once to contact him. Each time a secretary with an icy voice told him Sir Anthony was not in his office, or Sir Anthony was in a meeting, or Sir Anthony had just stepped out of the building, and would Mr Laing please ring back later? He gave up ringing in the end. Try as he might, he could not stop thoughts of Farrar and Elizabeth from forming in his brain. When he thought of them now, they were sweating and naked, writhing together on a hot bed.

He sneezed several times and went back to room number seven.

'No luck,' he said. 'The great man's still out and about.'

'He'll have to speak to you.' Pauline was adamant. She disapproved of Farrar, she'd never made a secret of it. He wasn't qualified to run the China Desk, she argued. Just because he'd spent a few years as First Secretary in Peking, taken a year off to learn something rudimentary which he called Chinese, and licked every upper-class backside in sight, did not make him desk head material. In her opinion. And, though he was never so forthright, in David's as well.

'I've asked him to ring back.' He sneezed again. His hay fever had been late in coming on this year. Rain had kept the pollen at bay until a week ago. But now he could feel it marshalling its strength to make the summer miserable.

'He could be on his way,' suggested Donaldson. Pauline gave him a withering look.

There were several sessions with Tursun, each more frustrating than the one before. The boy knew a great deal, that became more and more obvious as the day wore on; but not everything he said made sense, and a lot of the information he passed to them was self-contradictory.

He gave them a place name – Karakhoto – but could not locate it on any map of the region. Nor could anyone else. When asked for the names of the generals responsible for liaison with the Iraqi scientists and military men, he could only name two – Wang Chigang and Zhao Chingyu – neither of whom rang bells with David, who knew the names of everyone in the provincial military hierarchy. There were several map co-ordinates, but when David pressed for details of what they referred to, the boy became visibly confused and started contradicting what he'd already said.

At times it was hard to pin him down. He would allude to things in an imprecise, airy fashion, as if he were a medium at a travelling fair.

'There's a man with thin hair,' he said. 'In the Taklamakan. Be careful of him.'

'What's his name?' asked David. Tursun shook his head sadly and said he did not know.

'Black walls,' he said. 'There are black walls without windows or doors. They are hiding something behind them.'

'Hiding what?' The boy shook his head again and lowered his eyes.

To David, the whole affair had a bad smell about it, an overpowering odour of incense sticks and tarot cards, cheap horoscopes cast in old bazaars, oracles murmured darkly at wayside shrines. He'd seen it all in his day – sleight of hand and sleight of tongue, old men touched by madness more than holiness, little boys with large eyes and outstretched hands. The only thing was, this time he couldn't for the life of him work out how it was done.

By mid-afternoon, the boy began to flag. His confidence was leaving him. He said he was tired, that he'd travelled a long way, and had had little sleep. They were all exhausted by then anyway, so David called an early halt to the last session. Mrs Hughes took the boy back to his room, where he went straight to sleep. His parents were being kept in a separate suite on the top floor for as long as the debriefing lasted. They were frightened and, without Tursun to interpret, they talked to no one.

David went upstairs and knocked on their door. The father opened it, a small man with a permanently pained expression on a face that looked years older than it could possibly have been.

'*As-salamu alaykum. Kirishka rukhsatmu?*' David greeted him. He expected some sort of pretence, a masquerade to chime with Tursun's, but there was none.

'*Wa alaykum as-salamu. Kirin. Olturup biraz chay ichin.*' The man's invitation was spoken in plain Uighur. As he asked David inside, a half-smile crossed his lips, and he seemed to stand a little straighter.

'My name's David Laing. I'm in charge of your son.'

'Yes, Mr David. Please. Please come in.'

David followed him inside, along a short corridor to the living room. Tursun's father introduced himself as Osmanjan. His wife was sitting on the sofa watching the cartoon channel, her lips moving silently as though following the words. She got up when David was introduced, and bowed shyly. When he spoke to her in Uighur, her eyes almost popped out of her head, as if it was the last thing in the world she might have expected. Osmanjan introduced her. Her name was Rotsemi.

'Our guest would like some tea.' Osmanjan sent her off to the little galley kitchen where Britain's most notorious traitors had brewed endless cups of PG Tips.

'I would like to speak to her as well,' said David as she left. 'You understand that, don't you?'

Osmanjan nodded. What little trace there had been of a smile on his face had gone. He knew he was not among friends. Just because a stranger came speaking Uighur . . .

'She knows nothing of all this.'

'And you – what do you know?'

The man shrugged and invited David to sit down. In the corner, the television continued to make a nuisance of itself. The garish colours and jerking movements of a Looney Tunes cartoon flickered and gyrated on the edge of vision. Screeches and whoops boomed from the set.

'You are Muslims,' David said. 'Why all this talk of reincarnation? Shouldn't you leave that to the Hindus and the Buddhists?'

Osmanjan reddened. It was as if David had accused him of sleeping with other men's wives. Or betraying his people.

'It is the boy's story, not mine.'

'Then you say you do not believe it?'

'It is not for me to say. It is his story.'

'He *is* your son, isn't he?'

Osmanjan nodded. Behind him, a new cartoon had started. Road Runner zoomed through the desert, pursued by Wile E. Coyote. Every few seconds, the room was rocked by an explosion.

'How old is he? He says he is twelve, but I don't think he can be more than ten.'

'No, twelve is correct. He has always looked younger than his real age.'

'And he was born in Sinkiang?'

Another nod.

'Where in Sinkiang?'

'Khotan.'

'Have you always lived there? You don't have a southern accent.'

'No, we have lived many places. Urumchi. Charkhliq. Turfan. Kashgar. Many places.'

'And you got to India through Ladakh?'

'Yes. It was a long journey. I thought we would die. It was cold. The snow was like demons.'

'Who told you to make that journey? Who told you to go to India?'

'The boy.'

'You take orders from your son?'

Behind him, a woman's voice answered.

'You don't know him. You don't understand.'

David turned to find Rotsemi standing in the doorway. She held a tray on which a sturdy brown teapot and three china cups were balanced precariously. David recognized them: British Home Stores, Swansea. There were little crowded tears in the woman's eyes.

David got up and went to her.

'Let me take that,' he said. She shook her head and came in, fighting the tears back, and set the tray down on a low pine table. In her world, it was unthinkable for a guest to help his hostess.

'My son has done nothing wrong,' she said. 'All this is to help us, his father and mother. He seeks nothing for himself.'

'I wouldn't suggest such a thing. I only want to know what is happening.'

She poured tea into the cups, Uighur-style, without milk, very sweet. The tea was golden-brown, more suited to Chinese than Uighur taste. David thought there'd be little point in having a word with Arwel or his good lady. He'd get a couple of black tea bricks in London and bring them down. And give Glynis some pointers about traditional Uighur cuisine.

'We have come here with our son,' said Rotsemi. David took a closer look at her. She couldn't be more than thirty, but her face was white and drained, and her eyes held a vacant look, as though both curiosity and terror had been wiped from them.

'Is he your only child?'

'Yes.'

'I have other children,' said Osmanjan. 'From my first wife.'

'Where is she?'

'Dead.' He said it in a flat voice, as though to tame an emotion more acid than simple grief. 'They took her from me. She died in prison. Then they took the children. There are three of them. Perhaps they are alive. Perhaps dead.'

David did not need to ask who 'they' were. Only the Han Chinese authorities could have put a wife in prison and taken children away by force.

He looked at Rotsemi.

'And you? Do you want more children?'

Her pale face coloured gently, and she nodded.

'Now, perhaps. Now that we are safe.'

'Why were you in danger? What did you do that made Sinkiang dangerous for you?'

Rotsemi shrank back visibly. She'd said too much already. Osmanjan sipped from his cup, holding it from behind, as though it had no handle.

'You must speak to my son,' he said. 'He knows everything. He will tell you.'

'Was it on account of a man called Hyde? Matthew Hyde?'

Osmanjan did not answer. But David could see he recognized the name.

He spent half an hour with them, and at the end he was no further forward. The son had led them here, the son knew everything. They were just his hangers-on. When he finished his tea, he made his excuses and left. The last thing he heard as the door closed was Woody Woodpecker's insane laugh. Stepping on to the landing, he sneezed loudly.

Chris Donaldson was waiting for him downstairs.

'I'm told you came down by car.'

'That's right.'

'Any chance of a lift back?'

'Where are you going?'

'Hampstead.'

'Well, that's not too far out of my way.'

'You don't have to take me all the way there.'

'May as well. But you'll have to pay your way.'

'I thought you'd say that.'

David fished in his pocket for his keys, and tossed them to Donaldson.

'You drive. I'm bushed. But I've a few questions I'd like to ask you.'

CHAPTER EIGHT

People's Republic of China
Western Region Military Installation 14
(Chaofe Ling)
[Co-ordinates classified]
Level 3, Corridor 13

The corridor was almost two and a half miles long. Four kilometres, to be precise. Four thousand metres. Engineer Zhang Fengsuo said it was the longest corridor in China, maybe the world, and he should have known – he'd designed it, costed it, and supervised its construction. It never turned, never wavered, never altered, not for an inch of its length. In the ceiling, two thousand light units burned day and night. A team of fitters replaced those in each section on a week-by-week schedule. The corridor was divided into twelve sections, so it took three months to work through the corridor before starting all over again.

There were forty-one corridors like it in the installation, six on each level, crossing and crisscrossing, one hundred and sixty-seven kilometres in all. Each corridor on level three had a minimum of five hundred doors, and each door . . .

Karim Hasanoglu shook his head in bewilderment and kept his eyes fixed straight ahead. Thinking about this place didn't help your nerves. He'd been here three weeks now, and still dreaded these long drives through the white, brightly lit corridors, each one exactly like the rest, with no landmarks or markers apart from the Chinese signs that he could not decipher.

He pressed down on the pedal and his little electric buggy picked up speed to its maximum of ten miles an hour. He didn't bother looking, but he knew that, right behind him, his state security tail would be accelerating to exactly the same rate. Karim gave an inward shrug. He'd been brought up in what one writer had called Iraq's Republic of Fear, and it was never much of a surprise to find yourself shadowed by a dead-faced secret policeman trying to be inconspicuous.

Here in the installation, of course, there wasn't much point in pretending, so his shadow just went along with him everywhere. Since Karim didn't speak a word of Chinese and his tail knew not a word of Arabic or Turkish, communications between them were extremely limited.

They'd told him to drive down the corridor until the tripometer on his buggy reached the figure 2850, where-upon he was to stop and ask permission to enter a door numbered 74:6 (3). At least the numbers were written in characters he could understand. When he slept, he had bad dreams about being lost down here, dreams in which he rode round and round for hour after hour, never seeing a way out, never coming across anyone he could ask for help. He shivered and looked at the dial in front of him. It read 2789. Another sixty metres would bring him to the door.

He knew what was behind the door, and didn't relish the thought of passing it. He hadn't a clue about details, of course, but he did have a shrewd notion as to what awaited him. They wanted him to help question a man, someone who knew more than he should about the weapons being developed here. Karim was a scientist, and he spoke Turkish, which was as close to the Uighur spoken in Sinkiang as you could get, so they'd fingered him as a help and comfort in present peril.

Karim was a Turkman from the mountains north of Mosul. His father had brought the family to Baghdad soon after the Baathists took power in 1968, had opened a successful business trading in agricultural equipment with Istanbul, and had eventually sent his three sons to university. Karim had gone to Baghdad's University of Technology to study chemistry. He'd come top of his class, made a good impression on the dean, and gone on to study for a doctorate at MIT. He'd been tempted to marry an American girl, stay in the States, and settle down in a comfortable job with a petrochemical company in the Mid-West.

Then one day he'd arrived back at his rooms to find a man from the Iraqi embassy waiting for him. A big man with prowling eyes. Sally had been there: she'd been the one to let the man in. He could still remember her eyes, the look of raw fear in them. It hadn't been anything the man had done or said. All it had needed was his presence. Karim learned later that the man's name was Hamza, and that he was the embassy's dog, the one they set on dissidents.

By then he'd packed his bags, and signed all the papers he needed to sign, and bought a one-way ticket from New York to Baghdad. One ticket. He'd cried silently all the way home, and when he'd stepped down from the plane his family had been waiting for him. They hadn't been alone. A man in shades had watched him back to their house. The following morning, he'd reported to the State Establishment for Phosphates Production, where a quiet-spoken man in a neat military uniform had handed him papers posting him to the giant fertilizer complex at al-Qa'im on the Euphrates. Long before he got there, Karim knew that phosphoric acid wouldn't be the only thing produced at his new place of work.

At 2850 he took his foot off the pedal and the buggy stopped. There was a grey door to his left. It looked exactly like all the other doors he'd passed. The number on it read 74:6 (3). Unlike most other doors, it bore no logograms spelling out the identity of whatever activity went on behind it. He smiled at his shadow and invited him to introduce them. The security man smiled back. He looked animated for once. Karim cringed inside. It was a hard and fast rule back in Iraq to dive for cover the moment you saw so much as a flicker of amusement cross a *mukhabarat* agent's face.

The little man spoke into a grille set in the wall next to the door.

'Wo shi Kao Shien-nun. Zhe wei shi Karim shiansheng.'

The door opened soundlessly. Karim stepped inside, followed by his tail. The door closed, leaving them in a small vestibule. There were photographs on the walls. Karim tried not to look, he knew what they were, but it was hard to avoid them. Over the years, he'd learned how to prevent himself being sick. He took a deep, slow breath and waited for the next door to open. It was heavier than the first, and he knew it would be soundproof.

There was a click and a soft whirring sound, and the second door rolled back. Waiting for him a few feet across the threshold was a familiar face. Huang Zhengmei smiled and held out her hand. Karim smiled back. It almost made him feel better to see her here. Perhaps things wouldn't turn out as bad as he feared. Huang Zhengmei was aged about thirty, pretty, with a musical voice and frighteningly intelligent eyes. You couldn't imagine anything remotely unpleasant happening while she was around. He took her hand in his. It was no larger than a child's.

'Miss Huang. It's good to see you again.'

She'd been responsible for settling him in over the first couple of days he'd spent in the complex. They communicated in English, which she spoke fluently: he'd been impressed to learn that she'd spent several years studying at London University.

'And you, Dr Hasanoglu. I'd like you to meet someone we all admire. Allow me to introduce Colonel Chang Zhangyi.'

A man stepped forward from a cluster of shadows on Huang Zhengmei's left. He'd been watching them all along, hidden. Now, as he came forward, Karim realized that he'd been foolish ever to think that the presence of a pretty woman might be allowed to get in the way of what happened here.

'Colonel Chang Zhangyi is head of security for Sinkiang Province.'

Karim felt the familiar chill, the instinctive lowering of emotional temperature he experienced every time he met men like Chang Zhangyi. Today, he thought, he was an honoured guest. Tomorrow, he could be served up to the colonel as a wholly different form of humanity. All it would take would be a word out of place, a hint of betrayal, or too great a degree of curiosity. He reached out his hand for a second time and tried to smile.

The colonel was like a statue come partially to life. Animate, but only in so far as there was movement in his face and limbs. Otherwise dead. No heart, no proper feelings, no remorse, no love, no depth, no fear, no compassion, no true hate – just the mechanics of life, without the essence. The perfect servant of a state system predicated on obedience. It was all there in the face, Karim thought, as though a fine calligrapher's brush had painted letters of the true man across his pockmarked skin.

'I'm grateful to you for coming today, Doctor. I know you're a very busy man and that you're engaged on important work here. But I assure you, this won't be wasted time.'

'You speak very good English, Colonel. You've been to England like Miss Huang?'

'Hong Kong. I spent some years there very early in my career, working for a British finance company. Now, if you don't mind, I'd like to get this over with.'

Chang Zhangyi gestured casually, and a guard standing near the door flicked a switch, turning on more overhead lights. Huang Zhengmei stood aside, allowing Karim to look past her into the rest of the room. It was a long, narrow room. The walls were painted black, a very deep, matt black that seemed almost to swallow the light as rapidly as the lamps threw it out. Karim felt a bitter taste in his mouth and swallowed hard. Chang Zhangyi led the way to the other end of the room.

There were several pieces of apparatus set against the walls. Karim tried not to look at them. He could guess their function well enough. He'd never been in a torture chamber before, but he knew enough people who had. Some had been tortured, some had done the torturing. One of his best friends at university had been a Kurd. They'd lost touch for several years after Karim went to MIT, then made contact again about three years ago. On their second meeting, Dara had taken off his shirt and shown Karim the knotted scars that ran like tramlines across his back. It had happened during the year and more he'd spent in the Red Security Building in Sulaymaniyya. In a room like this.

The prisoner was at the far end. The apparatus that held him resembled nothing Karim had ever seen or heard of. It was a cage with widely spaced bars, in which the man was standing upright. His head emerged through the top of the contraption, and his feet were supported on wooden boards that were covered in faeces and urine. He was naked and dirty, and his hair and beard were long and unkempt, straggling across the top of the cage like a weed that threatened to choke him. His features were masked, but Karim could see nevertheless that he was not Han Chinese.

'We have been questioning him for a very long time,' said Huang Zhengmei. 'We want to find out what he knows.'

'Does it matter?' asked Karim. 'He's hardly in a position to tell anyone.'

'He has not always been in this position,' said Chang Zhangyi. 'He may have told others before he came here. I need to know what sort of information they might possess.'

'Information about what?'

'About your project. Our joint project.' Huang Zhengmei walked up to the cage and stood in front of it, staring at the trapped man as if he was an exhibit at the regional museum in Urumchi. 'That's what he was being paid to ask about. He was a professional, he did a very good job before Colonel Chang Zhangyi's men found him. If we know what he has passed on, we may be able to do something to limit the damage.'

Karim took a closer look at the man. He was clearly in a lot of pain. The cage was stretching his neck, forcing him to stand on tiptoe to hold himself high enough to go on breathing.

'Can he talk? He seems . . .'

'He can tell us "yes" and "no". If we need anything more detailed than that, we can raise him.'

'I don't understand what the cage is for.'

Chang Zhangyi reached out a stubby-fingered hand and took one of the bars.

'It's an old punishment,' he said. 'The name for it is *kapas*. Our old masters had great ingenuity. To cut a man's head off takes no more than seconds. Even to flog him to death is a matter of hours at the most. But this cage is exquisite, don't you see? It will take about eight days to kill a man. Sometimes longer if the victim is strong. The neck is stretched, but as long as he can keep himself upright, he will not completely choke. Each day one of these thin boards is removed, and he is forced to stretch a little more. He can never sleep, he can never move. All his energy must go into standing and breathing.'

He shook the cage gently, and the man inside moaned.

'It's a form of execution, really,' said Huang Zhengmei, 'but we've found it useful as a means of extracting information. A few days in the cage does wonders for someone's vocal powers. Dull pheasants become songbirds almost overnight. They understand what is happening, and they know that, if they talk, they can stop it. They will either be sent back to their cells, or given a swift end. The penalty for not talking is an eternity in the cage.'

'And this one has not talked?' Karim tried to look into the man's eyes, but they were glazed over with pain. He wondered if the man knew they were there. He wished he could do something to put him out of his misery. Get him to talk, at least.

'He's told us nothing of any value.'

'Then why do you think he'll talk to me?'

'He probably won't. But you know better than I what questions to ask.' Chang Zhangyi tried to inflect his voice with flattery, but it came out more like a threat: Ask the right questions, or else.

'I'll do what I can. What are you most concerned about?'

'The M80 and M90 stages of the project. I don't understand it, but I'm told that information about these aspects might make it possible for the British or the Americans to develop counter-measures. Is that so?'

Karim nodded. There were elements in both those stages, and in a few others, that would suggest useful neutralization techniques to a scientist of the proper calibre. He turned to the man.

'Can you hear me?'

'Don't worry,' said Huang Zhengmei, 'he can hear you. Just ask your questions.'

'Did you know that the M80 experimental stage of the weapons project had five protocols?'

No answer.

'Did you know that only three of those were followed?'

No answer.

'Did you know that M80 was a multiple-level stage within a much larger experiment called Hsiao Ch'u, within a project known as Hong Cha?'

No answer. He turned to Huang Zhengmei.

'He's not responding,' he said. 'I think he's too far gone to answer, maybe even to understand.'

'Tell him that, if he answers, we will let him out of the cage. Tell him death will be very slow and very painful if he refuses to reply to your questions. He can be given drugs to keep him alert for as long as it takes to die. But if he answers, I will see to it that he suffers no longer. Tell him that.'

Karim felt the bile rise in his throat, and grew afraid he would throw up in front of them. This was unfair.

He'd been brought here as a scientist, not an interrogator. He succeeded in fighting the acid back, and told the prisoner everything Huang Zhengmei had said. He would have risked telling the prisoner just to nod, whatever the question; but he wasn't sure how much Uighur Chang Zhangyi understood. Or the woman.

'Please, try to answer this as well as you can. It will help us both. Hsiao Ch'u refers to sub-atomic particles. I think you must know that. But do you know what sort of particles were involved in the experiment?'

No answer.

Huang Zhengmei pushed him aside. She snapped at the prisoner in Chinese, but there was no response. Again she shouted at him, still there was no response. The man was breathing stertorously, and when Karim looked into his eyes he saw more than a flicker of recognition. He looked at the woman's face and saw it changed. He'd been wrong to think that nothing terrible could happen in her presence. Very wrong indeed.

'Send him out of here!' she snapped at Chang Zhangyi, indicating the guard, who stood a few yards away, watching impassively. Chang Zhangyi grunted, and the guard walked back down the room and through the door.

'You,' she said, looking at Karim. 'I want you to stay here. But I want you to understand that this is not for your pleasure.' To Karim's surprise and confusion, she started to unbutton her jacket. Carefully and methodically, she undid the buttons from top to bottom, then unfastened the sleeves and removed the jacket, handing it to Chang Zhangyi. Next came her boots, then her trousers. Underneath, she wore an army-issue bra and pants, but not even the tired green underwear of the People's Liberation Army could conceal the perfection of her body. Karim did not know which way to look. He wanted to close his eyes, but try as he might, he could not tear them from Huang Zhengmei. As though stripping in the shower-room among a hundred other women, she removed her bra and pants and passed them to Chang Zhangyi.

'He can see me,' she said. 'Somewhere in his mind, he finds me attractive. He can't help that. Beneath all the filth he's still a man. Watch.'

She took a step forward and put her hand inside the cage. Softly, she began to stroke the prisoner's thigh, then his genitals. It was the most grotesque thing Karim had ever witnessed. He looked at her face, the pretty face he had so much admired when he first caught sight of her, and found it ugly. To his horror, the man's penis began to stiffen.

'He may be nearly dead,' she said, 'but his nerve-endings still have life in them. Instinct takes over. He becomes excited, in spite of everything. The heart begins to beat faster. The lungs pull in more air. It gets harder to keep still, harder to conserve energy. Watch.'

And her fingers moved cunningly back and forth, bringing the man's organ slowly and painfully to new life. Karim could hear the laboured breathing grow harder and tighter. There was a moan, and as he looked the man struggled to keep what little control he had. Huang Zhengmei stroked and feathered and tickled his swelling penis, like a cheap prostitute hurrying her john to climax.

'Ask him again,' she said. 'From the beginning. If he gives straight answers, I'll stop. If not, I'll make him come.'

She remained intent on what she was doing. Karim looked at her, at her small breasts and perfectly rounded backside, at her thin arms and well-toned legs. He should have felt desire, he should have felt his own genitals urging him; but all he could feel was revulsion.

'The M80 stage of the weapons project had five protocols. Did you know that?'

The prisoner turned his eyes full on Karim. And for a moment Karim was sure he smiled at him. Then, with an effort of will that later seemed to Karim past belief, he pushed himself back and his feet forward, knocking the top board out of position. All his weight was taken suddenly by his neck.

Chang Zhangyi shouted and tried to get the cage open in order to stop his victim slipping out of his clutches. But by the time he had him upright again, it was too late. Swearing, Chang Zhangyi released the bolt that held the upper part of the cage in place, and the body swung forward, collapsing on the floor.

Huang Zhengmei had already started to dress again. She saw Karim eyeing her.

'You will not talk about this to anyone,' she said. 'Do you understand?'

He nodded.

'Of course,' he said. 'I'm not a fool.'

'Some of the biggest fools here are the scientists. Try not to be like them. You are not at home. You are not in a safe place.'

He nodded and turned to Chang Zhangyi.

'Did he have a name?' he asked. It seemed important to him to know.

'Why do you want to know?'

'I watched him die. I would like to know what he called himself.'

Huang Zhengmei's voice broke in.

'Hyde,' she said. 'His name was Matthew Hyde. He was a British agent. Now do you understand why it was so important to find out what he knew?'

RADIANT BLACK SKY

CHAPTER NINE

Elizabeth Laing took a long sip from her gin and tonic, and made a face only she could see, reflected back from the long mirror facing her. She felt friendless and at odds with the world. Sex always made her feel disrupted. Her drink tasted foul. She'd stepped up the gin recently, and was finding excuses to imbibe at the most inappropriate times. 'Maybe I'm developing an alcohol problem,' she thought, and as usual scolded herself for being a baby. Her need for booze was nothing more than a reaction to having broken free from her husband of twenty-six years.

She still didn't know why she'd stayed with David so long. After all, she told herself, nobody could describe her as clinging, and she wasn't exactly the loyal type. Anthony wasn't her first affair, and wouldn't be her last. She looked herself up and down in the cheval glass and almost smirked.

Not bad for forty-six, she thought. A bit of cellulite on the bum, a spot of sagging in the chest, but nothing to worry about yet. Maybe the menopause would change everything, but she was convinced she had quite a few years yet before it came. And when it did, she had her programme worked out: daily doses of HRT, silicone in bucketfuls, plastic surgery as and when, yoga with Vimla and Jerry at the Harbour, and five years' supply of the funny little yellow pills Dr Ramesh had given Sarah. And she'd stay off the booze. No problem. She took another sip.

'Admiring yourself again?'

Anthony's lazy voice pulled her back to the room and the afternoon. A scarf of sunlight had worked its way through the blinds and across her breasts. She didn't move. If he wanted her again, he could bloody well get off the bed and come over. The curtains lent the sunlight their weave. The scarf lay on her like real silk, so warm she could believe she felt it lie against her skin. She would not move, not even an inch.

'That's the third drink you've had since lunch,' he murmured. Not interfering, not even concerned. Just stating a bald fact.

She took another sip and rotated the glass so that the ice chinked gently inside.

'I feel like it. Sex and gin go very well together.'

'Do they?'

'Sex gets me worked up, gin calms me down. Don't know where I'd be without it.'

He said nothing, knowing that any remark, however carefully put, would lead to a massive over-reaction. She was defensive about her drinking. And what did he care anyway? He hadn't started his affair with her for love, after all. He looked round the vast hotel room. It was soulless and dreary, just a tired room that held too many secrets. They'd been coming here for years, furtively at first, and openly since she left David. There wasn't much need for it any more, but it was convenient when he wanted sex in the afternoon. The hotel was just a ten-minute walk from the office. Outside the window, a heavy boat made its way doggedly up the Thames. She still kept her back to him.

'Your ex-husband's been trying to get me all afternoon,' he said.

'Don't call him my ex-husband. That won't be official for absolutely ages, if it ever is.'

'You aren't thinking of going back to him, are you?'

'Oh, for heaven's sake, Anthony. Don't be so bloody bourgeois.'

He looked at her naked back, at the sunlight inching over it like silk, and felt the beginnings of another erection. It had been the same with Penelope at first. They'd been married for almost twenty years, had two lovely daughters, pursued separate careers, but sex had never been the problem for them it became for most people.

He wondered why on earth it was that thoughts of his beloved Penelope always seemed to come at the most inappropriate moments, as though he harboured guilty thoughts. And yet, he mused, guilty thoughts of what, exactly? He'd loved Penelope, more than it's given to most people to love someone. He hadn't had so much as a whiff of an affair while they lived together. And even afterwards, well, there'd been a long gap before he'd started his relationship with Elizabeth.

Was it easier if you split up first? he wondered. With Penelope there hadn't been the slightest lessening of affection. It had made it seem all the more unfair at the time.

They'd owned a place in France, and flew out there several times a year. There was enough money to mean they didn't have to rent it, which meant in turn that any of them could go over at a moment's notice for a weekend or a week or longer.

One weekend in spring, when the girls had a little time before school restarted, Penelope had made a last-minute reservation with a small airline operating out of Gatwick.

They'd taken off in high winds – 'well within the limits of operating safety', according to the subsequent inquiry – and flown up into a storm much too violent for such a tiny plane. The pilot had done his best to get back down again, but he'd lost control at two thousand feet, and the craft, a Shorts 360, had gone into a long nose-dive that ended in the face of a cliff. No one on board had survived. The girls had been called Emma and Suzie. They'd been sixteen and fourteen.

He'd never recovered, never expected to. In some ways, never needed to. All feelings of tenderness and joy had been swallowed up in him by darker emotions, sometimes visible, mostly well concealed. Out of private tragedy, he'd made himself what he now was. It wasn't Penelope's death that disfigured him; he'd never had a chance to grow out of love with her, to experience the disenchantment that allowed hope of something different. He was that rare thing, a man who kept his mistress in the public eye without caring about scandal or notoriety, yet who maintained his wife as a well-hidden secret, a phantom in the truest sense.

With her long back and sloping buttocks and God knows what other spurs to desire, Elizabeth seemed to think men owed her a living. She was keen on sex, but controlled herself, and knew how to turn it to her advantage.

Which suited him down to the ground, since he had his own reasons for making her his mistress, which he was sure never to reveal to her or anyone else.

'He's going to be a very busy man soon.'

'Really?' Her voice had a bored edge to it. He felt himself go limp again. Bored was dangerous. Bored was tantrums and tears and spending sprees and drinking till well after midnight. She was a child, he thought, an expensive, lustful, angry child. But she could use him as cunningly as he used her, for her own ends, in her own ways.

'Elizabeth, turn round. I can't talk to the back of your head.'

She spun to face him, and for a moment he thought he'd angered her, but instead she smiled, a huge, disarming smile that put her beyond any criticism. It was a tactic, of course, he knew that even as he felt relief not to have to cope with another outburst; but it was at least a familiar tactic.

'What I'm saying . . .' He paused, asking himself exactly what it was he *was* saying. He couldn't tell her everything, but he wanted to protect her. Not because he loved her, but because she was of more use to him now than ever. 'I'm saying that you should keep away from him at the moment. He may be tied up. I just don't think you should be around him, that's all.'

'I'd no intention to. Why would you think I had?'

'I didn't mean that. Just that it's . . . not entirely safe.'

'It was never safe, Anthony. You know that as well as I do. Nothing's changed.'

'Then why did you leave him? If nothing's changed.'

'He was too nice, Tony dear. A poppet. A sweetie-pie. He doted on me, did you know that? He'd have done anything for me. Or Maddie.'

'How is Maddie?'

'I'm not entirely sure, to tell you the truth. There was a bit of a scene after I told her I was leaving her precious father. Bit of an upset. You know how bloody unstable she is.'

'She is your daughter.'

'You don't have to remind me.'

'I see nothing particularly wrong with her. A bit woolly-headed, bit lefty in her politics.'

'She never got over that awful Chinese boy. But for that she'd be all right.'

'But for that . . . Indeed. That's what undoes us all, isn't it?'

He looked frankly at her body. She was right to admire herself, he thought. He'd seen twenty-year-olds who would have envied her firm breasts and flat stomach.

'I've got to get back to the office,' he said. 'Things are brewing.'

'So I see,' she said. She stood up gracefully, and poised herself like a cat, and moved towards the bed.

The phone rang angrily. Farrar swore. The only person who had his number here was his secretary. He rolled over, reached for the phone, and dragged it off the hook.

'Farrar.'

'Sir Anthony, it's Linda. I'm sorry to disturb you, but it's somewhat urgent. I have Mrs Laing's daughter on the other line. She wants to speak with her mother.'

'Oh, for God's sake, can't you ask her to wait?'

Elizabeth was kneeling on the bed now, smiling at him invitingly.

'Not really, sir, no. She's a little distraught. Apparently, she's been trying to get hold of her mother for some time. That's why she rang me. She says it's an emergency.'

'Where is she?'

'At a clinic in Esher. I can get the number, if you like.'

He put his hand over the mouthpiece.

'It's Maddie,' he said. 'She's in some sort of clinic. She wants you to ring back. Shall I get the number?'

Her face seemed to crumple. Behind her, against the open window, the curtain flapped and flapped like a trapped bird's wing. She shook her head.

'No,' she said in her quietest voice. 'That's all right. I know it by heart.'

He murmured a quick explanation and put the phone down. When he looked at her again, her face had gone rigid, and her arms were folded, tight as a baby's swaddling, across her unprotected breasts.

CHAPTER TEN

There was a tailback six miles long and three lanes broad on the other carriageway. The late afternoon sun beat down mercilessly on the roofs of the slowly crawling cars. Hot, frustrated drivers, eager to be home, fumed and fretted in their narrow metal cages. An air-conditioning salesman could have spent the rest of his life on a sun-licked beach had there been world enough and time to pitch his wares to each and every one of those sweat-tormented souls. For once, David felt he was headed in the right direction.

'Your people use Arwel's place a lot, do they?' he asked.

Chris Donaldson popped a mint in his mouth and sucked hard. He offered one to David, who shook his head and started sneezing.

When the sneezing petered out, he glanced briefly at his companion. Donaldson was in his mid-thirties, suntanned, fit, probably very attractive to women. His clothes fitted him as they might have done a model on a catwalk. David wondered where they'd found him. Maybe he was the first of a new breed, designed to be impervious to the lure of tainted women deployed by foreign agencies.

'Section Six, you mean? We go down there all the time. It's a wonder our paths haven't crossed before. I've had them all down at one time or another: dissidents, Kurds, Shi'ites, defectors, would-be defectors. Sometimes I think we've had half the population of Mesopotamia down there enjoying Welsh cooking and English scenery.'

'There's no such thing as Welsh cooking. Watch out!' Chris overtook a white Mercedes.

'All they're fit for is rugby and bloody awful choirs singing "*Ar Hyd y Nôs*".'

'That's a bit hard. There's Joe's ice-cream.'

'Italian.'

Donaldson smiled and glanced to the right. The tailback had stopped moving now. What if one of the drivers had a heart attack? he wondered. Or a woman could go into labour.

'There used to be Jews,' he said. 'Lots of Jews. In Baghdad. Did you know that?'

'Yes, I knew that.'

'All gone now. All driven out.'

'What's going on there? You didn't hitch a lift just to chat about the disillusioned hordes of Iraq pouring their mangled hearts out to you over the ice-cream.'

Donaldson heaved a sigh and slipped another mint into his mouth.

'What do you know about a man called Umar al-Hani?'

'Never heard of him.'

'Hardan Wandawi? Muhammad Slaibi?'

David shook his head.

'Look,' he said. 'I'm feeling out of my depth already. Don't you think we should have a joint meeting?'

'I really wouldn't know. That's for our bosses to decide. To be perfectly honest, the fewer involved in this, the better I'll like it.'

David knew what Donaldson meant. At joint meetings, everybody kept his own counsel, and nobody gave away any information that might actually be of benefit.

'Go ahead,' he said. As he spoke, he glanced in the vanity mirror. The Mercedes had pulled out from behind a red Sierra and was keeping pace. Chris stepped down hard and pulled ahead, then slipped in ahead of a Jaguar cruising at ninety.

'Uncle Saddam is getting itchy fingers again. Seriously itchy. After the almighty cock-up that was made of intelligence before the Gulf War, we've all been on our best behaviour.'

David nodded. He had not been directly involved, but, like everyone in the service, he knew only too well that Western intelligence agencies had messed up badly back in 1990. They'd got just about everything wrong they could have done. A few days before Iraqi troops crossed the border into Kuwait, MI6 stated magisterially that the possibility of an invasion was 'very remote'. A few heads had rolled, others had eaten copious quantities of humble pie, and the machinery had gone on much as before.

'This time I think we've got it right. We've got some people on the ground, good people. There's regular feedback – I won't say how, you don't need to know. Three weeks ago, Zircon came in with radio signals between Baghdad High Command and five divisional commanders stationed between Najaf and Basra. They all received orders to move troops south to an area round the naval base at Umm Qasr, right on the Kuwaiti border.

'Since then, we've been receiving daily satellite photographs. Kennan, Crystal and Lacrosse have all been programmed to home in on southern Iraq, and the Keyhole satellites are doing broader sweeps. There's a lot of move-ment, in all directions. We think he's doing what he can to confuse us.'

'Do the Kuwaitis know?' David glanced in his mirror to see the Jaguar swing out and flex his muscles as he heaped on more speed and cut away in the outside lane. He could almost imagine the driver's nostrils flaring as he moved past. The Mercedes was right behind again.

'Tail?' asked Donaldson.

'Could be.'

'One of yours or one of mine?' Chris asked.

David shrugged.

'Ring Central for me, will you?' asked Chris. 'I'm going to pull off at these services. Any minute now.'

David lifted the car's telephone and keyed in a five-digit number. He could feel another sneeze starting.

'Monitor, please.'

He was patched through immediately to MI6's Agent Monitoring Unit.

'The number's K775 KYD,' said David. If they slowed, the other car fell back, if they picked up speed, it did too. A blue van pulled in between them.

David repeated the number. He could hear a keyboard being tapped at the other end. Ten seconds later he had his answer.

'It's legitimate. Belongs to a man called Scudamore. He owns an antique shop in Bristol. He's quite clean.'

David shrugged and keyed off. He passed on the infor-mation.

'He's a tail,' insisted Chris. 'Not a very good one, but a tail.'

The slip road appeared on their left, and Chris swung gently in. He headed down to the cars-only park and found a space. Moments later, he saw the Mercedes pull in behind them. There were few spaces, and the driver had to cross through to the next set of bays before finding room. They waited. No one got out.

'Let's have a word with Mr Scudamore,' David said, opening his door. Donaldson got out with him, and they walked directly towards the Mercedes. A middle-aged man dressed in a white linen suit, blue shirt, and vibrant bow tie sat behind the wheel. He saw them coming, switched on his engine again, and pulled out quickly, driving off towards the exit.

They watched him go, amused at the silliness of it. David resolved to find out more about Mr Scudamore when he had the chance.

'Since we're here, let's at least get some coffee,' said Donaldson.

'Any idea where we can get that at a motorway cafeteria?'

'Don't be so cynical. Some of the best coffee in the world is brewed in places like this.' Donaldson grabbed his arm and steered him towards the entrance.

They found a table in a corner away from the main eating area, next to a loud fruit machine that seemed quite happy to play itself over and over while waiting for customers who never showed up.

Donaldson cradled a cup of espresso.

'Real china,' he said. 'Real coffee. Britain is growing up.'

David pulled out his handkerchief just in time to block the enormous sneeze that had been brewing for several minutes.

'Britain is buggered. What's going on in Iraq?'

Donaldson smiled.

'Hay fever?'

David nodded.

'What do you take? Antihistamines?'

'Yes. But I'd rather not. Nasty side-effects.'

'You should see a homoeopath.'

David nodded politely, but he hadn't the least intention of seeing one. People had been recommending all sorts of weird and wonderful cures to him for years, but he'd bothered with none of them. Better the devil you know . . . He sneezed again and blew his nose.

'In answer to your question,' said Donaldson, 'a week ago, all communications between Baghdad High Command and field units ceased. We assume that they're now talking through the hard-wired fibre optics system they laid down before the Gulf War. We can't intercept anything they decide to put through that.'

'Why make the shift? Why alert us in the first place?'

'We think he's playing games. It wouldn't be the first time. Current reading of the situation says Kuwait is a bluff. The trouble is, there's no sure way of knowing what else he might try.'

'Surely he's had his fingers burnt too many times?'

Donaldson shook his head.

'Not really. He thinks he's invincible, because he always gets away with things. He came out of the Gulf War with almost everything intact. We let him stick it into the Shi'ites, we let him do almost anything he wanted with the Kurds . . . He goes quiet for a while, then . . .'

He sipped his coffee. It had been stewed senseless.

'Look, keep this to yourself, David. It's supposed to be seriously hush-hush. So far, the only person outside our section who knows is your desk head, Farrar. If he decides to brief you, just look suitably surprised.'

'Does he know you were there today?'

Donaldson set his coffee down, barely touched.

'Not drinking yours?'

'I asked if Farrar knew you were there today.'

'I really can't say. Let's say that, had he turned up, I'd have made a sharp exit. He'll hear eventually.'

'He's not a man to cross.'

'I'm aware of that.' Donaldson paused and took a cigarette from a pack in his shirt pocket. He offered one to David.

'No thanks. If I smoke, I prefer . . .'

'Don't we all?' Donaldson lit his cigarette. He sucked on it thoughtfully, and exhaled a slow cloud of pale blue smoke.

'Speaking of Farrar,' he said, 'I hear you and he aren't on speaking terms.'

'No, we speak. It's just . . .'

'A little bother with your wife.'

'Not a little bother, no. She's been having an affair with him for three years. I found out a few weeks ago when she left me and moved in with him. I'd rather not talk about this, if you don't mind.'

'Actually, I do mind. We're talking about national security. If you and Farrar aren't able to communicate . . .'

'Don't worry. It's all intensely civilized. I'd like to strangle him, and no doubt he finds me a bit of an embarrassment. But if anything happens, it'll be in the waste ground behind my local, not in the office.'

'I can depend on that?'

David hesitated. Donaldson was a total stranger.

'Shall I tell you the truth?' he asked. 'I'm not sorry she's gone. She was an unkind woman, self-centred and vain, and she made life miserable for all of us. If Farrar wants her, he's welcome to her. They suit one another. Now, you were about to tell me something hush-hush.'

Beside them, the fruit machine galloped through a new routine, beeping and whirring its little heart out. But nobody came to play it.

Donaldson laid down his cigarette and cleared his throat.

'Diogenes scored a hit last week. Five past four on Thursday afternoon.'

Though David never had recourse to its intercepts, he was familiar with Diogenes, a listening post based at Sinop in Turkey, run by Americans, and manned by British technicians from GCHQ.

'Somebody in Baghdad was careless. One of the men I mentioned earlier, Muhammad Slaibi. He's a civilian with the military rank of colonel. A Baath Party bigwig with responsibility for foreign exchange. He was using a car-phone without a scrambler, and he and the other party were speaking in English. The other man was the Chinese ambassador. Li Shuo. Is that right?'

'Yes. He was very close to Deng. Some people think the ambassadorship was a means of putting him out to grass.'

'I don't think so. It wasn't a long conversation, but it told us a lot more than either man would like us to know. A meeting is being set up for next week. Do you know someone called – I can't pronounce this properly – Chen Tiaoyuan?'

'Not personally. He's the Chinese Minister for Minerals and Petroleum. A tough customer. One of the most powerful men in the Chinese politburo. He's a chain smoker who practises *chi gong* regularly. They say he's inordinately fond of the Peking Opera: he attends every performance of *The Dream of the Red Chamber*. They even come to his house and put on special performances for him and his family. He's probably got more *guanshi* than the rest of the politburo put together.'

'*Guanshi?*'

'Pull. Contacts. Knowing people in the right places. I'm

sure you've got plenty of Arabic words for it. Chen's been to Baghdad a few times, hasn't he?'

'Mainly for conferences. But this isn't a conference. He's going to be the guest of honour, but attendance will be strictly limited. Saddam, the Iraqi Petroleum Minister, Li Shuo, Slaibi, and a handful of very private secretaries from both sides.'

'I don't see . . .'

'It was a long conversation. Slaibi's a talkative man. They argued a little.'

'About what?'

'About whether Iraq could supply China with four hundred million barrels of oil over the next ten years.'

'Four hundred? That's . . .'

'It's about half Iraq's annual production.'

'Is it? I was going to say it's a bit under half of what China produces. What's going on? The Chinese don't need to import anything like that much.'

'But they do need to import?'

'Increasingly, yes. All the same, they have enormous reserves. They just need to up production.'

David had ordered an Earl Grey tea with a sticky bun. He poured the tea into his cup and added a slice of lemon. Once upon a time, they'd called places like this transport cafés. Now they'd grown posh, all bright plastic and stainless steel. He sipped the tea. Nothing had changed.

'I'm having difficulty tying all this together,' he said. 'In the car, you told me about troop movements. Now it's a meeting to discuss oil exports.'

'Our analysts think they're connected. I mentioned two other names. One was Umar al-Hani. His name came up. Your man Chen wants to meet him while he's in Baghdad. Al-Hani's a general. To be precise, he's the general in overall charge of weapons development within the Iraqi

republic. The ambassador made a curious remark. He said "It's only a matter of weeks now. Put everything in place. There'll be no time to lose once the test is completed."

'We think they're ready to supply a weapon to Saddam. Not just parts. A complete weapon. We think that's what the troop movements are all about. He's going to start another war. And this time he plans to win.'

CHAPTER ELEVEN

'You might have waited for me.'

Sam nodded and continued eating. He'd heated up some sort of pie and chips in the microwave. Ever since his mother's departure, the boy had grown ferociously independent. It worried David a little: if he was cooking his own meals now, what else might he demand to do in a year's time?

'I suppose there's more food in the fridge?'

Another nod, another mouthful of chips.

David went to the fridge and pulled out a Marks and Spencer's Chinese platter.

'You want to share some of this?' He waved the box at Sam. Another nod, a forkful of pie.

'You realize you haven't said a word to me since I got in. Not even "I had a good day."'

'You didn't ask. You only complained about me starting before you.'

'Very well: did you have a good day?'

Sam shrugged.

'So-so.'

'So-so?'

'Billy fell in the lake. We had to fish him out. His mum was mad.'

'I should think so. Is he all right?'

'He spewed up some weeds and stuff, but he's fine. How about your friend, is he alive?'

David started unpacking the individual items and putting them in the oven.

'I don't know. It's a bit complicated. I may know more tomorrow.'

'You're going down again?'

'Afraid so. There's a boy there. He looks about your age, but he's twelve. Or so he says. Maybe, after this is all over, you can meet him.'

'I don't know. I've got plenty of friends.'

'Believe me, you can always do with more. He speaks Uighur.'

Sam snorted. 'Oh, that!' His father's repeated efforts to give him Uighur as his second language, just as his own mother had passed it to him, had been dismal failures.

Just as David slipped the last packet into the oven, the phone rang.

'Bugger.'

He turned the oven on and headed for the phone.

'Laing.'

'David, this is Elizabeth. Remember? Your ex-wife. Where the hell have you been?'

'Good evening, Elizabeth. It's always charming to hear your cheerful voice.'

'Don't be so bloody banal. I've been trying to get you all day.'

'I've been at work. Remember that? It's what some of us do for a living.'

'For God's sake, stop bickering. This is urgent. I had a phone call this afternoon from Maddie. Well, not actually from Maddie. She asked me to ring her back, so I did. I don't suppose you've spoken to her in weeks.'

'As a matter of fact, I spoke to her this morning.'

'What? She didn't tell me. And, for that matter, why didn't you tell me?'

'I did. I left a message on the great man's answering machine. I presume you haven't been home all day.'

'Not yet, no.'

'Where are you?'

The brief silence before she answered told him everything.

'I'm . . . not quite sure. Well, it's a hotel, actually.'

'And you're in the bar.'

'Lounge, actually. Quite a nice lounge, as a matter of fact.'

'Elizabeth, what did Maddie say?'

'Oh, you know it all already. You always know things before anybody else does. Regular little secret agent, aren't we?'

'Elizabeth, I asked you what your daughter said.'

'Did she tell you she's at that man Rose's clinic again?'

'Yes. I spoke with Rose myself.'

'Well, the cheap little bastard's on the scrounge again. Will I pay for Maddie's treatment? Then there's the room, and the food, and lab tests, and medication, and God knows what. It's a stinking rip-off. He –'

'Elizabeth, stop right there. If you don't pay, I will make such a public stink about you and your boyfriend it'll be all over next week's tabloids. So please wise up. Maddie's in trouble. And, frankly, she's in trouble this time because of you and your dangerous liaison. Now, tell me what she said and what you said to her.'

They talked for another five minutes, but Elizabeth told him nothing he did not know already. When she hung up, he felt as though someone had just wrapped a tight wet rope about his body, constricting him and hampering his breath.

'Was that Mum?'

'Yes.'

'What's all that about Maddie?'

'Maddie's ill again, Sam. She's in a clinic.'

Despite the vast gulf of years between them, Maddie and Sam had formed close bonds. She cared for him as deeply as though he had been her son and not her brother, and he had made of her a surrogate mother, even before Elizabeth's disappearance. He barely remembered her previous illness.

'Can I visit her?'

'Not yet. But probably in a week or two.'

'What's wrong with her?'

'She's just a bit upset about things. Some people find they can't cope when things go wrong in their lives.'

'Has she had a breakdown?'

'Who told you about breakdowns?'

'I don't know. One of the boys at school. I think his dad had one.'

'Well, what Maddie has is something like that. She needs to be looked after properly.'

'Is it because of Mum? What she did?'

'Partly, yes.'

Sam remained silent for a couple of minutes. Then suddenly bellowed 'They're burning!' and dashed to the oven to retrieve the meal.

After dinner, while Sam watched *Emmerdale*, David went upstairs to his computer and dialled in to the server at headquarters. He used Telnet to access Central Records, and in less than a minute had a file on Barry Scudamore, the proprietor of Celadon Antiques, Bristol.

There wasn't much. Mr Scudamore had lived a prosperous but quiet life. He was fifty-four years old, and he'd been in the antiques business for thirty-three of those. His father had started the business, and Barry had kept it on and made it what it now was. He had never married, but had lived for over seventeen years now with a man called Norman Cunliffe, his business partner and, presumably, lover.

None of this was of the remotest interest to David. What did grab his attention was the revelation – almost a footnote – that Celadon Antiques dealt, not in general objects of age and value, but specifically in wares of Chinese origin. Scudamore was the travelling partner: he made two or three business trips to China every year. Peking mostly, but other cities on a rotating basis. Recently, he'd paid a visit to Sinkiang, and then gone on to Lhasa, where he'd paid high prices for a trunkful of sixteenth-century *thangkas*. Taking pre-1795 antiques out of China was strictly illegal. Barry Scudamore must have had *guanshi* – bags of the stuff.

David printed out the file and shut down. As the screen blanked, he decided that it might be worth paying a visit to Mr Scudamore. He looked at his watch. It was too late for tonight. On the other hand, the Cotswolds were well within reach. He was beginning to think that a late-night visit to Matthew Hyde's incarnation would make a lot of sense.

'Sam, I have to go out again. More work.'

'Are you planning to kill someone this time? Is that why it has to be by night?'

'I wish I'd never told you about what I do. No, I'm not going to kill anybody. I just want to talk to someone.'

'The boy?'

'Yes, the boy. I may be back late, so I've asked Nicky if she'll stay with you. Is that OK?'

'I'm all right on my own.'

'You most certainly are not.'

'All right. But only if you promise you'll ask Nicky out on a date.'

'For God's sake, Sam: your mother's only been gone six weeks, and you're trying to match-make.'

'Nicky's pretty, though, isn't she?'

'Yes, very pretty. She's also half my age.'

'It happens.'

'Yes, Granddad. I'm well aware it happens. But how much time would you like to spend with a five-year-old girl?'

There was no answer to that. The doorbell rang, and he let Nicky in. She was looking nicer than ever. He cursed Sam for having even started the thoughts that took hold of him as he watched her shapely figure walk ahead of him towards the kitchen. One thing was certain: Nicky wasn't five years old.

CHAPTER TWELVE

Carstairs was set in darkness, like a ship in a troubled and unlit sea. Thick curtains of yews and poplars shut it away on four sides from the eyes of the curious, and at night lights were never lit in more than two or three windows. It was a house rule strictly adhered to, and there were locks on the shutters in the guest bedrooms to ensure that visitors made no unauthorized attempts to reveal their presence.

David turned off the road – it was more a farm track than anything – that passed the front of the house, and steered into the even narrower path that would take him half a mile between high clipped hedges down to the gate.

To the unpractised eye – a casual tourist turning up in a Range Rover with family and labrador, an experienced walker drawn there by what was marked on his Ordnance Survey map of the region as 'Forest' – the gate would seem no more than a typical farm gate. But any attempt to open it would prove futile. The car driver would quickly execute a three-point turn and head back to whatever vestige of civilization remained out there. The walker, on the other hand, had he chosen to climb over the gate, as walkers are inclined to do, would have been confronted less than half a minute later by a polite but firm man in a tweed cap and Barbour jacket, telling him he was on private property, and asking if he would mind awfully going back over the gate again.

Anyone trying harder to penetrate Carstairs' perimeter fence would have found himself face to face with one of the most impenetrable security systems in England. A network of sensors, light-sensitive Vidicon cameras, geophones, infra-red beams, and some carefully placed Barr & Stroud thermal-imaging units made the house unreachable to anyone without a permit.

David drew up at the gate and switched off his headlights. He hadn't rung ahead, so they wouldn't be expecting him. He wanted it that way. They'd have heard his engine, of course, and he knew he'd have been spotted on half a dozen cameras all the way down the lane. He honked five times. Moments later, he heard the gate open and close again. His own eyes were blinded by the sudden blackness, but he knew the man approaching would be wearing night-vision glasses.

The window was already open. He'd driven the whole way with it down: outside, the night was still warm, unable to shake off the stifling heat of the day.

'Can I do anything for you, sir?'

'You can let me in, if it's no trouble.'

'Yes, sir. May I see your permit, sir?'

David held out a credit-card-sized slip, which the man ran through a hand-held scanner.

'Thank you, Mr Laing. Shall I phone through for you?'

'I think you'd better, otherwise one of your boys may try to turn me into an Eccles cake.'

'Now, that would be a gross waste of Ministry of Defence raisins, sir. Would you like me to tell Mr Hughes you're here?'

'Yes, and tell Mrs Hughes I'd like a cup of tea and some of the cake she baked earlier, if there's any left.'

'Right-ho, sir. You'd better leave the motor in the yellow car-park. That's the one . . .'

'I know where it is. See you on the way out.'

Glynis was waiting for him at the front door, dressed in a heavy red woollen dressing-gown. David had seen her wear it in all seasons. She called it her pillar-box and claimed that a Soviet dissident had once tried to post letters in her mouth.

'Cake, please, Mrs Hughes, and a large pot of very hot tea.'

'Yes, sir. May I ask what brings you down here again at this time of night?'

'I want to speak to Tursun. I take it he's still up?'

'He's in the games room watching television. Arwel was teaching him to play snooker earlier on.'

'Could you tell him I'm here and that I'll see him in the library. Bring the tea there, if you don't mind.'

'Is something up, sir?'

'You know better than to ask, Glynis.'

'He's a lovely boy,' she said, ignoring him. 'So well-mannered, and considerate about his parents.'

'A paragon.'

'Well, I wouldn't know, sir. I'm not sure the boy's nationality comes into it. Though, mind you, Arwel says the Welsh . . .'

'Hot tea, Glynis. And two large slices of cake.'

Tursun came in with a huge smile on his face. David had to admit that it was hard not to like the lad. He'd obviously won Glynis Hughes over, and, in spite of appearances, she wasn't easily wooed.

'Come in, Tursun. Been watching telly?'

'Yes. *The Simpsons*. It's extremely funny.'

'My son likes it.'

'Do you have a son?'

'Yes, his name's Sam. He's nearly ten. About your height. He looks a bit like you. His grandmother was Uighur. My mother.'

'Yes, I remember your telling me.'

'I'm sure I did. Now, why don't you sit down? Over there. Mrs Hughes will be bringing tea in a moment. Or perhaps you'd prefer something different? Cocoa, or Horlicks.'

'A Horlicks, please.'

'Hot or cold?'

For a moment he saw the confusion on the boy's face. It was one thing to know a name like Horlicks, even to know it was a drink. But if you'd never drunk it . . .

'Have it hot. I hear Arwel Hughes has been teaching you snooker.'

'Yes, we had a terrific game. He showed me how to play a good safety shot. More important than potting, he says.'

There was a knock on the door, followed by a vision in red carrying a large tea-tray. David helped her set it on the table.

'Would you mind bringing Tursun a mug of Horlicks, please? Make it a strong one.'

'All milk?'

'Good Lord, yes. It never tastes right with water. Does it, Tursun?'

The boy shook his head. David fancied he was adept at picking up cues.

When Glynis had gone, David poured himself a cup of tea.

'You don't mind me starting before you, do you?'

Tursun shook his head again.

David sipped his tea. Earl Grey: he didn't have to spell it out any longer.

'We used to have some great games of snooker in there, didn't we?'

Tursun looked up at him, sensing danger.

'Yes,' he beamed. 'I always won.'

'Not always. But you were very good. Which makes me wonder why you have to take lessons from Arwel Hughes.'

Tursun's face tightened. David could almost see the cogs turning.

'I'm a lot smaller. And Tursun's body has to relearn everything Matthew knew.'

'Tursun, why don't we stop playing games? I don't know how you're doing this, though I have to say I'm very impressed indeed. But the fact is, I'll catch you out in the end. I have one hundred and one ways, believe me. I could ask you intimate questions about things men and women do together in bed – things Matthew would know, but a boy your age would not. I could pretend that Matthew and I did this, that or the other, and in the end you'd give the wrong answer. Shall I go on?'

The door opened again. The pillar-box appeared, delivered a mug into Tursun's hands, and vanished again without a word.

Tursun shook his head. He clutched the mug in both hands, suddenly a small boy out of his depth in an adult world. As David looked at him, he thought he saw all the affectation of adulthood simply fall away. In a matter of seconds, Tursun became a child again, and the look on his face was one of pure relief.

'I would have told you,' he whispered. 'But I had to keep up the story as long as possible. He told me to.'

'He?'

'Matthew. Mr Hyde.'

'Yes, I thought as much. Where did you meet him?'

'In Sinkiang Province Number Five Labour Reform Camp.'

'Near Khotan?'

'Yes. Do you know it?'

David shivered.

'By reputation. What were you doing there?'

'My father was arrested, and they made me go with him. My mother too. Our family are Muslims. To the Chinese, that means we're rebels. As far as they're concerned, the entire population of Sinkiang is made up of counter-revolutionaries.'

'They may not be entirely wrong. What did your father do to be put in the camp?'

Tursun looked down glumly at his mug of Horlicks. He had recovered the small boy who'd been hiding behind Hyde's facade all these months, and with him all the buried emotions of a child.

'Drink it,' said David. 'Don't worry, it's just a kind of malted milk. Try it and see.'

The boy sipped tentatively at the liquid, frowned in puzzlement, then took another, longer sip. Satisfied, he looked up at David.

'He had a workmate who was the leader of a Muslim faction. They had jobs in the same brigade at the Silk and Mulberry Research Centre. My father used to supervise the mulberry trees. He knew everything there was to know about the trees: which ones grew best in shade, which ones needed regular pruning. He once showed me how trees with dark leaves were best if you wanted silk for dyeing. His father taught him all those things. Grandfather died when I was three. My father worked very hard, and he kept himself out of trouble. Politics meant nothing to him.'

Tursun paused. Something was troubling him.

'Mr Laing, my parents know nothing of all this – the deception, my coming here. Matthew Hyde told my father that he should follow my directions, that they would be given a house in England, and work. You must promise me that. They went through terrible things in the camp, and afterwards, in order to get me to India.'

David had already worked out that the last thing anybody wanted was to send the family back to China. The boy, in particular, whatever his real story, knew far too much ever to be allowed within a mile of anyone with so much as a drop of Chinese blood in their veins. No sooner had the thought formed than it was followed by another: who had asked Barry Scudamore to tail him that afternoon? Had David himself been the antique dealer's target, or the twelve-year-old boy drinking Horlicks in front of him?

'I need to speak to some important people, Tursun. It won't be my decision. But you can rest assured that you won't be sent back to China. I'm certain of that. Now, tell me how your father came to be arrested.'

Tursun took another mouthful of his drink. It was so cosy, David thought, as all these meetings were. He'd sat in this library with a succession of men and women, and sipped tea or coffee, and talked about the weather for a while. And from the weather they'd pass on to horrors beyond belief. He wondered if Glynis Hughes had the slightest idea of the things that were said in these rooms. Torture, rape, sexual infidelity, betrayal, murder, suicide, darkness of any and every kind. This boy sipping Horlicks for the first time knew secrets that could affect the lives of millions.

'One day, the police raided the house belonging to my father's workmate. His name was Abdul Wahhab. There were weapons in a pit under the floor. They arrested everyone connected to him. My father had a Koran in our house. He never read it – he can't read. But the police said it was a sign of subversion. The court sentenced him to fourteen years in a labour camp. They sent my mother as well. I wasn't at home then, but I was sent to the camp a month later.'

David stopped him.

'Before you go on, Tursun, I'd like to know one thing: how do you come to speak such good English? You're not going to tell me Matthew Hyde taught you.'

'Is my English good?'

'You know perfectly well it is. Even if you've never tasted Horlicks in your young life, you could pass as an English child.'

'That was the idea.'

'Whose idea? Matthew's idea?'

The boy shook his head slowly. He finished the drink and put the mug on the table between them.

'No,' he said, 'that came later. There is a school, a very special school in the east, near Shanghai. There's a lake called Tai Hu.'

'Yes, I know of it.'

'It has almost fifty islands. One of them is called Chinghua Dao, Jade Island. You will not find it on any map. Chinghua Dao used to house a Buddhist monastery called Lingyin Si. It was shut down shortly after the revolution, and the monks never returned. Fifteen years ago the buildings were converted into a school. Its name is less poetic than the one the Buddhists gave it: Kiangsu Elite School Number Three.'

He paused, smiling as though something about the name or an image it conjured up amused him.

'Have you heard of the elite schools?' he asked.

David shook his head.

'I'm not surprised. They're a very well-guarded secret. Matthew Hyde had never heard of them either. They were established by the Chinese intelligence services in the sixties. The aim of the first school was to produce Chinese men and women who could pass themselves off as fully assimilated second- or third- or even fourth-generation Americans.

'They took boys and girls at the earliest possible age and immersed them in American life and culture. They were brought up like Americans, in every respect. They spoke English every day. Their teachers were Americans who'd been well paid to do the job and keep quiet about it. The children watched American films and read American books and ate American food. Television programmes were recorded on primitive video machines. The latest records from the States or Britain were flown in. By the time they reached their teens, these were Chinese children only in spirit.'

'Tursun, you're not remotely like an American.'

'I'm sorry, I should have explained. That was the first school. I think four American schools were set up in the end. They still exist, but I don't know where they are. When they saw how successful the experiment was, they began to open other schools. There was a school for German, another for French, another for Spanish. That was when they started bringing in children from minority races, like myself. Han Chinese can't pass themselves off as second- or third-generation everywhere.

'I was discovered when I was four years old. Most Uighur children don't try to speak Chinese until they're taught it at school, and even then very few become fluent. By the age of four I'd learned as much Mandarin as a Chinese boy of my age. I had an ability for languages. One of the local cadres heard about me and notified Peking.

One week later, I was on a plane to Shanghai. The school I lived at was designed to train children for a life in Great Britain. Mostly, we were supposed to pass ourselves off as the children or grandchildren of Hong Kong Chinese. I was to pretend to be descended from Turkish Cypriots.'

'You'd have done it perfectly, believe me. I'd like to know more about this later. But now I'd like you to tell me about Matthew Hyde.'

CHAPTER THIRTEEN

The heat had gone from the night. A faint ghost of it remained in corners, among the roots of trees, beneath the eaves of the house, or swathed about clumps of hollyhock and fern. David shivered and stepped to the French window. He looked out into the darkness briefly, then drew the curtains. Suddenly he sneezed, then several times more.

'I'm sorry,' he said, turning to Tursun. 'Hay fever.'

'You should try some Chinese medicine.'

David smiled.

'Are you cold?' he asked.

Tursun shook his head. He had crossed from Sinkiang to Ladakh at the end of winter, he knew what cold was.

David returned to his seat.

'How did you meet Matthew?'

'He was in the camp. I met him about a week after he was brought there. He was arrested by a man called Chang Zhangyi. Chang Zhangyi is . . .'

'I know who he is. Only too well.'

'Your friend was in a queue for food. He muttered something in English when they handed him a plateful of muck, and I went up to him and said there were ways to get hold of better food. We became friends, of course. They treated him very brutally, much worse than the Chinese or the Uighurs. I did what I could to help, but it was very little. He was a good man. I liked him. Even when things were very hard for him, he would cheer me up.'

'He always was a bit of a cheery blighter. There were times I felt like thumping him. How come he ended up in a labour camp?'

'He told me he thought it was a trick to see what he might say if he was caught off guard. The camps are full of informers. It usually involves a deal to take a year or two off someone's sentence. You can never be sure who's genuine, who's working for the party.'

'Matthew would never have fallen for something like that. I'm surprised they even bothered trying.'

'That's what he told me. He and I had long chats during the first week after we met. I told him all about the school. He took a great interest in that. And then, one day he came to me and said he wanted to make a deal. He would tell me a bunch of lies about himself, which I could use to negotiate an early release for my parents and myself. I could have a letter written by him, in which he would request the British authorities to provide my father with a job and a house.'

'Do you have that letter?'

'Of course.'

Tursun slipped his hand inside his shirt and brought it out again with a badly crumpled sheet of Chinese writing paper. He unfolded it carefully and passed it to David. Outside, a nightjar called, its lonely cry echoing briefly among the trees. Tursun looked up, unsettled by the bird's call.

'This is Matthew's handwriting all right,' David said. He glanced through the note. 'And here's a little message for me. "David, you bastard – if you don't set Tursun's mum and dad up properly, I'll come back and haunt you." Doesn't leave me much choice, does he? I'll have to keep this. Do you understand? It's evidence you met Matthew.'

'You will give it to the right people?'

'You can be sure of that. You're a precious asset, Tursun. The state can spare a few thousand to see you're treated properly.'

'He said he wanted to train me to be him. To know everything there was about him. He said I was to claim to be a reincarnation, that it would draw less attention to me once I got to India. We spent weeks going over everything I had to know. Names, dates, places – all the things I've told you. And more there hasn't been time for yet.'

'I don't see how . . .'

'I have a perfect memory. Like a tape recorder. He only had to tell me something once or twice, and I'd have it in my memory for good. Have you got people who can do that?'

'There are people like you, yes. Some of them do amazing feats with numbers.'

'He told me how to pass myself off as him, so I could be sure of getting attention, and then he gave me details of Operation Hong Cha. I wasn't supposed to know what it was all about, just to be able to pass on what he'd found out.'

'Do you know more?'

'Yes. A lot more.'

'We'll start on it again tomorrow, then.'

The nightjar called again, just once. David looked up. He wondered where Matthew was. They'd been good friends. They'd worked together twice in Sinkiang, and Matthew had saved his life once in Lop Nor. Back home, he'd saved Matthew after the break-up of a long-term relationship. They'd been close. And now? Now, the only link between them was a twelve-year-old boy with frightened eyes and the memories of another man.

CHAPTER FOURTEEN

The journey home was swift and lonely. David checked more than once, but he was sure there was no tail. It was an elegiac return, like a lover's homecoming when he has left a much-loved mistress behind. He had lost Matthew Hyde for ever, of that he was now sure. Chang Zhangyi would not have left him in that camp for long. And after that . . . ?

Everything shook as a jet fighter whizzed past overhead. As the crashing faded, he wondered what was going on. Night flights were ordinarily banned. There'd be a flurry of complaints tomorrow. David guessed the plane had flown out of Brize Norton, an air force base that normally plagued the country to the west of Oxford. Either someone had made an almighty mistake that they wouldn't be allowed to forget in a hurry, or orders had come from very high up requesting night-flying practice within British airspace.

He pressed on, exhausted after a long day. It might almost have been better if he'd just stayed on at Carstairs, in order to get an early start with Tursun in the morning. But he had to see that Sam was all right, had to find a way of making up to him about today. And he needed to speak to Dr Rose as soon as possible.

He didn't care much what happened to Elizabeth any longer. Her drinking, her infidelities, her abrasive behaviour were all Anthony Farrar's concern now. Not for the first time, he wondered what Farrar really saw in her, beyond a good figure and a draining enthusiasm for sex. She was rich, of course, with heaps of shares in the family business, Royle International. Did Farrar want to get a foothold there? It seemed a painful way to go about something that might have been more easily accomplished on the old-boy network or the club circuit.

Another jet came thundering out of the empty sky. This one was following the course of the motorway, like a bomber following a river to its target. Surely it was way off the rule book to buzz traffic like that? David thought a discreet phone call might turn up some answers to match the uneasy feeling he was starting to get in the pit of his stomach.

The city appeared slowly, growing about him as though seeded out there in the dark. He remembered the first time his father had taken him abroad, to Central Asia. David had been nine, almost the age Sam was now. They'd gone to attend an academic conference in Samarkand.

Until then, David had never been very far from London. There'd been holidays in Devon or the Lakes, visits to an aunt in Scotland, and a school trip to the Wedgwood Potteries. And now, in a matter of hours, he was transported to a world straight out of the *Thousand and One Nights*.

On the last day, they'd been driven out into the Kizil Kum Desert, a place of fantastic shapes and unnameable colours, as different from London as the moon. What had struck David more than anything had been the silence. That, above all, had changed him. Stopping in the midst of a vast expanse of dark red dunes, their driver had extinguished the engine, and such a silence had flooded the jeep as David, in all his years of noise and traffic fumes, could never have imagined. On his return to London, he'd found the city brash and desperately loud.

Now, nearly forty years on, the city's embrace seemed somehow comforting. Deserts, for all their silence, could conceal horrors no city could ever match.

When he reached the house, the lights were still on upstairs. David muttered under his breath. Even in the holidays, Sam was expected to keep civilized hours. He looked up at the house and thought it had suddenly grown ridiculously big. It was a three-storey Victorian town-house, bought for them by Elizabeth's mother when they married, and now worth massively more than had been paid for it. He'd have a word with Sam, and if the boy was happy with the idea, they could start looking for a smaller place as soon as he'd finished debriefing Tursun. As he climbed out of the car, he thought of Maddie. When she came out of the clinic, wouldn't she need some sense of stability? It could so easily knock her back again to come home and find a 'For Sale' sign in the front garden.

He made to put the key in the front door, but as he did so, the door opened and swung back into the darkened hall. This time he swore aloud. He'd lost count of the number of times he'd had to tell Sam to close the door behind him properly. Surely Nicky hadn't gone already? She'd always stayed with Sam until David or Elizabeth got back. Had she sensed his passing sexual interest in her and decided to clear off before he got home?

He fastened the lock and snibbed it, then put the hall light on. Right in front of him, Sam's slippers lay on the floor. He felt a dull prickle of alarm. For the past year, Sam had been wearing his slippers on the way to bed and leaving them on top of a trunk in his room. He'd wear them in bed if allowed to. Ordinarily, when David came back this late, the television would still be playing in the living room, but tonight there was total silence.

No, he thought, not quite total. A muffled sound was coming from the front room, a sound he didn't like. He hurried to the door, then paused. In the few feet he'd crossed, he had changed from worried father to something none of his friends would have recognized, something he had trained to become in places that did not exist.

He went down to the kitchen and took a knife from the block, a well-made knife with a ten-inch blade. Holding it carefully, he crept back to the living room. He pushed down the handle and gave the door a shove. The room was in darkness, save for the flickering of the television, which showed nothing but a mesh of black and white lines.

He pressed the light switch and blinked as the room came leaping into life. At first, nothing seemed out of place. The furniture was exactly as he'd left it, the paintings on the walls were untouched, the ornaments on the mantelpiece had not been moved.

The smell was the first thing he really noticed. A beautiful smell made up of jasmine, lily, and rose. It filled the room, and he breathed it in deeply, wondering at its delicacy. There was something of the erotic in it. He thought of a bedchamber hung with silk, and a bed strewn with dark red petals. On the mantelpiece, two incense cones smoked silently, sending spirals of blue smoke into the congealing air.

He took a step forward. That was when he caught sight of her, on the sofa. She was naked, and for a horrible moment he thought it was all a clumsy attempt to seduce him. Then he saw the tape over her mouth and heard her groan and sob in an attempt to speak. Her arms had been tied behind her back, and her ankles fastened with more tape.

He went up to her and peeled the tape gently from her mouth.

'Nicky, what happened? Are you hurt?'

She shook her head. All her terror was in her eyes. Her body had gone rigid with fear.

'Sam? Is he . . . ?'

He could not get the words out. She shook her head.

'He's upstairs. I don't know . . . Two men, they . . .'

He bent as though to untie her. That was when he noticed what they'd done to her body. He stood back to see more clearly. Her attackers had written on her naked flesh with a pen of some sort. The message was in Chinese characters. On her left breast they'd written: 美人 *Meiren* – Beautiful Woman. On her right breast: 帅男孩儿 *Shuai nanhair* – Handsome Boy. Then along her belly: 别是一般滋味在心头 *Bie shi yiban ziwei zai shintou.*

He recognized the last words. They were the last line of a well-known poem by the Emperor Li Yu. Like an owl screeching, they ran through his mind even as he got to his feet and hurried to the door: 'Parting lies in the heart like a bitter taste.'

He ran up the stairs two at a time. *Bie shi yiban.* The words of the poem rang at every step like a bell in his head. Sam's room was at the end of the corridor on the first floor. *Ziwei zai shintou.* The door was wide open, and light spilled into the passage. David knew he was taking an enormous risk going into the room without a gun, but his gun was in his bedroom on the next floor, and he wasn't prepared to waste another second getting to Sam.

He dashed through the door and pulled up hard.

Bie shi yiban ziwei zai shintou.

They hadn't stripped him naked, they hadn't beaten him, they hadn't so much as disturbed a hair on his head. David moved into the room carefully, inching his way forward, feeling the hair start to move on his neck, straining to understand what they had done.

The boy was sitting on a large wooden stool, to which he was fastened by thick leather straps.

'Sam, what's wrong? What have they done?'

Sam turned a distressed face to him.

'I have to keep tight hold, Dad. They said . . .'

'Yes, I see, son. Don't move. Just stay as you are. Can you do that? Can you hold on a little longer?'

Sam nodded. He was holding a rope and pulling back on it very hard with both hands. The other end of the rope was attached to a spring mechanism that fed into the trigger of a large crossbow whose bolt was directed exactly at Sam's heart. By holding the rope he ensured that the spring remained taut. If he slackened his hold by a mere fraction, the spring would catapult the bolt straight into his chest.

David had had little experience with them, but he knew that crossbows were not toys but serious weapons that could inflict frightening injuries. At this short range, the bolt would not only pierce Sam's slim body but would tear through it and embed itself in the wall behind.

In his long experience with weapons, the one thing he'd learnt was to do nothing hastily. The crossbow had been set up as a booby trap of sorts, and well-made booby traps often had more than one way of being sprung. The obvious thing to do was check the bolt. If nothing stood in his way, he could simply lift it from the groove and disarm the weapon. The moment he looked at it, he knew that wasn't an option. Someone had designed a long cage to fit over the bolt. It held it firmly in place, and would only release it when the trigger fired.

His next thought was to move the whole crossbow. It

was screwed down firmly to a metal stand, and the stand was bolted to the floor. Someone had gone to a lot of trouble.

'Dad, my arms are sore. I can't hold it much longer.'

'Don't worry, Sam. If I can't find a way of disarming this thing quickly, I'll take over.'

'You've got to hurry, Dad. I'm really tired. I've been holding this thing for hours.'

'OK, Sam, I'm coming now. I'll get hold of it, then I want you to make a phone call. I'll give you the number.'

He turned and smiled at the boy. Sam was trembling, straining to keep the tension in the rope. He smiled back at him bravely, but David could see he was terrified.

Suddenly, he saw Sam's head turn, drawn by something at the door. It was Gromit. David remembered noticing her in the living room when he'd gone in to find Nicky. The cat ran in and headed straight for Sam.

David let out a cry and lunged for the cat, but it was too late. She jumped up at Sam, expecting him to catch her, clawing his face as her attempt failed, throwing his delicate balance off. The boy threw up his hands, and the spring thudded back, releasing the trigger and sending eight inches of steel bolt into the centre of Sam's chest, hurling him backwards and smashing him against the bedroom wall. A smear of blood washed the wallpaper. It was an image David could never expunge from his mind: Sam's blood, red on a poster of the Arsenal football team, his passion and his ambition.

He did not cry out. There was no time. By the time David reached him, he was already dead.

CHAPTER FIFTEEN

The sun shone as brightly as a winter fire all through the day of the funeral. Trees caught the light in the furrows of their branches, and juggled it between their leaves, dappling and undappling the grass at their feet. Row upon row of white headstones lay bedazzled in the brightness, and here and there a golden name would shout aloud, or a sequence of dates, carved deep in the stone, would tug at the attention of passers-by.

Sam's dates, when they came to be carved, would plead for notice. Nine years, seven months, five days. Until then, a wooden cross served to mark his head. The grave was heaped with flowers, more flowers than David had ever seen in his life. He walked about among them for a while, reading cards, struggling to remember the host of names, until it was too much, and he stood to one side, fighting back the darkest tears of his life.

Elizabeth was there, as she had every right to be. David could not have turned her away. He gave her what little comfort he could; she made herself a sort of hostess to the occasion, and said nothing to comfort or quieten him. It was not that she did not grieve, merely that she coped with her grief by turning it into something else: resentment or self-pity, and frequently anger. Every so often she would remove a little bottle from her handbag and take a not-too-surreptitious sip from its neck. He pitied her then, and might almost have loved her had she not looked at him, all love extinguished, and shaken someone else's hand.

She held him responsible, of course; he'd expected that. She said nothing directly, but it came out again and again in little meaningful phrases against which he could not defend himself. 'If he hadn't been . . .' 'Surely, if there'd been the slightest risk . . .' 'Did you really have to leave him on his own . . . ?' She stopped short of blaming the service, knowing that any accusation there would come too close to home.

Anthony Farrar stayed away, knowing his presence would have caused an unwelcome stir. As David's boss, of course, he was morally bound to be present, not least because there was every reason to believe Sam had been killed in error for the boy being kept down in the Cotswolds. David couldn't decide whether Farrar's absence was out of delicacy on account of his relationship with the dead child's mother, or because he wanted to avoid drawing attention to the link between Sam's death and his father's occupation.

There were others there from the China Desk and elsewhere in the service, close friends and acquaintances of David's who'd made a point of turning up. They hadn't all known Sam, but those who hadn't knew of him. Privately, they'd sworn that whoever was responsible would pay a high price for the boy's murder. They'd already stepped up surveillance of the Chinese embassy to the point where they knew if a toothpick went missing from the refectory.

Elizabeth's older brother, Laurence Royle, was there, of course, looking rich and healthy and completely detached. A bevy of lesser Royles had come with him, curiosity-seekers from a world that knew little of grief or any raw emotion. Laurence shook hands on all sides, picking his careful way through his fellow guests like a surgeon among prospective patients. The 1997 election had lost him his previously comfortable seat in the shires, but he had not thrown off the patronizing manner of a member of the political elite.

David's parents were there, still devastated by the news. His mother seemed to have shrunk, like a fruit that has dried from within, shrivelling the flesh. His father held himself stiff and still throughout the interment, gazing out over the trees into a distance whose ends were invisible to anyone but himself. Later, when they went back to the house for food, he kept to himself while David's mother helped Elizabeth. David found him sitting on a high stool in the kitchen, an undrunk cup of tea in hand.

'Why don't we go out to the garden?' David suggested.

His father said nothing, but followed him out. It was a large garden, full of Canterbury bells and hollyhocks and tall trees covered in moss and thick clumps of ivy. Up above, the branches were patrolled by convoys of dipping and turning birds. The old man looked up at them for a minute or more, then turned to David.

'"The oriole cries, as though it were its own tears
Which damp even the topmost blossoms on the tree."'

David knew the poem, a brief, four-line piece by Li Shang-Yin.

'No orioles here, Father.' He sneezed once, assailed by the garden's thick pollens.

The old man sighed, and they walked on. Guests watched them go, but no one intruded on their grief.

David looked at his father, as though seeing him for the first time in years. Age had settled on him like a deposit of white ash, transforming his skin to parchment and his hair to thin strands of gossamer. His shoulders were stooped, but he refused to use a stick. Mentally, he seemed as sharp as ever.

'Why isn't Maddie here?' he asked.

David had expected the question, dreaded it.

'She doesn't know, Father. She isn't well again.'

'Is she in hospital?'

'Yes. Dr Rose's clinic.'

'I hope that bitch is paying.'

'Not today, Dad, please.'

'When will you tell her?'

'I don't know. Rose says it could do irreparable damage to tell her now. Her breakdown was a reaction to Elizabeth's leaving. If she learned that Sam . . .'

'I'm sorry, David. You've got too much to cope with. Why don't you close the house for a while, come and live with us? You'll be no good here on your own.'

'I'll get by.'

'You never get by. You're not self-sufficient. Your mother spoilt you.'

'Father, there's something I need to tell you. Please don't mention it to anyone, especially not Mother.'

'I never mention anything to her. Here, let's sit down. I'm tired, standing all day.'

A wooden bench stood in the green shade of a tall ash tree. Two cousins hovering nearby smiled awkwardly and moved away, leaving David and his father alone. They sat down side by side, father and son, both bereft. All David could do suddenly was cry, deep, all-engulfing washes of silent tears that tore his heart. His father sat with him patiently, saying nothing, with one arm round his son's shoulders. Above them, the birds sang and flew in and out, chirruping as though their hearts would burst.

In the house, in the unlit upstairs bathroom, Elizabeth sat on the toilet with her head in her hands, weeping uncontrollably. She'd been to Sam's bedroom and found the toy rabbit he'd loved so much when he was three. It had been enough to trigger this crying jag. She held it by the ears, between the fingers of her left hand, a token of her grief, and a reminder that Sam had been lost to her long before death intervened.

Somewhere outside, she heard her name being called. In her absence, her sister Ann had started to show people round, taking friends to Sam's room, pointing out the spot where he had died. People began leaving after that, one after the other, unable to bear the strangeness of this grief.

The garden emptied too, for no one had the heart to stand in the sunshine watching the ghost of a little boy run and climb and shout among the shrubs and flowers. David, his tears exhausted, watched them go, half-familiar figures moving back to the house. He heard his mother's voice through an open window, sing-song, intoning an Uighur prayer, very quiet and subdued, locked more and more into the world of her youth.

'Father,' he said, 'I have to leave London tomorrow.'

'Leave?'

'I've been ordered to Sinkiang. I'm flying to Urumchi in the morning.'

The old man nodded. He understood too little and too much.

'Will it be dangerous?' he asked.

'Yes. It's not routine. I can't tell you any more. I shouldn't really be telling you this much. You must keep it to yourself. If word got out, my life would be in even greater danger.'

'You have my word, you know that.'

'I know.'

A cloud passed like a sponge over the sun. David shivered. Up at the house, his mother's voice dipped and died, and there was silence over everything.

'David, before you leave, promise you'll come to visit your mother and myself.'

David tensed. He'd wanted to get clean away, without tears or regrets.

'Dad, I'm not sure I . . .'

'There's something I want to give you, David. It may be of use where you're going.'

'What is it?'

His father gave him a cat-like look, knowing, yet expressionless.

'You'll see,' the old man said. 'Promise me you won't leave without it.'

David hesitated for a moment, then nodded.

'I promise,' he said. 'Now, isn't it time we went in?'

'In a moment. I like sitting here. I've always liked this garden.' A leaf fell into his lap, as though bringing notice of the autumn to come. 'They were Chinese?'

David nodded.

'I think so, yes.'

'Han?'

'Probably, but I can't be sure. They were able to write characters.'

He told his father about the girl, what they had done to her.

'It's meant to be erotic. To write on a naked woman's body. Was she very beautiful?'

'Yes. In another setting I would have found it erotic. This was ugly.'

'It is such a beautiful poem. To put it to such use . . .'

He shook his head. David looked at the sky.

117

'*Wu yan du shang Shilou . . .*' he began.

'"I climb West Tower alone in silence,
While above my head the moon moves like a sickle.
The Yutong tree is lonely,
Bright autumn is locked in a dark courtyard.
You can slice away the pain of separation, but it will not
    leave you,
For your mind will still be in turmoil.
Separation is nothing but melancholy.
Parting lies in the heart like a bitter taste."'

His voice grew still. The cloud still sat on the sun, and a
dark shadow lay across the lawn. Autumn was months
away, but David could feel it in his heart already, locked
inside it for ever.

'Let's go in,' he said. 'It's getting cold.'

And Elizabeth sat in her pale bathroom, that she had decorated years ago with her own hands, and felt the weeping
subside, but not the pain. To live the life she lived, she had
no choice but to fight down all feelings of tenderness or
pity. She could not admit, even to herself, that a part of
her still loved David, that little Sam had meant everything
to her, and that Maddie awoke in her maternal instincts
nobody would have guessed she had. And because part of
her also hated David and pretended indifference to Sam,
and despised Maddie for her weaknesses, she was able to
bottle her other feelings inside and go on being the hard
bitch she thought the world wanted her to be.

CHAPTER SIXTEEN

It was raining heavily by the time David reached the clinic. Everything was depressingly familiar: the tree-lined avenue, the drive up to the main house, the door with its discreet plaque. He rang the bell, and listened to its notes fading on the evening air. All round him he felt the weight of understated opulence. His life with Elizabeth had never quite accustomed him to real luxury. She'd always mocked him for it, good-naturedly at first, in recent years with genuine spite.

He'd met her shortly after finishing his degree, at a reception in the Chinese embassy. The Cultural Revolution had been officially over for a few years, but its effects still lingered, particularly within institutions like the diplomatic corps. The reception had been the first event in the embassy for years at which outsiders had been present. David's father had been invited, one of several academics who the Chinese hoped might breathe a little life back into their universities after their long closure. He'd brought David in order to introduce him to a Uighur professor who had somehow survived the worst of the purges.

And Elizabeth? She'd been there with the rest of her expensive clan: Laurence, her older brother, groomed to be head of the family firm; Bernard, a younger brother, recently made a director, with responsibility for foreign sales; and their mother, Cassandra, head of the firm, a monster at seventy-five, with a captivating smile and eyes that would have frozen steel.

He ought to have taken his cue from the mother. But at twenty-two he'd found her fascinating and charming. And Elizabeth had knocked him off his feet. At twenty, she'd been beautiful, funny, and winningly sad. They didn't make women like her where he came from; in fact, they didn't make women like her anywhere else on earth. He spent most of that evening with her, and before they left asked her out. Now, nearly thirty years on, he could still taste the pleasure of that moment when she'd said yes.

Soft footsteps crossed the hall, and the door swung open. A young woman in a nurse's uniform smiled at him.

'Mr Laing?'

He nodded and stepped inside. It smelled familiar.

Rose was waiting for him in his office on the ground floor. Everything in the room was exactly as it had been three years earlier. Row upon row of hunting prints on the back wall, a wide mahogany desk against the window, a tall blue-and-white vase in one corner that David had explained patiently was not Ming Dynasty, but Ching. Rose came forward with a smile on his slim face identical to that of the nurse.

He was a small, dapper man with wiry white hair brushed back behind a high forehead, as if to convey strength and intelligence. David found him affable enough, and immensely skilled at his job; but he could never quite like him. The doctor held out a pale smooth hand and took David's, as though reaching for a fragile ornament.

'How's Maddie?'

'Maddie is fine. The hysteria has calmed down a great

deal, and the drugs are slowly modifying her other symptoms. It won't be fast, but we've started to make progress. I started her on lithium yesterday. Just 200 milligrams, but I'd like to move her up to 800 or 1,000 in the next couple of weeks.'

'What about psychotherapy? If she's stabilizing . . . ?'

Rose shook his head sharply. His neatly packed little skull seemed to vibrate. A thin strand of hair fell away from the central pile.

'Many of my patients see psychotherapists. I have an excellent man for hypnosis, he gets good results. But I would not recommend either approach for Maddie under any circumstances. Psychotherapists have to dismantle someone's personality before putting it back together again. I think Maddie is too fragile for that. It might not be possible to rebuild her once she has been taken apart. Let me do what I can with the drugs. They'll give her whatever support she needs to do what she must do.'

'Can I see her?'

'Of course. But not for long. Your wife was here earlier.'

'Elizabeth? What the hell? You know what we did today?'

'Yes. I'm very sorry. Your wife was . . . not well when she arrived.'

'She'd been drinking?'

'Oh, yes. But it wasn't the drink. Her grief expresses itself in . . . unhealthy ways.'

'Such as?'

'She wasn't alone. She had someone with her, a – well, what I would call a guru. Perhaps I'm not being accurate. Perhaps he's a shaman, or a channeller, or whatever. You know what I mean. Long robes. A peculiar hat.'

'Oh, Lord. I think I've heard about this man. He does the

rounds. Elderly widows, young girls. Tell me you didn't let her take him up to Maddie.'

'That's what she wanted. She claimed he could "set her chakras" right. I told her, he was free to do what he liked, but he wasn't going within fifty yards of your daughter.'

'I don't suppose she was any too keen on that.'

'There was a little confrontation, yes. But she saw sense in the end.'

'And did she see Maddie?'

'Yes, for a few minutes. I left the guru with Tim Bowles, my assistant, and went upstairs with her.'

'Did she say anything . . . ? I mean, did she mention Sam or the funeral?'

'No. Absolutely nothing. I was there the whole time. I thought it best. Mrs Laing seemed . . . not quite in control.'

'What about Maddie? How did she handle it?'

'Very well, considering. Look, why don't we pay her a visit? She often talks of you. I told her you were coming today.'

More than anything, David disliked the clinic for its suffocating silences. Everything seemed shut in behind walls and doors and drugs. All the cries of grief and howls of pain, all the tears and sobs of pure misery were blocked up, shut down, concealed. There were no rattling trolleys, no slamming doors, no whistling orderlies, no televisions blaring: just white-clothed nurses moving in rubber shoes across thick carpet, doors that opened with a soft hiss at the press of a button, and every so often the quiet passage of a doctor in a dark suit and pastel tie, come to minister in silence to the manic and deranged.

As he paused to open the door of Maddie's room, Dr Rose turned to David.

'Forgive me, but I need to know. When I spoke to her yesterday, Maddie said you . . . I don't know how to put this. She suggested you had killed people. That this was in some way connected to your work. I told her you were a civil servant, that it was highly unlikely you would go round killing people. But it seems to distress her, and I need to get at the root of it. Is there any connection? Perhaps you work for the Ministry of Defence?'

He'd never told her; she'd guessed from chance remarks he'd made, from hints and clues. It had been just before her boyfriend, Zheng Juntao, had been killed, and somehow the two events had locked together in her mind: her father's career in intelligence, and her lover's disappearance.

'I must be certain this is covered by your obligation to confidentiality.'

'Of course.'

'All I can tell you is that Maddie is telling the truth. I think she's frightened I may be killed in the same way. What happened to her brother was connected. I work in a very dangerous trade.'

'And your departure tomorrow?'

He hesitated. Too much depended on this trip for anyone to know about it.

'I'm going to Scotland,' he said. 'To train some new employees. To put them through their paces. Unfortunately . . . I won't be able to make any phone calls. Perhaps you can help me with that.'

'I'll see what I can do.'

He pressed a red button on the wall, and the door slid open.

'Call me when you want out,' he said. 'You know the routine.'

David stepped inside, and the door sighed shut behind

him. Maddie was sitting in a comfortable armchair beside the bed. She looked up and, when she saw who it was, broke into a broad smile.

'Come in, Dad,' she said. 'I'll ask them to give us tea. Why didn't you bring Sam along?'

RADIANT RED SKY

CHAPTER SEVENTEEN

Sinkiang Province
Western China

The plane dipped through the burnt air like a diver shearing water. There were no clouds, but layers of hot, swelling air tossed the fragile casing with its human cargo like a paper cup in a high, incautious wind.

They came in low across the Turfan Depression, the second lowest place on the earth's surface. David looked through the window. Below him, an expanse of green tumbled away to the horizon. Then, abruptly, the land lifted and they were flying across a desert of stone. At an angle ahead of them, the Huozhou Shan hills shimmered like crimson flames against the blue air. And then, as the plane banked in its descent to Urumchi, through the window opposite he caught sight of the Tien Shan range, white-topped and lyrical, its peaks swirling like jade dancers among veils of cloud and mist. The Heavenly Mountains. He'd climbed there several times, almost died in a blizzard once on the slopes of Pik Pobedy, slap on the border with what had been the USSR.

He winced inwardly as a fearful sound of crunching and grinding rocked the plane. It shook loose its landing gear, wobbled, and straightened again. David offered up a silent prayer that the landing apparatus had not fallen off in the process. China's air safety record was enough to make even Bruce Willis take the bus. But David had been left no choice. He had to be at a medical conference in the morning, and the four-hour flight from Peking beat days on a train.

He glanced through the window again. It was a perpetual mystery to him how anyone, even the modern Chinese administration, could have taken such a beautiful situation and created the city of Urumchi. Below him, a sprawl of industrial plants stretched unbroken across the landscape. He closed his eyes to prepare for the landing.

'Come in, Dad. I'll ask them to give us tea. Why didn't you bring Sam along?'

'Oh, he's busy at the moment. He was given a project for the holidays, and it's reaching a peak. Though, to be honest, love, I'd rather he didn't see you in hospital. It might upset him.'

She'd looked at him oddly, almost as if she'd known. Her face hung before his thoughts, obliterating everything with its lines of pain and its aching green eyes. Maddie had inherited her mother's looks, but not her character. Or perhaps some of it. One day she might become an alcoholic, or turn to drugs. If she ever came out of hospital.

He opened his eyes. Someone had remembered to switch on the seat-belt sign. Maybe they knew they had a *waiguoren* on board. Looking around, he noticed a few others. They'd all be going to the conference. He hoped he wouldn't end up in conversation with any of them. That wasn't the idea.

They hit the ground with a thump and a whoosh of racing engines. The woman next to David threw up neatly into a paper bag, turned to him apologetically, and said, '*Women yijing zai di shang ma?*'

He nodded.

'No question,' he said, and pointed to the runway skidding by outside. She craned past him, then, reassured, sank back in her seat. Wearily, he reached for the briefcase he'd crammed beneath his seat four hours earlier.

'Come in, Dad. I'll ask them to give us tea. Why didn't you bring Sam along?'

'Come in, Dad. I'll ask them to give us tea. Why didn't you bring Sam along?'

'Come in, Dad. I'll ask them to give us tea. Why didn't you bring Sam along?'

He closed his eyes tightly and held his breath until it all went away.

'Dr Khan?'

He looked round to see a slim woman of about thirty approaching him from the rear of the hall. He wondered how she'd recognized him.

'You must be Dr Muhammadju,' he said. '*Al-salam alaykum.*'

She held out her hand in Western fashion and he took it firmly.

'*Alaykum al-salam,*' she replied. 'I'm very pleased to meet you. Here, let me take your bag.'

Her long hair was tied behind and covered by a smart headscarf.

'My case hasn't come through yet. I'm beginning to wonder if it isn't in Lanzhou or Hsi'an by now.'

'It won't have gone that far. There's a place right here in Urumchi where lost bags have a habit of turning up. Usually a bit lighter than when they started.'

'You're from Urumchi?'

She shook her head.

'Kashgar. Didn't they tell you that in London?'

'I've been a bit rushed. I was told you'd be meeting me at the airport and then sorting me out for the conference tomorrow. By the way, how'd you recognize me?'

'I was sent a photograph. It was a good likeness.'

'Lovely.' He saw his bag break through the opening and come wobbling towards him on a conveyor belt that seemed to have been built on bricks. As it came within range, he pushed through a crowd of soldiers and grabbed for it, only to see it zip past as the belt inexplicably picked up speed. He extricated himself from the milling soldiers, heading round the carousel, then he saw her standing in front of him, smiling, his case in hand. He made to take it from her, but she shook her head firmly and led the way to the exit.

'Were you warned that the photograph at the conference administration will bear considerably less resemblance to me than the one you were sent?'

'I was aware of that. And, in case you're wondering, I don't want to know. As long as you can help me out, I don't care if you've got a criminal record as long as the Great Wall. By the way, where did you learn to speak such good Uighur?'

'My mother was Uighur. From Urumchi. I've been here before.'

'I'm sure you have.'

She found a taxi outside and told the driver to take them to the Huachao Hotel on Shinhua Lu. The conference was being held in the new Holiday Inn, but David, knowing it would be packed with delegates, had cancelled the real Dr Khan's reservation and booked himself a room in a hotel that catered mainly for Muslims coming from Central Asia. It was the beginning of a process that would end in his vanishing as though he had never been here.

The driver was Han Chinese, a rat-faced man who spoke with a thick Yunnan accent. David could not make out who he resented most: the rich foreigner in a tailored suit, or the independent Uighur woman giving him orders. Or was it something else?

He took the back way out of the airport, bouncing them over rutted tracks and bare fields before finding the tarmacked road again.

'He's trying to save money on the parking fee,' said Dr Muhammadju, making light of the escapade. But David could see she wasn't smiling.

'What do you do in Kashgar?' he asked.

'I work at the Uighur Medical Hospital. We've been looking at ways to integrate our system with Chinese medicine. Is that something that interests you?'

'Well, in principle, of course. I know very little about Chinese medicine.'

'Naturally. Well, perhaps I should tell you about my work.'

As the little taxi ploughed its way through crowds of cyclists making their way home from the factories on either side of the road, Dr Muhammadju launched into a detailed discourse on moxibustion and the triple heater, and their relation to Yunani concepts of the elements . . .

David smiled and nodded every so often, understanding nothing. He was totally out of his depth, and he suspected she knew it, or was testing him in some way. The trouble was, he simply hadn't a clue how much she knew about him. The whole mission had been hammered together at the last minute, and his own preoccupations had made it impossible for him to get involved. He'd had to leave everything to other people, and he didn't like that. It left him exposed, constantly on the brink of dangerous mistakes.

What he did know was that she'd been told he could help her with some problems down in Kashgar, that he had expertise that would benefit her and her patients. That was to be his pretext for leaving Urumchi and turning up a couple of days later in the little desert town. But if it meant keeping up an effective front as a doctor, he was beginning to doubt his chances of getting past a single evening.

The real Dr Khan had been one of six British doctors registered for the conference, the 'First International Conference on Traditional and Scientific Medicine', being held under the auspices of Sinkiang University. To get him off the plane and David on had been relatively simple. Naughty Dr Khan wasn't really a doctor at all, though he had made a little fortune in a clinic off Harley Street, selling interesting potions for the treatment of impotence. His file had been kept for years in Central Archives just waiting for the right moment to pop out, and pop out it had done. A mild word had sufficed to extract a vow of silence, a promise to keep away from any future conferences, and a copy of the paper he had been booked to read in Urumchi.

David stared out of the window, watching the city as it braced itself for night. His eyes were watering, and he kept wiping them with tissues. His hay fever had chased him half the way across the world.

'You suffer from hay fever?'

He nodded.

'It's all right,' he said. 'I brought plenty of antihistamines with me.'

She smiled and said nothing. The sun shivered as it

dipped through the evening sky, and shadows leapt from the corners of buildings and the domes of mosques. Suddenly the sky became blood red, and in the distance a man's voice lifted from the Shaanshi Mosque, the first of innumerable calls to evening prayer, and David thought the voice itself was reddened by the sinking sun.

They entered the first of the city's wide, tree-lined avenues. In the growing darkness, it looked almost romantic. The taxi drew up outside the Huachao, and the driver, still surly, dumped David's luggage on the ground. He proceeded to hang about, as if waiting for a tip, but Dr Muhammadju stepped up to him and spoke sharply in Chinese, reminding him that tipping was still technically illegal. He climbed back into his car, leaned out of the window, and spat expertly within a couple of feet of where she was standing, before driving off at high speed.

'I'm sorry,' she said. 'He was very rude.'

'I've seen worse in London.'

'This isn't London, this is the back of beyond. The Chinese used to be polite. Now they're becoming wealthy, and this is what we get.'

She helped him in and waited while he registered with the *fuwuyuan*. He handed over his passport and watched while it was locked up in the safe behind the desk. When the long form had been filled in properly and checked thoroughly by three clerks, he walked back to where she was waiting.

She had taken off her headscarf and let her dark hair fall softly to her shoulders. Her face, that had seemed pretty enough when confined by the scarf, was quite beautiful without it.

'Shall we have a drink?' she asked.

'I thought you were a Muslim?'

'I am. But I'm quite emancipated. Here in Urumchi I can let my hair down.'

'Literally.'

She smiled and led the way to the little bar. He asked for a Sinkiang Pijiu, the local beer, she had a Scotch.

'I'm sorry about the monologue,' she said.

'No, that's all right. I found it very interesting.'

'You didn't understand a word. Look, I had to do that to avoid getting into a conversation about . . . Well, like this one.'

'Because of the driver?'

She nodded.

'But he was from Yunnan. I'm sure he didn't speak a word of Uighur.'

She sipped her Scotch thoughtfully and put the glass down.

'Probably. But the government has been planting spies in all the main towns, especially here in Urumchi. Han Chinese, so you don't think they understand anything. But they've been taught Uighur in Peking, for the very purpose of overhearing conversations and reporting on people. Taxi drivers are the worst. They take people to hotels or private addresses. An hour later, a couple of plain-clothes police turn up.'

'I saw some plain-clothes men outside the hotel as we drove up just now.'

She nodded, unsurprised.

'They're keeping a high profile during the conference. Foreigners in town means potential trouble. I'm taking a risk just sitting in here with you.'

'Even though you're a delegate?'

'Especially because I'm a delegate. It puts me in close contact with people like you. You should be careful too. A Han Chinese will take you for a Uighur.'

'You said you knew I didn't understand a word of your fascinating discussion of traditional medicine. Just what have you been told?'

She shrugged.

'About you? Not so much. A man approached me before I left Kashgar, someone I didn't know. He came to the hospital, pretended to be a patient.'

'A Uighur?'

'Yes. He said there was someone who needed to leave the conference in Urumchi and make his way to Kashgar as inconspicuously as possible. He said that if I could help, this person might prove useful to me in return. And he explained that you were not a medical doctor.'

David took a mouthful of beer. It was heavier than he remembered it. He looked at her face. For the first time, he noticed she was wearing make-up. On another day, in a different place, he might have longed for her. She was very beautiful, very poised. Something told him she was not happy. No, not unhappy, just sad.

'I'd like your help,' he said. 'I've got to deliver my paper tomorrow afternoon. Now, I've gone over it several times, but I want to be sure I've got it right. Once that's over with I mean to leave for Kashgar. Someone else will take my place on the plane back to London.'

'You want me to go over the paper with you?'

'Please.'

'And you want me to leave the conference and go with you to Kashgar?'

He hesitated. It was what he would have liked, but he didn't know yet how far he could push her.

'Either that or . . . maybe you know someone there who could put me up until you get back. Are you giving a paper?'

'Day after tomorrow, in the afternoon. I was planning

135

to get a bus back the day after that. Can't you stay till then? It won't look too convincing if you just disappear.'

He shook his head. A man was watching her surreptitiously, raking his eyes across her face every minute or so. David looked straight at him, and he turned away.

'The sooner I get to Kashgar, the better.'

'Are you staying there, or do you plan to move on?'

'Dr Muhammadju . . .'

She smiled mischievously.

'Nabila,' she said. 'My given name is Nabila. What's yours?'

'Aziz,' he said.

She went on smiling. On any other day, in any other place . . .

'And your real name?' she asked very quietly.

'I . . . My name is David,' he said.

She looked as though he'd said something to hurt her.

'David . . . is the same as Da'ud?'

He nodded.

'That was my husband's name,' she said. 'He was called Da'ud.'

'Was?'

She did not answer at once. Behind the bar, the barman put on a record. It was dark outside now, and people were coming to the hotel, singles and couples. A woman's voice sang of emptiness and the false promises of love.

'He died,' she said, her voice flat, shorn of all emotion. He looked into her eyes again, but this time he did not find her there.

'How did he die?' Even as he asked, he knew she was not going to answer.

'Not now,' she said. 'We don't know one another. I shouldn't have mentioned him.'

136

'I'm sorry. I didn't mean . . .' His voice fell away.

'Was that a lie?' she asked.

'I'm sorry?'

'About helping me in Kashgar. Are you planning to go down there without me? What was the point of all this subterfuge? Can you help me at all?'

He finished his beer and put the glass aside.

'Perhaps you should tell me what it is you need help with.'

She sighed. He realized that she seemed tired, like someone who has been fighting a long battle and can barely continue the struggle.

'People are dying,' she said. 'In Kashgar. Karghalik. Khotan. In oases all along the southern edge of the desert. I see them every day now. Each death is reported, an autopsy is done, a record is made. But we don't know the cause of death, and the government makes excuses and sends no one. If you can't help, I don't want you in Kashgar.'

She got up and, without another word, walked out of the bar. He watched her go. Then he was alone again, and the song beat against him like a stone, and he saw Sam's face among the shadows, and heard his voice as if the dead could speak.

CHAPTER EIGHTEEN

Carstairs
Gloucestershire

The sun struggled for a bit with a giant patch of cloud, then gave up the struggle and went to sleep for the rest of the day. From the window they could see sheep grazing, cloudlike, against the drab green of nearby fields.

Tursun was tired and tense. He fretted, wanting his long interrogation to end. After all, he'd told them everything – well, almost everything – and they still weren't willing to call it a day. Matthew had promised him and his parents a new life in England, and Tursun was eager to take it up. So far, all he'd seen of his promised haven had been an airport, a motorway, and these extraordinary green fields. He'd asked several times for a chance to go out walking, but the answer had always been the same: 'Not today, not today.'

'Tursun, you really must try harder. I know it isn't always easy remembering, but what Matthew Hyde told you is important, and we have to be sure we get every-thing.'

Pauline Potter sounded exasperated. She too was begin-ning to wonder whether it might not be time to let the boy go. Except that it wasn't that easy. She'd filled in a huge form for Requisitions, setting out the case for

Tursun and his parents to be granted a modest house and an annual stipend in return for important services on behalf of Britain.

Since then, there'd been five new forms, and any amount of letters from Treasury officials, all taking the line that Britain owed the family nothing (no written agreement, no evidence of contact with the late Mr Hyde; the document supposedly penned by Hyde could have been stolen, and did not, in any case, commit the Treasury to payment of any kind) and that Immigration officials were eager to look into the case, since it appeared that the subject, his father, and his mother had entered the country without official authorization, and that current regulations required their repatriation to China.

'He isn't listening, Pauline. This whole thing's gone on too long. He's only a child, for God's sake.' Chris Donaldson leaned back in his chair and lit up yet another strong cigarette.

'He's more intelligent than a lot of adults I know. He doesn't smoke, for one thing.'

'Intelligence doesn't equal maturity.'

'It really doesn't matter. He knows things only an adult could know. God, I wish you'd stop blowing that smoke in my face.'

On the table, a tape recorder turned slowly, picking up everything. It could not be switched off without the fact being noted, together with a record of how long it had been switched off for. There were just two of them with Tursun today. Most departments had got what they wanted from him, but Potter and Donaldson hung on in the hope of bringing to light some tiny nuggets squirrelled away in the boy's memory.

'I'll finish it off outside,' said Donaldson. 'That should keep you happy.'

Strictly speaking, there were always meant to be at least two individuals in charge of the debriefing. But Tursun wasn't exactly a double agent on the run. Pauline nodded, and Donaldson went out.

Tursun looked at her, as though seeing her for the first time. She had a kind face, though he knew she could badger him as hard as anyone in an effort to extract more answers. How old was she? Fifty or so, he guessed. But he'd heard that women here aged better than they did in Sinkiang, where the hot sun and heavy work laid years on them before they'd even grown up.

'Tell me more about your school,' she said, 'the special school where you were trained in English.'

He began to talk about the different compounds, the English enclosure that had everything down to Andrex toilet paper and Bovril. While he talked, he reached for a pad of paper and began writing. She watched his hand move. His gestures and facial expressions fascinated her, made her wish she'd had a child of her own. Instead, she had a nephew up in Yorkshire called Brian. Brian did not fascinate her. He was dull and surly, and his infrequent visits left her cold.

Tursun tore the sheet off the pad and pushed it across the table. He went on talking all the time.

'We used to watch English television programmes. Some were on satellite. The others had been recorded. I used to like *Fawlty Towers*.'

She picked up the paper. Seven words, that was all. She read them in an instant, but it took several seconds more for their significance to sink in, and when it did she felt sick. 'There is a traitor within China Desk,' the note read. That was all.

She looked at Tursun, and he looked at her, very serious now, not a little boy any longer. She wanted

140

to take him out of here, and hold him in her arms, and comfort him. What had he been through, what was he going through now?

'Some of the other children liked the music programmes, but I thought they were rubbish.'

'Did you ever watch any soap operas? *Coronation Street*? *EastEnders*?'

'When I could, yes, I . . .'

The door opened, and Donaldson came back in. Pauline crumpled the sheet of paper in one hand and slid the ball into her jacket pocket.

'Tursun's been telling me about his school,' she said.

'Let's get back to Operation Hong Cha, if you don't mind,' said Donaldson. He sat down and smiled at Tursun.

There was a booming sound as a jet fighter rushed past overhead, followed by a second and a third. They were much lower than usual.

CHAPTER NINETEEN

Urumchi
Sinkiang Province

At two o'clock, David delivered his paper to a soporific audience, most of whom had drunk copious amounts of alcohol over lunch. When his ordeal was over, there was another short break, during which he politely walked away from anyone who showed more than a passing interest in the paper and its arcane contents. He thought himself very lucky when one of the participants chose the next session to have a heart attack. Considering that the room was full of doctors, it was astonishing just how much panic ensued when the man keeled over. David took the opportunity to slip outside unnoticed.

He was still at the entrance, making up his mind where to go next, when Nabila appeared out of nowhere. She'd been in the room, smiling appreciatively throughout his paper, clapping loudly at the end.

'How do you think it went?' he asked, offering her a cigarette. It was the last in a packet of Benson & Hedges. There wouldn't be any more unless a miracle happened.

'No thanks,' she said, shaking her head. He slipped the packet back into his pocket.

'The paper was dreadful,' she said. 'You mispronounced "hepatosplenomegaly". And you forgot to point out that

142

shu-hsin-mu and *hsiao la-liu* are just synonyms for a plant called *nu-chen*.'

'Waxy privet.'

She smiled broadly.

'So, you do know something.'

'A little. That wasn't my fault anyway. Dr Khan didn't bother to put it in his paper. Did I tell you he's actually a fraud?'

'Really? That explains quite a few things about what he wrote.'

'I'm sure I improved on it. My Chinese must be better than his.'

She looked round. A soldier on a motorcycle went past. In the sky above, a helicopter moved back and forwards slowly.

'Shall we go for a walk?' she asked.

He looked at her, mildly surprised. It was hardly considered proper for a Uighur Muslim woman to issue casual invitations to strange men. Sinkiang wasn't Iran or Afghanistan, but the fundamentalists were gaining ground in the south, and veils had started to appear even here in Urumchi.

'Why not?' he said. 'I'd like to get away from the conference for a while.'

They set off together, walking down to the market streets that ran east off the city's main drag. The Uighur traders were concentrated in and around a street called Jiefang Nan Lu. David remembered it vividly from previous visits. Something about it had changed, he wasn't sure what. The markets were as animated as ever, the traders' cries as sharp; but something in their manner or their eyes was different.

'How *did* you come to learn Chinese?' she asked. They were looking over a little stall selling Pakistani cloth. 'I mean, I can understand your knowing Uighur if your mother came from Sinkiang. But very few Uighurs your age speak Mandarin. I bet your mother didn't.'

'Let's just say . . .'

'Let's just say you're a spy and be done with it.'

'I'd say you're very quick to jump to conclusions.'

'You have to be because . . .' Her voice changed suddenly. She picked up a length of fabric. 'Have you seen this? The pattern's originally from Persia. It travelled here from Central Asia along the Silk Road. Now they make it in Lahore for the Sinkiang market.'

'It's very pretty,' he said, thinking it over-coloured and vulgar. He wondered why she'd changed the subject so abruptly. Then he caught sight of the plain-clothes policeman sauntering towards them. He didn't smile or otherwise show any sign of recognition, but David was sure he was one of the two men who'd watched Nabila and himself enter the hotel the night before. Despite the heat, he wore the regulation trenchcoat and a pair of sunglasses. David was convinced that China's secret police had kitted themselves out with props from a bad gangster movie.

They walked on to a stand selling Yengisar knives. The bright blades shivered in the light. David took a single backward glance. The plain-clothes man was standing still now, watching them. The stalls near him had grown silent. No one bought or sold.

'I'm sorry,' Nabila said.

'Sorry?'

'The policeman. It's not you he's interested in, it's me.'

'You? How can you know that?'

'I'm used to being followed. It hasn't been too bad recently, but . . .' Her lips tightened into a grimace. 'They know about my paper for the conference. My office has been broken into three times since I registered. They've never found anything, because I've kept my draft somewhere else. I submitted a different paper to the regional Security Bureau, but that's not what I'll be reading tomorrow. I think they're expecting me to smuggle in a few extra pages.'

'I don't understand this. What possible interest would a medical paper have for the security apparatus? Are you planning to give away state secrets?'

She led him away from the stalls, away from the market, strolling east towards Nanmen Square and the Shaanshi Mosque.

'I'm not sure. My paper deals with the deaths I mentioned. I discuss various treatments I've tried with patients showing that range of symptoms. It's disastrous, really, because not one patient has ever survived. I think the cause of the condition may be man-made. Emissions from a factory, perhaps. That would get the authorities interested in what I had to say, especially if the factory had paid a lot of money to the local authorities.'

She looked at him sadly, half-expecting him to rebuff her. When he still said nothing, she tackled him directly.

'You said you might be able to help. Was that true? Or were you just saying it so I'd still take you to Kashgar?'

The mosque appeared ahead of them, its Chinese roof of green tiles topped by a high crescent. Out of nowhere, a cloud came wandering across the sky, utterly lost, utterly pointless.

'Nabila, I honestly don't know whether I can help you or not. Maybe. I hope so. But it all depends. I have an idea your deaths could be linked to my reason for being in Sinkiang, but . . .'

'Then you are a spy.'

'I didn't say that. I think that's something better left

alone. For both our sakes. One thing I can promise you. Back in England, I have access to the best laboratories. I can have your findings examined by people who can help you, whatever the problem. That's a promise.'

She looked at him, still uncertain whether she could trust him or not. But what did it matter? She'd learned that you didn't get very far by worrying whether somebody was going to keep their promises.

'Do you really speak much Chinese?' she asked.

'*Tian bu pa,*' he said, '*di bu pa, jiu pa yangguizi shuo Zhongguohua.*'

She burst out laughing and clapped noisily, drawing the attention of several passers-by. He'd quoted an old proverb, 'I'm not afraid of heaven, I'm not afraid of earth: the only thing I am afraid of is foreign devils speaking Chinese.'

'*Ni zhen shi didao de Zhongguotong!* You're a real China hand,' she exclaimed. 'But you still haven't told me where all this erudition came from.'

He laughed and told her about his father. There seemed to be more people than usual milling about the mosque, but it wasn't even one of the five times for prayer. The stallholders outside, selling Korans, *tafsirs*, and books on religious law were doing a roaring trade. One old man sat a little apart selling piddling-tubes, little pipes that mothers used to let their infants pee down their trouser leg. David had always considered them a wonderful invention. He sneezed twice and decided to take another tablet.

They made for a small café nearby, and sat down to have cold drinks. There was no beer available this close to the mosque. David ordered a glass of *bingshui*, Nabila asked for a drink of ice, yoghurt, and honey.

As they sat and talked, a mood came stealing over the

city, quietly, as if a curtain was falling all around. David looked into the street from time to time, and he sensed a tension in the air, like the tension before thunder. He felt that others were aware of it as well. One old man kept glancing into the street, another, his eyes hidden behind large quartz glasses, would lift his head occasionally and stare ahead of him. Their glances were not casual, but intent, as though they expected something.

David ordered chrysanthemum tea, and Nabila dark tea from a pressed brick. The *kutkuchi* brought little cakes on a patterned plate. David bit into one and felt it tremble in his mouth as it crumbled and dissolved. It tasted sweet, then there was nothing.

'Are you married?' Nabila asked.

He followed her gaze and realized he'd kept his wedding ring on.

He shook his head.

'Technically, yes. The divorce proceedings have already started.'

'Does that take long in England?'

'Not very.'

He twisted the ring idly for a few moments, then pulled at it. It would not pass over his knuckle at first, but a few more gentle tugs and it was free. He hesitated for a second, then put it down on the table in front of her.

'Here,' he said. 'It's yours. It means nothing to me any more. I'm sure you can have it made into something decent.'

She shook her head violently. Her cheeks had reddened, and she seemed upset.

'No,' she said, her voice firm. 'I can't take such a thing. I don't want a present that means nothing to you.'

She pushed the little ring back across the table, and he picked it up, embarrassed, and put it in his pocket.

There was a palpable stillness over everything, as though every door and roof and wall had been painted with it. Glancing out again, David noticed that the street was no longer filled with bustling crowds. Behind a window on the other side, he saw a Chinese face peering out nervously.

'What's wrong?' he asked.

'I don't know. But you're right, there is something. I've been aware of it myself. What day is it?'

He glanced up at a calendar behind the counter.

'Seventh of July,' he said.

'It can't be that. Unless. What's the Muslim date?'

'Let me see. Eleventh of Rabiyul Awwal.'

She nodded and stared out into the street.

'I've been so busy getting ready for the conference, I've been doing everything in Chinese dates. I'd completely forgotten that tomorrow's the birthday of the Prophet. I think there may be trouble.'

He knew what she was referring to by 'trouble'. The Muslims of Sinkiang had been struggling for a long time to put an end to Chinese rule, and to create a Republic of East Turkestan. In the past few years, there had been small rebellions, and any number of riots in the towns, all of them put down violently.

For over a year now, Muslim resistance had been hardening. One of David's colleagues had monitored five heavy-arms shipments in the past six months, three via Pakistan, over the tightly guarded Khunjerab Pass, two from Tajikistan. The weapons had been bought in Afghanistan with Iranian money.

'Nice little weapons, David,' his friend had said, drooling over the computer printout. 'Assault rifles, night-sights, grenade launchers, sniper's rifles. State of the art, straight from Belgium and France, a doddle to use if you've got the skill, and who hasn't these days?'

Now, he wondered how many had turned up in Urumchi.

'I think we should head back to the conference,' he said.

She hesitated, reluctant to leave what seemed to be a safe haven. But as yet there was no sound of angry crowds, no vibration from heavy engines, and she thought his suggestion might be a good one.

They paid and hurried out.

CHAPTER TWENTY

The street outside was almost deserted now. David decided that the best thing to do was head for the main Chinese thoroughfare, which would take them away from the Uighur district and back up towards the Holiday Inn.

A loudspeaker was droning a few streets away. David could make out very little. The language was Uighur, the voice a man's. It was not a young voice. As they turned a corner, the sound suddenly clarified, and David realized there must be more than one speaker.

'It's coming from the mosque,' said Nabila. 'I think it's just some sort of event in preparation for tomorrow's festival.'

They turned another corner and saw the Shaanshi Mosque ahead of them at one end of a broad square. All the Koran-vendors and sellers of piddling-tubes had vanished. The square was empty, but for pigeons strutting back and forwards in search of bread. David sensed that the mosque itself must be filled to overflowing.

The loudspeakers were perfectly audible here. The voice was that of the *ahun*, rising and falling in the lilting manner peculiar to his profession.

'They do not pray, they do not fast, they do not give alms. Their only pilgrimage is to the village of Mao Tsetung. Their only marriage is with prostitutes and lewd women. They call themselves Communists and atheists, and mock their Creator. They bring their vices with them from Peking and Shanghai to the land of Islam. Gambling, alcohol, prostitution, contraception.

'People of Islam, do not let yourselves be deceived. Do not let the feet of the unbelievers trample on the sacred Koran. Do not let men of depravity violate your women. Do not let Satan and his minions ridicule God's laws in order to steal your property.'

The voice boomed from every side, the words clear and precise.

'The moment has come to strike back. The moment has come to declare holy war on the forces of evil. The moment has come to send the Chinese back to the land of unbelief. Let them hear your voices in the street. Let them tremble as you march to victory.'

The preacher continued to incite his listeners. His words were not veiled in the least. He was calling on them to rise up against the Chinese, to cast the unbelievers out from their midst, to create an Islamic state.

'I think it's time we got away from here,' said Nabila. 'There's going to be trouble.'

She had hardly spoken than they became aware of the sound of heavy engines on every side. In less than half a minute, the shouting of the loudspeaker was drowned by the rumble of approaching vehicles. A lorry appeared in the mouth of one of the streets leading into the square. Moments later, a second appeared just north of it.

'They can't attack the mosque,' said Nabila. 'Not even they would dare.'

But as they watched, masses of green-uniformed soldiers started moving into the square. They were all Han Chinese, possibly shipped in from other provinces. David strained to see their uniforms more clearly.

'They're from a special force regiment. Lingdao ba or Yingshiang chi. The bastards mean business.'

Every exit was blocked. They ran along a row of closed shops, in the hope of finding somewhere to hide. But every door and every window had been locked or shuttered. David remembered that his passport was still in the possession of the hotel reception. He didn't think any of the soldiers moving into the square would have the patience to listen to protestations of innocence.

'I'm sorry,' he said. 'We should have stayed in the café.'

'We don't know what's happening back there. Can't we break one of these doors?'

Suddenly, there was a hissing sound on their right. They turned to see an old man holding the door of his shop open and waving urgently at them.

'*Kirinlar!*' he urged. '*Kirinlar!*' all the while beckoning them frantically inside. They didn't ask any questions, but tumbled gratefully through the shabby wooden door. The old man slammed a heavy metal bar back over its stanchions, then turned a key in a large old-fashioned lock.

David glanced round. The shop belonged to a Chinese apothecary. Even on a day of bright sunshine, it exuded darkness from every crevice. The smell was overpowering: a mixture of senna, liquorice, and moss, mixed with the peculiar aromas of one thousand and one other herbs, plants, toadstools, roots, berries, and dried fruits. Everywhere, large wooden boxes bulged with specimens of what looked like every herb known to man. A long glass counter ran the length of the room at the rear. Behind it, rows of dusty wooden shelves rose to the ceiling, crammed with glass jars containing an extraordinary variety of substances. David could make out snake skins, whole snakes wound up like firecrackers, dried monkeys, toads, centipedes, grasshoppers, rhinoceros horns, elephants' penises, shrivelled tortoises. From the ceiling hung bundles of dried plants, a baby crocodile, a bag of scorpions, another bag of roasted silkworms, and a dozen buffalo horns.

The old man introduced himself as Lao Wu – Old Wu – and tried to draw them to the rear of the shop, out of sight of the troops now flooding into the square. David shook his head.

'I want to see what's happening out there.'

Nabila came towards him.

'David, you don't need to watch. It's much too dangerous. This old man is risking his life to get us out of here.'

'You go with him. Please. I've got to stay here. It's my job.'

He knew that wasn't exactly true: if he stayed, he would endanger his mission, and that was what counted most. But he couldn't tear himself away. He was an eyewitness of whatever was about to happen. He crept to the window and crouched down low, out of sight behind a box of dried marigolds.

The square was swollen now with green uniforms. The troops were heavily armed. David felt his heart beat unpleasantly fast: he was certain they were planning to make an assault on the mosque itself.

Two soldiers appeared carrying a long ladder, which they laid against the wall of the building. The loudspeakers still blared out their message of resistance, the *ahun*'s voice mingling with the rumbling of the motors. As David watched, a young officer shinned up the ladder with a pair of wirecutters in one hand, found the wire powering the loudspeakers, and sheared through it with a single motion. A shower of sparks signalled the death of the speakers.

An older man in a neat blue Mao suit stepped to the

centre of the square. David thought there was something familiar about him. He carried an electronic megaphone casually in his right hand. As he reached the centre of the square, he turned to signal to someone behind him, and David caught sight of his face. It was Chang Zhangyi. They were old enemies, bonded by indifference and pain. David did not like to see him here.

Chang Zhangyi raised the loudspeaker to his lips and spoke sharply into it. His voice lifted above the lorries' gentle roar, penetrating the wood and brick of the mosque.

'Come out quietly and you will not be harmed. We are here to help you. Don't be afraid. You can only come out through the doors to the square. Put your hands on top of your heads and come out peacefully.'

David turned round. Nabila and the pharmacist were still waiting at the back of the shop.

'Why haven't you gone? I told you to go.'

'If you're caught without us you'll be in serious danger,' Nabila said. 'I'm waiting for you, and Old Wu says he won't go without me.'

'I have to stay.' He paused. 'How many people does the mosque hold?'

'I don't know.' She turned to Old Wu.

'Five hundred,' the old man said. 'Maybe more than that today.'

'Is it full?'

'I saw them going in. It's packed. All men today. No women.'

'Are they armed, do you think?'

Old Wu shrugged. '*Keneng*,' he said, '*keneng bu.*' Perhaps. Perhaps not.

David looked out again. The cordon of military had tightened round the square. Only a very thin mouse could have squeezed past. So far no one had appeared from the mosque. Chang Zhangyi continued to bellow his instructions through the loudhailer.

'It will go much harder for you if we are forced to enter the mosque. Use your sense and come out now. Come out and disperse. That is all we ask.'

A figure appeared in the central door, a young man in T-shirt and jeans, his hands clasped nervously behind the back of his head. He came out into the square and started walking forward slowly. Behind him, others came out, and in moments worshippers were spilling from every doorway. David guessed that the soldiers had breached the doors on the other side, and were pushing those inside out into the square.

Without warning, the cordon moved in on the Uighurs as they struggled through the narrow doorways. People had started to panic at the sight of the soldiers. David saw youths and boys as young as five or six desperately looking round for an exit. Once out, there was no going back inside.

And now the soldiers struck. Two at a time, they advanced on anyone in the open, dragging or frogmarching him to the waiting lorries. Some tripped and fell to the ground, whereupon the soldiers started kicking them. The kicking was systematic and designed to cause internal injury.

Some of the younger men tried to fight back. One tried to punch a soldier who was pulling him by the hair. Chang Zhangyi walked up to him and shot him through the head at point-blank range. With the first shot, panic grew. Shouts and cries came from every direction.

A man of about twenty tried to run, hoping perhaps to break through the cordon and squeeze out past the lorries. He'd gone twenty yards or so when a short burst of sub-machine-gun fire stopped him in his tracks. He collapsed to his knees, clutching his riddled chest, then tried to steady himself on one arm. David saw Chang Zhangyi stroll across to him, raise his pistol, and shoot him in the back of the head.

David looked round. Nabila had joined him, watching in terror as the square, so peaceful fifteen minutes earlier, was overtaken by a mass of screaming, beaten humanity. They saw legs broken, arms wrenched from their sockets, heads smashed with truncheons, collarbones fractured, flesh kicked and pounded and torn.

An old man was seized by the beard and hurled backwards on to a waiting bayonet. The *ahun* came out in his traditional green cloak, a frail old creature supported by two younger men. He was knocked to his knees and punched repeatedly in the face. Someone snatched the Koran from his hands and shredded it into small pieces. One of the young men tried to intervene and was knocked unconscious with a rifle butt. The old man tried to retrieve the holy book: a soldier knocked him back down and stamped hard on his hands again and again.

'Oh, no, David!' Nabila's hand grabbed his tightly. He tried to follow her line of sight. 'There,' she said, 'near that lorry.'

He caught sight of a small child, separated from its father or brother, crying loudly and staggering in a daze of fright among the fighting and bewildered crowd. Chang Zhangyi appeared from the side, grabbed the boy with one hand, and threw him head first against the back of the lorry. A dark stain appeared on the tailgate as the child slumped to the ground. He did not move again.

Old Wu grabbed David's jacket from behind and pulled it hard.

'Sir,' he said, 'if we don't leave now there will be a curfew. They'll cut off all the streets round here until this is tidied up. If you don't come with me now you'll end up in the same state as those people out there.'

David turned to Nabila. She was still clutching his hand, and all the while tears were pouring down her cheeks.

'They're not human,' she said.

'I'm sorry,' said a voice behind her, 'but they are human. That is why they do what they do.'

She stood up and looked at Old Wu. His frightened, tired face brought her to herself.

'Take us out of here,' she said. 'We've seen all we need to see.'

CHAPTER TWENTY-ONE

The Rose Clinic
Esher

When Elizabeth turned up on the arm of a tall, grey-haired man, Maurice Rose's stomach performed a speeded-up version of the hokey-cokey. He knew the Laings had separated, of course. After all, that's what had driven the unfortunate Maddie back to him in the first place. He looked them both up and down, and decided that 'unfortunate' was not an epithet that would sit easily on either pair of shoulders.

'Dr Rose, this is my partner,' she began, broadening her smile beyond what was strictly human. He watched her, wondering when she would crack. 'Anthony Farrar. I brought him along for moral support.'

Farrar stretched out a lovingly manicured hand. Outside, the light dwindled from the sky as hope from a bereft heart. In the corridor, a trolley shuddered past.

'I'm pleased to meet you,' Rose said, though he was not.

'Likewise.' Farrar seemed to carry the Mandate of Heaven on his person. Rose was used to dealing with powerful men, from politicians to gangsters, but he'd never felt vulnerable until now.

'I take it you've come to see your daughter, Mrs Laing.'

'Quite right. And Sir Anthony –'

'Goes nowhere near her.'

She started and looked round her, as though a suitable retort lay near to hand. She'd been here before, she'd been here many times; but the room had frozen solid around her, there was nothing she could get a grip on. What she found was lame enough; but she'd never been particular or wise.

'I don't think I like your tone, Doctor.'

'It's the only one I have. Your daughter is my patient, which means I'm one hundred per cent responsible for her.'

'Look, I don't know who you think you are, but Anthony . . .'

'Is part of the reason Maddie's in here. I think we should talk about that. Let's start with the evening she arrived here.'

He talked at her until she tired. Elizabeth had no powers of endurance. She wilted at every mention of the problems Maddie was facing, and refused to accept any responsibility for her condition. Anthony watched the proceedings with an air of resigned remoteness.

'Have you quite finished, Doctor?' she said when Rose came to an end.

The light slipped and slipped. All things were leaching into an uncertain darkness. In the clinic, no one sang or screamed or cried out of love. But behind closed doors they contemplated suicide and the imperfection of their lives.

'For the moment, yes,' he said.

She looked at him steadily.

'Then I insist on seeing my daughter now.'

'That's out of the question,' Rose replied, shaking his head sadly. 'You do not insist here. This is my clinic. Only I can insist here.'

'Well, if that's how you want to play it, I'm off. But you can be the one to tell Maddie that she's out of here tomorrow, because that's when I stop paying your bills.'

'That's your privilege. But Maddie's father has insisted she be treated here, and I rather think . . .'

Farrar broke in, as though this was no more than a fractious meeting of desk heads he'd been asked to chair.

'For God's sake, why don't you two stop bickering? Doctor, if you would kindly allow Elizabeth to have a word or two with the troubled soul upstairs, perhaps you and I could have a little chat about how to get on. Like yourself, I'd like to make sure the bills for Maddie's stay get paid regularly.'

With a few well-modulated sentences, Rose was pacified. Strong in his own sphere, the doctor lacked the finesse to resist a man like Farrar. A quick phone call brought a nurse, a small Japanese girl with frightened eyes. Her name was on a blue badge above her small right breast, Keiko. She bowed ingratiatingly.

'Nurse, will you please take Mrs Laing upstairs? She's Maddie Laing's mother. Let her have five minutes with her daughter. Then bring her down again. Five minutes, remember. Tell Maddie I'll be up with her soon.'

Elizabeth got to her feet like a snake shedding its skin.

'Thank you, Doctor,' she said. 'I'll see you later, Anthony.'

At the door, Rose called to her.

'Mrs Laing, be sure you say nothing about your son. Be very sure of that. I consider it important.'

She turned and gave a smile, as if to say, 'Don't take me for an imbecile,' and proceeded through the door. The nurse followed her, and they went upstairs.

Maddie was sleeping, her face turned from the soft light that burned on the bedside table. The nurse made to wake her, but Elizabeth prevented her.

'Just leave me with her,' she said. 'I don't want to wake her.'

The nurse did not really understand, but she took the sense of Elizabeth's directions and went out to wait in the corridor.

Elizabeth went across to Maddie and knelt beside her. With one hand, she reached up and moved a long tress of auburn hair out of Maddie's face. She was desperate for Maddie's love, but frightened of the intensity of the younger woman's rejection of her. For her five minutes, she sat with the back of her hand against Maddie's cheek. When the nurse returned, nothing had been said, nothing had been changed. Elizabeth went back downstairs and left as she had come, on Anthony's arm.

CHAPTER TWENTY-TWO

Urumchi
Sinkiang Province

He woke abruptly, already struggling to fight off whatever was pushing his head back against the pillow. It
was pitch dark; he could see nothing, but he could feel
a hand pressing against his mouth. Fully awake now, he
swung with one hand, grabbing his attacker's wrist and
pulling down hard. He came up and round, grateful that
the stifling heat had forced him to sleep without covers. A
second quick movement brought his arm round to catch
beneath his assailant's chin.

'*Bie nuo!*' he snapped. As he did so, he reached behind
his back, scrabbling beneath the pillow to find the gun
he'd placed there before going to sleep. 'I said, don't
move,' he repeated, bringing the gun up and holding it
hard against the stranger's temple.

'David? Please let me go. I didn't mean to startle you.'

He took a deep breath and released it, fighting back the
adrenaline that was flooding his system.

'Nabila?'

'You're still choking me. Please.'

He took his arm away, and she moved back into the
room. A moment later, the light went on. David's heart
was still slamming against the wall of his chest as if intent

on killing him. He looked down at the gun in his hand, and dropped it back on the bed.

'I think you'd better put on some clothes,' she said. Only then did it sink in that he was stark naked.

'Keep your eyes closed,' he ordered as he leapt off the bed, trying to find his trousers. When he'd put them on, along with the shirt he'd tossed over the chair a few hours earlier, he went back to the bed and sat down.

'Perhaps you'd better explain to me what all this is about,' he said, nodding to the chair as though they were about to have a friendly chat at two in the morning.

She didn't move. He noticed that her hair was a mess, that her clothes weren't half as neat as they'd been earlier.

'I need your help,' she said.

'Look, I've already explained . . .'

She shook her head vigorously.

'Not that,' she said. 'I don't mean that. Something has happened at my hotel, something that could put me in great danger. I want you to come there with me.'

He sensed a trap. This was a woman he hardly knew, and here she was in his hotel room, inviting him back to hers. There was nothing overtly sexual about the invitation, but in China there didn't need to be. Even as things stood, they could both be arrested for flagrant immorality.

'What's wrong?'

She shook her head. For the first time, he noticed she was visibly upset. Something *had* happened, and he didn't think she was setting him up.

'Will I need this?' he asked, holding up the gun.

The sight of the gun seemed to terrify her.

'I . . . I don't know,' she stammered. 'It's up to you. But maybe it's best. You shouldn't leave it here.'

They were about to leave when she turned to him, a worried look on her face.

'Do you have any other identification with you? Other than the passport you handed in here?'

He hesitated, not knowing if it was wise to let her know just what he did and did not have.

'Please,' she said. 'It's important. You have to get into my hotel.'

'Very well. But if anything happens . . .'

'It's all right. No one else will know. But, please hurry.'

He went to his suitcase and found a second passport in the lining. It was an Australian passport in the name 'Harry Kirim' and was filled with stamps and visas from the Central Asian republics. Next to it were some identity cards. He slipped them all into his back pocket and followed Nabila through the door.

The door to the rear exit was halfway along his corridor. It led on to what was really no more than a service stair. For a lot of residents, it represented the only way in and out that was not supervised either by the reception desk downstairs or the *furen* on each floor.

Suddenly, his earlier suspicions returned.

'How did you get past the *furen*?' he demanded, stopping her on the next landing down. 'And how the hell did you get into my room?' Room keys were kept by the *furen*, who let guests into their room every time. This was a police state, and very strict controls were kept over who could handle dangerous objects like hotel keys.

'Don't be so suspicious,' she said. 'Obviously you've never been a real doctor. It does things to the mind, lets you see solutions to the strangest things. I could have gone straight to the *furen*, had her wake you up, talked with you in the corridor. But she'd have asked for my ID, and she'd have remembered me afterwards. That could have got you in a lot of trouble.

'So all I did was show her my ID with my name covered up. I told her her mother had been taken to the Minorities Hospital out past the reservoir. I made it sound urgent, and she hared off, leaving her keys. Sometimes being a doctor has its uses.'

He laughed.

'What if she hadn't had a mother?'

'Everybody here has some sort of mother. It was a risk, but it paid off.'

He looked at her, impressed by her resourcefulness. Uighur girls weren't brought up to be resourceful. His own mother couldn't have walked past a blind and deaf *furen* if her life had depended on it. As they made to set off again, he caught her wrist.

'Have you been crying?' he asked.

She bent her head, turning her face away from him, then nodded silently.

'Has someone hurt you? A man?'

He was frightened that this unknown woman might be pulling him into something unpleasant, something that could compromise him and his mission. He felt himself drawn to her, and he wanted to do what he could to help her. But lives depended on the success or failure of his mission here, and he could not afford to take unnecessary risks.

She straightened up and looked at him.

'A man, yes,' she said. 'I think he's dead. I think I killed him.'

'How did this happen?' he asked, but she was already hurrying down the stairs again ahead of him. He gave up and followed her.

Outside, she led him through a maze of back alleys.

He noticed that she didn't ask about the pistol. Had she expected it? How much did she really know about him? They finally came out at the other end of Shinhua Lu right under the shadow of Hong Shan, the three-thousand-foot-high mountain that squatted in the heart of the city.

'This is my hotel,' she said, pointing to a tall building named after the mountain. 'My room's on the fourth floor.'

He looked at the hotel entrance and saw two men in trenchcoats, smoking and chatting, as though waiting for someone. Plain-clothes policemen, ostensibly there to keep an eye on conference delegates, but more probably to watch out for anyone who might have been involved in the meeting at the Shaanshi Mosque earlier in the day.

'I'll go in first,' she said. 'Come in about ten minutes. Make sure they don't see you before that. Say your transport broke down on the way in from Turfan. You went there earlier today and you're just getting back now. Your case is on the minibus, but you've got to be at the conference in the morning.'

'I get the idea.'

'My room's number four thirty. As soon as the *furen* leaves, come round.'

'What if . . . ?'

'All the empty rooms are at the rear.'

She started off, then turned back.

'Thank you,' she said. 'Thank you for trusting me.'

This time she went straight in. The two policemen followed her with their eyes. When she was gone, he saw them making ribald gestures, and heard them laughing. He went back down the alley and cut through so he came out lower down the main street. As it was, he wasn't quite sure where he was supposed to be coming from.

Taking him for a Uighur, the two policemen tried to harass him as he made for the entrance, but he pulled out his passport and hung it open in front of them. They pulled back apologetically, and one held the door open for him. After all, the conference was about building good international relations. And showing how well minorities were treated in the People's Republic.

The large foyer showed clear signs of moving in the reverse direction to China's economic boom. The colour scheme was built around dark brown and sickly green, and everything that should have been wood or leather was plastic. Over the entrance to the restaurant, silver and red decorations screamed sixties glamour. He trudged to the desk and banged loudly on the bell until someone came.

The clerk, a bleary-eyed Chinese woman with rotten teeth, looked at him as though he was an offence against nature.

'I need a room,' he said. All the time, he was thinking about Nabila and what was happening in her room. If she had really killed someone, mustn't he still be in there?

'No rooms. Too late for rooms.'

It was tempting to launch into a tirade of fluent Mandarin, but his best bet here was to play the dumb *waiguoren* and hope he could wear her down. On second thoughts, his best hope was to play the rich dumb *waiguoren*. That would wear her down a lot faster. And it did.

He slipped a thick wad of hundred-yuan notes from his wallet and asked how much she required. She glanced round and decided that this was as good a chance as any to make a small profit for herself. The price she quoted was almost double the going rate. He handed it over without a quibble.

'I want a fourth-floor room,' he said. 'It's too noisy lower down, and I get dizzy anywhere higher.'

She was about to protest when he produced another hundred-yuan note. Without a word, she produced the registration form, and he filled it in carefully in English, making several deliberate mistakes.

Upstairs, the *furen* handed him his key, and he made his way straight to his room, opening and closing the door again before darting round the corner to number 430.

He knocked gently, and the door opened at once. All in all, it had taken him nearly half an hour to make it here, and Nabila's face showed the strain of waiting.

A man was lying motionless on the bed, face down, his trousers round his ankles.

'Is he dead?' asked Nabila.

'You're a doctor. Haven't you examined him?'

'I can't touch him. I can scarcely bear to look at him.'

David went to the bed and put his finger to the man's neck.

'He's dead.' He turned and looked at her. Now she was here again with the body, all her defences had collapsed. Her face was empty, her eyes frightened, her movements short and quick and nervous. 'Suppose you tell me who he is and what it is you want me to do.'

She pointed to a corner in which a crumpled rain-coat lay.

'Plain clothes,' she said. 'Just like the ones downstairs. They've been all over the city tonight. This one . . .' She made for the room's only chair and sat in it, breathing quickly, then forced herself to breathe more slowly and more deeply. The dizziness passed. She looked up at him.

'I'm sorry,' she said. 'I've never been in a situation like this before. I'm frightened . . . I'm afraid they could come knocking on the door any minute now. It must be two hours since he turned up. He . . . said he wanted to question me. I don't know if that was true or not . . .'

'Did he say about what? About me? Did he know about me?'

She shook her head.

'No, nothing about you. He was interested in my paper for the conference. And he asked about my family. My father mostly.'

'I think you'd better explain.'

'There isn't time. We have to do something about him.'

'He'll wait. What about your father?'

'His name is Azad Muhammadju. He's an *ahun*, a Muslim holy man. He was involved in a rising a few years ago. It was only his holiness that kept him out of a camp. He's been under close surveillance ever since. That includes members of his family. Everywhere I go I get calls from the police.'

'Like tonight.'

'Yes.' She looked at the body on the bed. 'Except that this one was different. He tried to rape me. He told me that if I protested he'd make a lot of trouble for me, a lot of trouble for my father. I tried to fight him off. He . . . He pulled down his trousers. He was . . . he tried to pull up my nightdress, but I struggled. I reached up for something to hit him with. I thought it was the water flask. But . . .'

Her voice fell away, and her eyes led him to the object she'd picked up in her terror. A plaster model of the city's mountain, that she'd bought as a souvenir for her mother. She'd taken hold of it and struck him on the temple before she even noticed the weight.

David got up and examined the body. There was no blood, but his temple had been cracked by the blow. He sat down on the bed and tried to think. This was his second night in China, and already things seemed to be running out of his control.

'We need to get him out of here,' he said. 'You can say he left when he should have left.'

'Yes, but where can we leave him? Once they find him, they'll examine him. We've got no transport. And we can't call the police.'

'You're right,' he said. 'You're in serious trouble. And it looks like I'm in it with you.'

CHAPTER TWENTY-THREE

Getting him out of the hotel was the easy part. They dressed him in his trenchcoat and glasses, and tied his ankles to theirs, one on each side, and smuggled him down the rear stairs. As they passed the *furen*, Nabila hastily pointed out that their friend had drunk more Maotaijiu than he could handle.

'We're taking him down the back way,' she said, 'in case his friends at the front see what he's been up to.'

The *furen* just nodded and turned her head away. In matters involving the secret police, discretion was always the better part of staying alive and out of prison. By tomorrow, she'd have seen nothing and heard nothing she was not supposed to.

Once they were in the stairwell, it was easy going. As long as they didn't bump into other wayward guests, their coast was clear. Except that this was always going to be the easy bit. Outside, they got him to a dark corner, between a colony of rubbish bins and the hotel truck. Nabila sank to her haunches. Since bringing David over, her confidence had doubled; but the dark and the cold night air were starting to undermine it again.

'Tell me about the rape attempt,' David said.

She shook her head.

'I'd rather not say anything about it.'

'You'll have to. I need to know whether you would

have been his first rape, or whether he habitually made advances to his female suspects.'

'Why's that important?'

'If he did it habitually, the chances are he has a reputation among his colleagues. They may know about the rapes, or just that he likes sex a lot.'

She looked off into the darkness, where it collected above the city, squatting like a black toad. Words were redundant. Acceptance was everything. The city was unnaturally silent.

'Please, Nabila. This could be important.'

'I don't see how.'

'Trust me.'

She could not trust anyone, she thought. Not even herself.

'He said . . . I was in a lot of trouble. My paper could lead to my arrest. If I wasn't careful, I'd end up in a prison camp. Unless . . .' Her face froze. She could still see the policeman, his eyes brightening, his voice growing heavy.

'Unless what?'

'He said he wanted to be kind to me, that he liked me. He said it would be a pity if a pretty woman like me disappeared into one of those hell-holes; I'd come out a wreck, if I ever came out at all.'

'So he offered to save you from a fate worse than death if you co-operated. By having sex with him.'

She didn't answer at once. Day after day she'd sat in her room at the hospital in Kashgar, listening to stories like this. Women raped by their brothers and fathers, women forced to have sex with husbands whom they'd been made to marry, women whose whole existence was compliance with male demands. Nothing could ever be made public. In Sinkiang, as in other Muslim societies,

172

dishonour was the greatest sin. Being raped invited dishonour. A dishonoured woman risked death.

'He touched me after that. He ran his hand down my cheek. Very gently.'

'I don't need to know this, Nabila. I just want to know if it was you in particular, or every woman he could victimize.'

'He started to stroke my breasts. I tried to stop him, but he was getting excited, I couldn't hold him back.'

'Why didn't you cry out?'

'Who would they have believed? He pushed me back, but I kept struggling. That made him angry. "Why are you making trouble for yourself?" he said. "Other women are grateful to me for helping them. They know how to show their gratitude."'

'Then he did this sort of thing regularly.'

'Not with me.'

'No, not with you. You have strength of will. All the same, it may be better you killed him. Once you started struggling, you gave him a reason to fight back.' He paused and looked hard at her. He wanted to comfort her, to stroke her back or head as he might have done with a child. But he sensed that the last thing she wanted was for a man to touch her. That was the beginning of his love for her, though he barely recognized it at the time.

'How well do you know Urumchi?' he asked.

'Reasonably well. I studied at Sinkiang University. What do you want to know?'

'I'd like to know where I can find a brothel.'

She felt herself go cold. Was he mocking her? She'd barely known him twenty-four hours, knew him little better than she'd known the man who tried to rape her. Had he been asking all those questions just as a pretence? Or as some vile form of self-gratification?

'A man like this would frequent brothels,' he said. 'For all we know, he may be a regular visitor at one or two. That's where his colleagues have to find him. Do you see?'

The cold left her as quickly as it had come. Something in his voice reassured her. From the moment she'd called him, she'd felt safe. He could be trusted, she was growing sure of that. And what he said was right: a brothel could serve as the perfect cover for her crime.

'I don't know anywhere,' she said. 'But I know some-one who might do. He's a doctor at the Minorities Hospital. His name is Liu Yaobang.' She paused.

'Is there a problem?'

'Maybe. I'll have to be very careful how I approach him. He was . . . In his youth he decided to specialize in venereal diseases. He'd found a lot of people going untreated, so he suggested setting up a clinic where they could be referred. A few days after the meeting in which he made his proposal he was arrested. This was just before the Cultural Revolution. He spent the next fifteen years digging potatoes in a labour camp.'

'What did he do?'

'I already told you. He suggested setting up a clinic for sexually transmitted diseases. The local authorities had already decreed that they had eliminated such diseases throughout the province. The workers, peasants, cadres, and patriotic health workers had loosened the grip of a centuries-old horror and given the people of Sinkiang health and prosperity.'

'What does your friend do now?'

'He runs the venereal diseases clinic here in Urumchi. He's a new socialist person. VD is a new socialist concept.'

'Will he help you?'

'Yes, he'll tell me what I need. But it's very late.'

'This is urgent, Nabila. Your life's at stake. We don't have much time.'

'All right. I'll go back up to my room and ring him now.'

He shook his head.

'Not from your room. After what happened at the Shaanshi Mosque today, they'll be monitoring every call. The police could make a connection. Go through the back entrance to reception. Tell them your phone's out of order, and say you have an urgent call.' He paused. 'Where does your friend live?'

'At the hospital. I don't know if I can get them to call him at this time.'

'You're a doctor. Make something up. When you've got full directions, come back here.'

She nodded and turned to go. He called her back.

'Nabila – can you try to get hold of a pen? A felt-tip would be ideal, otherwise a ballpoint.'

'I'll do what I can.'

She returned ten minutes later, looking ill at ease.

'Well?'

'They let me ring, but they weren't happy about it. I had to make a thing about being a doctor, about it being an emergency. I spoke in Uighur, I don't think they understood.'

'Did your friend have the information we want?'

'He wasn't too happy about being woken at this time just to be asked where the nearest brothel is.'

'I'm sure he wasn't. Did he know?'

She nodded.

'There's an establishment called Shie Chu Tian Tang – the Paradise of Joy and Harmony.'

'That's a very nice name.'

'It's very popular with policemen and military officers, apparently.'

'Is it far?'

'It's in an alleyway between Tuanjie Lu and Yan'an Lu, south of here. How are we getting there?'

He pointed to a small van used by the hotel for bringing food from the markets.

'Did you get the pen?'

She held out a large ballpoint pen.

'Go easy with it,' she said. 'It cost me two yuan.'

He had already found some sheets of cardboard in one of the rubbish bins. On the back of the first, he wrote: *Jiuhuche* in large Chinese characters. Ambulance. On a second, he wrote *Az Sanliq Millätlär Dukhturkhana* in Uighur: Minorities Hospital, with a Chinese translation next to it. These he fixed to the windscreen. A third sheet he likewise inscribed in Chinese and Uighur, and positioned on the door separating the body of the van from the driving compartment. It read: *Ganran/Yalluq* – Infection. To be on the safe side, he added a very plausible skull and crossbones.

'You write Chinese very nicely,' Nabila said. 'Better than most Chinese.'

'My father started me on my first characters when I was four. By the time I was ten I wrote it better than English. Not that that's saying much.'

'Where's . . . ?' she asked.

'I've put him in the back. You'll see.'

They drove off five minutes later, slowly and carefully. The moon had appeared, and the sky was crackling with stars. But off in the mountains thunder rolled slowly from peak to unillumined peak, boding storms to come.

CHAPTER TWENTY-FOUR

Getting the van to go had been easy, David reflected. Getting to the other side of the city was anything but. The authorities had imposed a curfew on all Uighurs, and had set up checkpoints at almost every corner in order to impose it. Anyone found on the street without a permit would be arrested. Anyone attempting to run would be shot. It was standard policy.

He drove down a maze of back alleys, lights extinguished, foot poised over the brake pedal, ready to slam down at any sign of life ahead. At Renmin Lu, he crossed westwards, keeping away from the area around the Shaanshi Mosque. There was no need to keep his lights off here. Twice, he passed groups of soldiers patrolling, but there was no checkpoint till the next crossroads, south of the main market.

He called into the back, alerting Nabila. At any moment now, they could be arrested, perhaps even shot on the spot.

He drove down to the checkpoint slowly, knowing that too much speed could be deadly. No Chinese soldier was likely to forget the incident, two years earlier, when a young student named Nur Hodja had driven a small delivery truck slowly and directly towards a military post in Turfan. Fifty soldiers had watched him come. He'd smiled at them and stopped and smiled again, then pressed a button detonating two hundred pounds of high explosive in the back.

The checkpoint was made up of two armed jeeps, each furnished with a light machine-gun. They were Chinese versions of the Soviet RPK, capable of firing 660 rounds a minute. David eyed them cautiously. A nervous trigger-finger could turn the van and its occupants into a bloody cheese-grater in seconds. At least two of the occupants would be upset. He put his foot gently on the brake and slid to a halt near a soldier carrying a Type 56 Assault Rifle. It wasn't as powerful as a machine-gun. But it could leave you just as dead.

'You! Switch off your lights! *Kuai dianr!* Drive over here! *Zai nar.*'

There were six of them, all young, all on edge. Two sat at the back of each jeep, holding on to their machine-guns as if their lives depended on them. Further back, an officer stood watching languidly with careful, intelligent eyes.

The first soldier held his hand out stiffly, like a school-boy waiting to be caned.

'*Gongzuozheng!*' he barked.

David shook his head.

'I don't have an ordinary ID,' he said. 'You'll have to take this.'

He reached into his pocket. The soldier watched his hand, as though it might suddenly grow thorns. The officer remained where he was. He seemed mildly amused. David produced a card and held it under the soldier's nose. He flashed a torch on it and sniffed in puzzlement. David's ID was a *zhuanjiazheng*, the 'expert certificate' issued to foreign experts brought in by the Chinese government. The soldier held it as though it had just bitten him, and thrust it at his superior.

The officer scrutinized the card very carefully.

'This certificate says you work in Kashgar. What are you doing in Urumchi?'

'Not understand good. Chinese not speak good.'

The officer glanced back at the card. It described David as Australian.

'Do you speak English?' he asked.

David nodded, and the officer asked him his first question again in English.

'I'm attending the conference on traditional medicine.'

'And what brings you out here so late?'

David pointed at the sign saying 'Ambulance'.

'There's a shortage of ambulances at the military hospital.'

'I hadn't heard of it.'

'Would I be driving this if there was any choice?'

'I want to see inside. Will you open the back, please?'

'There's a very sick man in there.'

'What's wrong with him?'

'I'm afraid I'm not allowed to divulge that information. He may be very contagious. I'm willing to open the rear door, but I am warning you not to go too close.'

He stepped down and walked slowly to the rear. The officer followed him. Behind them stood the soldier with the assault rifle. David opened the door.

Inside, Nabila sat on the floor of the van. Across her lap, covered in a long blanket, was China's least promising police officer. She wore a medical mask over her face, improvised from strips torn from the lining of her skirt. With one hand she was raising the dead man's head, while with the other she was pouring water from a bottle. Some of the water slipped down, the rest came back up, making a catching sound. She lowered the body and removed her mask.

'He's deteriorating rapidly,' she said. 'We have to get him to the Minorities Hospital. Please don't hold us up longer than you have to.'

'*Gongzuozheng*,' snapped the officer.

She pulled out her ID, and David took it and handed it to the captain. Everything seemed in order.

'We really have to hurry,' said David. 'He could die before we get him there.'

'You know there's a curfew? You know I could have you both shot?'

'I think,' said David, stepping up very close to the young man, 'that it would be the last order you ever gave. I think you and your family would regret it every day for the rest of your miserable lives.'

David saw the man's hand move towards the holster where he kept his side weapon. As he did so, David moved in closer. He heard a bolt being drawn behind him. He froze, then, keeping a smile on his face, he whispered to the officer. The young man's face lost its composure, and his hand fell from the holster as though suddenly numb. He motioned to the soldier behind David, who dropped back as though stung.

'Go on,' he said. 'I'll say nothing more about this. If he dies . . .'

'Then our lives are even more at risk than yours. I know that.'

He got back into the driving seat and switched on the engine. Slowly, using only side-lights, he began to pull away. Suddenly, a voice from the checkpoint brought them to a halt again. David turned and wound down the window. The captain strode up to the door.

'You should be careful,' he said. 'You look very like a Uighur.'

'So I've been told.'

'Then you should take care what company you keep, *waiguoren*.'

David said nothing and wound the window up. The street stretched ahead of him, empty of traffic, empty of lights.

He drove past his hotel. It was dark. An old man stood outside in defiance of the curfew, smoking a wooden pipe. At the next turning, David swung left and doubled back towards Yan'an Lu.

'What did you whisper to him?' called Nabila. She remained in the back in case they were stopped again.

'The captain? Oh, I just said our friend in the rear is General Wan Yaobang, and that if he died because of a delay there'd be one less captain in the People's Liberation Army tomorrow.' He sneezed loudly, swerving the van.

She laughed, the first time since he'd known her. A light, unselfconscious laugh that echoed briefly in the tinny interior of the van. He drove on, cursing the little engine for its roughness.

He turned right on to Yan'an Lu.

'It's the second on the left after the New China Bookstore,' said Nabila from the back.

'I can hardly make out anything in this light.'

'Drive more slowly.'

'How's our patient?'

'He'll live!'

The headlights scraped across a tall painted sign reading *Shinhua Shudian*. David counted the next two openings, switched off the lights, and turned into the little alleyway.

Ahead of him, the fronts of tiny houses swept away into darkness. A patina of moonlight glazed green tiles and blue doors with a wash of pearl. They were tawdry houses, undistinguished, built by committee, but in the dreamy accents of the new moon they had grown almost beautiful.

David stepped out and started to walk along the house-fronts, wondering how he was supposed to find the brothel among so many identical facades. He walked softly, avoiding the water channel that ran down the centre of the *hutong*. In the mountains, the thunder still rolled in sullen arrhythmic beats. He shivered with sudden cold.

A house on the left stood out from the rest. Its door was painted bright red, and on it someone had painted in exquisite calligraphy the two characters that make up the word Heaven. Somewhere a small bell chimed. The sound carried a few feet and fell exhausted.

He walked back to the van and opened the back door. 'Found it,' he said. 'Let's leave the van here. I don't want to make any noise.'

Together, they lifted the body from the van and carried it awkwardly along the alley. The windows on all sides were blank. David didn't bother checking whether any-one was peering out at them or not. No one would risk their neck by volunteering information. The three wise monkeys were stamped on the forehead of every man or woman born in China.

They laid him down at the door of the brothel. David fumbled inside the man's jacket and brought out a thin wallet. It contained his ID – his name was Luo Lianying, he was a lieutenant with the Urumchi Gongan Bu, he was thirty-two years old – and photographs of a woman and two children. David replaced the wallet in Lianying's jacket, but kept the photographs, placing them as well as he could into the dead man's left hand.

'Do you think . . . ?' Nabila began, then fell silent.

'Do I think he loved them? I hope so. Feeling guilty won't make this any better, believe me.'

He took a bottle of whisky from his pocket. He'd found it in his hotel room, and taken it with him. He lifted the dead man's head with one hand, and with the other poured whisky into the open mouth. Very little went into the throat, but it hardly mattered. What mattered was that whoever found the body should say the dead man had been drinking, that he smelt strongly of alcohol.

David opened the dead man's coat again and took out a Type 51, Tokarov-style pistol. Bending down, he fired a single round into Lianying's right temple, then pressed the pistol into his right hand.

'This is sordid,' said Nabila, looking down at him. She had seen the photographs, seen what use David made of them.

'Yes, it is sordid,' David answered. So much of what he did fitted that category. In his scale of things sordid, brothels scarcely figured.

'Will it be enough?' she asked.

'I don't know,' he said. 'This is all improvisation. My hope is that the whole thing looks embarrassing enough to prompt a cover-up.'

'And if not?'

'Come on, let's get back to the van. I don't want to hang around here any longer than I need to.'

'I asked what would happen if they don't opt for a cover-up.'

'There's nothing to tie him to you or your hotel. He's a policeman shot in an alley by Muslim separatists in retaliation for today's massacre. Open and closed.'

'It could provoke another massacre.'

'Please, Nabila. Once you start thinking that way, it'll go on until you're out of your head. They don't need excuses to kill people.'

They shut the rear door and got into the van.

'I'll take you to your hotel, then I'll walk back to mine. The van has to be left where we found it.'

He drove off. In order to avoid the checkpoint they'd been stopped at, Nabila directed him along rough tracks out on the east of the city, well away from the Shaanshi Mosque.

They were stopped again at the crossroads just above the People's Theatre. This time they said they were on their way to the Military Hospital to operate on a badly injured hero of the day's struggle.

'I've been in Daheyan,' said David. 'It's taken until now to get me here. If any more time's wasted . . .'

And he was waved through.

They got into the hotel yard as they'd left, and David parked the van, removing the cardboard signs that had given it its brief legitimacy.

'Get to your room as quickly as possible,' he said.

'Aren't you staying here as well?'

'I'd like to. But I've left too much in my hotel. I need to retrieve it. It won't take me long to walk back there.'

'What if you run into another checkpoint or a patrol?'

'They won't shoot a foreigner. You know that. Take care.' He was on the brink of leaning forward to kiss her on the cheek, as he might have done a Western woman. Then he thought better of it, and moved away from her across the bare concrete of the tiny yard. He saw her walk to the door that led back to the rear staircase. As she reached it, she turned to look for him. Moonlight fell on her, opalescent and strange, and for a long moment her face and hands gleamed in it, like the face and hands of a ghost.

Much later that morning, David stirred from a dreamless sleep. He looked at his watch and saw he was already late. Dressing quickly, he hurried outside and walked at top speed to a shop three streets away. It was a bookshop selling both Uighur and Chinese titles. Taking his time now, he browsed through the shelves until he found a copy of the *Ben cao gang mu*, the classic medical text of the Ming period. As he took it to the counter, he slipped something between the covers, the British passport he had carried in the name of Dr Aziz Khan. The hotel reception had handed it back without objection.

The woman at the counter looked closely at him as he handed the book over.

'This copy is damaged,' she said. 'I'll just go inside and get you one from stock.'

She disappeared, taking the original copy together with the passport. When she returned a few minutes later, she still held the same copy in her hand, but the passport had gone. David smiled as he took delivery of the book. It would make a fine present for Nabila.

CHAPTER TWENTY-FIVE

Carstairs
Gloucestershire

Tursun came awake startled. He'd been sitting in his armchair, reading *The Lord of the Rings*, and he must have fallen asleep, book in hand. It took a few seconds to realize that another plane had gone by, lower and faster than any so far. They'd been at it all day, hurtling past low enough to be seen from his bedroom window. Mrs H. said they were in the middle of an important training region, and promised him a visit to Brize Norton once his debriefing was over. He'd smiled his thanks, and looked forward to visiting the air base; but he knew it wasn't routine when they flew after midnight. They were practising to fight in the dark, somewhere thousands of miles from here. Sometimes when he heard them screech past, Tursun entertained a brief fantasy of flying one himself, faster than the fastest thing alive. And then the fantasy would flicker and die, and he'd think about what it would be like to be in such a plane when a missile tore it apart.

He got up and went to the window, pulling aside the curtains to look out. All he saw was blackness wrapped over blackness, night spilled over night. If the plane returned, he wondered if he would see it. Sleep left him, and he sat watching, waiting for the roar of the jets to crash through the darkness again.

He'd started to worry about how long it would be before they called a halt to his debriefing, and what would happen to him and his parents after that. He didn't really know his mother and father very well, but they were the only family he had, and he'd learned to feel affection for them during their long escape from China. The woman who handled his debriefings had said it might be a while yet before a house could be allocated to them. He'd asked her about starting school, about finding somewhere that could accommodate itself to his peculiar abilities.

'That's much more difficult, Tursun,' she'd said. 'We don't have schools like the one you went to in China. But wherever you go, you'll be speaking English all day long. And you'll get a chance to learn other languages. French, German . . .'

He'd looked at her, a little surprised.

'What if I want to learn Japanese? Or Arabic. Or . . .'

She'd laughed and shaken her head.

'Not in a British school, I'm afraid. Later, when you go to university.'

'I'm ready now,' he said, and she looked at him and nodded. Yes, he was ready. She reckoned he could polish off Japanese in a year or two, then Arabic in about the same time, and then move on to Norwegian or Portuguese.

They'd talked for a long time that day about his future, and what shape it might take. He'd been confused. Part of him wanted to fly a jet-plane or command a submarine, another part wanted to teach Asian languages at a great university, somewhere like Oxford or Cambridge or Wales, which Mrs H. had told him was the greatest university in the world.

Now, the future seemed infinitely far off, somewhere

at the end of a very uncertain road, a dusty road full of hidden holes, and steep drops on either side.

There was a knock on the door. He got up to answer it. Mrs Hughes always brought him a late supper, some sandwiches and a mug of Horlicks. Living here, he'd discovered that he was naturally a late-night person. David Laing had told him that. He'd got on well with Laing, found him honest and genuinely concerned for his well-being. The news that his son had been killed had upset Tursun badly. He'd already got used to thinking about Sam as his first English friend, had imagined going places with him once he was free, maybe even attending the same school.

'No ham tonight, love; but I've cut some nice chicken breast.' Mrs Hughes eased her way into the room, squeezing her ample figure through the door-frame. 'Lovely with a fresh salad, it is, lovely.' The plate on her tray held a chicken-and-salad sandwich big enough to feed seven cats.

'*Diolch yn fawr, Mrs Hughes*,' he said. '*Rwy'n hoff iawn o gyw ia.*'

'Oh, no, dear,' she corrected him, 'not *ia*. That would mean you like frozen chicken. *Gyw iâr* is what you want.' She set the tray down on the foot of his bed. She'd been teaching him Welsh – 'proper' Welsh, not like that rubbish they speak in Caernarvon – almost from the day of his arrival. A trip to next year's eisteddfod was already on the agenda.

'Soon be seeing the back of you, I hear,' she said, placing his Horlicks on the dresser. Steam lifted from the heavy china mug, thick and comforting.

'What's that?'

'I'm told you won't be with us much longer, *bach*. Couple of days and you'll be heading on. I hope you'll remember your old friends when you go. Come and visit us. Keep your Welsh up.'

He was upset to hear he'd be leaving so soon: he'd started feeling at home at Carstairs, and he'd grown very fond of Mrs Hughes. He'd miss his mug of Horlicks every night, and the little aimless chats that went with it. At the same time, he was excited to think he'd soon be on his way. A new school in September, new friends, a proper life for his parents. He might even go to Wales and enrol in a Welsh-speaking school. His father would be happy there, he could find a job repairing cars – something he'd done in his spare time in Sinkiang. He didn't expect there'd be many mulberry trees in Swansea.

'Will they let me visit you, Mrs H.? I just ask because . . . well, you know this is a very private place. I don't think people just come and go.'

'That's to make sure you're safe, love. We'll ask Mr Laing and see if he can fix you up with a pass. I mean, it's not as if you've been like some of our guests, have you? And if Carstairs is out of bounds, there's plenty of towns round here where we can meet. Not to mention Swansea.'

'And St David's.'

'Yes,' she said, hiding the faraway look in her eyes, biting down memories that were no concern of the boy's, no concern of anyone but herself. The sorrowing cathedral, and the small town like a trap.

'I'll show you the coast,' she said, as she always did. 'We'll go to Solva together. We'll have tea in Narberth. Now, eat up your sandwich. Arwel will be wondering what's become of me.'

She left him alone, stranded between thoughts of quiet bays and the recent memory of a warplane booming through the quick darkness outside. He ate his sandwich, the bread home-baked, the meat salted just so, the salad fresh from the garden at the back. In all his life he'd never known such comfort, and it saddened him that a good man had had to die in order to bring him to this.

He lifted the Horlicks. It was at exactly the right temperature for drinking. His first sip left a white moustache across his upper lip. As he raised a finger to wipe it away, there was a knock on the door. Mrs H. must have forgotten something.

'Come in,' he said.

The door opened. It was not Mrs Hughes. When the man stepped into the room, Tursun thought he did not know him. The stranger closed the door and turned, his face caught in the light from Tursun's bedside lamp. Now Tursun thought he recognized him. He'd seen him somewhere before. Or had he? Perhaps it was just another false memory, not his own memory, but Matthew Hyde's.

'It's you,' he said, not knowing who he meant. Another plane chose that moment to rip the darkness apart.

'Nasty buggers, aren't they?' said the man. He was tall and slim, and everything about him fitted perfectly.

'What do you want?' asked Tursun.

The man's finger went to his lips.

'Silence,' he said. 'Just silence.'

And he put his hand into his pocket and brought out a short blade that had been sharpened until it was silver-bright.

'I promise I'll be quick,' he said.

And he was.

CHAPTER TWENTY-SIX

Kashgar lay grey and sullen beneath a yellow sky. Sand from the desert blew across its heart like smoke, turning and spiralling until everything was covered in a pale ochre haze. And higher than that, in their own atmosphere, cradled between city and sky, a flock of hoopoes dipped and soared, feeding in mid-air.

She touched his arm and pointed ahead through the window of the coach.

'Look,' she said. He leaned across her and gazed out.

Above the soft, hanging dust there rose a line of mountains, their white peaks imperfectly outlined against the most distant horizon. A faint nimbus floated about some of them, a trick of the sunlight, cast slantwise through cloud upon their eastern flanks.

'The Pamirs,' he said. He'd seen them before, many times; but he'd never forgotten the thrill of that first sighting. He'd been eighteen, and he'd come to Sinkiang for the first time. That night, he'd sat in a torch-lit courtyard in Tashmalik, listening to a young girl sing a lament to the accompaniment of a single *dutar*. The perfect, long-drawn-out notes, and the face of the young girl, shimmering in the light of torches, had made a lasting impression on him. The following morning, looking through his window soon after waking, he'd seen them at close quarters, giants of ice and snow.

From the Tien Shan in the north to the Altun Shan in the south-east, great mountain ranges encircled Sinkiang like a necklace of ice. Except in the east, where the Jade Gate and the Sun Gate protected the roads into China, no one could enter or leave the province unless they crept through one of the high passes, at the mercy of cutting winds and freezing snow. The mountains seemed impossibly remote to David, smothered down here on the desert's edge, choking on warm sand, sweating and aching from the long journey.

They'd been on the coach for what seemed half a lifetime. Apart from overnight stops at Korla and Aksu, they'd spent three days on board, thumped and shaken and pummelled all along the northern rim of the desert. David felt like a lump of dough that was ready for the oven.

He and Nabila had hung on at the conference to the very end, leaving just before the dinner to take the first available coach to the south-west. The police had been everywhere, stopping people, checking papers, and from time to time arresting anyone whose face didn't quite add up.

They'd hurried to the coach station to find it horrendously overcrowded. Everyone who could – and quite a few who couldn't – was trying to get on a bus out of Urumchi. It was easier said than done. Every coach had two or three policemen waiting to scrutinize travel documents and send off those whose papers didn't measure up.

For the first hundred miles they'd been stopped regularly by military patrols, but after that things returned to normal. In Sinkiang, security checks were rare, unless you took a wrong turning and wandered into one of the many forbidden zones. Go too far, and there'd be no check: just a bullet in the back of the head.

They splashed across an irrigation ditch and headed down into the town. Slowly, the faceless concrete slabs of Communist rule gave way to traditional buildings fashioned from mud brick. Almost everyone on the streets was Uighur. David stretched his legs and began to feel more comfortable.

'Have you been to Kashgar before?'

It was strange, he thought, that she hadn't asked him the question earlier.

'Once,' he said, 'when I was much younger. I don't think anyone will remember me.'

He'd taken on a fresh identity, calling himself Ruzi Osmanop, a university researcher from Kazakhstan with unspecified qualifications, currently employed by the Chinese government to write a report on medical developments in the south of the province.

The coach pulled in to the bus station off Tian Nan Lu and pulled in to a narrow bay, where it wheezed and clattered to a halt next to a yellow-painted mule cart piled high with hessian sacks. Three uniformed policemen were standing waiting by the bay. One was cleaning his teeth with a small stick. David felt a knot form in his stomach and tighten into a ball as he caught sight of them.

Ordinarily, the arrival of a coach would have been a signal for bedlam to break out. Now, everyone went about the routine of clambering over seats, pulling down luggage, and struggling for the door as quietly as though they were children ordered to silence by a strict teacher.

As they stepped down from the coach, each passenger was stopped and questioned. Two young men in front of David were arrested and dragged off by two policemen who'd been waiting at the back. A woman in her seventies had her veil ripped off.

David's papers were examined closely.

'Where did you board the coach?'

'It's on my ticket: Urumchi.'

'What were you doing there?'

The questions were routine, but the attention being paid to the answers by the policeman was not. David could almost see his brain scanning and analysing everything he said.

'Who spoke on the second day of the conference?'

David rattled off a list of names.

'What was Professor Liu's paper about?'

'The use of Ilex cornuta in kidney-deficient backache.'

It was all noted down, to be checked later against some master-list, or by telephone with someone in Urumchi itself.

He got through and waited for Nabila. When her turn came, he saw her arguing and expostulating with one of the policemen, and he grew anxious that he was about to strike her or arrest her on the spot. Neither happened. She calmed down, slammed shut the suitcase he'd asked her to open, and stormed off in David's direction.

'What happened there?'

'Happened? What do you think happened?' She was still furious.

'Keep your cool. I'm not the one you're angry with, remember?'

She took a deep breath and nodded.

'I'm sorry. It's just that . . . something like this happens every time I go away.'

'Not just to you . . .' He glanced back at the line of their fellow-passengers who were waiting to be let past.

'To me in particular,' she insisted. 'They know my name. The moment I say who I am, I can see little lights going on behind their eyes: "Nabila Muhammadju, isn't that old Azad's kid? I wonder what she's been up to."

194

That's how it starts. I told this one to fuck himself. I was at a legitimate conference with official approval. If his mates decide to start a massacre in Urumchi at the same time, that's not my responsibility.'

'You shouldn't take risks.'

She was about to answer, then he saw her mouth close and her eyes set.

'David, go to the Chini Bagh. I'll meet you there later, then we can make proper arrangements about where you're to stay.'

'Nabila, what's wrong?'

He followed her gaze. A tall man was standing a little way off, near the exit. He was dressed in traditional Muslim costume, but all in black, even his *dopa* hat. The knife at his belt was long and lacking in ornament. He stood without movement, and no one jostled or pushed him. His eyes were fixed on Nabila.

'I have to go,' she said. And, picking up her suitcase, she hurried to the waiting figure. They exchanged no greeting. David saw him take her case, then go ahead of her through the doors. She followed him closely, and she did not once look round.

CHAPTER TWENTY-SEVEN

Urumchi Airport

Professor Kirim Ishmail coughed and looked round the little departure lounge apprehensively. He hoped no one would recognize him. Urumchi was such a small place, however, that it was hard not to be recognized ten times a day. He didn't mind that usually, except when the person doing the recognizing was employed in some capacity by the Public Security Bureau. Today of all days and here of all places, he could not afford to be recognized. He wasn't supposed to leave Urumchi on foot, much less by air. Much less carry a one-way ticket in a false name to London.

For several years now, the little professor had been Sinkiang's leading dissident, a thorn in the flesh of the authorities, protected only by the fact that he had a reputation outside China as an economist and that the same authorities who loved to keep him shut up also beat their way to his door every so often for counsel.

He was not a likely-looking dissident. In the event of an uprising or a protest, he'd have stood at the back looking on. Kirim was not a rabble-rouser. Normally, he wore thick quartz glasses, a thin moustache that did him no favours, and a straggle of white hair that had lost all sense of purpose or direction.

The day before, his wife Roshan had got rid of all that for him, giving him dark hair and greenish contact lenses, and shaving his moustache completely off. He kept putting his hand up to stroke it now, only to let it fall back to his lap disappointed. He was nervous, but he knew it was vital to keep control. If anyone asked, he would say he was afraid of flying. It was true enough.

But flying wasn't his real fear. His real fear was being sent back to a labour camp, and he'd heard rumours that moves were afoot to have him packed off to one in the desert around Lop Nor. He knew he wouldn't survive even another year in a camp. That was why he was here, clutching his ticket to London via Peking and keeping a close watch on the flight bag that contained his British passport under the name of Dr Aziz Khan. He also carried papers, a badge, and a brightly printed folder from the Conference on Traditional and Scientific Medicine that had just been held in Urumchi. It had all been left at the house of a friend by the real Dr Khan. Assuming there had been a real one.

He knew British intelligence was behind the whole thing. They'd been in touch with him before. After all, no one knew more than he did about the economy of western China. His ideas had formed the basis for more than one Western research paper on the subject, and for dozens of crudely-printed leaflets issued by other dissidents. Despite being a pariah, he had access to classified information, culled from pages left by late-night visitors.

The British had initially made contact with him after his release from his first prison camp. His students had denounced him soon after the Cultural Revolution, he'd been condemned as a rightist, and he'd spent several years in a camp near Korla making amends for his past and learning the humble virtues of ignorance. He'd gone back to the university in Urumchi after its reopening and the rehabilitation of staff, and gone on teaching quite happily for three or four years. And then he'd started arguing for separatism for Sinkiang and Tibet. The authorities hadn't liked that. Holding rightist views on economics was one thing – combining them with calls for the liberation of vast chunks of the Communist empire was quite another.

So now he sat in a flea-bitten airport lounge, clutching a badly stitched flight bag and wondering when, if ever, he would see his wife again.

A bell chimed softly and a voice announced in Chinese that Flight AC17 for Peking would be boarding in fifteen minutes. Professor Ishmail looked round again, scanning the faces of his fellow-passengers. They were all strangers. He planned to keep it that way.

CHAPTER TWENTY-EIGHT

Kashgar

The warm amber sunlight that had caressed the city all day like a cat's paw lifted itself up at last and, with a quiet exhalation of breath, vanished behind the mountains hard against the western sky.

David had been in his hotel room ever since his arrival, chafing for Nabila to come. He felt alone and out of sorts. Now, darkness crashed down like a huge stone lid, shutting him in more narrowly than ever. He looked round the shabby, coffee-coloured room. They'd put him in the old building. The new block out front was packed with Gilgiti wheelers and dealers who'd come down along the Karakoram Highway from Pakistan. They'd stay a night or two, sell what they could, buy what they could, and split at first light the next morning.

A snatch of *qawwali* music wafted down the long corridor outside, losing itself in the high ceiling and intricate, dusty mouldings. The Sabri Brothers praised God and extolled the Prophet, and their audience responded with enthusiastic cries of 'Allah' as the music grew in pace and volume.

David put down his pen. He was having trouble with the letter he'd started to write. He wanted Maddie to know he was all right, and he'd got off to a good enough start, giving her a heavily sanitized account of his first few days.

I'm in Sinkiang investigating traditional forms of medicine. Don't laugh! I just collect data and samples, stuff they can analyse properly back home. Who knows? Maybe I'll come up with something that could help you, get you off those drugs. I'll ask Nabila about it – she's my guide and teacher, a doctor in Uighur medicine. She's a Muslim, so you can be sure your old Dad's safe from any risk of hanky panky . . .

But the more he wrote, the more he wanted to tell her about Sam. He could tolerate the small, necessary lies that covered him and his mission: he'd been telling them most of his life and had learned to live with them. But pretending Sam was still alive was more than he could do, and he knew Maddie would notice if he didn't mention him.

He sighed and began again, wondering if there was some way round the problem. A tiny breeze touched him from the open window, and he sneezed, then sneezed several more times. In the few hours since his arrival in Kashgar, his hay fever had grown steadily worse. His eyes were permanently red and puffy, his nose streamed. Almost all his antihistamines had gone, not that they seemed to be doing any good.

He looked up at the enormous light fitting above his head, a relic of the old days. It looked as though it hadn't been dusted since the Communist takeover. He picked up his pen again.

Darling, there's something I need to tell you . . . He crossed it out and started again. *Darling, there's something you ought to know. You must have wondered why Sam didn't come to visit you at the clinic . . .* He put down the pen again. His own emotions about Sam were still too raw. And, on reflection, he knew Dr Rose would vet any letters before they got to Maddie. He looked round the room again.

His father had told him about life here in the late thirties. The Chini Bagh had been the old British consulate. Since the imperialists left in 1949, it had decayed slowly to its present state, a dilapidated relic of worse and better times. Birds nested on its flat roof, insects walked with invisible hushed feet along its dark corridors, its walls were crumbled and torn like ancient silk.

Someone knocked on the door. David looked up and shouted 'Come in.' No one answered. A second knock followed. He got up and went to the door.

A man was standing patiently in the corridor, a young man dressed in a long black *chapan*.

'Ruzi Osmanop?'

David nodded.

'Come with me, please.'

'I'm sorry – how can I come with you? I don't know who you are, or what you want.'

The young man looked at him as if he was mentally retarded.

'I've been sent by Dr Muhammadju. She says you are to come right away.'

'Does she? I have to get my jacket first.'

The young man took a step closer and looked into the room. David almost felt ashamed of it. It had been grand in its day, but now paint and carpet and woodwork looked worn and shabby, as if the life had gone out of them.

'This is not a good hotel,' the young man said. 'If you have anything of value, don't leave it in your room.'

David had had no intention of doing so.

'Wait for me there,' he said. The stranger nodded, and took a couple of steps back. David closed the door. Unwatched, he hurriedly gathered together anything valuable or potentially incriminating and put it in a small shoulder bag.

A pony cart was waiting outside, not many yards from the Public Security Bureau. Holding the reins was an old man wearing a white *dopa*, his long beard falling to his chest. He turned as David and his companion approached, and his eyes fixed on David for a moment; but he said nothing. David climbed on to the seat next to the driver. They set off in silence broken only by the clip clop of the pony's feet and the rhythmic tinkling of the little bells round its thin neck. The driver urged it on with gentle clicks of his tongue. A bicycle with a dim light passed them and vanished behind the old city walls. There were no cars or buses. They turned left into a narrower street that led towards the Idgah Mosque and the Old City. Bit by bit, the modern world let go its grip on things.

As they approached the bazaar, a haze of fluorescent lamps illuminated a scene that had not changed since the middle ages. The stalls and booths that lined the streets were swarming with customers. Barbers worked on the pavement, lathering, scissoring, razoring and pummelling, attacking their victims' heads with vicious-looking knives and cleavers that seemed to have been dug up from some ancient battlefield. Behind them, stalls offered ripe yellow melons, fat peaches, and swollen grapes. Others displayed tall leather boots or hand-crafted silverware, bolts of silk, or layers of carpet. All lit with a high, naked light.

Among them, small restaurants drew a constant stream of flagging shoppers inside. There was not a Chinese face in sight.

They left the mosque and the bazaar behind. The noise faded, and they came to an alleyway that was too narrow for the cart to pass through. David and the young man got down, and the old man drove off, still saying nothing, and they were left standing in the unlit street while the moon worked its slow way between the roofs above.

'Down here,' said the young man, plunging into a lane that snaked its way between high blank walls. The moonlight made a brief appearance as they turned a corner, then disappeared again. Their feet were loud on the broken cobblestones. David fingered the gun in his pocket.

They reached a tall, dark door, and the man in black reached up to pull on a bell-handle set high on the right-hand side. A bell jangled somewhere far within.

A bent creature with slow, blank eyes opened the door and stepped aside to let them in. They waited while he closed the door, then he led the way along a short passageway and into the courtyard.

David halted, struck with amazement. All in front of him, the courtyard sang with light. The moon, trembling high above, seemed as though bought and hung there, to bring light each evening into this little space. Great trees soared to the roof – palms and cedars and poplars, their branches frosted by light. At their feet lay a pool of sparkling water in which the moon floated like a swollen fruit. In the pool, brightly coloured carp and goldfish darted in and out of the silver disc. Everywhere, tall glazed pots stood filled with flowers. He stood entranced, as though he'd been brought to some sort of paradise, a place of rest. He thought of Sam, and he thought of Maddie, and the moonlight seemed to shake, as though on the point of breaking. And on a thin breeze, music wafted across the stars, an old waltz tune from another time and another place.

He looked up. His escort had gone, leaving him standing alone by the pool's narrow edge. On the other side of the courtyard stood Nabila, watching him, her face half-hidden in a shadow that fell from a wind tower high on the corbelled roof. As she stepped forward, her features formed quickly in the light, and he caught his breath and held it tight inside him for a while.

'What do you think of the Chini Bagh?' she asked. She sounded very different here. He guessed it was her father's house.

'Not much,' he said.

'I haven't been inside,' she said, 'but I've heard it's a little grim.'

'Why'd you send me there, then?'

'History,' she said. 'Let's go inside. My father's waiting.'

She led him from the courtyard through a low door in a mud-brick wall.

'Your father?' he asked.

'He wants to see you. I explained you'd be working with me at the hospital.'

'But why . . . ?'

An intricate brass lamp hung from the ceiling overhead. The walls were bare, devoid of any ornament.

Nabila stopped and turned to him.

'My father gives me a great deal of freedom,' she said. 'I was allowed to study medicine, to practise in the hospital. I'm even allowed to live in quarters supplied by the authorities for medical staff. To travel alone to Urumchi. But my father is still a sheikh, he still has the right to make demands on me. A strange man is a potential threat to his honour.'

'It's not your father I'm falling for.'

The words were out almost before he knew what he was saying. Nabila looked at him, her eyes startled. He could not tell if she was angry or moved or frightened.

'Please,' she said, 'don't joke about it. My father is a very serious man.'

'Why did you tell him about me in the first place?'

She looked at him as though he'd asked why the grass was green.

'Nothing happens in Kashgar that my father doesn't know about.'

'I thought he was just a holy man.'

Her eyes grew wide. High on the wall above her head, a light flickered and became still.

'Much more than that,' she said. 'He is the pivot. If he crooked his finger, the people of Kashgar would rise up against the Chinese. And after them all the people of Sinkiang. My father can decide whether there will be war or peace. You should be careful of him.'

A few yards more brought them to a green-painted door. Above it, in Chinese-Arabic lettering, hung an inscription. It was a verse from the Koran: 'O you that believe. Fight those who are not believers, dwelling near to you, and let them find you harsh towards them. Know that God is with those who fear Him.'

A man approached them out of shadows further down the corridor. He bowed to Nabila, then turned to David, explaining that he had to frisk him.

'That isn't necessary,' Nabila said. 'Dr Osmanop is a friend of mine.'

'I'm sorry, Miss Nabila, but your father gave explicit orders. You know I can't go against his instructions.'

The frisking was fast and thorough, and David realized that Nabila's father must have surrounded himself with professionals. Both the young man who had picked him up at the Chini Bagh and this one had that unmistakable quality of men trained to kill. He hoped they would not notice the same thing in himself.

'I'll have to hold on to this,' said the guard, holding up the pistol he'd found in David's waistband. 'You can have it back when you leave.'

'I heard it can be . . . dangerous here in Sinkiang.'

The man did not answer, but put the gun away and opened the door. David stepped inside, followed by Nabila. The door closed behind them.

Sheikh Azad sat on cushions arranged on a high *kang* projecting from the wall facing the door. The *kang* was a platform used for sitting, eating, and sleeping: in the winter, a fire would be lit underneath, making it the perfect place to pass the day. Round the walls, several of his followers sat, neither hostile nor friendly, waiting to see what their leader would make of the new arrival.

The old man waved David forward, welcoming him.

'Al-salam alaykum. Marhaba! Marhaba!

'Sit down here,' said the sheikh, motioning David to join him on the *kang*. Nabila remained standing near the door.

Sheikh Azad was a man of about seventy, dressed, like his followers, in simple black garments. His wrinkled skin hung to his face like a mask that has been worn too long. But the eyes that looked back from it were black and shining, and danced like a twelve-year-old's. Except that the brain behind them was that of a man, not a child.

'You do me honour,' said David, 'asking me here.'

'On the contrary, you honour me by your visit.'

'And you honoured me by sending such a fine pony to carry me here.'

Sheikh Azad smiled.

'I'm pleased to see you know the difference between a pony and a donkey,' he said. 'Now, tell me if you know the difference between a man and an ape.'

The conversation moved circuitously through a maze

of subjects, and however David tried to introduce his own topics, his host made sure he was always the one to initiate or close. They talked of God and His prophets, of Alma-Ata and Kazakhstan, of medicine and the curing of souls. Politics was not mentioned once. Nor the Chinese. Only David and Sheikh Azad spoke. Nabila remained standing by the door, listening.

Over an hour later, the sheikh grew silent. He nodded his head several times, muttered 'good' to himself once or twice, and turned abruptly to the men on either side of him, telling them to leave. No one acted surprised. David made to go with them, half-rising from the *kang*, but the old man grabbed him by the wrist and pulled him down.

'Not you,' he whispered, 'not you.'

When the other men had gone, David noticed that Nabila still remained in her position by the doorway. She smiled at him, and her father gestured to her to join them. She sat on his other side, away from David.

'I would like you to join us at our meal this evening, Dr Osmanop,' Sheikh Azad said. 'I hope that is no inconvenience.'

David shook his head. Even if it had been, he'd hardly have turned down the invitation.

'Excellent. There will be *poshkal* and *jarkop*. Made in the Kashgar way. Perhaps it won't be to your taste.'

'I think it will suit me very well.'

'Good. Now, I wish you to tell me something. My daughter here is a very great doctor. Perhaps that is just the opinion of her father. But I hear she does good.' He paused. Between his fingers, the amber beads of his *tasbih* glided like thoughts. 'She tells me you may know how to stop the deaths.'

David found it hard to answer.

'I . . . don't know. That's not what I said to her. I said I might be able to help. I can have her data analysed at an important laboratory. If their findings allow us to take action, perhaps we can stop the deaths.'

The old man looked at him. The merriment had gone from his eyes. Now, there was only sadness. A great burden was weighing him down.

'Dr Osmanop,' he said, 'I have watched you tonight and listened to you. I have no wish to pry. But I do know that you are not from Alma-Ata. I do know that only half of you is Uighur. I do know that there were ten more deaths today, in Karghalik. And I know that earlier today the Chinese authorities increased the number of closed zones in this region from five to seventeen. Now, perhaps you can tell me – what is causing these deaths?'

David did not hesitate. He knew that, before all this was over, he would need the old man's help. Azad Muhammadju would not betray him.

'A weapon,' David said.

'A nuclear weapon?'

David shook his head.

'Perhaps. But not a conventional one. At this stage it seems to be poisoning the atmosphere. If it were possible to perform autopsies . . .'

Nabila shook her head.

'The hospitals have strict instructions. All the bodies are shipped to Urumchi, then returned for burial in sealed coffins. The burials take place under police guard.'

They talked for a little longer, then it was time for dinner. Sheikh Azad led the way to the family quarters, where a large cloth had been laid on the floor of the main room. The house was not large or grand in any way, just adequate for the needs of Sheikh Azad's household and his wider family of followers when they came to seek his

208

blessing or ask his opinion. Nabila's brothers, Omar and Osman, were there. David regaled them with stories of Alma-Ata and a trip he'd made to Moscow. Everyone was happy. Nabila's mother did not appear.

It was after midnight when he left.

'Stay at the Chini Bagh tonight,' said Nabila. 'Tomorrow we'll find you somewhere more congenial, with a friend.'

She walked with him as far as the courtyard. A light had come on to take the place of the vanished moon. Its weak light softened and remoulded everything, giving the courtyard a sense of diminished scale, of peace and intimacy. David heard footsteps behind them. A guard, his face hidden by shadow, handed his gun back to David, and apologized for its confiscation. No one asked why a doctor should want to go about armed.

He stepped down to the level of the pond. Someone had scattered water about, and it was very cool. She stepped down beside him, almost close enough to touch.

'I liked your father very much,' he said. 'He's down to earth. I imagine he's extremely popular.'

'Be careful of him, David,' Nabila cautioned. 'Trust him only as long as you do nothing to offend or hinder him. He's completely devoted to one thing: Islam. That's why he wants Sinkiang to be free, so he and his followers can set up an Islamic Republic.'

'And what about you? Is that what you want?' His eyes were growing accustomed to the light; he could make out her face.

'I don't know.' She paused. 'I'd like my father to be happy, I'd like my people to have the final say in their own lives. If that means having an Islamic Republic, I'll go along with it. Anything would be better than Communist

209

rule. But . . . Islamic rule will mean restrictions. Women like myself won't be able to have careers, maybe not even lives apart from being daughters, wives, and mothers. I don't want that.'

'What did your husband want?'

'Da'ud?' She hesitated, and he thought she might close the subject again. They were standing close together at the edge of the pool. A fish darted silently between water-lily pads.

'Da'ud is a martyr,' she said. 'He was killed three years ago, during a raid on a government arms store. He was my father's right-hand man. The possibility of an Islamic state meant everything to him. I don't have such aspirations. I'd live in Peking if it meant I could have him back again.'

'Did you have children?'

She shook her head. A soft desert wind fanned the leaves high above them.

'What about you?' she asked.

He was about to tell her about Elizabeth when a window opened on the second floor.

'Miss Nabila! Miss Nabila, it's getting late. Your mother is asking for you.'

'I have to go. Mehmed will take you back to the Chini Bagh. I'll call for you first thing in the morning.'

'Nabila Khenim!'

'I'm coming!' She accompanied him to the door.

'Until tomorrow, then,' he said.

'Yes,' she answered. 'Take care.'

A small red flower grew in a pot at his feet. He bent down and plucked it, then held it out to her.

'It's not much,' he said.

She took it from him, and as she did so their fingers grazed, and she looked into his eyes.

'Thank you,' she whispered, before turning and running back to the house.

He went outside into the alley. Mehmed, the man who had come for him at the Chini Bagh, was waiting a few yards away.

CHAPTER TWENTY-NINE

Peking Airport

'Passenger announcement.'

The little bell that followed struck everyone into immobility and silence.

'Will Dr Az Kung, travelling to London on flight AC105, please make himself known at one of the Air China desks?'

The announcement faded and everyone relaxed. The departure lounge was filled with an extraordinary mixture of humanity. Professor Kirim Ishmail had never been abroad in his life before, had never seen so many people on the move. He was growing excited. Take-off was half an hour away. Every time he glanced up at the clock, the hand was a little closer to its destination. He'd be on the plane by then, of course. The bell rang again.

'Will Dr Azez Haun, passenger for London, please make himself known to Air China in the departure lounge?'

They'd been making the announcement for something like ten minutes, always varying the name, until now he realized he was the object of their search. He felt his heart go cold. Why had he been singled out?

He considered sitting tight and brazening it out, to see if he could still make it on to the plane. Surely, once they'd taken off . . .

On reflection, he could hardly avoid detection. They'd want to check his papers before letting him on the plane. With a sigh he got up and went to a small desk at the far end of the room.

'I'm Dr Khan,' he said, speaking English. The girl behind the desk didn't speak the language much better.

'Ah, Dr Huan. You were a member of International Conference on Traditional and Scientific Medicine, yes?'

He acknowledged that he was. She smiled and asked him for his boarding pass.

'All members of International Conference are to be upgraded to first class. This is your new boarding pass. When you board, you will be directed upstairs to first class. I hope you enjoy your flight.'

Bewildered, his heart still fluttering, he returned to his seat. A few minutes later, an announcement came, asking standard-class passengers to make their way to gate number seven. Slowly, the departure lounge emptied. Finally, half a dozen first-class passengers were left, including himself.

'Will passengers Zhang, Evans, and Genscher please proceed to gate seven.'

The first three picked up their jackets and bags and headed for the plane with the weariness of long-experienced travellers. Kirim did not know how to judge them. This would be only his second time on a plane. It seemed a comfortable enough way to travel. He'd heard that you could even sleep well in first class.

'Passengers Macey and Lu to board now, please.'

He watched them go, then glanced round and discovered that he was all alone. The fear returned then, and with it the knowledge. They'd found out about him late, and somebody high up had vetoed an open arrest that might cause embarrassment, maybe even get into foreign newspapers. So this elaborate game with a first-class transfer had been arranged.

For a moment, he thought of walking down towards the gate, trusting to the proximity of the other passengers. Maybe he could get on board that way, maybe they'd be forced to let him go.

He looked back at the lounge entrance. The first PSB man had arrived. And down at the doors leading out to the gate, an airport security guard carrying a sub-machine-gun.

He sat tight and waited for someone more senior to arrive. And he wondered who had tipped them off.

CHAPTER THIRTY

She arrived at the Chini Bagh at half-past eight, dressed in a white medical coat and flowered headscarf.

'I've got to be at the hospital in a few minutes. Would you like to come?'

'I don't have a white coat.'

'I'll get you one. What colour would you like?'

'What colour?'

'Of white coat.'

'What have you got?'

'Anything you like. We generally take a white coat, smear it with a herbal concoction, and leave to dry. They usually come out in shades of brown, but I once had a fetching purple.' He laughed and said he'd take white.

The hospital was less than a thousand yards from the hotel, a small, unimposing building. A large red cross above the door proclaimed its identity, otherwise it might have been anything from a school to a silk factory.

Inside, Nabila led him on a rambling journey along green-painted corridors in which trolleys and drip-stands and dirty laundry jostled for space with staff and patients. Several white-coated figures passed, greeting Nabila warmly. No one seemed in a hurry. A middle-aged man stopped to chat with her briefly. He showed absolutely no interest in David. Further along the corridor, several patients lay on narrow beds.

'We're running out of space. The People's Hospital over the river has started sending us their overflow. We have to take them if someone over there prescribes Uighur medicine. You'd be surprised how many of their patients have started suffering from conditions that will only respond to traditional remedies.'

David glanced at the inert forms on the beds.

'The only thing this lot would respond to would be a shot of electricity.'

'I'll bear that in mind.'

Round the next turning, they came to a scuffed dark brown door that bore Nabila's name. It had been painted carefully on a rectangular plaque of lighter wood. She took a long key from her pocket and opened the door with what looked to David suspiciously like a flourish, as if to say, 'This is my territory'.

One of the walls was covered in posters showing the various acupuncture points and meridians, the major therapeutic flowers and herbs, and optical charts.

The other walls held glass-fronted wooden cabinets of a type David remembered from his schooldays. They'd pursued him from one lab or classroom to another, tall and ugly, crammed full of dark jars that held unnameable substances. A quick glance showed him that these were little different. He could make out what looked very like a giant centipede in one, staring out at him with frightened disdain.

'Pop yourself down,' said Nabila, pointing to a typing chair.

'I'm quite comfortable standing, if you . . .'

'I said, sit down.' Her voice had turned peremptory. He sat down. As he did so, he noticed with interest a desk and some filing cabinets hard against the back wall. He wondered if they contained Nabila's records of the mysterious outbreaks of illness.

'Is that where you keep . . . ?'

'Roll up your sleeve,' she ordered, cutting him off.

Bemused, he did as he was told. She came and stood beside him and began to feel his pulses, all six of them. It took several minutes, during which time she said absolutely nothing. When she was done, she wrote down her findings on a sheet of white paper.

'Very good,' she said. 'You're alive. Now, tongue, please.'

'What's all this in aid of?'

'No questions. Tongue.'

There was nothing for it. He stuck his tongue out as far as it would go. Nabila pulled it out half an inch further, took a long, hard look at it, and nodded.

'Tongue back,' she said. He hoped she wouldn't want to examine much more of him.

She went to her desk, consulted a couple of leather-bound books, and wrote out a prescription. Holding it in one hand, she went round the cupboards, taking down jars of dark liquid and decocting a little from each one into a tall measuring jar. When it was half-full, she handed it to him.

'This is for you,' she said.

'But I'm not ill.'

'No?'

She took a mirror from the desk and held it in front of him. The face that looked back was red-eyed, red-nosed, and crack-lipped.

'It's hay fever,' he said. 'You can't do anything . . .'

'Drink the medicine.'

'It looks disgusting.'

'It is disgusting. You'll have to get used to it. I'll give you a prescription for the hospital pharmacy. They'll give you a bag of herbs, and you can boil them up later.'

He sipped from the jar.

217

'Oh, my God,' he gasped, pushing it away from him.

'Don't sip it. Just drink it down in one go.'

He closed his eyes, pretended it was whisky, and poured it down his throat.

She smiled.

'Good boy.'

He shuddered.

'I hope that isn't all you brought me in here for.'

'Meaning?'

'Well, I quite enjoyed having my pulses read.'

'Good. I'll read them again tomorrow. You should be a lot better by then anyway.'

'You have very delicate fingers.'

'Actually,' she said, 'they're quite coarse. I know a Chinese doctor who can detect the sex of an unborn baby just by reading the mother's pulses.'

'I'm sure his fingers weren't quite as graceful as yours.'

This time she blushed. To cover her embarrassment, she turned and went to a cupboard containing three shelves of wide-necked jars.

'I've had enough, thank you,' said David. Surely she couldn't be planning to dose him again?

'This isn't medicine,' she said. She took down a huge jar from the second shelf and brought it over to the desk. It had a cork stopper in its mouth, which Nabila removed with no little difficulty. Once it was out, she laid it to one side and rolled up her sleeve. David wondered what disgusting specimen of preserved livestock she was about to fish out. She plunged her hand into the jar, swished about a little, then drew out a roll of something wrapped tightly in polythene and secured with corroded elastic bands.

She wiped the roll with a small towel, and set it on the desk. Before touching it further, she resealed the jar and returned it to the cupboard.

218

The elastic bands had rotted. They fell away in pieces as Nabila started to undo them. She brushed them aside, then unrolled the polythene. Inside it was a tube of paper, tightly rolled. Carefully, she unrolled it across her desk.

It was a map of southern Sinkiang, showing the desert rim oases and part of the Taklamakan itself. The colours used to designate contour ran from bright yellow to dark brown. Across this expanse, someone had drawn a series of perfect red circles. Each circle had a number attached, the smallest being two, the largest eleven. Beside these were dates in proper Arabic numerals.

'These are the deaths,' said Nabila, taking a red pen from her pocket and uncapping it. 'I learned last night that there have been others. Here . . .' On the map she placed a clear plastic rectangle punched full of circles, ovals, curves, and other shapes. Centring the rectangle on a spot near Chira, she quickly inscribed another little circle. 'And here . . . and here.' Against the first circle, she wrote '7', against the second '4', and against the third, '9'; 20 deaths in all.

'Do you have more details?' he asked, sitting to study the map.

She extracted a file of patient notes from a drawer under the desk.

'These are photocopies,' she said. 'The originals are kept in a safer place.'

He began to pore over the map.

'I have to be at a clinic,' said Nabila. 'I'll leave you here. I'll lock the room behind me, so if you need anything, speak up now.'

'I'm fine. You'd better get going before they send somebody looking for you.'

When she was gone, he sat for a while, just to get his bearings. It took him several minutes to realize his feelings of unreality had nothing to do with the hospital or the mysterious objects he found himself surrounded with. It was Nabila. He was starting to have feelings for her that could ruin everything if he didn't check them right away.

He examined the map, building up rough patterns from the positions and dates of the deaths. The patient files suggested possible patterns of severity. Using a pencil and ruler, he drew lines between some of the circles, and from the circles towards a series of vanishing points that might have been the origin of the toxin which was causing the deaths. Whatever it was, he felt certain it was coming from somewhere along a line about four hundred miles into the desert. The line was several hundred miles long, an impossible distance to search.

She returned in just over an hour. The clinic had gone well, one of her patients had been fit enough to go home, and her professor had congratulated her on her paper at Urumchi. She came in smiling and dropped a heap of files on a chair.

'You look happy,' he said.

She explained why.

'My patient is the wife of the deputy chairman for the county,' she said. 'She went away very pleased with my treatment. Next thing, she'll send her husband. I'm sure of it.'

'He doesn't have hay fever, does he?'

'No idea. What about you?'

'I . . .'

She held the mirror in front of him again. No redness, no puffiness, no nasal discharge.

'Don't think that lets you off more treatment,' she said. 'Getting fully better requires hard work. Now, have you ever been to Lake Karakul?'

The name evoked more memories of his first visit. He'd only spent half a day there, but he still remembered it as the most beautiful place he'd ever been.

'Briefly,' he said.

'Good. That means you can drive. I go there once a year, in July. It's already late, and I daren't leave it any longer.'

'Exactly what do you go there for?'

'The Snow Lotus. It blooms the same time every year. It's extremely rare. You can find specimens at Heaven Lake, near Urumchi. I was very tempted to go when I was there, but there was the problem of getting the flowers back. I know where they grow around Karakul.'

'This is more medicine, I suppose.'

'Yes, more medicine. It's very helpful for rheumatism or arthritis. Also menstrual cramps. I use it quite a lot.'

'Sounds like fun,' he said. 'Karakul.' He thought for a moment, then looked up, tapping the map in front of him.

'Nabila, have you ever heard of a place called Karakhoto?'

She nodded quietly.

'The Black City,' she said. Her voice was low, as though she did not want to be overheard. 'Yes, I've heard of it.'

'Is it in the desert?'

'Perhaps. People say it is, I wouldn't know.'

'But you could find out?'

'It's not that simple, David. Karakhoto is a buried city. It lies beneath the sands. No one has seen it in centuries. But everyone knows the name. It is the Devil's city.'

He took a slow breath and looked at her.

'I want to go there,' he said. 'I think it's where our weapons are being stored.'

'Then the Devil hasn't gone away,' she whispered.

He ran his hand softly across the surface of the map, as

though by some process of divination he could locate a city that had been hidden for generations. And that was when he understood that he would have to venture into the Taklamakan alone.

CHAPTER THIRTY-ONE

Nabila called for him early the next morning in a battered Suzuki 4X4 with 'Traditional Uighur Medical Hospital' inscribed in tall red letters across both sides in Uighur and Chinese. Her arrival took him by surprise. He was still writing his letter to Maddie. In the end, he'd decided against saying anything about Sam.

'Just let me finish this,' he said, scribbling a few last endearments.

Nabila watched him impatiently, wanting to get on the road before it was too hot. The previous evening, she'd taken David to the apartment of one of her cousins, Momin, who was a musician with a local troupe that played at weddings and festivals. Momin turned out to be first-class company. He refused to take a penny in rent, and said he was honoured to have a colleague of Nabila's as a guest. David sensed that Nabila was held in high esteem by her family, and was treated very differently to most Uighur women as a result.

Momin was a Muslim, but a lot less severe than Nabila's part of the family. He laughed when she turned up to take the doctor from Kazakhstan on a herb-hunting expedition. It was the sort of thing she did all the time.

'Would you like musical accompaniment?' he asked.

Nabila, sensing that she was about to be chaperoned, told him to mind his own business.

'Get her to sing for you,' he said to David as they prepared to leave. 'She has a wonderful voice.'

She took her headscarf off as they left Kashgar, and put it into a glove compartment stuffed full of glass jars. Her hair was black and fine, and it caught the sun as they drove.

'We won't just be looking for Snow Lotuses,' Nabila said. 'That whole area's thick with healing plants.'

'It's nice to know,' he said, 'but I'm worried about losing a day. I don't think we have much time in which to find this weapons plant.'

'Who are we?'

'You and I.'

'No, you meant somebody else. If I can find it, there's nothing I can do about it except smuggle the documents I've got outside. Maybe I can get some campaigning group in the West to make a lot of noise about it. From my point of view, a day or two doesn't make such a difference. But for you . . .'

'I can't tell you why, Nabila, but if the weapon they're testing now goes into full production, it could entail loss of life on a tremendous scale.'

'I rather guessed that. Don't worry. We aren't just looking for flowers at Karakul.'

They drove on rapidly. The jeep's official name was 'Spirit of Revolution', but Nabila called it the Camel and banged it every time it gave them trouble, which was often.

It took them several hours to get to their destination. They stopped at Upal for a quick breakfast of samosas. At Ghez, a weary soldier laid his gun aside and checked their permits. Handing them back, he waved them through without a word. David looked back at the tiny outpost and watched it dwindle until it faded from sight entirely.

Technically speaking, they were on the great Karakoram Highway that led through the Khunjerab Pass into Pakistan. For the moment, though, it was just a dirt track that appeared to be going nowhere. Sometimes a heavy truck passed them filled with tourists or traders. The gaudily painted Pakistani lorries seemed to have been sent there from a different world. When they passed, the drab landscape reverted to its hues of grey and ochre. Nothing seemed to live here. At times, they seemed the only moving thing on the face of a dead planet.

And then they came to Karakul.

They mounted a steep rise, and topping it came upon a carpet of grass wider than half the world. These were the high pastures, the lush *pamirs* where the Kirghiz horsemen rode among their herds. The mountains towered above them, steep and white, and their summits were cradled by high, never-ending winds. Nabila pointed upwards to where snow-banners drifted against a dark blue sky. Grey mist clung like a shroud to the shoulders of the nearest peak, so high it took their breath away to watch it turn and twist.

Nabila pointed beyond it to the highest peak of all.

'That's Muztagata,' she said. 'The Father of Ice Mountains. There's an ancient city hidden deep in the ice. They say its inhabitants cannot die, but live for ever in peace and happiness. Sometimes I wish I could be one of them.'

'Would it be cold, do you think, to be inside all that ice?'

She shrugged.

'I don't expect so, otherwise how could they be happy? They experience no discomfort, they can't feel anything.'

'Poor people,' he said, looking at the ice. But he knew why she was tempted, all the same.

*　　*　　*

Pauline Potter looked out of her bedroom window at the dark street. The people in the top flat opposite were holding a party, and every now and then a snatch of music would escape and hurry to her side of the road. She didn't go to parties herself much. Museums and art galleries were more in her line. She'd had a dull life, she didn't mind admitting it. If her mother hadn't died when she did, it would have been even duller. It didn't cause her much concern, though, just as it didn't bother her that she was still unmarried at the age of forty-seven and a half. She was discreet in her liaisons, in control of their outcomes, and, on the whole, preferred solitude to smelly socks and inarticulate cries of 'Break his leg, Shearer!' Other people made a fuss, other people worried about her being on her own when it came time to draw her pension. 'I'll get a cat,' she said. 'Or a snake.'

Nervously she fingered the slip of paper in her pocket, the one Tursun had passed to her in the debriefing chamber. All this time, and she still hadn't made up her mind what to do about it. All she knew was that, if there really was a traitor in the China Desk as the boy claimed, it wasn't her. That left fourteen other people, not counting the desk head himself. Whoever she shared the message with, she'd be taking a gamble.

The only course of action open to her was to take it higher, go above desk level, but keep it in the service. Internal Security would take it seriously. But that was a gamble too. Once they started poking their noses into everything, nobody's life would be worth living. If the leak was traced back to her, she might as well resign the service on the spot. Nobody would forgive her, least of all that bastard Farrar.

It couldn't have come at a worse time. This Sinkiang

business was about as serious as things got, and from the sound of it, they were getting worse.

She'd been trying to make contact with Carstairs on and off all day, the last time around ten o'clock. It wasn't good practice to keep the house out of touch for so long. She'd looked at her watch. Just after midnight. She'd check again, then ring Dan McGuire at Safe House Control, see what was going on. She wanted to talk to Tursun again. On her own.

Somebody smashed a bottle against the kerb three storeys below. Pauline glanced out again. It looked as though the party was starting to turn rowdy. A sports car pulled away and tore off up the street with a screeching of over-inflated tyres.

Any more of this and she'd go over to protest. There was no point in ringing the police unless things got seriously out of hand.

Somebody knocked something over. She looked out again, then a chill went through her as she registered that it hadn't been in the street. It had been in her kitchen.

Someone must be in her flat. A burglar who'd chosen his moment badly. Except that the alarm, which was of very good quality, had already been set. No ordinary burglar could have got past without triggering it. She went to the door and listened hard. Silence. But she knew he was there. Or more than one, perhaps. Not a burglar, something else.

There were six rooms in her flat: two bedrooms, a kitchen, a bathroom, a living room, and a cubby hole she called her study. That meant he'd find her within seconds. She hurried to the sofa and pushed it with all her strength across the door. He wouldn't take long to push it back, but it might give her time. Time for what, she didn't know.

She remembered the panic button. It came with the

alarm, a little round box with a red button that you could press if you thought something was going on that shouldn't be. Like the alarm itself, it connected directly to her local police station. Her alarms took priority over other people's (except, presumably, for the MP who lived in the next street, or the up-and-coming TV show host at number seventeen).

The box was on a cord that she was supposed to keep draped round her neck whenever she was in the flat. She'd done that for the first week or two after getting it; but slowly it had faded from consciousness, and in the end she'd shoved the whole thing in a drawer somewhere. Somewhere in here, she hoped, running frantically to the desk under the window.

As she pulled out the first drawer, she heard something behind her. She turned and saw that the door was being pushed hard against the sofa. Not a burglar, then, she thought. Not here to nick the family silver. She tipped the contents of the drawer wholesale on to the floor and watched despairingly as a bottle of ink unscrewed itself and covered the pink carpet with a slowly spreading pool of black.

The lake was a shifting mirror across whose surface the tall peaks all around were forever reflected. They left the jeep and strolled to the water's edge. She walked close to him, carrying a wicker box. Reeds fringed the edge of the lake like tiny flagpoles, swaying in the light breeze that came in across the water. A little further out, a fleet of blue-headed ducks moved at a leisurely pace across the lightly ruffled surface.

'It can be terrible here in winter,' said Nabila. 'Storms start up in the mountains, and the wind fights its way down here and tears the lake to shreds.'

She had brought tea in a flask, and a box of *biao* stuffed with mutton and onions. With quick fingers she unwrapped a slab of goat's cheese and laid it on a cloth upon the grass.

'It's best we eat a little now,' she said. 'Lunch is still a while away.'

She filled their tea-glasses with steaming black *chai* that she'd strained before putting it in the flask.

He took his cup and sat for a while in silence, waiting for it to cool, gazing out over the long expanse of the grey lake.

'Tell me about your wife,' Nabila said. 'There wasn't time the other night.'

'Is it important?' He took some bread and tore it in half.

'Yes,' she said.

'How important?'

'Very important,' she said. She wasn't looking at him. Her eyes were fixed on a small boat that floated far out on the lake.

He drank a little tea and ate a little of the bread, and wiped his lips, then told her about Elizabeth. He told her everything, he left out nothing important. She listened to him carefully, and without comment. A cormorant swooped low across the lake's surface, and darted suddenly into the blue water to seize a fish. It re-emerged, glistening, leaving a trail of sparkling water in the air as it flew back to the shore.

'What about children?' she asked. 'Do you have any?'

He didn't know what to say. 'Yes' and 'No' were both lies in their way, evasions at best. She did not press him. A cool wind came from the mountains, lifting her hair to one side. She caught it up with her right hand and pinned it back in place.

'I have a daughter called Maddie,' he said. And he went on to talk about a little girl with her hair tied in a blue ribbon. Every time he paused, he looked round at her, and he saw that she was looking directly at him, that all her attention was focused on him. And he told her what had happened to the little girl. That she'd grown up and gone to China, where she'd fallen in love. That her lover had been a student and a dissident called Zheng Juntao. And that one night the security forces had come for him and made him vanish as if he'd never been, and the little girl had not seen him since.

When he next looked, her gaze had turned from him and was fixed on the far shore of the lake.

'I had a son as well,' he said.

'Tell me,' she said. And her voice spun away across the lake's expanse until it was lost on the air.

A voice spoke to her through the crack of the open door. The sofa was heavy, but it was giving way inch by inch. She looked at the wall opposite the sofa. The bookcase she'd inherited from Uncle Simon stood against it, its upper half tilted by one or two inches outwards from the wall. She'd always meant to have it properly fastened. The case was tall and heavy and full of huge books, some hers, some relics of the late Simon Masters.

Mentally, she measured the width of the room against the height of the case. Much depended on how it chose to fall, but she reckoned it would span the gap almost perfectly.

'Miss Potter,' came the voice, a man's voice, very hard, very insistent. 'Please don't make this difficult. Please don't force us to break down the door.'

'Clear off,' she said. 'Nobody asked you to come here.'

'As a matter of fact, they did, Mrs P. This is out of your hands. Other people are making the big decisions. Now, please let us in and we'll get it over quick.'

Her answer was an extraordinary crash. She dreaded to think what the couple downstairs must think. With any luck they'd ring the police. The bookcase, glass shattered and contents thrown all over its insides, lay like a bridge between the sofa and the wall. Pauline stuck an old sewing machine in the little gap that remained, and reckoned she'd be safe for a bit longer.

She hurried back to the table and extracted the second drawer. She turned it upside down, and its contents bounced and skittered across the carpet. The panic button rolled beneath the television stand.

She snatched it up and pressed the button. There was no light to show whether the little box had sent its signal or not. She hoped the battery hadn't gone dead.

There was a crashing sound behind her. She looked round to see a great gash in the door, and an axe-head sticking through it. As the axe-head was drawn back, ready for another swing, the door-bell sounded.

Small flowers dotted the meadow, their red and blue and yellow petals bright in the late morning sunshine. She'd gone ahead of him a hundred yards or more, and every time he straightened he could see her slender figure, bent over the grass, and the basket in her hand. He would look at her for a while, and she would sense his eyes on her, and turn and wave, then bend again to her search.

He could not believe that he was in a flower-filled meadow and not sneezing. Her medicine had worked a miracle.

High up, an eagle lifted through currents of empty sky,

and turned, and drifted as if in a silent dance. He'd heard that the Kirghiz hunted with them, training them like falcons.

Just ahead of him he saw a cream-coloured flower. It was like a lotus, but larger.

'Nabila!' he called.

She looked round and saw him beckoning. She put down her basket and came across.

'Is this what you've been looking for?' he asked.

She bent down, nodding, then looked up at him, and smiled.

'Let me have your knife,' she said.

She didn't cut the flower at the stem, but dug it out carefully from the earth, exposing its roots. She held it up before him, its perfect whiteness like bone against the tanned skin of her hand.

'Well done,' she said. 'You've got very sharp eyes.'

He shook his head.

'Not really,' he said. 'I was just lucky. It was right in front of me – I couldn't have missed it.'

'Well, here it is anyway. It may be the only one we find today.'

She held it out to him, and he cupped his hands and let her drop the flower into them. He was astonished by how soft its petals felt. He looked into her eyes. There were tears in them.

He bent and put the flower gently in the basket. Then he straightened.

'Nabila,' he said.

She looked at him, but she did not move. He took a tentative step towards her, and reached for her hand, and held it in both of his. She smiled awkwardly.

'Tell me . . . what to do,' she said.

'It's all right,' he said. 'You don't need to worry.' But

his heart was beating behind his ribcage like an animal trying to tear free.

He reached out and wiped away the tears that had gathered on her cheeks. He did not ask what they were for. For him, perhaps, or for herself, he had no way of knowing. She'd tell him in the end, he wouldn't push.

'I love you,' he said. Words almost forgotten, like a phrase in a foreign language learned years ago and not used since. 'Do you understand?'

She nodded and said nothing.

'It's not because I'm here alone,' he said, 'not because I need a woman. There's nothing like that in it.'

'I know,' she said.

'If you tell me to leave, I'll go. I would understand. I know how difficult this is for you . . .'

He stopped talking as she reached up and put her hands behind his head, and drew his face close to hers, and kissed him, gently, then hard. And he pulled her close, her whole body touching his. She was like someone who has been asleep for months or years, and then woken to find the whole world changed. Drawing her head back, she looked at him and stroked his cheek.

'God forgive me,' she said, 'but I love you too.'

'What has God to forgive you for?' he asked.

'For being a woman. For being a Muslim woman in love with an unbeliever. If my father knew of it, he would kill me.'

'And do you truly love me?'

She put her lips against his and began to kiss him again. Not hastily as before, but softly and slowly now, and with real intention. The simple movement of her tongue in his mouth excited him more deeply than Elizabeth and her bedroom games had ever done. He put his hands behind her and sank slowly with her to the soft grass.

*　　*　　*

Wham! The axe tore away another chunk of door. She could already see the face of the man wielding it. *Crash!* The sharp blade tore into the wood as if it were straw.

She pressed the panic button several more times, then ran for the window. The sash rolled up without effort, and she looked down into the street, three storeys below.

'Don't even think about it, Miss Potter. You don't have the strength or the training. You'll just kill yourself.'

'What's the difference?' she shouted back as she stepped through the window.

He smashed down the rest of the door and started climbing through the gap. He was dressed from head to foot in black, and in one hand he held a semiautomatic pistol equipped with a silencer. The sofa got in his way, giving her time to move away from the open window. He was right about her not having the strength or training. Not in the sense he meant. But she worked out in her local gym most evenings. She went on long walks at weekends. The drainpipe didn't look too safe, but it was the only way down. She started her descent.

He sauntered across to the window, gun in hand. This was less tidy than he'd planned, but in the end it made no difference to him where she ended up. She was the last one they needed to eliminate, and after this he could have a little rest.

At the window, he stared down, trying to pick her out. A single bullet in the head would send her down into the area below. He'd be gone by the time anyone came to investigate. Her head came into view just to the left of the drainpipe. He admired her pluck. As he raised the gun, she looked up, right in his eyes. It didn't put him off, but it distracted him.

At that moment, a police car came screaming down the

street, its blue light flashing, and its siren competing with the party opposite. Faces appeared at several windows. He drew back inside the room, cursing his bad luck. How could she possibly have brought the police here in such a short time?

Behind him, the door-bell rang again. He removed his balaclava and opened the door. The downstairs neighbours were standing there, a gay couple, one middle-aged and paunchy, the other young and slim.

'Is Pauline all right?'

'We heard a crash.'

'And then all that banging.'

He brought the pistol round from behind his back and shot them, one shot each, in the forehead. As he stepped back to let the second one fall, he saw a policeman appear at the head of the stairs. Stepping across the bodies, he walked towards the policeman, gun in hand.

'Put the gun down,' ordered the policeman.

'I'm doing my job,' he said. 'If you'd just let me get on with it.'

The policeman was frightened. Well, he had a right to be. But he did his best to stay on top of it.

'You'll only make things worse. Believe me.'

'In my case, it couldn't be further from the truth.'

He pointed and fired in as much time as it took to say 'Bang'.

At the bottom of the stairs, he saw the second policeman running for the door. He let him go. After all, he hadn't seen his face.

Outside, partygoers had gathered to watch what was going on. Windows had been opened, letting loud music out into the street.

He checked the area, but she wasn't there. He shrugged

and slipped his pistol back into his pocket. She wouldn't get far. Where was there for her to go?

The frightened policeman was in his car frantically radioing for reinforcements. A red sports car moved away from the kerb opposite.

He walked to his motorbike, pulled it straight, and sped off in the opposite direction. What an absolute shambles, he thought. The traffic and the night swallowed him up.

They lay naked on the grass. He picked small flowers idly and strewed them across her breasts and belly.

'I love your body,' he said.

'Men are supposed to love women for their minds or their souls.'

He shook his head.

'That isn't true,' he said. 'It's just what women want to be true. When a woman has a body like yours, it's impossible to do anything but love it.'

'Were you loving my body just now, or loving me?'

'Oh, that? I was certainly enjoying your body. And I was loving you as well.'

She rolled closer to him and ran her fingers gently from his chest to his groin and up again.

'Just a moment,' he said. He reached for his jacket and fumbled in the pocket, then brought out a tiny object that caught the sun.

'Here,' he said. It was his wedding ring. 'Will you take this now? It meant nothing when I gave it to you before. Now it means everything.'

She held out her hand and he dropped it on to her palm.

'I can't wear it,' she said. 'Not on my finger.'

'That isn't important. I just want you to have it. And perhaps one day . . .'

She slipped the ring on her right hand, then moved across and straddled him, and put her fingers on his mouth.

'Just today,' she said. 'Not tomorrow or the day after tomorrow or the day after that. Just today.'

CHAPTER THIRTY-TWO

The East China Club
London

'What do you mean, she got away? How the hell could she get away? She was in London. She was in her flat. There was nowhere to get away to.'

Laurence Royle still looked the shining picture of urbanity he'd been at Sam's funeral, but his mood was a lot less detached. The Hyde business had him severely rattled.

Anthony Farrar shrugged.

'Nevertheless, she escaped. I don't know exactly how. I don't altogether care. All I got was some garbled excuse from the agency I paid to do the job. A total imbecile. Do you know, he actually succeeded in killing Potter's neighbours and a policeman? God knows how we're ever going to hush it all up. It's a bloody nuisance.'

'It could be more than a nuisance if the police make a thing of it.'

'Laurence, will you please trust me on this? I've been doing this sort of thing for years. A clear-up operation involves cut-out mechanisms. None of the people we used has the remotest connection to Six or special services.'

Royle scratched one side of his nose gently. A lot hinged on keeping this business under wraps.

In exchange for the weapons technology and parts that

his company had been able to smuggle to the Chinese, they'd been offered near-exclusivity for oil rights in the Tarim Basin. By 2010 it would make Aladdin the number one oil firm in the world. And he was nearly certain the Iraqis would play ball as well. If Saddam got his weapon and it did what he wanted it to, there was nothing he wouldn't do for those responsible.

The beauty of it was, of course, that no one would ever be able to link Aladdin Oil to Royle International, or Royle International to Pacific Arms, or Pacific Arms to Anthony Farrar. Yes, he thought, that really was the beauty of it. On the other hand, that triple-dyed bastard Matthew Hyde had managed to get wind of the scheme, and had succeeded in getting word out in the most bizarre manner possible.

'Who got into Carstairs, Anthony? It wasn't some local lad chancing his arm. I've run a few ops in my time. Not just army ops, Anthony. The real world. Carstairs was impregnable. If somebody got in there, they were insiders. That's too close for comfort.'

'That's not quite how it's being interpreted by Security. You may not know it, but Carstairs had another guest that night. A man called Abd al-Reza Khodadust. Iranian. Head of a terrorist ring with branches throughout Europe. The French were particularly keen to get their hands on him. Something about those Métro bombings. Anyway, that's unlikely now. Mr Khodadust is a free man. I believe he's already back in Tehran celebrating his release.'

'Are you telling me the towel-heads had the expertise to break into a place like Carstairs?'

Farrar shook his head like a teacher resignedly working his way through a lesson with a dull child.

'I doubt it. Mr Khodadust owes his freedom to an ex-SAS team known as System 11. They went in and out like a dose of salts, and the only thing they brought in and left behind was half a page torn from a Koran.'

'I hope you're right. You guarantee the boy is dead? Your little gang took care of everything?'

Farrar coughed. He had long, well-groomed fingernails that he drummed lightly on the arms of his chair. He knew the sound irritated Laurence.

'I guarantee it. His parents. And Mr and Mrs "Have you ever been to Wales?" Hughes. Every trace has been wiped out.'

'Except this woman.'

'She won't last long. She was never a field agent. After all, where can she go? She'll try to return to the fold, cosy up to our security people. Once she does that, she'll be history.'

'You sound like a banal Yank film, Anthony.'

'Do I?' He was tempted to call Royle a pompous twat, but thought better of it, as he'd thought better of it ten thousand times in the past.

Royle reached for the enormous globe of brandy he'd insisted on having brought up. Farrar considered it vulgar and pretentious, like most things associated with Royle. Royle was a showman, and the last person in the world Farrar would normally want to be seen associating with. Even after four generations, the Royles were still trade. Wealthy trade, sophisticated trade, but they hadn't managed to throw off that grubby taint of the self-made man.

But he put up with it because he had to put up with Royle. Without Royle, his reward for smoothing things with the Chinese would amount to very little. One or two million at the most. But their agreement – signed by them both and locked in a very solid safe at the back of a very big vault in a Swiss bank – guaranteed him more money than he'd ever wished for. Once that was in his hands, he could take a fresh look at his relations with Royle's little sister.

'I was upset by what happened to young Sam.' Royle put his nose into the glass and made a show of relishing its contents.

'Yes, I regretted that too.'

'Don't those Chinese know what they're doing? It wasn't your SAS lads again was it? What did you call them? System 11?'

'Most of the time they're very good. How on earth they got their wires crossed on this one, I honestly couldn't tell you.'

'He was my favourite nephew, in a way. I could have done without that.'

They were in a private room at the club they shared. It was a room Royle used frequently. Oak walls, oak furniture, any number of culinary delights preserved in oak. His brandy had spent most of its life in a barrel. Sometimes Royle felt like a culinary delight himself, well preserved and smelling of old wood. He would be fifty-five next week, almost the same age as Farrar. His entire life had been spent building up the family business, then finding a niche for himself in politics.

He knew he had not been terribly well liked at the House, but it hadn't bothered him. The party's defeat in '97 had left him without a seat or much hope of finding another one, but by then he'd been thinking of turning it all in anyway. Politics, he'd decided, was a game for wankers. The new anti-corruption climate made it even more so. He was a businessman at heart, and he'd got about as far as he'd ever get with his political connections. If the Chinese thing came off, he'd have all the connections he could ever need and all the money he could ever spend.

'How's Lizzie?' he asked. Just being friendly. All part

of the game. In reality, he couldn't have cared less how his tight-sphinctered little sister was.

'Well enough. I've been talking to her about her drinking. With David gone and Sam dead, I want to keep her occupied. She says she wants to take a more active part in the firm . . .'

'We've been through this already, Anthony. Lizzie's a bit of a loose cannon. I mean, we keep her on the board because she has a right to be there, but honestly, it's only on condition she keeps away from everything but the AGM.'

'I know that. But things have changed. The reason she drinks is because she has nothing else to do. She's an intelligent woman, Laurence, probably more intelligent than any of you give her credit for. Let her sit in on a few board meetings. Give her responsibility for some project or other. She can't do any harm, believe me.'

'What's this about? I hope to God you haven't let her in on the Karakhoto Project, Farrar . . .'

'Do you really think I'd do that?'

'Sometimes I'm not sure.'

'I keep my mouth shut, Laurence. It's my business, remember. I was trained in how to keep a secret. I've spent my life keeping them. And Karakhoto represents all I've ever worked for.'

'And you think Lizzie's capable of doing more than just sitting on her beautiful backside looking regal?'

'I think you have a lot to learn about your sister, Laurence. Give her a go, if only for my sake. I actually think it'll help the drink problem.'

'Very well. I'll sound out the other directors. But the first hint of going off the rails . . .' He downed a mouthful of brandy in a single, practised motion. It seemed to mellow him as it coursed through the tubes and channels of his inner self.

'There won't be any hints. I promise you.'

'What about David?' Royle started the brandy process again. Farrar sipped meditatively on a very old Scotch in a very fine crystal glass. No soda, no water, just the simple amber liquid.

'I'm sorry?'

'You know perfectly well. My brother-in-law. I believe he packed himself off to Chinky-land.'

'The Chinese call it *Zhongguo*, the Middle Land.'

'Didn't know that. Clever buggers, the Chinkies. I sometimes think . . .'

'Yes?'

'If there is a God, he'd be Chinese. Slitty eyes, yellow skin, the lot.'

'Odd thing for you to say.'

'Yes. But I do sometimes think that. The Royles owe a lot to the Chinkies. We've been dealing with them for four generations now, us and the Morrises.'

The Morrises were a family related to the Royles who'd been brought into the business forty or fifty years earlier. A marriage of convenience had brought some very useful Pacific markets within the sphere of Royle International.

'You didn't know that, did you, Anthony?'

'Four generations? I'd guessed it must be about that.'

'My great-grandfather, Thomas Royle. Got his portrait in the library. Dull bit of work. He was a Shanghai trader from soon after the place got opened up. Didn't have two pennies to his name when he started. Well, who has? He got it all going, then my grandfather took over. He was the one who knocked it all into shape. Phased out the opium, started a proper import–export routine. Very jolly. He went into Hong Kong at the first chance, which helped when Mr Mao and his chums came on the scene.'

'I'm sure it did.'

'Did, absolutely, that and getting the main show back to London. But, then, you'd know all about it, wouldn't you? An old China hand like yourself.'

'A little. Nothing to what you've got locked up in your little black boxes back in head office.'

'Like to get your hands on those, would you?'

'Naturally. My guess is you've got more in there about the Chinese Communist Party than we've got in London and Washington combined.'

'Forget it, old boy. They're just boring trading records. You'd find them frightfully dull.'

'I'd take the risk.'

Royle shook his head.

'Not on, old son. I don't have the authority. Trade secrets – there'd be hell to pay if the board heard of it.'

'Laurence, I take it your black boxes don't contain any information about Karakhoto? I mean, I wouldn't like to think that some clerk or other might just stumble across your notes.'

Royle looked suitably horrified.

'Good Lord, you don't think I'd be such a fool as to leave something like that lying around where any Tom, Dick or Harry could lay his mitts on it? I keep my notes and things where I can find them, and nobody else.' He looked round. 'It's a touch chilly, don't you think?'

Farrar shrugged.

'Hard to say . . .'

'Anthony, I rather got sidetracked there. I was asking about our mutual friend David Laing. He is in Chinky-land, isn't he?'

'If you insist.'

'Well, as a matter of fact, I *do* insist. You would, in my position.'

'The answer is, Yes, he is. I'm very well aware of the fact.'

'And do you intend doing anything about it?'

'I've lost track of him. He was in Urumchi, now he could be almost anywhere.'

'Didn't he have a contact, for God's sake?'

Farrar nodded.

'He did. But the file with all the details has been removed.'

Royle's hand thumped the table, almost knocking his brandy glass over.

'Who the hell would do that?'

'There's only one person who could. Pimpernel Potter.'

'Oh, for God's sake. This is a shambles. You're supposed to be a professional. Can't you do anything?'

'Perhaps. My worry is that Potter may have made contact with him, alerted him to certain . . . irregularities back here. I'm planning to send a very discreet message to our old friend Colonel Chang Zhangyi. He'll get a description of David and details of any names he may be using.'

'What are you going to tell him David's out there for?'

'To bring financial and military aid to the Sinkiang rebels. It's something very close to Chang Zhangyi's heart. He'll be only too delighted to provide help.'

'And the boy? Are you planning to mention him?'

'No, I rather thought that might be indiscreet. I want this whole Hyde business buried. The last thing I want is for Chang Zhangyi to get wind of the fact that London has a lead on the Karakhoto Project.'

'Can he find Laing?'

'Chang Zhangyi? Good God, yes. He's never let me down yet. Chang Zhangyi could find a single brick in the Great Wall if you asked him to. David Laing is as good as dead.'

245

CHAPTER THIRTY-THREE

Sinkiang Province
Western China

On the journey back, everything seemed changed. The road, the rocks, even the bleak and isolated checkpoint at Ghez all looked different, as though a world had ended, and they were driving back through another one that had taken its place. They spoke very little, but from time to time they would look at one another before turning back to the road. It had grown oppressively hot.

'We only found that one Snow Lotus,' said Nabila. 'You were very observant.'

David changed gear. 'Just lucky. Till today, I thought luck had deserted me.'

'So, you think finding me was like finding a Snow Lotus, a matter of luck?'

'Not luck exactly, but . . .'

'Watch out for that pothole.' They swerved. 'I don't believe in chance,' she said. 'I believe God writes our fates. I believe my meeting you was destined. Don't you feel that?'

'I think my whole life was just a preparation for it, but I don't think it was written down.'

'You don't believe in God?'

'Not like you, no. Aren't you afraid God will be angry with you for making love to me?'

'Perhaps. My father would be even angrier if he knew.' She turned her face to him. 'David, you must be careful. If my father wanted you killed, he could do it at the snap of a finger.'

It was a sombre thought, and one that briefly over-clouded them. But not even the threat of an angry *ahun* could spoil what they had found. As they came within sight of the outskirts of Kashgar, David drew the jeep in to the side of the road and kissed her. It was a long kiss, and both knew it might be their last for some time.

'I want to go to the hospital,' said Nabila as they drove off again. 'I'd like to leave what we've collected in the dispensary with Dr Khalla. And I want to give you some more medicine. And – oh, yes – I'd like to introduce you to other members of staff.'

Seeing the look of alarm on his face, she put a hand out and stroked his cheek.

'Don't worry,' she said. 'Just a general chat, then I'll whisk you off.'

'Is it really necessary?'

'We can't have you drifting in and out of the hospital like a ghost, can we?'

Little concrete houses began to congregate on both sides of the road. They'd been thrown up in the sixties and seventies to provide cheap housing, in the process building a cordon of misery around the medieval city.

'Home,' Nabila said.

'How quaint.'

'Have you noticed something, David?'

'I'm driving beside the most beautiful woman in the world.'

'No, look again.'

He looked round and caught sight of a PLA jeep parked

on a corner. In it, two tired-looking soldiers were surveying the cheerless landscape and eating noodles.

'Army,' David said.

'Observant of you. The point is, they usually keep off the street in Kashgar. There are fewer Chinese here than anywhere else in Sinkiang. Something's going on.'

Ten minutes later, they were walking through the front door of the hospital. The calm orderliness that had characterized the place the day before had gone, to be replaced by bustle bordering on controlled panic. White-coated members of staff were hurrying up and down the corridors, bumping into one another or weaving more skilfully past. Patients stood about in clusters outside their ward doors, talking animatedly, or hovered at the edges alone, as though waiting for some sort of doom to descend.

Nabila made several attempts to grab hold of passing colleagues, but each time she was brushed aside, not always gently. Then she saw someone she knew well disappearing down a side corridor, towards the children's ward.

'Elyashar!' she called out, pitching her voice to reach him above the hubbub. He hesitated, looking round, then caught sight of her and ran to where she was standing.

Elyashar was a thin, bearded man in his early forties, a head or two taller than David. Little spectacles twinkled on a thin nose that he scratched repeatedly. Two tufts of hair that could not be controlled stuck out at either temple, and his eyebrows seemed to be leaping off his head in terror.

'Nabila – where on earth have you been? I've been looking for you since twelve o'clock. You were supposed to do a paediatric clinic for Dr Salan.'

'I left a message about that. Didn't you get it? I went out to Karakul. We were looking for Snow Lotuses.'

'We?'

She introduced him to David.

'Elyashar Mehmeduli, the hospital taskmaster. Elyashar, this is Dr Ruzi Osmanop, from Alma-Ata. He's come to look at some of our work on the anti-depressant properties of Hypericum.'

They shook hands, then Elyashar turned back to Nabila.

'Your message is probably still waiting on my desk. There's been a bit of a panic on for the past few hours.'

'So I can see. What's up?'

Elyashar realized they were trying to make themselves heard over an impossible din.

'The paediatric records office is just down here,' he said. 'Why don't we go there?'

Squeezing past a group of patients dressed in thin towelling robes – lime green, pink, powder blue, and white – they found a door bearing the one word 'Records'.

Inside, it was stifling hot, but mercifully quiet. In front of them stood a long desk, and behind it row upon row of steel filing cabinets.

'What's going on?' asked Nabila again, the moment the door was closed.

'You mean, you don't know?' Elyashar looked genuinely surprised.

'I told you, we were out at Karakul. That's where we got these plants – which will have to be put in the refrigerator soon if we want to keep them.'

'Sorry, I forgot. Everything's in such a muddle. Look, the authorities announced fresh restrictions just before twelve o'clock, three –' He glanced at his watch. 'Yes, three hours ago. There's to be a curfew in Kashgar from eight o'clock tonight. What's worse, no one's to go out of the city. After seven, nobody gets in either.'

'What? No one?'

Elyashar nodded glumly.

'That's not all. The airport's been closed until further notice. All travel south of the Taklamakan has been banned. Any foreigners in Kashgar or any of the oasis towns to the east have to travel direct to Urumchi tonight.'

'Why all this panic in the hospital?' asked David.

'That all started about an hour ago. We're trying to cool it down. A rumour got out that there was going to be a repeat of the massacre in Urumchi. Somebody said Colonel Chang was in charge of the operation. Somebody else said there'd been wind of an insurrection.'

'How would that affect the hospital?' Nabila asked.

'After the shootings in Urumchi, the hospitals were filled up. A lot of the ordinary patients were thrown out to make room for the injured.'

'I didn't know there were any survivors,' said David.

'My sources say there were. Not many, but enough to cause chaos for a while. Of course, if it happened here, this isn't the hospital they'd head for. They'd use the People's Hospital up the road. But try telling that to this lot.'

'This insurrection business,' Nabila butted in. 'How reliable is that?'

Elyashar shrugged.

'I thought you'd know that better than me, Nabila. If there's going to be one, your father's likely to be at the head of it.'

'Don't go saying things like that too loudly, Elyashar. It's dangerous talk. But I'll have a word with my father, see what he knows.'

They passed into the corridor again, and were again confronted with a gaggle of anxious patients. Elyashar hurried off to the meeting he was due to attend.

'Let's dump these in the dispensary quickly,' Nabila said, 'then let's clear out of here.'

The plants were taken off to a refrigerated vault some-where. Just as the assistant was about to take them away, Nabila leaned over and took something from the nearest basket. It was the Snow Lotus.

'I think I'll hold on to this,' she said, glancing shyly at David. She slipped the lotus into a pocket, then turned to another assistant, and ordered a bottle made up from herbal decoctions.

'Here,' she said when it was ready. 'This is for you.'

'But it tastes awful.'

'You've been out in the country today. How many times have you sneezed?'

'Three, I think, but . . .'

'How many times do you normally sneeze?'

'More than that, I suppose. I don't mind sneezing, really. This stuff is absolutely foul.' All thought of miracles had vanished when brought face to face with the medicine bottle.

The assistants had all gone to the back to unpack the plants.

'David, you may be big, you may be virile, you may have the looks of Adonis and the organ of a stallion, but underneath you're just a little boy.'

'All men are little boys at heart. It's no reason to criti-cize them.'

'You can't protect me as long as you're a little boy. You can't love me as long as you're a little boy. What's more, until you start taking your medicine every day, you can forget about my gorgeous female body and its myriad delights.'

He smiled and swallowed the draught, and they started to leave. Then David turned back to her.

'Nabila, is there anything that might help Maddie? Some herb, some root?'

Nabila frowned.

'From what you've told me, it isn't that easy. I'd really need to see her, take her pulses, and so on. But we can talk about her case, and I'll do my best to prescribe something.'

Nabila wanted to find a pony cart and go straight to her father's house. Elyashar had been right: if anyone knew about a threatened uprising, it would be Sheikh Azad.

They headed down to the Chini Bagh, where cart drivers often collected. A couple were parked near the entrance. Further along, a large Pakistani bus was being loaded. The passengers, mostly Pakistani men who'd been staying in the hotel, were standing around, sending luggage up to the roof rack, eating kebabs, or just idling until the journey started. They didn't seem in the least concerned at being sent out of Kashgar so arbitrarily.

A few yards away stood another group intending to board the bus. Five men and four women, all Western backpackers who had, presumably, been travelling the Silk Road. Kashgar was a famous spot to hang out.

David went up close and overheard some Australian accents. Then, out of the blue, a young man spoke in a broad Scottish accent, saying they might all be faster hiring some donkey carts.

The idea came into David's head ready formed. Something about the closure of Kashgar had made him feel fenced in. The letter for Maddie was still in his pocket. He couldn't send it from anywhere in Sinkiang. But what if . . . ?

'Can I please have a word with you?' he asked the Scot. He spoke in English, but with an accent straight out of the bazaars of Central Asia.

'Fuck off,' said the backpacker.

'Please – I like to ask you something.'

'Ah've changed all the money Ah need. So fuck on off.'

David wanted to hit him, but thought better of it and merely shook his head.

'Not change money,' he said. 'Pay you money.'

The Scotsman looked him up and down with thinly disguised disgust.

'If you're talkin' aboot what Ah think you're talkin' aboot, ye can gae fuck yoursel' twice, ye wee shite.'

The temptation to knock the youth insensate grew hard to resist. The unnamed Scottish rover looked as though he'd been on the road a long time and collected most of it on himself. He also seemed to have spent a long time with camels of the smelliest variety. A sweet nature would have compensated a lot.

David was about to try again when Nabila appeared from the side.

'Having trouble, Ruzi?'

'Not me,' he said. 'Our friend here.'

'Ah'm no' havin' trouble, missis, but yir boyfrien' here's in big trouble if he disnae fuck on off.'

Nabila stepped up to the traveller and stared him straight in the eyes. Then, whipping one hand between his legs, she grabbed his balls in a potentially agonizing grip.

'Listen,' she said, 'if you don't want me to squeeze these to a pulp. He does not want to fuck you, believe me; he does not want to sell you drugs or change your money. All he wants is to pay you to do him a small favour. Now, go over there and talk to him about it politely.'

'And if Ah don't?' The threat to his testicles notwithstanding, the stout representative of Scottish manhood was unwilling to shift his ground.

'Let me tell you,' Nabila went on. 'The bus will leave with all your things on board. You will stay behind.

You will never leave Kashgar. Believe me, that is the truth.'

Something in her voice, something in her face made a light come on in his eyes.

'Aye, maybe so, likes. All right. If you'd kindly take yir han' off ma privates. Thank you. Not that Ah havnae enjoyed the wee stroke tremendously.'

He looked round with a surly expression at David and nodded towards an empty area near the hotel entrance. Further down, armed soldiers were observing the loading of the Pakistan-bound bus.

'Where you going now?' asked David.

'Where the fuck d'ye think? Karachi. You want tae come along? Is that it? Is that the wee favour?'

David shook his head.

'I stay here. But I have letter I like posted. You stay in Karachi?'

The Scot shook his head.

'Fuck Karachi. Ye cannae even find decent booze. Ah've been on the road too bloody long anyway. It's all fucked, ken. India's fucked, China's fucked. Even the hash is crap. Ah'm takin' the first plane oot tae London. Then it's straight up the M1 for me.'

David's eyes lit up.

'Take this,' he said, shoving a substantial bundle of Renminbi in the Scot's direction. An initial reluctance to take Chinese currency was checked as he noticed just how much there was. Even at an unfavourable rate, he'd still come out on top.

'A letter, eh?'

'In London. First-class stamp. You have to buy that yourself.'

'How d'ye know Ah willnae dump the whole thing oot the windae?'

'You will lose more money.'

David held out the letter, which was still unsealed, and took a pen from his pocket. 'Fifty pounds for you if you see it posted or delivered. If you give me name and address . . .'

For a moment the dusty Scot looked at David as though he'd just been thumped. Finally it sank in. So many Renminbi now, so many pounds on safe arrival of the letter. He dictated his name, Calum Kilbride, and an address in Edinburgh, and saw them written down and sealed into the envelope.

There was a shout from the bus. The passengers had started to climb on board. Five o'clock wasn't far off.

David handed the letter over.

'It is important,' he said. 'For somebody important.'

'Ah make no promises, but Ah'll do ma best.'

David watched him go, and for some reason he believed him.

CHAPTER THIRTY-FOUR

London

He walked back through discontented streets, lulled by the sound of so many human voices in a stir. London pleased and tormented him. It had such a range of vices to offer the lonely and the unsure, and sometimes the thought that so much was available here worked in his veins like a drug. He'd tried almost everything at one time or another, from sex to gambling to mind-altering substances. Tonight he wanted something more, something out of the ordinary.

He headed down to Chinatown, round Gerrard Street. The restaurants were still clattering and chattering away, each one filled with its gaggle of tourists and a sprinkling of London Chinese. He was not known here, and he enjoyed just walking about, catching snatches of rapidly spoken Mandarin or Cantonese, half-pretending to himself he was back in Shanghai or Peking.

He cut off down a back lane, and from it to another, until he was deep inside a little maze running between back doors and kitchen windows. Huge bins stood everywhere, waiting to be filled and picked up later in the morning by trucks. A grey cat scampered away, surprised with its head inside a rubbish bin.

The door was on his right, where he remembered it:

a black door without number or name. He rang a bell up high by the lintel and waited. Minutes passed. He knew they had a camera, very well concealed. They were checking him, then the alley.

A man's voice came from a hidden grille.

'*Shei?*'

He gave his name.

'Wait there.'

Another minute.

The door opened and a small Chinese woman dressed in black beamed at him.

'*Fah-la Shiansheng, ni hai huozhe?*'

He laughed and bent to kiss her on both cheeks.

'Yes, still alive. Has it been that long?'

'Not so long. But when you not get in touch, old friends . . .'

'I'm sorry, I've been terribly busy.'

'No excuse. Come inside, can't leave door open.'

He followed along a short corridor, then up a steep flight of steps. It was so familiar, he could have taken every step blindfolded. If he remembered rightly, that's what they had done to him the first time. Later, they'd discovered who he was, and that he'd let them stay in business. From then on he could have entered almost any room on the premises. He paid well, too, better than most of their clients. It guaranteed him the best of everything. After all, as he often said, what was the point of coming to a place like this if you couldn't have the best?

'Is anyone else using the place tonight?' he asked. He knew there were others, of course. But it was polite to ask.

'You not worry, Mista Fah-la. All taken care of. You got place to you self.'

He knew what that meant. Whoever else was here

would be hurried along. There was time. There were enough rooms.

'Have you anything special for me, Zhou Furen?'

Her mouth opened, exposing rows of diamond-capped teeth. She'd make an expensive corpse, thought Farrar. Or a toothless one.

'She come yesterday, Mista Fah-la. You never see one so beautiful. Take you breath away.'

'You always say that, Madame Zhou.'

She looked at him quickly, almost sternly.

'No,' she said, and her voice was no longer bantering. 'This one make you want to live for ever. Or maybe die.'

'What age?'

'Not so old. Sixteen, maybe. Little breasts like small *minzu gua*.'

'Still a virgin?'

'Of course. We make sure of that.'

'And properly trained?'

'As much as you could wish, Fah-la Shiansheng.'

Her girls were trained from about the age of eight in music, poetry, the *I Ching*, deportment, conversation, and other elementary arts. At the age of sixteen, the most attractive were taken to the house in Guangzhou for four months, during which time they were introduced to a wide range of sexual and sensory experiences. They learned every possible way to pleasure a man short of intercourse – for it was vital that they remain virgins until they met their first clients – and how to receive pleasure in the same way.

'Then let me see her. I warn you, I'm very tense tonight. My mind is wandering. My thoughts are in China. I can't rest. I need something to restore my serenity. Do you understand? I won't have her if she isn't as you say. I'll

258

settle for something else. Don't promise me perfection if you can't provide it.'

She smiled.

'Believe me,' she said. She spoke in Chinese now, knowing he would follow suit, knowing it would be easier for the girl, who spoke no English. 'Believe me.'

He followed her down a corridor to more stairs, and climbed with her to the next floor. He'd been here before, perhaps nineteen times in his life. It wasn't very often when you came to think about it. But that did not matter. The Hui Hou did not much like their clients to come more often than that. A single day in one of their lotus houses was meant to resonate in a man's memory for months, even years afterwards. If all a man wanted was simple satiation of the flesh, he would generally be directed to one of their blue houses, the well-known *hong fangzi*. These latter were brothels of good quality, no more. For many men, they were all that was required. The girls were attractive and well looked after, the surroundings comfortable.

The lotus houses, on the other hand, were not brothels. There were seven of them, one each in Hong Kong, Tokyo, Paris, London, Cairo, New York, and Los Angeles. Clients were known to fly thousands of miles to their nearest house. Entry was by invitation only. The lotus houses appeared in no handbooks or directories. The cost alone meant that they were open to only a very small elite. But not even money could guarantee entry. Large numbers of extremely wealthy men had been turned down. One or two had tried to use muscle to get in: each had been found strangled the next morning. The Hui Hou brooked no form of defiance.

Anthony Farrar had always paid in coin and in kind. His protection had saved the London house from discovery and closure many times. And more than once he'd alerted the Hui Hou to threats to their trade routes. Getting the girls out of China was their biggest headache.

Coming to the second floor always took his breath away. It was not just that it was luxurious. He could have found that in any top-grade hotel. But this was harmonious. The rooms and their contents had been laid out according to the rules of Feng Shui, with one aim in mind: to produce inner peace, harmony, and refinement of the senses.

Madame Zhou showed him to a small antechamber.

'Wait here,' she said. 'I have to make the rooms ready. Master Lu will be with you presently.'

She went out, bowing low, as she had been trained to do sixty years ago. He was left behind in silence. With a deep sigh, he sat down on a low lacquered stool. Alone, he felt the pressure fall on him like an axe. He slumped on the stool, head in hands, sunk in a confusion of dark thoughts. The meeting with Royle had depressed him. He knew David Laing in many ways better than he knew Elizabeth. David was the smartest field agent ever to set foot in western China. He was dangerous, and he could turn the Karakhoto scheme upside down if he was allowed to.

He felt drained. It was at such times that he came here, in search of replenishment. But tonight, for the first time, he could not be sure of being brought back to life. He was too grey, too tired, under too much pressure.

The room had eight walls, a perfect octagon. It had been painted black and furnished with the utmost simplicity. He got up and went to the wall behind him. It opened to reveal a small wardrobe. He removed his clothes and folded them carefully on boards from which they would later be taken to be cleaned and pressed.

From a board at the top he took down a silk robe, an antique from the middle Ching Dynasty, black silk embroidered in black. The same motif was repeated in various sizes across front and back: the circle of *yin* and *yang*, male and female, day and night. He tied the slender waist-cord and returned to the seat.

Facing him was a long calligraphic scroll, white paper painted with jet-black letters, the brushmarks bold and precise. The quotation was from the 'Analects': 'The Master spoke of the Shao music. It was, he said, perfectly beautiful in form and perfectly good in its influence.'

He sat and meditated on the words. All the time, his thoughts came back to the girl. Would she truly take his breath away? he wondered.

The door opened without a sound, and the Master Lu entered. He knelt in one corner and unwrapped the *ch'in*, a long, zither-like instrument in whose art he was a master. Anthony observed him closely. In all the years he had been coming here, the Master seemed never to have changed. They had never addressed a single word to one another, though Farrar had numerous questions he wanted to put to him. It was reputed that, within the narrow circle of scholar-musicians who played the *ch'in*, Master Lu was undisputedly supreme. Farrar had also heard it rumoured that the salary he received from the Hui Hou was several times that of a well-known film star who had been turned down more than once for entry to the lotus house in Los Angeles.

It was well known that the Hui Hou treated their servants well. In return they demanded nothing less than absolute devotion, absolute loyalty. While they lived, they and their families received all they needed, according to their status. If they broke their vows of allegiance, the penalty was swift and condign. The Hui Hou made grim use of the ancient punishment known as *mie jiuzu*: not only would the traitor be painfully killed, but his family to the ninth degree, and his friends, his teachers, his students, his pets.

Of the thirteen living masters of the *ch'in*, seven lived in the lotus houses of the Hui Hou. They seldom played anywhere else, unless one of the ruling circle asked them to perform for them, or for a specially invited guest.

Without preamble, Master Lu began to play in the pitch of the Ming Dynasty. Farrar sat still, blotting out from his mind everything but the gentle, dulcimer-like tones of the instrument. He lost track of time. In the lotus houses of the Hui Hou, time was of no importance.

CHAPTER THIRTY-FIVE

Cadogan Place
London

'What a surprise. And what has wafted you so fragrantly to my door, Laurence?'

'You might let me in, Lizzie. I've walked bloody miles to get here.'

'Weren't there any taxis?'

'At this time of night?'

She peered out into the dark street.

'Where's Anthony?'

He looked surprised.

'I thought he was here with you. He's been gone long enough.'

'I thought he was out boozing with you. Oh, come on in, for God's sake.'

They went to the living room. A cigarette still burned on a marble ashtray set on an enormous coffee table in the shape of an upturned hand. Near it stood an almost-empty glass and, on top of the Chinese drinks cabinet, an odd-looking bottle.

'What the hell's that?' asked Laurence, nodding in the direction of the bottle.

'Marc de Bourgogne, of course. Freddie brings it back with him. You know Freddie, don't you, dear?'

He flung himself down on a sofa. Over the years he'd only been here before with Farrar, and found it odd to be in the room with his sister. Freddie Poole was an old friend of their father's, a doddering old roué who kept a crumbling house in Burgundy, complete with a French mistress of about the same age. She wore amazingly scarlet lipstick and tight skirts, and it was said she'd been a chanteuse in Paris before the War.

'I most certainly do. He's a bloody fool. And you're a bloody fool to drink that stuff. It must be a hundred and twenty per cent at least.'

'That's why I drink it. Do you have any idea how pure this is?'

'No, I don't.'

'Like a virgin's inner tubing.' She sat down in a Mackintosh chair opposite him. It was her favourite chair. It wasn't just an original. It was *the* original.

'Not something you'd know much about.' He paused. Sometimes banter like this could go on for hours. 'As a matter of fact,' he said, 'I did see Anthony tonight. We had dinner at the East China.'

'Yes, I rather thought that was it. And how did you boys get on? You weren't nasty to one another, were you?'

'Not in the least. Why would you think that? Fact is, we got on awfully well. Anthony was in good form. Pity they won't let women into the club: you'd have enjoyed the meal.'

'I doubt it. And, speaking of Anthony, where the hell is the bastard?'

'Not sure, really. I rather thought he'd headed on home. He'll be back soon, I imagine.'

'Probably gone off to some whorehouse. He does that from time to time, you know. You do know that, don't you?'

The Marc de Bourgogne had trickled down all her little red lanes a bit too fast.

'Lizzie, I'd rather not know about Anthony's peccadilloes.'

'Don't see why not, he's got enough of them. He'll pick up a peccadillo at the least opportunity. He hasn't fucked me in days, but he's happy enough to put his pecker in a pickled peccadillo.'

She stepped to the table and picked up her glass.

'For God's sake, Lizzie, put down the bloody glass. If anyone's pickled round here, you are. I want to have a proper conversation with you. There are some serious things we have to talk about.'

'Really?' Her hand hovered near the glass, then drifted away, and she resumed her seat. The tall back made her appear regal, or so she thought.

He told her about his conversation with Anthony, how he had been urged to put her back on the board and give her some real work to do. Laurence was not altogether a fool. He knew his sister had abilities that were seriously under-used, and he knew that, if she made a fuss about it, she was legally entitled to use her seat on the board. Royle International was still a family firm, and it was Laurence's intention that it stay that way.

She listened with only half her mind. She'd expected the conversation, but not quite so soon. Anthony must have done his work well.

'But you have to agree to go easy on the sauce. I mean it, Lizzie. They won't stand for it.'

'Who won't stand for it?'

'The board. You know perfectly well. You're not popular, Lizzie. If you want to impress them, you have to turn up sober and stay sober all day. If you're given responsibilities, you'll carry them out, and you won't let Anthony's peccadilloes or your own peccadilloes get in your way.'

'You know, Laurence, I never did like your lecturing. You got in a year or two ahead of me, and you've never stopped rubbing it in my face since. I'm a big girl now. I can handle my sex-life and my drink-life and my drug-life, without any help from anybody.'

She stood and made for the table. Her hand went to the glass. No more hesitation. She was in control.

'I'm not preaching, Lizzie. I just want this to work out for you. You don't always handle things that smartly. Maddie, for one thing.'

'What the precise fuck do you mean?'

She lifted the glass and downed a mouthful of the spirit without flinching. He watched her and said nothing.

'I mean, if you think there's something wrong with Maddie, why don't you come out and say it? Maddie's fine, she's over her trouble. Rose got her over it.'

'Calm down, Lizzie. I'm not accusing you of anything. Forget I said anything.'

'No, you did say something. You said I didn't handle things too smartly. Maddie for one. That's what you said.'

Laurence sighed. He was having very serious doubts about bringing Lizzie back. But he made allowances for the fact that she'd been left alone all night, and that Anthony still hadn't made an appearance by the early hours of the morning.

'Anthony told me about this recent problem. I asked him why Maddie hadn't been at Sam's funeral, and he was very honest with me.'

'Was he?'

'He's actually quite concerned for the girl. He says she's back with that man Rose.'

'As a matter of fact, yes. He's not a bad man, Rose. His prices are a bit steep, but they say he's the business. Maddie signed herself in.'

'Anthony said it might have been because of you leaving David. You think that could be true?'

'How should I know? I saw her a few nights ago. She was fine. I expect she'll be out in a day or two. Bugger all wrong with her, really.'

She took the bottle and filled her glass again.

'Sure you don't want some of this, Laurie? It's first class.'

He shook his head.

'No, thanks. I've got to get home.'

'I'd drive you over, only I've got to hang on for Anthony. He can't be much longer. Even the best whore couldn't keep him on the boil indefinitely. Actually, he comes quite quickly, you know. Too bloody quick for me, I can tell you. What about you, Laurie? How long's it take you?'

Laurence got to his feet.

'Where's your car, Lizzie?'

'The Merc? God knows. No, He doesn't. It's at the front. Why?'

'Give us the keys like a love. I'll have somebody bring it round in the morning.'

'They're over there,' she said. 'In the fruit dish.'

He fished them out and thanked her. There was a stillness between them. He hated Elizabeth, but he was sorry for her too, sorry for all her unhappiness. And Sam's death had unhinged her a little. Maybe Anthony was right. She needed responsibility, and she needed to get out and see people.

'Come over tomorrow for lunch,' he said. 'Come on your own. Tamsin's invited a couple of old friends. You don't know them, nobody special. But we could have a proper chat about the board. When you're feeling more yourself.'

'I'd like that, Laurie. That's a very good idea. Take care driving back.'

She got up and kissed him on both cheeks, rather in the French style, which he abhorred. But he stood his ground, and she sent him on his way.

She leaned against the door after it closed.

'Ta ta,' she said. 'Toodle-oo. Bye-bye. Cheerio.' And slowly she slid down the door until she was crumpled at its foot. She'd wait until Anthony came home, and give him a piece of her mind. And then she'd see about Maddie.

CHAPTER THIRTY-SIX

Although it was late, he did not fall asleep. The purpose of
the music was to calm without actually dulling the senses.
Master Lu plucked the strings with the greatest precision,
interpreting the successive pieces in a cautious manner,
dampening desire, yet priming it for the night and day
to come.

'*Lo mei hsi wu sheng,*' the Master sang in a low voice.
'*Yu ch'ih hsi ch'en sheng.*'

No more her silken sleeves rustle and brush the ground.
In the Courtyard of Jade, dust lies thick as fallen leaves.

It was a lament by the Emperor Wu of Han, for a dead
concubine. Farrar knew it by heart. It was one of the first
Chinese poems he had learned. The Master Lu had never
sung it for him before.

The music went on. A girl with a rose in her hair came
in and set a small table before Farrar. A second brought
a cup and poured chrysanthemum tea into it from a
Yishing-ware pot. When the tea had settled in the pot,
the first girl returned, bringing incense on a small stand.
She set it to Farrar's left, and lit it. The girls left him and
the Master alone again.

He drank the tea slowly, meditating on the poem. 'Her
empty room lies cold and still.'

When the pot had been emptied, Master Lu bowed and

stopped playing. He wrapped his instrument and got to his feet. As he went to the door, he turned, and for the first time spoke to Farrar.

'I have seen her,' he said. 'There has never been one like her here before. Take care she does not bewitch you.'

He drew the door shut behind him, and for a time there was silence. Then the girls came and took away the pot, the cup, and the lacquered table.

He sat alone, waiting.

The door opened, and Master Wei entered, carrying a wooden box. He was a small man, slightly plump, quite different in personality to the music master.

'How you been, Mista Fah-la? Maybe two years since you last here.'

'Longer than that.'

'You performing your exercises like I tell you?'

'Sometimes.'

'Sometimes not good enough. Tai ch'i chu'an every morning. Ch'iang chuang kung every evening. Most important. Show tongue, please.'

Farrar let the doctor examine his tongue, then his pulses. Wei Chiao was reputed to be able to diagnose an illness two years before it made its first appearance. He had treated more ailing heads of state than any of the world's hospitals. He was a humble, unassuming man, the last in a long line of court physicians. His personal fortune was reputed to amount to more than that of most of the great men he treated.

'What pitch Master Lu play in?'

'Ming.'

'And what did he sing?'

'The lament of the Emperor Wu of Han.'

'Spit in bowl, please.'

Farrar spat.

'When you last make love?'

'Four days ago, I think.'

'You worried about something?'

'Yes.'

'Liver *ch'i* very weak. Will strengthen. Remove robe.'

Farrar took off the black robe. Chiao took four needles from the box and inserted them in the points named *ch'u-ch'ih*, *pai-hui*, *feng-ch'ih*, and *tsu-san-li*.

'I make herbs. You wait here.'

The doctor left. Farrar relaxed, letting the needles do their work. Already he could feel the *ch'i* moving through his body, relaxing and revitalizing him at the same time.

Half an hour later, when the needles had been removed and he had taken his herbs, Farrar stood and replaced his robe. He already felt much better than he had on leaving the East China Club. There was a loud click, and the third door opened. Smiling, he passed through.

A pink-coloured corridor led him down to a green door on which the single character *yu* had been written. He placed his hand on the character, and the door opened of its own accord.

The door closed softly behind him. Two stools faced one another. The walls were dressed in jade-coloured silk. Soft concealed lighting filled every corner. He counted the walls. Six. Cones of *moxa* herbs burned in each corner.

He sat down on the couch bearing the characters *nan ren*, signifying 'man'. Nothing here was left to chance. He forced himself to breathe slowly. She would not appear yet. He was not ready for her.

Somewhere, perhaps in the next room, a *shiao* flute began to play. Its gentle notes rose and fell like the wings of a butterfly crossing a broad lawn. He closed his eyes and let the music waft over him. Someone laughed, a young woman. He opened his eyes, but the room was still empty. He knew he was not listening to a recording. He sat quietly and waited.

The girl laughed again, and her voice crossed that of a second, hushing her. It would be the two girls who had brought him tea, he thought. There was a brief silence, then her voice came again, amplified this time, a laugh, then a quick intake of breath, then the sound of steady breathing. Slowly, her breathing grew heavy and ragged, and soon it changed its pattern, acquiring the unmistakable tones of a woman being brought skilfully towards orgasm. The flute continued to play, its notes weaving in and out of her breath like a butterfly playing in the branches of a tall tree.

She did not come quickly. The other woman knew how to hang her out, keep her on edge, and all the while she grew steadily more frantic, building and building, not in one crescendo, but several.

As the girl's last cries died down to gentle moans, Farrar became aware that the sound of her pleasure had given him a large erection. He stood in order to straighten his robe. The fluttering of the flute faded to silence.

At that moment, the door opened.

She came in without ceremony, while he was still standing, and he looked at her and felt his heart break. Madame Zhou had not lied. He had never seen anyone so beautiful in his entire life. Not seen, not touched, not imagined, not dreamed. No one. No one like her.

She stood just inside the doorway, so he could continue looking at her. Madame Zhou had been right about her age. Her face and body lay exactly poised between childhood and adulthood. She was tall and slim, and dressed in a long dress of black silk that accentuated her figure perfectly. A single glance told him she was naked underneath. Her long black hair had been lifted and combed into a low chignon, leaving her neck absolutely bare.

'May I come in?' she asked in Chinese, using the formal style.

'Yes,' he answered.

She sat on the other couch, and Farrar returned to his.

'My name is Meihua,' she said. Her voice was soft and melodious.

'Was that you playing?' he asked.

She smiled and nodded.

'Did you watch?'

She nodded again.

'Who cried out?'

'The one with the rose. Her name is Junying. Would you like her to be with you instead of me?'

'No,' he smiled, 'you will do very well.'

She stood and went to a cupboard in the third wall, and from it she took a copy of the *I Ching* and a jar containing fifty long yarrow stalks. A low lacquer table followed, and this she set on the floor with the book resting on it. Beside it, she placed a slip of white paper. She knelt and removed the stalks from the jar, setting one aside – it would not be used again – and dividing the remainder.

She took one stalk from the heap on her right hand and placed it between her ring finger and the little finger of her left hand.

He watched her perform the ritual of consulting the oracle, but he barely noticed yarrow stalks or book. He could not take his eyes off her, her face above all. His erection was as hard as ever, and he felt feverish, desperate to have her.

She took the left-hand heap in her left hand and took from it bundles of four. Three stalks were left in the end. These were placed between her fingers with the other stalk.

He watched her fingers manipulate the stalks. Her hands were long and graceful, their movements economical. The stalks moved in and out, were divided and sub-divided. The results were counted off and written down on the slip of paper. Slowly, the hexagram took shape.

She looked up.

'*Hsien*,' she said, speaking the name of the hexagram. She opened the book and leafed through the pages. 'The judgement reads: "Influence. Success. Perseverance furthers. To take a maiden to wife brings good fortune."' She paused, passing her eye down the lines. '"Nine in the fourth place means: Perseverance brings good fortune. Remorse disappears."'

It seemed a good omen. He smiled. She put away the book and stalks and jar, then closed the cupboard. She returned to the couch and reached up and let down her hair. It fell into place softly, with a gentle shake of her head.

'Shall I recite for you?' she asked.

He nodded.

'What shall I recite?'

He was impressed. Only the most intelligent girl would ever open herself to the charge of not knowing a poem selected by a guest. At the same time, only a boorish or pedantic guest would choose a poem by a little-known writer.

'Do you know the poetry of Li Shang-Yin?' he asked.

'Very well. He is often recited here.'

'Do you know "The Walls of Emerald"?'

'Of course. It is my favourite poem.'

'Do you mean that, Meihua?'

'Yes. It frightens me. However often I read it, its meaning still escapes me. Yet I'm sure it has meaning.'

'I believe it has. But not for the likes of you or me.' He paused. 'You are very beautiful, Meihua.'

'I am glad I please you.'

'You do more than please me.'

'Shall I undress for you?'

He shook his head. There was an order in all this. It was why he came.

'Not in this room,' he said. 'This room's pleasures are all I ask of it.'

'Would you like to smoke while I recite?'

He nodded.

She clapped her hands once, and the door opened. The girl with the rose entered. She was completely naked now. In her hands she held a large opium pipe and a bowl containing pure opium mixed with three other drugs and seven powerful herbs. She set these down on a low table next to him, and went out again. He put the pipe to his lips and began to smoke. Very softly, a scented smoke wreathed itself about his head.

'"Twelve turns of the rail on walls of emerald,"' she began.

'A sea-beast's horn repels the dust, a jade repels the
    cold.
Letters from Mount Lang-yüan have cranes for
    messengers . . .'

Her long dress was fastened with tiny buttons from neck to hem. As she recited the poem, her right hand fell to the lowest button and undid it. He felt himself harden again.

She would not undress. Some, coming to a lotus house for the first time, found this strange. They had used escort

275

agencies before, and they thought this just a more expensive version. They were very wrong. This was only the first room, Farrar reflected. The essence of what happened here was that nothing should be done in haste. In lovemaking, delay is everything. He'd been to a cricket match earlier that day, losing himself in the slow pace and finely tuned cadences of the game.

Meihua recited another line from the poem and opened the second button. He watched her face. He thought of Elizabeth, and wondered why he'd stayed with her so long.

'"To glimpse her shadow, to hear her voice, is to love her,"' recited Meihua. '"On the pool of jade the lotus leaves spread out across the water."'

The dress was open as far as her knees now, but she kept it in place so he could not see her legs. The opium mixture began to take effect, making him relaxed while keeping his senses sharp. Her voice lulled him further, swaying through the stanzas with practised ease. Perhaps it really was her favourite poem.

He thought of David Laing in Sinkiang. How precise had the directions given by the boy Tursun been? He'd heard what the boy had said on tape. But there'd been a few times when he'd been left alone with Laing. In the time available, how likely was it that David could really track down something as well concealed as the weapons centre? He'd received hard confirmation that the first full-scale prototype would be ready for testing in a week to two weeks.

Her hands moved slowly up her thighs, opening buttons quietly until she reached her pubic region. He caught a brief glimpse of dark hair, then her fingers slipped inside and began to move backwards and forwards between her legs; all the time she continued to recite the poem.

But her voice was already growing rough and hard to control. When she recited the last line, it was with a sense of relief for them both. Her fingers moved back and forth rhythmically, and he watched, now her face, now her hand, intent on every movement. Her face and neck reddened, and her left hand clutched the edge of the couch. He could see nothing but the back of her long white hand, now slow, now fast. Her eyes rolled back, as if she were on the verge of fainting, and her breath came in tearing gasps. He wanted to take two simple steps across the room and take her. But this was only the first room.

She was very skilful. She knew when to increase and when to slacken the pressure, when to slow down and when to hurry, when to use her fingers and when the palm of her hand. Every time she seemed about to come, her hand would relax and she would look at him and smile the most innocent smile in the world. He would smile back, admiring how well she had been taught.

When she came, it was explosive, her entire body arching as spasm after spasm passed through her, making her cry out again and again. And he watched and felt himself more aroused than he'd been in years.

She grew calm again, and rearranged her dress, and smiled.

'Are you ready yet?' she asked. 'Or shall I do it again? There are many methods.'

He shook his head, and, opening his robe, took his erect penis in one hand. She got up and went to a cupboard, from which she brought a small porcelain bowl. It was so thin he could see her fingers through it.

She placed the bowl on the floor, then knelt in front of him while he masturbated. He lacked her training, and in her presence he felt like a schoolboy again, discovering sex for the first time. Even dressed, she roused him as no other woman had done. He tried to hold back, and the drugs did help a little, but in the end he came quite soon. Very skilfully, she caught his semen in her cupped hands, then let what she could fall into the little bowl.

He put his robe back in place, and the door opened, admitting Master Wei. The master took the bowl from Meihua, dipped his index finger in the semen, and brought it to his lips.

'Salty,' he said. 'A little tired. You sleep now.'

Meihua led him to a small, beautifully furnished bedroom. He could not work out how it related to any of the other rooms: it was like a maze up here. Master Wei brought him a pot of herbal tea and left him with Meihua. He took off his robe and lay naked on the bed.

'Stay with me,' he said, 'while I sleep.'

CHAPTER THIRTY-SEVEN

Kashgar

The city centre was in chaos. Half of Kashgar was out ransacking the bazaars, while the other half was at home making secure what they had bought earlier. The traders were happy, but only up to a point. Stock was dwindling or gone, and with the city closed, there seemed no hope of replenishing any of it.

You couldn't buy a sack of rice anywhere, regardless of quality or price. The butchers were down to their last joints of lamb, the bakers had baked their last batches of *biao*, nobody had bags of flour, the last cans of cooking oil had gone an hour ago. But the crowds continued to work their way in and out of the stalls, ready to haggle and buy the moment they saw the least sign of something that might see them through the coming siege. David saw one man struggling past with a wooden trolley heaped with jars of honey, and another with more watermelons than he and his family could hope to eat in a month.

Two young men stood guard outside Nabila's father's house. Inside, armed men stood in small groups everywhere. One, who did not know Nabila, tried to stop her crossing the courtyard, but was quickly pulled off by his colleagues. In another corner, Nabila's brother Osman was talking to one of the commanders. Turning, he caught sight of Nabila. He walked across the courtyard and greeted her warmly.

'What's going on, Osman? We only just heard about the curfew at the hospital.'

'Some security people arrived here about an hour ago. They took Father and Omar. I was at the mosque when it happened. By the time I got back, they'd gone.'

Nabila's face went white.

'But why on earth should they want to take Father? That could spark off precisely the sort of insurrection they say they want to prevent.'

'Well, I think that may be exactly what they're after. I think they want a repeat of Urumchi.'

'But why? It doesn't make any sense.'

'I agree. But I think Chang Zhangyi wants to provoke us. The international press won't criticize him for putting down an insurrection that threatens people's lives and property. Father has issued specific instructions. There are to be no further prayers in the mosques. In fact, no meetings of any kind, especially in the Idgah. We're to submit unless our women and children are threatened. And in the meantime, the *jihad* commanders have been instructed to get ready to launch an all-out campaign once the word is given.'

'I don't think that's wise,' said David.

'And just what do you know about it? Please, I know you're working with Nabila. But you'd be best to stick to your herbs and potions.'

Nabila hardly knew what to do.

'Osman, he knows more about this than you think.'

'What can he possibly know? He's not even from Sinkiang.'

'Nabila . . .' David beckoned her to one side. 'Nabila, I'm trusting you with my life. If it wasn't for this morning, I couldn't do this. You have to speak to your brother, or make him speak to me. Back in London, I'm a senior intelligence officer.'

'I'd guessed that much.'

'Very likely. Anyway, my job is to analyse military activity in western China. In the past few months, things have been very busy. The PLA's been moving tanks, guns, even whole regiments right along the border with Gansu. They've also been bringing in troops disguised as workmen, in civilian lorries. Have you heard of Baoguo Barracks in Huocheng County?'

She nodded.

'Baoguo now has an entire tank regiment in residence. Our assessment of your manpower indicates that any rising you undertake at this point will be crushed out of existence within twenty-four hours. There'll be massive loss of life. They may even bulldoze Kashgar to the ground. Believe me, this is not the time.'

She did not question anything he said. That too was a heritage of the morning. Thoughtfully, she went back to her brother. She needed to communicate David's fears without actually saying how he knew what he did. When she finished, Osman came over to where David was standing by the pool.

'It's a beautiful pool,' David said. 'I only saw it at night before.'

Fish darted in and out of the deep shadows among which they lived their lives.

'There have been fish in this pool since the time of Yakub Beg. My great-grandfather built this house. He was also *ahun* at the Idgah Mosque. I am told he brought the fish here from the tomb of Abakh Hoja. Have you been there yet?'

David shook his head.

'Nabila says you think they might destroy the city.'

David hesitated. How much could he, in honesty, tell this man?

'They have the power to do it, and I believe they have orders to do it under certain circumstances.'

'What circumstances?'

'A rising, however unsuccessful. As revenge, assuming you killed Han officials or military men.'

'How do you know this? You sound suspiciously like a government agent.'

Again, David paused.

'Would I sound like that', he said, 'if I were to give you a complete breakdown of their military disposition in Sinkiang as of last week?'

'You could make that up.'

'You have men out there. Let them check everything I tell you. Believe me, I'm trying to help you. And I'm trying to prevent unnecessary bloodshed.'

'I hope that's true. If not, your own blood will be the first. Now, forgive me. I have a lot to do.'

'I'll have the breakdown ready in an hour.'

Osman headed off to the main gate. Nabila led David upstairs, and he told her what he'd promised Osman.

'I'm going to do this from memory,' he said. 'I just need a table and some paper.'

'I'll have that arranged for you. David, Osman mentioned something else to me. He said I'm not to leave the house again. And you're to stay as well. I'm sorry, but my father left strict instructions. If there's an invasion, the *mujahidin* can defend the family better here.'

'Surely your father didn't mention me.'

'No, that was Osman. He wants to keep an eye on you.'

'In that case, I'm going to need my things from your cousin's place.'

282

'I'll send somebody round before the curfew.'

'No, I have to go myself. There are things in those bags . . .'

'I'm sure there are, but Osman won't let you go. I'll go myself, if that suits you. I can have an escort, I'll be quite safe.'

'All right. I don't want to cause you trouble, love.'

They were on the second floor. A balcony gave out on to the courtyard, where the fish still swam in the pool.

'David, you have to be very careful in this house. Especially in what you say. Any hint of improper familiarity between us could lead to your death, perhaps both our deaths. I'm not just Sheikh Azad's daughter. I'm also the widow of a holy martyr. There are plenty here who'd like to see me in a veil.

'I'll get your paper now. You can sit out here: it'll be pleasant for you.' She looked yearningly into his eyes. 'I like things to be pleasant for you.'

He smiled and watched her walk down the corridor and out of sight. When she was gone, he went to the rail and looked down. From somewhere, a light breeze had sprung up, rippling the surface of the pool and lifting the lightest parts of the foliage.

A servant came, carrying a light wooden table, followed by another with a chair. David thanked them and sat down. A few minutes passed, and he got up and went to the rail again. The breeze still worked its way in and out.

At that moment, a door opened somewhere further down the corridor. A babble of voices sounded loudly and was shut off again as the door closed. Nabila appeared, carrying sheets of white paper.

'Thank you,' he said.

'I have to go,' she said. 'My mother's very agitated. She

thinks they may torture my father again, or kill him. I want to try to calm her down, then go to the hospital for some medication.'

'Nabila, how can I find out about winds?'

'I'm sorry?'

'Winds. Prevailing winds, winds on certain days. If your victims really were killed by something in the atmosphere, they must have been downwind of a test. If I can establish the wind directions for each group of victims, I can get a bearing on the test site.'

She looked at him and smiled.

'I already did that,' she said. 'After the first few times, when I realized what might be going on, I started asking about which way the wind had been blowing. I've got all the notes back in my room at the hospital.'

CHAPTER THIRTY-EIGHT

He woke to a gentle pressure from Meihua on his left shoulder.

'Master Wei told me it is time to wake you now,' she said. 'You are to drink this.' She held out a fresh pot, a Yishing-ware pot in the shape of a pomegranate. He had seen one like it in a museum in Peking, an extremely rare specimen.

A chair and table had been set up at the foot of the bed. Meihua placed the teapot on the table, then the door opened and the first two girls came in, each carrying a tray on which covered bowls had been set. Like Meihua, who must have changed while he slept, they were wearing coral-coloured dresses. They placed the bowls on the table, together with a pair of chopsticks.

The girls left, and he got off the bed. A fresh robe was waiting for him on a stand, a coral robe. Meihua began to serve him. He felt ravenously hungry suddenly, though he had eaten well at the club. The combination of sexual excitement, drugs, and medicinal herbs was slowly altering his body chemistry. It had happened before, but not like this. At his invitation, Meihua ate with him. He could hardly stop looking at her.

He ate a little of everything: Whampoa eggs, chicken livers, pickled cabbage, twice-cooked pork, beef with red-in-snow, Phoenix in the Nest, braised ox-tongue, *ma po tau fu* beancurd, eight-treasure bean curd, yin-yang rice, Yi noodles, oysters with hair seaweed. He lifted some of the last dish and offered it to Meihua on his chopsticks.

'Good deeds and prosperity,' he said, and she laughed. It was an old pun, for the name of the dish and the words of the New Year greeting were almost identical.

Each dish had been liberally sprinkled with aphrodisiac substances. Herbs like Asiatic ginseng and damiana, a powdered preparation of Spanish fly, powdered rhinoceros horn, the flaked meat from a tiger's penis, and *lu chong*, the wind-dried inner part of a stag's genitals. Horny goat weed had been powdered and mixed with the wine, a bottle of Latour '59 which had been opened just the right length of time before.

'Are you ready now?' she asked when he put his chopsticks down for the last time.

He nodded and got to his feet.

She took him further through the maze, a long way this time, until they came to a door bearing the character for 'coral'.

The room was decorated in dark pink, more lavish than the jade room. He had been in the coral room once before, many years before, and he and a girl named Yingmei had spent two hours exploring one another's bodies before reaching their separate climaxes. He'd had intercourse with her later, several times, but however good that had been, it was those first encounters in the coral room that had most enchanted him. In his dreams he still thought of her. She'd been fourteen, with a tiny mole beneath her left breast.

Meihua stood in front of him.

'I enjoyed our meal,' she said. 'The cook is called Li Jung Chuan. Madame Zhou had him brought from Peking, where he cooked for the Prime Minister.'

'I can well believe it. The Phoenix in the Nest was the best I've ever tasted.'

She ran her tongue slowly round her lips. He watched it inscribe its long oval, red as though flushed from the wine. Her eyes were bright.

'Shall I undress for you now?' she asked.

He nodded once.

Swiftly, she lifted her hair and tied it high with a comb and a ribbon, to leave her neck and shoulders bare. Then she unfastened her robe and let it fall to the ground. Underneath it she wore a long white shift that reached from her bare shoulders to her ankles. Her small breasts pushed the soft fabric out gently.

He felt his heart pounding. Her arms and shoulders and neck were the most perfect expressions of the human form he'd ever seen.

She pulled a ribbon high up on the shift, and it ran out in a single motion. For a moment, she held the ribbon between her fingers, then let it fall, and it dropped spinning to the floor. And she looked at him and smiled shyly, then moved her left shoulder and her right shoulder in turn, and the shift cascaded to the floor.

Her body was more perfect than he had ever dared imagine it. He'd slept with many women in his life, but none of them like this.

For the next three hours, they touched and withdrew, touched and withdrew. She came a dozen times, effortlessly, sometimes on her own, sometimes with his help. He could not manage that, but using a Taoist technique he had learned many years before, he reached orgasm three times without ejaculating. For the fourth time, Meihua played with him for almost an hour before finally giving him release.

So they continued through a long day, moving from

room to room, pacing themselves carefully. Each room brought them closer, and the longer they went on the more passionate grew their lovemaking. In the sixth room, the peacock feather room, Meihua finally lost her virginity to him. He remained inside her for over an hour while she climaxed repeatedly. Then Master Wei changed his prescription, and in the seventh room she sat astride him, lightly moving her hips in a smooth rhythm that brought him to a climax time after time.

Afterwards, they lay in each other's arms and fell asleep at last.

He woke sometime after midnight. Meihua was still asleep on the large bed beside him. Even now he was not sated. He wanted more of her, much more. She was the loveliest creature he had ever set eyes on, and he could not bear to part with her.

Quietly, he went into the corridor. Madame Zhou was there, waiting on a little stool. She had nodded off, but the moment the door opened, she looked up and greeted him brightly.

'Well, Mista Fah-La. Did I speak truth?'

'You've never been so honest in your life, you old scoundrel. I'd like to know all about her.'

'Not permitted.'

'Well, is Meihua her real name?'

'Not know.'

'Can I see her again? I've never asked that before. Perhaps even . . .'

The little woman was on her feet now. She lifted a finger and set it gently against his lips, shaking her grey head.

'Not permitted,' she said, then paused. She frowned, as though pondering something hard. 'Mista Fah-La . . .'

'Yes?'

'There is an eighth room, Mista Fah-La. White

chrysanthemum. Would you like to see?'

He felt a slow chill pass through him. His breath caught in his chest. He'd always guessed there was an eighth room, often wondered if he had the courage.

'How much?' he asked.

The price she demanded was very steep, more than all he'd paid already. But he understood why.

'Show me the room,' he said.

It was the most beautiful room of all, utterly white, filled with white silk and leather and ivory. The only interruptions were on two walls, where poems had been executed in black ink on white paper.

Madame Zhou showed him through the room and its cupboards.

'Is it used often?' he asked.

She smiled crookedly.

'Maybe once a year,' she said. 'Maybe less.'

'I'll wait here,' he said. 'When she wakes, bring her to me.'

'I send Master Wei first. Most essential.'

When all that was done, and he'd taken the right drugs and herbs, and *moxa* had been lit in every corner, he sat down and waited. His heart was beating fast. Every inch of him was excited. And slowly, as the herbs began to work, he felt he had the courage.

The door opened and Meihua stepped into the room. She was still naked, and the moment he saw her his body responded. She saw his penis harden and smiled.

'What is this room?' she asked. 'I didn't know there was another room.'

'I always thought there was, but this is the first time I've seen it myself. Do you like it?'

'It's a little cold. But very beautiful.'

'Just like you.'

'You don't find me cold, do you?'

'Cold? No, it's just a way of talking.'

She started to read the poems on the wall.

'What sad poems,' she said. 'I wonder who put them here.'

'Madame Zhou, perhaps.'

She laughed.

'I'm not even sure she can read.'

'Well, I can read.' He stood and went to a cupboard. From it he took a large pot of ink and a calligraphic brush. Next to them he found a small ivory box. He brought them all across to her and placed them on the floor.

'Darling,' he said, 'why don't you lie down there? It's very comfortable.'

She knew at once what he planned to do. The tradition of writing poems on a woman's body was an old one.

She lay down at once.

'Will it tickle?' she asked.

'Just a little,' he said.

'What will you write on me?'

'First turn over on to your front. I want to write on your back.'

'A poem?'

'Yes.'

'Is it one I know?'

'I think so. The poem of Li Yu before he died.'

'Yes,' she whispered. 'I know it.'

'Recite it, then.'

He knelt over her, and as she recited he painted the characters on her back and buttocks and legs, the strokes shortening and lengthening to accommodate the fluctuations and creases of her skin. He thought she looked exquisite from behind. Her proportions were perfect, more perfect than any poem.

290

'*Wu yan du shang Shilou* . . . ' she began.

'"I climb West Tower alone in silence . . ."'

He knew his calligraphic skills were limited, but for the first time in his life he felt his fingers relax into the brush, felt the strokes come under his control. He wrote the last line of nine characters along the length of her left leg, and as he came to the final stroke of the last character, *tou*, her voice died away. He sat and looked at her, at her white skin, at the ebony ink drying across it. He wanted to run his hands across her, wanted to tell her everything was all right. She tormented him more than any woman had ever done.

'Turn over,' he said when the ink had finally dried. She rolled on to her back, and he caught his breath once more, seeing her face.

'When are we going to make love again?' she asked.

'In a moment, love. You have to be patient.'

'I never thought actually making love could be so fantastic.'

He stroked her cheek. Her use of the word 'fantastic' brought home to him just how young she was.

'Poor Meihua,' he said.

'Are you very rich?' she asked. She wasn't supposed to ask such questions, but he sensed something irrepressible about her, an instinct for fun or mischief that was locked inside her by the rules and regulations of the house.

'Not very rich,' he said. 'At least, not yet.' He looked down at her breasts, and ran the palm of his right hand across them. She arched her back as his hand grazed her nipples. 'A few weeks more, perhaps. Then I may be very rich indeed.'

She smiled and held his hand to her left breast.

'When you are very rich, can I come and live with you always? Make love every day?'

He shook his head sadly.

'You belong to the Hui Hou,' he said.

'Perhaps you can buy me from them.'

It was a shocking thing for her to say. The Hui Hou considered even a hint of treachery a major crime. Farrar looked at her and frowned.

'I already have done,' he said.

Her mouth opened to ask another question, but he bent forward and closed it with a kiss. He was in love with her, truly in love with her.

He picked up the brush and wrote across her breasts and belly the first seven characters of a poem by Li Shang-Yin, the poet whose words she had read to him in the jade room.

'It is always hard to meet, unbearable to part.'

As his hand moved across her body, slanting, sloping, sliding in practised gestures, evoking a dead poet's yearning on a living woman's flesh, tears began to run from his eyes. She did not notice at first, then a drop fell near her navel.

She reached a hand up and put it behind his head, drawing him down on to her. The floor was soft, almost like a bed. He lay on her like that, pressed close to her, the ink from her skin transferring itself to his. And as he lay, he became aroused again, suddenly, unendurably.

They began to make love again, this time with a passion lovers might have felt only after long experience, at a time of parting, or when coming together again after a painful separation. Every part of her body had become sensitive to his caresses. He only had to kiss or stroke her anywhere, and she would cry out and cling to him hotly. Her sweat and his sweat combined to wash the ink slowly into incomprehensible smears, leaving great stains across the white carpet.

292

He entered her, holding her hard against him, and began moving slowly inside her, rousing her yet further. As he did so, he reached out for the little ivory box and pulled back the lid. Inside lay a thin cord of silk, about two feet long.

Lifting her head, he slipped the cord behind her neck, then brought the ends to the front.

She paused.

'What are you doing?'

He made a simple knot in the cord, then turned his fingers almost languidly in its ends, shortening it.

'Fah-La? What are you doing?'

'Shhhhh,' he said. 'Relax. This will make you come harder than you've ever come.' And he started to tighten the cord, just enough to constrict her breathing. As he did so, he began to move inside her again. She relaxed briefly, and let him move and tighten and relax the cord, and as the minutes passed her body grew hot, and her breath grew hard to catch, and her head started spinning, and everything, everything was concentrated between her legs until the sensation grew and widened, spreading to every part of her body, consuming her, tightening her like a bow, and she came, and kept coming time after time until she sank back exhausted to the floor.

He bent and kissed her.

'Poor Meihua,' he said. And she smiled up at him, her first lover.

He pulled on the cord tighter now, watching it cut into her throat. Too late, she realized what was happening. Her body fought against him, but he was too heavy for her, and the cord was cutting the breath out of her quicker and quicker every second. Her eyes, that he'd called beautiful before, bulged in their sockets, her hands, that he'd praised earlier, flapped awkwardly in her effort to grab hold of something, her legs, that he'd admired so often, kicked out at all angles, her face, that he'd thought the most beautiful face in the world, began to grow red, then purple.

And the whole thing came to an end in a moment. All her movements stopped, and the eyes that stared up at him were as lifeless as eggs. He let the cord fall from his hands. Then he started moving inside her again. She was still warm and moist, and he was excited beyond measure.

When he came, it was the most perfect orgasm of his life. And he came again and again, eight times in all.

When he was finished, he lay down beside her, cradling her body in his arms as though trying to bring her back to life. The door opened and Master Lu entered. He sat down and stroked the *ch'in*, bringing the instrument to life. Then he began to sing, a poem of Meng Chiao, dead nearly twelve centuries.

'Keep away from sharp swords,
Don't go near a lovely woman.
A sharp sword too close will wound your hand,
Woman's beauty too close will wound your life.
The danger of the road is not in the distance,
Ten yards is far enough to break a wheel.
The peril of love is not in loving too often,
A single evening can leave its wound in the soul.'

Farrar looked at him and remembered the words of the oracle she had cast:

'"Remorse disappears."'

And he put his head in his hands and wondered how long that would take.

RADIANT WHITE SKY

CHAPTER THIRTY-NINE

Kashgar

Something felt wrong. It had started with the silence that attended sunset. No call to prayer, no voice raised anywhere in the twilit city to summon men to God. Later, the silence had revealed the sound of engines somewhere in the distance, heavy engines whose rumbling continued late into the night.

'Tanks,' David had said. 'T59s and T69s, and maybe some long-range artillery. They're circling the city.'

He looked up and caught Nabila's eyes. He could tell she was frightened. The atmosphere in the house was a mixture of fear and defiance. One group of firebrands was at that very moment planning how to rescue Sheikh Azad from captivity. An informant at the local garrison had told them the old man was being held just outside the city at a military barracks called Kizilkara. Now, they were thinking of ignoring all advice and disregarding the sheikh's own instructions in order to prove their manhood or their religious commitment. Osman was doing his best to keep them under control.

'Your father will be all right,' David said. 'I know Chang Zhangyi. I've watched him for years. He can be brutal. But he uses brutality as a means to an end. It isn't in his interest to hurt your father at the moment, or kill him.'

'How can you be so sure?'

'I told you: he plans to his own advantage. If Chang Zhangyi discovered that being kind to people achieved better results, he'd be the kindest man in the world.'

'I disagree. Even if it damaged him, Chang Zhangyi would go on being cruel. It's his nature. You don't expect a cat to be kind to mice.'

'That's not the point. Chang Zhangyi could kill your father in order to be rid of him, but he knows that would only turn the rage over Urumchi into something beyond all reason. I think he believes that, as long as he holds your father hostage, it gives him some sort of power over the population. And I personally think he's right.'

They were sitting in a room on the second floor, next door to Nabila's mother's room. The old woman was resting at last, lulled to sleep by a concoction made by Nabila, who had brought a supply of herbs back to the house. Every now and then, Nabila would pop into her mother's bedroom to check how she was. David, as an outsider, could not meet any of the female members of the family except Nabila.

In one corner of their room sat Asiyeh, a plump Hui Muslim from Gansu. Now in her mid-fifties, she had arrived in Kashgar during the Cultural Revolution and stayed on as a seamstress in Sheikh Azad's household. She had never married, partly because she was as ugly as sin, and partly because men gave her a nasty feeling. 'I get a horrible feeling if one comes close,' she used to say. 'Very nasty. God's hand slipped when he made men.' Osman had planted her in the room to act as a chaperone. While David and Nabila talked, she sewed elaborate embroideries on silk. She never missed a stitch, and she never missed a movement of the couple she'd been set to watch.

They were sitting facing one another across a long table on which Nabila's map had been spread. She would read out results from her records, and watch as David marked them carefully on the landscape.

'I'm afraid of Chang Zhangyi,' she said. She looked down at the map, then up at David and across at Asiyeh. 'I had a sister,' she went on. 'Her name was Rabbia, she was sixteen years old. I was very close to her. One day, when I was at university, Chang Zhangyi's men came here. They took my father to prison, and they took my sister to a place they call Hei Juyuan. Do you know of it?'

He nodded. He knew it only too well.

'I don't know exactly what happened there,' she said. 'But I have been told that Chang Zhangyi raped my sister. She was very beautiful.'

She saw Asiyeh watching her closely, on the verge of speaking.

'Some say he fell in love with her, some that it was simple lust. He had sex with her many times.'

'Miss Nabila, you should not talk about such things.' To Asiyeh, talking about sex in front of men was almost as bad as doing it.

'Not now, Asiyeh. Dr Osmanop is a medical doctor. He understands such delicate matters.'

A surly look was her only reply.

'This took place over a week or two. He would have her taken to a comfortable bed each evening. He would rape her, then he would have her sent back to her cell to lie on a heap of straw until it was time for him to make use of her again. One of the guards who came on duty in the second week was a secret Muslim. He kept his conversion to himself in order to infiltrate Chang Zhangyi's headquarters. Chang Zhangyi's treatment of Rabbia made him very angry. He smuggled in a knife with her food, a very beautiful knife from the country of the Baoan. It was his intention that she should use the knife on Chang Zhangyi when he next came for her. Instead, she used it on herself. She must have stabbed herself twenty or thirty times before she found the fatal spot.'

'I'm sorry, very sorry.'

'Yes. She was a lovely sister. My father loved her more than me, I think. Everyone loved Rabbia.'

They sat in silence for a long time. The sound of tanks came across the darkness with such clarity that they thought at times they must have entered the city and started along its alleyways.

'Let's go on,' said Nabila. 'I want to finish this.'

It took only a few minutes more, and the calculations were finished.

'It coincides with part of my original estimate,' said David. 'Look, this line meets mine at several points. The problem is, we're still looking at a stretch some fifty miles long, probably longer. In the desert, that's a long distance.'

'What do you plan to do?'

He looked across at Asiyeh.

'Can we go somewhere else?' he asked. 'I don't want to talk about this in front of her.'

'She has to stay with us, you know that.'

'Let's go down to the courtyard. There are guards out there, and Asiyeh can watch us from up here, over the rail.'

Asiyeh gave a grudging acceptance, as long as they kept within sight.

It was hard not to. They strolled back and forth, breathing in the scented night air, listening to the small sounds of the household as it made ready for sleep.

'I have to get out of Kashgar, Nabila. I have to get to a suitable point at which to enter the Taklamakan, find a guide, some food and equipment. If I can locate the centre, I can get word back to England to send in a raiding party to sort it out.'

'How can you do that?'

'I've got an Ultralite satellite communications set in one of my cases. If all else fails, I can get out of the desert again and use something more conventional.'

'And if you can't get out of the desert?'

He hesitated. High above their heads, an angry bird scolded its mate.

'A lot of people will die,' he said.

'Have you ever been in the Taklamakan?'

He shook his head.

'Ever ridden a camel?'

'Once when I was twelve, at Whipsnade Zoo.'

'Do you know how much water you will need, how much food, where to find water for the camels?'

'I was hoping the guide would tell me that.'

She looked at him softly. There was moonlight in her eyes, and moonlight on her cheeks.

'And if you lost your guide? What would you do then?'

'Make my way as best I could.'

She shook her head.

'You would die. The Taklamakan is the desert of death. Remember what its name means in Uighur: "You go in, but you don't come out". The old people didn't call it that for nothing. There are dunes in there over one thousand feet in height. Whole ranges of them, mountains of sand. It is the worst desert in the world, and you will be going into the harshest part of it. If you lose your way, you will die. If you lose too much water, you will die. If your camels die, you will die. It is unforgiving. Hedin barely

301

escaped with his life, and he went in no distance at all. Almost all his companions died.'

He wanted to hold her, reassure her that he knew what he was doing. But to touch her would be fatal to both of them.

'I have to go,' he said. 'What's there has to be found on the ground, not by a satellite or a plane. There's no one else to do it, I have no choice.'

'I realize that,' she said. 'But you must be fully aware of what you face. You'll need a companion.'

'A companion?'

'I'm coming with you,' she said. 'I've been riding camels since the age of five. And they weren't in a zoo.'

CHAPTER FORTY

The Rose Clinic
London

It was early evening when she turned up, a little bedraggled, about half an hour after the last dinner trays had been cleared away. It had been raining hard outside, but the heat remained in the air, making the atmosphere humid and oppressive. She was angry, and he could see she'd been crying.

He took her into his office, wondering if he had the courage to suggest she might benefit from a short stay on the premises. An irrepressible thought grinned at him like a monkey behind bars, that he could offer her a package deal for mother and daughter.

He closed the door and smiled his thinnest smile.

'Mrs Laing. Always a pleasure to see you. And what can I do for you?'

He thought he sounded too much like an unctuous shopkeeper showing his wares, or, God forbid, an undertaker.

'A little sherry, Doctor? Shall we?'

Elizabeth had barely touched alcohol all day. She'd woken with a blinding hangover, spent the rest of the morning drinking prairie oysters and waiting for Anthony, downed a couple of Prozac, which she got from her dear friend Frances, taken delivery of the Merc from some dreadful adolescent who'd scowled when she handed him five pounds and then hared off to the nearest Tube station on God knows what unspeakable enterprise.

Laurence had telephoned soon after that to remind her about lunch, which had been with a ghastly little couple called Price-Enright, newly returned from Seattle, and awfully wrapped up in Feng Shui and 'psychic harmonies', neither of which they had the slightest clue about. Their dog, a monstrous pug with bandy legs and an impossibly large penis, was sick under the table just when the caviare and blinis were being served.

Then there'd been a 'chat' with Laurence in the round library, during which she'd agreed to turn up at the office in two days' time – at nine in the morning, for heaven's sake!

She'd expected Anthony to be there when she got home, but the moment she slipped her key in the lock, she knew the house was still empty. It had been a great temptation to run back to the bottle, but she had other thoughts to occupy her. She went to bed for a couple of hours, cried herself silly at first, and then slept till six.

She'd been woken by the sound of the front door closing. She felt rather groggy, something she put down to the Prozac. It took her a few minutes to orientate herself, then she called out.

'Anthony? Is that you? I'm in the bedroom. Where the hell have you been?'

He didn't come in straight away. She waited, straightening herself in the dressing-table mirror.

'Anthony, what the fuck are you doing? I'm in here.'

She didn't yet know whether to be angry with him, or understanding. She couldn't throw him out, it was his flat, and she daren't antagonize him too much, or he might sling her out instead. He still didn't come.

So she went to him.

He was sitting at the kitchen table with his head in his hands, mumbling to himself. She'd never seen him like this before.

'It's not like you to knock them back so hard, Anthony. She must have been something, eh? Must have been a knockout. Or was there more than one? You've been gone long enough to shag every tart from here to King's Cross silly as a drunk rat. Just amazed you've got the stamina, that's all.'

She sat down opposite him, and he raised his head, and she wished she hadn't said a word. She'd never seen a look on a man's face like that before, composed of so much grief and despair. He'd been crying. Something was very wrong.

'Darling, I didn't realize,' she started. 'What's wrong?'

'Nothing's wrong. There's no use asking questions. I'll be all right in a while if you leave me.'

'Is it something to do with work?'

'Work? Yes, in a way. I brought a present back for you, Lizzie. It's in the hall.'

It was not like him to bring home presents. Did that indicate a guilty conscience? Or growing fondness? David had always brought her little presents back after work.

'I don't need presents, Anthony. I just want to know you're all right.'

'How I am is my business. Now, please, leave me alone. I'm going to bed early anyway.'

Stung, she got to her feet.

'I may be going out myself,' she said. 'On personal business. Don't wait up.'

She went to the bedroom and dressed. The rain had

already started, but she planned to take the car. The keys were in the bowl again. She went out without even saying goodbye to Anthony.

On the way, she paused in the hall. There was a box on the Chinese table. No Harvey Nick's or Harrods bag in sight. Just a plain red box. She lifted the top. Inside was a doll on a wooden stand, a Chinese doll dressed in a coral dress and holding a fan. When Elizabeth stood it up, she noticed that a small plastic lever jutted out from the base. She pushed the lever to 'on', and the doll began to dance, moving the fan from side to side, raising and lowering her other arm, and twisting her slim body. It was a gimcrack thing, the sort of souvenir knick-knack you might find in the cheap shops in Hong Kong, or in some of the supermarkets near Soho.

She left it on the table. As she opened the door, the doll halted and bowed. As it straightened, a squeaky voice came from a speaker in the base. 'My name is Meihua. *Nin hao.*'

And then it began to move again in its odd, laboured dance.

He poured her a sherry and made to put the bottle away.

'You too, Doc. Don't want to drink alone. Only the truly sozzled do that, eh?'

He sighed wearily and poured half a glass for himself.

'Bloody good sherry, too,' she said.

'Apostoles,' he said.

'Sort of in-between.'

'Yes.'

'You don't like me much, do you, Doctor?'

Her question startled him, as did the coolness with which it was put.

'I'm trained not to put personal judgements between me and my patients, or their relatives. I don't like or dislike you.'

'Bollocks. That's like saying I don't fancy you or not fancy you. If I took my clothes off, you'd have a hard-on inside five seconds. If I said all the things I'd like to say, you'd have me out of the door and in the street.'

'Mrs Laing, you seem to be getting the wrong end of several sticks.'

'Yes, well, I'm sure that's true. But at the moment I get the distinct impression that someone's been shoving the sticks hard up my backside. I'd like to see What's-her-name, if you don't mind.'

'Has your husband come back from his travels yet?'

'No idea. Could have been gobbled up by tigers, for all I know.'

'I don't think they have tigers in Scotland.'

'Is that where he told you he is? He must think we're all a pack of idiots.'

'Perhaps we are. If you'd care to wait here, I'll ask Maddie if she'd like to see you.'

'Why the hell wouldn't she? I'm her mother, for God's sake. And I pay the fucking bills.'

'I'm sure there's no reason at all. But as long as Maddie's in my care, I really can't introduce visitors without her permission.'

He hared off before she could stop him. She sat, savouring her sherry, gazing at the well-tended lawn below. They must have been having tea outside when the rain began, she thought, noticing the forlorn tables with their cups and plates that no one had yet come to clear away. What was Anthony doing now? she wondered. Each time she thought of the face that had looked up at her, showing such naked anguish, her mind flinched away from it and all it implied. But it couldn't be ignored. She'd have to go back to him in the end.

Rose returned. He was showing signs of fraying at the edges, Elizabeth thought. She wondered if she had such a bad effect on him. But no doubt running a clinic like this was a cocktail of stresses.

'Well, Doctor?'

'She'll see you if you go up now. Try not to tire her. She's been getting on quite well over the past few days.'

In her room, Maddie waited patiently. She'd finished her chicken, and she'd finished her dessert. The rain outside had grown gentle, and she could sit now and listen to it fall across the garden. She could remember their garden at home, remember it vividly. There'd been a wooden bench beneath an ash tree. And birds in the high branches, and in the summer hollyhocks and Canterbury bells. She'd played there with Sam when he was younger. If she went home now, she'd play with him again. She wondered why he hadn't come to visit her.

That bloody man Rose had had the effrontery to suggest his being present while Elizabeth paid her visit to Maddie. Bloody cheek. She'd soon seen that one off.

She pushed open the door and fastened her sights on Maddie, who was sitting in her chair as usual. Elizabeth smiled and closed the door. She felt a wave of over-powering love for her daughter, but other passions pushed it aside. She did not move any closer, not at first. She wanted to weigh up the strange being fate had bestowed on her.

Maddie was nothing like her mother. Had it been the father, eyebrows would have been raised. But Maddie did resemble David. She was a feminized version of the man, very slim, very petite, very vulnerable. She had auburn hair, and a face that would have been beautiful had it not been haggard.

She looked up.

'Hello, Mummy. I thought Daddy might have come along as well.'

'Afraid not, sweetheart. He's still in China. Serving his country.'

'Don't make fun of him.'

'No intention. Maddie, I've come to take you home.'

'But Dr Rose . . .'

'Forget about Rose. Your father agrees. Staying in this place isn't doing you any good. You need to get out with people.'

'But the nurses take me out.'

'I'll get you a nurse, dear. Not one of these Filipinas, wouldn't know if they were nursing or waiting on tables. Proper nurse. I actually believe we have some company nurses. Laurence will know. He's been asking about you. And Max.'

'How is Granddad?'

'Not so well since the fune– . . . He'd like to see you.'

'The funeral?'

'Oh, one of his friends died. It happens a great deal at that age apparently. Shook him a bit.'

'And what about Sam? He hasn't been to visit me.'

'Sam? He's been quite poorly, actually. Nothing serious, but it has kept him indoors a lot.'

'Poor thing. What is it? Flu or something?'

'I'll tell you all about it once we get home. Now, we're going to go downstairs together and tell that nice Dr Rose you're off.'

'Why's your hair so wet, Mummy? You haven't been out in that, have you?'

Elizabeth ground her teeth together.

'Some bastard stole the Merc. The little imbecile who brought it home must have forgotten to set the alarm. I had to get a taxi over, and we'll have to get one back.'

Maddie burst into giggles.

'I can't help it, Mummy, really I can't. You look just like Mrs Robinson in *The Graduate*. You know, the scene where she's been outside in the rain and then comes in, and Elaine knows she's the woman Benjamin was sleeping with. Remember?'

Elizabeth shook her head.

'Probably. We saw lots of films back then. I rather fancied myself as Audrey Hepburn.'

'Never heard of her.'

'You will, dear. Now, come on, let's get out of this morbid place before we all get suicidal.'

CHAPTER FORTY-ONE

Kashgar

The cordon round the city had grown tighter and more ominous by the hour. The sound of tanks had stopped, and a hush lay over everything, as though everyone was just waiting.

David and Nabila spent the day making plans. As far as possible, they worked separately, to avoid any hint of scandal. The maid Asiyeh haunted them pitilessly, clearly disappointed that they gave her so little to do. On occasion, there was nothing for it but to consult one another, whereupon Asiyeh was whipped into service, watching and sewing as they pored over maps or went though one another's lists.

Around noon, they ate lunch with the family. Nabila's mother stayed in her room, but her brothers and some of the fighting men stayed. Osman said nothing to them over lunch, but afterwards he followed them into the courtyard.

'I wish you'd let me in on what you're doing,' he said. 'I don't like things going on without my knowledge.'

'Too bad,' said Nabila. She held a glass of tea in her hand, tenderly, as though it would crack.

'When the time is right, you'll know everything,' David

said. 'We may need your help. You may need ours.' He paused. 'Have your men decided whether or not to attempt a rescue?'

Osman shook his head.

'I managed to talk them round. They know it's pointless. They won't even get out of the city.'

Nabila looked at her brother eagerly.

'Surely there must be more than one way out.'

He shook his head wearily. He'd been up most of the night, talking, arguing, trying to reason with unreasonable men. And all the while, worry about his father had eaten away at his self-control.

'No,' he said. 'And it gets worse every hour. There was a young girl from Shule this morning. Her family live there, and she comes into Kashgar every few days with eggs to sell. She got desperate when she found she'd been trapped in the city, so she tried to get back to the village. Some soldiers found her and shot her. Just before lunch, I heard of a family of Kirghiz who'd tried to return to their pastures. They were attacked and beaten, and now they're being held at a camp on the Tashkurgan road. The animals are gone, of course. It's as if there's a ring of steel round the whole city.'

David nodded. It was beginning to fit only too ominously into a pattern he'd begun to perceive.

'Are they holding everyone,' he asked, 'or only Uighurs?'

'Anyone who's not Chinese. The Han Chinese have already gone. They sent a delegation up to the checkpoint before the river. That was this morning, about eight o'clock. About an hour ago, they sent soldiers into the Chinese quarters. They've been escorted out of the city, and I hear they're being flown out this afternoon. Where to, I don't know. But it leaves the city completely in our hands.'

312

'What about the city officials?' asked Nabila. 'Or the police?'

'The Gongan Bu? They cleared out hours ago, even before the rest of the Chinese. They'd been briefed well in advance, you can bet. The officials have gone too.'

'Who takes their place?' asked David.

'I do.' He said it without pride or self-assertiveness. It was a simple fact. 'Where there is an absence of power, it's proper for Muslims to set up their own rule. I've already given orders to prevent looting. Some young men broke into the houses left by the Han. I'm ordering their execution. A notice is going up, warning everyone that looting or stealing during the period of the siege will be punished by death.'

He looked at his watch. A few yards away, his escort was waiting, impatient to be on their way.

'I have to go now,' he said. 'Our biggest worry is food. Without it, we can't survive. And we still don't know what they want.'

David shook his hand. He watched Osman go, feeling sorry for him. He could have answered his biggest question if he'd chosen: he knew what they wanted, why they'd locked the inhabitants of Kashgar into their own city. But he knew that, if the least rumour was started, the result would be mass panic and who could guess how many deaths?

They set up a trestle table in the courtyard, and laid out a map of the city. David flattened it with one hand. Nabila's hand grazed his as he did so.

They faced two major problems: how to get out of Kashgar, and how to make their way to a suitable point on the southern rim of the Taklamakan to enter the desert safely. The ring round the city was solid, and over lunch they'd heard of individuals whom desperation had led

313

to try a dash across the fields, where there were no checkpoints. None had got through alive.

'I can't come up with anything,' Nabila said at last. They were sitting in the courtyard, drinking tea. Asiyeh sat ten yards away, sipping black tea with sugar as if her life depended on it, which it probably did. Her daily intake threatened to leave the house with nothing to see it through the siege.

'If we could disguise ourselves as Han Chinese, we could just walk on out of here,' said David.

'What about flying out?'

'No use. Those tanks carry anti-aircraft missiles.'

They laughed at the absurdity of it.

'Or we could dig a tunnel to the outside. It would only need to be a couple of miles long and come out in a safe spot.'

David sipped his tea and watched the wings of a tiny bird as it played through the branches of the mulberry tree.

'We wouldn't have to go that far,' he said. 'If we could start inside a house at the very edge of town, we'd only have to dig underneath the cordon. If we exited when it was dark . . .'

'Is it possible, do you think?'

'I'm not sure. There'd be a lot of digging. If we had help, we could dig right through the day. Even so, it could take a week or two to get there.'

'We can't get help.'

'Are you sure? I'd have thought a tunnel would be some help to Osman and his men.'

'I'm sure it would. But then it would be their tunnel, and they'd control who went through it. I wouldn't be allowed.'

'Well, perhaps . . .'

'No, David. I meant it when I said I'd go into the desert

with you. I'm not afraid of that, but I am afraid of sitting here not knowing what might be happening to you.'

'Can we get help from someone else? I've got enough money to pay some boys to dig for us.'

'That might work. There's plenty of cheap labour at the best of times. But you'd have to be able to depend on every single labourer. Some of them wouldn't be above visiting one of the checkpoints late at night and giving them exact details in exchange for a new pair of shoes.'

'Perhaps we could keep them in one spot . . .'

'We'd have to think about it carefully. If only . . .'

She put down her glass. Cardamom seeds floated on the surface of the golden tea like tiny barrels.

'Come with me,' she said, pushing her chair back and heading for the door. David followed.

Nabila muttered something to the guard at the entrance, then shooed David into the alleyway.

'Where are we going?' he asked.

'Officially, to the hospital. In fact, you and I are off to meet one of my neighbours.'

She hurried him through a tortuous maze of dusty lanes, where each turning seemed only to lead into three or four passages, where what seemed a cul-de-sac would suddenly open to reveal a narrow gap between high, windowless walls. However dark and bewildering it all became, she did not hesitate once, or retrace her steps, or dither. She forged ahead as though she could have done it all blindfolded.

They came at last to a high wooden door whose only distinguishing marks were the Chinese character for 'peace', and next to it a calligraphic version of its Arabic translation.

'Chinese?' asked David, surprised to find any Han this deep inside the Old City.

Nabila shook her head.

'Hui,' she said. 'This house has belonged to my neighbour's family for over one hundred years.'

The Hui were Chinese in appearance and language, but Muslim by religion. Officially, they formed a separate ethnic group.

Nabila rang a bell, and within minutes they were ushered inside and asked to wait in a little room by the gate. David looked round. Quotations from the Koran, some in Chinese, some in the original Arabic, lined the walls.

The door opened again, and a man in Muslim dress came in, leaning on a cane with a brightly polished silver head. He bowed politely to David, then fixed a pair of mischievous eyes on Nabila. David guessed he was about fifty years old. He was very thin, and his posture suggested some form of wasting illness.

'Nabila,' he said. He spoke in Uighur, with a flawless accent. 'How unexpected, and how kind of you to come to visit me. And to bring a friend.'

She introduced them. Hot tea was ordered, and they all retired to a small shaded room where shadows hung in every corner. Here too, the plaster had been painted with swirling arabesques of Chinese and Arabic lettering, now in red, now in green, now in black.

'The calligraphy's extraordinarily fine,' said David. 'Was it done very long ago?'

'Not very.'

'Does the calligrapher still live in Kashgar? If he does I'd like to meet him.'

'Yes, he lives in Kashgar. But he does not like to meet people.'

Their host was Ma Jenwen. He lived with his wife and his aged father, and Nabila said she had known him all her life, since they were children together.

316

Seeing David's puzzled face, Ma Jenwen explained.

'How old do you think I am? Fifty, fifty-five?'

David hesitated. He was aware that the truth lay outside perception.

'Yes,' he said, 'perhaps. I really don't know.'

'Jenwen and I were born five days apart,' said Nabila. 'Our fathers were close friends. Still are.'

'I have an illness that kills me very slowly,' Ma Jenwen said. 'It's no more than the same disease that is killing you, killing my beautiful Nabila here. But its signs are less visible on her face. In my case, the disease has not progressed as rapidly as was once feared. But by the time I am forty, I will seem seventy and more. If it speeds up even more, I may not reach forty. Now, I don't think Nabila brought you here to talk about this. Or to drink tea.'

Nabila put her teacup down and looked at David. Shadows spidered about them, dipped and swerved as the light shifted outside. In a corner of the room, someone had placed a solitary rose, bright red, with emerald leaves.

'Ma Jenwen is a civil engineer. He qualified at Sinkiang University a year before I did. I won't recite his biography. But he has worked with sewage construction in several places, and with mines.'

'I see.'

David ran his hand through his hair. A light dusting of sand was sprinkled through it.

'Nabila and I have a problem,' he began.

Ma Jenwen sat listening. Now David spoke, now Nabila, each setting out the difficulties they envisaged in tunnelling out of the city. When they finished, there was a long silence. Sounds came from the alleyway outside. Little boys were kicking a football back and forwards. Someone was playing music on a gramophone, a Uighur pop song whose scratchy words seemed to faint away on the dry air.

'It can be done,' said Ma Jenwen at last. 'But it will be very difficult, it will take a lot of time, and it will entail considerable risk. You cannot use street boys to dig: they can't be trusted. You'll have to use your father's men.'

'I've already told you,' said Nabila. 'If Osman or my father get one word of this, they'll lock me inside till the siege is lifted.'

Ma Jenwen looked very hard at her.

'What makes you think it will be lifted?'

'Nothing, I . . .'

'Just assumed? I think you assumed wrong.'

'What makes you so sure?' asked David.

'Instinct,' he said. 'Sometimes, I feel as though I'm living ahead of time, as though I'm already several years in the future.'

'You're not,' said David. 'You're with us now.'

'My mind goes anywhere it pleases. Believe me, they don't mean to lift this siege and walk away.'

'All the more reason for us to get out,' said Nabila.

'You want to escape? Perhaps it is all in aid of a little romance? I really can't help you if that's so. We would all like to escape, for all sorts of reasons. But no one can claim special privileges. Not even if they're the daughter of our beloved Sheikh Azad.'

'Or a very dear friend of yours?'

He hesitated, then shook his head.

'Nabila, I've already explained. None of us can expect special treatment.'

'I'm not asking for special treatment. I can't tell you why we want to get out. But you know me well enough. Quite honestly, our lives will be in more danger outside than they could ever be in Kashgar.'

318

He frowned and ran his hand uneasily along his stick.

'What about other lives?' he asked. 'How many will be put in danger if you are found outside?'

'I don't know. None, I hope. But you must believe me, Jenwen – if my friend and I succeed in what we plan to do, a lot of lives will be saved.'

'How many?'

Nabila did not answer. Her friend's interrogation was upsetting her. She'd never seen him so serious before. It was David who replied.

'All of Kashgar,' he said. 'Every man, woman, and child. And after that? Tens of thousands more. Perhaps millions.'

'This is the truth?'

'I have no reason to lie to you.'

'Nor has Nabila. But she lied to me before.'

Nabila looked up, shocked.

'When . . . ?'

'When you ate my melon and threw away the rind.'

Her mouth opened and closed again. Ma Jenwen sat facing her, smiling broadly. Nabila's face turned as red as the rose in the corner.

'But . . . You knew that was me?'

'Yes. And the time with the yellow plums. And that other time with the seedless grapes I'd bought in the market.'

'How old were we then?' she asked.

'You'd have been eight, I think. I was anywhere between eight and sixteen. But you mustn't worry, I won't tell your father.' He burst into loud laughter, and they joined him. 'But we must get you out of Kashgar.' He paused. 'Nabila, I think there may be an easier way. But I can't be sure. You haven't seen my father in some time, have you?'

'No, but . . .'

'I think you should. And I think we should introduce Ruzi here to him.'

With surprising energy, Jenwen got to his feet and led them out of the room into the house.

It was as though someone had stopped a large clock, and with it frozen parts of time itself. David could not say exactly what gave that impression. It was not a single thing, but a combination of presences and absences. The house had been so constructed that they passed from room directly to room, through open doors. There was nothing modern anywhere, no newness, no polish, just age upon age of dust. No radios, no electric lights, no barometers, no clocks, no photographs. As though the living were not living, and the dead were not dead.

It was a large house. Wherever they went, they encountered the frozen air of a world that had stopped at some point: with the fall of the Ching Dynasty, perhaps. Or the demise of the Republic. Or a small death in the family, it was impossible to say.

At the very last, they came to a broad staircase that led to a wide wooden landing. Ma Jenwen led them up. The wood was varnished and highly polished, like a frozen lake at dawn. They crossed the landing and came to a door on which someone had traced in a very competent hand the characters for 'truth' and 'eternity'.

'He's waiting,' Ma Jenwen said as he opened the door.

They walked inside, and he closed the door behind them. David took Nabila's empty hand, for they seemed lost in a place not quite of this world, and he was afraid to lose her. It was a large room, filled with shadow and sunshine in almost equal proportion.

They should have known something was wrong almost from the start. Perhaps it was the plainness of the room that lowered their guard, or the incense that covered any smell. The walls were pure white, and the curtains that billowed in at the windows were of white muslin. There was no furniture, except for a bed at the far end.

Everything around the bed was plain. The wall behind it was blank, save for a phrase from the Koran that ran across the head of the bed. The floor was bare of carpets. The bed itself was dressed in the starkest white, with covers that hung almost to the floor.

Nabila thought there was something strange about the bed, but she couldn't see clearly from where she stood.

'What is it, David?' she asked.

He went a step nearer.

'Flies,' he said.

There had been a sound from the beginning, but until now it had been impossible to identify it: a low, buzzing sound, the accumulated arousal of thousands of blowflies come to feed. But what were they feeding on?

They walked forward as far as their stomachs could bear it. Slowly, the dense black cloud seemed to lift, as though the flies sensed their nearing presence, or, sated, rose to hover before once again descending. And for a moment they saw the old man lying with his back to the wall, and what had been his mouth wide open and full of buzzing flies, and what had been his eyes wide open, blinded with flies.

Nabila put her hand to her mouth and staggered back, then turned and made for the door. The others followed her. Behind them, the buzzing intensified, and the black cloud fell again on the thing on the bed.

Outside, Nabila leaned for a few minutes against the wall. As she recovered herself, her stomach heaved, and she ran to the corner to throw up. Straightening, she looked at Ma Jenwen.

'How long?' she asked.

'Two days ago. The day before yesterday.'

'Before the siege?'

'Yes. He said he sensed something bad coming, said he was afraid to wait for it.'

'And then he died?'

'That night. I was alone with him. He seemed to be sleeping, then . . . I noticed that his breathing had stopped.'

'Why did you leave him? You realize he could be a health hazard in a city like this? Good God, Jenwen, you're an engineer, you know about public health measures. What you've done is unforgivable.'

'I had no choice.'

'What do you mean "no choice"?'

'He made me promise. He said he was not to be buried in the public cemetery but in the sanctuary of the Abakh Hoja Tomb. I thought I would arrange it on the following day, then . . .' His voice stilled.

'He has to be buried. Abakh Hoja is six miles beyond the city limits. We can't take him there. It will have to be one of the sacred tombs inside the city, the Sayyid Ali Tomb or . . .'

Ma Jenwen shook his head.

'It doesn't have to be. I couldn't take him, but you can. He knew a way to Abakh Hoja's Tomb. In the days of Yakub Beg's rebellion, when the city's fortifications were strengthened and everyone feared there would be long sieges, my great-grandfather vowed that the people of Kashgar must never be cut off from the tomb of Abakh Hoja. He and his sons and servants dug a tunnel beneath the city walls and out all the way to the tomb. I'm too weak to carry my father there. But you can.'

CHAPTER FORTY-TWO

London

> Polly Potter, Polly Potter
> Fell off her perch, and Pussy got 'er.

She clasped cold hands round her steaming cup of coffee. For some reason, the window of the café was misted over. She didn't mind not being able to see out, in fact it quite suited her. It provided further concealment, kept prying eyes away. The old schoolgirl jingles ran through her head like thread in a bobbin. She'd been Polly all those years, and hated every minute of it. Being plain and brainy hadn't helped.

> Polly Potter, Polly Potter,
> Potty Potter's potty daughter.

She sighed, remembering. They'd called her all sorts of names, cruel, thoughtless names and senseless gibes she'd done her best to ignore; but what resources do you have at thirteen? Her years at Dumbarton College had been unremittingly awful. She'd often thought that entering the Secret Service had been an unconscious means of getting her revenge.

Polly Potter, Polly Potter
Never did what she had oughter.

She'd telephoned the service earlier in the day, once she'd
got herself set up: some money from her cash machine,
a change of underwear, a bit of make-up, a hip flask of
whisky, and she felt ready to face the world. Or, if not
the world, a little bit of it.

The attack on her flat had terrified the life out of her.
Twenty-five years in the service, with a couple of postings abroad, had never put her in a position like this.
But the attack had been nothing compared to what had
happened since.

She'd been put through to Security right away, and
they'd been very kind at first, promising immediate back-
up, tutting and clicking their tongues at every mention of
mayhem and her pulse-racing getaway.

'Any idea why, Miss Potter?'

'Why?'

'Why they're after you.'

'I haven't the slightest fucking idea. For all I know their
mothers brought them up badly. Shame on them.'

There'd been a few suggestions, none of which she'd
given house room to.

'Are you in debt to loan sharks?'

'No.'

'Have you ever handled hard drugs?'

'What do you think?'

'Does someone hold a grudge against you? An old
victim of the service, perhaps? Somebody we shopped,
somebody you laid a trap for? A relative? A friend? Friend
of a friend?'

'How the bloody hell should I know?'

'Just thought I'd ask.'

He'd sounded hurt. They often did, they were sensitive souls, wore their hearts on their sleeves. Agents didn't call them the Social Workers for nothing.

'If you want to know the truth . . .' she'd said, thinking it was time she told them, conscious that this disembodied voice on the other end, however cool, however hurt, was the voice of Security. The Social Workers were her way out of this. And Tursun's refuge too. They had the safe houses, the new identities, the hope. She did not know if the boy was alive or dead, but she had to do what she could to guarantee his protection if Farrar hadn't got to him yet.

She knew it was Farrar, of course. No, not knew, not really. Common sense told her it was just her long dislike of the man implanting suggestions. His name had popped into her head the moment Tursun had slipped the note across the table to her; but she'd forced it out of her mind as too wild, too implausible. Then instinct had prevailed again and she'd settled for Farrar as her best bet.

Prejudice could not be ruled out, but mostly it was an accumulation of little incidents over the years since he'd taken charge of China Desk – trivial things that had meant nothing at the time, but which gained in significance the more she thought back over them. She realized she'd had them filed away for just such a moment as this.

'If you want to know the truth,' she'd said, her voice held calm and reasonable to fool the voice-analysis machines, 'we've got a traitor in-house.'

There'd been a frozen silence, and for a moment she'd felt naked, inadvertently exposed.

Polly Potter, Polly Potter
Red worms eat 'er and maggots rot 'er.

'Could you be more specific, Miss Potter?'

There'd never been a Mr Potter, as it were. Plenty of men, several of whom had offered to change her name to Pride or Orpington or suchlike. Such nice men, but quite useless to her, every one.

'Please, Miss Potter. We need your help.'

'Well, as a matter of fact, I'd . . . rather not be. Specific. Not till I'm in a safe house. Or somewhere more secure than that.'

Another silence, as though Central Operations was slipping away from her down some sort of slippery grey tunnel. She knew them, they could wipe you out with a word or its omission.

'This isn't very helpful of you. If you don't tell us . . .'

'As a matter of bloody fact, I've told you all I actually know. I don't think it's a coincidence that I receive information about a traitor, and next thing a big man with a gun starts smashing my flat to pieces. I want you to take me out of here and put me somewhere he can't get at me. I also need a communications link to China so I can pass on a warning to one of our agents. Then I want you to send someone to Carstairs pdq. There's a boy in there who may be at risk.'

'We know about the boy.'

'What do you mean, you know about him?'

'We know who goes in and out of Carstairs, Miss Potter. Wouldn't be right, our not knowing.'

'Then you'll get him out?'

'If he's there.'

She didn't like that 'if'. It clung to her afterwards like a rebuke. They took down some details, but even as she spoke, she overheard a man's voice in the background, murmuring words she could not make out. Had he been there in the room with them all along, or was this just a phantom voice on the line, a listener-in, an appraiser, a reckoner? It had been an insecure line anyway – where was she going to find a secure one at two in the morning?

They'd told her where they wanted her to go: a warehouse in Ponders End, down near the ballast works. It was a place where the service stored boxes of shredded paper before incinerating it. Or so they said. 'How long will it take you to get there from where you are now?' they'd asked. 'At least an hour,' she'd said. Taxis were too clumsy and unreliable, so she stole a bicycle and left a wad of banknotes to mark its disappearance.

She'd turned up well ahead of them and found a vantage point from which to watch. She'd not lost her field skills, what few she'd ever learned, watching, listening, observing (which was quite different to watching), waiting, anticipating. She'd added a few of her own, not that anyone had ever paid much heed: intuiting, blending, ignoring appearances.

They came in four cars, and she didn't like the look of any of it. Least of all did she like the heavies they'd wheeled in. She knew their names, Stuart and Stevie. The Bouncers were big lads from the North-east, very sweet-natured, but remarkably strong and welded to duty like ice to skin. They had not been brought out to Ponders End to comfort or reassure her. She was a loose cannon, and in the handbook loose cannons needed more than a little ballast.

She'd slipped away on her bicycle, back down the Hertford Road, and slowly into town. A cheap hotel had loomed into sight just as she was on the verge of collapse and wondering how much further she could go. She'd booked a room and slept well into the afternoon. The hotel was near Hackney Downs, about as near the bottom of the star-rating system as it was possible to get without falling into a black hole and staying there. Most of her fellow-guests were professional women turning tricks. She'd been awakened about two in the afternoon by a couple in the next room engaging in vigorous and noisy physical exercise.

Now it was nearly eleven at night. She'd spent much of the day in cheap cafés and pizza parlours, drinking oily coffee and thinking it all through. The file on David Laing which she had stolen was now destroyed. Even so, she desperately wanted to get in touch with David, but she couldn't think how. It only occurred to her as she'd been about to finish her last drink and shuffle back to the hotel.

She'd found the café on her first foray: it was a few doors away from the hotel. There'd been a telephone behind the counter, so she'd made her mind up there and then and rung Chris Donaldson from Section Six. He knew David, he knew Tursun, he would understand the problem.

He told her he'd be there in an hour or two.

'Don't tell anyone else,' she said.

'I won't.'

'Not even in the service.'

'Especially not in the service.' He'd laughed gently and replaced the receiver.

So she ordered a coffee and a KitKat, and sat down at an empty table in the corner. Apart from herself and a balding man behind the counter, the place was deserted. She'd asked the man earlier when he closed, and he'd answered that it was an all-night café, that there'd be customers in and out till morning: taxi drivers, nurses from the maternity hospital at the end of Jew's Cemetery, prostitutes from Dorking Road, firemen, spongers, creeps.

'No druggies, though. I can't stand that. Got no time for that, I haven't. Drugs.' And he'd spat on the floor as if to say that hygiene was king.

It had suited her down to the ground. A Camp coffee and a KitKat and a long wait, it was what she wanted.

He turned up fifty minutes later, dressed in pitch black, as though he'd come for a funeral. A cigarette hung on his lower lip, his eyes looked tired. The café had filled a little. Cigarette smoke hung on the air, blue and drifting, the drug of choice in here. There was a night watchman from a nearby building site, a few loaders from the freightliner terminal, a couple of the girls from the far end of Dorking Road. They looked up hopefully as he came in, then dropped their eyes again, seeing him focused on her table.

'I see the cavalry has finally arrived,' she said as he sat down next to her, scraping his chair over the torn linoleum.

He lifted an imaginary trumpet to his lips and tooted.

'I see you've found the most salubrious place in London to hide out in,' he said, glancing round. The coffee machine coughed and spluttered. One of the girls laughed, and briefly the place seemed charmed.

'I didn't know places like this still existed,' she said. 'There's something timeless about it. They know one another, the regulars that is, and there's a sort of camaraderie. But it's all surface. They don't really know one another at all. They're just passing in time. The night goes by, and they drift in and out, and nothing changes.'

'You sound depressed.'

'Wouldn't you be?'

'I'll take you out of it,' he said. 'Not just the café, the whole thing. But first I need to talk. I need to know exactly what's going on.'

He stood up and walked to a jukebox on the wall

opposite. The man behind the counter watched him go. He made a selection of five records, then turned back to the table, pausing to buy a coffee on the way. The first record came on, Tom Waits singing 'Downtown Train' in a dirge-like voice that seemed somehow appropriate.

'Go through it from the beginning,' he said, settling back into his seat. Steam rose from his coffee cup, making a faint veil between them. 'Don't leave anything out.'

She was tired, but she knew she'd not get any sleep until she told him what little she knew. She told him, and he listened, frowning.

'That's all?'

She nodded.

'You don't actually know who this traitor is?'

'Tursun didn't name him. Not in my presence, anyway.'

'But you must have your thoughts. Your suspicions. Ideas spun at home.'

'I have ideas, yes. But nothing certain.'

'Have you told anyone else?'

'You. Security, of course. That's it.'

'Why didn't you just turn yourself in to Security? They'd have looked after you, it's what they're good at.'

She glanced round the café in its trembling fluorescent light. Its all-pervading desolation caused her real discomfort. She'd been here so long, she felt part of it already.

'Someone sent the Bouncers,' she said, hugging the words to herself. 'I didn't like the look of them. There's no need for that.'

'So you ended up here?'

'As you can see.'

'Did you telephone anyone else from here?'

Her head moved from side to side. She wanted to sleep, to sleep for a long time.

'I've no one left to phone,' she said.

'No friends?'

'What would be the point? It would only land them in trouble.'

'You've had discreet liaisons from time to time. Would one of them . . . ?'

'Take my word for it.'

'Very well, I do.'

She looked up then, as though his questions had alerted her. The café had emptied. Even the man behind the counter had made himself scarce. The coffee machine gurgled unattended, throwing out clouds of steam in all directions.

The door opened and Anthony Farrar came in, dressed in a light coat. He looked tired, thought Pauline, and his cheeks and eyelids were pale. He did not smile when he caught sight of her. She did not smile back.

'I'm sorry . . .' said Donaldson, the only apology she'd ever get.

They'd always mocked her. What happened now would be no exception. As she got to her feet she felt Farrar take her elbow.

> Polly Potter, Polly Potter,
> First they got 'er, then they shot 'er . . .

CHAPTER FORTY-THREE

Ma Jenwen instructed Yusup and Zunun, the two under-takers who lived in the next alley but one, to deal with his father's rapidly decaying remains. They demanded payment well above the standard rate, and Jenwen handed over every penny without quibble. The body was embalmed – quite against usual practice – and wrapped tightly in the best bandages. Downstairs, they placed the old man in the light wood coffin that had been prepared for him ten years earlier, and filled the spaces with camphor before nailing down the lid.

The old man's Muslim name was Shams al-Din, and his Chinese name was Ma Deming. He had been ninety-seven years old, he had married seven wives, divorcing four and outliving three, and he had had a single child, who had spent his entire life dying. Ma Jenwen had never thought to outlive his father, in spite of the old man's great age. His own life had been such a helter-skelter race towards death, and his father's such a sedate journey.

Just on the edge of the old town, between a bakery and a shop selling translations of Arabic texts on law, there stood a small neighbourhood mosque.

'Take the coffin to the Molena Ashidin Mosque,' Ma Jenwen said. 'Leave it there till morning. I still have to notify some of the family.'

'We can't bury him in the cemetery outside the city. You understand that, don't you?'

'I'm speaking to the family of Sheikh Azad. They have space.'

David and Nabila had been given strict instructions to return when it was dark. The Chinese curfew had been lifted, because no one remained to enforce it. But Osman had imposed one of his own, and his men were scattered across the city to see no one used the crisis to rob and steal.

David spent the evening at Momin's, sorting out what he needed to take with him and what he could leave behind. Of prime importance was his Magellan GPS, a small hand-held device weighing just over one and a half pounds, that would allow him to navigate using the twenty-one Global Positioning System satellites. In theory, GPS in hand, he'd be able to navigate his way through pea soup, thick-cut marmalade, and molasses.

He also packed his pistol, a sub-machine-gun, and several boxes of ammunition for both. The gun was an Uzi. He'd been forced to choose between it, with a 10-inch barrel, and a Sterling Mark 7 in its 4-inch version; the Uzi had won because it was so reliable in desert conditions.

He pulled the last strap tight and looked at his watch. There were still a few hours to go, and suddenly he felt desperately tired. He'd barely slept the night before. And he'd be lucky to find much time to sleep for a long time to come.

He said goodnight to Momin and went to bed, setting his alarm for two o'clock Peking time. Within minutes of his head touching the bolster, sleep was sucking him down into a deep pit that seemed to have neither bottom nor top. He felt himself spinning helplessly within it, then he and the pit had become one thing, and there was nothing but spinning, and nothing but darkness.

And then there was no darkness, and everything grew still. He was in a great forest, and above him the trunks of giant trees seemed to go up for ever. He walked and walked, trying to find a way out, but the further he went, the more all-encompassing the maze of trees became. It was as though the whole world had grown green. What sunlight came through the tangle of branches above had lost its original colour and acquired an emerald tinge.

He sat down on a tree-stump, tired and lost, and suddenly he caught sight of a doorway, and a staircase going up behind it, and proper light coming down from somewhere out of sight.

He passed through the doorway and started climbing the stairs. It seemed to take days to climb to their very top. The last step took him on to a short landing of polished ebony, where he came at last upon a fanciful door, embossed with dragons and wonderful trees and birds, and painted in red and gold. A huge lock of polished brass took up a great chunk of one side, and silken tassels as big as giant artichokes hung on the other.

David opened the door silently and stepped into a vast room scented with lilies and ambergris. Everywhere heavy curtains hung, embroidered with silk and gold thread. Beneath their feet, thick carpets had been laid, Chinese and Indian and Central Asian, all mixed together lavishly, their colours and their patterns clashing and harmonizing without rhyme or reason. From the ceiling hung thousands upon thousands of paper lanterns, each lit from deep within by a single candle, each with its own colour – now amaranth, now sapphire, now celadon, now carmine, now magenta and heliotrope and amethyst, now azure and indigo and ultramarine, now citron and fallow and jonquil and nankeen. Hundreds of colours, no two ever quite alike. And from each lantern hung ribbons and tassels that moved in the gentlest of breezes.

There was a sudden ringing of a child's laughter. He turned incautiously and caught sight of a small figure vanishing behind a curtain.

'Sam?' he called. 'Sam.' His voice echoed round the room for a moment, then was stopped dead by the heavy hangings.

He ran in the direction in which he had seen the small form disappear, and just past the curtain he saw him again, a little boy like Sam, in the midst of a game.

'Sam!' he cried. 'Sam!'

The boy turned, and he saw it was Sam, then he turned again and ran between more curtains. From nowhere, a man's voice spoke two lines of poetry:

> Separation is nothing but melancholy.
> Parting lies in the heart like a bitter taste.

He rushed forward and saw the boy running for a tall black door. The door opened and shut, and when David reached it, it was part of a long black wall without opening or breach.

He turned and saw a second door behind him, a white door that stood open to reveal a white room. When he reached it, he found he was naked. He could hear his heart beating loudly. Somewhere, a master musician was playing on the *ch'in*. The door closed behind him, and he looked to his right.

A naked woman was standing facing him, smiling. She was young and very beautiful. She opened her lips to speak, and in the sweetest of voices said, 'Remorse disappears.'

335

He made to step towards her, but as he did so she became pale and began to shrink, like an unhappy ghost.

Suddenly, the walls of the room began to crumble, and he found himself standing in sand, and there were dunes all round him, and beyond them mountains of sand. When he tried to walk he found himself trapped up to his knees, and no amount of struggling would allow him to break free.

And then he woke, calling Sam's name loudly into a darkness he did not recognize.

FLAME OF A BUTTER-LAMP

CHAPTER FORTY-FOUR

The tunnel lay beneath the *minbar*, a short wooden stair-case built to serve as a pulpit. From a wreathing pattern of arabesques, a tiny handle emerged to give purchase on a little door with grimy, creaking hinges. It had not been opened in a very long time. A mass of cobwebs filled the opening, and as the door pulled back, tearing them, dozens of black bodies scurried in all directions, fleeing back down into the darkness and solitude beneath.

'There are steps down to the tunnel itself,' said Jenwen. 'They were built of wood, so be careful. Nobody's been down there in a century and a half, and for all I know they've rotted away completely.'

'What about the tunnel?' asked Nabila. 'What keeps that in place?'

'I'm not sure. My father never told me. But the chances are it was wooden struts. It's a long tunnel, they wouldn't have used stone.'

'So they could have rotted away as well?' said David.

'I suppose so.' Jenwen looked downcast. Only now was it dawning on him that the route to the tomb might be closed, and that his father's last wishes might not be capable of fulfilment. The old man's body lay behind them on a trailer. Dark stains had already started to appear here and there on the tight bandages that strapped him about, little messages from the world of corruption to the world of light.

At the moment, David wasn't sure just how bright things were looking for himself or Nabila. He didn't know how they were going to get out of the city if the tunnel had collapsed. And if his guess was right, staying in Kashgar wasn't such a clever idea.

He took a large torch from one of his bags and swung a powerful beam of white light into the opening. More cobwebs everywhere, and steps staggering down into the blackness.

'They don't look all that straight to me,' he said. 'I don't see much point in risking our necks just to find out.' He switched off the torch and turned to Jenwen. 'Any chance of finding a ladder in here?'

Jenwen nodded.

'This way,' he said.

The mosque had a small minaret. Five times every day, the muezzin would climb to its top by means of a long ladder. It could be dismantled if it ever needed repair, and it took Jenwen and David only minutes to uncouple the long bottom section from the rest and drag it to the tunnel entrance. It hit the ground with about a yard to spare.

'Thank you, Jenwen,' David said. 'You've been more helpful than I could have hoped for. I promise we'll get your father buried as close to the shrine as possible. You can visit his grave once this is over.'

Jenwen thanked them, but he still looked glum.

'Something's going to happen here in Kashgar, isn't it?' he asked.

'I don't know,' David answered. 'I have no way of knowing. But, yes, it is a possibility. Later, when we're clear away, let Osman know about this tunnel, and tell him to start sending as many people out as possible, provided he can do it without starting a panic.'

They embraced quickly, then David climbed into the opening. The ladder held steady, and once he had negotiated his way past the opening, the rest was easy. The descent could not have been much more than twenty feet, but by the time he reached the bottom, he was covered in spiders' webs and, as far as he could tell, every spider from here to the tomb. He had a revulsion, bordering on a phobia, for the creatures, and once down he beat and shook and jumped to rid himself of them. They scampered off, heading back into the darkness, leaving him shivering.

Nabila lowered the four-wheeled trailer on a rope. It bumped and grated as it went down, then thumped to the ground and crouched there like a cat waiting to pounce on the next passer-by. It was followed by the old man's body. David shone his torch on the mummified figure as it twisted down, scratching and banging on the ladder's rungs as the rope holding it slackened and tightened, turned now this way, now that. It too hit the floor less smoothly than intended. David grabbed it by the shoulders and manhandled it on to the trailer. He stepped back quickly. The old man stank abominably.

Next came the bags holding their basic equipment. They'd have to find anything else they needed outside, once they had camels on which to carry the load. David straightened them, manoeuvring a couple on to the trailer next to the body. At the same time, he heard Nabila's feet in the space above him.

Moments later, she appeared at the foot of the ladder. There wasn't much room for them to stand together. Jenwen called from above, checking they were safely down.

'Everything's fine,' shouted Nabila. 'Get back to your house. And take care. There's still a curfew.'

A muffled farewell came from above. Then the ladder was pulled up, a few rungs at a time. When it was clear of the opening, Jenwen closed the door. It slammed down heavily, blotting out the little light there had been to connect them to the outside world.

David shone the torch up along the way they had come. About twelve feet above their heads, the rotten steps had given way. They were trapped. The only way out lay ahead, down the tunnel. If the tunnel hadn't caved in years ago.

CHAPTER FORTY-FIVE

Western Region Military Installation 14
(Chaofe Ling)
[Co-ordinates classified]
Level 7
Security Classification: Maximum

'Lock in five!'

A heavy bolt shot into place. A voice incanted, '*Suo-shang le*.'

'Lock in six!'

The regulator's finger pressed an illuminated button and there was a sound of a bolt slamming, followed by a hiss of escaping gas.

'*Suoshang le*.'

The routine continued. Right across the operations room a buzz of concentration kept everyone bowed over his terminal or display screen. Lights flashed and dimmed, screens filled with information and grew still, there would be bursts of conversations, then absolute silence that seemed to go on for ever. It would take over two hours to complete the installation, and they all knew that a single mistake could disrupt the procedure for hours more, or even days. Some mistakes could be fatal. Some could wipe out the entire complex at a stroke.

Chang Zhangyi stood at the back of the room. He was

only an observer here. His men were scattered through the complex, asking questions, double-checking answers. The entire security operation for Chaofe Ling was in his hands, and he liked to pay regular visits just to make sure everything was running smoothly, or, if it wasn't, to find out why.

He frowned and thrust a long toothpick between his upper incisors, hunting out what remained of his supper. Things had not been going forward very easily in the past couple of weeks. Each of the last three tests had been delayed, one for no less than four days.

The Iraqis were growing impatient. They'd already started troop movements and could not now pull back. Their battle plan rested on accurate use of the new weapon: if it went well, Saddam Hussein would seize control of the entire Middle East, from Israel to Pakistan; if it went badly, he had opened himself wide to defeat on a scale unparalleled in modern military history.

And that, thought Chang Zhangyi, would spell disaster for China. He wasn't supposed to know that, and he was well aware that, if he so much as breathed a word about it to anyone, he'd end up in one of his own dungeons.

All the same, he knew it was true. He'd seen estimates that the oil reserves in the Tarim Basin, covering the Taklamakan and some of the region beyond, amounted to between twenty and forty million tons. That was still the official line: some Western oilmen were talking about potential reserves as big as Saudi Arabia's. He'd met them when they came over to carry out surveys on the fringes of the desert. Big men, strong men; but easily deceived.

In fact, the Tarim Basin was almost empty, and it was getting emptier with every day that passed. The oil was leaking away, into God alone knew what unreachable depths. Decades of nuclear testing in the nearby Lop Nor had produced the most undesirable of results. Across both deserts, the bedrock had cracked and, in places, sheared across. Vast oil pools had started to drain away entirely. Visitors were shown only carefully selected sites, and sent away with promises for future development that were sown with procrastination.

Chang Zhangyi watched the composite screen overhead, on which each stage of the operation was being plotted. So far, so good. First, they had to pump a series of biochemical agents into the shell of the bomb, then they had to mount it on to the delivery vehicle. This would be the first time they had been deployed together. The big challenge would come the following week, when they would carry out their first live test on the population of a large town.

Without the oil, he thought, China would begin to die. A little at first, then with increasing rapidity. The country needed to be self-sufficient in oil if it was to drag itself out of the last century. Now, as it was beginning to develop a solid industrial base, the dream of wealth and security was once more slipping from its grasp. To import oil, it would have to sell something. There was plenty of coal, but countries with oil didn't want it, and middlemen would rake off more than they were worth.

Hence the project. Hence the urgency to ensure that Saddam did not lose his last war. They'd sold him weapons in the past – who hadn't? – but this would put him in permanent debt to the People's Republic. And when he had control of all the oilfields of the Middle East, he could dictate terms to the West and provide all the oil China wanted for less than it would have cost to extract it at home in the first place.

There was a bleeping noise. At first he thought it came from the console in front of him, then he remembered his pager. He hated it, just as he'd hated his mother's voice summoning him as a child. He'd never married for that reason; he wanted no wife to call him home, or scold him, or bicker with him. He'd devoted his life to the service, and risen in it faster than any of his fellow-graduates. Whatever the political climate, he'd stood alone, and he'd ridden the storm. A wife and a family would have got in his way, like compassion or guilt.

He told the security officer beside him to keep an eye on things, then slipped through the door into the short corridor that gave access to the main throughways of Level 7.

An elevator took him to Level 1, and a buggy to his office. Pan was waiting inside, a little impatient.

'It better be important.'

Pan withered, but rallied as he thought of his reason for calling his superior from the test preparations.

'I think so, sir. There was a call from London. Secure satellite. He'll try again in a few minutes: I said you had a little way to come.'

'Farrar?'

'He didn't say, sir.'

Just then the phone rang again. Chang Zhangyi picked it up this time. Farrar's voice came on the line, sharp and clear. Chang Zhangyi waved impatiently at Pan, telling him to clear off.

'How are you, my old friend?' he said.

Farrar got straight to the point. Chang Zhangyi listened carefully, jotting down notes. When Farrar came to an end, he smiled to himself, anticipating the coming manhunt.

'I'm exceedingly glad to hear it, old chap. Because, if you don't stop Laing, you and I most definitely will be dead.'

'Rest assured, Mr Farrar, he's as good as dead.'

CHAPTER FORTY-SIX

There was a scent in the tunnel like the breath of long-dead roses, something that would not wash out of the soil or vanish from the air. David breathed it in unwillingly. It smelt corrupt, almost infected, and yet it had in it the sweetness of recently laid flowers piled high on one another over centuries.

The tunnel roof was not high enough to allow either of them to walk unbent. The walls and the wood-slatted ceiling pressed in on them, and at times the floor itself seemed to rise, as though to lift them yet closer to the roof. David hauled the trailer and its load along by means of a coarse rope that had partly unravelled in several places. The rope cut into his hands, drawing blood, its irritating fibres slipping beneath his skin.

In numerous places the walls sagged: they were astonished that there had not been several cave-ins. Struts were bowed or half-broken, and here and there the soil behind them had broken free.

Nabila went a little in front of him, shining the torch-beam down into the plummeting dark. He could see her only as a rupture of the light ahead, and he felt an appalling guilt, knowing what he was bringing her to.

'Why does the tunnel smell of flowers?' he asked.

She paused and breathed in deeply.

'Roses,' she said. She shook her head. 'It doesn't make

much sense. My father once told me about this tunnel. He said that, in the days of Yakub Beg, the ground was strewn with roses. They grew them all year round, in great quantities, then they brought them down here and laid them on the ground all the way from Kashgar to Abakh Hoja's Tomb. The practice continued for almost fifteen years, then Yakub Beg was defeated and the tunnel sealed. It was known as the "Velvet Path". Others called it the *Tariqat Allah* or the *Sabil al-Firdaus*, the "Path to Paradise". They used to carry the sick along it. Some went all the way on their knees. There are stories of miracles.'

David looked round him at the naked walls and uneven floor. He saw no miracles. Yet something in the soil or the air conspired to hold the last traces of the flowers that had been left there by a short generation of pilgrims. He glanced up. Every so often, he could see glass lamps hanging from the struts, grimy now and without light; but in every one a candle still waited for the touch of flame.

Less frequently, he could see the ends of narrow ventilation shafts. Putting his hand to one, he could feel a faint touch of fresh air. They must have been skilfully hidden in the fields above, and angled or cowled in some way to allow rain to run off without flooding the tunnel.

He halted for breath. Nabila waited for him a few yards ahead. At first he could hear only his own breath, rasping a little in the close atmosphere. Then, as his head cleared, he heard something else. It sounded like footsteps. Behind him. Even as he strained to listen, it stopped.

'Did you hear that?' he asked.

'Hear what?'

'That sound behind us. Here, let me have the torch.'

She passed it to him, and he swung the beam back into the tunnel the way they had come. There was nothing visible but the trailer and the frail bundle on it, walls and floor, the marks of the little vehicle's wheels.

He passed the torch back to Nabila, and they headed on. David had calculated that roughly two yards separated one set of struts from the next. Keeping a mental record of how many they had passed, he stopped when they had reached an estimated mile. He glanced at his watch. Just over half an hour had elapsed since they entered the tunnel.

'Would you like me to take the trailer?' asked Nabila.

'No, I'm all right. Another mile, perhaps – then you can take over.'

They did not talk much as they progressed through the tunnel. The thick air made breathing difficult, and talking a struggle.

They paused to manoeuvre the trailer round a heap of earth that had fallen into the tunnel. As they did so, David heard the sound again, soft footsteps cushioned by the soil. Nabila turned too.

'Yes,' she said. 'I heard it that time.'

David took the torch and went back several yards.

'Jenwen?' he called. 'Is that you, Jenwen?'

There was no answer. He called again, but his voice was swallowed up by the thick walls and the darkness and the stillness.

'It must be Jenwen,' he said to Nabila. 'There's no one else back there, surely.'

'He may be following his father's corpse.'

'Then why doesn't he just stay with us?'

'I . . . I'm not sure.'

He sensed the hesitation in her voice, but did not pursue the matter. If Jenwen wanted to dog their footsteps, it could do no harm to let him. It was irritating, no more than that.

They went on. Half an hour took them another mile. Feet followed them all the way: feet that kept pace yet never caught up. It was hard to tell whether it was one pair of feet or more. Sometimes David stopped suddenly, and then, for half a second, he would catch it behind him.

They halted at the end of the second mile, and Nabila walked back to take the trailer. As she did so, she looked back down the tunnel.

'Look,' she whispered.

David turned. Everything was silent. The scent of long-dead roses multiplied. Nabila switched off the torch.

Along the tunnel behind them, as far back as they could see, candles were burning inside the little lamps. The flames flickered and grew still, flickered and grew still. David held his breath. He expected to see someone at last, to catch sight of their pursuer – or pursuers – stepping into the light like an actor on to an illuminated stage. But no one moved.

'Don't be frightened,' he said. 'We won't harm you.' He said it in Uighur, then in Chinese, but no one stirred. Out there, on the edge of the dark shadow, where the light ended, he saw what might have been movement and equally might have been a candle bending with the weight of its own flame.

'Let me have the torch again,' he said. Nabila put it in his hand, and he switched it on. For a quick moment, he was certain he saw something move, a low, crouching figure, very pale. But it had been no more than a flash, and within moments his certainty had faded.

'Let's keep moving,' he said.

They pressed on as before, their feet thick against the soft soil.

'I think I know who they are,' whispered Nabila. 'My

father once told me a story about the people who live in the tunnels beneath Kashgar.'

'Tunnels? You mean this isn't the only one?'

'I don't know. I've sometimes heard other people refer to them. They're supposed to have been built a long time ago, during a siege, to let people move about in safety. But I can't be sure. They may just be a legend.'

'Like the people who live in them?'

'I don't know. What would they live on? Where would they find water? They'd go blind without light.'

'But someone or something is in here with us, there can be no doubt of that.'

'No. Perhaps they aren't a legend after all. My father said that when the Chinese defeated Yakub Beg some of his soldiers took their wives and children down to the tunnels, and that they stayed there and grew old and died, and that the children had children of their own.'

'Is that what you think?'

She shook her head.

'There are people in every city who drop behind, like someone at the rear of a camel train in the desert. Who knows where they go, what they do to survive?'

They walked on in silence, not knowing what to make of any of this. There were footsteps, certainly, and other tiny noises they could not interpret. The tunnel stretched out in front of them, as though it meant to swallow them.

They passed an opening to one side. David stopped and shone the torch inside. Another, narrower tunnel had been dug through the earth, its sides strengthened by rough mud-bricks that must have been made down here and dried somewhere on the surface.

'It seems to go back quite a distance,' said David. 'I wish there was a chance to explore, but we've no time to waste.'

They passed two more tunnels. Though they stopped and looked inside only to find them empty, each time they were assailed by a sense of watching eyes somewhere back in the darkness. Had they learned to see in the dark after all? When David looked back down the main tunnel, the lamps had been extinguished.

Three hours after stepping into the tunnel, they came to a square door built of heavy timber and studded with enormous iron nails. A huge brass lock occupied about a quarter of each wing. Koranic verses had been inlaid along the sides, in Arabic and Chinese. In the centre, an inscription had been engraved in a lozenge-shaped sheet of copper: 'The Shrine of Abakh Hoja, may God have compassion on him'.

David dropped the rope, and he and Nabila set to work on the lock. Though untended all this time, the door was still in good shape, and the lock as hard to break open as it had been when a key was last turned in it.

'What do we do?' asked Nabila. In spite of her equilibrium, she was beginning to find the tunnel claustrophobic and unnerving, and the discovery that they might find themselves trapped at the very end of their journey had brought her close to panic.

'It's a beautiful door,' said David, 'but we have no choice. I'll have to break the hinges.'

'With what?'

In reply, he opened one of his rucksacks and drew out a short crowbar.

It wasn't easy to slip the flat end of the crowbar between the door and the jamb, but the wood had softened a lot, and, once he had forced an opening, the rest was simple. Under pressure, the wood and screws gave way, and the door fell in at the back.

Laying one wing of the door to one side, they pushed

the other back on its hinges. Ahead of them stood a steep flight of steps, cobweb-choked like those at the other end.

'I'll go up first,' said Nabila. Suddenly, she wanted to be free of the darkness. 'Will you be all right on your own?'

'Yes, I'll be fine. You'll have to haul the old man up. We'll leave the trailer down here, though – there's no need for it now. Here's the rope.'

She climbed up, choking on dust and cobwebs, striking out at spiders as they fell on her hair and face. Ten steps. Twenty steps. And then, quite abruptly, a ceiling above her head. She must be under the floor of the shrine. Careful not to stumble backwards, she reached up and placed one hand against the ceiling, fearful that it would be as stoutly locked against her as the door had been. She pushed upwards, and at first it seemed that it was locked on the other side, or that heavy weights had been laid on top of it; but another push persuaded the flooring above her to give way, and a last shove sent it flying back with a crash.

'Are you all right up there?' called David. His voice sounded weak and lost, as though it already belonged to a different world.

'I'm fine,' she called back. 'How are our friends?'

'Very quiet.'

She took a deep breath and climbed out of the opening. Her eyes felt blurred. The air up here seemed entirely fresh after the tunnel, and she drank it in greedily. She hadn't a clue where she was. Taking the torch from her belt, she snapped it on.

Her head was just above a tiled floor, and her first guess was that she was in one of the many rooms of the shrine complex. Then the torch moved on, and she picked up a clutter of strange shapes. Slowly, she brought the light back and focused on the shapes one by one. They were nothing more than pieces of rubble, some large, some tiny, scattered everywhere across the floor. The further out she looked, the more there seemed to be.

'David,' she shouted down, 'I think you should come up here.'

She scrabbled out on to the floor and waited for him. There was a scuffling sound, then he was with her. Carefully, she pointed out to him what she had seen.

He took the torch from her and switched it off. No need to draw attention to themselves. He then looked up. An open sky with the faintest hint of dawn, sprinkled with stars, with Venus rising. And far off against the horizon, the setting moon.

'They've destroyed it,' he said. 'They've demolished the shrine.'

Even as he spoke, a heavy engine burst into life not far away.

'That's a tank engine,' he said. He walked a little in the direction from which the sound was coming.

Lined up in rows, a division of heavy tanks stood waiting for dawn. Their crews were sleeping on the ground beside their vehicles. Someone laughed nearby, then a gruff voice told him to be quiet.

'Let's haul our equipment up and see if we can get out of here before light. I don't give much for our chances if they clap eyes on us.'

'What about Ma Deming?' Nabila asked.

'I think it's best if we leave him where he is. He's right underneath where the shrine used to be. This rubble is probably packed full with old bones. If there's any blessing here, he'll get his share.'

'And what about them?' she asked.

'Our friends in the tunnel?'

'Yes. Do we leave this doorway open for them to find a way out of here, or do we close it to stop the army finding a secret way in to Kashgar?'

'I don't think the army needs secret entrances. Let's leave it open, let them do what they choose with it.'

He went back down and started attaching bags to the rope. Nabila hauled them up and stacked them to one side. It would be a lot to carry for the first phase of their journey.

David's head appeared at last above the entrance hole. Nabila helped him up. Her hand remained in his. He could barely see her amid so much blackness.

'I'm glad you came,' he said. 'I couldn't do this without you.'

She drew him to her and kissed him. Here and there around them, tank drivers set their engines racing.

She brushed a tangle of cobwebs from his hair and stroked his cheek, then kissed him harder. That was when the voice came.

'Step apart slowly, keep your hands in the air. Don't even breathe.' The language was Chinese, the dialect Cantonese.

As they pulled away, David looked round. A single guard holding a heavy-duty sub-machine-gun.

'Kneel down,' commanded the guard. 'I'm getting help.'

CHAPTER FORTY-SEVEN

David looked round in desperation. Their only weapons were in the bags. He still held the torch: it was a long Maglite, made of metal and capable of being used as a club. But how the hell was he going to get close enough to have half a chance?

The soldier made up his mind for him.

'*Shoudiantong!*' he barked.

David had no choice. He lowered his arm and let the torch fall to the ground. He did not think the guard would shoot them unless provoked by a direct assault. But once he examined the contents of the bags neither his life nor Nabila's would be worth anything.

David's Chinese accent was far from perfect; but he realized that the soldier, probably away from Canton for the first time in his life, would most likely take it for a regional dialect of Mandarin, which he would know only imperfectly, if at all. In the dark, he and Nabila could pass as Han Chinese.

'We've just got here from Yengisar,' he said. 'The Uighurs started attacking us. Our children were killed, and my wife and I just got away with our lives.' He hoped the remark about dead children would make its mark.

'There's been no word of trouble in Yengisar.'

David took a step towards him.

'What do you mean, "There's no word of trouble"?' he

asked. 'They're killing Chinese children. There's blood everywhere. Can't you take our word for it? We got out with a few possessions, and we headed this way hoping the army would look after us. We want to go back to Peking. I was a senior cadre, I was due for promotion and a one-way ticket back home, and now look at me.' He took another step in the soldier's direction, arms raised in a gesture of supplication, a picture of harmlessness.

'You'll have to speak to my captain. I'm just here as a guard. It's my job to keep the Muslims out of here. If you're a cadre, you'll be all right.'

But David knew that, once the sun came up, their fate would be sealed. He took another step towards the guard. The man prodded him hard with the barrel of his gun, knocking him back several paces.

'Stay where you are, and don't move again unless I tell you.'

With his free hand, he reached into a pouch on his waist and pulled out a handset. The light was growing. David wondered if the guard would distract himself enough to make a rugby tackle a reasonable risk.

At that moment, the handset fell from the guard's hand, smashing against the marble floor at his feet. David looked round, astonished, thinking Nabila had intervened somehow, but she was still behind him, unmoving as before, her hands on her head. The next instant, David looked back at the guard. He was staggering, trying to keep his balance. The machine-gun dropped with a loud clatter to the ground.

David heard a hissing sound, then a dozen more, and each time the guard seemed to stagger or spin a little, until finally he fell to the ground, crumpled, jerking, coughing and moaning in an attempt to cry out. David bent down beside him.

'What is it? What's wrong?'

But the only answer came in the form of wheezes and gurgles.

Nabila joined them. She had brought the torch, and while David shielded the light from the nearest tanks, she shone it on the man. His face and throat were peppered with tiny darts, forty or fifty of them in all. She pulled one out and sniffed it.

'Scorpion,' she said. 'But this has been concentrated. I can make out some vegetable poisons as well. It's hard to be sure . . .'

The guard started to convulse. Nabila tried to hold him down, while David looked round desperately for something to put him out of his misery.

'I have a knife,' he said. 'It's in one of the rucksacks.'

Nabila shook her head.

'Help me here. He's almost dead.'

Behind them, another tank sang out, as though playing its part in a ritual to summon the dawn. Still, the only true light was from the moon and stars; but at any moment the first faint strokes of the coming day might appear on the eastern horizon.

The guard cried out in a choked and garbled voice, calling perhaps on his mother or his friends for help, or simply calling out against whatever simple thing had turned his life to agony. The cry seemed to pass through all his limbs. Suddenly everything in him went rigid, and his back arched incredibly, like a bow, and a great cry started to come from him, which Nabila had to stifle, and they both held him like farmers with a steer, and for a moment there was overwhelming panic in his eyes. He died like that, with blood in his eyes and in his ears. Nabila let his head fall back against the ground, and set about removing the darts from his neck and face, very carefully.

David relaxed the grip he'd kept on the man's legs. As he did so, he glanced round. He caught sight of their bags, and a few yards away, the opening to the steps leading down to the tunnel. There, in the opening, a small shadow was standing, watching. David got up and made to go to it, but it vanished.

'We have to get rid of the body,' he said. 'If his friends find him like this, there'll be a manhunt from here to the Pamirs.'

They carried him to the tunnel entrance. David shone the torch down; as far as he could see, there was no one at the bottom.

They manhandled the guard to the opening, then let him fall. There was a heavy crunch, then silence.

They closed the wooden doors, and moved some of the rubble over them, so that the spot was well covered.

'Let's get out of here,' said David.

Nabila looked up. Beyond the tanks, she could see trees on the horizon. A star hung, luminous and diamond-hard, near the head of a tall cypress. And from the horizon itself there appeared a thin glow that signalled the coming day.

CHAPTER FORTY-EIGHT

Cadogan Place
London

'Fuck on oota' it! Ah said, fuck off.'

The *Big Issue* seller looked again at the six-foot excuse for a human being. He decided he was wasting his time in return for nothing but insults, made a gesture and went off in search of someone more in harmony with the coming millennium of love and universal brotherhood.

Calum Kilbride glowered after him. He hated beggars. He couldn't see the point of them. Or understand why they gravitated towards him as a possible source of bounty and goodwill. Perhaps they were all blind. Or mentally crippled. During the months he'd spent in India and Pakistan he'd seen more than his fair share. He'd never given any of them a penny, however hideous their deformities or pitiful their aspect. 'Ah'm fucking poor mahself!' had been his constant cry, sometimes punctuated by pulling out the empty linings of his trouser pockets. 'All Ah keep in ma troosers is ma balls. So fuck off, ye radge wee turd.' Beggars in India and Pakistan never believed this. You didn't get to travel thousands of miles across the globe on what they earned.

He looked up at the house. Whoever lived here wasn't

poor, wasn't even moderately well off. If they kept anything in their trousers, it was hand-made designer underpants that they wore once and threw away. He'd sniffed them when he'd turned up at the clinic. Not designer underpants, but pound coins, a hell of a lot of them, all sloshing about this kid Maddie.

In his dreams, he often imagined that a big London publisher had offered him a million-pound advance for a book of raw Scottish ravings. 'Just talk dirty,' the publisher said, dealing out the fifty-pound notes, 'and make sure you write it in Scottish.' Dirty Scottish words were the in thing, apparently. And drugs. He'd have to put in lots of the white stuff and have loads of characters in severe mental trouble on account of it. Calum already considered himself a master of the Dirty Scottish genre. He knew that one day the big screen in the Edinburgh Odeon would be shouting his own words back at him in stereo. Fuck the beggars then, eh? Fuck everybody.

In the meantime, he reckoned he could pick up a couple of hundred here if he played his cards right. He had it all worked out in his head. 'Ah'm down tae ma last fifty pee.' 'Ah've had a gruellin' trip, Ah'm near dead wi' the fatigue.' 'Ah wis robbed by loonies gettin' ootay China.' If only he could get to the wee dame in person, he was sure he could exert his charm and charisma, perhaps even his sexual allure to make an impact on her emotions and her pocket. He'd cleaned himself up and changed his clothes since getting back. Nothing spectacular, but he'd caught sight of himself in a couple of shop windows. He didn't doubt for a moment that he could still pull the birds.

He reached up and pressed the bell.

He waited. A little time passed, then unhurried footsteps approached.

'Sorry,' was Elizabeth's first expression on seeing him

on her doorstep. 'We have a rule. No hawkers. I thought you all knew. You're wasting your time here.'

He caught her just as she was closing the door.

'You're no' Maddie Laing are you?'

'Maddie? I don't understand, what's wrong?'

'Ah cannae tell you. All Ah know is Ah wis given this address by a man called Rose. Ah have a letter fir this Maddie. Fae China.'

Elizabeth's chin went up. There were only two possibilities.

'You'd better come in.'

'It's no' you, is it?'

'No, it isn't me.'

'But she's here, eh?'

'We'll see, we'll see. For God's sake, wipe your feet on the rug.'

It had been raining most of the day. He'd let himself get wet in the hope of extracting a few more drops of compassion out of them.

She took him to the living room. He gawped once or twice and collapsed into a large armchair.

'Drink?'

'Wha'?'

'Would you like a drink? Sherry – no, perhaps not – gin, whisky? Ah, yes, you seem like a whisky sort of person.'

'Maybe a wee . . .'

'Yes, I know. Dram. Certainly. I'll join you. I scarcely touch the stuff nowadays. How about you?'

'Ah . . . Ah've been on ma feet. Travellin', likes.'

'Yes. You suggested that. I seem to remember the booze in China leaves something to be desired. A pale imitation, if you can get it at all.'

'It's a' fuckin' . . .'

362

'Don't say it. This is a tranquil house.' She smiled wickedly at him. He seemed like fun. Not the sort of person she met every day.

She thrust a thick cut-glass tower at him and he took it. His hand shook and his nose threatened to spill on the carpet. He wiped it on his sleeve and tried to smile.

'Tissue?' she said, aiming a large box of Kleenex at him.

'Right. Aye. Just the thing.'

'Now,' said Lizzie, 'I'm Elizabeth Laing. Tell me all about it. But do leave out the swear-words. They're my prerogative.'

Upstairs, Maddie lay in an untidy ball on her unmade bed, humming. The notes of her humming hunted for perfect pitch but invariably failed to find it. At times the hum became a sort of wail. Her dead brother's name sang through it all, like the steady thrum at the heart of a mantra. The bitch her mother was taking her to a guru, some sort of Indian Rasputin in a hand-stitched turban and bare feet who made a comfortable living battening on the gullible souls of Knightsbridge and all areas adjacent.

She lay on her back and screamed at the ceiling, then put her hands over her head when it screamed back. Why had Lizzie told her about Sam? She wasn't ready, she couldn't cope, not with this much grief, not all at once.

Her mother had started to cut back on her tablets. When she was leaving the clinic, she'd overheard Dr Rose pleading with her mother not to reduce the dosage under any circumstances, not without his express permission or that of another psychiatrist. Now, her lithium was way down, her Prozac was being slashed, and her other drugs had been flushed down the toilet pan. She desperately wanted to get to a telephone and ring Rose, check what he thought, ask him to get her out of here – she was well over eighteen, after all, and not even her mother had the right to keep her here against her will; but the door was locked night and day.

'And what did he look like? This man, the one you say handed you the letter?'

'Ye dinnae believe me?' Calum was growing to dislike this pompous woman, with her serious hair and alcoholic eyes.

'No, Good Lord, of course I do. It's not that at all. Why should I disbelieve you? I'm sure you're very honest. You look very honest from head to toe. If you shaved and had some decent clothes, you might even look quite presentable. Physically.'

It had not taken Lizzie long to see that beneath Calum's rough exterior there lurked an even rougher interior. Wash him, put him in Boss underpants, and he'd grace any catwalk. Or bedroom.

'Cut out the crap, will ye? Ah've brought the fuckin' letter. All Ah want is ma reward and Ah'm oot o' here.'

'Such impatience. Look, McGonagall, I'm not running a nursery for the totally deranged here – though, considering what I've got upstairs, I might as well be. Before I part with good money, I want to know this extra thing: What did he look like?'

Calum gave a rather wooden description. His memory of David was hazy. He'd been stoned at the time, and the wee wanker with the envelope had been just another native.

'Oh, for God's sake!' exclaimed Elizabeth. 'Stay there.'

She flounced off, and came back half a minute later carrying a framed photograph.

'Is this him?' she asked, pointing to a man on the right of a group that included herself and Maddie.

Calum took the photograph and squinted at it. It was a good likeness. And he could see the resemblance between him and the girl.

'Ay, likesay, that's him. Was this taken oot there, then? Was the wee man your guide or somethin'?'

'Don't be such a bloody retard. The "wee man" is the girl's father. The girl is Maddie Laing. She is David Laing's daughter and my daughter too, which makes me his bloody wife, though as you can currently see, he and I are not exactly living a marital existence.'

'How'd you come tae get hitched tae a Chinese guide?'

'Forget about it, Hamish. You say this was in Kashgar?'

'Ah dinnae take kindly tae bein' called Hamish. It wis ootside the Chini Bagh.'

'That means nothing to me. And I'll call you what I damn well like. You say it was on the day a curfew was imposed? Nothing in, nothing out, except for the bus you were on?'

'The Karachi Express. It's what we called the squits all the time we wis on it. Ah've been overtook by the Karachi Express in more toilets than you've set foot in.'

'Don't be so sure about that. You're certain he stayed behind, the man who gave you the letter?'

'That's why he handed me the letter in the first place. The Chinese wirnae lettin' the natives oot. An' he was well hitched up tae a wumman. Nice wee thing, fancied her masel'.'

'I see. A woman. Well, I'm not surprised. Good luck to them both.' She basked in the thought that Anthony would be pleased with her, rotten pleased. He'd be pleasantly submissive tonight in bed, she thought. Which brought her back to David and his 'wumman'. One of his own type, no doubt, an ending he richly deserved.

The thought of David's infidelity – as she deemed it – had a curious effect on Elizabeth.

'Not bad, this whisky, eh?' she said, draining the last mouthful from her glass. 'Shall I top you up?'

'Ah've got tae be goin'. Maybe Ah should take the letter tae the wee girl now.'

'Oh, no, out of the question. Look – what did you say your name was?'

'Calum. Calum Kilbride.'

'Well, Calum, I have a distinct impression your clothes are on the wet side. Why don't you stay for a shower and brush-up while I get the girl to dry them out? Then we can see about this wretched letter.'

'Well, Ah . . . Ah dunno. He said . . .'

'Who, David?'

'Ah dinnae ken. The man who handed me the letter. Said there'd be somethin' for bringin' it here. Ah widnae bring the matter up, likes, except . . . The fact is, likesay, Ah'm doon tae ma last fifty pee. And Ah'm near dead wi' the fatigue and all.'

'You poor man.' She reached out and gave his knee a reassuring stroke.

'There wis . . . loonies on the road oot of China.'

'Good heavens. Well, would five pounds help?'

He shook his head. Now he'd started, he was getting into his stride.

'He wis talkin' more than five pound. More like . . .' He took a deep breath and smiled. 'Two hundred. Or so.'

She looked hard at him for about a minute, sizing up one reward against another. Inside her brain, a little screen read 'What the hell?'

'Calum, sweetheart,' she began. 'Two hundred is a lot

of money, even for me. Postmen don't often get to see sums like that, much less scruffy Scots hot off the hippie trail. My feeling is that I'm entitled to a few more services than that. Don't you agree?'

She fell silent, but her fingers played with the buttons of her shirt, opening two more than was really modest. She looked at Calum. He was looking her up and down, uncertain where to go from here. She opened another button.

'Ah think Ah'd better have that wee shower,' he said in an awkward voice.

'Damn right. And brush your teeth.'

'An' after that, Ah have tae deliver the letter.'

'Not right after, dearie. You have a pressing appointment just then.'

'The trip wis gruellin', y'unnerstan'? Ah'm near wore oot. Ah may no' be up tae much.'

'My dear man, getting your Celtic backside from the western frontiers of China to Cadogan Place won't have been half as gruelling as the next three hours are going to be. And God help you if you don't perform, Hamish. This is not a clinic for sexual inadequates.'

'Ah dinnae ken about you, missus, but Ah could do wi' another wee bracer.'

She smiled and poured two long ones.

The first thought that struck him was that there'd been a mistake. The kid in the photograph downstairs had only been thirteen or fourteen. The dame on the bed had to be twenty-something. The door had been locked. He didn't like that, couldn't see the need for it. It had started to occur to him that this was a family to be avoided at all costs.

Maddie watched him from the bed, on which she'd been lying in an attempt to doze off. She opened her eyes warily and took note of the stranger standing in the doorway. The door closed behind him of its own accord, and there was the sound of a key turning in it.

'Who the fuck are you?' she asked.

'You askin' me, doll? Ah'm Calum, an' Ah'm completely spent. Would ye mind if Ah sat doon on that chair?'

'What are you doing here? Who sent you?'

'Your daddy. Can Ah sit doon? Ma back's killin' me somethin' terrible.'

'My father? Did you say my father sent you?'

He ignored her and sat down on the armchair.

'Nice chair,' he grunted. 'Good springs. Ye'd never believe the half-sprung monsters Ah've sat on in ma time.'

'You said my father sent you.' She felt herself growing angry again. The anger could get unbearable, could drive her into hysteria or plummeting despair.

'He did.'

'Rubbish. My father's out of the country. A long way out. I don't know what you told my mother, but it won't wash with me.'

'Look, doll, Ah didnae come here tae be insulted.' He had, in fact, had exactly what he came for, two hundred smackeroos for bugger all. Well, on reflection, the money had been for sexual services. He'd made her come four and a half times. That was worth a bob or two.

She rolled to the side of the bed and swung her legs over.

'Just get the fuck out,' she screamed. It was hurting her. Something was coming up inside her, something from depths Rose didn't know about, from the dark hours between coming awake at dawn and final consciousness around noon. Final waking was knowledge, final waking was the bitterness of reality. 'My father's dead,' she said. 'They killed my brother, and then they killed him. Now they want to kill me too. Is that what you're here for? Is that what you've come to do? Who sent you? Six?'

'Aaah, fuck this, Jimmy.' He drew the bent and travel-stained letter from his pocket. He'd insisted that it remain unopened until it was in her hands. There'd been a long argument with the missus about that. But he hadn't budged. 'Yer father's no' dead. At least, he didnae look dead when Ah saw him. Ah wis in Kashgar. Have ye heard of it?'

She took the letter with shaking fingers. Kashgar? Maybe it wasn't a trick. She tore open the envelope and pulled out the thin sheet of paper inside.

'Take yir time, dinnae mind us.'

She began to read. For a while, the words and sentences fell apart in a desperate vortex of deconstruction that left nothing to make sense. Then everything steadied, and she felt herself become calm. The words snapped into place, and it was almost as though she could hear her father's voice.

Maddie, I honestly couldn't get out of this. You know I'm not allowed to tell you why, but you must believe me when I say it was important, more important than any of my other trips. Darling, I'm desperately concerned about you, more than you can guess. All I want is for this to be over so I can catch the first plane out and be back in London with you as soon as I can.

I hope Dr Rose is taking good care of you. He's a bit of a stick and very fussy, and, of course, he's terribly keen on money, but, actually, I think there's quite a good psychiatrist under all that.

Darling, your mother and I are still good friends in spite of anything you may think at the moment. She has her own problems, some of which you know about. Try not to mind Anthony too much. I don't like him, but he's not a bad man, so why not give him the benefit of the doubt?

The main thing is for you to get better. It's all I live for, honestly. When I get back, I want to see you on form again. Between ourselves, I've been thinking of quitting the service, taking a job where I can spend more time with you and Sam. But first of all, I've got some leave due, a lot of leave. If you're up to it – and I'm depending on you – we'll head off somewhere together, just the two of us. Scotland, maybe, or Ireland. Maybe we could go down to Cornwall for a while. Your choice.

So you don't think I'm holding out on the gossip, I'm . . . Oh damn, I don't know how to say this, but I can't write nothing now, can I, or you'd smell a rat. As you always do. Maddie, I've fallen in love. I was going to write 'I think . . .' there, but that would have been a lie, and I never want to lie to you. Her name is Nabila, she's a doctor of Uighur medicine, and she's much more glamorous than I am. You needn't worry, it won't go anywhere. She's a Muslim, I'm not, and there's an end to it. Mind you, it's nice to dream sometimes.

Maddie set down the letter, leaving unread the hastily scribbled notes at the end. Two tears formed in her eyes and found their way slowly down her cheeks. She wiped them away clumsily with the back of her hand, but more came to take their place.

'He shouldn't have lied about Sam. He knew about it

all the time, knew he was dead. Why did he have to lie about it?'

'Look, doll, Ah'm a bit oot of ma depth here, know what Ah mean?'

She looked at him as if seeing him for the first time.

'How'd you get this letter?' she asked.

'Your auld man gave it tae me.'

'Then he's in Scotland after all? That's what Rose said. But he told me he was going to China.'

'It's all the same fuckin' thing, believe me.'

Somebody banged on the door. He groaned. Surely he'd scratched her itch enough for one day. He stood, casting another glance at the girl on the bed.

'You goin' cold turkey, hen, is that it?'

'Not what you think.'

'No, but – what are ye on? Crack? The Big C?'

She shook her head.

'Just prescription drugs,' she said. 'My mother's trying to wean me off them.'

'Fuck that. Ye look like shite, beggin' your pardon. Ye need help, doll.'

More banging.

'All right,' he shouted. 'Ah'm no' raping the bastard.'

He got to his feet and went to the door.

'Ah'll be back,' he said. 'Dinnae fall asleep on us.'

Lizzie stretched out naked on the bed, and yawned deeply. It had been a satisfying afternoon, in ways she wouldn't have thought possible. If only life could be that fulfilling in general. She yawned again and hugged herself, and felt the inevitable onset of depression.

She wondered why she did it. Years ago, she'd made excuses – David went off for long periods on his own, Anthony had his own flings – but none of them really matched the sordid reality. She'd discovered by the time she was in her mid-twenties that it was possible to obtain sexual satisfaction while remaining empty inside. But with the passing of time the emptiness had grown while the satisfaction was increasingly hard to find. She might as well have said she wanted love and been done with it. Lots of people confused sex with love, she wasn't alone, she comforted herself in the sense of belonging it gave her.

One thing she was sure of. If she had her way, her precious Maddie would never be a prey for gigolos like Calum Kilbride. She'd see to that, she promised herself.

CHAPTER FORTY-NINE

Sand came from nowhere and went back to nowhere. A small breeze moved with it among the dunes, picking it up, casting it down again, as if in slavish performance of some ritual so ancient it had no name and no purpose. However often the sand moved, nothing changed. The dunes were undiminished. They rose up and sank down, driven by their own secret tides. It was like an electric power in them, an energy older than anything else, older than stone, older than the caverns in stone.

David wiped a film of sand and sweat from his forehead. Moments later, it had started to form again, slick and repellent against his skin. He could make out the top of the dune, then another, higher still, beyond it. These were low dunes, three or four hundred feet at most. Before long they would reach the mountains of sand, dune piled on dune for a thousand feet and more.

He glanced behind him. Their train of camels was still fractious, and from time to time an animal would stop dead, or throw its load, braying loudly as it shook it off, or another would try to break from the caravan. Sometimes one would try to do all three in quick succession.

'They'll settle down in time,' Mehmet, their guide, had said. 'It's always like this at first. Give them three or four days.'

'What's the longest journey you've done in the desert?'

'Two days.'

There were nine camels in all, seven males and two females, each one joined to the other by a short length of rope that stretched from one beast's tail to the next one's nose. They were fat Bactrians with long manes and thickly padded humps, well-preserved against the hardships of the coming journey, but edgy beasts all the same, inclined to snarl at unlikely moments, or bite, or kick out.

'Just how used to desert work are they, anyhow?' David had asked Mehmet on the second day.

The guide had shrugged. He was a man in his early thirties, with a large moustache and a disconcerting tendency to scratch himself anywhere and everywhere, for hours at a time.

'Not a lot,' he said. 'Nobody goes into the desert much. What's the point? There's nothing to buy or sell.'

'So these camels have never actually made a desert crossing of any kind before this?'

'I imagine not.'

'But you have at least worked with them round the fringes?'

Mehmet scratched his belly and shrugged eloquently.

'Not these camels, no. I'd never set eyes on them before yesterday. My brother bought them from friends in the next village.'

He gave them names, Uighur and Arabic names like Khoja, Latif, Aziz, and Abdu'l-Kerim. David couldn't get on with the names, at least he couldn't match them to individual camels very well; so he did a naming of his own on the second day, just before they pitched camp for the night. He gave them solid English names, as if to tie the poor beasts to a different reality than the one they walked through: Bill and Ben, Woolly, Elvis, Rag,

Tag, and Bobtail, Doris and Mabel. It amused him at first, until they snapped at him or refused to budge at a critical moment. Doris and Mabel were particularly nasty.

Nabila gave them names of her own, names she admitted to but refused to divulge. They were most at their ease with her, and as the days passed David and Mehmet both called her to the front when a camel needed talking round. When she spoke to them, it was not in Uighur or Chinese or English, but in a language of her own devising. She'd found herbs and other medicines in Tazgun, the village where they'd bought the camels, and every night after they'd been unloaded, she tended to their saddle sores and infestations.

They had so many names in the end, it scarcely seemed to matter what you called them. Except that they responded to Nabila's names and ignored the rest.

'You mustn't call them silly names,' she said to David one day when they'd stopped at the bottom of a high dune to recuperate a little. 'Or childish names.' She gestured to Mehmet. 'He gives them Muslim names, but they aren't Muslims, they wouldn't recognize the Prophet if he walked right past. And you give them names from old television characters.'

'I wish I hadn't told you that.'

'They have their own names. In a little while, you'll see.'

He looked round again. Woolly was in the lead as usual, a huge brown animal with a long matted coat and a crew-cut head.

'Come on, Woolly,' he urged, 'get a move on.'

But Woolly just plodded on as before, miserable as sin beneath a sun that had lifted the temperature to over a hundred degrees Fahrenheit. His friends plodded after him, equally miserable. So far none of them had come up with a way out of the mess they were in.

By the time the journey finished, David reflected, they would be skin and bone – if they made it that far. They stretched behind him, their heat-soaked bodies dotted like frail dinghies along the steep leeward flank of the dune. Far at the rear, he could make out Nabila's diminutive figure as she moved in and out among them. He looked up to see Mehmet cheerily waving from the top of the dune. Another one down, only another ten thousand nine hundred and forty-one to go. Roughly.

David wondered if they had not made a mistake in coming into the desert this early. It had been a hard decision, the only really difficult decision he'd been forced to take during this entire mission. The Taklamakan is an oval of sand squashed between the Tien Shan and the Kun Lun. It is an almost uniform mass of ochre sand that runs for eight hundred miles west to east and three hundred and fifty north to south. The bare figures conceal a nightmare. There is no life in it. To move across it in any direction takes superhuman will and effort. The desert prohibits life, smothers it, wrecks it, blocks it at every turn. To enter the Taklamakan is to die, quickly or slowly, it makes no difference to the sand or the stone a thousand feet beneath.

The sector David and Nabila were headed for lay somewhere around the centre of the oval. It was no coincidence: the centre was the logical place to put such a site. Ideally, they should have headed east by road, entering the sands only when they were directly south of their presumed target. But the fierce restrictions on road travel along the desert's southern rim made it an unacceptable risk to go very far in any direction. After leaving the Abakh Hoja shrine, they'd spent much of their time ducking out of sight of military convoys and isolated trucks and jeeps. From time to time, they'd seen donkey carts go crawling over the semi-lunar landscape of the desert's edge, and they'd seen the occupants pulled to the side and searched.

In the desert, there were no patrols. No soldiers, no jeeps, no helicopters, no searchlights, no barbed wire. The dunes would guarantee their safety. David had made his decision, and they'd gone in.

He sighed, looking up at the dune they were climbing. It only made matters worse that they were walking in the wrong direction. He'd caught on to the problem soon after they set foot in the sand. Travelling as they were from west to east, they were climbing the dunes on the leeward side, where the sand was softest and hardest to get a grip on. It felt like walking through treacle.

'Mehmet,' he called, feeling the grit enter his mouth as he did so. 'We'll stop at the bottom of this dune. It's time we had a rest.'

They'd been up since first light, loading the animals before breakfast, then setting off at the slow but steady pace they'd grown accustomed to. Noon was the time of fiercest heat. They took what shelter they could inside their little tents while the camels rested, still fully laden, mouths agape with thirst. They would not be watered until that evening. If they were watered at all. It all depended on whether they found underground water or not.

They made their little camp at the bottom of the dune, leaving the camels spread out untidily where they'd knelt to rest. The sun was still too high to make it worthwhile looking for water, let alone digging a five- or six-foot hole to get at it.

Mehmet made tea, using water from one of the drums

they'd carried from Tazgun. David had taken a dislike to them the moment they'd been trundled out of the store in which they'd been kept: dumpy metal barrels, square and squat, each one capable of holding around eighty litres. They'd seemed quite sturdy to look at, but when David inspected them he found they'd been welded together from smaller pieces of metal – parts of old oil cans, vegetable-oil containers, even imported beer cans from heaven knew where. In places, the metal was thin enough to pierce with a light blow, and everywhere the welding seemed no more than the work of moments.

'One of these barrels is going to get smashed open,' he said. But he didn't think one, he thought four or five or more.

Mehmet said nothing. He'd heard this before. His younger brother had obtained the barrels from an uncle in Kumkesha. They'd been the best available. Well, all that was available. His uncle made them for households along the narrow corridor of fertile land that flanked the desert's western edge, and he'd never had a complaint before this. Of course, none of his barrels had ever been used on a camel before.

'Drink your tea, love, and stop fretting,' said Nabila. She spoke to David frequently in English, in spite of Mehmet's evident disapproval. Their guide seemed to suspect them of God knows what improprieties. They'd said they were man and wife in order to ward off awkward questions at Kizilawat; but Nabila was known in the area from her regular travelling clinics, and the sudden appearance of a husband provoked raised eyebrows here and there.

'What's our safety margin?' she asked, sipping her own tea from a chipped cup. 'How long before it's just as far to get out as it was to come in?'

'Quite wide. I'd say ten or eleven days before we reach

that stage. That's without accidents. The moment we have an accident, the margin narrows, maybe a little, maybe a lot. Each time something goes wrong, each time we stray from the route, each time someone sprains an ankle or a camel collapses, the margin narrows even more. You can count on accidents in a place like this. I'm surprised there haven't been any already.'

'I didn't know we had a route.'

David shrugged, but she sensed he was being guarded about something. She'd caught him more than once, standing atop a dune, taking bearings with his compass.

'It's somewhere out there,' he said, sweeping his hand in a wide semicircle; but they were hemmed in by dunes, and any direction might have been as good as another.

Nabila worried less about their struggle to cross the desert than she did about Kashgar and her father and the rest of her family.

'They're planning to use Kashgar as a test site for this new weapon, aren't they?' She sipped her tea calmly, as though at home, quiet in the afternoon. It was already full of irritating grains of fine sand.

'I think so, yes,' David answered. Nabila nodded and said no more, staring out along the valley between the nearest dunes.

'Is there any chance of our getting to this place, this . . . Karakhoto, before they carry out the test?'

He shrugged again.

'Maybe. I don't really know. Perhaps it's already taken place. How would we know out here?'

'But what if we do get there in time? What can we possibly do, just the two of us?'

'Nothing directly. Our advantage is that no one will be expecting us. They won't have defences or guard posts out in the desert. But the weapons centre must be huge.

It doesn't show up on satellite photographs – this region's very closely studied, believe me. I think it might have been built under the bedrock, using equipment brought in from one of the Lop Nor centres.'

'Brought in? Brought in how? You're talking about very heavy equipment. Wouldn't it have shown up on your spy photos?'

'They won't have brought the equipment in overland, Nabila. The desert alone would have made that impossible. No, they must have dug a tunnel and brought it in underground.'

'But that . . . that would have cost a fortune.'

'Probably a lot less than the Channel Tunnel. They'd have used slave labour, cut corners on safety, built for limited use. They'll have thought it worth the effort if it gave them a chance to build and test a weapon capable of doing what we think this can do.'

There was silence for a while. Nabila looked up. Wind touched the ridge of the dune they were about to climb, like a playful finger tossing sand. The whole place seemed like a playground, a huge sandpit fit for giant children. Somewhere out of sight, she thought, lurked faceless demons, monsters that could turn a desert to glass or mountains to the finest sand.

'What do you think it can do?' she asked.

'There isn't much hard data on which to hazard even a wild theory, but . . . my guess is that this is a nuclear device based on the latest weapons built at Lop Nor V and VI. I think you'll find they've succeeded in compacting the central device. That will mean concentrating the blast so that a single weapon destroys no more than a street or two, maybe less, maybe just the building it falls on.'

'Why not just drop a conventional bomb?'

He raised a hand.

'You're missing the point,' he said. 'They don't want to destroy the street or the building. But when the bomb explodes, all the force goes into the radiation. Even from such a tiny blast, a very wide area would be saturated with radiation hundreds of times more deadly than that released by ordinary nuclear bombs. Nothing could shield against it. Nothing.'

'But what's the use of it?'

He looked almost surprised.

'The use of it? Like any weapon. To kill people. The problem with most nuclear weapons is that they generally kill too many people. They make a mess, they wipe out entire cities. This one's designed differently, or so we think. The Iraqis want it because it's a perfect battlefield weapon. You can calibrate it so you either get a small blast and massive radiation with a very short half life, or you choose a large blast if that suits your strategy better.'

'But . . . my patients aren't showing radiation symptoms.'

'Aren't they? Remember, this isn't ordinary radiation. And what you've seen until now has been the early experimental stage. What they're looking for is radiation that can kill its victims in a matter of hours, even minutes.'

The sand was like a dream nothing could pass. Nabila took a fistful of it in her hand and let it sift slowly to the ground. Dust to dust. A camel bayed behind them and was silent. Mehmet rose to his feet and strode to the first animal. It was time to go.

CHAPTER FIFTY

Laurence Royle's Office
London

'It's like a bloody desert in here. Can't a person have a drink, for God's sake?' Elizabeth flung open a cupboard door only to find two shelves of glasses and a cocktail mixer. 'Bloody hell!' She slammed the door shut, but it bounced open again, shaking the glasses.

'Cut it out, Lizzie. You're on the wagon as far as I'm concerned. And you're on probation as far as the rest of the board goes. Don't, for God's sake, look so petulant. You agreed to stay sober, so do me a favour and pack it in. You can have a small brandy after lunch. A Hine Antique. Very old, almost as old as me.'

She didn't laugh. How he wished she would. Even as a child she'd been too serious, too domineering to be much of a friend. It struck him suddenly that that was what he'd always wanted of her: companionship, humour, some sort of recognition that they were siblings. He looked at her now. Did she ever loosen up? he wondered. Did she laugh in bed?

He looked at his watch. The board was due to convene in ten minutes. He was expecting a stormy ride on two counts – first, his decision to reinstate his sister on the board, and secondly for the escalating costs incurred in setting up the Aladdin Oil deal. None of the rest of the board knew the first thing about it, of course, and Laurence had no intention of telling them. But money was shifting about between accounts, and some explanations would have to be given.

'You could at least give me a ginger ale, you creep. I'm parched.'

'Why didn't you say so in the first place?'

He opened the drinks cupboard, found a small can of ginger ale, and poured it into a glass.

'Ice?'

She shook her head. He handed the glass to her and closed the cupboard.

'Nothing for yourself?' Her voice carried a hint of danger. Her cheeks were flushed, her eyes a little too sharp.

'Afraid not. Look, there are things we have to talk about. But I've just remembered there are figures that have to be crunched before the meeting gets under way. Norton's working on them upstairs, but I'd like to see just how he's getting on. D'you mind if I leave you here for a few minutes? I won't be long.'

'Of course not, why the hell should I mind? Don't worry – you don't have to keep an eye on me: I won't touch your precious booze.'

'Yes, I'd far rather you didn't.'

'It's a nice office, Laurie. Smarter than the old one. Not as tarty.'

'Man called Forshaw. Very well thought of. He designed the whole thing.'

'You'd better toddle along. People will be arriving any minute.'

He pursed his lips and made for the door. It closed behind him softly, as if layers of hot air had been placed between it and the jamb.

Elizabeth listened to the door, then set her ginger ale down on the table nearest her.

'Bugger,' she said. 'Bugger, bugger, bugger.'

He hadn't given her any time. It was just like Laurence to do that. She remembered, when she'd been a schoolgirl, with pubescent breasts and knickers from hell, she'd fancied him out of all proportion to his real usefulness as romp material. He'd never responded. When they were alone together – which was often enough – she'd take ages to work herself up to whatever it was she thought might get things going, only for him to make a sharp exit with an excuse about polishing his cricket bat or preparing for tomorrow's Latin class. He'd been a wanker then, she thought, and he was a wanker now.

Still, she could try to make a start. She reckoned he'd be gone ten minutes at least. Even if the others arrived, they'd be shown straight to the boardroom.

Anthony had given her clues as to what to look for. She went about her task systematically: cupboards first of all, testing inside to see if any suggested a false front, paintings next. Laurence had never been one to skimp on art – the room had two Modiglianis, a Balthus, two very well-known De Chiricos, and a Matisse that had, if she was any judge, found its way to its present location by somewhat dubious means. But none of them concealed anything but wallpaper.

Her eye was attracted by a sturdy rosewood bookcase on the wall nearest the door. It fitted the decor perfectly, and it was filled with colour-coordinated books, all hand bound and arranged by size. It was a title on the middle shelf that caught her attention: James Joyce, *Finnegans Wake*.

She almost burst out laughing. Her eyes ran over some of the other titles. They amounted to a compilation of the most bought, least read novels of the past hundred years. Unless he'd picked up nasty habits since she last visited him, Laurence had always been innocent of the sins of intellectual pretension and reading. No doubt the man called Forshaw had recommended these to go with the Modiglianis and the Matisse. She was surprised there wasn't a signed copy of *Miss Smilla's Feeling for Snow*, her own candidate for the Pretentious, Moi? Award.

She reached for a large copy of *Foucault's Pendulum*. It stayed put. She pulled harder, but it remained stuck fast where it was. Of course, she thought – they're all fakes. That made it even worse. Just to confirm her suspicion, she reached right to the back and ran her fingers along the fronts of the fake books. The back of her hand raked along something metallic, and with a leap of comprehension she knew she'd found what she was looking for.

It took half a minute more to work out that pressing in the two outermost spines allowed the entire centre section, along with the shelf on which it rested, to tilt forward. The safe sat perfectly smugly at the rear, a difficult-looking bugger with three sets of combination wheels.

Elizabeth froze at the sound of footsteps in the corridor outside. She heard raised voices, and started to fold the shelf away; but the voices continued down towards Fusspot Finch's office. She let the shelf down once more and hurried for her handbag.

The little device Anthony had given her snuggled comfortably alongside her atomizer and compact mirror as though it too had no more than a cosmetic use. She snatched it up and hurried back to the safe.

One by one she worked the dials through the device, turning them while it read the results into a series of computerized calculations. She felt her palms sweating as her fingers twisted and turned. She should have waited until the next visit, found a pretext to send him out for longer, or maybe found a way of getting herself in late at night.

A series of quick beeps told her the first dial had been fully decoded. She read off three numbers, twisted the dial, and pulled the handle. It clicked down with a satisfying thud. She started on the second dial. It seemed to take twice as long. More voices in the corridor, more footsteps. Anyone could pop their head round the door. The little green digits whirred. She was sweating all over now. Beep, beep, beep. She dialled three more digits, pulled down the second handle. Click.

The telephone rang. She froze. Not many people had Laurence's direct number. Was Finch passing a call on to him, thinking he was in his office? The phone kept ringing. Elizabeth didn't know what to do. She couldn't just leave the safe as it was. She thought she was losing her nerve. The telephone stopped. She realized she was holding her breath tightly, that her bottom lip was trapped by her front teeth, that her fingernails were digging into her right palm.

She set the device for the third dial. Digits whirring faster than a fairground wheel of fortune, the clicking of the dial as it moved through its circumference. She couldn't bear to turn her head and look at the door. Beep, beep, beep. Three more digits, clunk. The door swung open and a small light went on inside the safe.

Her instructions had been vague. 'Anything to do with oil, anything with the name Aladdin, anything linked to China or Iraq.' She foraged about among the contents of the little cavity. Bonds. Boxes that looked as though they held jewellery – that probably explained where Mother's best pieces had gone. Deeds to a string of villas in France and Italy. Patents. Some private letters. A sheaf of papers marked 'Aladdin Oil: Survey Findings'.

Underneath this last were five more sets of papers relating to Aladdin, and behind them two envelopes marked in Chinese 'Diaochabu' – the name for the Central Committee's own intelligence service.

Her nerve very nearly failed her at the end. Laurence could open the safe at almost any time, and surely he would miss the Aladdin papers and the envelopes before anything else. They were in her hand. She glanced at them and put them down.

At that moment, there was a scuffling of footsteps in the corridor again, and Laurence's voice, rising in a greeting. She made her mind up instantly. Her jacket had an inside pocket like a man's, so she swept up the papers and stuffed them into it. It took a matter of seconds to close the door, snap shut the handles, spin the dials, and flip the shelf back into place. She sat down and reached for her handbag.

The door opened and Laurence bounded in. He loved to appear spry, as though the affectation of athleticism served as a talisman against the creeping advent of old age. She looked up and smiled at him, at the same time pushing Anthony's ever-so-useful device back into the recesses of her bag.

'God, I hate board meetings,' he said. 'There's always so much to do. And most of it boring.'

'A bit like life, Laurie.'

'You haven't drunk your ginger ale. Would you like some ice?'

'No, thanks. I just didn't ... It's not the same on one's own.'

'You said you were parched.'

'Parched? Of course I'm bloody parched. Not half as parched as that little bitch Madeleine, mind you.'

He flung her a hurt look.

'There's no need for that, Lizzie. The poor girl's ill.'

'Don't you believe it. These doctors could make anyone ill. Once they start doping you, it's downhill all the way. There's nothing wrong with Maddie a spot of fresh air and sunshine won't put right. And it'll be a damned sight cheaper.'

'Cheaper?'

'Didn't I tell you? I've taken her out of the clinic. They can't just force you to stay in those places, you know. They don't want you to if you don't pay.'

'What the hell are you up to, Lizzie? You can't just go round hauling somebody in Maddie's state out of reach of medical help.'

'Don't be so bloody po-faced. She's perfectly happy to be with me. I love her, I want the best for her. I'm her mother, after all.'

'You're living with Anthony.'

'We get on very well. We're a little family.'

He sighed. He hated contretemps like these in his office. He'd made the room as perfect as possible: every colour co-ordinated, everything in its place. Raised voices, arguments, dissonance of any kind felt rough and out of keeping.

'You said she was parched. What did you mean?'

'Oh, that's one of the drugs. Lithium or something. Don't worry, I'm getting her off the lot. She's seeing Rajiv Mahareshi every afternoon. He does readings of her chakras. Marvellous man. He cleared up my sinusitis in a matter of weeks.'

'Lizzie, you can't just take someone off lithium like that. It could be dangerous.'

'Not with Rajiv at the controls. He communicates with the higher powers.' She picked up the glass of ginger ale and downed it in a single swallow.

'Now, Laurie, I think we're keeping them all waiting.'

CHAPTER FIFTY-ONE

Nothing moved. In the first days of the crossing he had expected birds, their black or white wings effortless above the silent dunes. They would cry out from time to time, he thought, or spin in circles endlessly, like moths spinning in the night. The silence was absolute. In the west, the reddening sun tumbled towards the highest peaks of the Tien Shan, a haze of blue on the horizon.

David closed his compass, and skidded and stumbled his way back down the dune to where Nabila and Mehmet were already setting up camp. At one end, the camels were kneeling in a long line, patiently waiting to be unloaded. Nabila and Mehmet had already removed the loads from the front two beasts and were working on the third. Nabila looked up and waved. David waved back. As he did so, he lost his balance and pitched forward on to the sand.

He must have shouted. He couldn't remember, but as he straightened there was almost the echo of a cry in the air.

He looked down towards the camp. The sudden cry had panicked two camels at the rear. They were on their feet, running between the dunes in search of some sort of safety. Mehmet and Nabila's animal, still bowed down with a stack of boxes and sacks, lurched to its feet baying raucously, its neck outstretched, its eyes wide with unreasoning terror. The sight of its mates haring off across the sand had filled it with dread.

Nabila dashed to pacify the remaining animals. She had already developed a rapport with them, and called them by the private names she had given them, to which they seemed to respond. She called in a soft voice, trying to soothe them while they cut and reared, shaking their great heads from side to side, like children refusing a teacher's admonitions.

In the meantime, Mehmet tried to make the third camel secure. He already had it marked down as a troublesome animal. It was very nervous, and inclined to be fractious at the slightest provocation. He approached it carefully, trying not to frighten it further, yet all too aware of how easily it could injure itself.

It was already on its hind legs, throwing its baggage askew on to its neck. Mehmet made a grab for the beast's bridle, and as he did so its front legs straightened, and it reared up unsteadily, braying again. One of the camels ahead responded to the sound, sending its own low-pitched lament back across the sand.

That triggered off a second panic in the jumpy animal Mehmet was trying to help. It jerked forwards, at the same time snapping its head back as if to dislodge some of the slipping load that was holding it back, and tearing the bridle from Mehmet's hand. He reached round in a clumsy effort to retrieve the bridle, and thus pull the camel's head back in line. His hand missed, but the camel, irritated by his unwanted attentions, pulled back suddenly. Before Mehmet could react, the huge jaws opened and shut viciously round his hand.

He screamed once, then the camel bit down hard, and Mehmet dragged what was left of his hand out from between the inexorable teeth, and collapsed in a heap on the sand. The camel, prodded further by the scream, went lurching forward after its mates, trampling Mehmet's legs as it went.

David reached him almost at the same moment as Nabila. Mehmet wasn't unconscious, but he had nearly passed out from the pain. David looked down at his hand and turned his face away, wanting to be sick. The fingers had been severely crushed, dragging both skin and flesh away. Two fingers dangled, almost severed. The back of the hand was mangled badly.

'I'll deal with this,' said Nabila. 'You go after the camel.'

'It can't get far. I'll hold him for you.'

She looked at him angrily.

'David, I can handle this. If these camels drop their loads we could lose important items of equipment. They have six water barrels between them. For God's sake, try to catch them and get them to hunker down again.'

Stung, he ran off after the nearest beast. To his left, the sun was falling rapidly, far out of sight behind the dunes that hemmed him in on every side. It would be dark in a few minutes. He knew he could end up losing the camels for good in the blackness, or, even worse, losing his own way, not just for one night, but for all time. In moments, the margin for error had narrowed to a thin line.

He twisted round the piled-up wall of a dune that had spread its skirts into the valley, and there ahead of him was the third camel. None of its load had broken free, but the jolting it had received made it seem more precarious than ever. David came in behind it quietly, but even as he did so, the camel shied. Suddenly, the ropes holding everything in place gave way, and the entire load toppled heavily from the beast's back to the ground. The water drums, built for much lighter treatment, buckled along the side weldings, and David watched with anguish as water broke through and spilled in streams on to the sand. It continued to pour out for half a minute, then the sand drank it down eagerly. Soon there was nothing to see but two shrinking patches of damp.

The shock of losing its load had, paradoxically, brought the shivering camel to a complete standstill. David walked up to it gingerly, fearing it might attack him as it had gone for Mehmet. But it just stood rooted to the spot. He coaxed it, using the words Nabila used to get it to sit, and to his surprise, it did.

He didn't know what to do next. There was no way for him to reload the animal on his own – it was a two-person job at the best of times. He was concerned about the first two camels, who seemed to have done a disappearing act. He was toying with the idea of going after them when darkness slammed down and he was lost between sand and stars. He carried no torch, he had no other means of making light.

With the darkness came the beginnings of a bitter cold that could not be easily endured. David rummaged blindly among the fallen baggage, feeling with numb fingers for cloth of any kind. Above him, starlight filtered down through a blatantly clear sky. No moonlight yet, but when it came he might risk the walk back along the valley, bringing the camel with him. He looked up at a long wedge of black thickly packed with stars. There were no constellations he recognized, no planets he could trust. All a stillness and a mystery. But as he watched, he noticed small lights creeping across the surface of things. Spy satellites, each in its own orbit, arcing over China down towards East Asia or up towards the Arctic.

He managed to pull the packing cloth from one bundle and to wrap himself in it. If he hunkered down by the camel he might be able to pass the night in some degree of comfort, and he'd know if it tried to get up and walk away. He was desperately thirsty, and pangs of hunger had started gnawing away at his shrivelling innards.

Mehmet had been badly hurt, he was sure of that. But what the hell could Nabila do for him, out here in the middle of a wasteland? Perhaps she could bandage the hand in some way, and tie it up so it could be tended to as soon as they got out of the desert. But in the meantime, what could be done to stop Mehmet's pain?

The camel had not touched water in two days. There'd been signs of underground water at the spot they'd chosen to camp in, and the plan had been to dig down once camp was set up. Now, God alone knew when there'd be a chance. As though aware of David's thoughts, the camel moaned gently. Its stomach made sympathetic noises, and it belched loudly, filling the air around it with an unbearable stench.

Out in the darkness he heard his name being called. He stumbled hurriedly to his feet.

'Nabila!' he called. 'I'm over here. I'm with the camel. Try not to startle him.'

There was silence for a while, then footsteps sounded along the gully, and suddenly a light became visible in the darkness, bobbing and weaving its way towards him.

He stood up to greet her. The light dazzled him for a moment, then she was there beside him, her arms round him, clinging to him. She seemed lifeless, like someone who has been pushed beyond all limits. He ran his hand over her hair.

'You're exhausted,' he said.

'I'll be more exhausted by the time this is over. So will you.'

She shone the torch over the camel, then across the scattered pieces of baggage it had dumped.

'What a bloody mess,' she said. 'What about the water? Did you manage to save any?'

'Not a drop.'

'All right,' she said. 'We'll hobble this one and leave her till the morning. She'll be safe enough.'

'She?'

'Didn't you know? Your precious Bobtail's a woman. And I'd guess she's about two months pregnant. I think that's what's been making her so jumpy. Better we don't risk her with a normal load again. Certainly not water.'

They hobbled the animal with cord that had slipped loose from the baggage. It complained, but made no attempt to struggle or to bite.

They made their way back along the narrow defile between the dunes. It was bitterly cold now, and a small breeze had somehow managed to sneak through the gaps in order to torment them.

'How's Mehmet?' David asked.

'Not too good, I'm afraid. I've treated people with camel bites before, but nothing like this. He needs to be in a modern hospital, not stuck out here in the wilderness.'

'Is there nothing you can do for him?'

'A certain amount, but not very much. At the moment, I've got the hand anaesthetized using acupuncture, but the effect won't last for very long unless something else is done. At least two of the fingers require amputation.'

'Can't you do that?'

'I'm not a surgeon, David. I know the principles, but that's all. I've never actually cut anyone open or amputated a limb. If I had an operating theatre and proper equipment . . .'

They walked the rest of the way in silence. When they got to the camp they found Mehmet propped up against one of the saddles taken from the remaining animals. David greeted him. He seemed restful, but his face betrayed the apprehension he felt underneath. His hand rested on his lap.

Nabila knelt down beside him and shone the torch on it. It looked hideous. Bone had been exposed across four fingers, and on the end two the skin had been racked back away from the palm. Apart from that, everything from just below the knuckles to the fingertips had been badly crushed. In several places, the bone had splintered, and bits poked out jaggedly, defying easy treatment.

Nabila turned to David, speaking in English.

'I don't think I have any choice. I have to amputate. The end fingers are too badly damaged to even dream of repairing them.'

'Can't you stitch it all up until he gets to a hospital?'

'The simple answer is no. I've gone over this every way I can, and I come back to amputation each time. He won't see the inside of a hospital for God knows how long. I may not be a surgeon, but I have treated plenty of surgical cases. Limited amputation offers him the best chance, believe me.'

Mehmet broke in.

'I'm sorry, Doctor, but I don't understand Chinese. Are you saying that you want to cut my hand off?'

She shook her head and tried to smile.

'I hope not, Mehmet. But I think we may have to amputate those two fingers. I'm sorry, there's not much choice.'

He nodded heavily. Nabila knew that the loss of two fingers could prove a serious blow to someone like Mehmet, who earned his living by hard labour. He'd adjust in time, but at first it would be difficult for him. The chances of anyone providing him with a prosthesis or anything else to compensate for the fingers were zero.

396

'We've got a couple of additional problems,' Nabila said. 'One is the other six camels. Only two have been unloaded, and they're getting restless. We need a fire if possible. It's going to get extremely cold here without one. I thought I saw some tamarisks on the way in.'

'Yes, I noticed them too. Let's get the camels unloaded, then we can get enough wood for a fire.'

It seemed to take for ever, working in the dark, but by and by they got through their tasks and got a small fire burning next to Mehmet.

Nabila set up one of the water drums to form a low table, and covered it with a cloth, almost like a small altar. She opened a small leather bag and took a number of instruments from it, which she laid on the makeshift table. Picking one up, she showed it to David.

'Take a look at this,' she said. 'Do you know what this is? It's an instrument for working on camels' feet. I can't even tell you its proper name. The whole set came from a vet who works in our hospital. They're all I have. Now, you tell me how I'm supposed to cut through human bone without crushing it, splintering it, or snapping it. I need a saw, David, a proper surgical saw. I need proper equipment. Otherwise this is just going to be so much butchery.'

She was close to tears. It seemed that, no matter what she did, she would cause Mehmet more pain and lasting disfigurement. David took the implements one by one and examined them. Nabila was right. None of them was designed for surgical work.

'Is this all he gave you?' he asked. 'Does he never have to carry out amputations on animals?'

'I expect he does, I don't know. But this is all he gave me.'

'You're sure you can't just stitch him up, bandage the

397

whole thing together till we reach somewhere he can have proper help?'

She shook her head.

'Those fingers are too badly damaged. If I don't amputate, they could end up gangrenous or worse, and that could start spreading.'

'That leaves us no choice.' He nodded towards Mehmet. 'Get him ready as best you can. There's a bottle of brandy in that bag. I'd recommend about as much as the poor bastard can swallow.'

'What are you planning to do?'

'I'll show you in a minute.'

He went off into the darkness and sat down by the flank of one of the camels. Nabila could hear him working while she prepared Mehmet. A steady scraping sound came from the darkness: David was sharpening something.

'He's ready,' Nabila called at last. She'd forced Mehmet to drink a foul-tasting tea of concentrated herbs, and by careful placing of acupuncture needles, she'd made his damaged hand and wrist go numb again.

David arrived. He was carrying a large hunting knife. Nabila looked at him in horror.

'David, you can't . . .'

'It's a good quality knife. The blade isn't going to break on us, and it isn't going to slip. It's the best we've got.' He looked at Mehmet, then back at Nabila. 'We have to tie his hand down.'

'David . . .'

'The knife is very sharp indeed. It's an Ek survival knife, and it can do a lot of damage if it isn't handled carefully. I don't want Mehmet pulling out when he sees me start to cut.'

'He won't pull out. Trust me.'

'I have to trust Mehmet.'

'Then ask him directly.'

David hesitated, then turned to Mehmet. He spoke to him briefly in Uighur.

'I will not move. God has willed that I should lose some fingers. Moving will change nothing. Wherever my hand goes, there will be God.'

'Very well,' said David. 'Let's get this over with.'

They helped Mehmet arrange himself so that his hand lay firmly on the narrow operating table. Nabila spoke to him gently, and David could see how he relaxed, as though bewitched by her voice.

He brought the sharpened knife to the table and laid it across the back of Mehmet's hand. Nabila held the torch steady over it.

'Show me where to cut,' David said.

She guided the blade to the right place and indicated the correct angle at which to cut.

David took a deep breath. Beside him, Mehmet had closed his eyes and was murmuring a prayer, rapidly. David held the knife ready. Nabila nodded. He cut down, and there was a cry so piercing it ripped the black tent of the night from pole to pole, and then silence fell, and there was blood pouring out on everything.

CHAPTER FIFTY-TWO

Around midnight, Mehmet fell into a very deep sleep. Nabila had done what she could with the hand, stitching flesh together where possible, packing and bandaging it where not. His three remaining fingers were badly crushed, and the bones broken. About an hour after the amputation, he'd been wracked by sudden spasms of shivering. In part they were a delayed after-effect of the double shock he'd sustained, in part the result of having to sit in the freezing cold after losing so much blood. Nabila gave him her sleeping bag and made him drink something foul-tasting that finally made him sleep.

She lay back against a heap of camel-bags and closed her eyes. There was no wind, no sound except for the grunting of the camels and Mehmet's fractured snoring. She opened her eyes and saw a black sky so filled with stars no one but God could ever possibly count them. A shooting star dashed suddenly across her view, incandescent for a moment, then gone for ever. It had, for that moment, been the brightest thing in its universe.

She shuddered. David had gone away on his own to check on the camel that had bolted. He'd had no hopes of finding the others, but they both knew they'd have to look for them at first light. If they remained lost, that meant they were down nearly five hundred litres of water at a single stroke. Even if they found water under ground in the morning, it would be brackish, fit only for the camels. Without the barrels, they would have no means of storing any.

The desert was a truly awful place, she thought. It had always been on the edge of her consciousness as a girl and a young woman, a place of stories and legends, a stony wilderness where the *jinn* walked, and ghouls, and the ghosts of children who'd lived in the ancient silk cities, now lost and buried under the sand. Later, she'd ridden or driven along the desert's edge and gazed out over it warily, thinking of what might be hidden out there. Or not hidden.

Now, shivering in a hollow defile between towers of white sand, watching the stars revolve indifferently, she felt the full horror of the emptiness she was in creep upon her and bury her, like sand burying a fortress or a long caravan whose bells are at first dimmed, then silenced for all time.

What was the horror exactly? Was it the sense of so much empty space, or the almost total absence of life, or the feeling that, whichever way she went, she would still be lost? Or was it the silence, or the sound of sand moving against sand, or a ghostly memory of sounds that had once been here and were gone for ever?

She decided it was none of these things. There was something else, a more powerful feeling than all the others, a sense that, far from being dead, the desert was intensely alive. Death was only an appearance. Reality was a form of life in which the desert – watchful, listening, alert – preyed on all other forms of life that came within it. She could think of no other place on earth that had made such a success of death. Every step she took, she could feel the desert couching, very like a beast of prey.

She fetched the torch and headed on down to where

David was watching the camel. He'd taken some blankets and a little food, and when she found him, he was propped up against the animal's side. He'd lit a small fire, and when she came up he was trying to read something in its light. It looked like a map, very torn and tattered, with inscriptions in Chinese. When he noticed her standing by the fire, he folded the sheet up and shoved it inside his coat.

She slipped down beside him, saying nothing, pausing only to whisper something in the camel's ear.

'What have you been saying to Bobtail?' he asked.

'None of your business.'

'I don't want any agitation in this caravan. I won't stand for that. You're not one of those foreign agitators, are you?'

She put her arm round him, and they sat together in silence while Bobtail digested the food David had brought her.

'Why'd you come down here on your own?' she asked.

'I'm not sure. I just wanted to listen to my own thoughts, I suppose. I'm sorry. I've neglected you.'

'No, I've been busy. Mehmet's asleep. He should stay that way until dawn. I don't want to give him too many herbs: they can be toxic in too large a quantity. The acupuncture may help for a while tomorrow, but it won't stand much of a chance when he's moving.'

'It's between him and God now, Nabila. There's nothing more you can do.'

'Haven't you eaten? It doesn't look as though you've touched anything.'

'No, I'm not really very hungry.'

'Nevertheless, you have to eat.'

'Who says?' He was snappish, almost aggressive.

'I say. I'm a doctor, you have to listen to me.'

'I'd like to know the hell why.'

'I already told you, because I'm a doctor.'

'You're not my bloody doctor.'

She took her arm away gently, retreating from whatever was burning him up.

'No? And just who else is your doctor out here? Bobtail? Mehmet maybe? Listen, David. It's time you wised up. You're the expedition leader, and I'm sticking my neck on the line to follow you and do whatever you say I should do, even when I think you don't have a clue what you're doing. But when it comes to what concerns the health and well-being of this little party, I have the final say. If I tell you to eat, you will eat; if I tell you not to eat, you will not let a morsel pass your lips until further word. The reason is quite simple. If you play the little boy and get petulant and push your dinner to the other side of the table, you will get weak and dehydrated tomorrow. If that makes you ill so you can't eat tomorrow, we're heading for trouble. Mehmet isn't out of danger yet. He'll need careful watching for a few days. If I could make a phone call and have him lifted out of here by air, I'd do it this minute.'

She stopped suddenly. The truth was, she wished she could have them all lifted out. They'd been fools to get themselves this far inside the desert in the first place.

'Very well, I'll eat if it makes you happy.'

'No, you'll eat because it helps keep us alive. Thank you for what you did back there.'

'Mehmet? I hated doing that. I've seen men lose limbs before, but only in combat. This was a bit too personal.'

She put her arm round him again, and this time he settled against her beatifically, and reached up and held her hand.

'Is that what you were thinking about when you came out here?' she asked.

'A little, yes. But mostly Sam. I can't get him out of my mind these past few days. It's being out here in the bloody sand, with nothing else to do but think. Don't you find that?'

'Yes, I know what you mean. I find myself thinking about my sister Rabbia a lot.' She paused and squeezed his hand. 'And about us. Do you think . . . Do you think we'll come out of this alive?'

'I honestly don't know. I wouldn't think it very likely.'

'Do you think, if we did survive . . . Would you just go back to England?'

'Oh, God, Nabila, I don't know. I couldn't stay here, you know that. I wouldn't last a day. And I couldn't bear to leave you behind.'

'But I have my work here.'

'Not any more you don't. They know who you are, and if our mission succeeds, you'll be the most wanted woman in China.'

She laughed aloud at the thought, at the absurdity of it.

'Me? The most wanted woman?'

'Why not?' he said, laughing. He reached up and drew her round and kissed her softly. 'You're already the most wanted woman in the Taklamakan.'

'I'm the only one.'

'You're forgetting Bobtail and a few others.'

'Do you want me?'

He drew her close to him again. No more jokes now, just the comfort of holding her.

'Very much,' he said, and kissed her again, not a short kiss this time, but one that seemed to go on through a time of its own creation.

'Nabila, it's far too cold . . .'

'Shhhh. Just follow my instructions, and you'll be all right.'

She unzipped his trousers and reached inside.

'I could catch frostbite,' he protested. 'I'd have to . . . You know, like Mehmet . . .'

She warmed him with another kiss.

'Don't worry,' she said, 'this isn't going to catch frost-bite. Not where it's going.'

CHAPTER FIFTY-THREE

They found the two missing camels around noon the following day. The beasts were exhausted and looked very sorry for themselves. Unable to dislodge their loads, they'd settled down in the shelter of a dune and spent a miserable night, unwatered, unfed, and unable to snatch more than a few winks of sleep.

David and Nabila stayed close together, not just because it made them feel better, but because separation could prove fatal. The high walls of the dunes made it almost impossible to navigate. Even from the summits, other high dunes still contrived to block the view, and the best anyone could do most of the time was to steer a fairly straight course with the help of a compass, two feet of twine, and a strong sense of smell.

On the ground, a turning of a few feet here or a distraction of a yard or two there could lead to a widening maze in which all sense of true direction was lost. Two people could part, agreeing to meet again in half an hour, and never see one another again. The desert made no concessions to human weakness. Out here, orienteering was not a sport, but the most vital part of staying alive.

They'd left Mehmet behind with the main body of camels. He was conscious, but still traumatized. Nabila had been reluctant to leave him at all.

'Ordinarily, I'd just say, "He'll live." I've seen men much

more badly injured take it in their stride and get on with their lives. But that injury weakens him and makes it hard for him to do the most elementary things. That means he may not live. Unless he can make adjustments very quickly, the desert won't let him. And we can't afford to let him hold us back or weaken us in any way. We can help him: but the moment he shows signs of holding us back . . .'

She broke off, hating what she was saying, knowing it had to be said.

They'd followed hoofprints in order to track down the camels. Now, coming back, they followed exactly the same course. The camels had been two miles away, a dangerous distance, maybe a quarter of a day's march. The journey back doubled the distance. All the time, David felt vulnerable, knowing how hard it could be to rejoin the main caravan if they strayed from the path even a short way.

The weather felt oppressive, the heat more clinging than normal, the air denser. David wrapped his scarf round his mouth. Nabila walked ahead with Doris, saying nothing.

Suddenly, she stopped and pointed with her stick towards an opening to one side, angled so it was now visible on the return trip. David came up, leading the other camels. He looked inside.

Between two enormous dunes a large space had been eroded from the sand, like a giant grotto, smooth-edged yet grotesque. It was bowed, like a chapel carved out of light, unpolished stone, its sides so high and rounded that David wondered for a moment if any of it was sand at all.

But it was not the sand that Nabila had been pointing at. Not the sand, not the great swoop it made over their heads. He stepped further inside and lowered his gaze.

At first, it could have been almost anything. David squinted, trying to make the object out against the bright sunlight that surrounded it. It might have been an outcrop of rock, or a strange formation of sand sculpted by the wind, or perhaps something half-angelic, dropped from the sky – part of a helicopter, say, or the wing of a light plane.

But as he looked it became clear that it was none of these. For one thing, it seemed to have been made from cloth. Parts of it fluttered loosely in the springing breeze, and a biggish section flapped back to reveal a dark interior before swinging shut again, the gesture of an erotic dancer or a butcher stripping back flesh.

'It's a tent,' whispered David, 'a bell tent. Look, that's the centre pole . . .'

'But . . . who . . . ?'

The tent was half buried in sand, and a fine coating had covered the canvas on all sides. David took a step closer.

'Who? Don't you know?' He stopped then, puzzled, and a little afraid of this unexpected thing. 'Give me a moment.'

He went back to Doris and found his torch in a pack towards her rear. She watched him impassively as he rejoined Nabila, carrying the torch like a small club. He approached the tent again, tentative and wary, as though it might rear up and attack him.

Holding the torch at an angle, he gripped the large flap and drew it back. He shone the light down into the hole this created, then looked inside.

'Well, what do you see?' asked Nabila impatiently. By now she had a premonition of what it would turn out to be.

'Two men,' he said, then, turning, he spoke with greater exactitude. 'What's left of two men. Some sand has got in, but not enough to cover them. Not yet.'

'They must have been trapped in a storm. Or grown too ill to go any further. How recent was it, do you think? Can you tell from . . . ?'

He switched off the torch and looked round. What was in the tent had not been very pretty.

'They're not skeletons,' he said. 'More like mummies, really. It's this dry air, it preserves things amazingly well. By my reckoning, they've been here over a hundred years.'

'And exactly what do you base that reckoning on?'

He smiled.

'I can do better than that, I can tell you their names: one was called Yolchi, the other Muhammad Shah.'

'Now you're just playing games. I don't think it's so nice to poke fun at the dead.'

'Poke fun? Nabila, haven't you heard of Sven Hedin?'

'The Swedish explorer? Yes, of course. Everybody in these parts has heard of his adventures. But he died in the fifties, David, back home in Sweden, not out here.'

'He tried to make the crossing from Merket to the Mazartagh Mountains back in 1895. He went into the Taklamakan with four men, eight camels, three sheep, and two dogs, and he barely made it out with two of the camel-handlers. The last he saw of Yolchi and Muhammad Shah, they were sitting in this tent, waiting for the inevitable. They both knew they had no strength left. God knows how Hedin and the others survived.'

They hurried away from the tent as though it was cursed or contaminated, leaving behind not even a prayer for the spirits of the two men trapped for ever inside it. The tent itself was of no use to them: the canvas was rotten, the ropes were nearly gone. They preferred to leave it as a shrine. As they plodded on, the dunes on every side seemed to weigh more heavily on the narrow path they were treading between them.

Neither of them noticed anything much out of the ordinary until they reached a spot about halfway back to the camp. They had just started to turn the corner of a low dune when David noticed something.

'Can you feel it?' he asked.

'The breeze?'

'Yes. It's getting fresher all the time.'

'And the fresher it gets the faster it becomes.'

He looked down at his feet. The wind was scuffing the sand along in small puffs. Further off, it was raising it in little plumes, their feathered tops spinning, then fading off into nothing.

'Look,' David said.

'It's wiping out the track.'

'We don't have time to get back to Mehmet before the hoofprints are completely wiped out. There's a real risk we could make a wrong turning.'

Nabila looked up. The round disc of the sun was reddening, but all around it, like a murky halo, a grey haze was forming. On the tops of the higher dunes, sand-spouts were performing a crazy dance. The horizon was veiled in a yellow-grey mist.

'It's blowing up into a full-scale sandstorm, David – I was caught at the edge of one years ago. It's stupid to think of trying to push on. Let's put ourselves and the camels into the lee of that dune.'

She pointed to a dune of red sand some three hundred feet high. All along its edges, sand lifted in a thin red veil, as though mocking them.

'What about Mehmet?'

'We'll get lost if we push on. He'll just have to fend for himself as long as the storm continues. He knows the desert well enough. There's plenty of food and water for him.'

The sombre image of the sand-choked tent and its gnarled inhabitants rose up in David's mind.

'How long do these storms usually last?' he asked.

'There's no saying. A few hours sometimes. Often a day or more.'

'That's all?'

Nabila hesitated. The camel she was leading was growing fractious.

'No,' she answered. 'Sometimes they can go on for a week. In the city it's never very bad, we're too far from the heavy sands. But in the desert . . . I've heard patients speak of it. You can survive a week in the *karaburan* if you have enough water with you. Provided the wind doesn't drive you mad first and send you wandering in circles.'

'Have you known of that happening?'

'Oh, yes. A man was brought to us about a year ago. There'd been a big storm along the southern sector of the Taklamakan. It went on for four or five days. This man was a goatherd from Tongguzbasti. He'd gone out into the desert in search of tamarisk, along with a camel for the load. At midday he had some bread and water and lay down for a sleep. When he woke there was a storm the like of which he'd never seen before. There was nothing for it but to hunker down and make the best of it; but at some point – whether it was day or night he couldn't say – he found himself on his feet, shouting and screaming at the noise, and walking for what must have been miles.'

'He must have been hopelessly lost.'

'Should have been. His camel never turned up again. But he was incredibly lucky. When the storm cleared he started walking west, and by a sheer miracle he hit the northern tip of the valley Tongguzbasti's in. He was in a bad state by the time he reached us. I wouldn't have given him another day.'

They selected their spot carefully, unloading the camels in a hurry and using the bales and boxes they carried to build an improvised barrier that might in a pinch keep some of the sand from them.

The day darkened rapidly. As the wind spiralled in force, the sun was bit by bit eclipsed until it became nothing but a dim ember glowing behind endless ashes of sand.

'What happened to him?' asked David as they placed the last sack on the barricade.

'Who?'

'The man who got lost beyond Tongguzbasti. You didn't mention his name.'

'Atik,' she whispered, her voice barely audible above the roaring of the wind. 'He was called Atik.'

'And was he all right? Did he recover?'

She looked into the face of the wind.

'No,' she said. 'He lasted two days. We thought we'd saved him, but he kept running away from us.'

'Running away? But surely . . .'

'Not in body. He was too weak even to get out of his bed. In his mind. He ran away from us in his mind. We couldn't catch up with him. He died with his face unchanged. It was the face he'd brought in from the desert.'

With the dune to their backs and the camels ahead of them, David and Nabila watched the storm take hold of the world. Piece by piece, everything was wiped out. They held one another's hands tightly and wondered if, when they next saw clear daylight, they might ever find their way again in the darkness of the desert.

And David wondered if the faces he had glimpsed in that

rotting tent had been like the face of the madman caught on the edge of all things lunatic. And whether his own face might not soon grow the features of his own madness. He thought of Sam, and he thought of Maddie, and he felt the madness grow in him like another storm.

CHAPTER FIFTY-FOUR

'Ah said, Ah'm jist mindin' ma own business. If you dinna mind.'

'Actually, Hamish, I do mind. If you don't move on, I'll be forced to arrest you for loitering.'

Calum looked the policeman up and down. He hadn't yet reached the age when all policemen look young. But he was long past the point when they all looked like the enemy. This London Bobby was proving a considerable pain in the arse.

'Am Ah offendin' you or somethin'? Ah mean, lookit all these other folk walkin' up and doon. You're no' arrestin' them, are ye? Ah dinnae see you threatenin' them wi' the handcuffs an' a night doon the slammer.'

'Oh, for God's sake, you know what this is all about. I daresay it's not the first time you've been asked to move on. Your face doesn't fit, Hamish. Your clothes don't fit. Your accent doesn't fit. Now, I'm asking you for the last time: are you going to move, or do I have to move you?'

Calum took one last look at the house and smiled.

'Nae bother,' he said. 'Why didn't ye ask me nicely the first time?'

He dipped his head and strolled away comfortably, feeling the street around him like a long, bright coat. His feet barely touched the paving stones, his head felt elevated, like it was up there among the clouds, like it was part of the sky. A less astute observer might have assumed he was on a high. Well, perhaps he was: but it wasn't the high the policeman thought, or the passers-by if they so much as noticed him.

He could feel the policeman's watchful eyes hang on him as he walked away, and he formed his fingers behind his back into a V-sign. He didn't mind being chased off. For the moment, he'd seen all he needed to, found out all he wanted.

The house was owned by a man called Farrar. Some sort of bigwig in a government ministry. Fair do's. This Farrar was shacked up with the woman Calum had recently been shagging senseless on the biggest bed this side of the Channel. Nobody had known a thing about the girl, which probably made his life easier. He guessed that Farrar was the live-in lover, Elizabeth the sex-starved mistress, and Maddie Elizabeth's daughter. He had a shrewd idea what Maddie's problem was; he thought he had the means to solve it while solving some of his own problems at the same time.

'How much tae King's Cross, Jimmy?'

The cab driver looked at Calum as though he'd just stumbled off an *X-Files* set.

'What?'

'The train station. Chuff chuff. Ye ken?'

'You want to know 'ow much is it to King's Fuckin' Cross?'

'Ye catch on quick, likesay, Jimmy.'

'Well, 'ow the 'ell do I know? Depends on the traffic. Could be around ten quid, could be eight, could be more. Depends. Why don't you take the Tube, mate? Do us all a favour.'

'Gie us a break, Jimmy. Ah'll give ye twenty if ye take the scenic route.'

The heavy door closed behind him with a satisfying clunk.

He didn't feel out of place in King's Cross. Nobody would have done unless they were dressed in a fur coat and sporting a tiara. Out on the street, he started trawling. He was looking for someone he knew. If he was going to deal, he wanted to deal with a face he'd seen before. As the dark began to close in, he concentrated less on the streets than the bars and cafés. Sometimes he went in and out again, scanning the faces, watching the watching eyes. Pale, sad faces, red eyes with red rims.

He didn't need to ask who this one was or that. Their names didn't matter. They were prostitutes, pimps, dealers, sharks, users, trip-hop kids, speed garage freaks waiting out the hours till their clubs got under way, exhausted social workers, AIDS counsellors, poor immigrants, homeless refugees, travellers without a bed. He'd seen every face a thousand times. They looked at him, recognizing him as one of themselves.

He found his mark about ten o'clock, in a fluorescent dive off Cromer Street. A small-time dealer in a grubby green suit, about five foot eight, sporting a gangsta beard and dark shades. Summer and winter, he looked the same. His front teeth were blackened where smack had left its unmistakable deposit. Calum had him down as dangerous, maybe deranged. He dredged deep into his memory and came up with a name.

'Y'aw reet, Murray? Eh? Long time no see.'

He sat down opposite the other man and stretched a big hand across the table. Murray did not respond. Next to him sat a girl of sixteen or seventeen, glassed into a world of her own.

'Ye've no' forgot me, have ye, Murray? Try tae remember

aboot six months back. You and I did us a wee deal before Ah flew oot on the big silver burd tae Pakistan.'

Murray turned and spat on the floor. Calum wondered if he could actually see him from behind those sunglasses.

'What are you looking for, Scottie? A woman is it? Is that what you had last time? What about sweet little Linda, here? Cunt like the palm o' your hand. She'll make you come twice while you're waitin' to start.'

Calum looked at Linda's sad, unrevealing face. He'd had sex with more dolls like her than he cared to remember, but he'd never once been stirred. They were all stretched flesh and needle tracks and emptiness.

'Ah'm shagged oota ma brain today, Murray. Ah couldnae do justice tae the doll's charms even if God wis tae gie me a dick like the Scott Monument as compensation. What Ah need fae you, Murray, is a pocketful of illegal substances.'

'I don't carry illegal substances, Jock.'

'Ay, that's cool, likes. That's what ye told us the last time too. Dinna worry, Murray, Ah've been in this game longer than yersel'. If Ah canna score wi' you, Ah'll fuckin' score wi' some cunt else. Some cunt who disnae waste ma time fobbin' me off wi' a burd who couldnae fuck a stick o' rhubarb if it wis covered in butter an' flavoured wi' guacamole an' re-fried beans.'

Murray pretended to reflect. He'd grown up near Dover Harbour, learned his trade peddling to and from tourists arriving from the Continent. It had been easy enough in the good old days, then the big boys muscled in and pushed petty criminals like himself off the scene. He'd hopped on the first coach out, and washed up at King's Cross, where he had a friend with a floor to sleep on. Now, a couple of years on, he'd created a small business for himself, a franchise he rented from a man called Bernie 'the Diary' Lett.

Murray, who considered himself a growing force in the drug world around the Cross, now calculated across three feet of cigarette-scarred Formica how much of a fool the big Scotsman might turn out to be.

'How much?' he asked.

'How much what? Ah want tae see what ye've got. Ah want tae know how fuckin' pure it is, and Ah want tae know up front how much yer askin'.'

'I told you, sweetheart, I don't carry.'

'Ah didnae think ye did. Did ye take me for a total moron? Ye'll have tae take me tae yer stash. Only, one thing, Murraymint: Ah'm nae fool, an' Ah suffer fae a radge bad temper. Y'unnerstan'?'

'Come on. We're wasting time in here. And just so's you and I understand one another, the name isn't Murray, it's Maurice.'

An old man walked along Harrison Street, his coat buttoned, his face turned in against the vagrant chill of the cooling night. His feet made no sound on the uneven paving stones. Once he looked up. On the wall of a boarded-up house someone had written the letters 'C' and 'E'. He had no idea what they meant, he no longer wanted to know. What did letters matter at his age?

A girl watched him from a doorway opposite. She couldn't read or write. Letters meant nothing to her either. She'd seen him a dozen times before, shuffling down the street. Sometimes he was carrying groceries from the corner shop, sometimes he paused to have a sly cigarette.

'Hey, Granddad,' she called, catching his attention. As his eyes swung round, she put her hands on her thin top and pulled it up to her armpits. She was naked underneath.

He looked at her breasts and looked away again. What did naked women matter at his age?

'When did you say we met?'

'What?'

'You said we met before. Did a deal. When was that, eh? My fucking memory's a fucking blank.'

Calum looked at his new chum and smiled. For a pusher, Maurice had dipped his fingers many times too often into his own bag of goodies. But Calum didn't care about that. In a way, it made him feel relieved. If Maurice was taking sneak previews from his own stash, it made it all the more likely that the basic supply hadn't been heavily cut.

They were in a sleazy upstairs room five minutes' walk from the café. The furniture consisted of two chairs, a low North African table, and a bed with a quilted headboard. Two mournful Chinese prints hung on one wall, snatched from a nearby dim-sum house. On the bed, the girl called Linda lay stark naked, staring at the prints, at the grey monkeys in their tall trees. Maurice had ordered her to strip the moment they got inside. It was one of the ways he used to keep his girls under control. Judging by the bruises on Linda's body, Calum reckoned it was not the only one.

'Chrismus,' he said. 'It wis just before Chrismus last year. Ah told ya already, Ah wis off tae Pakistan by Hogmanay. Ah met you in a wee bar called McNally's. Remember that? It wis a friend up in Paisley sed Ah'd find you there. Ah only had tae ask fir Murray.'

'Maurice.'

'Aye, likesay, Maurice. There wis a wumman wi' us. Nice wee number called Nancy. Big eyes. Bigger knockers. She had a tartan tattoo on her right arm. Mibbe you

419

remember that. Not many burds have one ay those. It wis a MacLeish tartan. That wis her name, Nancy MacLeish. Ye must remember a burd like that.'

'Maybe I do. Maybe if you had a photograph. My fucking memory plays awful tricks all the same. So, what are you looking for? Charlie? E? Puff? Scag?'

'Got a weebit everything, dae ye, Jimmy?'

'I can get you what you want. If I don't have it, my business colleagues will turn some up. As long as you've got the dosh.'

'Dinna fash yersel' aboot that. Jis' make sure the gear's up tae scratch.'

'All right, all right. I've only got the best. But I need to know what you want.'

'Charlie. An' a wee bottle of linctus, if ye have any.'

'Right. Stay here. Keep an eye on Linda here. If you fancy a screw, be my guest. Despite appearances, she's hardly been used. I'd be sure to roll on a rubber, though. If you see what I mean.'

Maurice went out, locking the door behind him. Calum got to his feet. He didn't like this place, didn't like the feeling he got from Maurice. The room smelled of corruption: rotting wood, damp plaster, old drugs, unwashed skin, dried vomit. And cheap perfume overlying everything . . . He'd been in too many rooms like this. Maybe this one would be the last.

He went to the window and drew aside the grimy curtain that hung skewed in front of it. The street below sweated in darkness. Carved by a streetlamp, an old man shuffled across the pavement, as though uncertain where his awkward steps were leading him. To reach that age, and still to be walking streets like these. The thought made Calum shiver deep inside.

CHAPTER FIFTY-FIVE

He let the curtain fall. His fingers felt grimy from years of dust. When he turned back to the dingy room, Linda was looking fixedly at him from the bed. Their eyes met for a brief instant, then Linda went back inside her head.

Maurice returned carrying a brown-glass bottle in one hand and a sample bag in the other. He was trying to smile, but the distortion made his face look wrong. Calum smiled back.

'Did you ever hear tell of a lad called Roger?' Maurice frowned, as though the effort of remembering another human being was too much for his limited resources. 'He was from Belfast. We used to call him Rajjer the Dajjer round here. He was always dodging the police. There was a spot of trouble, and he went to Paki-land last year. Skived off, and nobody's heard from him since. I wondered if you'd seen him out there. The shit owes me money.'

Calum shook his head.

'Never set eyes on him, but Ah heard he fell off a cliff in the Karakorams. Terrible lang wey doon. Ye could be five minutes in freefall before ye felt a butt in the head. Forget aboot yer money. A vulture's had it long since. In the beak and oot the bum, along wi' most of Roger. Now, show us what ye've got.'

The bottle of methadone was fully sealed. Maurice

ripped off the white plastic that covered the neck and top, unscrewed the cap, and handed it over. Calum sniffed it, then put his little finger inside and sucked. For a moment or two, he savoured it like someone trying a new wine. He recognized the unmistakable odour and flavour of Balsam of Tolu that had been added to make the linctus palatable. In some, it might have evoked images of South American forests, but Calum was reminded only of his own pained efforts to come off heroin.

'Fine,' he said. 'This'll dae fine.'

'Taste OK? Funny, you don't look like a linctus man to me.'

'Ah'm no'. This isnae fir me. What d'ye think Ah am? Some kind of loser, sippin' linctus and beggin' a quick shag offa some stringy wee doll wi' breasts the size o' mushrooms?'

'Look, no offence, eh? Do you want to try the powder?'

'Ah'm no' fuckin' stupid, am Ah?'

He dipped two wet fingers into the tiny bag and extracted enough of the contents to constitute a fair sample. Slipping the fingers into his mouth, he rubbed the powder round his gums and across his tongue. Then he sat and waited, slowly working the paste round his gums and dental cavities. When a couple of minutes had passed, he sucked it all up and spat it out evenly on the carpet.

'What the fuck wis that?'

'Ch-Charlie. The real thing, mister, the real thing.'

'That wis as real as yir beautiful, Jimmy. Ah've tasted more buzz in a deid wasp. Now, lemme tell ya this just the once. If ye fuck aroon' wi' me a secon' time, ye'll no' be a wee prick any longer. Ye willnae have a prick. Ah've cut off more dicks in ma time than Ah've had white puddin's fir breakfast. Unnerstan'?'

'How much do you want?' Maurice had handled difficult clients day in and day out for years; but something about the big Scotsman gave him pause.

'Ten bags this size. Bring 'em in empty an' bring the mummy bag with them.'

For a moment, Maurice seemed about to protest; but instead he opted for a course of prudence. He went out and returned in less than a minute. His hand shook as he held out the plastic bag of cocaine. It wasn't very big, a few ounces at most; but if he cut it often enough he could make it stretch a long way.

They repeated the test, and this time Calum pronounced himself satisfied.

'Fine,' he said. 'Yir bollocks are safe. Now, tell me how much an' Ah'll be scootin' on oot o' here.'

Like two traders in an Arab *suq*, they haggled their way to an acceptable price. Calum unfastened his money-belt from round his waist and unzipped it. That was when he realized he'd made a mistake, one so elementary he couldn't believe he'd made it. He'd put all his money into a single wad, and now he was forced to draw off single notes in order to make up the price he'd been asked. He saw Maurice watching him closely as he did so.

He handed the money over, a note at a time. Maurice counted it, and when it was done, he handed over the bag and the bottle.

'Loadsa dough for fuck all, isn't it?' said Maurice.

'Ah told you already, Jimbo, it's no' for maself.'

Calum got to his feet. He wanted to be out of here like a shot. Maurice stood too. He seemed on edge. A tic at the side of his mouth flickered a message of unease.

'Maybe Ah'll see ye round aboot Christmas. Buy you a wee dram. Ah ken where tae find ye now.'

He started to tie the money-belt back in place. Before he

could finish, Maurice had pulled a gun and was pointing it at him.

'Just nice and easy, son. Drop it on the floor next to me. Real gentle, mind.'

'Are you pointin' that stupid wee thing at me, Maurice? Ah cannae believe it. Ah thought ye had more sense in that wee head o' yours. Do Ah look like some wee runaway fae Aberdeen or Peebles that disnae ken what he's aboot?'

'I don't give a fuck where you're from, Scottie. Just hand it over and clear on out.'

Calum looked at the gun, then at Maurice, half in anger, half in pity.

'Ye realize what ye've done? Do ye? Ye realize you're dead? Ye realize that, d'ye no'?'

'Shut the fuck up. If you think I don't know how to use this, you're badly wrong. I spent a year in the fucking army. I was taught to shoot by professionals. I've fired more guns than you've had Chinese takeaways. Now, do yourself a favour and hand the fucking dosh over.'

Calum continued to stare at him. He was feeling decidedly pissed off. He doubted if Maurice had ever fired this or any other gun in anger. His only purpose in carrying a gun in the first place would be to put the frighteners on those of his clients whom he needed to impress. That would be the length and breadth of it.

Maurice didn't really see what happened next. He saw the disputed money-belt fall to the floor, and felt gratified that common sense had prevailed. Next thing, Calum's right arm swung round. Maurice felt something hit him hard. When he looked down, he saw a large kitchen knife protruding from his belly. He looked at it as if it was a joke of some kind, then it started hurting and he tried to pull it out. The pain as he did so was so severe he screamed out loud and collapsed backward into a sitting posture on the bed. The knife stayed where it was. The gun dropped from his hand.

Calum walked over slowly and picked up the gun.

'Ye'll no' be needin' this, likes?' he said, and slipped the gun into a pocket.

He put his hand over Maurice's mouth and pulled the knife out of his belly with a yank. The other man let out a second, muffled scream. He was bleeding badly, his blood leaking on to his clothes and the grubby bed linen.

'Oh, Jesus. Fucking Jesus,' cried Maurice. His cheeks had turned horribly pale. His lips trembled as he spoke. Behind him, Linda lay huddled in a small heap, as if she could shrink into something so insignificant it would not be seen. 'You've killed me. Look. You've fuckin' done for me.'

'No' yet, Jimmy. Ah'm a professional. Ah take ma time. Did ye know Ah wis in the Paras? Did ye?' He balanced the knife in his hand as if it was a bayonet. He'd bought it in Harrods before catching the taxi. A nice-looking assistant called Eileen had sold it to him. She'd had a lovely smile. He'd been tempted to ask her out. Maybe he would when all this was over.

'Look, I'm . . . sorry I . . . put the gun . . . on you. I wasn't serious, though. I mean, I . . . wasn't going to . . . shoot you or anything.' Maurice sensed that he was pleading for his life. The big Scotsman frightened him. He should have known better than to mess about with him in the first place. If it hadn't been for the overly tempting glimpse of the wad he carried, he'd have done the deal and let him go.

'Ah did warn you,' Calum said, 'but ye didnae listen. Ah said, if ye fucked wi' me a secon' time, ye'd be mincemeat. Ah might as well hae been gabbin' tae masel'.'

'I'm listening now, aren't I? You tell me what to do, and I'll fucking do it, honest I will. You didn't have to stick a fucking knife in me. Christ's sake!'

'Look, Ah'll tell ye whit Ah want ye tae dae. Ah want ye tae unzip your troosers an' take oot your prick if ye can manage tae find it in there.'

'What? Fuckin' hell, I'm not some poofter, you know. If you want to suck someone's dick, I'll find one for you.'

'Ah'm nae poofter masel'. Ah'm a man o' ma word. Now, come on – ye dae it half a dozen times a day.'

Calum looked at Linda, white and shivering, crouched on the thin pillows.

'C'moan, doll, this is more in your line o' work. Get yoursel' doon here an' treat our wee friend tae a hand job.'

She shook her head, frightened beyond belief. But Calum just stepped over to her, grabbed her by a scrawny wrist, and pulled her down to where Maurice was slowly bleeding to death. He wasn't her boyfriend, at least not exclusively. They had sex from time to time. The truth was, he was her pimp, and the pimp of several other women, all supplied by Bernie. She had no feelings for Maurice, but she didn't want to see him die, and she was scared to death that the Scotsman would kill her as well.

'Ah willnae say it again, doll. A hand job or a blow job, whatever takes yir fancy. Jist get the wee fucker hard.'

She sat on the bed beside Maurice and unzipped his trousers with trembling fingers. With difficulty, she extracted his limp penis from the tangle of his underpants. It had shrivelled to almost nothing.

She took her time, using all the techniques she'd picked up on the job. At first, she thought nothing would happen. He was too ill, too distracted, too frightened. And

426

then, as if by some miracle, she felt him stiffen just a little. She breathed a sigh of relief and went about her task with greater hope, and bit by bit the reluctant organ grew in her hand. She prayed she wouldn't be asked to have sex with Maurice. Not with that wound in his front.

'Thanks a lot, doll. Now, give it tae me.'

Calum pushed her aside and took hold of Maurice's half-erect penis in his left hand.

'You'll no' be needin' this any longer, will ye? Jist close your eyes an' it'll be over in a second.'

He drew the knife to the base of the organ and, before it shrank again, sliced it wholesale from Maurice's trunk. A quick fumble and another cut deprived him of his testicles as well.

Calum stood back, holding his trophies in one hand. Maurice had passed out. He lay prostrate on the bed while blood pumped freshly from his new wounds.

'He's gonna die,' protested Linda. 'You bastard, you've carved him up so much he's fuckin' bleedin' to death.'

'What's wrong wi' that?'

'Why don't you ring for an ambulance?'

'What fuckin' good would that do me, eh? Get some polis an' that tae turn up here, and him talkin' and you gabblin'. Not tae mention the waste o' taxpayers' money. Do ye realize the state the National Health Service is in? There's citizens oot there that needs a amblance more than this wee shite. Now, if ye dinnae mind, Ah'd like tae finish this off so's Ah can get back tae the big job Ah have on. Ye'd no' believe the money Ah stand tae make.'

Maurice had started to come round.

'Ye feelin' all right, Maurice? Ah'm sorry Ah called ye Murray, it wis careless of me. An' Ah'm sorry Ah cut your willy off. But Ah said Ah would, so Ah felt obliged tae stick tae ma promise. Here, you may as well huv them as a souvenir.'

He pressed the freshly severed organs into Maurice's limp hand.

'Where would ye like the *coup de grâce*, Maurice? Ah'm willin' tae entertain any suggestions. They reckon the throat's the best. But there's plenty o' good alternatives. Ah could gouge yer eyes oot. Shall Ah do that?'

'Ah, Christ, leave my fucking eyes alone. I'm asking you, please, just leave me alone. Let her go for an ambulance. Please.'

'Well, where would ye like me tae stick the knife in? Here any good?'

Calum thrust the knife hard into Maurice's side, taking care to put his hand over his victim's mouth while he did so. Maurice called out inarticulately, fighting now against the blow and the steel. Calum smiled at him and removed the knife, then plunged it into another part of his belly. He seemed to know exactly where to thrust in order to avoid a fatal wound. The knife went in and out, in and out, as though he was a doctor probing for a weak spot. Maurice started to go into convulsions. Froth and blood appeared at his lips, then he started to cough up thick gobbets of arterial blood.

'Tough wee bugger, isn't he, doll?'

Linda had gone into something like a trance.

'What d'ye think? Is Murraymint still conscious? D'ye think he can hear what Ah'm sayin'?'

She didn't answer. What was he saying, after all?

He picked up Maurice's head and cradled him. Knife in hand, he began to croon to the dying man, a soft song he'd learned as a child, when he still had no knives to play with.

428

Speed bonny boat like a bird on the wing,
Onward, the sailors cry.
Carry the lad that's born to be King,
Over the sea to Skye.

The knife dazzled his hand. He held it tight against Maurice's white throat as he sang, and he imagined blue seas, tall mountains and green hills. He remembered cold days in Northern Ireland, huddled in a ditch, or walking slowly down a sniper's run, his heart beating as though lubricated with hot oil.

'Dinnae be mad with me, Murray, son. Ye wir never a proper squaddie, ye cannae unnerstan'.'

He wiped blood away from Maurice's mouth with the back of his hand, then took the knife and let the blade slide across the waiting throat. Maurice's whole body jerked once and was still. Calum put his knife down on the bed.

'Well, Linda, our wee friend's gone tae meet his maker. Dae ye think it matters? Eh? D'ye think any bugger'll turn up at his funeral?'

She sat silently watching him out of the jungle of her trance. Her last fix was wearing off quickly, and she had nowhere to hide. She'd wet herself from fright, and she was frightened the smell might anger him.

He lifted his head and looked at her. He wanted to be merciful, compassionate, like some sort of God. There'd been days in the barracks when he'd sat out the rain and fancied himself Calum the merciful, receiver of accolades. Day after day he'd drive past them in the streets, a rifle in his hand, and never fire, and he came to count it an act of mercy on his part, and nothing to do with orders from above.

'They'd be quiet a long time,' he whispered, loud

enough for her to hear. 'Ye'd ken they wir oot there, watchin' ye, and ye'd know they wir waitin' their chance. Ah wis on patrol, an' they shot ma mate in front o' me, right in front o' ma eyes. Ye were never sure, ye could never be sure when it would come. It's nothin' tae do wi' mercy or humanity or that. It's just doon tae opportunity. Now it's his chance, now it's yours.'

'I've done nothing,' said the girl. 'You can have me as often as you like. Take me with you. Please.'

She'd always counted on men to settle her debts with them through sex. A blow job or a long-term commitment. It made little difference to her.

'Ye looked at me,' he said. 'Ye fuckin' looked at me. Ye ken ma face, ye ken ma name.' He paused, then suddenly exploded in inexplicable rage, a torrent of anger that ripped through her and curled her into a ball.

'You fuckin' looked right at me! Why the fuck did ye do that, eh?! Yer just a wee hoor, an' Ah've nae more need for ye than Ah have for the Queen of England.'

She lifted her head, pleading for her life. Her face was wet with tears, her lips were dry, she was gasping for breath. She opened her mouth and, as she did so, Calum pushed the knife into it all the way, until it hit the back of her skull. He didn't look at her again.

He found Maurice's stash before leaving and took everything in it. There were shirts in a wardrobe, and Calum changed into one that took his fancy, cutting his own bloodstained specimen into small pieces and flushing them down the toilet. It was time to head back to the digs he'd found, so he could change properly. Then he'd take a taxi to Knightsbridge. He wondered if Maddie would still be awake by the time he got there.

CHAPTER FIFTY-SIX

They would drowse and nod and fall into a fitful sleep that would last for minutes, then snatch themselves awake again into a dreadful darkness and a terrible roaring of sand. It was impossible to tell whether it was night or day. An inky darkness blotted everything out, and it felt as if the entire world had been erased, leaving them encased in what remained, until the sand swallowed it too.

David chafed at the indefinite delay the storm imposed on them. They were already under pressure to reach the weapons site before the first full-scale test. Every minute mattered, yet here they were, crouched in a prison of wind and sand, unable to move an inch.

He fell asleep again, and walked for miles through a dream of ancient cities ringed with stone, in search of something that had been lost centuries ago. When he woke, Nabila had gone.

He leaped to his feet, calling her name. Each time, the wind snatched it from his lips and tore it into tiny little pieces. 'Na . . .' he called, 'Na . . . Na . . .', but his voice tailed away and he was left with his own silence.

An unimaginable panic took hold of him. If she'd strayed even a few feet away, she would be irretrievably lost by now. No matter what direction he went in, he had only a fractional chance of finding her. And every false move she made would only compound her initial error.

By the time the storm lifted, they could be separated by a mile or more of blank sand.

He opened his mouth again, but this time he was facing directly into the wind. In seconds his mouth had filled with sand. He crumpled up, choking, coughing, spitting. But there was barely enough saliva to moisten the little grains and to clear his throat of them.

He staggered back to the camel behind him, and retrieved one of the water canteens. He drank and choked, and drank and choked again, simply grateful to get the sand out of his mouth. More careful now, he closed the canteen again. It was almost empty. In their hurry to get everything organized, they'd only drawn enough water for their immediate needs. Now, the two canteens needed filling again.

A rope joined their camel to the others, and David used it to trace his way to them. He found a water barrel, and managed to stand it on end in order to insert a tap. As he did so, he heard a muffled voice from somewhere to his right.

'David? David, is that you?'

He felt a wave of relief pass through him. He tried calling back, but the wind snatched his words away. Nabila was upwind of him, and her voice, though flattened by the noise, still reached him. He fought his way back towards her, pushing physically against the powerful tide of wind-carried sand that was doing its best to push him back or throw him reeling to the ground.

At last he caught sight of a shadow that might have been Nabila. He made a last effort and reached her. She pulled him to her, then made him hunker down beside her, so they could talk without shouting too much. Even so, it was an effort to get the words out.

'Where the . . . hell have you been?' David asked. 'I

woke up . . . and you were gone. No message . . . nothing –
I . . . thought you were lost.'

'I'm all right. I've been . . . Look, why don't you . . .
come over this way . . . and give me a hand?'

He followed her through the whirling sand. It was a
matter of only a few yards. Nabila knelt down in front
of a mound of packages that had been carried on one of
the runaway camels.

'If you can . . . hold that, I'll . . . pull this out from . . .
underneath. That's it. Now just . . . No, pull that . . .
back there.'

She switched on the torch and swung its beam in front
of him. All at once, he saw what she'd been up to.

'I remembered . . . that we'd packed . . . the tent on
one of the . . . two leading camels. So . . . it was just a
matter . . . of finding it.'

'And setting it up . . . in this wind.'

'That as well.'

'Didn't you think . . . I might have gone off . . . into
the storm . . . looking for you?'

'Of course not. You're . . . not a fool.'

'You don't think . . . I love you that much?'

'Yes, of course. You're . . . very sweet. But you're . . .
not a fool. And please stop . . . being so angry. You should
be . . . grateful I didn't wake you up.'

They found as good a spot as they could in which to
pitch the tent. It was an old People's Liberation Army tent,
the best Nabila had been able to find in the bazaar. She
had repaired several holes before packing it, but there'd
been nothing she could do to turn it from an unwieldy
mess of canvas into anything remotely resembling a
modern tent.

It took them over an hour to erect it. But once it was
up and they crawled in, zipping the opening firmly against

the wind, it transformed everything. The howling was still there, admittedly, but it was outside. Inside, there was no wind, no sand, no constant buffeting. And, in time, the interior grew warm. It felt the greatest thing in the world to have a tent, and to be inside it and to be alive.

They fell asleep soon afterwards, still in the darkness. David had fashioned earplugs for them both out of wadding that he'd found on one of the saddles. The storm vanished while they slept, as though its world and theirs were entirely separate.

David woke first. When he removed the plugs from his ears, he heard the same rushing sound as before. Nothing had changed. He stretched himself and reached for the torch. Reluctant as he was to go outside, the need to empty his bladder was overpowering. He unzipped the opening and slipped out, zipping it again behind him.

The wind was fiercer than ever. He thought they'd have to bed the tent down even more securely. With the help of the torch, he found Doris and, several yards further on, the spot where he'd made a latrine. Swearing loudly, he made use of it, then covered it with the help of a spade – not that he really needed to bother.

Back at the tent, he busied himself reinforcing the ropes and weighing down the sides with sand rammed into bags. If the wind rose any higher, they'd have to hold the tent down with their bare hands.

He went back inside and zipped the entrance tightly. The difference in temperature was remarkable. He swore not to venture out again without his jacket, which he'd taken off in order to sleep.

The soft light of an oil lamp filled the interior. It had come with the tent, a fifties PLA veteran that had graced a hundred mess halls and hung at the poles of a hundred tents. The zip had been an eighties improvement. Nabila looked up and smiled.

'What's that?' he asked.

'This?' She held up a broad sheet of paper that had been lying across her lap. 'It fell out of your jacket. I'm sorry if . . .'

He dashed across and snatched the paper from her hands. It was the map he'd been studying earlier.

'You have no right . . .' he started.

Nabila snapped back at him before he could go further.

'Right? What do you mean I have no right? This is a map, isn't it? I assume it's not intended as an exotic wall decoration. As far as I can see, it's a map of the Taklamakan – which by some incredible coincidence happens to be where we both are. You and – in case you're suffering from a lapse of memory – me. I think I have as much right as anyone to look at this.'

'I'm sorry, love, but . . .'

'Don't call me "love". If you don't trust me, then you certainly don't love me.'

'Nabila, please – let's not have an argument. This isn't the ideal place for one, is it?'

'I don't see that we have any choice.'

'Listen, it wasn't a case of my not trusting you. I . . . just thought the map might confuse things, that's all. But if you want to see it, that's fine by me.'

He sat down beside her and unrolled the map across the bumpy floor. Nabila bent down and stared at it for a couple of moments.

'How old is it?' she asked, trying to keep her voice calm.

'About one thousand three hundred years,' he said. 'In the early Tang Dynasty. It was drawn by a Buddhist monk named Zhang Hsueliang. He started work on it at the Hsiang Guo monastery in Kaifeng, and completed it in the course of a visit to the Da Yan pagoda in Chang'an. He was seventy-five years old then. It's all there, if you want to read it.'

He pointed to several lines of rapidly executed calligraphy along one edge of the map.

'Where did you come by this?' asked Nabila, impressed in spite of herself.

'From my father. He found it in the bazaar at Hami before the revolution. When he guessed where I was going, he handed it on to me. I think he meant it to be some sort of talisman.'

'But . . . You seemed to be reading it as if it was more than just that.'

'Did I?' He smiled. Outside, the wind shrieked darkly between the dunes. 'Actually, I didn't give it much thought at first. Then I started looking more closely. Here, let me show you.'

He ran his hand over the stiff paper, flattening it further.

'The map's drawn with the West to the top, North to the right. All we have to do is turn it like this' – he twisted it through ninety degrees – 'and it suddenly turns into something remarkably like a modern map. Over this way' – he pointed to a circle at the eastern end – 'he's indicated how many days' journey to Chang'an. The Taklamakan – he calls it the Liu Sha – looks much as it does now – these are the Kun Lun mountains down here, and these are the Tien Shan. You can see that he's familiar with the route down into India. My bet is he travelled the pilgrim route more than once himself, and that this map's the result. As you might expect, these little stupas all seem to be monasteries along the southern Silk Road.'

He ran his finger along a line that seemed to represent

the road joining China to the West. Caravans had taken this route from as far as Peking in the east to Persia and Rome in the distant west. Nabila traced the same road, from the opposite direction, and their fingers met and touched briefly.

'Now, look along the southern half of the desert,' David said. 'He's drawn three rivers, do you see, all formed by glacial meltwaters running down from the Kun Lun mountains. That's not entirely accurate, because we know the rivers had mostly dried up by the third century.'

'And these?' Nabila pointed to little circles along the edges of the streams.

'Ah, those are interesting. They weren't there either when he drew the map. They're oasis cities. Just sand and mud-brick now.'

'Dandan-Uilik, Endere . . .'

'Niya. As far as I can see he's got them all in exactly the right spots. If they hadn't already been discovered, this map could have led an expedition straight to them.'

He paused and straightened the map.

'But look up here.' He stabbed his finger at the northern sector of the desert. 'There shouldn't be any settlements here. The Tien Shan waters didn't drain into the desert the way those in the south did. No river valleys, no settlements. That's what I was always given to understand. But Zhang has marked five towns slap in the middle of the sands. He's added their names, the number of their houses, and a few other details.'

She looked, deciphering the name of each in turn.

'Pan T'ang, Chie Kiang, Ts'ang Mi . . .'

'That's right. But look more carefully. On the line after each name, he draws a circle within a circle, and inside them he writes the character for "well". These are oases with artesian wells.'

437

Nabila scanned the map. The style of calligraphy was rather strange, but if she strained she could make out most of it. She nodded.

'It does look like that, yes. But what are these?'

She pointed to a series of small triangles stretching between the oasis towns in the north, and at two straggling lines between the northern and southern cities.

'I'd be willing to bet those are just smaller wells, maybe tiny underground deposits. But they'd be just enough to allow for regular communications between the different settlements. What's more, I think those wells could all be there today.'

'But surely . . .' Nabila's forehead was creased with little furrows. 'Surely the cities died out long ago. The wells must have dried up.'

'Probably, yes. Or they may have been buried by sand. Or the northern towns may have suffered after the southern settlements dried up. I really don't know. There are too many possibilities. But I'm certain there's still enough water in any of these wells to satisfy the needs of three humans and nine camels. There's only one small problem . . .'

'How do we match all this up to the grids on a Tactical Pilotage Chart?'

He took her hand tightly.

'I'm beginning to think this whole thing was a big mistake,' he said.

He fell silent. Outside, the wind yammered its way across the never-ending dunes, as it had done for millennia, burying cities, erasing times and dates and places, the names of men and women, their habitations, their graveyards, their fortresses, their watering holes, their hopes, dreams, and memories. With every breath it took, it redrew the map of an entire region.

Nabila took her hand away.

'I've got to go out too,' she said.

She opened the tent door. A blast of raw sand was blown across everything.

'I'll not be long,' she said, and tied the flaps behind her.

CHAPTER FIFTY-SEVEN

Maddie sat straight up in bed. She'd been trying to sleep for over two hours now, with no success. If this went on much longer, she knew she'd lose it completely, she'd start screaming the house down, the way she'd done years ago. But her mother refused to let her go back to the clinic, saying this was something they'd have to work through together. It was a load of crap, and they both knew it, but Elizabeth couldn't bear to lose face.

She was sure she'd heard one of them creeping about out there in the corridor. Lying awake like this in the pitch darkness, she was sensitive to night sounds. She could lie for hours, listening to the house settle round her.

Even as she pondered on what the footsteps might mean, the door of her room opened and closed again. The corridor had been sunk in blackness. She strained to see, comparing one patch of black or grey with another. Yes, someone was standing in her room. Her brain spun. Shit! she thought, it has to be that slimy bastard Anthony, creeping in in the hope of stealing a furtive shag. He'd tried to feel her up before this. He must reckon I'm so out of it by now I won't care if he screws me silly all night. I think I'll scream my head off after all.

Just as she opened her mouth to do so, a heavy hand clamped over it and moist lips brushed her ear.

'Ah'm no' here tae hurt ye, doll. Ah've come tae take ye oota here, y'unnerstan'?'

For a minute or more, she thought she was going to die. Her heart launched a burst of wild throbbing spasms that were certain to knock fatal holes in her chest wall. Who was this? What did he want? Was he going to molest and murder her?

'Calm doon, pal,' he said. 'Yir in safe hands. It's yir mate, Calum. Remember? Ah wis in here before, Ah brought ye a letter fae yir auld man. Like Ah say, Ah'm no' here tae touch a hair o' yir head. Ah'm here tae take ye oot, an' tae get ye off this cold turkey. Can Ah put the light on an' take ma hand away withoot you screamin' yir pretty wee head off? Can Ah?'

She felt her heart slam on the brakes. Calum. The letter. He'd seemed a bit wild, but harmless; she'd no reason to be afraid of him. But how on earth had he managed to get into the house? Had they let him in? Surely not, if he was planning to take her out. And why all this tiptoeing around in the dark?

She made up her mind and nodded.

'You're sure now ye unnerstan' what Ah'm sayin' exactly? One scream an' we'll both be fucked. Yir mither's a nice woman, but she'll see they sen' me off tae prison fir five years an' keep you in this wee room till ye go out o' yir heid.'

She nodded more vigorously, and mumbled incoherently through his thick palm. His hand smelled of sweat and drugs. He took it away, very carefully, ever ready to slap it back down again at the first hint of a cry for help.

'Thank you,' Maddie whispered. He switched the bed-side light on, and she closed her eyes to block the terrible whiteness it threw against her. When she opened them

441

again, he was sitting on the side of the bed facing her. She remembered his rough face and smiled. He answered in a low voice.

'Yir no' upset Ah snuk in on ye, likes?'

She shook her head. Blood vessels too small to see or count were pumping up and down the contours of her brain. She felt dizzy and excited at the same time. A strange man in her room in the middle of the night. It was nothing sexual, just a visceral excitement about what might happen.

'Did you really come to take me out of here?'

'Better than that, doll. She's makin' ye go through cauld turkey here, isn't that right?'

'Cold turkey? Well, yes. Yes, I suppose that's exactly what it is.'

'Weel, let's see if Ah cannae do somethin' aboot that. What were ye on?'

'On? What drugs? Well, Valium, lithium carbonate, two different antidepressants, and . . .'

'Ah'm no' askin' what did ye get fae the chemist. That stuff'll fuck yir mind up an' turn ye into a drug addict. What were you gettin' on the street?'

'Oh, hell, no – I'm not withdrawing from street drugs. I haven't done drugs in years.'

'What did ye do the damage with when ye were takin' them?'

'Nothing much. Hash. I smoked a lot of hash. And I took some cocaine. Then . . . I got ill, so I never touched the stuff again.'

'Right, then.'

He rose and went to the dressing table. When he came back, he was carrying a small mirror in one hand. He took the bag of cocaine from his pocket and opened it. Later, he'd divide the contents up, hiding the main stash in his luggage and putting the little packets where the sun doesn't shine. He traced two lines of cocaine along the mirror's polished face, then produced a fresh fifty-pound note from his pocket.

'This is one Ah prepared earlier,' he said, and proceeded to roll the crisp note into a tube. 'Can ye use this?'

She nodded. The way things were going, she had little chance of getting hold of any drugs for days, so why the hell not go with the cocaine? Maybe her Scottish Lancelot would be able to supply the medications she needed.

One line disappeared up her left nostril, the other into the right. She coughed, then regained her composure.

'Gie that a few minutes,' he said, 'then we'll be on our way.'

'How'd you get in?' she asked. 'He has this place like bloody Fort Knox.'

He shook his head.

'That's where yir wrong,' he said. 'He's got great locks an' all that, an' a big alarm system on the ground floor, but once ye get up here there's next tae nothin'. Ah shimmied up a drainpipe at the back an' Ah wis in by a windae before Ah got oota the taxi, more or less. Yir door wis a doddle. Yir mither keeps the key in the lock.'

'How are we getting out? I can't climb down a drain-pipe, I'm not steady enough.'

'Ye'll be steady. But if ye know the password, we can cancel the alarm an' walk oot through the front door.'

She shook her head. This was the bastard Anthony's house: she'd never been here until her mother brought her from Rose's place.

'Ah, well. We'll do it another way. Help me make a dummy here in the bed.'

They worked quickly, using blankets and a pillow to create the semblance of a sleeping form. Maddie topped it off with a fur muff from the wardrobe that was close enough to her hair colour to pass muster in poor light. Calum removed all but one of the room's light bulbs, leaving only one 40-watt specimen to light if the wall switch was pressed.

'This is fun!' said Maddie, already feeling better than she had done in months.

'Dinna let yersel' get carried awa',' warned Calum. Too much euphoria could blow the whole thing. He wouldn't rest easy till he had her in Scotland, somewhere she wouldn't get out of so easily as this. He had the place all set. It was just a matter of getting her to believe he was the Pied Piper.

'Right,' he said. 'We go doon fast as we can, straight tae the front door. Once we're oot, we scoot fir the main road. If there's a taxi, we grab it. If no', we've a long walk ahead of us.'

'Turn your head,' she ordered. When he did so, she leapt out of bed. She'd been sleeping in her pants: it was still too hot for anything else. It took her moments to find jeans and a T-shirt, and a few more to pack a change of underwear and one or two other items.

'OK,' she said. 'I'm ready.'

They went out on to the landing, and closed and locked the bedroom door behind them. Maddie was well under the sway of the drug by now. He hoped he'd given her enough to keep her that way.

They crept down the stairs, one at a time. As they reached the half-landing, a sudden screech jolted them. Whatever else it was, the alarm system was rich in decibels. They hared down the rest of the stairs, along the hall, and out into the night.

CHAPTER FIFTY-EIGHT

They woke and slept, woke and slept. The tent had become their world. Outside, nothing altered, nothing changed. The wind drove as always across the dunes, thick sand blotted out any light, and the shrieking and wailing of the storm made it sound as though doors to hell had been torn from their hinges.

Life was made up of dreams and nightmares. Several times, David found himself in an ancient city of red stone. All around the city, tall dunes of white sand rose up like mountains, throwing shadows into every courtyard and public place. Men in black robes, their faces hidden by thick hoods of camel's hair, walked hurriedly from house to house and street to street.

The further David walked, the taller the houses grew, and before long it became very dark in the narrow spaces between them. On doors and windows he saw displayed the trophies of old executions and punishments: heads and hands and feet nailed to wooden boards.

He saw an open doorway on his left and went inside. On his left, a second opening led him into a small room. A pillow and a red quilt lay on the floor. From somewhere close by, the sound of a *ch'in* came to him, and a woman's voice singing a song from the harem of the palace of Wei.

All day the wind blew strong,

The sun was buried deep.
I have thought of him so long, so long,
I cannot sleep.

He laid himself down quietly on the quilt. As he did so, he noticed that the room was not a room, but a tent. And from somewhere a roaring came that wiped out the woman's voice and the delicate music of the *ch'in*. He closed his eyes and slept.

When he woke the roaring was gone. Light sieved through the canvas, and sharp needles of sunlight pierced it wherever they had a chance. Nabila was sitting facing him, humming softly, a soft smile on her lips. She held a needle and thread in her hand, and was repairing a sleeve that had been torn in the tussle with the camels.

'What are you humming?' he asked. Images of the red city were already fading from his mind. He didn't want to move.

'You wouldn't know it. An old Uighur song about men, and how they're always deceivers, and the revenge a young girl takes on her unfaithful lover.'

'Oh? What does she do to him?'

'There are two versions. I was humming the one we young Uighur women sing in private. In the polite version' – she held up the needle and thread – 'she sews his private parts to the tail of a mad camel. But in the version I was humming . . .'

'I don't think I want to know. And I'd appreciate it if you put that needle away. Am I right in thinking the sun has come out? And the storm has gone?'

'How clever you red-blooded Anglo-Saxon men are. If you'd care to follow me outside, I'll show you all there is to see.'

She put her sewing away, and stood up. Outside, the

world had turned to sunshine. David stood in astonishment, willing himself to believe it was all real. From the sun downwards, everything looked just like a film set. He imagined it all being rolled back on rubber wheels, revealing raw concrete underfoot, and white lines marking the contours of the dunes.

Nabila's voice broke into his reverie.

'Over here, David. Please, it's important.'

He stumbled through the sand towards her. As far as he could see, the high dunes were still in their original places, even if their shapes had changed. Navigating back might not be that difficult.

Nabila was bending down beside one of the camels. Doris, as far as he could tell. The poor beast was buried to her neck in sand.

'Is she . . . ?'

'Yes. I've checked,' said Nabila. 'I looked at the others earlier. They're all right, but they'll need watering quickly.'

'What happened to her?'

'Doris? It's hard to say. How long did the storm last?'

He shrugged.

'God knows. Three or four days at least.'

'Yes, that sounds about right. She'd already gone without water a couple of days before that. Even for a camel, that's stretching things a bit in these conditions.'

'And you say the other two are OK?'

'So far. But if we don't find water for them soon, they'll die as well.'

David looked round at the acres of sand that had been tossed and sifted by the wind, then set down softly again. The routine they'd followed so far for finding water the camels could drink had been to keep a sharp eye out for the tell-tale patches of white salt that betrayed the presence of moisture beneath the sand. The water, when it could be found, was five or six feet down and brackish; but it served the camels well, and saved the fresh water.

They roused the other camels and headed off, following a bearing taken with David's compass. Using that and the general contour of the dunes, they were sure it would take less than an hour to meet up again with Mehmet and the main caravans.

Two hours later, there was still no sign of them. Their own camels were weakening rapidly. David was sure they had been over the original camp site, but however closely he looked, he could see no sign of the missing man or his beasts, not even hoofprints.

'He may have gone to look for us,' said Nabila.

'Surely not while the storm was still at its height. Look, if this was the site, then he and the camels must have left during the storm, not after. Does that make any sense?'

Nabila frowned, then nodded.

'Perhaps,' she said. 'I've heard of men being driven half insane by the *karaburan* and setting off to walk home while it was still blowing. Mehmet must have been on the edge already, with the pain in his wrist. He could have just taken the camels off in an attempt to get out of the storm.'

'Then they could be almost anywhere by now.'

'Yes – within reason. In practice he can't have got far.'

'We need those camels, Nabila. They have our water, our equipment . . .'

'Why don't you climb that dune there and see what you can make out?'

'Right. Where are my binoculars?'

Nabila dug into one of the saddlebags and whipped out

a tatty pair of army surplus glasses she'd picked up in Korla many years earlier.

'You lent yours to Mehmet, if you remember. But you can have these if you like.'

He took them from her.

'These aren't exactly high-performance.'

'I liked them very much when I bought them. I thought they were the smartest thing . . .'

'Well, hardly . . .'

He broke off, sensing she was hurt.

'I only meant . . .' he started, then broke off again.

'In Kashgar we have a saying: However highly polished your spectacles, you will see through them only what you want to see.'

He laughed.

'Who made that nonsense up?'

'I did. And it isn't nonsense. Remember you're in the desert. It's easy to be misled by a mirage.'

'I'll do my best to keep out of their reach.' He bent and kissed her. 'Don't leave this spot, for God's sake. We can't afford to get split three ways.'

'I'm staying put whatever happens. Haven't you noticed the tamarisk bush over there? I'm going to dig down. There might be water.'

'Good luck.' He kissed her again and started up the dune.

The sand, softer than ever after the storm, made every step of the climb a torture. The dune must have been close on four hundred feet high. Each time David placed a foot on the slope ahead of him, it sank down, giving him little purchase. His legs ached intolerably before he'd gone fifty feet. The sun was high, not far short of noon, and the heat that blazed down on him from behind threatened to bake him dry. He kept his head down and plodded on, one hand on his stick, the other in free air, defying gravity, or so it seemed.

At the top, he looked behind him, all the way down the flank of the dune. A long diagonal trail of blurred footprints marked his passage. His eye flicked over it, then down to where Nabila and the two camels waited like insects.

The dune was high enough to give him a vantage point from which to see for several miles in most directions. Again and again, he swept his eyes over the deceptive landscape, a uniform carpet of ochre full of hollows and hummocks and great sweeping hills. He almost thought that, if he could strip it away, another landscape would be revealed, of green fields and gentle slopes and small river valleys. Nothing moved. No birds straddled the sky. No gazelles raced between the dunes.

Then, out of the corner of his eye, he caught sight of something. A series of black marks against the sand. It was hard to tell if it was moving at all at first. He raised Nabila's glasses and started to sweep. Where the hell were they? He altered the focus several times, but still the marks eluded him. Again he tried with his bare eyes. The marks were still there, but only just: in a moment they'd have passed out of his line of sight behind a dune.

This time he got the glasses in line and found what he was looking for. There was no sign of Mehmet, but the six camels disappearing from view were unmistakable.

He waved his arms and shouted at the top of his voice.

'Mehmet! Mehmet! Over here! Look up, Mehmet!'

But there was no answering cry, no waving figure acknowledging him.

He gave up at last and started back down the dune,

bumping and sliding and skiing his way down ten times faster than he'd gone up.

Nabila was waiting for him.

'I heard you call. Did you see Mehmet, or were you just trying to get his attention?'

'He was down there. I didn't see him, but I caught the tail end of the caravan moving in line. He must be at the front. We've got to act quickly, otherwise he could be lost for good.'

'Which direction's he heading in?'

'That's the funny thing. They were going due south.'

'He's taking the most direct route out of the desert, then. He must think we're dead.'

'He has no reason to think otherwise. Look, I'll take one of the camels and try to head him off.'

Nabila shook her head decisively.

'No point. You'll get no speed out of either animal.'

'But Mehmet . . .'

'You'll have to go on foot. But if you do that, I want you to make completely sure I can follow you. Wait.'

She went to the first camel, a gangly creature David had named Elvis. It took her a while to find what she was looking for, rummaging through the huge packs while Elvis snorted protests and moaned softly at the lack of water.

'Here,' she said, triumphantly pulling out a loosely wrapped bundle of thin wooden sticks that turned out to have Chinese flags glued to one end.

'Stick one in every five hundred yards or so, always well within sight of the one before. And pick them up again on your way back.'

'Wouldn't it be better if you followed me? Most of the camels are over there with Mehmet.'

'Then you'd better get a move on. I'm staying here.'

She thrust the flags at him. He took them and kissed her, then turned to go.

He had walked about six feet when her voice stopped him.

'David . . .'

He turned round and looked at her. She seemed small and tired. Her skin had dried, making it look as though she'd aged years since the storm started.

'Make sure you come back to me,' she said. 'Do you hear me?'

'I won't be long. I promise.'

He set off, skirting the tall dune and coming out into more open country. He'd memorized the terrain that he'd seen from above; but here on the ground, it all seemed confusingly different. He began to wonder if he would, after all, be able to find Mehmet and his charges.

The flags stood up reasonably well in the soft sand. The sticks were made of light wood, and the flags themselves were of flimsy material. David found himself glad that Nabila had had the foresight to bring them in the first place. Looking back the way he had come, David realized that even a moment's inadvertence could cause him to lose the way.

He thought he recognized the dune ahead. It was white, with a row of camel-thorn bushes bristling across one side. He made a turn at it, praying he was making better speed than Mehmet. When he looked round again, the view back to his starting-point was blocked. If another storm came, he would never make it back to Nabila.

CHAPTER FIFTY-NINE

Suddenly, some distance ahead, he saw them – a curving line of tired-looking camels plodding stoically across a burnt landscape. Their foreshortened forms shivered in and out of focus in the waves of heat that bounced off the hot sand. David focused his glasses on them. Mehmet was walking at the front, hunched and weary, his damaged arm dangling by his side like a lump of dead wood.

Glancing round quickly, David saw that he could reach them much more quickly if, instead of pushing on along the trail they'd left, he were to climb the dune on his left and slide down the other side. That way, he'd come out more or less facing them. It was a monstrous mistake, but there was no way he could have known it at the time.

His legs were still weak and rubbery after his recent climb, and they bore him to the top with great reluctance. When he got there, he found himself thoroughly out of breath. Looking down, he saw Mehmet and the camels at roughly the position he'd expected to find them in. They were heading for a clump of tamarisk bushes in the middle distance, probably with the intention of digging for water. David was facing them: the dune had brought him round ahead of them.

David thought at first of calling, but he still felt too winded to do more than pant for air. He started to slide down slowly, less anxious now, and aware of the danger that lay in spraining or breaking a leg or an ankle. He wondered if Mehmet could see him yet.

At the bottom, there was still some little distance between himself and the front camel, while the cut of the dune had placed David at an angle to his quarry, with the result that he was approaching them from in front rather than behind. He walked slowly towards them, knowing there was now no way Mehmet could miss him.

The first tamarisks came in sight. Even here, the heat haze lay over the ground, twisting everything into false and deceptive shapes. David squinted for a first sight of Mehmet.

Suddenly, there he was, a black figure walking unsteadily towards him, now visible, now concealed by the flank of the camel he walked beside.

'Mehmet! Mehmet! It's me, David! I'm over here! Can you see me?'

The camel-driver did not respond at once. He just kept trudging on. Then, as David's voice grew more insistent, he raised his head and opened his eyes, shading them with his good hand. When he caught sight of David, he leapt into the air and called out exultantly. Next thing, he was haring towards him with as much speed as his tired limbs could muster.

David glanced around with satisfaction. He'd found Mehmet, and it looked as though he'd found a substantial reserve of water at the same time. He started to walk forward. They were about two hundred yards apart. David waved again, and Mehmet, suddenly animated and full of energy, ran as fast as he could across the flat bed of the little arroyo.

What happened next was so frightening and so unexpected that David refused at first to believe it was happening at all. He blinked and looked again.

454

One moment, Mehmet was clearly visible, the next, it was as if he had slipped or fallen to his knees. David squinted, then lifted the glasses to his eyes.

Mehmet had sunk to his waist in a bed of quicksand. He was struggling to regain his balance in the hope of being able to swing back to the firm ground he'd just left, but the more he struggled, the more he was pulled down. Had he fallen with his good arm facing back to solid land, he might – just might – have succeeded in pulling himself back to safety. But his left arm, with its swollen and almost useless hand, would not give him the thin purchase he needed so badly.

David started to run towards him, then stopped. He'd just realized it would be the height of stupidity to blunder forward in a straight line without knowing where the pool of quicksand ended. The edge might be only feet away from him. There was no point in killing himself along with Mehmet, and leaving Nabila to die alone. Her words echoed in his head: 'Make sure you come back to me.'

He started walking more slowly, using one of the flags to prod the ground a couple of feet ahead of him. Mehmet was screaming now, yelling at the top of his voice for help, now calling on David, now on God, now on his mother. David reckoned he was the nearest, then remembered his own mother reading from the Koran when she prayed: 'God is closer to you than your neck vein.'

The stick sank suddenly into something very liquid. David almost overbalanced headlong into the waiting pool, then caught himself by executing an awkward twist at the hips that left him sprawling on firm ground. He struggled painfully to his feet and checked the distance between Mehmet and himself. Fifty yards at least.

Mehmet was up to his armpits.

'Try not to struggle, Mehmet,' shouted David. 'I'm coming round to get you.'

But how wide was the pool? For all David knew, it was irregularly shaped, with side-pockets extending on either side of him. Would he be faster going to the left or to the right? Did tamarisk bushes grow on dry land or quicksand? Or both?

He headed right, prodding to the side and front in the hope of telling where the quicksand began and ended. Mehmet was babbling rather than screaming now. David was glad he was too far away to see the man's face. Every time he looked, the camel-driver was in deeper than before.

'I'm coming, Mehmet,' he called, 'just hang on!' But he didn't know how he was going to get the man out, even if he did reach him in time. And his progress was so slow, he was beginning to doubt whether he could make it in time.

Mehmet responded with a series of frantic cries. David trained the glasses on him and saw he was already up to his shoulders. Not much more than three or four very short inches separated the sinking man's mouth from the surface of the quicksand.

David quickened his pace, desperate to get to Mehmet before he was wholly engulfed. The thought that he might be late by a matter of minutes or seconds lent urgency to his efforts. Urgency and a touch of recklessness.

He'd reached the side of the pool and was free, or so he thought, to head directly for Mehmet. He started to run, forgetting to use the flag to test the ground in front. Just as he came within range of Mehmet, the sand beneath his own feet gave way. There was a sucking sound, and David found himself dragged down into something that felt like wet porridge. There was a second slurping noise, and when he looked he saw that he was already up to his armpits in the stuff.

CHAPTER SIXTY

He'd given her a direct hit of cocaine in the taxi, making up the solution with mineral water he'd taken from her bedside table. By the time they reached their destination, she was bright-eyed and bushy-tailed, and madly in love with Calum and his wonder-drug. She hadn't felt as good as this in years.

'Well,' he drawled, smiling at her, 'well . . .'

She looked at the red mark on her forearm and grinned.

The cab left them in a cul-de-sac behind Paddington Station. Calum had an old friend there, a Hibs fan called Malcolm who allowed him to put up on his floor any time he was in London.

He let them in with a front-door key. This was where he always stayed whenever he was in London. He'd slept there the night before, and breakfasted heartily before setting forth for Knightsbridge. The living room was as he'd left it, the sofa-bed open, spilling sheets and a thin duvet on to the floor. His friend was the house DJ at a small club two streets away. He didn't have a girlfriend, just a string of nubile one-nighters, all aged about twelve, all spaced on E and wide open to his blandishments.

Calum glanced at his watch. Almost four o'clock. He wouldn't expect Malkie back for another hour or two.

'C'moan in, hen. It's no' the Ritz, but the way you feel, it's no' the Ritz you're after, is it?'

'Fuck the Ritz. Mother's always going there. Stupid place. Not as nice as this at all.'

He led her in, holding her lightly by the hand as though she was a precious substance he'd found and brought home. In her way, that was exactly what she was. He didn't plan to let her out of his sight until he had her tucked away safe and sound at their final destination. Given several more doses of cocaine, she'd never leave his side, not as long as he controlled all access to the drug. And where they were going, he'd be the only medicine show in town.

'Is this where we're staying?' she asked. He wondered if, in spite of her high, he'd seen her upper lip lift ever so slightly as she looked round at Malkie's faded walls and dingy furniture.

'Just for the night. We'll be oot o' here an' on our way agin tomorrow.'

She looked at him in surprise.

'Where to?'

'Better Ah dinnae say, likes. Careless talk could fuck us all. There'll be polis on the streets already, your face'll be on the telly before Richard and Judy hit the studio.'

'They'll think I got out myself, won't they? I mean, they've no reason to think there was anybody there but me.'

'Ay, likesays, more than likely. But when they have a wee think aboot the key an' the lock and all that, they're very likely tae reach a different conclusion. Now, will you be all right on the sofa-bed?'

'Oh, I don't feel like sleeping.'

'Me an' all, doll. But Ah want us tae get an early start. We've a long trip ahead tomorrow.'

'Oh, come on, we've plenty of time. The mood I'm in, I could stay up all week. We could go to a club, find a place playing Garage, do some serious dancing. How about it? There's Pure Silk – have you been there?'

Something was racing inside her. He could sense the imminent instability, the dangerous flux of mood and manner, the urgency that could lead to a crash if it were not controlled.

'Ah've been tae them all, believe me. Ah wis a DJ masel' once, back in Embra. That wis years ago, mind. Fir the moment, let's just concentrate on gettin' you tae sleep.'

He reached into his right-hand pocket and brought out four diazepam tablets. From the other pocket he took the small mineral water bottle he'd brought from her room.

'Look, doll, Ah dinnae have time tae argue. Ah want you relaxed an' fit fir the mornin'. So do me a big favour an' slip these doon.'

He handed her the tablets. For an extended moment, she hesitated, and he thought she was going to throw them in his face. But the chemicals lent their blessing to him, and she downed all four tranks in one go.

He helped her to the bed.

'Where are you sleeping?' she asked. 'Would you like to sleep with me?'

'Thanks very much, hen, but it's been a long day an' Ah'm bushed. Maybe another time, eh?'

'You may never get another offer.'

'No need tae worry, doll: Ah'm not aboot tae die fae sexual deprivation. Just you lie doon an' sleep.'

Unwillingly, she put her head on the pillow. He spread the duvet over her. Her feet stuck out at the other end, exposing a pair of Doc Martens that she'd been wearing when she turned up at Rose's clinic. He removed the boots and slipped her feet back under the cover.

He thought that he'd have to be careful about the drugs he was giving her. Drugs could have unwanted interactions, and the last thing he wanted was to turn her manic or violent. He'd just have to play it by ear until he saw which way she was bouncing.

He found a sleeping bag in a cupboard in Malkie's room. By the time he'd arranged it on the floor, Maddie was starting to drift off. Calum was worn out, but there was one thing to do before he too fell asleep. He went over to a large table that served Malkie as dining table and desk. A small PC took up one end. Calum turned it on, then located the ink-jet printer that lived on a nearby windowsill.

He quickly typed a letter, printed it on plain paper, and slipped the result into a white envelope. All it needed now was a stamp, and in a few days Calum Kilbride would be a rich man.

When he woke, Maddie was still out. That suited him perfectly. He got up and checked in Malkie's room: his friend was sleeping soundly in the company of two very naked young objects of desire whose warm and willing bodies seemed to have been moulded in a Japanese plastics factory. Calum, his exhaustion vanished, was greatly tempted to make himself known to them, but this morning his priorities had changed. He closed the door and left the flat.

He found a car-hire agency next to the railway station. It made things more difficult that he wanted a camper.

'You're sure you wouldn't like a Ford Sierra, sir? We have the complete range. Or a Mondeo? Any colour you like today . . .'

'What fuckin' use is a Ford Shitemobile tae someone who wants a camper? Will ye tell me that? Just make a few phone calls an' get me a camper roond here inside the hour.'

He whipped out a very large wad of money, his own supplemented by a packet he'd found at Maurice's the night before. Several notes passed over the counter in silence and disappeared in silence.

'I'm sure we can find a vehicle to your satisfaction, sir, if you'll just be patient a few minutes longer.'

He gave the address that was on his driving licence, paid in cash, and took delivery of a brand new Spacecruiser half an hour later. The girl behind the counter waved to him as he drove away. He smiled back at her as though she was somehow complicit in his plan.

Maddie was awake and waiting for him when he got back. Malkie still had not emerged from the bedroom. One of his naked conquests was sitting at the table munching on a slice of toast with marmalade.

'Shouldn't you be at school?' he said.

'This is school,' she murmured sleepily. 'You know?'

'What? School o' Life an' that?'

She nodded complacently.

'School o' Hard Knocks?'

'That's right.'

'That's nothin' but shite,' he said. He got Maddie to her feet and helped her to the door. While she waited on the landing, he collected his own bags, everything he'd brought from Pakistan. With her help, he got them downstairs.

When everything was stowed safely in the camper, he got Maddie inside. They were parked in the alleyway behind the flat, where no one was too likely to notice them. Maddie was still groggy from the combination of drugs she'd been given. He got out four more diazepam and, in spite of her protests, forced them down her throat. He was frightened of her OD'ing, but equally frightened that she might wake en route.

Once she was quiet, he took most of the cushions and things out of the space beneath one of the beds. Maddie fitted inside perfectly. He put a blanket over her, wedged her with cushions and bedclothes so she wouldn't be thrown about too much, and closed the upper half on top of her.

When that was done, he walked up to the street and put his envelope, now sporting a first-class stamp, into a pillar box on the corner. He sniffed the air. Petrol fumes and the smell of rotten eggs from catalytic converters. Where he was heading, there'd be nothing but pure air. He smiled to himself contentedly and walked back to the camper.

CHAPTER SIXTY-ONE

He closed his eyes tightly. Behind him, Mehmet's scream-ing continued for about a minute. It was followed by an abhorrent choking sound, then brutal silence.

When he opened his eyes again, he was all alone in the most unforgiving of landscapes. He was still sinking help-lessly into the quagmire, his body creeping downwards millimetre by millimetre. He didn't try to call out. What would have been the point? Even if Nabila had heard Mehmet's frantic cries and set off immediately, there was every chance she'd lose her way, or the very real likelihood – no, the certainty – that she'd arrive much too late.

He realized that he still had one flag in his left hand and the bundle of a dozen or more in his left. Holding on to them seemed pointless. He was about to let them drop out of sight for ever, when he froze. There was a slim chance that the flags could save his life.

He tightened his grip and slowly brought his left hand up out of the goo. Taking care not to disturb his precarious balance, he brought his right arm round and returned the single flag to the bundle.

Although any individual stick could be snapped in half with ease, the bundle had real strength in it. David flailed backwards, struggling to stay upright while lunging with the flags to strike dry land. Leaning with all his weight on the bundle, he tried to use it as a pivot to provide the leverage he needed to start his body turning. If he could only get his top half on to firm sand, there was a chance he could pull himself out.

The problem was that the bundle could not gain a proper purchase in the soft sand. It kept slipping out of place, forcing him to repeat the motion every few minutes. He'd managed to get himself a little round, but it was much harder than he'd thought at first. The quicksand was thick and gelatinous, and it resisted every effort David made to turn himself through ninety degrees. His shoulder was already starting to hurt badly. Before long it would become excruciating, and then he'd have to stop. One of the flags slipped and snapped, then another. He felt himself being pulled down further, and realized that he would soon be unable to keep his hold on dry land.

But still he did not let go. It was strange, he thought, that the human tendency was to hang on, however hopeless things looked. He concentrated his thoughts on good things, on Sam and Maddie, wishing one alive and the other in safer hands than Elizabeth's. And he thought of Nabila, left to a certain and painful death in the desert.

'David . . . Don't make any sudden movements.'

It seemed the most wonderful hallucination. At least he'd die content, he thought.

'I'm going to put a rope over your head and underneath your armpits. The other end is tied to one of the camels. Once you're secure, I'll pull you out. Is that all clear?'

He closed his eyes again, enjoying the illusion. Perhaps he was already dead and removed to paradise. The Muslims believed that the dead consorted with houris. Perhaps he'd been sent one with Nabila's voice.

He was brought out of his reverie by a rope slipping over his head and shoulders.

'Lift your arms. That's it. Just a little more. That's fine.'

He felt the rope tighten under his armpits, then pull him backwards and a little out of the gunge.

'Nabila? Is that really you?'

'Just how many strange women do you expect to meet out here?'

'Quite a few.'

He felt her arms grip him under his armpits.

'That hurts.'

'Don't worry. Once you're far enough up, I'll grab hold of something else.'

Squatting on the ground behind him, she went on pulling, then returned to the camel to tighten the rope a little. A few more pulls and he was out, covered in quicksand, but physically unhurt.

'Thank God for that,' he said. 'How did you . . . ?'

He broke off. Next to him, Nabila was in floods of tears. Her carefully maintained facade of imperturbability had collapsed once she'd pulled him to safety. There'd been so little time to spare, and she'd almost lost him.

'I didn't . . . really know . . . how much you meant to me . . . until now,' she said, and her words hung in the air about him like tiny, whirling sparrows. He was half delirious, half assailed by a desperate need for sleep. She clung to him, still gently weeping, afraid he might stop breathing at any moment.

'How did you know?' he asked.

'I was watching from that dune,' she said, 'the tall one, the one you climbed. I could see you and Mehmet heading for one another. Then something happened to Mehmet. He seemed hurt, but you weren't running straight for him. You started moving very slowly. That's when it dawned on me what it was. I was off that dune and running before I had time to think. And here I am.'

She'd settled now, secure of him again. And he was starting to come out of the fluctuation of mood that had gripped him since being rescued.

'You're going to have to take those clothes off,' she said.

He looked down at himself. From his feet almost to his neck, he was covered in a viscous coat of wet sand.

'They'll dry out,' he said. 'I'd give them half an hour in this heat. But I wouldn't mind taking them off. Why don't you do the same?'

She looked down at the pool. Mehmet was in there somewhere, sinking ever more deeply into his horrid grave. Nabila shook her head.

'Not now, love. It's just your hormones. You've been very agitated. And not here. Come on, we've got to get the camels joined up again, then we've got to get back en route.'

Before they set off, David got out the old map again, and spread it on the ground.

'Look,' he said. 'We've been heading almost due east until now. But what if we do this instead?'

He swept his finger along a diagonal line that would take them towards the city called Chie Kiang.

'It takes us further north than we want to go, but it puts us in line with likely water sources. Even a single well of clean water would be a tremendous help.'

'You realize we'll be heading straight for some of the highest dunes in the Taklamakan? There are whole ranges like that down there, David. There are dunes a thousand feet and more high.'

David was nonplussed. Surviving a sandstorm and a pool of quicksand one after the other had buoyed him up. He felt capable of tackling the highest dunes and the hardest treks. His good luck had produced a sense of self-confidence in him, a feeling of strength that was bordering on foolhardiness. He had started to forget that the desert offers no margins for error. He was like a cat with nine lives who can't count.

'We'll find a way round them, don't you worry,' he said.

'How do you plan to find these mysterious cities anyway? This map's not to scale. We could end up miles out, walking past them and not even aware of the fact.'

He unfolded one of the Tactical Pilotage Charts, which showed the precise locations for the buried cities of the southern rim.

'We can take precise co-ordinates for Dandan-Uilik and Endere from here. Every night from now on, I'll take satellite bearings for our own position. Zhang's map isn't to scale, but if you take some measurements you'll see that it's more or less in proportion. If I make adjustments, it should be possible to work out some rough co-ordinates for the northern cities.'

'It's a huge gamble, David . . .'

'Maybe. But look at this.'

He pointed at a dark line between Pan T'ang and Chie Kiang.

'I've been thinking a lot about that line,' he said. 'It joins two of the cities, but not the third. On the western side of it stands Ts'ang Mi. To the east the lines of triangles, which I think are wells. I think the dark line's a wall, built to connect Pan T'ang and Chie Kiang, and to keep the people of Ts'ang Mi from gaining access to their water. If I'm right, we'll hit the wall somewhere. After that, it has to be plain sailing.'

'I think it's time we were on our way,' she said. The lead camel lifted its head and wrinkled rubbery lips at her.

She bent over and whispered in its ear. David watched in wonderment as the animal struggled to its feet like a capsized boat trying to right itself.

He folded his maps and chivvied the other camels to their feet. As they started moving, he looked up. The sky was clear blue, and still full of heat. Almost out of sight, a tiny dot moved westwards. An aeroplane, very high up. An aeroplane leaving no contrail and making no noise. He watched it out of sight, then followed Nabila to the first dune.

FIREFLIES

CHAPTER SIXTY-TWO

Kashgar
Afternoon

Outside the Idgah Mosque stood women in long brown veils like figures who had just stepped out of a Symbolist painting. In their hands they held bowls of green grapes, proffering them to worshippers as they came out. The latter, pausing briefly, bent to spit on the grapes and murmur a quick blessing as they passed. That night, the grapes would be taken round the beds of the sick and the benches of the infirm in the hope that the *baraka* they had just accumulated would alleviate their suffering.

The men circulated in the square outside. Ordinarily, they might have passed on to the bazaars, or headed to a café with some friends, to smoke, drink tea, and chat. Not now, though. For one thing, people had started coming to the mosque outside the times of the five compulsory prayers. Some hardly left the building, a few holy men had taken to staying up all night reciting Naqshbandi prayers for the relief of the city and its people, and students from Kashgar's main religious seminary had set up a rota for the constant recitation of the Koran.

Eshak, the blind beggar, leaned against the second alcove to the right of the main door, his face skywards, his hand outstretched for alms. Alms were in short supply these days. Everyone was hoarding, and no amount of pleading could extract more than a few pennies. People, some intent on prayer, others too anxious to think straight, passed him by as though they, not he, were blind.

As a matter of fact, he reflected, that was closer to the truth than anyone knew. He was blind in only one eye, but for years now he'd earned his crust by pretending to be completely sightless. His right eye was fine, better, if anything, than it had been on the day its companion on the left had gone out of business.

He leaned back, gazing fixedly at the sky. No clouds, no trace at all of the storm that had rampaged through the city all these days. It would take weeks to clear the sand from buildings and streets and vehicles. He scratched his shin and stared at the perfect blue above him.

A little speck appeared in the corner of his vision. A black dot, moving slowly across the sky. It couldn't be a bird, he thought – it was moving in much too straight a line, and it seemed much higher up, though that was hard to judge.

Someone pressed a coin into his open hand. He bent his head and mumbled an Arabic blessing he'd learned from his father many years earlier: *baraka 'llah fik*.

His donor passed on, and Eshak let his gaze wander back to the swept and glimmering sky. The plane was passing straight overhead now, right over the centre of Kashgar. He thought it funny that he could not hear it.

In a little upper room at the back of the mosque, Yusup Beg was bending over a low table groaning with books. In the centre, its pages untouched by any of its companions, lay a large Koran from the mosque library, a *waqf* copy penned in elegant Arabic letters. Around it were dispersed *tafsirs*, concordances, dictionaries, manuals of holy law,

472

and a complete set of the traditions of al-Bukhari. He checked the wording of the Throne Verse against its citation in the commentary of al-Baidawi. Wrinkling his nose, he frowned, made a note on the pad on his lap, and leaned back on his haunches, yawning.

That was when he felt it begin. It was extremely muted at first, no more than a shiver in his spine and a faint tingling in his feet. Then it grew in strength. He thought it was an earthquake, he was sure it was an earthquake. The books on the table in front of him started to quiver. Volume 30 of Tabari's *Jami' al-Bayan* slithered its way to the edge and toppled to the floor. It was followed by several more.

Yusup leaped to his feet, anxious to retrieve the Koran before it suffered either indignity or damage. As he stood, he looked through the window. He blinked his eyes, then rubbed them. For as far as he could see, snow was falling on the city. He crossed to the window and looked out. The sky overhead was as blue as ever, yet snow was falling over everything, white and cold and perfect.

Asiyeh watched as the snow fell into the courtyard, white and cold and ominous. She'd known something bad was coming, known it from the moment she woke that morning. There'd been the aubergines, for one thing. There she'd been in the kitchen, slicing them up for the noonday meal, when she'd noticed that several of them had dark streaks through the white flesh, streaks that looked suspiciously like writing to her untutored eye. She'd remarked on it to Narges, who'd nodded and said, 'If we could read these, we'd know a thing or two about the Torment and when it's going to end.' 'The Torment' was what everybody called the blockade.

And then there was the matter of the Koran. Asiyeh

opened the Holy Book at random after waking every morning in order to see what it had to say about the day to come. The fact that she couldn't read it any more than she could an aubergine had never deflected her. She made her own intuitive readings, and indeed enjoyed something of a reputation with her friends as a woman to whom God had granted insights denied others. This morning's reading had been the darkest in a long time.

'Asiyeh!'

She started and looked to where the call had come from. Osman had just come through the gate and was waving to her. She'd seen him age thirty years in the past week. He staggered a little as he came through, and she wondered if he'd been taken ill. Or perhaps he wasn't getting enough to eat. In spite of his position in the city, and the near-absolute authority he exercised, he refused to take more than his proper share of everything, including food. His men were harsh on hoarders and looters, and Osman could not afford to have it even hinted that he himself was anything but scrupulously honest.

She stood watching him, thinking maybe it was best she went down to him. He could be an impatient man, and no wonder, given how busy he was. She waved back to him and started for the stairs. As she did so, she noticed with horror that the snow had started to change colour from white to grey to black. In a matter of moments, the courtyard, that had been so beautifully white and untarnished, looked as if it had been swept with a black brush.

She cried out in disgust, then noticed Osman stagger again. He looked up and caught sight of her on the balcony, and she saw that his face was creased with pain and some terrible inward agony. Before he could call out or gesture, he fell face forward into the pond. Asiyeh screamed and ran for the stairs, but he was dead long before she reached him. He was not the first, nor was he the last.

CHAPTER SIXTY-THREE

London

The day before had been a very long day, and it hadn't been improved or shortened for Elizabeth by Anthony's decision to spend most of it in the office.

'My child is missing!' she'd screamed at him that morning as he was on his way out. 'For God's sake, Anthony, she could be in a gutter by now, she could be desperate. Or in a hospital. My God, Anthony, she could be in an NHS hospital, in a ward full of homeless people and loonies. Do you have any idea what some of those places are like?'

'Well, yes, I do, as a matter of fact. Not very nice, as you say, and hopelessly overcrowded. Which is why I have comprehensive medical insurance, as do you. Now, if you'll excuse me, I do have to get to the office. My driver's waiting.'

'Fuck your driver. What about Maddie? What about my child?'

'Look, darling, Maddie will be perfectly all right. If she starts feeling unwell, as I'm sure she will, I'm quite sure she'll find a nice policeman and ask to be brought here, or back to Rose's establishment. You could always try ringing Rose later on. Now, I really do have to go. My country needs me.'

'You know, you really are totally pathetic, Anthony.

I mean to say, you virtually run an intelligence service, you spend your time with spooks and secret policemen, but you can't come up with a single idea as to how to find a missing child.'

'She's not a child, Lizzie. You know that perfectly well. Maybe this outing will be good for her, maybe it'll help her grow up properly. God knows what you did to her in the first place, to get her into this state.'

She'd spent the rest of that day looking for Maddie herself, in a rather desultory fashion. If Anthony had his office, she now had her own business commitments and, once they'd been attended to, there'd been a long-planned lunch at Le Caprice with Tiggy Althorpe, then her regular massage and workout at the Sanctuary. It had been late afternoon when she rang Rose, and he said he'd heard nothing at all from Maddie, but that he'd certainly ring Elizabeth the moment he did.

The evening had been spent indoors, watching TV and waiting for the door-bell to ring. Anthony had been out at one of his watering holes. The phone hadn't gone all night.

Now, as the second day was up and yelling 'Rise and shine' through her curtains, she was beginning to think that Maddie might have been serious about getting out and staying out. Lizzie woke with a hangover on all fronts, downed half a bottle of very old whisky, and made up her mind to tell her errant excuse for a daughter what she could do with herself if she dared to ring up for help or turned up at the front door pleading to be taken in again.

She picked up the house telephone and rang the long-suffering Filipina maid.

'Imelda? Listen – if my . . . If Miss Madeleine turns up, can you please tell her to fuck off?'

'Sorry? No understand.'

'Oh, for God's sake. Look, you know who Madeleine is. Maddie. Remember? The little slut who took up residence here and then did a midnight flit?'

'Yes, Maddie, yes. Understand.'

'If she should turn up at the front door asking for asylum, can you tell her this house is out of bounds? Can you do that?'

'Bounds?'

'She's not allowed in. If there's trouble, ask for me.'

'Yes. Not allowed.' There was a sigh at the other end, then, before Elizabeth could put down the receiver, a chilly voice. 'You want breakfast now, Mrs Laing?'

'Breakfast? No, I bloody well don't want breakfast. Why don't you just go and burn some toast? You sound like you could do with a diversion.'

She slammed down the phone and spent another hour rebuilding her face. When she felt able to face the world again, she slipped downstairs to the hall and picked up the mail from the table. It was always so ridiculously late these days, she thought, sifting through it as she wandered back to the kitchen.

'Bills as usual,' she murmured, echoing voices up and down the country. Always the same bills too: American Express, her Harvey Nichols account bill, her monthly bill from the Ritz. She paused, pulling out a plain white envelope addressed to her in rather clumsy handwriting. It carried a London postmark.

She sat down at the breakfast bar and slit the envelope with her forefinger. Who the hell did she know in Paddington? she wondered.

'Nobody lives in Paddington, absolutely nobody,' she murmured, taking a folded paper out of the envelope and straightening it. She read it, slowly at first, then rapidly as she grasped what it was about. It was quite short, in fact, but entirely to the point.

> I have your dotter, Maddie. If you want proof, tip out
> what's in the envellope.

She lifted the envelope and shook it. A ring fell out, a small ring set with a large sapphire. Elizabeth's mouth went dry. She recognized the ring at once. She'd bought it for Maddie as a birthday present five or six years earlier.

> You and your husband look fucking loaded, so Im going
> the whole way on this. I want a million, in cash. Ill be
> in touch to give you instruchions. You'd better believe
> Im capable of doing damage to her. If you dont obay
> my orders, youll find bits of Maddie coming through
> your letterbox. She has nice little tits. Id hate to see
> them come off.
> You can tell the police if you like. But if I were you
> Id keep the fuckers out of it. Ta-ta for now. Ill see you
> in my dreams.

CHAPTER SIXTY-FOUR

There was no way of telling one day from the next. The weather did not change, the sky remained the same, the landscape they passed through looked identical to the landscape of two or three days ago. Had it not been for the compass, they might have been going round in circles. Sometimes Nabila thought they were, sometimes she thought the compass just pointed at random. If there was radioactivity out there, wouldn't that be possible?

'You're forgetting about the GPS,' David said. 'According to it, we're making steady progress in the right direction. And if it fails, there's always the stars.'

In reality, navigating through the dunes was not as easy as David made it sound. There was simply no way of keeping to a straight line, and in the heat that clamped down on them throughout the hours of daylight, it was all too easy to forget to take bearings when they should.

Every day, the temperature rose to well over one hundred degrees Fahrenheit. Two days in a row, it reached one hundred and sixteen. Shade was hard to come by, and if any appeared it could only be enjoyed for a brief spell while they rested. The strain of walking and climbing would have been enervating even in a cool climate, but here the constant heat sapped what little energy they had. They could afford to take only the shortest of rests: once you stopped walking and sat down on the warm sand, every cell in your body would cry out to fall asleep; but if you did, you'd wake an hour or two later with the vilest of headaches, parched, giddy, sick, and rubber-legged.

They ploughed on in a silence that was broken only by the gentle clanging of the camels' bells. At times, David would look up, and for an instant he'd be exhilarated by what lay ahead: the knife-edge of a dune, slanted against the sky; the ripples on a dune's side, perfectly laid, like the sand ripples on a seashore at home; the line of camels behind him like a funeral cortège, or etched at sunset against the horizon, black and unexpectedly graceful.

Moments later, his exhilaration would evaporate in the heat. The sun beat down pitilessly, arching its back over them, whipping, scourging, flogging anything that drew breath. At times it felt as if there was no way to breathe, that there was too little air, and that they too had fallen into a vast quicksand from which every last trace of moisture had been removed.

They were in darkness among light. With their heads bowed and their faces swathed in bright cloths to keep out the sand and the sun's harsh rays, they moved like miners along tunnels of their own making. David found two pairs of dark glasses in one of the packs, and they wore them when they could.

A second camel died two days out from the quicksand. It had been weakening even before the storm, and afterwards it went into a severe decline. It started to have trouble keeping up with the others, and Nabila had forced it along using a combination of coaxing and pushing. Each night she examined it carefully and gave it what she could, which was little. Then, quite suddenly, its knees buckled and it collapsed to the ground. By the time they got to it, it was dead.

The death of the first camel had not caused much

difficulty. It had been easy enough to redistribute most of her load between the other animals. But this time it was out of the question: there simply wasn't anywhere for most of the food and equipment to go. If the other camels had been fresh, they might have taken some extra weight without complaining, but as things stood, every extra pound represented an additional risk.

A few essential items were swapped for others of less importance. They transferred as much water as they could, but more than half had to be jettisoned. It was given to the other camels, the first fresh water they'd tasted in a long time. Nabila poured it out, helping by helping, into a huge red plastic bowl from which the camels sucked great panting mouthfuls.

They moved on, leaving the dead camel buried beneath a shallow layer of sand, and its load scattered like litter around it. The next dune was the highest they had come to yet, but the camels, refreshed by their drink, climbed the slope with what almost seemed to be eagerness.

It was as they reached the razor-sharp ridge that David first noticed something out of the ordinary. It was a thin sound that he realized must have been building in his ears for the past minute or so. He shook his head, thinking it might be a blood vessel in his ear, or mere imagination; but, no, there was something there, and it was growing louder. It seemed familiar and somehow threatening, and he strained to make out what it was.

Slowly, the sound built itself in his head, taking on a discernible shape. Perhaps he would have recognized it earlier, had it not been so incongruous out here, all these miserable miles from nowhere.

He scurried back to where Nabila was manoeuvring the rear camels on to the blade of the dune.

'Take them back down,' he shouted.

'What?'

'The camels! We've got to get them right off the ridge, on to this side of the dune. Come on, help me turn the leaders round.'

Before she could ask, he was haring off to the front and tugging at the head of the lead camel. Puzzled by his odd behaviour, the beast bucked against his efforts; then Nabila arrived and whispered her blandishments in its ear. It halted and turned to go back on to the dune's western flank.

'What's wrong, David? What have you seen?'

'Nothing yet. It's what I can hear. Listen.'

She paused, listening intently.

'Yes,' she said, 'there is something. A sort of buzzing. Like a giant bee. Would a plane be flying this low?'

'It's a helicopter,' he replied, urging the camels on. 'Coming in from the east. He's flying slowly, which means he's on a surveillance run.'

'Can you see him yet?'

'I haven't tried. We've got to chivvy these camels down before he sees us. We're standing out here like robins on a Christmas cake.'

'Like . . . ?'

'I'll tell you later.'

They scrambled to hurry the camels as far down as possible. Once the last animal had been hunkered, David raced back up to the ridge and threw himself down just below the top. He pulled out his binoculars, then crept to the very edge.

The chopping noise was much louder now, amplified by the silence through which the helicopter was moving.

David scanned the sky in what he thought was roughly the right direction. He thought there was only one chopper, but it was always possible that there were others out there. The sun was behind him, putting him at an advantage. Nevertheless, finding a chopper at a distance in an empty sky wasn't as easy as it seemed.

And then he saw it, its whirling blades caught in a ray of sunshine long enough to catch his eye. He lifted the glasses to get a fix on the aircraft. It was flying at an angle to him, allowing him to get a reading of its flank. His first thought was that it was Russian, an Mi–8 Hip or an Mi–24 Hind C: an attack helicopter, anyway. China had bought a huge number of them after the collapse of the Soviet system. That hadn't made them any friendlier.

The copter was about half a mile away, approaching in a straight line. He watched it come, holding his breath. As he did so, he became aware of a second engine, some distance to his right. He swivelled and spotted a second helicopter some distance off, but flying parallel with the first. How many more were there, he wondered, spread over the vast expanse of the Taklamakan?

He knew that, if the nearest copter swept right overhead, there was nothing they could do to stop him spotting the camels or, more likely, the long line of hoofprints that punctuated their trail mile after mile into the distance.

To his relief, the pilot made his pass about half a mile to the north, and kept moving in a steady course away from them. He watched it until it passed wholly out of sight, then went back down to Nabila.

'He didn't see us,' he said.

'How can you be sure? Maybe he's flown on to his base to report what he saw.'

David shook his head.

'First of all, he must be based to the east. He won't have enough fuel to go right to the western end of the desert. That applies whether he started in the west or the east. I think he'll veer off to the north soon for refuelling.'

'What's he doing? Do you think he was looking for us?'

'It's hard to say. I don't really think so. I saw a second aircraft a few miles further south. There could be half a dozen or more, there's no way to tell. Just because we're the only living things in the desert doesn't necessarily mean we're being hunted. We're in range of whatever tests they've been carrying out: maybe the copters are monitoring fallout or something else specific to this weapon. I think that's a lot more likely than sending helicopters into a place like this just to find two people who escaped from Kashgar.'

'What if they come back? What if they catch us in an exposed position?'

'There's nothing we can do to prevent it. But you have to remember that we're really only specks from up there. If they stay high, they can see the terrain very well, but it's hard to make out individual objects or people. The minute they come down low enough to make naked eye identification, their command of the terrain is lost. That's what happened just now. By being on the lee side of a tall dune a mile or so south of his flight path, we were invisible.'

'That doesn't mean we're really safe, it just means we were lucky.'

'We'll try to keep it like that. Let's stay here for about half an hour, then move on. We're losing too much time.'

He returned to the lip of the dune and started scanning the sky for incoming helicopters. None followed the first two, not within his range of vision at least.

But he knew they were coming, that they'd come in again and again. They were looking for him. The helicopters themselves gave that away. Neither the army nor the air force possessed Mi–8s or Mi–24s. Only one agency had bought them from the Russians, the Guojia Anchuanbu, China's new Ministry for State Security. And David happened to know that the Guojia Anchuanbu owned a small air base somewhere on the eastern edge of the Taklamakan.

CHAPTER SIXTY-FIVE

Loch Monar

He watched her sleep. Da-da, dee-da, he hummed to himself as he bent over her, almost on tiptoes, watching her sleeping features. She was closed down, inert, stretched on the bed like a white bird washed up on an unwelcoming shore. Flotsam. Jetsam. Her hair was like seaweed from the bottom of a troubled sea. Dee-da, da-dee.

He'd no idea how long it would be before she regained consciousness. On the one hand, he wanted her awake to be able to talk down a phone and prove she was still alive. On the other, he wanted the minimum of fuss. This – he looked at Maddie – had all the potential of turning into a puking, bawling, cabbage-headed pain in the balls.

Being new to this kidnapping business, he'd no idea how best to handle his goods. He knew he might have to damage her in order to get what he wanted. He'd heard that cutting off ears and fingers could have a serious persuasive effect on reluctant relatives. If she'd been a man, he'd have started with his middle leg. He reckoned that, if you sent one of those in the post, next-day delivery, they'd know you meant business. And he did mean business. In her case . . .

He glanced at the rise and fall of her small breasts. She

hadn't put a bra on when she dressed. From time to time he could see the tiny mound of a nipple push through the fabric of her T-shirt. He'd been tempted to strip her more than once, give her the once over, maybe run his hands over her.

Her eyes swooped open. No preliminaries, no fluttering, no twitching of the lids. They stayed open, as she swivelled to take in her surroundings. He expected she wasn't able to see much, that what little she did see was blurred.

'Where . . . am . . . I?' she asked, her voice befuddled with something darker than sleep. There was pain in her eyes, and bewilderment, and loss. He ignored them, since in all honesty they were as much use to him as an attack of the trots.

'You're with me, hen,' he said, bending over her, a doctor but for the white coat and the educated voice. 'Ye remember me, eh? Calum Kilbride. Remember Ah brought a letter fae yir father, all the way fae China. Ah helped ye ootay yir hoose in London. The big hoose. Mind that?'

She nodded blankly, still in a fog.

'But where . . . ?'

'Ye fell asleep. Didnae wake up after London. Ah let ye stay like that while Ah drove. Best thing, likes.'

'Yes, but where exactly . . . ?' She was coming round rapidly now, taking account of her surroundings. He didn't want her to know where she was. She might have to speak to her mother, and he couldn't risk the possibility that she might tell them where to go looking for her.

'Maddie,' he said, 'ye ken yersel' ye havenae been very well. That's why ye were in that clinic. Since yir mother took ye oot, ye've gone badly doonhill. They fuckers wis puttin' you through hell, likesay. So Ah pulled ye oot and drove ye up here, where they cannae find ye. How ye feelin' now, doll?'

Maddie's head was still spinning, and a persistent grogginess threatened to pull her back down into the dark, dreamless sleep out of which she had only just awakened.

'I'm a bit woozy,' she said. 'Whatever you gave me must have been bloody strong. How long have I been out?'

Calum shrugged.

'Aboot a day an' a half. Ye can have some more in a wee while. But first ye need tae put some grub inside ye.'

She looked round the strange room. Almost everything was made from pine: the ceiling, the walls, the floor, the door. Her bed had a light quilt made up of patches in vibrant colours. Stuffed animals of all shapes and sizes populated a bay of shelves opposite. The lampshade was in the shape of a balloon, with a basket hanging below it filled with white mice. She looked round the room and speculated on why bad taste could sometimes be so comforting.

She swung herself round and planted her feet firmly on the floor.

'I'm not really hungry, thanks.'

He sniffed. All that politeness when he knew she was a swarm of maggots inside.

'Dinnae go makin' that mistake, hen. Ye havenae eaten in two days or more. Would ye no' like some bacon or a wee sawsidge?'

She shook her head.

'Neither, thanks. I'm a vegetarian.'

'Aw, Christ, Ah had tae get mixed up wi' a loony. Nae cunt in his right mind eats just vegetables. Nae wonder you're such a scraggy wee thing.'

489

'What about eggs? Everybody has eggs.'

She started towards the window. He did not try to get in her way.

'Ah've got fresh eggs, bread, marmalade, an' some cheese. No fancy French stuff, mind: just ordinary cheese.'

She drew back the curtains. It was broad daylight outside. For a moment her eyes shrank from the blazing sunlight, then she recovered and looked out. A long meadow ran down to a lake, a beautiful blue lake on which nothing moved. To the left, she could make out trees, the beginnings of a forest, perhaps. At the far end of the lake there were mountains, blue mountains topped with cloud, whose reflections lay on the flat water as though put there to still it. As she watched, an eagle plunged down towards the lake, and lifted again with a silver fish squirming in its beak. And everywhere she looked, she saw flowers.

'Where is this?' she asked again. 'It's beautiful.'

'Aye, it's no' bad. Better Ah don't tell ye where we are, though. Better not, eh?'

'But why . . . ? I don't . . .'

'Ma no' tellin' you is for your own good. Stay there an' watch, if ye fancy. Ah'll get ye your grub.'

He came back fifteen minutes later, carrying a folding table which he set up in front of the window.

'Ye'll find a chair over by the dressin' table. Ah thought ye might like tae watch oot the windy while ye eat. What will ye drink?'

'Orange juice. My throat's parched.'

'Ah've nae juice, but Ah've got squash.'

'Well, I . . .'

'It'll have tae do. Unless ye find water more satisfyin'. Or tea. Ah can make tea.'

She shook her head.

490

'Squash will do very nicely,' she said, thinking to herself that her Galahad would have to be trained. For the moment she was content to let herself be fed, and to wallow in this breathtaking scenery to which she'd been transported like a character in *Aladdin*.

It felt too good to be true. London, Farrar's house, Rose's clinic were all bad dreams, as far away as China. She thought about her father, and wondered if she'd ever see him alive again. And all at once the demons came, rustling their heavy wings, mocking her, telling her there was nowhere she could run to in order to escape them. But she thought that perhaps she had just found such a place.

Calum came in, carrying a plate of scrambled eggs and mushrooms. He wasn't absolutely sure they were mushrooms, but he'd found them that morning, growing next to the trees. He'd fried them in butter and tried one. It had tasted close enough. The smell they exuded awakened what little appetite Maddie had.

'Calum,' she asked, taking the plate from him and setting it on the table, 'can I have some more of whatever it was you gave me when you came to the house?'

'Finish your breakfast first, then we'll see.'

A ribbon of sunlight tied itself through her long hair, and the brightness of it drew his eyes. He noticed that she had narrow shoulders, and that her breasts were exactly as he would have wanted them to be.

'Is this your place, Calum?' she asked.

He shook his head.

'It's no' mine, no' exactly. This is kinday what ye might call a holiday residence. It belongs tae ma Uncle Hamish an' ma Auntie Morag. Morag's ma mother's sister, likes, only she disnae call hersel' Morag any more. It's Charlene. That's because she's so keen on this Country an' Western rubbish. "Stand by yoo-oor maaaan", an' all that. Goes

491

line dancin' evra Friday night in Kirkcudbright. Can you believe that? Woman ay fifty plus wi' five bairns an' a figure like Roseanne Barr. Mean tae say . . .

'Well, she and Hamish bought this wee dive fir fuck all years an' years ago, when Ah wis nae bigger than that table. Ah spent most o' ma summers here till Ah grew up and pushed off. Ah wisnae gonna be Scotland's answer tae Tammy Wynette. They're no' so very keen on us now, ma aunt an' uncle. But Ah said this wis an emergency, an' could Ah have the place fir a week or two. They were very good aboot it, actually. Said Ah could have the bothy free o' charge so long's Ah looked after it. So, here we are.'

'Is it very remote? I mean, it looks very cut off here.'

'Aye, we're well oot the way here. Ah wis here in the winter once. We wis snowed up three months, and nae shite came tae get us oot. Couldnae get in, likes. Three months wi' fuck all tae eat but baked beans an' frozen sawsidges. It's a fair bit oot fae anywheres here.'

'But it is Scotland, isn't it? If you got snowed in like that. Or the Lake District, I suppose.'

He said no more, but watched her eat. She was hungry now, but handled her food gently, taking small mouthfuls at a time. In all honesty, he'd expected her to wolf it down. He would have done so. Anyone he knew would have done so.

He glanced at her again. He'd never seen a woman like her before, or if he had it had been at a distance, out of his grubby reach. Even sick, she looked better than any of the women he'd ever met or slept with.

When she finished, he cleared the table and folded it away. It was a card table, really, but the baize had been stripped off and the top replaced with wood veneer. Maddie rose and returned to the window, to gaze out at the lake.

'Can I go down to it?' she asked.

'Doon? Doon tae what?'

'The lake, of course. Or is it a loch? Would I be able to walk round it? Or go for a swim? I've no costume, but perhaps you can come up with something.'

'Ah'm not sure. Ah used tae go for walks when Ah wis a bairn, with ma cousin Jimmy and his sister. Well, maybe later on.'

'Why later? Why not this moment?'

'Ah ... well, for one thing Ah've got tae make a telephone call. Ah need you tae say a few words tae yir folks.'

Her face lit up with alarm.

'I don't understand. What on earth are you up to? I don't want to speak to anybody, let alone –'

'Ah'm just plannin' tae give yir mother a wee bell. Her and her – what's his job description? – boyfriend.'

'Boyfriend's a bit . . . Have you met Anthony?'

'No, but the cunt starred in a number o' portraits artfully displayed roond the auld place.'

'Then you have some idea. Why the hell would you want to speak to them?' Panic had seeped into her voice. Maybe her rough Galahad was having second thoughts.

'It's no' for you tae fret yir pretty head aboot.'

He whipped a small mobile telephone from his pocket and waved it at her.

'Nokia,' he proclaimed, making it sound like a football chant. 'It's got all the functions. An', believe it or no', Ah git next-tae-perfect reception oot here. Ah mean, it's fuckin' radge, eh? There's nae shoaps, there's nae polis, there's nae church, an' there's nae pub, but Ah get better fuckin' reception on this wee gadget here than in parts o' London. Fuckin' radge, eh?'

She looked at him and smiled. He seemed a loose

cannon, but she thought he was harmless, really. All the time, a need was growing in her for the drug.

'What's "radge"?' she asked.

'Crazy, likes. Now, where's yir mother's number?'

He fumbled in his pocket and brought out a crumpled piece of paper with a scribbled telephone number on it. He switched the phone on and punched in the number. There was a single ring at the other end, then a woman's voice answered, harsh and fragile.

'Hello? Who's this?'

'Hello, Lizzie. Remember me? Ah'd say it wasnae a matter of "Who?" so much as "How much?" wouldn't you?'

'How is Maddie? I want to speak to her. I don't think you realize what you've got yourself into. There'll be hell to pay if you've harmed her in any way.'

'Ah think we'll take things in the right order. What aboot the polis? Has either o' you told the blueberry muffins anything aboot this? Are they listenin' in tae this conversation?'

'Oh, don't be such a pillock. Who do you think I've got here, Inspector fucking Morse? I've as little wish to see the police here as you do. All I want is to get my daughter back. Put her on the line.'

Calum pressed the 'Mute' button and turned to Maddie.

'Yir mother wants tae have a word. Tell her ye're all right, but say nae more than ye have tae.'

She looked at him coldly. Thoughts of gallant knights had entirely left her.

'Would you like to tell me what the fuck is going on here? "How much?" "What about the police?" Have I just been kidnapped? Is that what this is all about?'

'No, but Ah'd like yir mother tae think so. Ah'd appreciate it if ye'd just play along wi' the charade. You'll come tae nae harm fae me, Ah promise.'

494

She glared at him for several moments, then snatched the phone.

'Mother? Are you all right?'

'I think it's I who should be asking that question, dear. Just what the hell do you think you're up to?'

'I'm not up to anything, Mother. Jesus, does somebody have to be up to something just because they've run out on you?'

'Of course not, dear. It's just that . . .'

'Let's get this straight, Mother. You pulled me out of a clinic where I was being given essential treatment, and you refused to get me the drugs I needed. So I decided to get as far away from you and that two-faced bastard Farrar as I could. Once Dad gets back, I'm moving in with him. End of story.'

'Darling, has he hurt you?'

'Hurt me? Quite the opposite. I'm feeling better than I have in years.'

'Well . . . Has he laid hands on you?'

'Laid hands . . . ?'

'You know perfectly well what I mean.'

'He's been a perfect gentleman.'

She felt the handset lifted from her. Calum sat down and crossed his legs.

'Hear that, Lizzie? Yir daughter is unharmed an' unfucked. If ye'd prefer tae keep her in that condition, a wee donation tae ma trust fund would be appreciated. Ah'm no' greedy, but Ah dinnae intend tae haggle over this. You'll pay the price Ah ask – nae discounts, nae reductions, nae bargain offers.'

Elizabeth sighed.

'How much?'

He hesitated at the last moment, wondering if he shouldn't raise his demand after all. What if she had more money than he thought? He almost doubled his original price, then reasoned that there were ways of raising it further down the line. A package with a finger in it would go down a treat. Or a nose.

'One million,' he said.

'Pounds?'

'What the fuck else?'

'I'm sorry, I'll have to talk about this with . . .'

'Ah wouldnae waste much time, hen. Ah'm no' runnin' a Billy Butlins here. You an' Spiderman have two days. One tae get the money, one tae get it tae me. Otherwise . . .' His voice fell away. He looked at Maddie, raising his eyebrows as if to say it was all a joke. But that wasn't what he was thinking. Inside he was contemplating his options.

'Otherwise what?' Anthony Farrar's voice hurtled down the line like an angry rocket.

For a moment, Calum was knocked off course, but it took only seconds for him to regain his equilibrium.

'Ah leave all that tae yir imagination. The chief thing is that ye've only got two days.'

'Fine. Two days. Now, listen carefully to me, you numskull. I take it you've never dealt in amounts like a million before, so you will hardly be aware that we will need a good deal more than twenty-four hours to put a sum like that together. People like Elizabeth don't just leave their money in a Post Office savings account or the Co-op Bank. Money gets tied up in shares, trust funds, bonds – and a lot of it lives abroad. For her to realize one million will take at least three days. Do you understand that?'

'If Ah said you'd get Maddie's head in a Damien Hirst box if Ah didnae see ma money, what would ye do?'

'Do? Frankly, I'd think you were the greatest buffoon who ever lived. If you kill her, you get nothing. If you wait a day or two longer, you get all you want. We haven't even disputed your price, so we can expect a bit of co-operation from you. Now, when the money's ready, where do you want it left?'

'Dinnae push me. Ah'll leave you know nearer the time. An' Ah want you tae swear there'll be not a word said aboot this tae the polis.'

'Very well, you have my word on that if I have your agreement on the question of time.'

'Good. Three days. Ah'll keep in touch.'

He pressed the 'End' button and switched off the phone. As he put it down, he looked at Maddie and winked.

'Are you serious?' she asked. 'I mean . . . you could go to jail for a scam like this.'

'Only if they get me. It's worth a go. Half a million each – that isnae bad.'

'They'll never cough up. They know I ran off with you.'

He shook his head.

'No' the way Ah sees it. For all they know, Ah could have hit you over the head and dragged ye ootay the hoose. For all they know, Ah could be a fuckin' psychopath, Ah could be oota ma head.'

'Are you?' Maddie didn't know if she asked the question seriously or in jest.

'Ah do a good imitation. Now . . .' He looked at her empty plate. 'D'ye feel like dessert?'

She shook her head.

'No, thanks. That was lovely. But . . . I'm feeling a bit sicky. If I could have . . .' The craving was eating her from somewhere deep inside.

'Ay, Ah ken what ye want. Wait here, Ah'll see what Ah can rustle up.'

He came back smiling, in his hand a shiny hypodermic filled with glistening liquid. She sat down on the bed and rolled her sleeve up meekly while he injected straight into her blue and waiting vein.

She talked animatedly for a while, then fell like a snowdrop down through gulfs of darkness to her own resting place, in her own silence.

He straightened her on the bed, with her head on the pillow and her hair arrayed behind it, copper hair flecked with sunlight. She seemed at rest, but he could not pull himself away. He moved a long lock of hair from her forehead to the side, and gently traced the line of her eyebrows. Her eyelids fluttered softly as he did so. His hand moved to her cheek, and on to her lips.

He wanted to leave before something awkward happened, but she seemed to exercise a hold over him. His right hand moved quietly down to her breasts, and for several moments he held her left breast in his palm. The fabric of her T-shirt shifted, and he let his hand move with it, round and round, against the softness of her body.

Something stopped him from going further. He cupped her breast with both hands, then kissed it.

He stood and went to the door, making sure to lock it behind him. Inside the room, Maddie opened her eyes with a flicker, and brought her hand to her breast, where the sense of another hand could still be felt. She smiled softly to herself, and fell asleep again.

CHAPTER SIXTY-SIX

Judaidat al-Hamir
20 miles north of the Saudi/Iraqi border

Looking about him, Captain Peter Terry had a distinct sense of déjà vu. He'd been cut off about two hundred miles north of here during the Gulf War, and bloody lucky to sneak back to his own side of the border again. Back at Bradbury Lines barracks, he'd been decorated and slapped on the back; but he'd never forgiven his political masters for their failure to topple Saddam Hussein. His sense of déjà vu was intimately tied up with some very strong feelings of betrayal.

He wasn't alone. His three companions had spent time in an Iraqi jail and had only come out again as a result of concessions made by the UK to Baghdad. They'd been over the moon to get out of their hell-hole alive, but they couldn't help feeling that an unacceptably high price had been paid for their freedom. They'd volunteered to help bring a tyrant to his knees, only to see him, years later, still cocking a snook at anybody and everybody who got in his way.

Peter looked his men over. They were a dusty-looking bunch already: the Syrian Desert did not waste time in putting its mark on intruders. He'd chosen them very carefully, regardless of the SAS and its internal politics, under conditions of absolute secrecy. He himself had been picked as team leader by someone very high up the military hierarchy. And details of the mission had been handed to him on the plane only minutes before he and his team had set off to cross the Saudi/Iraqi border.

A special flight had taken them from England to Saudi Arabia the night before. Neither the plane's departure nor its arrival had been recorded. They'd landed at a desert airfield that had been constructed during the Gulf War, abandoned, and now brought back to covert life for a single operation.

The flight had been tense, tinged with irony. The drone of the heavy engines had intertwined with the steady hum of worries and fears that vibrated through each man's head.

Bill Burroughs, the youngest of the team at thirty-six, hated flying. He'd sat hunched up at the back of the cabin, counting off the minutes to touchdown. Barry Dobson, a Geordie from Whitley Bay who was reckoned the hardest, fastest, and most dangerous of them, showed round photographs of his youngest child, Mary, aged two weeks and three days. Dai Matthias, currently the only Taffie serving under the SAS cap-badge, had grumbled about the horrors of canteen food, and played chess with Peter.

They'd landed in darkness, without lights, while Burroughs muttered fervent prayers in the rear. The Hercules – a C.Mk 1 – had been night-camouflaged and equipped with an automatic landing device called Charles (the airfield had been designated Camilla). The second they hit the ground, he changed completely. In a matter of moments, the flying phobic surrendered place to someone who could keep a cool head even under the heaviest fire. No one who knew him would have thought to sneer at his fear of flying. He'd made over three thousand parachute jumps, seventeen of them at the North Pole, and his leave weekends were spent hang-gliding in Scotland.

They'd unloaded the plane by themselves, and unpacked their equipment by the light of heavy-duty torches: two Landrover 110s, a short-range Longline Light Strike Vehicle that was to be used for the last stage of the mission, four M72 anti-tank weapons, two Stinger surface-to-air missile systems, a Milan anti-tank weapon, two Minimi light machine-guns, two Browning 0.5-in machine-guns, M16 assault rifles with attached M203 grenade-launchers, and any number of bits and pieces deemed to enhance the joy of combat.

The moment the last bullet had been de-planed, the impatient aircraft turned and scrambled back up the little runway, taking off as effortlessly as if it had been broad daylight, en route for King Khalid Military City, sleep, and fresh fuel. Its low hum came back to them for half a minute, then disappeared in the night.

They'd paused for a moment then, savouring this familiar, unfamiliar night world in which every sense was heightened. Nobody much liked being out here again. It was too quiet, too cold at night, too hot by day, too open, too closed. There were no landscapes here, no peaks or rivers or lakes or forests to rest the eye or the mind on.

Then their training had taken over, and Peter Terry called them over to one side.

'I've just been handed our mission orders,' he said. He took a map from his pocket and unfolded it on the ground while Burroughs trained a light on it.

'Our target is here,' he said, stabbing his forefinger at a spot about forty miles west of Baghdad. Someone behind him groaned.

'Al-Falluja. Jesus Christ, they're sending four poor

bastards in to smash up al-Falluja. I've got a better suggestion – why don't we just top ourselves here? It'll save fuel and we'll be repatriated in a better class of box.'

The speaker was Dai Matthias – the Dai Lama. His precise Neath vowels hung on the desert air like invisible moths. Peter did not bother to look at him or the others. Dai's reaction was reasonable. Al-Falluja was one of Saddam Hussein's largest weapons complexes, which included plants for the manufacture of nerve gas and Scud missiles, all constructed by German and Austrian firms in the eighties. It was among the most tightly guarded sites in the Middle East, way out of the league of a troop of soldiers, however tough, however Welsh.

'Give me a chance, Dai. If you aren't interested in this job, there's a chip shop down the road.'

'I'm off chips, me. Bad for the heart, see.'

'Let's get on with this briefing, then. We're not heading for al-Falluja proper. Intelligence have got wind of something a few miles further south. Another weapons centre. A holding base for weapons being shipped in.'

'Shipped in? Where the hell from?' Barry sounded indignant, as though the thought of imported weaponry threatened to taint the purity of the operation.

'That's classified. If I knew I'd tell you, but I don't. I don't even know what sort of weapons they are.'

'Nukes?' Bill leaned forward and scrutinized the map as if it held the answer.

'I honestly don't know, but at a guess I'd say you're spot on. Somebody back in London is willing to go to war just for the chance to take these buggers out.'

'Which is where we come in.'

'Broadly speaking. We've got mugshots of the suspect area. You'll get to see them in a minute. But all you'll see is industrial clutter, camouflage, and desert. The real thing's underground, in a series of bunkers going very deep. It's impossible to pin it down to within less than a mile or two. London wants it within yards. The plan is for us to go in, locate it, and call in an air strike.'

'And get away.' Barry did not let so much as a hint of a question enter his voice.

'Yes. We give the word "Go" and get the fuck out.'

'Or perhaps we get the fuck out and then tell them they can go in.'

'If circumstances permit, that might be an option.'

'Not unless . . .'

Peter looked round.

'Unless what, Dai?'

'Unless they plan on using nukes themselves.'

'Nukes?'

'That's what I said, boyo. Nuclear fucking missiles. They'd be bloody fools not to.'

CHAPTER SIXTY-SEVEN

One moment, there was only desert, the next an expanse of golden trees running away as far as the eye could see. A light breeze had come up suddenly that morning, and even before he stumbled on the trees, David heard their leaves rustling, as though he had fallen on a hive of bees or a colony of larks.

'Nabila!' he called. 'Darling, come here quickly.'

She hurried up the side of the dune and stared down with him at the little forest below. Bright yellow leaves fluttered along a sand-pressed valley, waiting for birds that never came.

'Let's go down,' she shouted. 'Oh, let's go down.'

Next minute she had vanished in a storm of sand and whirling limbs, tearing off her head-covering, leaping like a small gazelle through the hot air. David smiled and followed more slowly, bringing the camels with him. He knew there would be water for them, not far beneath the surface, for it was obvious that the trees must be growing along an old river valley, and that water must still be coming down from the mountains in the north.

'What sort of trees are they?' he asked.

'I've no idea. I've never seen anything quite like them before.'

'They're a bit like a gingko, don't you think?'

'Could be. Why do you think the leaves are yellow? It's only August.'

'Climate change. The nights are colder than they should be.'

She went up to one of the trees and stroked its trunk. The bark was a pale burnt colour, striated with light blue, and hard to the touch. Nabila found a crack and forced her nail inside, pulling back a tiny section of bark. She bent and sniffed hard at the spot she'd uncovered.

'David, come and smell this.'

He bent down beside her and sniffed. A faint, resinous smell filled his nostrils briefly, then something else, a fleeting, jasmine-like odour that haunted him for days afterwards.

Leaving the camels tethered, they walked through the little forest hand in hand. Underfoot lay a carpet of soft mulch, set down over who could say how many centuries by the drop of leaves in autumn.

Once, Nabila looked up and saw a white butterfly flitting between the trees. Moments after it had vanished, she caught another movement to her left. When she turned, she found herself staring straight into the startled gaze of a young gazelle. Its huge green eyes were fixed on her in astonishment. She stood stock still and whispered to David to do the same.

'This can't be happening,' David said, unable to see how such a creature could live in the heart of such a vast wilderness.

'I've heard of them appearing further south, near the desert's edge. No one knows how they survive, but they do. We must be the only other living things this poor creature's seen.'

'Or is ever likely to see. Except perhaps for a lady gazelle. Provided they use the same dating agency.'

505

Whether at the thought of coming face to face with a member of the opposite sex, or the realization that he was already seriously outnumbered, the gazelle took fright and skipped off through the trees. Nabila laughed.

'What's a dating agency?' she asked.

'You don't want to know,' he said, then told her.

'We have dating agencies too,' she said. 'We call them mothers.'

'Would they have matched us, do you think?'

'Not in a million years. You're far too ugly for one thing. For another, you aren't a Muslim. That's a big problem. And you like sex too much.'

'I don't think I can take the blame for that. The sex is all your fault. Those big eyes, those curves, those legs . . . No man's safe.'

'Those are very sexist remarks. Even in Sinkiang.'

'This isn't Sinkiang. This is the Taklamakan. At least I have you all to myself out here.'

'Let's make love here,' she said. 'Beneath the trees.'

'Now?'

She nodded and started to undress.

'What if somebody comes along?' he asked.

'We'll just have to be polite and ask them to look the other way.'

She lay down on the soft earth and watched the sun filter its way through the high branches, its heat broken, its glare fragmented into a million shards of light. Then David was beside her. She pulled him to her, blotting out the sunlight with his body, blotting out the past and the future.

Afterwards, they lay together in silence broken only by the sound of the leaves high above their heads. The sun moved down across the sky, forming an intricate shadow play across the ground and over the surface of their skin.

'There are people watching us,' whispered Nabila.

'Well, they'll just have to be polite,' laughed David.

'No, not like that,' she said. 'I can hear voices all round us. Can't you?'

David looked round. A faint chill passed across his skin. He could see no one and hear no one.

'It's just the leaves,' he said.

She shook her head.

'No, it's not that. I think they were here before, centuries ago. Maybe they came out here from one of your cities.'

'Ghosts?'

'No. I don't really believe in ghosts. Presences, perhaps. Memories.'

He pulled her to him tightly. Their bodies fitted so perfectly together, it seemed like another form of magic. He had too many presences of his own, too many memories.

'Will you marry me?' he asked.

'I don't know.'

'Why not? Don't you love me?'

'I love you more than you guess. But it's not that simple. I have to ask my father's permission.'

'But surely . . .'

'It would break his heart if I did anything else. I can't be responsible for that.'

'Is there any reason he shouldn't give his blessing?'

'You're not a Muslim. A Muslim man can marry a Christian or a Jew. But not the other way.'

'Then I'll become a Muslim.'

She looked at his face, so close it was almost blurred.

'Be careful, David. That could prove a very dangerous

thing. Islam is like the Taklamakan: you can get in, but you can't get out again.'

They spent the night in the forest. David dug a well at random, and found water six feet down. It was cold and fresher than any water they'd uncovered in the desert before this. The camels drank it down greedily, luxuriating in the coolness. David thought it might have been the best water they'd ever had in their lives.

That night they camped on the edge of the forest, afraid to light a fire beneath the trees. David brought out his map and spread it on the floor of the tent.

'I've just taken fresh co-ordinates,' he said. 'Going by my earlier calculations, this forest should be slap on top of this river valley.'

He stabbed his finger at a meandering line that indicated a river and bore the name Hsiao Shui: 'Little River'.

'It's possible,' Nabila said. 'But what about one of these others?' She pointed to another three lines coming down from the mountains into the desert.

'Maybe. But comparing old Zhang's map with the modern one, I'm reasonably certain this is it. It fits better than the others. Now, if we head due east we should hit this –' He pointed to a square surmounted by a triangle. Beside it small red characters read 'The Old Tombs'.

'Anything strike you as odd about these tombs?' he asked.

'They're . . . not attached to any of the cities. Yes, that is strange – they're miles from anywhere. Who would want to bury their dead all that distance away? I mean, they're not exactly within visiting distance, are they?'

'I have a feeling that . . .'

'Yes?'

'Well, that whoever built the tombs was afraid of ghosts.

Maybe they thought it would be enough to keep unwelcome visitors at bay if they just buried their bodies a couple of days' journey away.'

'You think that's who my ghosts are?'

'Here? No, I doubt that. Your ghosts belong to you. But there may be another explanation for the position of the tombs. Look.'

He pointed to a small circle without characters.

'He's indicated the location of a city, but he hasn't given it a name. Instead, he's written "He who enters will die." I don't know what that means. But I'm ninety per cent sure this is Karakhoto. The Black City.'

CHAPTER SIXTY-EIGHT

He took her for a walk twice a day, down by the loch. He taught her its name, Loch Monar, and the names of the forests that hemmed it in from three sides, Monar, and Strathconon, and Glencannich, and the names of the two highest mountains to the north and south, Sgurr a'Chaorachain and Sgurr na Lapaich. In truth, he didn't know a word of Gaelic, but his accent made the names sound believable to her, and set a presence on the strange landscape.

The walks were Maddie's idea. Calum didn't really want to know, but he went with her to keep her placid and in sight. The thought of long walks in the fresh air made him feel distinctly uneasy. It wasn't that he was a stranger to physical exercise: in his days in the Parachute Regiment he'd gone on more long hikes than a Stuart tartan. It was just that he thought he'd left all that behind him, and now here was a girl with green eyes drawing him back to it again.

He pretended to himself that the walks were really an excuse to get away from the house, where day-time television competed with Auntie Charlene's record collection as the sole distraction from mind-numbing tedium. Charlene's taste in music was appalling enough to drive anyone outdoors: twenty or more Smurfs' albums, enough Tom Jones ballads to drive Glasgow insane, and every cover version ever made of 'Jolene'. It was an excuse, of course, and a good one, and he made what he could of it.

Maddie loved the walks. He was giving her less of the drug now, keeping her malleable but awake. She knew she needed him now, knew he held the only supply in heather-covered miles of what she craved. That didn't worry her for the moment: Calum was always ready and willing to dole it out as necessary.

After a while, he started enjoying the walks for their own sake. It wasn't that he was falling in love with her – he'd never have done a thing like that, it wasn't on his agenda. He had never really been with a woman like her before. From the age of thirteen, when he'd had his first sexual experience, his encounters with the opposite sex had been casual, his relationships strictly limited to short episodes of intercourse with few preliminaries and no afterthoughts whatever.

Maddie wasn't like that. He could always have used force, of course, only he reckoned that might put her off him in the end. But he was finding her more and more attractive, not just physically, but – as one of his old girlfriends had once put it – 'as a person'. He'd catch her gazing out over the lake, or watching a butterfly, or holding her breath while a rabbit passed through the undergrowth, and he'd find himself unable to take his eyes away. Once, she'd caught him looking at her like that, and she'd smiled briefly, then gone back to whatever it was.

At night he gave her a slightly higher dose, to make sure she slept soundly. He didn't want her sneaking off while he was in the land of Nod. She knew all about the ransom scheme now, and he didn't want her having second thoughts or feelings of sympathy for her creep of a mother. Sometimes he'd come into the bedroom to watch her sleep. He'd unbutton her nightdress and put his hand on a soft breast and pretend they were lovers playing a game of sleepers and wakers. Or that she was a sleeping vampire whom he'd come to pacify.

He'd sorted out the trick of getting the money safely into his hands long before the police turned up. He didn't doubt for a moment that Farrar had brought in Special Branch or whoever handled this sort of business the moment he'd set eyes on the original ransom note.

On his way up, he'd opened a bank account at a biggish branch of the Bank of Scotland in Stirling. The name he used was Anthony Farrar. If all went according to plan, Elizabeth would pay the ransom into that account (for which she'd be given just the number). In the meantime, Calum had obtained details of Elizabeth's bank account from Maddie, and had found out the account number by ringing and asking what it was.

There was a branch of his own bank in Inverness. He'd already spoken with the manager at length, alerting him to the possibility that Stirling would shortly be transmitting substantial funds from his account there to Inverness, and that he would require payment in cash straight away. He had everything set up, and very proud he was of it. Now it was just a matter of making sure that Maddie's nearest and dearest paid up in time. Otherwise he reckoned he'd have to rework Maddie's face a bit.

'How long can we stay here?' Maddie asked. She was sitting beside Calum on a stretch of grass that ran down to the loch. It was utterly deserted. Nobody came to sail on the lake or hike past it. A cry for help would have been long drowned in the silence before it ever reached human ear.

'Half an hour, likesays.'

'Don't be so stupid. I mean, do we have to leave once you get your dirty little mitts on Mummy's loot, or can we stay on?'

'Ah hadnae thought.'

Her face lit up.

'Then let's stay. If we go to some town or try to leave the country, they'll find us a lot more quickly.'

'Who said anything aboot "us"? Ah could plug ye full o' bullets an' drop ye in the loch, nae bother. Ah could be ootay here an' on a plane tae Mexico wi' the stash.'

'Would you do that? Shoot me, I mean. Drop me in the lake.'

He got to his feet, troubled by her insistence. She'd got inside him, that was the trouble. He knew he'd shoot her or drown her if he had to – knife her most probably: there was a fair choice of blades in Charlene's kitchen. No way was he going to let a bird stand between him and a cool million.

The truth was, he didn't have a clue what to do with her. If he took her with him, they'd think he'd double-crossed them and that he'd be demanding yet more money within six months. No way they'd ease off then – he and the doll would be the most wanted pair in the country, like Bonnie and Clyde, their mugshots plastered over every post office from John o'Groats to Land's End.

If he killed her, on the other hand, every murder squad between Stornoway and Dover would be on his trail. All in all, maybe it would be best to leave her, let her find her own way back to civilization. But he didn't think she'd be left all that easily.

She walked down to the lochside with him. He held her hand in an almost unconscious gesture, and she let him hold it. The longer this went on, he thought, the more difficult it became. A golden eagle swooped from a great height, where it had been circling vigilantly on a current of warm air. It lifted with a rabbit in its talons, its wings beating hard to regain height and buoyancy as it swept towards the wooded slopes of Sgurr a'Chaorachain.

'You've never been kissed properly,' she said. 'Have you?'

'Kissed?' he said, as if hearing the word for the first time. He felt suddenly embarrassed. Women didn't speak to him like this. They knew their place and did what they were told.

'You know,' she said. 'Kissed on the lips. Slowly. With due care and attention.'

'Attention?'

'Here,' she said, bending towards him. 'Like this.'

Neither looked round. They were growing too engrossed in one another. Neither noticed the faint movement of foliage five hundred yards away, where Lookout Seven observed them through high-powered binoculars. There were no boats on the lake, and the sky above was empty of aircraft; but the undergrowth from the lake to the house was thick with silent watchers.

CHAPTER SIXTY-NINE

By the second day, David had started to worry that they had missed the tombs. The dunes were growing higher all round them, some rising now to dizzying heights of a thousand feet and more, real mountains. One morning, very early, as the sun rose without heat above them, David looked up and saw mist wreathe the heads of all the mountains within sight.

He used his binoculars constantly, scouring their trail back and forwards each time a dune was crossed or rounded. But he could never detect the least trace of ruins or tracks. If they were out there, they must be completely buried in the sand by now. And if they were buried, would not Karakhoto be buried also?

One of the camels fell, breaking its leg and crushing two water barrels. Nabila wanted to shoot it, but David pointed out the risk of using firearms this near to the complex: one shot echoing out here where nothing moved would surely bring the search helicopters right down their necks. David put it out of its misery by cutting its throat.

They saw helicopters several times, making passes to the south. After that, they started coming by night as well.

'They're equipped with night-vision pods,' said David. Nabila laughed.

'Back at the hospital, we'd have brewed those up and given them to short-sighted cats.'

'Not these ones, you wouldn't. They're massive things that fit on small struts on the helicopter's side. The one I was trained with is called a LANTIRN: Low Altitude Navigation and Targeting Infra-Red for Night. It uses two pods, one for navigation, using a wide-field infra-red sensor and a radar that can map out the terrain you're flying over, and a second pod for targeting. It uses a narrow-field infra-red and a laser designator. Both the . . .'

'Cut it out, David. You sound like an arms salesman at some dreadful weapons fair. I think I prefer my pods. They never had anything as complicated inside them. Just seeds.'

'The point is, they can track us down by the traces of heat we give out. We and the camels. What makes it worse is the speed with which the sand loses its heat once the sun goes down. When it's dark, we're the only warm things in the desert.'

'How come they haven't spotted us yet?'

'I think the high dunes are foxing them. We always camp in the lee of a dune, which means the sensors can only pick up the dead zone all round us. Added to which, a great deal depends on the skill of the operators.'

'So, provided we stick close in to the dunes . . .'

'Provided nothing. As long as we're out here, they'll get us in the end. Even a bad operator can get results if he's patient. He only has to turn a corner and catch a glimpse of something that shouldn't be there. Between the camels and ourselves we're presenting a very visible heat trail.'

Nabila said nothing more. She wrapped her scarf about her face and retreated to the rear of the caravan, urging the last six camels on. The dune they were climbing was very steep, and there was a constant risk that another of the animals would lose its footing and crash to the ground.

The thought of the heat-seeking devices high in the air above them made Nabila's flesh crawl. She felt horribly exposed. The sky seemed less an open space than a lens for a giant, roving eye. As they reached the crest, she almost recoiled from the sense of openness. If a helicopter passed near them now, how could it miss them or the string of beasts they carried in their trail?

They camped three miles further on, getting everything in place before darkness fell. David suggested it might be safer if they didn't light a fire. It meant shivering in the dark and eating cold food, but neither regretted it. Once, towards midnight, they heard a chopper in the air above, a mile or two away to the south. David said nothing, but he had almost given up hope. He knew his enemy too well. The Guojia Anchuanbu would not let up until it had him and Nabila firmly within its grasp. He went to sleep, shivering. It felt like the coldest night he had ever known. The tent hemmed him in with walls of ice.

When he next woke, it was an hour before dawn. His dreams had left him limp and trembling, and he rummaged in his mind for the twigs and dust of reality, piecing them together until he had the strength to open his eyes.

Nabila was not in her sleeping bag. Was that why he had woken? he wondered. He waited for a few minutes, but she did not return. The delay grew, and he became anxious that something might have happened to her. No sounds reached him from outside. It was as if reality had less of a hold out here.

The tent flap was still untied. He pushed it back and stepped into the bitter pre-dawn air. Above him, stars loomed like grapes, bulging with light.

He swung the beam of his torch in a wide arc. Something was wrong, but he could not take it in at first. Next to his feet, one of the camels lay curiously slumped. He stepped up to it, and this time he could see it was dead. Bending down, he examined it: a long, ragged gash glistened in its neck.

He stood, doing his best not to panic. His entire body had started to go into overdrive. Chemicals were flooding his system, making it hard for him to think or act clearly. He stumbled forward and found a second camel, its throat cut wide open in the same manner.

'Nabila!' he shouted, not caring who heard him, only wanting to find her, to know she was alive. The desert made no answer. A couple of yards further, he stumbled on a third camel, its head lolling lifelessly in a pool of blood and sand. He bent down, pressing his palm on to the blood: it was barely warm.

Suddenly, he heard a sound. He'd never heard anything like it in his life. His first thought was that another camel was being slaughtered, that it was bellowing against the knife. But the cry continued, rising and falling, moving in an almost rhythmic pattern from low murmurings to high banshee shrieks, and he realized it was not an animal but a human being.

He snapped the torch up and round, turning it in every direction, trying to locate the sound. And then he saw.

Nabila stood several yards away, beside the last camel left alive. Two other dead camels lay on the ground behind her. She was naked, and her hair fell around her shoulders like a veil, and she was drenched in blood. As he watched in limitless horror, she stooped and placed a long knife against the beast's neck, and it cried out in sudden fear until she bent close and whispered in its ear, whereupon it fell quiet.

David was still too horrified for movement or speech, and he watched as she manipulated the blade to suit the camel's neck, then tore a ragged line across its soft, beseeching neck. It tried to stand, but the strength had already ebbed from its body, like water from a pool that the tide has left behind, so that it merely rocked and slumped and was still. Nabila caressed it, then drew away, letting the knife fall and standing back, her naked skin glistening with wet blood.

'Nabila . . .' He went up to her, bewildered and out of his depth. 'Nabila . . .'

She seemed not to recognize him. Her eyes were filled with something he had not seen in them before. It suddenly struck him that he knew her very little indeed, that she was a stranger to him in most matters.

'Nabila . . .'

Her eyes seemed glazed, focused perhaps on something he could not see or guess at. He came up close and took her by the shoulders, shaking her. She seemed to have no volition, like a puppet suddenly cut free of its strings. Her face and limbs were slack.

'What made you do this?' he shouted. 'Why did you kill them? Come on, answer me! You know this will kill us as well, don't you? Or didn't you think about that? Look at me, for God's sake. Do you understand what you've just done? They were our only way out of here.'

He stopped speaking, suddenly aware that there was no point in going on. Nabila had closed in on herself, and no amount of shouting or coaxing would bring her out again easily.

He managed to get her back to the tent, half guiding, half pulling her. It wasn't that she was reluctant: she just didn't seem to care. But he wanted to get her inside, out of the cold, before she came to harm.

Once inside, he wrapped her in her sleeping bag and threw his own over her. She was shivering horribly, and he knew there was no time to be lost in getting some kind of heat back into her body. Leaving her staring at the roof of the tent, he went outside and, with the help of the torch, found a bundle of tamarisk wood they had stashed away a couple of days before. It took only a minute or so for him to pass from camel to camel, confirming his original fear, that none had survived. It was still utterly beyond his comprehension that Nabila could have done what she had done.

He lit a fire outside the entrance to the tent, and fed it with dry twigs and thicker branches until it crackled and blazed. It didn't matter now that the heat might show up on some Chinese pilot's tracking equipment. At the moment, all he cared about was getting Nabila properly warm. In spite of what she had just done, he still loved her with a passion that lifted him beyond all this pettiness, this sand and blood and incurable desperation.

When the fire was well settled, he carried her out, still wrapped in the sleeping bag, and sat her in front of it. He heated water in a pan and, unzipping the bag, slowly washed the sticky blood from her skin, bending low from time to time to kiss her cheek or forehead or mouth, and to whisper words of reassurance. When she was clean, he helped her dress, then took her back inside, where she curled up inside the sleeping bag like a child. Exhausted, he went outside and sat by the fire, feeding it fresh wood every time it died down, and waited for morning.

Dawn was a cortège of red and gold and silver that danced for long minutes on the summit of the high dune opposite before turning to a faint tinsel glow. The world re-emerged from darkness like a snake shedding an old skin. David woke, bleary-eyed, and surveyed the camp-site. The humped bodies of the dead camels announced the death of all he had come here for.

There was a rustle behind him. He turned and saw Nabila, tousle-haired, emerging from the tent.

'David . . . What happened? I must have blacked out or something. My sleeping bag's covered in blood, there's blood on my clothes. Are you all right?'

He got up quickly and caught her before she could catch a glimpse of the dead animals. She pushed against him, but her strength had not fully returned, and he drew her back inside the tent and closed the flap.

'It's all right,' he said. 'You're not hurt, nor am I.'

'But this blood . . .'

'You don't remember?'

'Remember what? When I woke up I couldn't remember going to bed. There was dinner, then we talked – I'm not sure what about. I remember a dream about the camels, that I was slaughtering them. And then . . . this.'

'Listen to me, Nabila. Listen very carefully.'

He explained what he had found on leaving the tent the night before. Horror-struck, she listened, scarcely believing a word of what he said, yet unable to deny any of it. It seemed that what she remembered had not been a dream after all.

She did not move for a long time. Outside, the light grew, sending a warm, opalescent glow into the tent.

'Has anything like this happened to you before?' he asked.

'Yes . . . No . . . The truth is, I don't know. There's been nothing like this before. But I have had spells, lapses, breaks . . . My mother found me when I was five, just sitting by the pool, staring. She put me to bed, and I woke up several hours later with a headache, but no memory of having been outside at all. There were some episodes in my teens. It's a form of epilepsy.'

'Except that you're capable of doing things even while you're absent.'

'Yes, but never anything like . . .'

He put his arms round her and held her to him tightly.

'Have you any idea at all what might have prompted . . . what you did?'

'I'm not sure. I remember we were talking about the helicopters tracking us down because of the heat trail thrown off by the camels. I remember being frightened by that. It made me feel terribly vulnerable. There was a point – I remember this clearly now – when I started to think about slaughtering the camels. I must have gone blank soon after that.'

They went outside to inspect the damage. Flies had already started to gather about the heads of the dead animals, huge black clouds that seethed and chattered, growing larger every minute as invisible signals went out through the dunes.

'I think we should bury them,' said David.

'But that'll take for ever . . .'

He shook his head.

'All we need to do is camouflage them with sand. If we leave them on the surface, they'll be spotted before long.'

They set to work, using shovels they'd brought to do any digging that might be necessary once they reached their destination.

'Do we really need to do this, David?'

'Why shouldn't we?'

'Well, you said we're finished anyway. You said we can't get out of the desert without transport.'

'Did I?'

'Yes. But you're wrong, you know. We can walk. We carry what we can on our backs. We find some of these wells you've been talking about. If we're lucky, we come across Karakhoto or the complex. After that . . .'

She shrugged and stirred her shovel in the sand.

'You may be right . . .'

'You know I am. Whatever you intend to do, I'm not sitting here to watch the camels rot. We can walk out of this, David. It's up to you.'

He leaned back on his shovel and smiled at her.

'Very well, we walk. But in the meantime, we still have to cover these buggers with sand.'

CHAPTER SEVENTY

The Landrovers had been camouflaged to look like Iraqi army vehicles. To the camouflage, dollops of mud and sand had been added with a liberal hand. How helpful either of those devices might be should they be sighted by nomads or spotted by shepherd boys, no one really knew. The men themselves had been kitted out in Iraqi uniform, though the equipment they carried, from bergens to anti-tank weapons, was British or American.

They'd chosen the Landrovers quite deliberately. One of the lessons the SAS had learned in the Gulf War was the foolishness of sending men into western Iraq without vehicles. Tabbing with full bergens across open hostile country had taken its toll back then, during a winter war; to attempt it again in the full heat of summer would have been lethal. The greater risk of being spotted had been set against the near certainty of physical collapse and the inability to carry more than light weapons and limited ammunition.

Not that anyone wanted to use the weapons or the ammunition they carried. If the mission went off smoothly, they'd be in and out like fig-seeds. If it did not, they'd be up against half the Iraqi army, armed to the teeth and seriously pissed off.

They were driving in single file, using dipped and masked headlights. Peter Terry drove the first Landrover, with Bill Burroughs as his lookout. Behind came the Dai Lama in the other Landrover, which he'd christened Blodwen, in which most of the troop's weapons were carried; and after that came Barry Dobson in the Longline LSV, a souped-up beach buggy similar to ones used by US Special Forces units. Back in the Gulf War, they'd tried the LSVs out, only to find that their lack of range and their inability to take heavy weapons on board made them too limited for cross-border expeditions. But with two Landrovers for back-up, Barry's little number offered speed and manoeuvrability over difficult terrain. He'd called it Jennifer, after his daughter.

A light flashed on the jeep in front, and all three vehicles came to a halt. It was not yet dawn, but they could sense it just out of sight, creeping towards them.

'Are we all here?' asked Peter Terry. The others sang out their names in turn.

'Right, listen up. I calculate we're about sixteen miles south of al-Falluja, which probably puts us a mile or two away from our objective. Most of the traffic we passed last night was military, as far as I could tell. By dawn this road's going to be swarming with the bastards. I'd like to suggest we haul ourselves off-road and get our heads under camouflage for the rest of the day. I don't know about you, but I could do with some shut-eye.'

He strolled back to the rear vehicle, the LSV, where Dobson was already getting out the PG Tips.

'Leave the tea for now, Barry. I want to be sure we aren't in the middle of some bloody camping site before we get under cover.'

'Oh, come on, sir, we're all parched. We've been breathing sand all bloody night.'

'You can have as much tea as you like once we're settled. But I'm serious about the danger. We're not many miles from al-Falluja, and for all I know we could be on top of the bloody weapons base already.'

Terry had been with D Squadron, hunting Scuds during the Gulf War. Caution was second nature to him. He was already worried that they'd come this far without incident. It seemed almost too good to be true.

While they waited for dawn to come to the horizon, Terry took his Magellan GPS from the front vehicle and set about establishing their co-ordinates. He marked their position as nearly as he could on the map: as far as he could tell, they were not near any inhabited areas, military installations, or known tribal pasturing grounds. But sometimes things on the ground changed like lightning. Especially in Iraq. Especially anywhere in the vicinity of a major Iraqi weapons store.

Dai Matthias came across. He sniffed the air and glanced towards the eastern horizon. That was the nice thing about being out here in the desert, he thought, you had an uninterrupted view in every direction.

'Where are we, sir?'

'About where I expected. We'll have some kip, then make the first reconnaissance in Jennifer.'

'Looks quiet enough, sir. About as much life in it as Neath on a busy Saturday night, which is fuck all, as my Aunt Nerys used to say. Mind you, the only life in my Aunt Nerys on a Saturday night was my Uncle Andy.'

'It's starting to get light. I just want to report in our co-ordinates to London.'

He lifted the unit's Mobilfone from the rear seat and keyed in a number. Moments later, a handset was lifted in an office halfway across the world.

'Babylon Five,' Peter murmured.

'Star Trek on line. Go ahead, Babylon.'

'Is that you, Spock?'

Each of the base team used a code-name based on the TV series. The team in Iraq just used numbers, from one to four. Back in Cheltenham, where the expedition was being controlled by an SAS team, Spock was the alien: an MI6 field officer who knew more about the seamy side of Iraq than anyone at Stirling Lines. He had given them briefings for over a week before their departure, he would debrief them on their return, and in the meantime he was attached to one end of their satellite link on a twenty-four-hour basis. All he lacked was pointed ears.

'It is indeed. But I warn you, I'm not exactly a match for my namesake. Do you know what time it is here? Anyway, what can I do for you, Number One?'

'It's almost light here. I want to get the vehicles under cover as soon as possible. But I have a question. We passed some heavy traffic last night. It was moving south on our road. Several of the vehicles were carrying yellow lights. I've got nothing like that on record.'

'Does it worry you?'

'Of course it bloody worries me. What if they're using light codes?'

'OK, were there any green lights?'

'On the rear if we looked back, yes. I know about those.'

'I know you do. Tell me more about these yellow lights.'

'I've told you all I know.'

'No, you haven't. Were they high up or low down? Single or double?'

'Single. But it's hard to say how high up they were without getting a proper look at the vehicles in daylight.'

'You must have formed some idea.'

'All right, lowish.'

'Fine. Babylon, I'd like to know your most recent co-ordinates. I assume you're stationary. Have you checked your position yet?'

'Yes, I've got the co-ordinates here.'

He read out the figures just supplied by the Global Positioning Satellite.

'Great. OK, that's fine, we've got you. Babylon, will you please stay put where you are? You could be in serious danger if you move.'

'What the hell's going on, Spock? If there's danger ahead, let me pull back. At least let me get off this fucking road.'

'No, for God's sake, don't do that. That could be disastrous. Stay where you are, and don't move until you hear from me again.'

The connection was broken. Terry dropped his handset back on the unit. He turned to the others.

'OK, you lot. Spock says we've got to hang around here for the moment. Barry, you may as well brew some wet stuff after all.'

'Aren't we pulling off the road, sir?'

'No, I have orders not to do that.'

'I thought we made the decisions on the ground. Use our initiative, like.' Dai shook his head. His years of training and his battle instinct told him this was tempting fate.

Barry ambled back to his LSV and broke out the PG Tips again. He glanced up at the horizon. Dawn seemed slow in coming. At the edge of the sky, a few stars had started to pale.

Terry took Bill Burroughs and Dai Matthias off to one side.

'I don't like this,' he said. 'Get four bergens ready, and as much hardware as you think we can carry. We can tab in from here, but if we have to tab out again . . .'

They set to work, breaking off halfway to drink scalding cups of tea.

'I don't know how you all drink that rubbish,' said Dai. He had boiled a separate pot for himself, as he always did. 'Nothing like a nice jasmine tea or an oolong or a gunpowder to freshen you up.'

'I prefer a Japanese sencha myself,' said Barry.

'Well, you would do, you being a Geordie, see – all those Jappo factories up where you are, you'll be eating rice and seaweed next.'

'I'll leave that to you Welsh bastards. What's that muck you all eat? Laver bread? Looks like fucking seaweed stew, that.'

'So it is. Makes you tough, though, so my mam used to say.'

Peter Terry hushed them.

'Did you hear anything?' he asked.

'Yeah, something,' said Bill, who'd been giving only half an ear to the banter between the others.

They listened intently. Somewhere, not too far away, there was a sound of engines. It continued for a few moments, then stopped abruptly. They went on listening, wishing daylight would come. A minute or two passed, then more engines, from a different direction this time.

'Bill, back in the jeep with me. Barry, dump the LSV for now. Go with Dai, and get your weapons in order.'

'Are we going to move?'

'Yes. We're too bloody exposed here.'

'Shouldn't we get in touch with Star Trek, keep them informed?' Bill asked.

'What they don't know won't hurt them. We're on the ground. You can't run an operation like this from fucking Cheltenham. Come on, let's stop wasting time.'

But even as he spoke, dawn was at last pushing its way through the darkness, clearing it from the sky as though for ever. They hesitated then, knowing they'd missed whatever lingering cover darkness might have granted their departure. There was little point in setting off without assessing their surroundings. So they stayed put and watched the light grow second by second, and the landscape take on shape and colour.

It was Barry who made the first sighting. He was panning across the horizon with his binoculars. Suddenly, he froze, refocusing.

'Bloody hell,' he whispered.

'What is it?' asked Dai.

'Here, have a look for yourself.' Barry passed the binoculars to his companion.

Dai trained the binoculars in the same general direction as Barry. Several moments passed as he scanned the landscape, then a sharp breath escaped his lips.

'*Iesi blwdi Crist!*' he swore. He looked briefly at Barry, then turned to the front.

'Captain . . .'

'It's all right, Dai. I can see them. They're close enough now to see without glasses.'

Wherever Peter Terry looked, he could see them, armed men in black uniforms, moving at a steady walking pace towards them, hemming them in from every side – the Quwwa Khassa, Saddam Hussein's 'Special Force', recruited from the most loyal sections of the population, more highly favoured and better equipped than the Republican Guard.

Terry knew they had a simple choice: give themselves up to be imprisoned, tortured, and, in all likelihood, shot in the head in some Baghdad basement; or try to fight their way back to the Saudi border. He gave nothing for their chances of achieving the latter. Unless London could pull off a diplomatic coup.

He hesitated a few moments longer, then picked up the Mobilfone and keyed in the code for GCHQ Cheltenham. The phone rang at once. And went on ringing. Two minutes passed before he put down the handset. He knew there was no point in trying again.

In Cheltenham, Chris Donaldson listened to the phone ring. He knew why they were calling, and he knew they were wasting their time. Abbas was not a man to waste time. He had the British unit in his bag, and he would see to it none of them left that spot alive. They would be killed and buried, and the desert sand would cover their remains. It was too late now to prepare and send another unit. And in any case, the result would be exactly the same.

'It's like bloody *Zulu*,' said Dai Matthias, more or less to himself. 'Ivor Emmanuel singing "Men of Harlech" while the darkies come over the hill. What do you reckon, lads? Spot of the Spice Girls should see them off.'

No one laughed. Dying for your country isn't the easiest of things at any time, not least when it's all due to some slime-ball back home.

Peter Terry drew back the bolt on the heavy machine-gun. Johnny Arab would pay a very high price for today's victory. They'd go out, but they'd give Saddam a bloody nose on the way.

CHAPTER SEVENTY-ONE

'What was it like in the Army, Calum? Was it awful? You never talk about it.'

'Talk aboot it? Why the fuck should Ah talk aboot it? Ah didnae like the Army, an' the Army didnae like me. End o' story.'

They were inside, at opposite ends of the long sofa in Charlene's front room. The weather had taken a turn for the worse. Grey clouds slumbered over the mountains, and the lake was as dead as stone. Maddie felt down, as though the greyness and the deadness were intended for her alone. She was desperate to talk, desperate to make a real link with Calum. The thought that he might be no more than a petty criminal chancing his arm terrified her.

Calum had found a couple of CDs to play at last, old Joy Division albums he'd brought with him from Edinburgh one year in a futile attempt to stay sane. They hadn't gone down too well with his Aunt Charlene. 'What the Elvis is that, Calum? Is that what ye call music? Ah thought some friend o' yours had died, Ah thought you wis holdin' some sort o' wake.' They'd laughed a lot at that, and he'd smiled weakly, pretending to share their joke, and all the while he'd been black and violent inside.

He could do what he wanted now, Charlene wasn't around to interfere, and the music seemed to chime with Maddie's mood. He'd had them on all morning, track succeeding track, until a steady atmosphere of chill unease had been created.

'I just like to know about you, Calum – that's all. I've told you all there is to know about myself.'

'Look, Ah'm no' the Army, an' the Army's no' me. Ah wis in the Paras two or three years, and Ah came oot a sight dafter than Ah went in. Ah saw fuck all action, except what Ah created mysel' doon the barracks on a Setirday night. That whole bunch wis fuckin' radge. All they cared aboot wis goin' on long hikes an' how tae get intay the SAS. Everybody Ah met wis a headcase. It wis all Ah could do tae git ootay that place wi' a healthy brain.'

'Why'd you join in the first place?'

He looked at her pityingly, thinking he'd never come across anybody so out of touch. Like his Aunt Charlene reading a story that didn't have a happy ending. Where he came from, everybody knew why people went into the Army. Maddie didn't understand a thing, couldn't understand a thing. Birds like her were brought up well out of sight of it all. They had good homes, good schools, good holidays, good clothes, good boyfriends. She'd never seen Wester Hailes or Muirhouse on a black Saturday in December, never been in the sort of pub he'd learned to drink in, never made love in a toilet with her red knickers on the floor and her head against the cistern, never shot up in a derelict house, never given birth on her own to an illegitimate child, never . . .

He paused in his endless internal list of nevers, looking at her, as if by just being there she could somehow make all the negatives coalesce in a single, roaring positive. And so she would, he thought, if by just being there she brought in the million pounds he'd asked for. So she would, he thought for a second time, if she just went on sitting there, looking as pretty as she did now.

He slid a little closer to her.

'It's no' that easy,' he said. 'It disnae happen that way, likes. It's, well . . . Ye know some kids, they're in the same class at school, next thing ye're all on the dole queue together as well. One o' ma friends, a smart wee lad the name o' Gordon Stuart, wis the first o' the bunch tae join up. He went in the Paras an' loved every minute. First leave, he comes home an' tells me Ah've got tae join up masel'. Ah thought, why the fuck not? Ah had nae money, nae job, and nae way to get the one or the other. So Ah went in an' put ma stupid name doon on the line too.'

'Was that really the only choice you had?'

She inched closer to him, her forehead creased in concern for what he must have been. He was not conventionally attractive, she thought, but his candour and naïveté drew her to him.

'Where Ah come fae, choice is a girl's name,' he said. Humour apart, he realized he meant it, that he was no longer saying things just to amuse or impress her. He thought of all the things he'd said to women in the past, all the stale chat-up lines, the cheap endearments whose only purpose was to get your hand into someone's knickers. Not much chance they'd go down too well here. It left him dumb, trapped between his need for her and his fear of using force.

She touched his cheek. She knew it was a dangerous thing to do, since she already guessed he wanted her. At home, perhaps, she'd have sent him away, politely but firmly denying him any part in her. But she had no home any longer, nowhere to practise politeness and firmness in. She had neither touched nor been touched

534

by a man since Zheng Juntao's disappearance. His cheek felt hot and rough.

He did not move. Maddie let her hand stray across his stubbled cheek, then down to his mouth. He kissed it, then reached out himself, stroking her cheek in turn with his heavy, awkward hand, and she leaned closer to him while his fingers moved to her neck, to caress her and to feel the tight, naked pulse in her artery. Her breath moved in her throat like silk.

She was wearing a long white T-shirt emblazoned on the front with the slogan: 'Line Dancers Do It in Stetsons'. Without a word, she dropped her hands to its hem and lifted it over her head in a single motion.

At that moment, the music came to a halt, and they found one another in a silence that passed through every vein like smoke. His hand went blindly to her left breast, caressing it as a child's hand might stroke a small animal, and she came right up to him and kissed him full on the bloodless mouth while his shaking hand drew him to her.

She pulled off his shirt, uncovering a chest and arms that seemed to have been modelled on the Sistine Chapel.

'There wis a lad in barracks did these for fifty pee an hour. Nothin' he couldnae draw. It wis a way of passin' the time, likes. Ah went two or three times a week. Ah'd go tae sleep an' let him do what he wanted. Maybe that wis a mistake.'

'Nonsense, they're very nice. I'll look properly at them afterwards.'

And she kissed him hard, as though greedy for something she had been denied all her life, and he drew back once to look at her, small and naked beneath him, and laughed, as if he had no cares in the world.

*   *   *

They lay together afterwards on the floor, using cushions from the sofa to rest their heads on. Maddie felt an aching hole inside her, knowing that this was all a sham, that there could never be anything between Calum and herself outside these four walls. And she felt a terrible pang of guilt thinking about Zheng Juntao and how she had betrayed him.

'Wouldn't it be strange,' she said, 'if Charlene and Hamish were to come in right now.'

'Aye. Fuckin' marvellous. We could make oot again tae the strains o' Barry Manilow. Ever done that?'

She shook her head. Her soft copper hair lay like barley-sugar on her thin shoulders.

'Ah tried once. Gave me the droop. Ah couldnae get it up for weeks afterwards. There was a song aboot somebody called Mandy that kept goin' through ma head.'

'Was she nice?'

'Who, Mandy?'

'The girl you couldn't get it up for?'

'Tracey McBurney? She wis all right, Ah suppose. But for this Barry Manilow obsession.'

'Have you slept with a lot of women?'

'Well, burds like. Aye. More than ma fair share, Ah suppose.'

'Have you never tried for a long-term relationship?'

He tensed, sensing the direction she was trying to steer the conversation in.

'No' ma style, doll.'

'I'd only ever made love to one man before you.'

'That's nice. Bit of a waste, though, if ye dinna mind ma sayin' so. Body like your, likes . . .'

As if to emphasize his words, he reached out and stroked her breasts. As he did so, she sensed him tighten again. His hand stopped stroking.

536

'What's wrong, Calum, you . . .'

'Shhhh.'

She realized he was listening intently.

'What is it?' she whispered. 'What can you hear?'

'Ah'm no' sure. Could be some fuck's oot the back.'

He reached on to the sofa, where his jeans lay in a crumpled heap, and pulled a gun from one of the pockets.

'Calum, it's probably only . . .'

'Keep your mooth shut, and don't interfere. I'll pop ma kegs on an' . . .'

In the next few seconds, three or four things happened, virtually simultaneously.

A man in black abseiled from the roof to come crashing through the picture window.

Two more threw themselves through the smaller windows on either side of the bay, rolling to the floor and straightening, weapons pointing forward.

A fourth man kicked open the door of the living room and held it open, pointing a sub-machine-gun round it.

'Get on the floor! Drop your gun, and put your arms over your head! And make it quick!' he shouted.

Calum's reflexes were almost as fast. He wasn't as well trained as these intruders, perhaps, and he was a bit out of practice; but he hadn't lost his instinct. Before the others could recover from the force of their entry, he had pulled Maddie in front of him and rammed the barrel of his pistol into her mouth.

'Don't so much as fuckin' move!' he screamed. 'If Ah go, the doll goes too. More holes than Bonnie an' Clyde! Your boss wouldnae like that, would he? Two corpses when you came tae get one oot. No' much point tae that, is there?'

'Not a lot.'

The speaker walked into the room as though arriving for a dinner party. He wore a dark suit with a plain silk tie, cufflinks, not buttons, tightly laced Oxfords, and a smile that would have been disarming under other circumstances.

Farrar surveyed the scene with the detached air of an estate agent or an insurance assessor.

'I think you'll find that your hand will grow tired quite quickly in that position,' he went on. 'Far better to point at the back of her head.'

'Ah'll put ma gun where Ah choose. Who the fuck are you?'

Farrar stepped forward.

'I thought you might recognize my voice, Calum. Or have you forgotten our recent conversation?'

'It's you that's forgotten, Tony. Ah seem tae remember telling you tae keep the polis ootay this. If ma memory serves me properly you swore tae say nothin' tae the boys in blue.'

'You must be denser than I thought. Do you honestly think I'd employ Policeman Plod to carry out an operation like this? The lads with guns pointed at you, Calum, are members of an elite Hostage Rescue Unit. You, on the other hand, are a reject from the Paratroop Regiment who never learned to shoot straight and never will. Incidentally, I think the young lady might appreciate it if you allowed one of us to cover her up. She is rather naked.'

'Better naked than dead. From where Ah'm sittin', Ah cannae miss. In case ye cannae see, ma finger is so fuckin' tight on this trigger, a bairn could smell it. Shoot me an' the doll gets it too.'

Farrar inched forward a little more.

'Maddie,' he said, 'just try to relax. We aren't going to let you come to any harm.'

Maddie nodded imperceptibly. All her expression was in her eyes, wide and staring. She wasn't sure who frightened her most, Calum or Farrar.

'Now, Calum,' Farrar continued, 'I want you to listen very carefully. Your life may depend on it. The men you can see in this room are only my front team. There are two back-up teams, and I can bring others in with a single telephone call. I know what you're thinking. You want to get clothes for both of you, then you want transport – maybe a car with a driver – and a free passage out of here. Otherwise, you will threaten to shoot Maddie. The doll, as you say, will get it.

'I can certainly supply you with all that, but what I cannot do is promise to stand aside and let you vanish into the dead of night. This thing is out in the open now, and you will be pursued, whatever happens, wherever you go.

'If you kill Maddie, things really do get difficult. I could only give you a choice between being shot now or spending the rest of your life in jail. And I do mean the rest of your life. In solitary. You should have found out who I was before you started this whole stupid scheme.'

'Am Ah gettin' on your nerves or something? Or maybe it's the sight o' the burd wi' no clothes on. Ah've got a hard-on just tae feel her bum on ma dick. Ah cannae imagine what you've all got.'

'Is this true, Maddie? Has he got an erection?'

Maddie nodded. She wanted to scream, but her throat felt numb and out of her control.

'You are a vulgar little man, Calum. A gentleman never lets himself come to attention when the lady is in distress. Which your young woman is.'

'She'd no' be in distress if you hadnae burst in. She was no' in distress earlier when Ah made her come fae here tae John o' Groats. Ah expect you heard that.'

539

'It gave us a useful clue as to what was going on inside here, yes.'

'You jokers probably think Ah'm fakin'. Ah've never been more serious in my puff.'

'Your seriousness is not in question. It's your common sense I'm not so sure about. Let me run this past you again. If you kill Maddie, all your options run out. If you take her as a hostage, you will eventually fall asleep or make a mistake. We can be incredibly patient. And we can track you down wherever you go. You won't see a penny of your million pounds, and in a week or ten days or a month one of my men will put so many bullets into your body that your coffin, if they bother making one, will weigh a ton.

'However, there is an alternative which I believe may appeal to you. My only concern in this is Maddie's safety. Frankly, I couldn't care less about you. In order to settle this matter amicably, I am willing to make you a one-time payment of fifty thousand pounds, paid in unmarked bills, and a promise of free passage. You throw away your gun, you put on your clothes, and you walk outside. There's a car down by the road, a Grand Cherokee. That's thrown in free.' He paused and looked at Calum, the tattooed skin and the tangled hair. The youth was all Anthony detested. 'Well,' he went on, 'what do you think?'

'Show me the money. Show me you're no' just makin' this up.'

Anthony turned and went out of the room. Half a minute passed, then he returned carrying a small attaché case.

'Here,' he said, opening the case and tilting it towards Calum. Inside, rows of banknotes were held tightly by broad elastic straps. They seemed to glimmer in the artificial light, strangely coloured fish in a tank without glass.

Farrar went up close this time and laid the case next to Maddie's hip.

It was hard for Calum to keep up the nonchalant front he'd adopted. He'd never seen so much money in his life before. Packed together in a little case, with the Queen's tiaraed head repeated all the way across, fifty thousand looked like much more than his imaginary million. He did a quick switch of hands on the gun, put the barrel to the side of Maddie's head, and used his free hand to feel one of the wads.

'How do Ah know these arenae – what's the word?'

'Counterfeit? There's not a lot I can do about that. But you know where Maddie and I live. I imagine any cheating on my part would bring some form of reprisal from you. So, the answer is, no, they are not counterfeit. You have my word on that.'

'As in "A gentleman's word is his bond"?'

Farrar smiled tolerantly.

'If you like.'

'And are you?'

'I'm sorry?'

'A gentleman.'

'I'd certainly like to think so. It's not for me to say so, of course.'

Calum thought for a few moments longer.

'All right then, you've got a deal. Ah'll take the money an' the car. You can keep the burd. You'll no' be disappointed, she's a great screw. Maybe all your wee friends here can have a go as well. Make it worth their while comin' all the way oot here. But first, Ah'd like tae see your weapons on the floor.'

Farrar nodded. The HRU did as they were told, locking on their safety buttons and dropping everything they carried.

Calum hopped into his trousers, holding his pistol in one hand as he did so. It was trickier pulling his T-shirt over his head. Whatever way he did it, there was no avoiding that brief moment when his head went through the neck.

That was when they took him.

The man on the far left had his SMG up and firing in less time than it took Calum to squeeze his head through the ring of cloth. He fired several rounds, all directed at the centre of Calum's chest. The gun had not yet fallen from Calum's hand, nor his eyes quite stopped blinking before the other members of the unit finished the job.

Calum became a shooting-bag, an inert target of flesh and bone into which hundreds of rounds were pumped. His body erupted in bursts of red, spilling blood over Maddie until she was covered from head to foot in the stuff.

That was when she screamed. Her voice drowned out whatever echoes remained of the shooting, bringing people running from all directions. Elizabeth was there, one of the first. She staggered into the room, took one look at Maddie, and fainted clean away.

Farrar went to Maddie and tossed a blanket round her. It had been handed to him by a paramedic who'd accompanied the unit.

He put the blanket round her, and held her by the shoulders, and whispered in her ear. She was still shuddering with shock, and trying to shut out her horror and her fear. What he whispered was simple and to the point. 'Listen, Maddie, if you don't pull yourself together, your mother and I will have you bloody well certified and locked up somewhere from which you'll never resurface. Think about it very hard.'

He turned to the HRU men still in the room.

'Right, I want him taken out and dumped somewhere. Somebody get this place cleaned up. I'll take the girl upstairs.'

'What time are you planning to return to London, sir?'

Farrar looked surprised.

'London? You can take Lizzie back if you like. See she understands what happened. I'll speak to her later.'

'Very good, sir. What about the girl?'

'Maddie? She's staying here for a while longer. With me.'

He tightened the blanket round her shoulders and smiled. Maddie did not smile back. She was quiet, but inside she was still screaming.

CHAPTER SEVENTY-TWO

It was Nabila who came up with a method for locating water. Despite the heat of the sun's rays that baked the sand above them, the wells they had found previously had always contained cool water, and she reasoned that there might be a discernible difference between the area over a well and the surrounding desert.

She was proved right almost straight away. David used the infra-red scope to scan an area ahead of them and noticed a cool patch about twenty yards further along. Up close, it revealed the tell-tale salt crust of a small well. The brackish water was no use to them, but the experiment had opened up the possibility of their finding artesian wells, and perhaps wells whose water was still supplied by mountain streams to the north of the desert rim.

In the meantime, their own water was going down more quickly than they had anticipated. Carrying the weights they now did, each grew thirsty at a faster rate than usual. Daytime temperatures were still well above all that was reasonable or bearable, even for a desert, and they were baked hour after hour against the red sand as if they were joints of meat in the centre of a large oven.

The helicopters continued their daily passes, never quite close enough to make visual contact. Once, a green-painted chopper landed half a mile away from them.

David and Nabila watched, crouched behind the summit of a dune they had just climbed. A man got out and walked around for a while, then clambered back into the tiny craft and was whisked skywards again. They went to the spot afterwards, and found a dead gazelle and the pilot's footprints. It was a bit like being Robinson Crusoe and finding that solitary print by the water's edge.

Soon after that, David found his first proper well. It showed up on the scanner quite clearly, and when they scraped the sand away they found a circular stone cap bearing an inscription in Chinese characters. According to the inscription, this was well number seven in a series connecting the towns of the northern desert corridor. A hole about two inches in diameter and maybe a foot deep had been cut into the stone, and in it sat a length of broken wood, gnarled and twisted by the winds and sands of many centuries.

'I wonder how they found them in the first place,' said David as he pushed and pulled in an effort to dislodge the cap.

'By some form of dowsing, I expect,' suggested Nabila. 'I had a patient a few years ago, a farmer who used bent sticks to track down underground water on his farm and the farms of friends. Apparently he was very good at it. He was in great demand.'

'But out here?' He straightened for a moment.

'They'd come in winter, probably. Once they had one well, they could afford to take their time to find the next, then another one in the opposite direction.'

David bent again and tried to get the cap moving. It made a slight grinding noise, but still refused to budge. It had been perhaps two thousand years since it was last touched.

'Let me,' said Nabila.

David stood aside, still wincing from his efforts. Nabila stood astride the cap, bent down, and twisted it off in a single motion. David stared at her in disbelief.

'How did you do that?'

She shrugged.

'Girls' secrets,' she said.

They lowered a cup inside on a rope. When it came up, it was filled with the sweetest water they'd ever tasted. They drank and drank, then filled their water containers with as much as they would take. David replaced the stone cap and took a careful record of the well's position. Even if it were buried beneath ten feet of sand now, it would always be possible to dig straight down to it.

'What do you think the wooden post was for?' asked David.

'I don't think it was a post. I'd bet it was twenty or thirty feet high and that it had a flag on the top.'

'So travellers could find it.'

'Absolutely. What would be the point otherwise?'

The inscription said that the next wells lay ten miles to the east and fifteen to the west. Acting on the assumption that the wells must lie more or less in a straight line, and that the line must lead to a town, as shown on the map, they filled their water containers and headed due east.

'Ever get the feeling the ancient Chinese knew substantially more than we do even today?' David asked. He brushed more sweat from his forehead. His hair was matted to his scalp. He'd liked to have had it cut, but they'd forgotten to bring any scissors.

'You can bet the hard work was done by Uighurs.'

'Nonsense, you weren't even around then.'

'There is that.'

They walked more easily, knowing some sort of end was in sight. Shortly before sunset, in a moment of long shadows, they came to a valley with sharply pitched walls of sand.

'Do you want to go down?' asked David, 'or shall we wait until morning?'

'Better we go down and get ourselves out of sight somewhere. It's not worth checking for water, is it? We're not likely to find fresh so soon.'

'Not too likely, no. I'd rather use the energy to keep on towards the next well.'

The long descent was punishing, wracking every muscle in their legs and backs as they tried not to fall forward. David found himself pulling back constantly, using his bergen as a counterbalance to the force of gravity. Suddenly, about halfway down, the pull of the descent became too much for him. Just as he was about to fall forwards, Nabila caught his bergen and yanked him backwards. He sat for several moments, recovering his breath.

As he did so, he became aware of a regularity in the wall of the valley below that could not easily be explained as the work of the wind, chiselling the sand into shape. He looked round. The sun was getting close to the horizon, but there was still considerable heat in the sand. On an impulse, he reached into the bergen and pulled out his infra-red scanner.

Seconds later, he was looking at a wholly different place.

'What's wrong?' asked Nabila, coming up to him from below.

He just put out a hand, as though to brush her aside, to get her out of his field of vision.

'I don't believe this,' he said.

'What can you see?'

He handed the scope to her and pointed towards the dune opposite.

'Take a look at the dune. Can you see the way the sand falls quite naturally from its top down? Then it gets to a spot about halfway down where it slopes more steeply. Run the scope along that section.'

She did as he said, and moments later let out an excited yell.

'What do you see?'

'I don't know what it is. Long sections of cool, quite regular, horizontals mostly, with some perpendicular. Like . . . like building blocks.'

'That's exactly what they are. I'll bet anything those are stones. They don't hold the heat as well as the sand, so they show up as cooler areas. Those are houses, Nabila. We've found one of our cities.'

They hurried down to the bottom.

'We can't possibly hope to dig through this,' said David. 'But if we can get a fix on it, maybe we can get a message through. It could be a vital discovery.'

'Don't you think you could be making a mistake? If this is a town, how come the buildings are all under one dune?'

'Well, of course they aren't. They'll be under several dunes.'

'But why isn't anything showing on the surface between the dunes?'

'There could be low buildings. We don't know where the real ground level is. Anything would be covered with sand. Or if they were made from wood, they'd have rotted away.'

They looked round. It wasn't easy to form an impression of a city out here in the sands.

'Let's find a place to camp,' said Nabila. The light was

beginning to fade from the sky, and she wanted to choose a safe place before darkness set in.

Suddenly, she became aware of a sound, the chop, chop, chop of a helicopter's blade a little distance away. She looked up, and David raised his head too, but there was nothing to see. The engine noise faded as the copter moved away, then grew again until it was louder than before.

'Look, David – quickly!'

Nabila pointed along the valley to where a speck of colour had appeared just over the horizon. Even as they watched, it grew in size.

'It's coming in this direction,' shouted David. 'Let's get the hell out of here.'

'Wait. What's that?' She pointed back along the valley at the approaching aircraft.

David lifted the binoculars that he now carried round his neck. The helicopter sprang into sight, its outline softened by the deepening twilight.

'He's using searchlights,' he said. 'One on either side.'

They watched like rabbits on a dark road as the little craft drew nearer, two long pencils of light stabbing left and right through the deepening shadows.

'The bastard's got us trapped,' said David.

'He hasn't seen us yet. If we can get round the corner of this dune we'll make it. But we have to run.'

They started sprinting, and it seemed as though their feet bogged down in the deep sand at every step, and their legs felt like rubber. Nabila thought of jettisoning her bergen, but realized it would be a huge mistake to do so. Without water and basic provisions, they would quickly die.

The copter headed straight down the valley towards them, pausing every so often to allow the pilot to look more carefully at the ground beneath him. He'll be fully alert, thought David; there'll be a fat reward waiting for whoever brings us in.

Suddenly, he saw the terrain open up about a hundred yards on his left, revealing a broad opening where the dune ended.

'There,' he shouted. 'It's just up ahead.'

They dashed for the opening, desperately trying to get round to the other side of the dune. But it was already too late. The helicopter was on top of them, and before they could outrun it, one of the searchlights had them firmly in its grip.

The pilot could not stop all at once, but went on several hundred yards, then, with a graceful dip, danced and turned, then drove down hard to the gap. The searchlight swung round again, recapturing its prey and pinpointing them harshly against the sand. The pilot executed a slow turn until he was facing them, with the twin lights bright in their faces, forcing them to shut their eyes.

David regretted not having taken the pistol from his pack earlier. It was a Heckler & Koch P7, and at this range he could at least have put the lights out of action, maybe even done some real damage to the helicopter.

As if to mock him, the pilot opened up with a light machine-gun, peppering the ground right in front of them and sending huge plumes of sand like coloured smoke into the air.

'Keep running back!' shouted David.

He looked over his shoulder and almost fell. It was very nearly dark now, but the searchlights made visible what might have remained hidden had night fallen completely.

The dune did not slope down as it should have done. Instead, it ended abruptly in a high stone wall, a wall that towered fifty or sixty feet above their heads. It was carved and chiselled and ornamented, and in it was set a high door, gaping open and only partly filled with sand.

'Nabila! Up there!'

They ran together up the ramp leading to the opening, while bullets danced behind them. The helicopter bucked as the pilot attempted to keep them in sight and to fire accurately.

Exhausted, they flung themselves through the opening, not knowing and not caring what was on the other side. The firing continued, and the chopping of the rotors. The helicopter sank lower and lower, and the pilot began to fire wildly into the opening. If he could just pin them down long enough to radio for reinforcements, he'd be sure of his reward without actually taking too many risks.

David and Nabila found themselves on a gently sloping bank of sand leading into a vast unlit interior. Nabila threw her pack down and rummaged inside for a torch. With its help, she surveyed the area around the opening, while David hunted frantically for his pistol.

'Leave that for now, David. We've got to get out of his line of fire.'

They scrambled to one side of the opening, putting themselves out of reach of the bullets that still poured into the building.

Suddenly, the firing stopped. For a few seconds, all that could be heard was the drumming of the rotors, then there was a sound of grinding and screeching. The pilot, intent on firing into the opening, had let himself get too close to the wall.

There was an enormous crash, followed by an explosion. David rushed to the entrance to see the helicopter fall apart, its rotors spinning out of control then breaking up in what seemed like slow motion. The body of the helicopter seemed to crumple, then crashed to the ground in a ball of fire that gave out an intense heat.

An ominous silence followed.

'Thank God for that,' said David, turning to Nabila, who was now beside him, trying to make sense of the wreckage.

'Shhhh,' she said.

'What's . . . ?'

She put out a hand to silence him. Then he heard it too. A deep groaning, then a crunching sound.

'Get back from the doorway for God's sake, David!'

Nabila ran forward and grabbed his arm, pulling him back from the entrance. Moments later, there came a complicated sound made up of creaks, groans, and heavy bangs. The sound picked up volume quickly, then there followed a ghastly grating sound. They both looked up to see a great stone slab rush from its moorings, slipping downwards along well-chiselled grooves to slam with an almighty crash on to the threshold. It filled the opening precisely, as it had been intended to do all those years ago when it was first cut and set in its high place.

CHAPTER SEVENTY-THREE

Western Region Military Installation 14
(Chaofe Ling)
[Co-ordinates classified]
Level 3
Guojia Anchuanbu offices
Security Classification: Absolute

'I'm sorry to disturb you, sir, but I thought you should
see this right away.'

'Yes, what is it, Jia?' snapped the colonel.

Chang Zhangyi was busier than usual. The test had
gone satisfactorily, and the Iraqis were impatient to get
the warheads on board the plane that was waiting at
Lop Nor. That wasn't a problem in itself: the warheads
and other components could easily be moved down the
long tunnel that had been built deep beneath the desert
in order to allow building machinery and vehicles unseen
access to the Chaofe Ling site. But Chang Zhangyi was
worried about keeping the fate of Kashgar secret long
enough to get the bombs out of the country. That was
taking up all his time at the moment.

His aide, Jia Hsiujia, gingerly placed a sheet of flimsy
paper on the colonel's desk. The old man had been getting
increasingly tetchy, and Jia had had his head bitten off
more times in the past week than he cared to remember.

Chang Zhangyi grabbed the flimsy and threw it off his desk.

'I want you to tell me!' he nagged. 'That's what you're here for, isn't it? I don't have time to read this infernal rubbish you keep giving me.'

In the background, the air conditioning chuntered gently away, transforming the impossible atmosphere forty feet beneath a blistering desert into something cool and bearable. Further down, it worked a lot less efficiently. But up here in Chang Zhangyi's office it had never broken down. In spite of prominent notices to the contrary, the colonel insisted on smoking whenever possible, which meant most of the time in this, his private sanctuary. In acknowledgement of that fact, he slipped a long cigarette from a half-empty pack of Zhonghuas on his desk and lit up.

'A report has just come through that one of the helicopters involved in the desert search has had some sort of accident.'

'A serious one?'

'We don't yet know, sir. Possibly. All we know is that he was making an urgent radio report when contact was cut off.'

'I hardly see why you're disturbing me with this. Accidents like that happen in the desert. Sand gets into a vent . . .'

'Yes, sir. If he resumes contact, no doubt we'll find out. But . . . there is the matter of the actual radio message.'

Chang Zhangyi's eyes lit up. He sensed something peeping round the shadows.

'I take it you have the wording.'

'Yes, sir. On the . . . on the sheet I gave you.'

'I can't be bothered with that. Just give me a summary.'

554

'Well, he says he made visual contact with a man and a woman, and chased them into some sort of opening that ended in a cave. He opened fire on them, but found it hard to keep them in his sights. The last thing he transmitted was: "I'm going in closer, see if I can flush them out." Then we get some smashing sounds, him shouting . . .'

'Shouting what?'

Jia shook his head.

'We listened for several minutes. It wasn't intelligible.'

'And then?'

'The radio goes dead. They've been trying to raise him since then, but either his set is switched off or it's been smashed.'

'Was the pilot dependable?'

'Dependable?' Jia looked shocked, though he'd never have said so. 'Sir, the air crew selected for this mission were our top people.'

'Yes, but even top people make mistakes.'

Chang Zhangyi got up from his chair. He was smoking furiously, excited at the thought of being so close to Laing at last.

'Did he give co-ordinates?'

'There were none on the message, sir. But we do know the precise sector he was working through when this accident happened. If there's been a crash, we should be able to locate it quite quickly. The other crews have been ordered into that sector already.'

'Let's hope the idiots don't start crashing into one another. Tell them to pull out as many as possible and leave three or four to carry out the search. A helicopter can't be that hard to find. And order the pilots not to waste time trying to rescue their friend. They're to spread out and go on looking for our fugitives. They can't have got far. We'll launch a full-scale search in the morning.'

He waved a hand to dismiss Jia, then summoned him back.

'Jia, you said something about a cave.'

'The pilot mentioned it, sir.'

'Surely he was mistaken. There aren't any caves in the desert.'

'There are several mountain ranges. The Mazartagh, the Hamitagh . . .'

'They're all much too far south. I'm sure there's nothing in the northern region.'

'Sir, he said something about the cave being in a cliff . . .'

'That's just as unlikely. When did this happen?'

'Sunset, sir. It was almost totally dark when the helicopter crashed.'

'Then he could easily have been mistaken about what he saw.'

'I'm sure he was, sir.'

'All right, Jia, you've wasted enough of my time. Let me know the moment there's anything further to report. I want a helicopter and a sober pilot to stand by in case I need to fly out there.'

Jia saluted and went out, looking for a buggy to take him back to the central communications room. Set on auto, the almost silent buggies patrolled the rubber-lined corridors of the complex. You could almost set your watch by them.

Inside his office, Chang Zhangyi finished his Zhonghua and stubbed it out in a large ashtray littered with the corpses of its many predecessors. He drew another from the box and lit it. A thin twist of smoke made its way up to the ceiling, wreathing the white-and-red smoke alarm which Chang Zhangyi had long ago disabled.

He opened a drawer and pulled out a large map. Unfolding it as far as possible, he let it flop back over the desk.

He glanced at it for a few minutes, straightening it here, folding it there, until he was satisfied.

He picked up the phone and keyed in a short number.

'Helicopter control? Chang Zhangyi. I believe you've had an accident . . . So I understand . . . Now, do you have details of the sector covered by that particular craft? . . . I see . . .'

He wrote a series of numbers on the margin of his map, then some letters.

'No, I need nothing else. But let me know the moment further information comes in.'

He hung up almost absent-mindedly. All his attention was fixed on the map. It took him very little time to locate the crash sector and to mark it out in bright red ink. He had never imagined that Laing could make it this far. It made him all the more formidable an adversary.

'Well done,' he whispered. 'You very nearly made it. What a pity it has to end this way.'

He refolded the map and put it in its drawer. He paused to extinguish his cigarette, then got to his feet. For a moment, he felt a touch of disappointment at having outwitted Laing and his girlfriend. But there would be compensations, he reassured himself – untold compensations.

CHAPTER SEVENTY-FOUR

She was feeling bloody annoyed with Anthony, and she'd said so several times, in precisely those terms. Packing her back to London like that, and staying on up there just so he could help wean the precious Maddie off her drugs, as he put it. It was infernal cheek on both their parts.

To make things worse, she'd returned home to find her car as dead as a dodo, God alone knew why. While his, of course, was up there in the land of the fucking heather, enjoying the scenery. Bloody, bloody cheek.

She'd rung him straight away, vented her feelings, and demanded he find her something at once.

'I don't have anything, dearest. Why don't you just ring Hertz or one of those people? You only need something to tide you over. A little runabout.'

'I don't want a fucking Ford Sierra. I need a car, Anthony, a real car. Something with a bit of spunk in it. I've got to drive Laurence to the Lakes and back. We're entertaining major clients at the Sharrow Bay. We've taken over the hotel. I can't turn up at the Sharrow Bay in a Vauxhall, can I?'

'Well . . . do you have to drive?'

'That journey's hell by train, and it's even worse since privatization. Pooley Bridge is miles from anywhere, you should know that. It's why people go there. And there's that narrow road along the lake. Come on, now, you must have something in that bloody pool of yours.'

'Oh, all right. I'll have something sent round. But it's strictly irregular. You do know that?'

'I'll feed it some All Bran, dear – that should clear it up. How's the kid, by the way?'

'Your daughter? Wondered when you'd ask. She's fine. Rather better on cocaine than she was on the stuff Rose was giving her. At the moment she's a bit shaken by what happened up here. She'd grown quite fond of our young thug. She needs to take it easy. I'll stay here with her as long as I can. We've got plenty of provisions, if you like sausages and bacon and baked beans. And I'm treating myself to an introductory course in something called line dancing.'

'It sounds perfectly vile. You'll have to wear a stetson and high heels. Not your sort of thing at all. Now, when should I ring for the car?'

'No need, I'll have someone drive it round. Just give them a couple of hours. And, darling . . .'

'Mmmm?'

'Lighten up, do. Life can be great fun if you put your mind to it. Buy some records to take to the Sharrow Bay. Patsy Cline – that should loosen you up. Not to mention the staff.'

'Tony, do you love me?'

'Of course I do, why on earth should you ask?'

'No, I mean, really love me. You wouldn't just use me, would you?'

'Of course not. Darling, what is all this about?'

'Promise you won't leave me down here on my own much longer. I just have such a bad feeling about things.'

'I promise, really I do. Once Maddie's on the mend.'

'Can't I come up to visit?'

'Absolutely not. For both your sakes. But once this is over, we'll all go on a big holiday together. A cruise, maybe. Something worthwhile. Greece, possibly, with Swan Hellenic. We could have lectures on line dancing on Knossos.'

'Very droll. I'd sooner Disneyworld. Now, be sure it's a decent motor, dear. A Jag if they have one.'

'I'll do my best.'

And he did.

Lizzie enjoyed driving with automatic transmission. The racing green Jaguar responded to her touch like a dream, much to Laurence's alarm. He was a cautious driver who thought the speed limit far too high, and seldom drove above third gear.

They'd reached Pooley Bridge two hours early. Inordinately pleased with herself – she hadn't had a drink since just before leaving – Lizzie had insisted on taking her brother into Windermere to do some sightseeing before they drove back to the hotel. She thought she'd buy Laurence one of those sheep made from wool and wood that they sold in little gift shops; but she didn't think he'd see the joke, not even if she called the bloody thing Laurence.

In fact, she couldn't have cared less about Windermere. What she was after was the drive down this wonderfully steep, twisting road, and the sight of Windermere at the end, the lake and the town together, and the sun burning on glass and painted metal. And the chance of scaring the socks off Laurence.

'I wish you'd slow down a bit, Lizzie. We've got plenty of time. And Windermere's really a bit dull.'

'Don't be such a wimp, Laurie. Sit back and enjoy the scenery.'

'For God's sake, Lizzie, there are other cars on the road.'

'I'm perfectly well aware of that.'

'You don't seem it.'

She shaved past a Reliant Robin and pulled back in to her side to the sound of enraged honking. Seconds later, the local bus came in sight on the other side, huffing and puffing its weary way up the steep incline.

'Laurence, whose idea was it to hold this ruddy dinner up here? I didn't think you liked the Sharrow Bay.'

'I don't, if I'm to be honest. Too much chintz for my taste. If anything moves, they put a tassel on it.'

'But the food's first class. Even you have to admit that. And as for the view from the lounge . . .'

'Oh, yes, I know all that. Personally, I find the food a bit on the rich side. All those sauces.'

'So why on earth did you choose to entertain such important guests there?'

He squirmed, then winced as they flew through a double bend, barely holding the road as Lizzie pushed down hard on the accelerator pedal.

'Well, they're Japanese, you know. The Japs like this sort of thing. A couple of days in the Lakes, some guff about Wordsworth and daffodils, a few award-winning meals, one of those extraordinary afternoon teas in the lounge, and they're anybody's. Thought you'd know that.'

'Was this your idea, Laurence?'

'What do you mean? Oh, for God's sake, be careful.'

'I mean that it doesn't sound like you.'

Laurence hesitated, then nodded.

'No, you're perfectly right. It was Anthony's idea, actually.'

'Really? I don't remember him ever mentioning the place.'

'Oh, yes, he comes up here quite often. He knows the owners, gets them to put on special dishes for when he's up.'

'Did he know I was going to drive you up?'

'Yes, he was very keen on that. Said the trains were dreadful – which they are – and that you and I could have a long chat about things, which we've done. Jesus! Lizzie, go easy. Have you been drinking?'

'Not a lot, why?'

She twisted the wheel on a left-hand bend, scraping the mudguard heavily along some rocks until the road straightened.

'For God's sake, Lizzie, slow down. You're going to kill both of us.'

'Actually, dear, I can't. My foot's right off the pedal, but the machine's got too much speed up.'

'Well, use the brake, then! Oh, God!'

They careered at great speed into a right-hand bend. An oncoming car swerved widely to avoid them.

'The brake's not responding. I don't know what's wrong.'

A sharper turn to the right took them all the way across the road, and the car scraped hard down the rock wall until Lizzie managed to get it back to the left.

'Blow the horn, Lizzie! Warn people to get out of the way. Come on!'

'I can't steer and blow the fucking horn at the same time! Just let me get on with it.'

Suddenly, the road opened out in a straight stretch, flanked by steep rock-strewn banks. Sheep grazed above them, looking down detachedly on the fast-moving cars below. Their backs were painted with red dye, marking them for slaughter.

The straight stretch seemed to tilt, and suddenly they found themselves on a steep downward run, and the car was picking up more and more speed, completely out of control now, despite Lizzie's frantic efforts to steer it into submission.

It was just then that something clicked in the steering column. Lizzie looked down in horror as the wheel froze in her hands, locked in a single, immovable position.

The car went rushing on towards another, sharper bend. On the other side, climbing with great difficulty out of Windermere, chugged a whisky lorry. By an immense coincidence, the driver was a distant relation of Calum Kilbride. He'd come down that morning on the M6. He was only doing ten miles an hour when the collision occurred. The Jaguar was clocking over ninety.

In Bonnie Scotland, Maddie Laing slept and slept. Out on the silver loch, Sir Anthony Farrar drifted in a small boat. He wondered if Lizzie was dead yet. It might have been simpler, he thought, to have kept her up here, taken her out on the lake, and got her drunk. But that would have messed other things up, and at the moment all he cared about was simplifying his life. His recent experience with the Hui Hou had frightened and galvanized him.

He'd found a rod in the house, and he'd come out to fish for ferox trout. There was scarcely a ripple to mar the surface of the lake. A bird called far away, across an expanse of dim and sparkling water.

He looked across the loch at Charlene's chalet. Maddie was sleeping in one of the upstairs bedrooms. The mess downstairs had been cleared away, and a few repairs made. What was left of Calum had been wrapped in burlap, weighted, and deposited in a deep bog ten miles away.

He'd go in soon to check that Maddie hadn't woken. The moment she showed signs of consciousness, he'd send her to sleep again. Later, she could get up for food. Then back to bed.

He'd watched her just now as if for the first time, sat beside the bed and watched the rise and fall of her breasts. The image of her naked had not left him, nor the image of her skin splashed with blood. For some reason, she had made him think of Meihua, the girl in the Lotus House, the beautiful girl he'd loved and pleasured and killed.

Maddie was not as beautiful, or as light in her frame, or as sensual. But that was no more than anyone could expect – few women met the exacting standards of the Hui Hou. On the other hand, Maddie did have a quality of innocence and expectancy that drew him to her. And he suspected that, if she were properly taught, she could become as sensual as Meihua and more.

The boat swung a little as a breeze passed over the water. Anthony shifted in his seat and pulled on the line. Ripples ran from the little boat to the shore.

He wondered if David Laing was still alive. It hardly seemed possible. The last he'd heard from Chang Zhangyi, there'd been no sighting. But that could just as well mean that he'd died in the desert. In fact, it was the most likely outcome.

None of this, he thought, need have happened had that self-righteous idiot Matthew Hyde not poked about in matters that did not concern him and passed on that dangerous message through the boy. Laing was the last person left alive who could alert the right people to the fact that there was a traitor in MI6. Assuming Tursun or Potter had warned him. What then? If Laing did, by some fluke, return, Farrar settled back comfortably, secure in the knowledge that, if he did so, he had the means of silencing him to hand.

SMOKE

CHAPTER SEVENTY-FIVE

It was as if the lid of a stone sarcophagus had slammed shut, leaving them sightless and breathless, without hope of ever returning to the world above. One minute, the world had been at their backs, and sunset, and the night sky filling with stars, then it had all been cut off as if it had never existed.

'What is this place?' asked Nabila.

'A house. Part of the city of Ts'ang Mi, if I'm right.'

'That can't be right. It feels too large, too grand for a house in a desert town. Where did they bring so much stone from, for one thing? And that slab crashing down like that. I can't believe they had fixtures like that in the average home.'

'Yes, that is a point. Maybe they built them like that, maybe that was the last section of wall waiting to be slid into place.'

'In that case, there should be a door somewhere. Or windows.'

'Of course. But they're probably buried under several tons of sand. Darling, I think we really are trapped in here.'

It had begun to sink in on them both that there really might be no way out. Their food and water would last them another few days at most, the food longer than the water. After that, it would be the slowest of deaths, and possibly madness before unconsciousness set in. Perhaps they would end by hunting one another down in the dark, or beating their heads against dumb stone.

'At least we took one of them with us,' said David.

'That's not really very helpful, is it?'

He shook his head.

'No,' he said. 'I was just trying to think of something to say.'

'On the other hand, we can't be sure there isn't an entrance near the surface, something further in, perhaps.'

'Given what I can remember of the relative dimensions of the dune and what we saw of this place, I wouldn't hold out much hope, would you?'

'Not much, no.' Nabila felt her heart sink. 'But that's no excuse for not trying. I'd like to know what this place is in any case.'

'We don't have that much battery power left. The big torch burns it up very quickly. We didn't bring any extra batteries. Once these have been used up . . .'

'I brought a couple. I wasn't really thinking that clearly when I packed. Let's see just what we've discovered.'

David dug deep into his bergen and came up with a large 'million-candle-power' torch, the type used by coal miners in some of the northern provinces, and very effective as long as the batteries held out.

He switched it on. For a moment, they were dazzled by the brightness, then confused by what the light started to pick out.

High above their heads, a curved and painted ceiling twisted and turned, its beams carved into the most fabulous shapes. Staring down at them were the starkly carved faces of gods and demons, men and hovering angels, some benign, others malevolent, one or two the very embodiment of evil.

David played the light back and forth, picking out more and more features with every sweep, faces with red eyes and lolling tongues, dragons with unsheathed claws, birds with rapacious beaks, skulls, daggers, black-faced devils, yellow-faced heroes.

'I don't think this was ever somebody's little hideaway,' he whispered, slowly swinging the beam down to the walls. Nabila came up beside him and took his free hand in hers.

The walls were faded, the result of centuries of erosion as wind and sand, heat and cold worked on them. But they could make out the traces of paint, while everywhere carvings of men and gods created a theatre of shadows and light as the torch beam picked them out and passed on.

'It must have been a temple, or a . . .' Nabila paused, shivering in the cold that clung permanently to this place.

'Not a temple,' said David. 'Look.'

He had dropped the beam to ground level. Right in front of them was a carved block of stone.

'That looks like a sarcophagus.' Nabila switched on her own torch and walked up to the stone. David followed her.

'That's exactly what it is,' he said.

He swung the torch round, and there, next to the first, stood a second sarcophagus, and beyond it a third, and others running back into the pall of shadows where the torch's beam ended.

Together, they went to the first sarcophagus. It was about four feet high, carved with animal and human figures along the sides, with finely chiselled writing on its flat lid.

'Let me see if I can read this.'

He bent right over, straining to decipher the lettering. Brushing aside a veil of sand, he read the text in Chinese.

> Zhou Huangdi, vassal of Han Wudi, heaven-designated Emperor of North and South. Lord of Pan T'ang, Governor of Chie Kiang and Ts'ang Mi, ruler of Yuzhou, master of Gaochang, guardian of the roads from East to West, protector of the temples throughout Yangshuo District, patron of the Seven Poets of Changma, benefactor of the schools of music and philosophy . . .

'We seem to have stumbled on somebody important,' grunted Nabila. 'But I can't say I've ever heard of him.'

'Nor have I. But I imagine you'll find dozens like him in here. These tombs weren't exactly built for hoi polloi. Let's see how far they go on.'

He started to walk forward, but his half-blind feet stumbled over an object in the floor. Nabila caught him by the arm, just in time to stop him falling face forward. They turned their lights on the floor. At David's feet lay what looked at first like a heap of rusted metal. But when he bent down and examined it more closely, he sprang back in revulsion.

'It's armour,' he said. 'And its owner's still in it.'

Nabila swept her torch across the floor. She could make out the separate pieces of armour – plates of metal that had once been sewn to leather leggings, a breastplate that had slipped from its leather straps, a helmet with an empty fitting once graced by an elegant plume. And inside, the hard white bones of their long-dead occupant.

'This place is full of them,' said David, pointing with his torch to further heaps of old metal and unclaimed bone. There were several by every tomb, and others in the wide passages between them, and yet others by the walls, where they must have sat a while before Zhou Huangdi's executioner or some other executioner came to dispatch them, strictly in turn.

'When did Han Wudi reign?' asked Nabila. 'Do you know?'

'You don't know?'

'Well, only vaguely. History was never my subject.'

'He was the top notch Han emperor. Ruled for ages; I don't know the exact dates. Somewhere round about the second century BC to the beginning of the first. Pretty well a record for an emperor.'

'So some of these tombs have been here – what? – over two thousand years.'

'And the rest may be even older.'

They passed slowly between the tombs, avoiding the remains of the dead warriors and palace servants whose blood sacrifice had sealed the tombs and ensured the immortality and liberty of their masters and mistresses.

'So many ghosts,' whispered Nabila. The tombs seemed to go on for ever, back and further back into the dark sand. In the end she stopped and told David she was too tired to go on.

They took food from their packs and made themselves a small meal. It was bitterly cold among the grey stone tombs, and they missed a fire to warm them and heat their food.

They switched off their torches after that, and Nabila wondered how many times more they would see one another's faces. In the darkness, they held hands. They were both tired, but sleep would not come. It seemed an excess to use up precious time by sleeping anyway. It was too cold to make love, too dark to talk, too silent to listen.

But in the end, sleep did come, a heavy, fitful sleep that gave them no real rest. It was disturbed by the ghosts whose slumbers they had broken after so many years.

Once, Nabila woke to hear a noise, a rattling and

clicking somewhere in the dark, and she switched on her torch and shone its light in that direction. Facing her, startled by the sudden brightness, was a gazelle. Perhaps it was the one they had surprised in the forest, perhaps a companion. It stood blinking into the light for long, troubled seconds, then dashed away among the bones and clutter. Did it too know it was trapped in here, that there could be no escape back to the sand or the green trees?

Large grey spiders scuttled and strutted everywhere, their long agile legs using men's fingers as their ladders. They made nests in the empty skulls, and emerged like grey crabs through the eyes and mouths. They would sit very still at times, then run in a sudden jerking movement that made Nabila shiver. She wondered if this was their constant abode, if this was just the latest generation in a long line of tomb-dwelling spiders, or whether they knew ways to pass between this place and the world of sunlight above.

David woke shortly after dawn, reading the time from his twenty-four-hour watch. He'd been dreaming of long stretches of desert filled with armies, their golden and red banners stretched out high above their heads like floating pavilions.

Letting Nabila sleep, he switched on his torch and opened his pack to get some water. As he did so, he noticed the old map that his father had given him. The sight of it jogged something in his memory. It was too vague to pinpoint, but he thought that, if he looked carefully, he might remember what it was.

He got up and walked about a little, in order to stretch his limbs. He knew they were going to die in here. There was barely enough food and water for another two days. They could eat and drink it all at once, it would make next to no difference. He thought of Nabila, dead and staring here, with spiders walking through her hair, and in time nesting in her empty skull.

'Where are you, David? I can't see you.'

He turned and saw a light blinking at him.

'Over here,' he said.

He went back to her, and they sat together, making as good a breakfast as they could with what rations they had. Nothing hot, nothing particularly palatable, just the dull business of keeping the body alive no matter what.

'David, I've had a thought. Would your satellite communications thing work through all this stone and sand?'

'The Ultralite? I'm not sure.'

'Why don't you give it a try?'

'What's the point in that? Even if I could speak to somebody back in England, they could hardly come out here to rescue us. And even if there was a way of sending people out, how the hell would they get into this place? They'd need heavy equipment to dig us out. That bastard Chang Zhangyi isn't going to be content to sit around watching them, you know.'

'Oh, for God's sake, try,' Nabila snapped, not petulantly, but out of a sudden passion that denied the despair that had been gripping both of them. 'We can't sit here doing nothing,' she hurried on, 'or wait till we starve to death. If you could speak to someone, they might come up with a way round the problem. Why can't you just try?'

Stung, David said nothing, but found the Ultralite and set it up on the nearest tomb, a monument to a woman called Wu Zhengmei, who had lived out her life as the principal concubine of Sima Hsiarou, puppet ruler of Ts'ang Mi.

He keyed in a series of codes and passwords, then gave it

the number that would put him through to the all-day and all-night monitoring desk in London. Nothing happened. He tried again, several times, but each time the apparatus simply went dead on him. The signal simply could not penetrate all that sand and stone.

He put the little case away in silence. Nabila said nothing. Perhaps he'd been right, she thought, but that wasn't the point. She walked quietly away into the darkness, wondering if he would follow her, or stay where he was, nursing his wounded pride.

As she walked, she let the torch she carried play over the walls. Some of them had paintings, faded now, but still distinguishable, others held niches in which tall statues had been placed. It seemed an extravagance to walk past like this, letting the torch-beam play on dust-covered walls. Was not light now the most precious thing in existence, the only thing between them and eternal darkness? But what would she have saved the light for? To brighten her death? To let her see David's face as he breathed his last?

The thought of that suffocated her, and she turned abruptly, just to be sure he was there. The torch found him bending over the tomb, stooped, weary, packing the Ultralite back inside the bergen, as though that was important now. She decided to go up to him and kiss him and apologize.

Even as she watched, she saw him straighten and then, out of the corner of one eye, she caught sight of something moving. She thought it might be the gazelle again, drawn by the light. She turned her gaze and, for a moment, or perhaps two moments, she saw a woman, a young woman in long robes, crimson and beaten gold and copper, with her long hair falling almost to the floor. She seemed to be pointing with one arm towards the ceiling. Their eyes met, then the woman was gone, and David was standing alone, bent over the tomb like a runner at the end of a long run.

She was about to rush to him when, suddenly, she stood stock still. Something had just occurred to her. She swung the beam, letting light play on the wall, then up higher, across the ceiling. More paintings, more carvings, more shadows. And yet . . .

'David,' she shouted. 'David, come over here!'

His hurrying feet came skittering across the floor, narrowly missing the obstacles that lay in his path. She saw the light he carried dip and weave towards her, then he was there.

'What's wrong?'

'Nothing,' she said, 'not a thing. I've just figured out how we can get out of here.'

'Oh, Nabila . . .'

'No, listen. These tombs were built to stand on their own. They were never meant to be buried beneath tons of sand. Isn't that right?'

'Well, yes, obviously.'

'The ceilings are slightly vaulted, which is why they've been able to hold all this weight. But not even the best-built roof can resist pressure like that for very long. It would take very little to dislodge part of a roof, and then we'd see the whole thing give way.'

'You mean, let's pull the roof in, then stand around while a million tons of sand crashes in on top of our heads?'

'No, I don't mean that at all. Just listen for once, will you? This is the only chance we've got.'

'I'm sorry . . . Go on.'

'Take a proper look up there. Use your torch, it's better than mine. Here, let me show you.'

She swung the beam of her torch on to a central section of the ceiling, where stone beams intersected with a central boss.

'Can you see?' she asked. 'The keystone is coming loose already, so are some of the beams. It might take another hundred years, maybe more, but I guarantee it's going to give in the end. Look further down, and there – do you see? – a lot of the beams are skewed or sagging.'

'That still doesn't help us.'

'Of course it does. You're just not using your brain. We don't try to dislodge any of these, because, as you say, we'll end up crushed to death beneath whatever's up there. But there are places where only one section shows signs of potential collapse. If we choose our spot carefully enough, what we should get is a controlled opening, maybe something a yard across, maybe even less. Once it's open, sand will start pouring inside. Like an hour-glass. After a while, there'll be no more sand. We climb up to the hole and squeeze our way out.'

David hesitated, studying the ceiling, thinking over everything she'd said. He hated the rôle he'd come to play, deflating her hopes for escape. But what use were false hopes, in the end?

'You're forgetting one thing,' he said.

'What's that?'

'How the hell are we supposed to get up to the ceiling in the first place? I haven't noticed any ladders lying conveniently about, have you?'

CHAPTER SEVENTY-SIX

The water in the lake had cooled after a long hot day. The fish, sensing the coolness, swam up closer to the surface. Moonlight struck the water at an angle. There were more stars than he had ever seen in his life.

Drifting in the cool centre of the loch, Anthony felt himself cut off from everything, suspended on a pool of ink, waiting for a fish to snare itself on his line.

There were times when the killings became a little hard to cope with. Most of the time, he found he could keep them at a distance. The men in Iraq, for example, did not matter in the least to him. Matthew Hyde had not mattered to him.

But Meihua had disturbed his equilibrium, her beauty had got under his skin, and the sense of her dead made him shiver at night, in the solitary hours of the morning. Now Lizzie. Too many deaths, too close to home.

He wondered again whether David Laing was dead. In all likelihood, he would never know for sure. But he could be reasonably certain that Laing and his girlfriend were lying face down in the heart of the Taklamakan, drawing vultures from every direction. If so, it didn't bother him. He'd be more worried to learn that Laing was alive and still looking for Chaofe Ling.

He looked up at the house. One light was on downstairs, another in the bedroom where Maddie slept. If you could call it sleep. He'd undressed her, washed her, and dressed her again in a simple nightdress that he'd found hanging in a wardrobe. And finally put her to bed.

The lake was wide and deep and cold. How deep, he neither knew nor cared. Ducks and other water birds glided across its surface, and sometimes they dipped their heads down and dived far below, to come up with small fish in their beaks. At the bottom of the lake grew dark green weeds and waving fronds and willow moss. It was cold and dark at the bottom of the lake, and no one ever went there, and no one ever came back from there.

He returned his oars to the rowlocks and began to move slowly back to shore. Only a few more days, he thought; only a few more days.

CHAPTER SEVENTY-SEVEN

The solution might never have occurred to Nabila had it not been for the image she'd already conjured up, sand pouring through a hole in the ceiling to form a sort of cone that would lead them up to the breach and out into the open air.

'David, let's get our packs. I want to go back to the spot where we came in.'

'Darling, you saw how enormous that slab of rock was. There's no way out.'

'I'm not interested in the rock. I'm interested in the sand.'

She explained to him how it could be done, and for the first time he thought she might have cracked it after all.

'How do we transport the sand from the entrance to here or further back?'

'We'll think of something,' she said. 'First of all, I think we should choose our place in the ceiling very carefully. And I think we should hurry. These torches aren't going to last for ever.'

'I think we should start at the entrance,' David said.

'Won't the roof be badly damaged after that helicopter crashed into it?'

'It could be. But I still think we should examine that area first.'

Right at the front, there were visible signs of cracking

and collapsing masonry. But a little back from that they found exactly what they were looking for. About twenty yards from the way in, the ceilings showed fewer signs of stress. There was a stretch where everything seemed firm, followed by one ceiling with a keystone that had already slipped. They settled on it as their way out, and marked the spot by erecting several spears and flagpoles above the nearest tomb. In spite of the cold, David hung his jacket between two of the poles, where it would pick up the light from a distance. They could not afford the luxury of leaving one torch lit on the tomb.

On their way back to the sand piles, they paused to move any skeletons out of the path they meant to take once they started work. It felt like a terrible desecration to them both, to wreck bones that had stayed together for two thousand years.

Even though the distance was not particularly great, the task of moving a substantial amount of sand to where they wanted it was far from simple. David discovered two metal shields, each with slots through which straps had once been laced. He removed the straps from their bergens and managed to fit them to the shields, making two harnesses that enabled them to fill the insides of the shields and drag them over the floor to the spot they'd chosen.

Their biggest concern was light. Without it, they would have been in pitch darkness, forced to stumble about until exhaustion or despair dragged them down. It was impossible to guess how many hours there were left in the torch batteries, or how many hours it would take to build the hill of sand high enough to reach.

With practice, they established a clear route to the mound, and worked out that it was around thirty paces away. Slowly, the sand rose. It would grow more quickly as it got higher, but it would take a vast amount of sand.

They'd grow exhausted and fall asleep side by side on one or another mound of sand. It was worse than being out in the desert. Sand filled their hair and clothes. When they slept, they dreamed of it. When they woke, it was the first thing they became aware of.

'I thought I saw a girl standing by that tomb,' said Nabila.

'Really? Which one?'

'The tomb of Wu Zhengmei,' she whispered, almost frightened to speak the name out loud. 'The concubine.'

'Yes, I know.'

They were in darkness; she could not see his face or guess at his reaction.

'When was that?' he asked.

'Just before I told you how we could get out of here.'

'I see.'

'Did you . . . ?'

'See someone? No. No, I didn't.'

'I imagine it was a sort of hallucination. It was only for a few seconds. I thought she had long hair and a robe of silk, a robe of red and gold.'

'Yes, I'd imagined her like that myself.' He paused. 'I think it's time we got moving again.'

He switched on the torch so they could get their bearings. The light showed his face briefly. He had grown pale and haggard, not himself at all.

'I'm sorry I . . .' Nabila began, but he cut her off.

'I didn't see her,' he said. 'But I felt her presence. At that same moment.' He would not say more.

Work was harder on the second day. The backbreaking routine of dragging heavy shields full of sand across the stone floor was followed by the sheer agony of getting the loads up higher and higher as the day went on.

They finished their last food and water that night. The

mound was not even half complete. As their strength waned, the task would stretch out longer and longer, perhaps too long for both of them to survive.

'I looked at the map again yesterday,' David said before they slept. 'It makes sense now. These are the Tombs of Ts'ang Mi. I think Ts'ang Mi was Karakhoto. And I'm sure the tombs are no more than a mile or two from the city. We're nearly there, Nabila. All we have to do is break through that roof.'

But she was already fast asleep. He kissed her and lay down on his bed of sand. The last thing he heard was the rattle of a spider walking over old bones.

It was late when they woke. Their limbs were aching badly. David could barely move at first. He did some exercises to get a bit of flexibility into his back, then headed for the entrance, dragging his empty shield behind him.

Nabila worked out how to make steps in the mound by using metal plates from sets of armour. By employing enough of them, it was possible to create a shaky but reliable path from foot to summit. At this point, the mound was about twelve feet high.

Their strength was ebbing rapidly now. They rested more often, and went about their task more and more slowly. Carrying such heavy weights was wearing them out. Once, as they rested, Nabila turned to David.

'If I die in here, promise you'll leave me. Promise.'

'Darling . . .'

'I'm serious. Please don't argue with me. I feel perfectly safe here. Ever since I saw that woman.'

'There was no woman. And I won't let you die.'

'David, it's too late for that now. We may both die here. There were times I had to tell this to patients, now I have to tell it to you. And to myself. It could take some time, but frankly, I don't think it will. We need rest and we need food, and we've no way of getting either. Once our strength gives out . . .'

They got up after that and dragged ten more shields to the mound. Each time, the climb to the top was both higher and steeper. As David dumped the last load on top of the mound, he felt dizzy suddenly and slipped, falling on to the summit and sending all the sand they had just laid there tumbling back to the bottom.

They could do nothing after that. Instead, they lay together in the darkness, and in time they fell into a long sleep. When they woke, they found that one of the torches had been left switched on and would give no more light. With the remaining torch, they struggled back to the entrance.

They made the long journey to the mound on their hands and knees now, scraping their way along painfully through the dark, like Sisyphus. Before long, their hands were scraped red and their knees were bleeding. Climbing the mound had to be done in two or three passes, with a little sand at a time.

Then Nabila suggested that they should start shifting sand from the bottom of the heap directly to the top. Done carefully, it gave them a few more feet in height without the time-consuming journeys in between.

Checking with the remaining torch, they could see that they were now within a foot or two of making contact. While bringing more sand up, however, they noticed something else: the mound was now too narrow at the top to go any higher. They'd always reach this point just to see the sand slither away from them, down the side. If they wanted to lift it even another foot, they'd have to widen and thicken the whole thing considerably. The torch started flickering. David led the way slowly down to the bottom.

'Let's go back to sleep,' he said.

Nabila understood what he meant. She hadn't the strength to resist either him or the temptation of a last rest. She'd die with him here, and they'd be found centuries from now, their clothes and bodies eaten away. The only things to identify them would be their packs and their unusual contents. Would anyone guess who they'd been, would anyone care?

She reached out her hand and found David's in the dark. He had switched off the light. She closed her eyes, knowing she would never open them again.

CHAPTER SEVENTY-EIGHT

Helicopter Base No 3
General Air Base
Western Military Region Sector 17
Lop Nor

Chang Zhangyi's impatience had turned into bad temper, and his bad temper to rage.

'I don't care if they're disguised as rats, I just want them where I can see them. Do you understand that? Or are you a total numskull?'

The man wincing beneath the flails of Chang Zhangyi's verbal assault was not exactly a foot soldier. He was Ho Wenming, commander of the Eighth Helicopter Squadron, quite an important person in his way. But round here, nobody outranked Colonel Chang Zhangyi. The mere act of standing up to him had landed more than one senior officer in serious trouble.

'Colonel, we've scoured the place. We're still scouring it. There's nowhere they could have run to in the time available. In any case, I had a troop of commandos flown in to make a ground-level check around the crash site and beyond. They found footsteps coming in from the west, walking then running. They lead right up to the crash site. After that, there's nothing.'

'That's impossible. Were their bodies found at the site?'

'No, sir. Just the pilot's.'

'Then, where the hell are they?!'

'We don't know, sir. But they can't possibly have survived. There are no footprints leading away from the crash in any direction. I know the troop leader personally. His men are very, very good.'

'I don't give a damn how good they are. Somebody is missing something.'

'Sir, I visited the site myself several times. You can come out and see for yourself. There's an enormous sand dune, and there's a stone wall. That's all. There's nowhere for anyone to go.'

'What about this wall? Is there some sort of opening in the side of it? Could they have slipped between?'

'We've checked that, and the answer's no. And you have to consider something else: their footprints go up to the wall. It's a bit messy closer in, because of the crash. But as far as we can see, they were standing in front of the wall when the pilot hit it. That corresponds with his radio message.'

'If they were hit by the helicopter, their bodies would be there. Use some common sense, man!'

'I'm trying to, sir. I spoke to the military forensic examiner this morning.'

'Bai Juntao?'

'Yes. He was at the site yesterday.'

'And?'

'It's just that . . . He pointed out that the pilot's body was very badly burned, but that he had had the protection of the cabin. The worst heat was outside, and Bai Juntao thinks . . .' He paused, wondering how Chang Zhangyi would react to what he was about to say.

'Yes?'

'He thinks their bodies may have been cremated by the

extreme heat. They could have been sprayed in aviation fuel and then, well, ignited at a very high temperature. The stone would have prevented the heat escaping. Once we've had a chance to go properly through the debris . . .'

'You're telling me that Bai thinks they've been fried to a crisp? That there's nothing left, not even a thigh-bone?'

'I don't know, I'm just passing on what he said.'

'What do you want to do?'

Ho knew he had to take great care. He wanted to stand his men down: the squadron had been on this round-the-clock pursuit for longer than was good. That's why the crash had happened. Pilots were losing their concentration and their finer skills. But he knew Chang Zhangyi wanted to go on.

'You're the best judge of what we should do next, sir,' he said. 'But I would like to make a formal request to stand down my squadron. Perhaps Peking will allow you to requisition other helicopters.'

Chang Zhangyi sighed. The mystery was beyond all reason.

'Very well, stand your men down. But bear in mind that, if there is any sabotage, your head will roll, not mine. I'm placing our conversation on record: I hope you'll do the same.'

Ho saluted and walked back to his office. Chang Zhangyi watched him go. Tomorrow, the squadron leader would be demoted and sent back to his home province to await an inquiry into his conduct of the search. Chang Zhangyi had better people to call on. They were coming in this evening. He just hoped they wouldn't be too late.

He started to walk down to bay six, where his private helicopter was waiting. The sooner he got back to Chaofe Ling, the better.

By the time he got to the chopper, the engines were running. His pilot knew better than to cause Chang Zhangyi any delay.

'This just came in for you, sir,' the young man said, holding out a sheet of fax paper to him.

Chang Zhangyi took the paper and folded it out on his lap as the helicopter lifted from the tarmac. It fluttered in the downdraught from the rotors, then grew still as the aircraft steadied.

The final snags have now been overcome, and the first batch of warheads will be ready for shipment early tomorrow. Please reassure me that all necessary security measures are in place, and that the immediate threat you mentioned has been overcome.

The fax was signed by Wan Shunzhang, the general commanding the Chaofe Ling complex. Chang Zhangyi leaned back in his chair and watched the dun and featureless landscape roll past beneath them. He smiled to himself. It was almost over, he thought. Almost over.

CHAPTER SEVENTY-NINE

They slept for a very long time, a night and a morning, fifteen hours or more, and Nabila woke feeling terribly sick. Her head was spinning and pounding, her eyes felt on fire, her throat was parched beyond belief. She reached out and shook David awake, to find he was in little better shape.

'We can use the shields,' she said, her voice shearing off every other word. 'They'll stack on one another like plates. You only need a foot or two more.'

He was scornful at first, then saw the possibility in what she suggested. They scoured the tombs for shields, and brought them in pairs or three at a time to the mound. Slowly, they stacked them. When there seemed to be enough, David climbed on to them, leaning on Nabila's arm to keep his balance. He turned the torch on the ceiling, then swung his left arm up to catch hold of the boss on the keystone.

The stone was a thick mass of encrusted cobwebs, black, and sticky to the touch, dead and live spiders of all sizes, and God knows what other accumulations of two millennia. Fighting down his revulsion, David asked for a cloth and used it to clean the stone and the area around it.

He studied it for a long time, and finally gave up.

'It's no good,' he said. 'It hasn't come far enough down. The weight of the surrounding stones is still holding it in place. You'd need a drill or a hammer and chisel to make any impact on this thing.'

Nabila touched him on the elbow and switched off the torch.

'We can't find those,' she said, 'but what about an explosion?'

'Unfortunately, we don't have any explosives.'

There was only the briefest of pauses.

'You have ammunition, don't you? Plenty of it. Why can't you use that?'

'Bullets would be no use, but the gunpowder . . . Yes. Yes, why not?'

She helped him down, and they found the ammunition in his bergen, one thousand rounds of 9mm Glaser slugs.

'We won't need all of these,' he said. 'It has to be a fairly controlled explosion, enough to pop the keystone out without cracking anything round it.'

He showed her how to break away the case and extract the gunpowder. They started building a heap of it on one of the square plates.

'We'll have to keep the torch switched on while we do this,' he said, 'but I'm worried about the battery giving out. I can't place a charge and blow it without light. We'll just have to work as quickly as we can, and hope the battery's got more life in it than we do.'

The light took its time to fade, but fade it did. When an hour or so had passed, they found themselves squinting in half darkness.

'Right, let's stop here,' said David. The pile of gunpowder on the plate was smaller than he would have liked, but he knew they were running out of time.

'You'll only have one chance,' said Nabila. 'If it's not enough to blow the stone out, there won't be a second opportunity.'

'I'm all too aware of that. Now, I need something to pack this stuff in.'

'What about a sock?'

But when they removed their shoes, their socks had too many holes to make them of any use.

Nabila rummaged frantically through David's pack, then through her own, but there was nothing that might serve the purpose. Unless . . .

She laughed out loud, remembering something she'd noticed in a pocket in her pack when she'd bought it. Opening the pocket in question, she drew out a small rectangular packet.

'Best army issue,' she said. 'Contraception for the masses.'

She tore the packet and extracted a beige-coloured condom.

'Chinese condoms aren't designed to help you enjoy sex,' she said, 'but they're very effective at stopping you having babies.'

David poured the gunpowder slowly while Nabila held the mouth of the condom open. They could barely see to do it.

'This could prove to be the most explosive time any condom's had in the history of the world,' joked David.

'Speak for yourself.'

They tied the condom tightly, then wrapped it in two socks, in case it got snagged on a piece of sharp stone.

Finally, David climbed back up the mound, and once again ascended the pile of shields. Nabila helped him gain his balance, then passed the pack of gunpowder up to him. He had already decided on the best spot to place it. It slipped in easily.

'Bring up three feet of rope and my cigarette lighter. In my bergen, the front pocket.'

She found them and climbed back up the mound. A

591

quick slice with her knife cut the rope down to the right length.

'Soak the rope in the lighter fuel. Be careful, it has to go the whole way. And hurry up, this torch won't last many more minutes.'

Nabila shook the lighter gently down the rope and handed it over. David fitted one end into a sock and let the rest dangle down to the top of the mound. The torch went out. He shook it, but it refused to do more than flicker and die. He let it fall and reached into his trouser pocket for his box of matches.

'I've got three matches left. Take the bergens to the back of the nearest tomb and get down behind it. As soon as I light this, I'll join you.'

'Will you have enough time?'

'Let's hope so.'

He listened to her dragging the packs to safety. If they did succeed in getting out of here, they'd need them.

'Ready!' she called.

He took a deep breath. There would be no second chance. He struck the match and held it to the rope. For several seconds, nothing happened, then, abruptly, the cord burst into flame. David hurled himself down the mound and scurried to the nearest tomb he could remember. As he threw himself behind it, there was a terrifying bang, the volume intensified by the enclosed space they were in.

The sound of the explosion echoed loudly round and round the tombs, awakening who could say how many spirits from their long slumbers. As it faded away, David could hear the smack and crack of small stones striking the floor. He'd have given anything to see exactly how much damage had been done. For all he knew, the entire roof might come crashing in on their heads any moment.

The stones stopped falling. There were cracking sounds, and groans, as if stone under stress were preparing to give way. Then a long silence, then more stones clattering to the floor.

'What's happening?' shouted Nabila.

'I don't know.'

'Why don't you light a match?'

He was ready to do so when he heard a new sound. He could not quite make it out at first, and then he realized what it was.

'It's coming through,' he shouted. 'It worked!'

'What's coming through?' asked Nabila, standing to share in his excitement.

'Sand! That's sand pouring through the hole. We did it!'

They made their way as fast as possible to the mound, and started to climb up. Suddenly, they were standing in a steady stream of fine sand. The mound was growing in size every moment.

'Come on, we have to keep this under control.'

With only their hands as tools, they spread the sand, pushing it down from the top of the mound, and as widely out at the bottom as they could manage. Like grain pouring into a silo, the sand rushed down remorselessly.

It went on for a couple of hours, and then, in one instant stopped. The sound stopped, and the darkness in which it had been wrapped. Through the hole came sunlight, sunlight so pure and so bright they had trouble seeing.

It was easy now to climb the mound in order to reach the roof. David went up first. The hole was big enough to squeeze through. He put his head up and looked out on the most beautiful landscape he'd ever seen. Mile after mile of sand dunes, mile after mile of emptiness, mile after mile of light.

He climbed out. Nabila came behind and passed the bergens up to him. Then she climbed through herself. She sat for a long time, while her eyes filled with bitter tears.

He kissed her hard on her mouth, and she kissed him back as if for the first and last time. Their lips and tongues were dry, as though they'd turned to leather.

'We're filthy,' he said. 'I think we should find some water.'

CHAPTER EIGHTY

Hunger became something more than pain. It took everything – air, light, the desert, the open sky – and imbued it with the same sense of gnawing, nauseating hunger that filled their own bodies. And the thirst lay on top, like raw skin on top of a wound.

'Why don't you use the Mobilfone?' she demanded again and again. 'Ask them to take us out of here. You've done your best. It just isn't possible to go on.'

But he did not ring, he would not consider ringing, and somehow they did go on. Over this dune, then over that. Another night came, and they huddled on the sand, shivering, without even the strength to get inside their sleeping bags, thin things of silver foil that seemed incongruous amid such savagery.

Morning found them side by side, not quite touching, fitful in dreams of hunger. Not food, not water, but the lack of them filled their sleep. David dreamt that he was in his garden at home, with Sam and Maddie. They walked round and round, but could find neither vegetables nor water. The whole garden had turned to sand and pebbles. A vulture stirred its clumsy, ragged wings on a branch of the ash tree. The other trees had turned to tamarisk shrubs. In the next garden, camels with tall spindly legs like those of Dali elephants brayed among the chimneypots.

They woke to a grey sky and biting cold.

'David, wake up, something's wrong.'

Nabila shook him into consciousness. She could sense a deep change in the atmosphere.

'It's too early for winter,' David said, sitting up and staring at the shifting field of grey above their heads. In his mind, he could still see Sam scrabbling in the sand to find water.

'Early or not, those look very like clouds. This does happen from time to time, you know. Pressure builds up, clouds form, there's a thunderstorm, and everything clears.'

Even as they spoke, the sky grew more and more like slate. A wind was pushing hard, throwing sand into their faces with mounting force, herding thunderclouds together high above.

'We should get on to high ground,' urged Nabila. 'If it does rain there'll be a colossal downpour. It won't last long, but a lot of water will come down. That's when flash floods occur. They often sweep down gullies like this. We wouldn't stand a chance.'

They struggled to the top of the dune. Both knew there was no guarantee as to where it would rain, if it did. If the clouds opened up half a mile away, they might not be able to get there before the water had sunk into the ground.

'We should dig some trenches,' David said. 'We can line them with our sleeping bags.'

'The bags are quite narrow . . .'

'That doesn't matter. Slit them down one side and the bottom. They'll still be fine to sleep in. We can use them as blankets.'

They got to work, scooping out clumps of sand with the little trenching shovels that they'd used from the start to dig down to water for the camels. As David threw his first shovelful to one side, there was a crack of thunder some distance away, followed in due course by flashes of lightning.

'I'd say that was around five miles over that way,' he said, pointing off towards the north. 'It's coming in hard from the mountains.'

'Is it moving in this direction?'

'It's too soon to tell. It could be moving round in circles for all I know. But if we can go by this wind, I'd say it is coming our way. That's if it doesn't wear itself out before it gets here.'

In the distance, the storm head was building. Steep clouds like rock faces rose with dizzying speed into the seemingly endless sky, while blue and white flashes rushed through them excitedly, charged with enough energy to power a city. In the unnatural light, the desert jumped out of the darkness like a vista at the North Pole.

'It could pass us without raining – that sometimes happens. It could be circling round and round that spot out there.'

'Anything could happen. Let's get these holes dug, then we can wait and see.'

They scooped out four shallow trenches, each one the length and breadth of a man's grave, and they lined them carefully with the light silver material. They removed their shirts and used them to line two smaller holes. It was bitterly cold, but they'd grown used to that. The cloths were weighted down against the wind with a variety of objects from the packs: a gun, a shovel, a rescue beacon. And all the time the sky darkened, and the wind changed its pitch, and the sound of thunder grew until it was above their heads.

And then the wind stopped. They looked up to see

themselves enveloped in an inky darkness that stretched for mile upon mile. Somewhere far away, perhaps as far as the desert's edge, a violet light shivered like dawn. Next moment, a vast downpour of freezing rain crashed on to the desert all round them. A curtain of water washed over everything, and it quickly became difficult to breathe, as though they had fallen into a dark lake or a great inland sea. They crouched, frozen to the bone by the icy water, without any means to warm themselves in all that empty space. The rain fell without cease, and in the gully below, as Nabila had predicted, water rushed in torrents and tore at the sides of the dunes, eating away at them and threatening to send them tumbling.

They lost all measure of time. All that mattered was the cold and how to endure it. They huddled together, finding a thin shelter in one another.

Then it was finished. One moment the downpour, the next a blissful silence and a sky as clear as they could have hoped for. The sun came out, and before long their wet trousers were steaming in the sudden warmth and their skin had started to lose the deadly chill that had set in it.

The trenches were filled with water. They used cups to fill the water containers, and when that was done they drank and drank from what was left until their bellies had grown distended.

It was time to move on.

They made good speed at first, though the water they carried dragged them down. Now that the ache of thirst had been removed, hunger returned to gnaw at them. There was no way forward but to push one foot ahead of the other, no way to find the willpower to go on but to blot out all thoughts and all anticipations. David consulted the compass every mile or so, and with adjustments and bends they crept on towards their objective. He had only one purpose in remaining alive – to reach Karakhoto and make that one telephone call that would summon down death and destruction on the ruined city and whatever lay beneath it. The holocaust he would unleash would engulf himself and Nabila – but having come this far, and being so very close to death, what other choice did they have?

As they walked, the landscape around them began to alter perceptibly. Gradually, the sand started to turn a pale shade of green. Tiny seeds that had lain dormant just beneath the surface for long months or years, now suddenly drenched by rain, had rushed to germinate. They would flourish for a day or two, until the moisture was sucked back from the sand and the dead heat of the sun at noon-day shrivelled them.

They struggled on until mid-afternoon, by which time neither could move another muscle. Without food, they were dying inside. They drank copiously, only to regret it soon after. David developed severe cramps that tormented him until he threw up. Nabila went to her bergen and fetched some herbs to ease his stomach pain. She heated a little water in a metal cup, using tamarisk twigs to make a fire. David sipped the infusion, a foul-tasting mixture smelling strongly of yarrow, and his tight stomach muscles slowly relaxed.

While he drank, he looked out over the vista of soft green. If you half closed your eyes just so and moved your head this way, you could believe you were in an expanse of meadows and tall, sloping lawns.

He opened his eyes to see a gecko making its clumsy way across the ground vegetation. It paused to feed on tiny insects that had sprung to life on the newly grown leaves. David got to his knees and crept towards the little creature, but as he neared it, it glanced at him and ran off to bury itself in the sand.

'Do you still have the herbs you used to treat Mehmet?' he asked.

Nabila nodded.

'I had some left over. Why?'

'If we go on at this rate, one of us is going to have an accident.'

'Would it make any difference if we did?'

'It might.'

He fell silent after that, and sat a little apart from her, watching the day pass. A vulture was circling in the copper sky, a mile or so away, its ragged wings catching fire in the sun. David thought it was waiting for them to die, and that others would join it before long.

When the sun dropped low and the green valley they were in vanished, he remained seated as he had been. Nabila brought two sleeping bag halves and put them gently round his shoulders, and kissed him goodnight. He said nothing. He was making up his mind to do something terrible.

Dawn again, and dew heavy on the grass and shrubs. Nabila did not wake.

He stretched his limbs painfully, and rose from the position he had occupied all night without moving. He went to his bergen, and found the bits and pieces to build what he wanted. Some thin cord cannibalized from rope, the boards from the ammunition box, a spring from his pistol. It took over an hour, and looked a mess when it was done. He tested it several times until he was satisfied it would perform well. Nabila was still asleep.

He found a suitable spot on which to set it up. It was steady, and it operated smoothly.

'What's that?' a sleepy voice behind him asked.

He turned and smiled at her, a lopsided smile that had no connection to anything but itself.

'Lizard trap,' he said. He showed her how it worked.

'You'll need bait,' she said.

'We'll catch some flies.'

She smiled at him with her thin, parched lips, and he smiled back at her, wishing she'd stayed asleep.

She went off a little way to wash and brush her hair and defecate if her bowels permitted. David took the opportunity to go to his bergen again. This time he took out the Ek survival knife that he'd used to amputate Mehmet's hand, and that Nabila had used to slaughter the camels with.

The hardest surface he could put his hands on was a metal armour plate from the tombs: he'd taken it with him in a vain belief that it would somehow find its way back to London and the Chinese department in the British Museum. It was hard work getting his little finger correctly positioned on the plate. He wanted the operation to be as quick and painless as possible. Any slipping or last-second holding back could result in a nasty wound, all to no purpose. A half-severed finger was no earthly use to him.

He tied a tourniquet tightly round his wrist, and at once felt the flow of blood to his hand become constricted.

Taking deep breaths, he laid the finger as accurately as he could on the plate, which he rested on top of the box holding the Mobilfone. He brought the edge of the blade against his skin, and he told himself there was no choice, not if they wanted to live.

'David! What are you doing?'

He looked up to see her coming towards him. There was anxiety in her voice and movements. It had to be now or never. He bit his lip hard and sucked his breath in. His forehead was covered in sweat. He tensed himself, pretending it was not his finger, that it would not hurt.

'David?'

She was running to him. He gripped the knife as hard as he could and slammed down, slicing his finger through in a single motion.

'Oh God, David! What have you done?'

He looked up at her and smiled a tilted smile.

'It's all right,' he said. He nodded at his severed finger, at the blood pouring from it. 'It's done now.'

'Why? What's the point of it?'

'It's bait,' he said. 'We put this in the trap, it attracts flies, and the flies attract lizards.'

His right hand was shaking. He let the knife fall to the ground and clutched his right hand. After the first shock, pain had started to course through the stump.

'Keep your hand upright,' Nabila ordered. 'Press your finger on this spot. Like that.'

She went off to her bergen and returned with dressings and a small bundle of herbs.

'You're very lucky I still have these. I'm very angry with you. Here we are, already in danger, and you pull a stunt like this.'

'I'm sorry, but there was no choice. We can eat lizards. Some of the bigger ones are full of flesh. Edible flesh. We don't have to starve. We're a day or two from Karakhoto – this will get us there.'

'Just keep quiet and give me your hand. This is going to hurt, but like yourself, I have no choice.'

Soon, the stump was expertly cleaned and bandaged, and a concoction of bitter herbs was brewing in the cup.

'You should have spoken to me,' said Nabila.

'And what would you have said?'

'I'd have told you that I was to blame for what happened. I was the one who killed the camels.'

'You weren't to blame for that.'

'No? Then who was to blame?'

'I don't think blame matters, do you?'

She sank down facing him. The smell of new-sprung plants filled her nostrils. She felt tired and insecure. In the act of performing her accustomed skills, she realized how poorly equipped she was to survive in these conditions.

'You should have spoken to me,' she said. 'You should have confided in me.'

'I knew you wouldn't let me.'

'We are in this together, love.'

'No, you're in this because I wanted you to come.'

'I volunteered. I came because I loved you and would not be parted from you. And because they have been killing my people. If we destroy this thing, we will have destroyed it together. Do you understand?'

'Yes.'

'And do you understand how much I love you?'

'Not entirely. I'm glad you're with me. That we'll be together at the end.'

'I love you more than myself,' she said. She reached out her hand and stroked his cheek.

She lifted his severed finger and wrapped it in gauze.

'I hope this works,' she said.

'We have to get there,' he said. 'Somehow or other, we have to stay alive until we reach our destination.'

CHAPTER EIGHTY-ONE

The lizards came, heavy and wall-eyed, like small dinosaurs, sniffing the air in search of prey. They walked into the two traps – Nabila had built a second one – and by noon over a dozen had been captured. They skinned them, and Nabila roasted them slowly over an open fire. There'd been no sign of helicopters since they left the tombs, and neither of them could stomach raw flesh.

Once cooked, they tasted delicious, or so they told one another. David's hand still throbbed with incessant pain, and yet the mere fact of having something to fill their stomachs with made it seem a trivial thing.

'It's like a picnic,' David said, pulling a strip of flesh from his third lizard, and remembering the day they'd gone in search of the Snow Lotus.

When they finished, they stuffed four of the lizards into their bergens, and wrapped David's finger in strips cut from their sleeping blankets. With any luck, they'd get a day or two more of baiting out of it.

Nabila walked on ahead. She still had not quite forgiven him, and she needed time to understand. Perhaps, she thought, she would not live that long.

They made supper on the remaining lizards. David pretended they were chickens, but, to be honest, they tasted more like snakes. All the same, he'd paid more for his two meals than he might have handed over at a smart restaurant for two dozen. If he got back, he planned to recommend lizard steaks to The Ivy.

Nabila took two branches from a tamarisk shrub and tried to dowse.

'You're wasting your time,' said David, as she walked up and down. 'There's still too much moisture in the sand. You'll end up finding wells everywhere.'

But not even that was true. She walked through a wide radius, but the branches never stirred.

A little before the sun went down, David climbed to the top of the nearest dune and gazed out towards the east. There was something strange out there, something he could not identify. He lifted the binoculars and focused them on the horizon. There was something lying in wait for them, something black, without detail. He could not see it more clearly, however much he played with the glasses.

He went back down to where Nabila was resting.

'I've just seen Karakhoto,' he said.

She looked up, not knowing if he was joking or not.

'The Black City?'

'Yes,' he said. 'About seven miles from here. We'll be there tomorrow.'

They left at first light. At their back, a halo still circled an enormous moon dressed in sheets of pearl. As the sunlight strengthened, they noticed that some of the vegetation was already showing signs of withering. By the end of the day, the desert would have reclaimed itself.

Mid-way through the morning, they stopped to eat and drink. Nabila again went through her dowsing routine.

'Are you sure you know what you're doing?' David asked.

'Not really. But it can't be that hard.'

Like a soldier detecting land mines, she swept her twigs back and forward across the sand. Suddenly, the twigs jerked in her hand and pulled down hard. She drew back and the twigs at once grew lifeless. Again she swept them over the narrow patch, and again they leaped.

'David! Quickly, over here!'

He rushed over, and she handed the twigs to him.

'Try it. Go on, see what happens.'

'Where . . .'

'Don't worry about that. Just hold them like this and relax.'

Still sceptical, he walked in a straight line, holding the twigs in front of him. And suddenly they dipped, at the very spot Nabila had identified.

They fetched their shovels and dug down as far as they could. Because the tools had short handles, they were forced to make the hole as wide as possible, so they could climb down into it.

At five feet, they struck moisture; at six feet, cloudy water. Nabila dug a little further, and water gushed up, filling the bottom of the hole. She bent and scooped up a couple of handfuls of water, which she lifted to her mouth. Tilting her head back, she drank. A moment after, she choked and coughed and spat out every drop she could, and kept spitting and coughing, spitting and coughing.

'What is it? What's wrong?'

But Nabila could not answer. David bent and scooped up a little water and tasted it. He spat it out immediately, gagging. It wasn't salty, as he'd thought, but utterly foul, as though a clear chemical had been substituted for the real thing.

He hurried to bring a flask of rainwater down to Nabila. She drank it in great gulps, then spat some out, and very slowly recovered.

They filled in the hole again, and sat beside it, sipping rainwater and slowly recovering from the effects of the water that had not been water.

'Where did it come from?' Nabila asked.

'I'm not sure. But I'm willing to bet that the source is that way. In Karakhoto.'

They went on walking, like shadows passing between sand and sky. David sensed a terrible emptiness building inside him. He had achieved his goal, and there was nothing more to look forward to. He would die here, and that would be an end.

Shortly after noon, they reached a place unlike any other on the face of the planet. It began with small patches where the sand had turned black, or where something like pitch had been poured on to the surface. When David bent down to see what it was, he came up with what looked like an imperfect disc of plastic, rock hard, unbreakable.

The further they walked, the more complete the blackness grew. The landscape on every side now was flat, as though the dunes had melted away. David had often wondered in the past if anything could be more bleak or desolate than the desert; he had his answer here. The landscape through which they were walking was the bleakest on earth. It was as if the blackness had destroyed every trace of life.

About a mile off they could see some buildings. They trudged towards them, bowed down and subdued by the vista on every side.

'What's that over there?' asked Nabila, pointing at a small structure a little off to their right.

They walked across. It turned out to be something like an outsized bus shelter, open on all sides, and without a roof. From what looked like ropes, several objects were hanging from a rod along the top, and resting on a sort of bench below. David went up to one of them. He had a good idea what they were, but he wanted to be sure. He took the knife and prised lumps of the black stuff away from the upper part.

As if emerging from behind a mask, a half-decayed human face appeared out of the black shell.

'Leave it, David,' Nabila urged. 'We've seen enough.'

But he continued to chip away at the carapace, concentrating on the area of the chest. Underneath lay the grey cloth of a work camp prisoner's uniform, and on it a strip of white cloth with numbers.

'They used them as guinea pigs,' he said, stepping away from the stand to which the men had been tied. There had been seven of them. Their hands had been fastened behind their backs. 'Just tied them there and waited to see what would happen.'

Nabila was almost too preoccupied to hear anything he said. She was thinking about Kashgar. If she closed her eyes she could see the whole city turning the colour of ink, its people dead in the streets, its birds dead in the branches of black trees. The only colour was in the sky. There was no birdsong, no barking of dogs, no calling of the muezzins in their black minarets.

There were prisoners everywhere they walked now. Their bodies were black and twisted, as though a sculptor had tried to represent different types of agony, like stations of the Cross. David reckoned they were coming to some central point from which all this blackness had radiated. The buildings they had seen in the distance were only a few hundred yards away.

'I think this must have been the real Karakhoto,' David said. 'These are all ruins.'

'How do you know they weren't made like this by the blast?'

'Because there never was a blast. Not in the sense you mean. They didn't intend to destroy the buildings, just to kill these poor bastards.'

'Leaving the buildings intact.'

'Not exactly. But they may already have a method for getting rid of this stuff.'

'And what about the place where they make these bombs? Is it underneath here?'

'It could be. I have to assume they need some form of air conditioning, and that they take in fresh air from up here. If we could find a vent . . .'

She looked round.

'If they had vents, they'd never have risked coating them in this stuff. The complex must be further on.'

'In which direction?'

'If the link is with Lop Nor, it must be east of here.'

'Wait here,' he said.

He left his bergen with her, and went off, carrying only his binoculars. She watched him walk to the nearest ruin and vanish round the other side. A few minutes later, he reappeared on top of the far wall, and she could see him sweeping the ground in front with his glasses.

When he returned, he was sombre.

'They're camouflaged,' he said, 'but there's no mistaking them. The first ones are about two miles away. Let's get over there now. I want to take a reading on the GPS.'

Without dunes to cross, this last stage of their journey took only a short time. Nabila looked back from time to time, seeing again in the ancient city's disfigurement the fate of her home and everyone in it she loved. David faced forward, determined to see through what he had started.

609

He knelt down at the first vent and put his ear to it. A dull humming noise rose from unguessable depths.

'It's operational,' he said.

'Couldn't your people just parachute in some explosives? You could drop them down these vents. I've seen that sort of thing in films.'

He smiled ruefully, but shook his head.

'Look at it,' he said, looking out at the field across which vents were scattered. 'It's vast, and God knows how deep it is. Explosives would only tickle it. By the time I got to the second vent, they'd have a troop of their best security men up here.'

'What can you do, then?'

'Telephone the co-ordinates back to my base. They already have planes waiting at Dehra Dun in India. They'll open the place up with two or three passes of carpet bombing, then penetrate the rest with nukes. It's the only way, Nabila. Believe me.'

'Dare I ask what's supposed to happen to us?'

'We start walking. If we're very lucky, we'll be out of range when they drop the bombs. If we're too slow or they come in sooner, we won't even know what hit us.'

'And when do you think they'll come in?'

'Tonight,' he answered, looking up at the sun as it pressed down towards the western horizon. 'They'll fly in very high, release very high, and get the hell out before the entire Chinese air force comes on their tails.'

She looked at him, agonized. There seemed to be nowhere in any of this for people.

'They're fighting a war,' he said. 'In order to stop a war.'

CHAPTER EIGHTY-TWO

They spent about an hour calculating the rough dimensions of the complex. When that was done and the GPS reference obtained, all that remained was for David to make his call.

'Do you trust telephones?' he asked as he swung up the Mobilfone's lid.

'No. What about you?'

He shook his head.

'What if our problem back there wasn't the tomb or the sand, but the phone itself?'

'You can always call out an engineer.'

'On what?'

'Your other phone, of course.'

David picked up the receiver and slowly keyed in a number. His hand shook as he did so. He heard the key signals, then a long series of crackles, beeps, and buzzes that suggested he might be in business after all. Then silence. His heart sank. Please, he whispered, not after all this, not after coming so far. Not after what they did to Sam.

'*Welcome to Long Distance Communications,*' intoned a recorded message, a woman's voice. '*If you would like to speak to Vauxhall Central, press one. If you would like to speak to West Europe Desk, press two. If you would like to speak to East Europe Desk, press three. If you would like to speak to Africa Desk, press four . . .*'

He sat, nursing the receiver, watching the phone's LCD display, waiting impatiently to make contact, cursing the absurdities of so-called technological advances that made urgent calls take ten times as long.

'If you would like to speak to Middle East Desk, press eleven. If you would like to speak to China Desk, press twelve. If you would like . . .'

David keyed in twelve.

'Please wait,' commanded another, older woman, in tones about as maternal as an air-raid siren.

He looked round. It had occurred to him that they might have detectors somewhere on the surface, and that he might even now be making a guest appearance on a bank of security monitors several floors below.

'Please enter your password and personal ID number.'

He did so. Beeps and warbles received them. It was like playing some dumb computer game.

'Further identification is required. Please enter your mother's maiden name.'

He complied, growing more and more frustrated. At this rate, his batteries would run out before he got through.

'Your father's middle names.'

'Oh, for God's sake, hurry up,' he shouted into the mouthpiece, while beeping in the required information.

There was more warbling, then a man's voice came on the line. For a second, David thought he'd won, then he realized that this too was a recording. Had the word 'emergency' totally disappeared from the vocabulary of the British Secret Service, he wondered?

'This call has been diverted. Please wait while we patch you through to a secure outside line. When you are connected, please speak with confidence.'

What the hell was going on? The call should have been dealt with at headquarters, and without this ridiculous delay. An outside line? 'Speak with confidence'? Just who were they trying to fool?

'What's wrong, love? Can't you get through?'

He shrugged.

'I don't know. Something isn't right.'

There was a regular UK ringing tone that lasted some minutes. Then a receiver was picked up.

'Gilchrist. Who is this?'

He remembered Gilchrist, a junior officer who'd passed quickly through the maze of desk politics and become a senior official at the age of thirty-two.

'This is David Laing. How secure is this line?'

'Absolutely secure, Mr Laing. Your secrets are safe with me.'

'This particular secret is not for your personal consumption. I want you to access file number CJ4 9PWY X05. Shall I repeat that?'

'No, I have it. Just a moment.'

There was the sound of a keyboard being tapped.

'Yes, I have it here. It requires several passwords. I can enter the first three: do you have the others?'

David gave them to him.

'Fine. I'll just . . . Oh, excellent, we're in. Now, what do I have to do?'

'You will see that I have been given authority to order an air strike on co-ordinates in western China. I now have those co-ordinates, and I'm ordering you to press the buttons at your end. You are to contact the PM for authorization. He will issue orders directly to Air Chief Marshal Sir Thomas Wingrove, who will issue the order for the attack. You do not contact anyone else, you do not waste any time. Once the attack has been completed, you will destroy the file. Have you any questions?'

There was a short silence. David wondered if Gilchrist was on his own.

'Unfortunately, I do, sir.' His voice came back from a great distance. 'Do you have a place name for your location?'

'I'm in a place called Karakhoto. Or, to be more exact, two miles east of it.'

Another silence. This time the line filled with crackling.

'And the weapons complex?'

'I'm standing on top of it.'

'You can vouch for that? I mean, what exactly is it you've found?'

'I've found air vents. Hundreds of them, spread over a wide area. And we've found a sort of test site a couple of miles away to the west. That's the old city. They've been using political prisoners as guinea pigs there . . .'

Gilchrist broke in.

'You're telling me that so far you've found nothing but vents?'

'Of course I am. This complex is underground. The only things on the surface are vents.'

'And what exactly do you propose I should do?'

David breathed in hard. All he wanted to do was to take Nabila and walk out of this mad place, find a way out of Sinkiang, fly back to London, and see Maddie. But he knew he could not do that. It could be Maddie's face they chipped free from a black casing next time. If the devices were delivered to Saddam Hussein . . .

'I want you or someone more senior to order the strike as planned. I take it everything's still in place.'

'There are still planes at Dehra Dun, yes. But the Indians are getting a little stroppy. The repercussions for them could be serious.'

'Then use them before the whole thing gets tied up in some pointless diplomatic row.'

'I'm afraid it isn't that simple.'

'It was when I last talked about this. There was full agreement. I take it bombs have not yet been delivered to Hussein?'

'There have been no reports suggesting that. The man in charge of that end of the operation is someone called Donaldson. Do you know him?'

'Not well. Look, what are you trying to tell me? That this is all off? That I've just risked my life for absolutely nothing? That this complex is to be left alone and allowed to go on building weapons and exporting them so long as nobody gets upset in the Foreign Office?'

'Calm down, Mr Laing. Calm down and listen. I can't order a strike until I have positive confirmation that the site you've found is the weapons complex we've been after. A collection of air-conditioning vents isn't enough. We need more than that. I'm sure you can see why.'

'No, I can't see why. You have the boy's testimony and Matthew Hyde's evidence. You know about the Iraqi involvement, and the nature of the weapons they want to import. You've got dozens of reports from field agents. You've got a defector who'd seen written proof that the site had been built and made operational. And now I'm standing on top of the fucking thing telling you to drop some fucking bombs, because otherwise there are going to be a lot of dead soldiers out there who deserved better than to be sent out in their Noddy suits just to line up for Saddam Fucking Hussein to play games with.'

'Don't get beside yourself, Laing. And don't get above yourself. You're just the field agent. You don't make the decisions. Some other poor sod is going to have to push the button and take the consequences if there's a mistake.'

'There is no mistake. There is something buried beneath the spot on which I am standing. I can assure you personally that it has not been built as a factory for cute toys, Christmas decorations, or chopsticks. It has been buried and camouflaged for a reason, and if you can't guess what that reason is, you've no right to hold a senior position in Six, much less make decisions that affect real people's lives.'

'I'll accept that you've been under strain recently, Mr Laing. But, frankly, I don't think this attitude is getting you anywhere. I don't care if you're standing on the edge of Mount Doom with a ring in your hand, I want some hard evidence that will let me go to the Prime Minister for authorization. Unless you've forgotten, he is a simpering pinkie trotting dog with a Foreign Minister who thinks human rights are a fit basis on which to conduct foreign relations. He will need to be convinced.'

'Precisely how?'

'You're the agent on the ground, as you insist on telling me. You get the evidence and we're in business. Simple as that.'

'If I try to get in there, I'll be a dead man. I promise you that.'

'You've taken plenty of risks so far. Just one more to make it worthwhile.'

David sighed. It was worse than being trapped in a hospital ward where nobody believed you were sane.

'You'll need the co-ordinates,' he said. 'In case you decide I'm right after all.'

'The co-ordinates? You already gave me them.'

He read a string of numbers down the line.

'Where the hell did you get them? I've only just arrived here, and I know I didn't give them to you. How could you have them?'

'That's . . .' For the first time there was hesitation in Gilchrist's voice. He realized he'd said something he shouldn't have. 'That's classified,' he murmured, as though his merely saying so would close the matter.

'I don't care if it's a cosy secret between you and the Queen Mother, I think I have a right to know how you got hold of them – and how long you've had them. And why the hell I wasn't given them.'

'You sound like a petulant schoolboy. Let's keep this professional. I'll institute inquiries, and when I'm ready I'll get back to you.'

'"I'll get back to you"? What the fuck are you talking about? Maybe you've forgotten, but I'm not sitting in some leather-upholstered chair in a chic office overlooking the Thames. I'm in the middle of a fucking desert, I have no food and precious little water. If you don't intend to blow this stinking fleapit out of the ground, then at least say so and send somebody in to take us out of here.'

'Us?'

'I have a companion.'

'I see. A woman?'

'Yes. Her name is Nabila Muhammadju. She's a doctor of Uighur medicine.'

'I shall certainly give some thought to the feasibility of lifting you out. You're our agent and you're entitled to that privilege. I'm not sure about the woman. She isn't our responsibility.'

'She's my responsibility. If you want to be an arsehole, just go ahead. But I'm walking out of here with her, and when we get back to London . . .'

'Don't be such a moron. I said I'd look into the matter, and I will certainly raise the issue of the – shall I describe her as a woman or a girl?'

'Just send a helicopter in. I imagine you can come up with one that has more than room for two?'

David's finger was poised to terminate the conversation, when Gilchrist came in again, in a different tone.

'Mr Laing, before we go any further, there is something I have to tell you. Are you still there?'

'I'm listening.'

'I'm sorry to have to tell you this, but there was no other way. It's about your wife.'

'Lizzie?'

'She was killed in a car crash a few days ago, along with her brother Laurence. In the Lake District, I believe.'

'Oh, God. Is she . . . ? When's the funeral?'

'It took place yesterday. I understand Sir Anthony took care of it all.'

'What about Maddie?'

'Maddie? I don't . . .'

'My daughter, you idiot.'

'Please don't be rude. I'm doing my best here. This isn't easy for me.'

'I'm sorry. Is that all you can tell me?'

'That's all I know. I can try to find out more. Maybe if you ring later.'

'You're forgetting my present circumstances. Since we seem to agree about the co-ordinates for this place, I want you to make the necessary phone calls to obtain authorization for the air strike. If you can arrange to fly us out as well, I'd be grateful.'

'I'll get on to it right away.'

Gilchrist put the receiver down and pressed a button beside the phone to stop recording.

'How did he take the news about Lizzie?' Anthony Farrar strolled over from the sofa on which he had been sitting.

'I think it came as a bit of a shock.'

'Of course it did. Could I have the tape, please?'

Gilchrist handed over the cassette on which he'd made the recording of the conversation. It could go back again after a little careful editing.

'He sounded certain about this weapons complex.'

'He gets enthusiastic. The whole thing's nonsense, of course. What he's stumbled on is a water purification plant. It's part of a desert reclamation scheme. Now, I'll just take this and be on my way. I want you to handle all calls from Laing. And I'd prefer it if you said nothing to anyone else at this stage. Let's see how it develops.'

David pressed the redial button a few times, then dashed down the receiver in a rage.

'What's wrong, love?' Nabila asked. 'Has something happened?'

He pulled angrily away from her, then halted and came back, and she took him in her arms and held him. Haltingly, he told her the gist of his conversation.

'And he told you your wife is dead?'

'Lizzie? Yes, if he's telling the truth.'

'What do you want to do?'

He looked around him. It felt as though the world had come to an end, as though he and Nabila were the last human beings to survive in the ruins.

'I want to get back to Maddie,' he said.

'All right, that's what we'll do. We've got enough water to get us to a clean well. We can trap more lizards. All we have to do is head directly north. A hundred miles or so. We could do it in ten days. We could still make it out alive.'

'And this?' he asked. 'My mission. Whatever Gilchrist chooses to think, or pretend to think, it's still here.'

'Make a record of the co-ordinates. Sort it out when you get home. Bypass Gilchrist, go straight to the top. But let's get out of here before we die.'

'And you?' he asked. 'What will you do? What do you want to do?'

She hesitated. It really wasn't up to her. What freedom did she have? Her world and all the people in it had been destroyed. She could escape with her life, but what remained for her after that?

'Will you come to London with me?' he asked.

'London?'

'I can get you a passport. Once we're out of China, we'll see if you can have a permanent one.'

'But I don't want to leave China.'

He touched her cheek gently, pushing back a strand of hair that had strayed across her eyes.

'I think you have to, dear. Once they know who you are, the authorities will hunt you down and kill you.'

'I want to take revenge. For what was done to Kashgar.'

'Then leave China with me. You can do more with my help from outside than you could ever hope to do here. Believe me.'

'But . . . where will I live? What will I do?'

'You can live with me. I have a house. You could help me look after Maddie.'

'What do you mean? You think I want to be your private nurse? Give me a bed and a residence permit, and I'll put myself at your disposal . . .'

He shook his head. He meant nothing like that.

'I'm not asking you to be a nurse, or a home help, or a private clinic for Maddie.'

'What then?'

'I'm asking you to be my wife.'

She looked at him in amazement, then took him in her

arms, and held him tightly, as if there was a risk of his flying away. They remained locked in their embrace for a long time.

'Even though I'm not a Muslim?' he asked.

'Even though you're the blackest heathen on the face of the earth.'

'Even though I nearly killed you out here?'

She kissed him on the lips.

'It doesn't matter any longer. I would have died back home. No doubt of that.'

'It's starting to get dark,' he said. 'I think we should get out of this area before the sun goes down.'

She did not say anything. She seemed to have frozen. David shook her.

'Nabila, we've got to go.'

She pulled back slightly. Her hair stroked his cheek.

'It's already too late,' she said.

He drew away from her and turned to look in the direction she was facing.

The ground must have opened up somewhere to disgorge them. There must be twenty in all, he thought. They wore well-pressed grey uniforms with red insignia at the collars and red berets on their shaven heads, and in their hands they carried sub-machine-guns poised to shoot.

He raised his hands resignedly and waited for them to come.

CHAPTER EIGHTY-THREE

Chaofe Ling

There was a short flight of steps leading downwards, then a lift. They made him stand in the lift, two men behind him, two holding his arms. No one hit him, no one threatened him, no one spoke to him. He indulged himself in a little fantasy, that he'd been captured by aliens and was being taken aboard their ship. After what he'd seen outside, he wondered if the fantasy could possibly be worse than reality. Even little green men might have a code of ethics, or be burdened with consciences.

He counted the buttons and made seven levels. To his vague disappointment, they stopped at Level 3, and he was frogmarched out into a corridor that seemed never to end. As he stepped from the lift, he shouted 'Haberdashery!' at the top of his voice. The cry bounced and slid along the never-ending passage, and died back into the silence that was always there. He wondered what they were doing with Nabila.

He spoke to them after that in Uighur, for form's sake. He asked questions, made vociferous protests, but he doubted if even one of them could understand a word of the language. He planned to keep up his pretence as long as he could, though he didn't expect for a moment that they would let him go free as a result. His story was that he and Nabila, a paramedic, had been accompanying a British explorer who had died en route, along with six others of their companions. It was important to have a story during an interrogation, it provided something for the mind to fasten on, something to embroider, something to lay traps with.

One thing worried him, and that was how exactly they'd known that he and Nabila were there in the first place. There were no ground-level personnel detectors at the site, he'd have staked his life on it. Who, after all, was likely to approach the complex on foot?

He was made to sit on a small go-kart, and escorted on a long journey that took him to door number 74:7 (3). The number was like all the other numbers, the door was like all the other doors. Except for one thing: the tiny character painted in black lacquer, the character *p'u*, simplicity.

'What about Nabila?' he asked when they pushed him inside. 'The woman who was with me.' But they did not answer. He tried in Chinese, but they pretended not to understand. They left, closing the door behind them.

On the other side of the door he saw, not a room, but a wall, and for a moment he started to panic. Then he saw that it was a ghost wall painted in black. On it was painted in white lacquer the character *su*, the simple and unadorned self.

Ghost walls were built in order to keep evil spirits out of rooms or buildings. The spirits can travel only in a straight line, so the short wall impedes their movement, since they have no way of going round it. David hesitated briefly, then went round the wall to the right.

Before him lay a vast room, its walls painted black, and its only illumination coming from two long rows of paper lanterns that hung down from the ceiling like the bellies of incandescent white doves.

In the centre of the room stood a plain chair of lacquered wood. The finish of the lacquer was Japanese in its simplicity, but the contours of the chair were unmistakably Chinese. The chair was placed on a square of red silk, about six foot by six. The floor was lacquered perfectly, and if David looked down he could see himself reflected in it.

He began to work his way round the room, brushing the walls lightly with his hand. The pain in the stump on his left hand was growing distressing, like a throbbing ache in a rotten tooth. He found the door, marked only by a small red light that flashed every few seconds, and an electronically operated lock that gave way to neither blows nor caresses.

'You're wasting your time,' intoned a voice from behind. He swung round to see a grave-faced man sitting in the lacquered chair, watching him.

David strode up to him. He was about fifty years old, tall, with a strong chin and thick eyebrows. It was not a face so much as a palimpsest on which the grey devices of a lifetime had been written: hate and scorn and pride and contempt and murderous rage, the seven sins times seven. David looked into his eyes and away again. He had not forgotten the face. How could he have?

'Colonel Chang Zhangyi?'

Chang Zhangyi nodded. He was dressed in black, very simply, as though to blend with the room. 'Welcome to Chaofe Ling. Sit down next to me, here on the floor. I'd like to talk with you.'

'I'd prefer to stand.'

Chang Zhangyi looked at him as though about to order him to sit, then thought better of it.

'If that is your choice.'

'It is.' He paused. 'What is this place anyway?'

'This room? I thought you'd be intrigued. This is my

624

meditation room. I like to spend at least an hour each day quieting my inner self. Every year I spend a month at a monastery in the mountains north of Guilin. Does that surprise you?'

'Why should it surprise me? We all have our weaknesses.'

'You don't like me, do you, Mr Laing?'

'That's beside the point.'

'On the contrary, it is the point. Liking and hating wear us out. I've brought you here because I think I can spare you all that.'

'And if I prefer to keep my likes and dislikes as they are?' David asked.

The other man looked at him for a long time without answering. David watched him, perfectly still. Inside, he was screaming to know what had become of Nabila.

'You have come to the end of a very long journey, Laing Shiansheng,' Chang Zhangyi said finally. 'All your battles, all your journeyings, all your yearnings end here.'

'What exactly do you mean by that? I'm to be put to death, is that all you mean?'

'Not if you do not wish it. No one will threaten you while you are here. You've been very brave. You've survived great perils, you've endured intense deprivations. None of that should go unrecognized or unrewarded.'

'I don't understand. My purpose in coming here was to destroy this place. If my superiors in London give the go-ahead, it could still be bombed out of existence.'

Chang Zhangyi shook his head slowly. His gaze seemed fixed somewhere beyond the room.

'That will not happen. Please suffer no anxiety on that account.'

'Why not? You can't be sure . . .'

'Because Anthony Farrar will not pass your message on to anyone else. Because he will tell his colleagues he has had confirmation that you are dead, and that there is no Black City in the Taklamakan. That is why.'

David felt a surge of pure fury rise up in him. He could never have found words to express it. He knew now who had killed Sam and who had betrayed Matthew Hyde.

'Try not to think about revenge,' said Chang Zhangyi. 'It's futile. You will never see Anthony Farrar again. If you can reconcile yourself to that, you can get on with your own life.'

'I don't wish for reconciliation.'

'No, but you must. And in time you will.'

'You say I'm to be rewarded for what I've gone through. That makes very little sense. I came here as your enemy, I am still your enemy. Why don't you just have me taken out and shot? Why make an exception of me?'

'Laing Shiansheng, you are not my enemy. You and I have never been enemies, and we are not enemies now. Forget about the Chinese Politburo or the People's Liberation Army or the Guojia Anchuanbu.'

'Forget about them?'

'They are of no real importance.'

'Then why have you . . . ?'

'I am a member of the Concilium of the Hui Hou. You have heard of us, of course. You have, perhaps, thought of us from time to time. Fantasized about us.'

David went rigid. For the first time since entering this place, he felt frightened.

'I have heard . . . a little.'

'Yes. Everyone has heard a little. But we are much more than whatever you will have heard.'

'I've heard you are butchers.'

'Only when we have to be. We abhor violence unless it favours proper ends.'

'And what ends are those?'

'Order. Law. Security. The elimination of the weak.'

'What do you want with me?' David demanded. 'What are the Hui Hou doing out here? I thought you belonged in cities. Like cockroaches.'

Chang Zhangyi's eyebrows rose.

'I am truly surprised at you, Laing Shiansheng. You know so much about this country and its secrets, and yet you say you are ignorant of the true position the Hui Hou hold in Chinese society.'

The colonel's hair was brushed back from his head, leaving his forehead exposed. David noticed small pock marks near the hairline. Chang Zhangyi went on speaking.

'Did it never occur to you that the government in Peking could never have carried out a project like this on their own? Didn't you know that, whenever they face problems they cannot solve without help, they turn to us? The arrangement made between Chaofe Ling and Saddam Hussein will bring vast quantities of oil into China. Most of it will remain in the hands of the Hui Hou. We are also negotiating deals with Iran and Libya. In due course, the United States will want a bomb as well, and I assure you they will pay us anything we ask. Others will follow.

'Where do you imagine this complex obtained the raw materials it needed to make the warheads? How do you think they were able to attract foreign scientists to work on the programme? I suppose you don't even know that over a dozen British scientists have been working here since the project's inception.'

'And me?' asked David. 'What do you want with me? Do you expect me to work on your project as well?' His back and legs ached, and he longed to sit on the floor. But that would have made it seem that he was sitting at Chang Zhangyi's feet, like a disciple with his master. And David did not consider himself Chang Zhangyi's disciple.

627

The colonel looked at him as if seeing him for the first time. His gaze reminded David of a lizard's stare – cold, half-focused, potentially fatal.

'I told you that your prowess should not go unrewarded. You thought you were brought here to be punished. Instead, I propose to offer you a reward beyond your imagining.'

'If it can't be imagined, how can it . . . ?'

'Be quiet for a moment, and I will tell you. It can take as long as thirty years for an aspirant to be admitted within the ranks of the Hui Hou. Some men die while waiting. A man like Sir Anthony Farrar, for example, has been close to us for many years, but he has never been properly committed, and has not been offered entrance even to the *zhu yuanchuan*.'

David recognized the phrase, the 'bamboo circle', as one he'd heard whispered wherever a group of Chinese gathered for drink or food. It referred to the lowest level of the Hui Hou hierarchy. People spoke of joining it as others might speak of winning the lottery or marrying into money.

'You, however,' Chang Zhangyi continued, 'are the sort of man we actively seek. I am offering you admission directly to the *si yuanchuan*, the silk circle, the second level of allegiance. You will enter it at the seventh grade. Before long you will be able to qualify for admission to the *yu yuanchuan*, the feather circle. That is a rare honour. With that honour comes tangible reward and the beginnings of a new responsibility.'

'I don't expect you're offering any of this for nothing. The one thing I do know about the Hui Hou is that they exact a price for everything they give.'

The colonel nodded.

'If you are to have such privileges, we should have

something in return. You are now a dead man, Laing Shiansheng. In a few days or weeks, your death will be recorded officially. Your wife is dead, your son is dead, and it seems that it will not be very long before your daughter dies as well. You can never return to England, never go back anywhere as yourself.

'A man such as you needs help to start a new life, otherwise he really will find himself dead and buried. Some have to find huge sums of money to carry off such a thing. You don't have to. You only have to tell us what you know. You have spent years watching China, gathering information, sifting it, passing it on to your superiors. Your insights will be invaluable to us.'

'And to Chinese intelligence, no doubt.'

'Perhaps. They would certainly express an interest. If they pay a sufficiently high price, they may have all they ask for.'

'Why should you or anyone else be interested in what I know? You have that simpering bastard Farrar. He'll already have told you far more than I can.'

Chang Zhangyi shook his head.

'Farrar knows less than you imagine. We aren't interested in the sort of gossip he sniffs up from the floors inside Vauxhall House.'

'My answer is no. You should have known that. I have a loyalty to my colleagues. If Farrar's a traitor, it doesn't mean I have to be one.'

'No matter. I don't expect a positive answer inside a month or more. There's no rush. You will be well looked after. A surgeon will take care of that finger. You will find that life at Chaofe Ling can prove more pleasant than life in many other places.'

'What about Nabila? What's been done with her? I want to see her.'

'Is she important to you? We thought she was just your guide. And perhaps of some use as a receptacle for your sexual release.'

David fought down an impulse to hit him. If Chang Zhangyi was deliberately seeking to provoke him, he preferred to remain calm.

'I plan to marry her. If you want my compliance in anything, make sure she's safe. I'll rely on you for that.'

An amused light glinted briefly in Chang Zhangyi's eyes.

'I see,' he said. 'In that case, I'll have her brought to your quarters. Would you like me to conduct you there?'

'I don't seem to have much choice.'

'No, not much. Mr Laing, let me show you something. As a token of our goodwill.'

He reached into his tunic pocket and drew out a folded sheet of paper. Without unfolding it, he passed it to David.

'I shall arrange for this to be sent to your daughter,' he said. 'I know it will mean a lot to her.'

David unfolded the paper. It contained several lines in Chinese script. A name, followed by an address. Zheng Juntao, the student Maddie had loved, who had disappeared into some forgotten work camp, and who had now returned to life with an address in a small town in Chengdu Province.

'They can be reunited,' Chang Zhangyi said. 'He is not that important. I can arrange for him to be given a passport and an exit visa. If you want. It is up to you.'

'May I . . . keep this?'

Chang Zhangyi nodded, and David put it in his pocket. It would change Maddie's life to have this, he thought. Change it, and perhaps save it. The Hui Hou pressed a hard bargain. How could he deny his own daughter the gift of life?

CHAPTER EIGHTY-FOUR

His quarters turned out to be a suite of rooms as richly furnished as those you might find in a grand hotel. The bathroom, a place of tinted mirrors and hidden lights, boasted a huge sunken bath and a separate Jacuzzi. In the bedroom, a walk-in wardrobe took up two walls and was stuffed with shirts and trousers and a long rack of silk ties. There were books to read in seventeen languages, records to play, videos to watch, and a large wide-screen television. One room was fitted out as a gym, with state of the art equipment made by a company in Seattle. Not even the best Chinese hotels had fittings like these.

'You will get used to luxury,' said Chang Zhangyi.

David shook his head.

'What's the point of having fifty suits and a hundred ties and hand-made shoes if I have to wear them here?'

'You won't always be here. When enough time has passed, you will be given a new identity and a place to live. You don't have to stay in China unless you want to.'

'I couldn't live in China.'

'I do not mean China as you know it, Laing Shiansheng. Trust me, there is more to the Hui Hou than even you can guess. In a little while, you and I shall travel together. I want you to see the monastery I mentioned. The monks would make you at home. It is one of seven monasteries in that region belonging to the Hui Hou. You would be welcome at any one of them. After all you have endured, they will offer you a little peace.' He paused. 'But now is not the time to talk of this.'

Chang Zhangyi turned and opened the door. As he stood in the opening, he turned back to David.

'Laing Shiansheng, you will understand why you may not have a key. It is, I think, as much for your own safety as for ours.'

David bowed low.

'I have all I need here, thank you,' he said. 'Except for Nabila.'

'Of course. I will see to it that she is brought to you shortly. In the meantime, perhaps you would like two or three of our prettier girls to help you bathe. You must be tired and filthy after such a long journey.'

'No, thanks. I'd rather bathe alone.'

'Very well. I have some urgent paperwork to see to. It should take me about half an hour. Time enough for you to freshen yourself. Someone will bring you to me when I'm ready, and I'll show you round.'

The colonel looked hard at him for a moment, then bowed and was gone. The second the door closed, David started to search the suite. He was looking for three things: cameras, audio bugs, and anything he could turn into a weapon.

In the course of the next ten minutes, he located and destroyed eight bugs and three cameras. The weapon wasn't so easy. There were no blades anywhere, not even a blunt paper knife.

The bell rang. When he opened the door, Nabila was standing in the corridor with two guards. One of them grinned and said he'd been instructed by Colonel Chang Zhangyi to deliver this package.

'She stinks of camel's piss,' said the other. 'I'd give her a good wash if I were you.'

She stepped forward into the suite, and David took her and kissed her on the forehead. He used his foot to kick the door shut. It clicked, and Nabila fell into his arms, sobbing.

She had thought he was dead, she said between sobs, and wished she were dead herself. He told her about Chang Zhangyi and all he had said. About his promises, and his veiled threats. About the sheet of paper that could give life back to Maddie.

'I think you have a simple choice,' she said. 'Turn them down and be shot, and leave Maddie to whatever terrors her life has left. Let me be shot as well. Or give them what they want in return for her life.'

'You know it's not that simple . . .'

The telephone rang. He'd tried it earlier and found he could not ring out.

He picked up the receiver. A woman's voice came on the line, speaking in English. Her voice was well-educated, softly modulated. A mental image formed of the speaker: young, attractive, ambitious.

'Mr Laing, my name is Huang Zhengmei. I am the personal assistant to Colonel Chang Zhangyi. The colonel is still tied up with his paperwork, but he is eager to commence your tour of inspection as soon as possible. I will come to your suite in ten minutes and bring you to his offices. Please be ready, both yourself and Dr Muhammadju.'

David put down the telephone.

'Looks like Chang Zhangyi wants to see us both.'

Nabila shuddered. She remembered the massacre in

front of the Shaanshi Mosque, the growling tanks, the tall figure strutting among the dead and wounded. And Kashgar. She remembered Kashgar.

'I can't face him,' she said. 'I can't bear to look at him.'

'You have to. We both have to go through with this charade.'

'Why can't they just kill us and be done with it?'

'They may still do that. I'm more worried about you than myself – you're of no real use to them. We can't just sit about waiting for them to take you off, or shoot us in the back of the head when it suits them.'

'What can we do? We don't have any weapons. How on earth are we supposed to turn the tables? Even if we got out of here by some miracle, we'd just find ourselves back exactly where we started.'

She sank down on to a sofa and closed her eyes. She felt wrung out and drained of hope, like someone who has looked down a long street, waiting for someone to come, and seen only dust moving in spirals. With an effort, she opened her eyes.

'If you could make telephone contact again, ask your people to send a helicopter in at least.'

Briefly, he told her about Anthony Farrar and the cessation of hope from home.

She said nothing for a while, then looked up eagerly.

'We can make our own weapons,' she said. 'How long have we got?'

'About five minutes, I think. But I've already looked all over the place – there's nothing here we can use. There's a little kitchen, but all it has are blunt dinner knives.'

'Coat hangers?'

'Wooden. Built-in.'

'What about . . . ?'

She got up quickly and ran into the bathroom. Next to the washbasin stood several bottles of aftershave and toner. She took one and slipped it into her pocket, then tossed a second to David.

'Hit their eyes,' she said. 'This will blind somebody for a minute or two.'

Next to the main mirror was a round shaving mirror at the end of a crisscross extending arm.

'Quickly,' she yelled, 'have you got a screwdriver?'

'Of course not.'

But she was already on the move again, yanking open drawers, rifling through their contents. From the third she triumphantly pulled out a nail file. She used it to unscrew the circular steel band that held the mirror together, and pulled out two sheets of glass. With the help of a towel, she snapped off several large slivers.

David had gone back to the room that passed as a combination of study, library, and TV room. He pulled out several desk drawers and came running back to the bathroom with a roll of Sellotape. The tape wrapped again and again round the long glass slivers to make strong handles.

Nabila tore strips from the towel.

'Wrap the blade in this,' she said, passing one to David. 'You don't want to cut yourself walking along, or . . .'

The bell rang, an incongruous musical chime, the sort of thing David's Aunt Trudy would have loved.

A young woman was waiting. She was dressed in PLA fatigues, but contrived to make them look smart. A calculating face matched the voice. When introductions were completed, she looked him up and down.

'You haven't changed, Mr Laing?'

'My clothes? No, I'd prefer to wait until there's time for a proper soak. I've got a lot of sand and sweat to wash off. Fresh clothes will feel a lot better once I'm properly clean.'

'Is Dr Muhammadju here yet?'

'Yes, she's inside.'

'May I come in? I'd like to make her acquaintance.'

David smiled and ushered her in.

'I'm afraid she's in the bathroom,' he said.

'Colonel Chang Zhangyi will be growing impatient. I think we should leave soon. Would you mind asking her to hurry?'

'I'm not sure if . . .'

Huang Zhengmei went up to the door and knocked on it. Speaking in fluent Uighur, she asked Nabila to get a move on. A minute or two passed, then Nabila appeared.

'I'm afraid I left a bit of a mess in there,' she declared.

Huang Zhengmei looked at her appraisingly.

'You don't seem to have spent much time in any bathroom recently.' She hesitated. 'If you'll forgive me, I need to use the bathroom myself.'

Without another word, she strode past Nabila into the bathroom. There was a click as she locked the door behind her.

Nabila hurried across to David.

'I've done my best to tidy everything up. She can't possibly guess.'

'We might have been watched. I couldn't find a camera in there, but there has to be at least one.'

'She got here while we were still finishing off.'

'They could have telephoned her.'

'What if she . . . ?'

'We don't have any choice.'

There was the sound of a toilet flushing, then Huang Zhengmei appeared in the doorway.

'Thank you,' she said. Her eyes moved from one to the other of them. There was no warmth in her face, only cold intelligence. She brought her right hand out from behind her back. In it she was holding two small slivers of glass.

'I was most concerned to find these on the floor,' she said. 'You could very well have hurt yourself. Glass is extremely . . . dangerous. And I noticed that part of your shaving mirror has been broken. Do you have the rest of the glass? I'll make sure maintenance take care of it at once. And I think you need a fresh roll of Sellotape.'

She crossed to the telephone and picked up the receiver.

'*Wei*. This is Huang Zhengmei. Send two guards to the jade suite right away.' She dropped the receiver and looked round to see David standing a couple of feet from her.

'Why do you need two guards to deal with some broken glass?'

'I think you know, Mr Laing. I think . . .'

She froze. Nabila had come round behind her and was pressing something hard against her throat.

'I think you know more than you need to, Miss Huang,' Nabila said. 'It may prove very dangerous knowledge. Slitting your throat open would come very easily to me. Now, stand up slowly and go back to the bathroom.'

Once there, David cut a long strip from a bath towel, making a rope with which he could tie Huang Zhengmei's hands behind her back. He then gagged her, using a rolled-up face flannel and a shorter strip of towel. Once she was secured, they hurried to make stronger ropes from the bed-sheets. They'd barely finished when the doorbell rang again.

'Huang Zhengmei asked us to come here. Is something wrong?'

The guards were new faces, but they seemed no friendlier than their predecessors.

'She had to go back to her own quarters. A violent headache. But she rang to ask if you could take us to Colonel Chang Zhangyi's office. He's been expecting us for some time. In fact, Huang Zhengmei said he was getting impatient.'

The guard made a quick phone call and nodded.

'His secretary says I'm to get you there as fast as possible. Let's go.'

CHAPTER EIGHTY-FIVE

'Let me show you my realm. It will make your eyes pop out of your head.'

Chang Zhangyi sat aloof and alone on a high metallic chair, from which he looked down on David and Nabila. He had changed from black into the well-pressed tunic and trousers of a Guojia Anchuanbu official. A half-smoked cigarette hung from his mouth. At his back, a huge window of plate glass allowed him to gaze out over rows of desks at which functionaries worked, like restless fish in a vast freshwater tank.

'I'd like you to see as much as possible,' he said to David, marking him out as beyond the pale. He'd ceased to pose a threat, so why shouldn't he see everything?

'I know you came here to destroy this place,' he went on. 'I don't hold that against you; you had a job to do, just like myself.' He paused to take a pull on his cigarette, and David noticed a small vein beating sluggishly in his temple. 'Unfortunately, Dr Muhammadju is another matter. She is a Chinese citizen who has openly betrayed her country. The sentence for that is death. To commute that sentence would require a special effort on your part, Mr Laing. Do you understand me?'

'She's done nothing to . . .'

'She has helped a foreign agent. Slept with him. Conspired with him to destroy a Chinese military installation and its personnel. Plotted the overthrow of the legitimate government of this country.' He paused. 'Shall I go on? Even you in England have laws, even you treat treachery with the contempt it deserves. Be very careful, Mr Laing. I can accommodate you in most things. But to save Dr Muhammadju's life, I should have to pay off some very powerful people.'

He stepped down from the chair and crossed to Nabila. His eyes made what they could of her, of her emaciated body, tanned skin and torn clothes.

'You should take a bath, Doctor,' he said. 'It is unfitting for a doctor to be dirty. To smell. To offend.'

He reached out a hand and ran its back along her cheek and down to her neck. David stiffened. His hand slipped into his pocket and his fingers tightened around the handle of the makeshift knife.

Chang Zhangyi turned quickly, as though he'd sensed the threat. He looked at David, noting his posture.

'In spite of all that,' he said, 'I understand perfectly. I would sleep with her myself if I didn't think it would degrade me to do so.'

David bit back the retort that came so readily to his tongue, and the urge he had to hit the man harder than he'd ever been hit in his life.

'I thought you'd brought us here in order to show us round the sites.'

'Of course.' He looked at his wristwatch. 'We can talk about these matters later.'

He snapped his fingers, and two guards appeared.

'*Women zou ba!*' he said, holding the door open.

Buggies were waiting for them, little red ones that would go almost as fast as they wanted.

At first there seemed to be nothing but the endless corridors and the closed doors that appeared at regular intervals. But slowly each level opened out, and Chaofe Ling appeared to them for the first time in all its complexity as a city. Level 3, which was restricted to high officials, was laid out like a small town, with a piazza, gardens, fountains, even small trees and lawns. Exactly where the water came from to supply the needs of a place this size, David could not begin to guess.

They made their way from level to level, like a procession of grandees passing through a principality. To David, it was more reminiscent of Dante's *Inferno*, and the slow descent through the degrees of hell. When they walked about, Chang Zhangyi would take up the rear. He seemed as delighted by the glories of Chaofe Ling as though he was seeing them for the first time. Time and again, he would exclaim his pleasure out loud, or clap hands at what seemed inappropriate moments, or sigh or laugh or mutter that something could have been done with more taste. By the time they got to the third level, he had started to get on David's nerves.

On Level 4, they had built a small university, where any of the workers in Chaofe Ling could study for a degree or continue earlier studies. Inevitably, most of the courses were in scientific subjects; but Chang Zhangyi explained that they also offered modules in literature, calligraphy, fine art, and music.

'We have a young man who may one day become a master of music,' Chang Zhangyi said. 'When he finishes work here, I shall send him to the temple of Baiyun Si, to study under the Master Ah Shuji. His instrument is the *zheng*. Perhaps we shall go to hear him one day.'

He turned to Nabila.

'And what about you, Doctor? Do you know anything about music? Or just what you Uighurs use in your dances?'

'I'm not much of a musician, thank you. But I do enjoy the songs of Cui Jian.'

Chang Zhangyi pretended not to have heard. Cui was a popular singer whose lyrics castigated the government and called for reform.

On Level 6 they were shown round a supermarket so large admission was by timed ticket only. Men and women walked round it as though hypnotized. David noticed food items on the shelves that had been imported from Europe and the United States. Chaofe Ling's inmates did not go short of provisions.

When they came out of the low temperature environment of the supermarket, the heat at this level was immediately more noticeable.

'How is everything brought here?' David asked. 'There aren't any roads, there's no airstrip, no helicopter pad . . .'

'Nothing has ever come here on the surface,' Chang Zhangyi replied. 'Not even the materials for building the city. We built a tunnel between Lop Nor and the site selected for Chaofe Ling. An enormous tunnel, larger than the one that connects your country to France. We used it to bring in raw materials, equipment – all the supplies we needed, and we built Chaofe Ling up from the bottom.'

'Most impressive.'

'It's the world's biggest engineering project. It's just a pity we can't tell the rest of the world what we've achieved.' He hesitated. 'Would you like to see the tunnel, Laing Shiansheng?'

David nodded. In spite of himself, he was knocked out by the sheer scale and organization of the complex.

Chang Zhangyi led them down a very long corridor at the end of which stood a metal-plated door. He stubbed out his cigarette in a tall ashtray beside the door, inserted a key, and let them through into a small foyer. The door closed and locked itself automatically behind them. In front of them was a second door with a glass front.

'This is a private lift,' Chang Zhangyi explained. 'It's used by the Director of Chaofe Ling, General Wen Shunzhang, by myself, and half a dozen other senior cadres.'

Only one guard could get in with them: the other would have to wait till they sent the lift back up.

It took only seconds to make the rest of the descent. The door opened on to another foyer, identical to the first. A second door slid open, and they stepped out on to the shiny black floor of Level 7.

They could hardly take it all in at first. The scale of the whole enterprise was vast, unobscured here by walls or doors or corridors. The ceiling climbed up far above their heads, and was filled with bright lights, like an over-active sky.

The centre of the space was taken up by a large circular pool half the size of Texas, its water made purple by batteries of lights deep underneath. Ripples passed back and forwards across the surface, driven by some concealed mechanism.

To one side of the pool stood a huge silver sphere with steps leading up to a small entrance near the top. Off to the other side was an enormous glass dome in which sat a small black dome. Right ahead of them was the tunnel. It seemed like a gigantic mouth, stretched wide open and ready to swallow all that came within spitting distance. A large black locomotive with closed wagons sat half-in and half-out of the tunnel entrance. On the platform, a row of open trucks led to the wagons, and David had no doubt that the slim shiny objects stacked on them were warheads.

'About an hour or so, and we're ready to go,' said

Chang Zhangyi. 'The last warheads are in the dome at present, running through some final checks. That won't be possible when they get to Iraq, so we have to be sure they're ready to go the minute they leave here. The better use Saddam makes of them, the more likely other regimes will be to pay for their own.'

'Does that mean there's a risk of one of them exploding while they're en route?' David asked.

'Not really. They can only be triggered in two ways – either by a signal sent directly from the control room down there' – he pointed at the little black dome – 'or by an altimeter which is pre-set to trigger them once they drop to a certain height.'

David let his eyes wander across the vista. Not without honesty, he said, 'You're streets ahead of us. I'm biting my teeth off just looking at all this. Do you think I could have a look at the control room?'

Chang Zhangyi seemed hesitant, then nodded. 'Why not?' he said. 'You've seen almost everything else.'

They found four little buggies nearby and drove silently to the dome. Up close, it seemed enormous.

Chang Zhangyi used a key to let them inside. Everywhere, technicians were bustling about in the carefully controlled atmosphere.

'When these warheads leave, there will be more to build,' said Chang Zhangyi. 'This country needs a large number for its own use. And we're about to start work on our new project.'

'What's that?'

Chang Zhangyi smiled.

'Oh, I don't think I should tell you that. What I'm showing you now is nothing you don't already know about. If I tell you what's coming, it could seriously compromise your freedom if you choose to accept the Hui Hou's offer.'

They went inside the control room. Everything was bathed in a ghastly green glow. At panels on every side, technicians sat reading computer screens, keying in information, twiddling dials, and carrying out complex calculations on hand-held keypads. There was no sense of urgency, just a steady hum of controlled activity.

'Why so many?' asked David. 'Surely you aren't still carrying out tests.'

Chang Zhangyi raised his eyebrows in mock surprise. The light gave his skin a faint green tinge.

'Surely you don't think we sit about here idly?' he said. 'We're always looking to introduce new refinements. In this case, to the triggering mechanism. In the past, we've experienced problems when climatic conditions have created false atmospheric pressures. As a result, the warheads have detonated too high or too low. It's only happened a few times, but it is an irritant. Now, if we use a more reliable feedback mechanism, we can issue the detonation command from here.'

'You're carrying out a test this evening?'

'Of course. The Iraqis insisted on a random test of one of their warheads. Their people picked one out a couple of hours ago. It won't be long.'

David felt a long shiver trickle down his spine.

'Where?' he asked.

Chang Zhangyi sniffed.

'Urumchi. In half an hour. You're just in time to watch.'

The door opened and the second guard rejoined them. David looked at Nabila. She was rigid with anger and trepidation.

Chang Zhangyi pulled them over to one of the control panels.

'This is the main panel,' he said. 'Once we get final barometric readings, we place the correct settings in the firing computer. Once they've been correctly transmitted to the warhead itself, they're locked in. A radio signal sends the trigger command at precisely the right moment – and Urumchi becomes a prime site on the new business itinerary of Asia. I never liked it much anyway, did you?'

'And the people of Urumchi? Will they just end up like their relatives in Kashgar? Like the people we saw you mow down in the Shaanshi Mosque Square?' Nabila could not contain herself. She had friends in Urumchi, relatives, workmates, memories. She had found love there for the second and last time in her life.

'They'll be martyrs to the cause of international understanding,' answered Chang Zhangyi. 'And to the coming Iraqi victory in the Gulf.'

'Actually, they won't,' said David, leaning forward to bring the blade of mirror glass to rest hard on top of Chang Zhangyi's carotid artery.

Nabila had tied her knots well. Huang Zhengmei had almost been defeated by them. Then, at almost the last moment, she had rolled across the floor and found another sliver of broken glass stuck in the carpet. Close up, it was not really a sliver at all, more a shaving, but it served – with much gritting of teeth and furrowing of the brow – to cut through one of the strands that bound her wrists. The rest unravelled easily.

She pulled out her phone and punched in an emergency number.

'This is Huang Zhengmei. Where is Colonel Chang Zhangyi? . . . I see. Are the two intruders with him? . . . Very well. Send ten men and have them meet me at the main entrance to Level 7. In five minutes. And make sure they're armed. Give them sub-machine-guns: this is an emergency.'

CHAPTER EIGHTY-SIX

They sat huddled in a corner on the floor, fifteen technicians and the two guards, scared as rabbits. The guards, trained to kill, had caved in when Chang Zhangyi had ordered them to hand over their weapons. One of them glared at David, the other at Nabila, as though sizing them up to go with a dish of hot noodles and sauce.

Chang Zhangyi just sat on the chair where David had put him, smiling broadly and tut-tutting from time to time, as though this were all a game. Two of the technicians had reluctantly supplied belts which fastened together into a long strap that now held Chang Zhangyi tightly to the chair. Another technician had provided a pair of smelly socks; tied together, they made a tight bond for Chang Zhangyi's wrists.

David and Nabila had a sub-machine-gun apiece. While David examined the main console, Nabila tied up the two guards.

'I don't see why you're even wasting your time,' Chang Zhangyi said. He seemed quite relaxed, confident in his perfect realm. 'I can accept you're upset, but I can not accept your logic. You're at the foot of the biggest military complex in the world. You've seen some of it. There's no way you can get out. Even if you did, you'd be hunted down. All that's out there is desert, just like before. You won't even . . .'

David turned from the console and appealed to Nabila.

'Keep him quiet, will you, dear? I want to concentrate on what I'm doing.'

To loud protests, Nabila set about gagging the colonel. She didn't know what David was planning to do, but if he could delay or abort the test over Urumchi, that alone would make these last minutes worthwhile.

David clicked his way through file after file on the computer. He knew what he was looking for, but it constantly evaded him.

'What are you looking for?' Nabila asked. 'Is it a text file?'

He nodded.

'See if the system has something called "Find File" or the near equivalent. Look under the "File" menu if you're already in a document.'

'Got it.'

'Key in some text that should be in your file. Anything, as long as it's not in a million other files.'

He thought for a moment, then keyed in 'Ground Zero'. It took about a minute, then three files appeared in the left-hand window of the 'Find File' application. He glanced at them and chose the third.

A telephone started ringing. David ignored it.

'Darling,' he said, 'can you see if there's any sort of window near the door. Check if anyone's here yet.'

She found a small porthole that gave a wide-angle view over the entrance area. No one as yet.

David was already keying codes into the computer and rolling a row of dials to match the configuration he wanted.

'Check them for keys,' he said. 'Take what they have, and be sure you get all of Chang Zhangyi's.'

Nabila went round the technicians, and each in turn

gave up his key to her. The guards needed help. Chang Zhangyi refused to hand anything to her.

She knelt in front of him, looking up at his face. For most of her life she had hated this man.

'Colonel, I don't know if you are aware of exactly who I am.'

'On the contrary, I know you very well. Your father was always a thorn in my flesh.'

'In that case, you'll know that I had a sixteen-year-old sister, a sister called Rabbia. Does that name ring any bells?'

'Of course it does. She was a lovely little thing. It was a pity she chose to kill herself.'

'Did you rape her?'

'Of course not. I slept with her several times. She enjoyed every moment. She could have been my mistress if she'd allowed herself.'

'Do you remember how she died?'

'She stabbed herself. Thirty times, with a knife of the Baoan. She went on stabbing until she pierced her heart. As I said, a tragedy.'

'This', Nabila said, taking the sliver of mirror glass from her pocket, 'is not a Baoan knife. It comes from a cheap mirror in David's quarters upstairs.'

For the first time, Chang Zhangyi had no answer. His skin went white. He thought she was mad enough to do anything with the knife. Her whole family had been mad: he'd have done better if he'd had them shot. It did no good to pay heed to the religious scruples of minorities.

She bent forward and unzipped his trousers, bringing out a small and frightened penis.

'Please,' Chang Zhangyi said. 'Don't do something so stupid. Leave me unharmed and it will go in your favour. But if you hurt me . . .'

She laughed.

'I don't think anybody in this room gives a damn about what happens to your precious penis. Except me. It matters to me that my sister had to go through so much suffering merely to give a few moments' pleasure to this thing. Was it even worth it for you, I wonder?'

Chang Zhangyi did not answer. He had started to tremble. His eyes were bolted on the makeshift knife with which she threatened to mutilate him.

She held up the knife, then snapped it in half, then in half again. She tossed the bits at his feet, then spat into his lap.

David got up and pulled one of the technicians over to the console.

'Punch in the code to finalize the trigger setting.'

The frightened man shook his head. A little courage now, and his fortitude might be rewarded. Give in, and Chang Zhangyi would be sure to have him eaten whole.

David extracted his knife and held it in front of the man's throat. He knew he had no time to play with. Without the code, the whole thing was a waste of time. Without the code, Urumchi would join Kashgar, and the Allied forces in the Gulf would face total destruction.

The man shook his head a second time. David drew the blade hard across his artery. Blood spurted out, smearing the console like a libation. He pushed the man to the floor, strode over to the corner, and picked out a second. He untied his hands and placed him in front of the console.

'Please key in the code, and be sure to do it accurately.'

This time, there was no hesitation. The code was entered, an acknowledgement message flashed on the screen. David turned the key to lock in the computer instructions, and slipped it in his pocket.

'I've set the trigger to detonate all warheads at this level. I don't know what the effect will be, but I believe it will stop your trade with Iraq, and I'm sure it will leave a hole in the ground where Chaofe Ling is currently standing. I'm sorry if this clashes with any plans you may have had, but there's not much I can do about that. The detonation is set to take place in twenty minutes. I wouldn't bother struggling with your restraints, if I were you. Even if you do get free, I've got the key.'

Chang Zhangyi, momentarily emboldened by his reprieve, flared at him.

'You're a total idiot. The minute you set foot outside this sector, you'll be shot down and the key will be brought back here. You're only making things worse . . .'

'Oh, shut up,' said David. He took Nabila's arm and they went to the door.

'Anyone coming?'

She squinted through the porthole.

'Over to the right,' she said. 'They're still outside the transparent dome.'

They opened the door and dashed outside, locking it firmly behind them with Chang Zhangyi's private key.

CHAPTER EIGHTY-SEVEN

The wind rushed in hard from the north, blustering down from the high mountains of the Tien Shan, working its way into the desert like a stain in still water. Its fingers played with the sand, lifting it and tossing it down again. As yet, it had little strength, but it was coming, no doubt of it.

Chang Zhangyi's helicopter sat on a flat patch of ground near the concealed entrance to Chaofe Ling. The pilot sat in the rear, where the seats were more comfortable, legs up on the seat opposite, headphones on his head. He was listening to a bootleg copy of an old Rolling Stones album, trying desperately to sing along to words he did not understand.

He glanced out of the window and saw that the sand was starting to lift. Frowning, he glanced at his watch. Chang Zhangyi wouldn't be back for half an hour at least. But once he did turn up, he'd want to be flown to Urumchi. That was all very well, thought the pilot; but what if there was a fully-fledged sandstorm by then?

Then he forgot about Chang Zhangyi. He wondered instead what it would be like to see Mick and Keef in concert before they got too old. One thing was sure, they weren't going to be performing in China in the near future.

* * *

The moment they came through the door of the black dome, they were spotted. Huang Zhengmei and her team of security guards were only about fifty yards from the doorway that led in and out of the larger dome.

'There's no point in even trying to get out that way,' Nabila said.

'I don't think we'll need to.'

He turned and led the way as fast as possible to another section of the wall, making a short-cut that left their pursuers some way behind.

'Let's see if this works,' said David, raising the sub-machine-gun. There was no time for punching out a circle of carefully placed holes. He just set the firing mechanism on 'automatic' and pulled back on the trigger. The gun did everything for him, ripping a gash in the side of the dome big enough to climb through.

By now, the distance between them and their pursuers had shrunk perceptibly. Nabila crawled through the gap, followed by David. A burst of machine-gun fire greeted their exit. The bullets went high. Huang Zhengmei and her merry men skidded to a halt and knelt facing their intended victims.

'Throw away your weapons, and put your hands behind your heads,' she called. Her voice echoed around the great empty space. Down at the tunnel, heads turned. On a gantry high above the train, someone dropped a spanner.

'When I shout,' David whispered to Nabila, 'throw yourself flat.'

He reached into his pocket and drew out a gas grenade, one of two he'd taken from Chang Zhangyi's bodyguards.

'Drop your weapons! Do it now!' Without amplification, Huang Zhengmei's voice came to them as a thin, inglorious thing. She was reluctant to shoot, given the possible consequences of a stray bullet.

'Drop the gun, Nabila,' David whispered. 'But be ready to pick it up again quickly.'

The gun clattered to the ground. Within the dome, technicians rushed forward to see what was going on. They pressed their faces against the glass, like children outside a sweet shop; pale, worried faces snatched from a dream of absolute security.

'Now you, Mr Laing. Be sensible.'

David seemed to hesitate. Then, as though reaching a hard decision, he threw his gun to the ground, at the same time shouting 'Now!'

He pulled the pin, drew back his hand, and threw the grenade hard in the direction of their attackers. Nabila, seeing David still standing, had not yet thrown herself down. As the grenade landed, some of the guards started firing at random. David grabbed Nabila and pulled her down. The firing continued for another few seconds, then the gas took hold.

Guns fell to the ground in a series of dull crashes. Then there was silence that lasted only moments until the sound of coughing and choking started to grow and grow.

'Hurry, Nabila! They'll be free of the gas any minute. As soon as one of them uses his brains.' David leapt to his feet, picking up his sub-machine-gun as he did so.

When he turned, he noticed that Nabila was still on the floor.

'Nabila? Darling, are you all right?'

For a heart-stopping moment, she did not move or reply. David felt his heart turn like a plummeting bird. He bent down.

'Nabila? Are you all right, love?'

She opened her eyes.

'I've . . . been . . . hit.'

'Thank God for that.'

'What?'

'You're still alive. Where did it hit you?'

'My chest . . . I think. Turn . . . me over.'

Fearing the worst, he turned her over. Behind him, someone kicked the gas grenade out of reach.

Blood had already pooled on the floor. Tearing her shirt open, he located two bullet-holes above her right breast. There were two exit wounds just below her shoulder at the back.

'I don't think you're badly hurt,' he said, not having the slightest idea whether it was true or not. 'If you can hold on, we'll be out of here in a few minutes. But we've got to get going before they reorganize.'

He looked up. One of the guards, still spluttering, was picking up his gun. David took out the second grenade and threw it straight into the pack of guards, enveloping them in a second wave of coughing and choking and blinded eyes.

'It's . . . no use,' wheezed Nabila. Her breath was coming hard as wisps of gas reached her. 'For God's sake, David . . . just leave me here . . . and get out. You've . . . got Maddie to think about.'

'Stop blethering. I'm going nowhere without you. You're my only reason for wanting to get out of this place at all. Now, press this hard against the wound, and keep pressing till further notice.' He ripped off his shirt and handed it to her.

Slinging his gun over one shoulder, he picked up Nabila's in his left hand and pulled her to her feet with the right. She staggered, and for a moment he thought she was going to faint.

'Don't give up on me now. We can still do this. Believe me.'

Behind them there came a shout. One of the technicians had found a case full of little white masks, the sort they used when handling powders or working in a toxic environment. He started distributing them to the guards, who were still spluttering loudly, and stumbling about in their desperate efforts to escape the all-pervasive gas.

The shout came again. It was Huang Zhengmei. She was standing off to one side, rubbing her eyes and doing her best to ignore the effects the gas had had on her. The mask prevented fresh gas getting to her lungs, but it did not remove what was there already.

'Give yourselves up. Reinforcements are already on the way. There's no way out for you: you're only making things harder for yourselves.'

'Oh, shut up.' David fired from the hip at her: one bullet struck her in the arm, another in the hip.

'Time to get out of here,' said David. He led Nabila as fast as she could walk, helping her to the lift by which they'd entered the bottom level. The doors closed behind them with a satisfying clunk. Nabila groaned and slumped heavily to the floor.

David scanned the buttons and pressed one marked 'Exit to Ground Level'.

The lift shuddered and began to rise at speed. Nabila had started coughing. Above her head, little lights flashed. They arrived at Level 1, and without warning the lift slammed to a halt.

'Attention!' came a woman's voice from a small speaker set next to the row of buttons. 'You may not proceed to Ground Level without formal clearance.'

David bent down to Nabila.

'I don't think my accent's good enough for this,' he

whispered. 'Do you think . . . can you pretend to be Huang Zhengmei?'

She blinked painfully, struggling to keep from losing consciousness.

'Help me get up,' she said.

He pulled her up by the elbow and helped her stand facing the little grille.

'Ready?' he asked.

She took a deep breath and nodded. He pushed a red button that seemed to operate the intercom.

'Listen to me . . . This is Huang Zhengmei. I have to get . . . to Ground Level right away. Colonel Chang Zhangyi is with me. We have to get to his helicopter now.'

There was a brief silence, then the woman's voice returned, apologetic this time.

'Major Huang, my apologies. I didn't know it was you. Please wait while I unlock your lift.'

A few moments passed, then the lift shook into life again. David glanced at his watch. Eight minutes left. The ascent to Ground Level seemed interminable. Level 1 lay two hundred feet beneath the surface, with only a handful of lift shafts joining it to the ground. Chaofe Ling had been built to withstand a nuclear strike from above, not from below.

The intercom crackled into life again.

'Green lift? Can you hear me? We have to take you down again. Huang Zhengmei has just been in touch with Control. She is in Level 7 and says you are an impostor. Prepare to be taken down again.'

Nabila lay on the floor, barely moving. David felt total despair sweep through him like glass. He thought despairingly of his father, of the hours he'd spent giving him his first lessons in Chinese, his voice speaking the language with practised ease. And he thought of Chang Zhangyi, running the colonel's voice through his head, his intonations, his inflections, his drawn-out vowels.

He pressed the communications button.

'*Wo shi Chang Zhangyi*. Stop this nonsense at once. The woman with me is Huang Zhengmei. You heard her yourself. The woman on Level 7 is a Uighur and an impostor. If I was down there, she'd have brought me to the phone herself, but she hasn't. She and her companion have created a block in the tunnel. I have a helicopter ready to fly to Lop Nor in order to clear the tunnel from that end.'

He looked at his watch. Six minutes. The blast would drive up the lift shaft and tear them to pieces.

'I'm not sure if I can . . .'

'Listen to me very carefully indeed,' David said. 'If you do not get me to the surface within the next few seconds, I shall see to it personally that you are whipped senseless before being shot.'

There was silence, then a click. The lift began to rise again. Ten seconds later, it clanked to a stop at Ground Level. David turned his key in the door, and it opened without interference. The first thing he noticed was the sound of the wind somewhere above them.

He hurried to drag Nabila out of the lift before the girl below thought better of her decision. When he looked up, he saw that they were at the bottom of a shallow well, with steps that led up to the sands.

'Nabila, you've got to climb these. I'll give you a hand.'

She looked at the steps as if they had been carved there by the hands of giants. Wouldn't it be much easier if she just lay down where she was and waited for the blast to destroy her?

Without waiting for a response, he dragged her upright

and started pulling her to the top. She managed to walk with great difficulty, but he pushed and pulled until she was at the lip of the well. The wind was howling now. He looked down and saw that blood was soaking through the shirt that she held against her chest.

Up on top, the sandstorm had picked up momentum. Visibility was abysmal, but not yet anything like the pea-soup variety they'd experienced before. David blinked, feeling defeated at the last. Then he saw the helicopter.

It was only a few feet away, its dull, camouflaged surface almost shimmering in the heat and rushing sand. The pilot was still engrossed in the Rolling Stones, while awaiting the blinking light on his transceiver that would alert him to Chang Zhangyi's imminent return. He didn't look up and didn't notice anybody coming.

There was a sudden howling as the helicopter doorway opened. David stood in the opening, pointing a gun at the pilot's head.

'Out! Now! *Hsianzai!*'

The pilot swallowed hard, then dashed for the door. David kept the gun levelled at his head.

'You've got about three minutes to run as hard as you can in that direction. But first, help me get her safely on board.'

They took her like a rag doll, and lifted her on to the floor of the copter. The pilot looked at her softly and stroked her hair into place.

'Is she badly hurt?'

'I don't know. I think so.'

'There's a first-aid box in the rear. Field dressings, pain-killers, the lot.'

'You'd better get moving.' David did not want to risk letting the pilot fly the craft, knowing he would in all likelihood take them straight to his base.

'What's going on?'

'Chaofe Ling's going up any minute now.'

The pilot looked out across the flat expanse of wasted sand. The sandstorm blocked off much of it.

'I'll never make it,' he said. 'Not in this!'

There was a sound behind them. David spun and froze as he saw Huang Zhengmei and two guards standing at the exit from a second lift.

'Put your hands behind your back, Mr Laing. Pilot, take him into custody.'

David realized he had thrown the guns into the helicopter after Nabila. He saw the pilot take his pistol from a holster on his hip and raise it. There was no point in any of this now. They would all be dead anyway.

Suddenly, the pilot twisted, took aim and shot Huang Zhengmei and the guards in quick succession. He breathed in and out quickly, then turned to David, slipping the gun back into its holster.

'I never did like her much,' he said. 'Now, let's get out of here.'

'Look after her, will you? I'll get this thing in the air.'

'Can you fly it?'

David hesitated. He still saw the pilot as his enemy.

'We'll soon find out, won't we?'

They jumped aboard and David took the pilot's seat.

The rotors were just coming up to full thrust when he felt the first tremors. The helicopter lifted a fraction, and he applied more pressure, and then, beyond the howling of the rotors and the roaring of the storm, he could hear it, deep, deep below, like a monstrous beast goaded beyond all endurance. He struggled to pull the copter away, but it seemed frozen in one place.

The pilot stood beside him.

660

'Let me,' he said. 'Please. You can kill me later if I don't go where you want. But this way, we'll all die.'

David looked out and saw a column of fire rising through one of the lift shafts, high, high into the air.

The wounded beast groaned and struggled, then roared in its death throes. David changed places with the pilot, and moments later they were lifting through sand and wind and fire, lifting high, spiralling upwards in a tight circle to gain height.

David looked down. The ground below them was heaving into an obscene and dreadful life. Suddenly, the columns of fire were cut off, and the ground vanished from sight as they twisted higher, rising above the storm into high, clean air.

They raced forward and forward still, and in their ears the sounds of Chaofe Ling's deadly agony chimed like the chimes of hell.

David looked back only once. In a wide area a little larger than Chaofe Ling itself, the storm had been beaten aside by a flat cloud of debris and sand. A shock wave dashed them like a giant hand swatting a butterfly, then another, and another. David looked on in admiration as the pilot handled the copter through each of the buffetings it received, until all grew still around them. And a silence came, as though great guns had fallen to rest.

They continued like that for a little while. David fetched the first-aid kit and started dressing Nabila's wound properly. While he was doing that, the pilot turned to him.

'My name's Chen,' he said. 'Chen Hsiaodong.'

'David. David Laing.'

'American?'

'English.'

Chen's face lit up.

'You like the Rolling Stones?'

'Of course.'

'Oasis? The Verve?'

'I'm too old for that.'

'You ever meet Mick Jagger?'

'Not knowingly.'

Chen smiled.

'Which way would you like to go, David?'

'Any way, as long as it takes us out of China.'

'That's fine by me.'

And the chopper dipped, then rose again, heading into the growing darkness of the west, and the hibiscus-red glow of sunset.

MIRAGE

CHAPTER EIGHTY-EIGHT

'Farrar.'

There was silence, then a series of echoes bounced across gulfs of space.

'Who is this?'

More weird noises, then a clear line.

'Hello? You don't seem to be getting through.'

'Farrar? This is Chang Zhangyi.'

'Chang Zhangyi? How the hell did you get this number?'

'That's hardly important. I need to speak with you.'

'Do you? Well, why don't you just go ahead?'

Crackles and hisses, then the pure silence of emptiness.

'We're facing a setback at this end.'

'Don't I bloody know! Your shipment is late, and my people have been getting reports about an underground nuclear explosion west of the usual Lop Nor sites. I thought you'd tested this system to destruction long ago. So just what the hell's going on?'

'Nothing. You don't have to worry. Our arrangements still stand. Your money is safe.'

'Is it? I should most certainly hope so, otherwise you're in serious trouble. What happened, exactly?'

'Our scientific regulators insisted on an underground test of the weapon. For technical reasons. Don't ask me why.'

'And?'

'It was detonated too close to the complex. There was a mismeasurement. The tunnel was damaged, and we couldn't move the warheads out to Lop Nor. They're still there, waiting for shipment.'

'That's all very well, but where the blazes have you been all this time? Mmmm? I've been trying to get hold of you at your different numbers, and there's been no reply or no signal.'

'Sir Farrar, fond as I am of you, I don't sit around waiting for your delightful calls. I've been all over the place since the accident, talking to people, making fresh arrangements. We can ship the warheads out in another three to four days. Five at the most. But first I need more classified information from you.'

'More? I've given you just about every last scrap of classified material you could possibly want.'

'Nevertheless, there are things I vitally need to have at my disposal before I go ahead with the shipment.'

'I can't see what –'

'Let me be the judge of that.'

'All right. But don't take long. I have things to do.'

He looked down at Maddie's long limbs and tanned body, tracing the knobbed curve of her spine with his eyes. He'd bought her the sunbed as a present, to compensate for the loss of her days by the lake, following their return to London. The drugs he was giving her – courtesy of the late but unlamented Calum – made her drowsy, and there was always a risk that she might fall asleep while on the bed and receive bad burns.

She opened her eyes and rolled over on her back. He hadn't told her yet about her mother's death, not that he thought she'd care. Her body was very like Lizzie's, the same proportions, the same softness in the limbs. He looked down at the beads of sweat that had formed on her skin.

'Who was that on the phone?' she asked.

'Just a business colleague. Nobody you know.'

'Still no word about Daddy?'

'Not yet. But I'm still trying.'

She didn't like him, and she didn't trust him. But at the moment, he was all she had. She wished she was back at the lake, she wished she was naked and swimming in the deep cool water, she wished she could dive down until the darkness and the weeds swallowed her.

Chen Hsiaodong flew west for a while, then turned due north towards Urumchi. It was a risky option, but one they had to take: Alma-Ata was simply too far. Nabila would have died long before then. Urumchi was on the wrong side of the Chinese border, but it had a large hospital and teams of trained doctors.

It was still a very close thing. Her heart almost gave out twice on the way, and only emergency injections kept her going.

When they landed at the airport, Chen helped David unload Nabila from the helicopter, and took off again at once. David left his weapons on board – one sight of them, and every policeman and state security official within fifty miles would be breathing down their necks.

Somebody found a trolley, and they were soon wheeling her to the airport entrance. At the hospital, she was taken off straight to an operating theatre. She was in for ten hours.

While they operated, David made contact with Liu Yaobang, Nabila's friend at the Minorities Hospital, the one who'd given her the name of the brothel. He explained the situation to him and asked for assistance.

'I'll do what I can,' he said.

The following day, against the loud protests of her doctors, David wheeled Nabila to a van that had been found by Dr Liu. She was far from well, but David knew that another few hours would bring the police or the PSB or the Guojia Anchuanbu sniffing around.

David drove west to Kulja, a rough journey of about four hundred miles. The van had fewer springs than he'd have liked, but he'd tied Nabila down firmly to a low bed in the back, and he drove as carefully as he could, bearing in mind the need for haste. Liu had given him drugs and advice on what to do for Nabila. The rest was down to luck and blind faith.

He passed a few military convoys, all headed in the opposite direction. They'd be scurrying in from all directions on an abortive rescue mission to Chaofe Ling. Every so often, he'd allow himself a smile as he thought of their victory. He had never imagined it could be so complete, so injurious a blow. But then he'd look back at the still form of Nabila and drive on without thought of victory or triumph.

Chen Hsiaodong was waiting at Kulja as arranged. He told David he had a wife and two children, and he wanted to leave China more than anything. More than he loved his wife, more than he loved his children.

Still unconscious, Nabila was transferred from the van to the helicopter, which had been waiting on the edge of town. Kulja was a one-horse border town packed with Russians, Chinese, Kazakhs, Mongols, Kirghiz, Tajiks, Uzbeks, Tartars, Uighurs, and any other race that could find room in its narrow streets. Another face would not be noticed. No one would report them; no one would care. They were just more strays on the Silk Road, a couple more refugees trying their luck on the ancient trade routes.

668

Alma-Ata was another matter. With a population of one and a half million and a nervy sense of its giant neighbours to east and west, the capital of the Kazakh Republic was not a place to sneak into.

They got permission to land at the airport, but once they disembarked, they were hustled to an empty shed next to the transit lounge. A horde of customs and immigration officials descended on them. None of them looked happy. It took over an hour for David to persuade them to send for someone from the British embassy. He wrote a brief, cryptic note, and sealed it in an envelope.

Half an hour later, the door of the shed opened and a man in a white suit came in, ushered by two policemen.

'Laing? Is that you? Good God, man, I'd heard you were dead.'

It was then that David realized his luck had turned. He'd met Douglas Ross before, back in Carstairs, a few weeks ago. With Tursun, that was it: he'd been at some of the sessions with Tursun. He'd been the one to find the boy.

'Ross? I didn't think to find you here.'

'I was posted two weeks ago. Just getting my bearings really. To tell you the truth, it's a bit of a punishment posting. I seem to have cocked up in my last billet, though nobody's told me so.'

'I think I know exactly why. Let's have a talk, out of hearing distance.'

Ross left half an hour later, looking ashen-faced and queasy. He did not return for five hours. When he did, it was with a doctor and a file of papers.

'How is Dr Muhammadju?' he asked.

'I'm getting very worried about her. If I can't get her to London soon, she will die.'

'They have a decent hospital here. Soviet-built. Not very comfy, but the facilities are good.'

David shook his head.

'If I leave her here, they will find her and they will kill her. Believe me, there are interests involved in this that won't hesitate for you or the entire Kazakh police force and army combined. I have to get her to London as quickly as possible, that's the only option.'

From his file, Ross fished out three passports and three airline tickets.

'The tickets will take you to Moscow. There's a flight in half an hour. I've made arrangements for Dr Muhammadju to have three seats. There's a connection an hour after you land at Moscow. That will have you in London in a few hours.

'The passports are the best I could do. I've made Dr Muhammadju your wife. It seemed the best thing.'

David nodded wryly.

'And Chen?'

'Hong Kong Chinese with British citizenship, has been living in England for the past two years.'

'And still doesn't speak a word of English.'

'You'd better teach him.'

Ross stood.

'I'd better get back. Since I'm the only intelligence man over here, I don't need to report much back to my superiors in the embassy. And London, as you say, can find all this out for themselves. But I'm needed for some diplomatic thing in an hour's time, and I'd sooner not attract attention.'

'Thanks. Don't worry. If I can sort things out back home, I'll make sure you get your choice of postings.'

'Ask for Rome,' he said. 'Or Paris.'

The flight to London passed without incident. Nabila slept the whole way: her condition had stabilized after her brief treatment at Alma-Ata, and for the first time David felt the nightmare of the past few weeks pass away from him. He taught Chen a little English and promised to do what he could to find him a job.

'What would you like to do? Will you go on flying? I could probably find you a job with a commercial helicopter outfit.'

Chen shook his head decisively.

'No flying,' he said. 'I never wanted to fly in the first place. I actually hate flying.'

'You do a very good job.'

'That made it easier. It's a lot less frightening if you know what you're doing.'

'So, what do you want to do, then?'

Chen hesitated, then a wide, mischievous smile crossed his face. He'd been smiling a lot since they got to Alma-Ata.

'If I'm absolutely honest,' he said, 'I'd like to be an entertainer. It's what I did before I got conscripted.'

'Really? What sort of entertainer?'

Chen smiled even more widely, and explained. It was then that David realized he had Anthony Farrar in the palm of his hand.

'Maddie, why don't you grab a few things and pop them into a bag? Enough for a week or two.'

'Where are we going?'

'Up to Scotland. To the loch. You'd like that, wouldn't you?'

'You can't go back there. That's Calum's aunt's place.'

'Show some common sense. That lodge is in the hands of the security services until the case is closed. Which means we can use it when we like. Be a good girl and get your things packed. I'm leaving in half an hour.'

'I don't want to leave London.'

'Why the hell not?'

'What if Dad comes back? Eh? What if he comes looking for me and I'm not here?'

'You don't have to worry about that, Maddie. If he comes home, he'll go straight to our central office. I'll leave a message for him, saying where he can find you. How's that?'

She nodded. Only the cocaine kept her from screaming. She thought he was dead. He hadn't written since that letter from Kashgar.

'Maddie, you must be careful. Your father's on a very dangerous mission. He may not make it back. Do you understand?'

But she just shook her head again. He left her to it, sitting on the bed and shaking her head. He decided to give her another shot of cocaine before they headed north.

The telephone rang. He took the call downstairs. As before, it was preceded by half a minute of outer space.

'Hello. This is Farrar.'

'Chang Zhangyi. Are you busy?'

Chen put the phone down. He'd always been especially fond of his impersonation of Colonel Chang Zhangyi, and this had been his finest performance to date.

David grinned and shut off the little tape-recorder. He'd bought it in a shop selling surveillance and industrial espionage equipment, with the assurance that it would make a perfect clandestine recording every time. He wound the tape back and played a few seconds' worth, then switched it off again.

'We've got him,' he said. 'You were brilliant.'

Chen shrugged.

'Plenty of practice in the pilots' mess. You should see

me do Chairman Mao. What are you going to do with the recordings?'

'I'm holding on to them for the moment. They're partial evidence that Farrar had dealings with Chang Zhangyi. We'll make a couple more calls and see if we can't get something more explicit.'

They were in David's old house, in one of the back rooms, where the sun lay on the furniture and dust twisted its way through its soft beams. David looked out on to the garden. He'd not been out there since the day of Sam's funeral. Even as he looked, he thought he could see the same light and the same shadows on the grass.

He went outside, needing to remember and forget, not knowing how to do either. He walked in the sunshine, astonished by how weak it was. He remembered his father, and the poem they had recited together. It seemed mere words now, and he could no longer capture whatever meanings it had once held for him.

Inside again, he went through the rooms one by one, removing every photograph, large or small, from the walls and various surfaces. As though conjured away, faces disappeared, and he let them go as if for ever. The house felt empty for a while, then full, he did not know what of. Not ghosts, not memories. He wept for it all, and ended by wondering what it was he was weeping for. If nothing else, he was home once more.

She hung somewhere between life and death, like dust in a sunbeam, drifting in a world of light, sleeping and waking, walking only in her dreams. He brushed her cheek and bent down to whisper in her ear. He always said the same things. There were times when he thought she responded, others when he thought he was losing her. Seeing her attached to so many monitors, with dozens of wires and tubes sprouting from her flesh, he could not say that she was the woman he loved.

A doctor arrived, one he'd met earlier. He had bushy eyebrows and a day's worth of stubble on his chin, and his name was Blennerhassett. He spoke with the softest of Dublin accents, and his eyes were blue and wounded.

'Is she making any progress, Doctor? Or is this apparatus just keeping her going?'

'You mean, is she a vegetable? The answer is no. But the answer to your first question is the same as before: it's too early to say. It would help if I knew more about what happened. Exactly how long elapsed before she received proper treatment?'

David fudged as well as he could. Any mention of China could prove extremely dangerous.

Blennerhassett took David by the arm.

'Look, Mr . . .'

'Rodgers. Simon Rodgers.'

'Mr Rodgers, I'll be quite frank with you. We're not unaccustomed to seeing gunshot wounds in here. But two wounds from an automatic weapon raise a lot of questions. I'm under a great deal of pressure to notify the police, but I'd rather hear the whole story from you first.'

'You will. But not now. I'm going to have to turn the tables here, Doctor. If you or anyone else on your unit does notify the police, they will be jeopardizing national security. That's a very serious matter, and the consequences could be extremely unpleasant. If it's any comfort, the people who wounded my wife are far out of the reach of the British or any other police. For the moment, I'd like you to concentrate on getting her well.'

The doctor looked at him blankly. He wasn't very old, late twenties at the most. David felt it was unfair to place such responsibility on such young shoulders.

'I'll do my best,' he said.

'Anthony? Is that you?'

'Of course it is. And who are you? And how'd you get my mobile number?'

But even as he spoke, recognition started to trickle in.

'Don't you recognize my voice, Anthony? Don't you know your ghosts? Your little voices from hell? This is David. David Laing. Don't you remember me at all?'

There was a very long silence. David wished he could have done this looking into the other man's eyes.

'Listen, you . . . Whoever you are, you can't be David Laing. That isn't possible. He's dead.'

'Am I? In that case, what does that make me? An awkward piece of ectoplasm? I'm sorry to disappoint you, but I feel very much alive. A lot more alive than your old chum Chang Zhangyi. You do remember him, don't you?'

'Now you are talking nonsense. I spoke to Chang Zhangyi today. He sounded alive and well to me. Or perhaps you're thinking of some other Chang Zhangyi.'

'Not really. Listen to this.'

David started the little recorder. He let it play for about one minute, then shut it off again.

'There's lots more of that,' said David. 'I've got it all on microcassettes. They're not damning in themselves. I'm sure you can afford to hire the sort of lawyers who could prove they were fakes of some kind. But they would start suspicions. The press might get interested. I'd be bound to insist on a full internal investigation. I'd have the whole thing out of your grimy hands within minutes. I know the system as well as you, and you know I wouldn't hesitate.'

A shorter silence, then Farrar's voice under perfect control.

'What is it you want, Laing? Money? Is that it? I don't think Liz left you anything in her will, did she? You'll be feeling the need of a little cash before long. And all the time you're asking yourself, how come that bastard Farrar pulls in these staggering amounts from Chang Zhangyi, while I haven't two pennies to introduce to the joys of a good rub? Or perhaps it's even simpler than that, a mere matter of promotion. In either case . . .'

'Shut up and listen, Anthony. I want you exposed. Privately, if need be, publicly if possible. You've done real damage to this country, and probably to our allies as well. I want you to burn in every hell there is, I want you to squirm for every sin, every little misdeed. I will watch you. I will listen to every word, and I will see to it that there are no evasions.'

'David, old boy, will you just shut up for a moment? If you can stop being so bloody self-righteous, I'd like to tell you something you should know.'

A longer silence this time, a decided silence. Then a different extension was picked up.

'David, I think it's better if I just put someone else on the line. She can explain the rest.'

'Maddie? Do you mean Maddie?'

Her voice came to him suddenly, muddled by the echo from the other phone. She spoke with a slur, but he would have known her anywhere.

'Daddy, is that . . . you?'

'Maddie? Yes it's me. I'm all right. I'm back in England.'

'Oh, thank . . . God. When . . . can I . . . see you?'

'As soon as possible. What's wrong, Maddie? You don't sound too good. Haven't you . . . ?'

The phone was snatched from Maddie. Farrar's voice came back on the line.

'You'll have to continue with your mutual simperings

another time. For my part, I've got more important things to do than listen to them.'

There was a scream in the background.

'Farrar, what the hell's –'

'Listen very carefully, Laing. Your precious daughter is with me. She is at this moment sitting about one foot away from me. In my hand I am holding a P7 pistol. The pistol is about half an inch away from sweetheart's temple, and I don't have to tell you what would happen if I were to pull the trigger. I want the tapes, and I want anything else you think you have. By tomorrow. Is that clear?'

'Perfectly clear.'

'And remember – try to pull any stunts and you will lose another member of your family. You've got yourself into something too big and too dangerous. Don't try to play with big boys like me, Laing, or you'll get hurt. And you'll hurt everybody else you ever cared about. Tomorrow. And don't make copies.'

CHAPTER EIGHTY-NINE

The call from the hospital came just after midnight. David took it, thinking it might be Farrar.

'Hullo, Mr Rodgers?'

He didn't recognize the voice at first. Or perhaps, he told himself later, he hadn't wanted to recognize it.

'Yes?'

'This is Patrick Blennerhassett. Your wife's doctor.'

David felt his heart begin to die. In all his nightmares, it began this way.

'Yes,' he said, 'I know who you are. It's very late for you to be ringing. Is something wrong?'

'Mr Rodgers, I'm afraid . . . I'm afraid we're losing her. She may not last the night. I think you should come over right away.'

'I'll be there as soon as I can. Can you keep her alive till then?'

'Yes, I'm sure I can. But don't waste any time.'

Nabila had been moved to a private room. The windows on all sides were barred by white venetian blinds that let thin shafts of light in. Beside her, green lights dimmed and glowed.

'She's in a critical condition,' said Blennerhassett. He looked younger than ever, like a young priest. His eyes were soft and kind.

'Can you think of anything that might save her?'

The Irishman did not reply directly.

'She's been severely traumatized,' he said. 'I don't have to tell you that. Perhaps if . . . Mr Rodgers, what was your wife doing before she was shot? I ask because she's in very poor physical shape. She's weak, dehydrated, even shrunken. And if I'm frank, you're almost as bad yourself.'

David told him what he could. Not the details, but the heart of the thing. The desert. The spiders. The helicopters circling.

'Jesus, Mr Rodgers, you tell a grand story. I scarcely know whether to believe you or not. But she's been weakened by something, and lack of water seems a very plausible mechanism. The trouble is that whatever she went through out there hasn't made it easy for her to fight back. The one thing I can't give to her quickly is her strength.'

'Doctor, I'd give anything to stay here with her, but I have no choice. There are other lives at risk. Will you promise to do all you can? I'll try to get back in the morning.'

'You have my word. But try not to stay away too long. She may regain consciousness before the end.'

Maddie was not at Farrar's house. Nor was Farrar. The house was empty. Of people, of personal effects, of clues. The alarm hadn't even been set. He hunted high and low, but found nothing. Nothing remained to show that Lizzie had lived there for a while. Farrar must have thrown her possessions out soon after the funeral. Or handed them ceremoniously to the family. David could not even smell a lingering trace of her perfume on the bedroom air.

He went back home, despondent. Without an address,

he could do nothing. Unless, of course, he just handed over the paper as Farrar demanded. He could always hand Farrar in; but that would mean Maddie's death, which he couldn't begin to contemplate.

At five to three, the phone rang, waking him from an uncomfortable sleep. He let it ring at first, lacking the courage to pick it up. But it persisted, and in the end he answered.

It was Call Minder, to tell him he had messages waiting. He rang back with his heart in his mouth. A woman's voice told him he had one message, left at twelve ten, when he was on the phone with Blennerhassett.

Dad, it's Maddie. I don't know if you'll get this, or when you'll get it. Look, I don't have much time, he's just gone downstairs, but he'll be back any minute. I think he wants to take me back up to Scotland. It's not easy to find, but I'll tell you what to look for when you come home. I suppose you're home now, if you're listening to this. Have you got a pen and paper?

CHAPTER NINETY

He took the 6.15 train to Inverness. It would have been much faster to have flown, but that would have meant leaving his guns and other equipment behind. There was no point in going in against someone like Farrar without the right hardware.

He slept and woke, slept and woke. Sometimes he would open his eyes to see dark forest hemming the train in, sometimes he would look up to see mountains or the shimmering surface of a lake. His mobile phone was in his bag, and from time to time he felt an urge to use it, to ring the hospital and be done with it. But he knew that doing so might affect Maddie's chances, so he let the phone lie where it was.

There were two changes, one in Edinburgh and the other in Perth. A signal failure north of Edinburgh caused two hours' delay. He arrived just after five, swept along the platform by a crowd of holidaymakers, his gaunt figure and heavy bag marking him out as something different. Parents lifted their children out of his path, and watched him go as though he carried a taint. The station-master knocked his pipe out on to the palm of his hand and shook his head: he knew trouble when he saw it.

He hired a Landrover from a garage in Harbour Road, and drove to the town centre to buy provisions and to eat a proper meal. He wasn't hungry, but he didn't know how long he might have to stake out the house. When he finally drove out of town, it was nearly eight. He recited Maddie's directions like a mantra. At every moment, beneath all other thoughts, he kept imagining the circumstances of Nabila's death. It had become a reality to him now, a fixed point in his universe, around which everything else would revolve from now on.

This far north, the summer sun would not go down till ten or so. He needed darkness for his final approach, but in the meantime, the extra hours of sunlight could prove invaluable. They would give him time to scout the territory around the house before he made up his mind to go in. The first thing he had to make sure of was whether Farrar and Maddie were actually here. They could not have come up by plane or train, only by road – and that would have taken until now at least, even if Farrar had been able to drive straight through without any breaks.

He drove past the house, glancing at it quickly as he went by. There was no car in sight, no visible sign of occupancy. He continued on for several hundred yards, hemmed in on either side by thick forest. Getting the Landrover off the road wasn't going to be easy. And then he saw a small opening on his left, a private road used by Forestry Commission vehicles. He pulled in, and in seconds he was well out of sight.

Dressed like a hiker, he made his first approach, keeping himself as far as possible in the shadow of the trees. There was no sign of perimeter security that he could see. That made sense in a place as remote as this, crisscrossed every night by all manner of wild animals.

He made a full circuit of the house and decided no one was at home. There was no alarm system that he could see, and only a minimum of locks on either doors or windows. Letting himself in through the back door, he moved quickly through the house, disengaging locks here and there, so that he could effect a silent entry later if need be.

There was a car in the garage, a small 4x4 vehicle with local plates and a sticker from an Inverness garage. He didn't think they'd come up from London in this.

There was a sun terrace at the back, and below it a lawn sloping down to the lake. It was hard to believe that he'd been in the centre of the world's worst desert only a few days before, and that he was here now, watching sunlight dapple the bright belly of a lake like glass. If only . . . He shook himself, determined to keep his emotions under control a little longer.

Looking at the edge of the lake, he noticed a small boat tied up at a landing stage by the lawn's edge. It was tempting to go down and untie it, and go drifting out alone on the water's face. He walked down slowly, and sat on the landing stage: he'd hear any car arriving in good enough time to make himself scarce.

After the absolute silence of the desert, this place was full of sound. Birdsong shimmered like water all around the lake. Small animals chattered and cried, and a heron fished in the lonely water through red and gold and green light.

Looking out across the lake, he noticed what must have been a small boat. He watched it idly for a while, then decided to take a closer look. He took his binoculars from his bag and trained them at full magnification on the little bobbing object. It took a while to get the right justification, then, as the boat and its occupants sharpened into focus, he stiffened.

The distance was too great for him to be sure, but something about the two figures made him suspect that they could be Farrar and Maddie.

He laid down the binoculars. How the hell was that possible? he thought. And then he guessed part of the answer. He stood and got himself into the trees, out of sight from the lake. He wondered how he could have forgotten that Farrar had his own private plane, a Cessna that he flew out of Luton.

Over an hour passed. In the sky, the westering sun had started to change colour. The little boat began to pull for the shore.

He watched them disembark, Farrar and Maddie as large as life. The expression on her face was fixed, as though more than life had gone out of it. David was tempted to go in right away, to take Farrar unawares at the earliest opportunity. But Maddie was too close. Safer to wait. Farrar must be tired by now, he'd sleep soon – and then David would go in.

He watched lights go on in the house, upstairs and downstairs. Carefully, he crept round the house. Curtains had been drawn only on the first floor. Maddie sat downstairs in a long living room, watching TV. She flicked indolently from station to station, then back again, going round and round without any obvious interest. Twice she got up and walked around, and David was sure she was heavily drugged.

He wondered whether he shouldn't go in now, but he was at a disadvantage in not knowing exactly where Farrar was. Even if he succeeded in getting Maddie out of the house, he still had to get her to the car, and then away. And all the time Farrar would be on the loose.

Then Farrar appeared in the living-room door. He was wearing a long black dressing gown. He ignored Maddie at first, striding towards the TV and switching it off. Making for the CD player, he slipped a disc inside and started it playing. David recognized it at once: a recording of ch'in music by the late Master Hsu. It seemed perfectly pitched for the setting and the mysterious time of day. Outside, the sky was reddening, and the waters of the lake seemed as rich as blood.

David squeezed himself back out of sight as he saw Farrar come to the French window and look out. From where he stood, David could see that tears were running down the other man's cheeks. What the hell was going on?

Farrar went back inside, and David resumed his original position. The first thing he noticed was that Maddie had changed. She'd been wearing a simple mustard summer dress when she came in from the boat; now she had on a long robe not unlike Farrar's.

Before David could grasp what was happening, he saw Farrar gesture at Maddie, and saw her robe fall in one movement to the floor.

David felt an overwhelming sense of shame and anger sweep through him. Without thinking, he took out his pistol, then stepped to the window and pulled it open.

'Put your robe back on, love,' he said. He could hardly bear to look at Farrar. Maddie did not move. 'It's all right, love. It's me. I'm back.'

'Nice to see you, Laing. You've got to admit she's got better skin than Lizzie. Better arse too. Better all round.'

'All right, Farrar, put your hands behind your head.'

'Have you brought my tapes, Laing? I've been looking forward to those. Though I hadn't expected to receive them here. How on earth did you find this place? To be quite honest . . .'

'Shut up. I am having very great trouble not shooting you. Now, I would like you to kneel on the floor and put your arms behind your head.'

'Can't do that, Laing. You can't expect me to, can you?'

'Listen to me. If you don't put your hands on your head, I will shoot you. I won't kill you, but I will disable you. You're coming back with me. You're going to tell all our friends every last detail of what you've done.'

'I must say your timing is lousy. But then, it always was. When there's time, you must tell me exactly how you got out of China. It must have been terribly exciting. What a pity a memoir's out of the question.'

'Hands.'

Farrar grunted and put his hands behind his head.

'I don't suppose you got within sniffing distance of Chaofe Ling. I'm told it's most impressive.'

'On the contrary, it's just a lump of black tar by now. You can forget about arms for Iraq for at least ten years.'

Farrar's face went pale.

'No doubt you're going to tell me you accomplished all this single-handed.'

'No, not single-handed. I had help all the way. Now, stop wasting my time.'

What happened next happened too fast to be more than a blur. Farrar moved suddenly, putting himself behind Maddie and out of David's line of fire. Then he pulled her to him, and spun her round, one hand about her neck holding a long blade.

'I'd have used this on her sooner or later,' he said. 'Throw your gun this way. Gently, now.'

David looked at Maddie. He had not seen her naked since she was a small child. Now, seeing her like this, it brought home to him the fact that during his absences and failures of love, she had become a woman. She had her own torments, her own bleak vision of the future. But she was still his daughter. He wondered if Farrar had had sex with her very often, or had this been the first time?

He dropped the gun.

'Good. Now, kick it towards me. That's right.'

Farrar picked up the gun, then began to move backwards to the French windows, pulling Maddie with him. Once outside, he started running, holding Maddie by one hand. Too high to know what was happening, she struggled to keep pace with him.

David stepped out on to the terrace. There were three shots in quick succession, then the sound of a boat bumping against the landing stage. Silence, then oars being slipped into rowlocks, and finally blades dipping into water. All over the dim lake moonlight lay like snow. He walked to the water's edge and saw them, a dark shape thrusting through the darkness, made visible by the white light falling on everything. A second boat lay in the water a little along the landing stage, but even as David watched it was filling with water. It would last maybe fifteen minutes out on the lake.

He walked back to where he'd left his bag, and slung it over his shoulder.

CHAPTER NINETY-ONE

There was a rubber dinghy on a frame in the garage. David wheeled it round and manhandled it on to the landing stage. He pushed off into the silence, scarcely knowing which way to go. Farrar's boat was no longer visible, the sound of his oars no longer audible. David just headed out across the lake.

After a long time, he shipped his oars and let the little craft float in whichever direction it chose. He listened intently, waiting for the first hint of a creak or the plunge of an oar. He went on in silence like that, for half an hour or more. Above him, stars the size of tangerines brought back memories of the desert.

Sometimes a light breeze would blow from the direction of the house, bringing with it snatches of the ch'in music, faint and mournful. The tense, quivering strings made a slow, plangent music, hovering on the night air and falling away again.

He heard voices somewhere ahead of him. Looking hard, he made out the other boat. Farrar was sitting in the bow, with Maddie behind. Carefully, he inched his way towards them.

The voices shifted, blown across the water by the breeze, or caught up with the music from the shore. David would hear a snatch of coherent words, then lose them again as the wind changed direction. What he heard was angry, a torrent of tearful railing from Maddie fended off by Farrar's dry sarcasm. But though he could hear words and sometimes sentences, David could never make out the sense of the whole thing.

He shipped his oars without a sound and crouched in the front of the boat, resting his rifle on the gunnel. All he wanted was one clear shot. The night-sight gave him a clear image of Farrar. He pulled back gently on the trigger, getting ready to fire the moment the boat steadied.

Suddenly, Maddie grew agitated. The boat she was in began to shake violently as she threw herself on Farrar, pummelling him hard with her fists. David took his finger from the trigger; he had no wish to kill his daughter accidentally.

Farrar pushed Maddie back, punching her hard in the stomach. As she tumbled into the back of the boat, David put his eye to the sight and took aim quickly. But moments before he fired, Farrar moved, tipping the boat. The bullet went through the rear sheet without touching him. Turning his head, he caught sight of the dinghy, though it was too dark to make out David's figure crouched behind the front.

Farrar bent down and grabbed Maddie, pulling her upright. He took a gun from his pocket and rammed the barrel against her jaw.

'Put the rifle down, Laing. Shooting me won't solve anything. On the other hand, talking with me could pay off handsomely.'

'If you shoot her, you won't last more than a few seconds.'

'That won't bring her back. Just push the rifle to the back of the dinghy.'

'Take the gun away from her head.'

Farrar did as he asked. Cautiously, David slipped the rifle behind him and let it lie just within reach.

'I don't need your money,' he shouted. 'Contrary to what you said, Lizzie didn't get round to changing her will. There's no point in trying to bribe me.'

'You always did take things at face value, didn't you? If I didn't know better, I'd think you were a little stupid. However, neither of us is stupid, which is why I would like to talk with you. Perhaps you can tell me why you think I came up to this Godforsaken hole in the first place.'

'I don't know, Anthony, and I don't care. From the look of it, you came here to seduce my daughter.'

Farrar smiled deprecatingly.

'How sweet of you to imagine it. Your daughter is certainly very lovely. She may even grow into a beauty one day, like her mother. But I don't really think of her as anything but a harmless screw, a means of passing the time. I've seen one truly beautiful woman in my life. Seen her and made love to her. Her name was Meihua, and she made every other woman seem worthless. She was like a key, Laing, a password to unimaginable pleasures. If she was here now, you'd understand. You'd want her more than you've ever wanted anything. And I'd give her to you. She'd be your reward and your downfall.

'Now, don't you want to see the end of your great adventure?'

'My adventure?'

'In Sinkiang, man, in Sinkiang. You didn't think it was that simple, did you?'

'Simple? I never thought it simple for a moment.'

'I don't doubt it. Nevertheless, it isn't over yet. Not by a long chalk.'

'Meaning?'

'First of all, please get rid of that rifle.'

690

'I'd prefer to hang on to it.'

'I'm sure you would. But I'd like to even the odds a little. I'm not going to hurt Maddie, not unless she attacks me again. In fact, you may as well have her back once I've finished.'

'Finished?'

'Unveiling the mystery to you, of course. You didn't think for a moment that all there was to that business was destroying Chaofe Ling? Chaofe Ling was important, and the deal with Iraq was brilliantly conceived – until you came along. But it wasn't the only show in town. You don't really think I'd have left my back uncovered, do you?'

'I'm sure you didn't. But that's of no interest to me. I just want to take Maddie back home. I want to shut my front door on the lot of you and live some sort of normal existence.'

'That's not possible.' Farrar's voice had become hard. 'Like myself, you've been drawn too deeply into this thing. I need your help to sort it all through. In return, you can name your price, financial or otherwise.'

'I'm not interested.'

'You will be. Tell me, what can you see just over there? In the water.'

David strained. A pale sweep of moonlight lay on the surface of the water like cream. Ripples formed in it. And then he saw something about ten yards past Farrar's boat. A buoy.

'It has a little transmitter on board,' Farrar explained. 'I pick the signals up on a gadget in my pocket. Incidentally, if anyone tries to tamper with it without switching off the transmitter first, it will blow up in his hands.'

He took something from his pocket, and David could hear the beeps as he entered a string of commands.

'Now, I think it's safe to go in. Don't worry, I'm not about to fly off anywhere.'

He bent down and fumbled in the bottom of the boat, coming up with an oar, which he proceeded to fit in a rowlock. A few cautious strokes brought him alongside the buoy. He reached out and caught it, then put his hand in the water, pulling out the upper end of a nylon rope. Slowly he pulled the rope up, drawing on something heavy tied to the other end.

What emerged at last was a flat object, about the size and shape of a briefcase. Farrar hauled it over the gunnel and brought it round in front of him, balancing it on the thwart.

'There's no need to try guessing,' he said. 'You won't come within miles. If you're patient, I'll explain everything.'

He wiped his hand across the box, removing strings of water weeds and green slime.

'Totally waterproof,' he said. 'You could put a heap of gunpowder in here, take it out in ten years' time, and fire it seconds later.'

'This is all very interesting,' said David, 'but I'm losing my patience.'

'Don't worry, it will all make sense in the end. Let me continue. The removal of Chaofe Ling has created an enormous problem, particularly for Saddam Hussein. He can't pull out from his current positions in Kuwait and Jordan, but he can't win the war without the weapons he was promised. He's facing military defeat and political humiliation.'

He opened the box and took out a slim lap-top computer.

'But that could all change.'

He pressed a button, and the computer leapt into life.

He tapped some keys and figures started to scroll up the screen.

'Excuse me, Laing, but I have to pay attention to this thing. I heartily wish the computer had not been invented.'

He began to type in snatches of text – passwords, commands, confirmations. The computer beeped and warbled and twittered back at him.

When not keying in commands, he would look round him at the blackness of the night and the whiteness of the moon. Music lapped across the water, and he felt himself calmed and made whole by it. He placed his palm on the bright screen, and a brighter light read it and pronounced it genuine.

'I believe that sees everything in place,' he said. 'Now, as to its purpose. You're as aware as I am that weapons development is an ongoing process. Like this computer here, a modern weapon is out of date the moment it leaves the factory. What you destroyed at Chaofe Ling were finished devices designed for a battlefield situation.'

He placed the computer back inside the box and sealed it with a series of rubber fastenings. When it was secure, he dropped it over the edge of the boat and let the rope out slowly, returning it to its place at the bottom of the lake.

'What you did not destroy were the prototypes for a new generation of these wonderful devices. There are seventeen of them in all, and they were removed from Chaofe Ling several weeks ago. These weapons will detonate at ground level, and they will not require delivery by plane or missile. To be precise, they have been designed as terrorist weapons, although they would, of course, be completely outside the reach of any ordinary terrorist organization. Unless, of course, it turned out to be a state-sponsored organization.

'Several of these weapons have been taken to the United States, where they have been distributed to a number of major cities. One is in Paris, one in Moscow, one in Rome, one in Berlin, one in Sydney, one in Tokyo. The rest are being held in reserve, except for one currently in London.'

David felt his breath grow cold. The warm night turned to ice around him.

'Anthony, this is insane. You can't possibly . . .'

'I just have done.'

He clicked the little gadget he had used to control the anti-tamper device on the buoy. Several lights flickered then went off again, leaving one to show the device was live. Farrar tossed the remote control over his shoulder into the lake.

'When the bomb wipes out half of London, Saddam Hussein will become the world's most powerful man. I don't much like him, if the truth be told, but things being as they are, I reckon he's the man to go with. And this is where you come in. You . . .'

'How long? How long before it detonates?'

'I'm not really sure. Not very long. Half an hour, fifteen minutes. If you had a radio, you could try tuning in to a London station, let it play until it blanks out. Maybe it's gone already, though.'

Suddenly, Maddie let out a cry that would have torn the moon from its moorings had that been possible. David snapped his head up to catch sight of her leaping forward. She grabbed Farrar round the neck, then toppled sideways over the gunnel, her weight dragging him with her.

David rowed up quickly, but there was no sign of either of them near the boat. He threw down his oars and leaped into the water, taking in a deep breath before plunging downwards.

The water on the surface had been lukewarm after a long day's exposure to sunlight. But within a few feet it grew frighteningly cold, and colder still every foot he went down, and he knew he was at the top of a very deep lake, and if he drowned in it he would never rise to the light again.

It was pitch dark in the water, and he lost his bearings at once, and could scarcely tell up from down.

He sank further, and he thought he was dying. His lungs were growing desperate for air. He went further down and felt a skin of ice had covered him, and then there were thick weeds reaching out for him, tough and slimy. He kicked free, pushing up for the surface again.

He rose to the top, spluttering, gasping for air, and the moment he could open his eyes he looked all round in desperation, but there was nothing and no one. He dived again, and suddenly he saw her, not far from the surface, floating, her whiteness marking her out.

He caught her by the armpits and brought her fast to the surface, then kicked out till they were next to the dinghy. He hauled her on board, flattened her on her belly as best he could, and pumped the water from her lungs. She did not move or breathe. He bent down and put his mouth to hers, frantically trying to fill her dying lungs with his own breath.

He collapsed across her at last, unable to get any response. And for the first time, he began to cry without control or help, in pure agony for all he had lost, but above all for Nabila and Maddie.

'Dad?'

Her voice was very weak, but it was her voice. His

name was followed by a string of coughs and splutters. He straightened her and helped her throw up more water, and when that was done and her eyes were open, he held her so tightly that she might have died from that alone.

CHAPTER NINETY-TWO

He did not hold her long; dared not. Every moment counted, a second's delay could be fatal.

'Maddie, I have to try to stop the bomb exploding. Did he say anything at all about it to you?'

She shook her head, still coughing.

'All right. I'll have to get the computer up first. I want you to rest in the dinghy and wait till I come back.'

'I don't have much . . .' She started coughing again.

'Try not to exert yourself, love.' He squeezed her gently.

'. . . choice,' she said. She drew him to her, shivering. 'He said he'd . . . booby-trapped the buoy.'

'I'm going to have to take care of that.'

'Can't you . . . just go down for the briefcase . . . and leave the buoy alone?'

'I've thought of that, but it's too much of a risk. The moment I touch the case, the buoy will be triggered, and for all I know the box is wired to blow or send out an electric charge.'

He leaned back hard on the oars, pulling away from the other boat and the buoy behind it. When he reckoned they'd gone far enough, he shipped the oars and fetched the rifle from behind. He glanced at his watch. Fifteen minutes had passed since Farrar had pushed the button.

He lay down against the curved side of the dinghy

and brought the rifle back against his cheek. It took him moments to track and find the buoy. What would constitute 'interference'? he wondered. And then he had the anti-temper mechanism in his sights. What the hell? he thought, and pulled the trigger.

A deafening explosion ripped the night from end to end. What had been endless silence was for a moment the very embodiment of noise. Pieces of debris swept over their bowed heads and fell into the water in a sequence of splashes. The surface of the lake shook, and ripples appeared everywhere, rings of silver in the moonlight.

Quickly, David rowed the dinghy back to where the other boat still bobbed miraculously up and down. It was taking in water slowly through the bullet-hole he had made earlier and one or two gaps left by the explosion. The buoy was nowhere to be seen.

The dinghy carried an old killick anchor. David threw it in and told Maddie to do her best to keep both dinghy and boat steady.

He jumped in with a tremendous splash. He'd taken the night-sight from the rifle. He'd always heard this model was waterproof, and he hoped that extended to a little more than getting a few raindrops on the lens.

Taking a deep breath, he plunged down, sucked in at once by the darkness. Kicking hard, he felt himself drop through the smoothness of ancient water and draw nearer and nearer the awful bottom of the lake. His lungs were crushed by the depth and by the knowledge that he could not breathe. Every second brought an increase in the pain in his chest, and in the panic that mounted remorselessly in the back of his skull.

He knew he could lose the race by as little as a fraction of a second. But whether a second or ten minutes, the result would be the same. Perhaps one man in a car driving out of the city would be spared; and perhaps a family, driving in, would be caught up in the holocaust. He judged himself to be near the bottom. Bringing the sight to his eye, he struggled to make sense of the green world he saw through it. Fish startled him, scurrying away from his flailing left arm as he swept through their normally undisturbed habitat. Then he saw weeds flapping, and steadied himself to avoid becoming entangled in them. They were everywhere, rank, rotting, thick as mummy cloth, swaying like decaying silk, green and green and green. He could see nothing of the box among all this luxuriance, and he wondered how far from it he'd wandered in his descent.

He wanted to kick his way back up again, to burst out of the water and drag in all the air and sweetness between here and the mountains. Instead, he swam in a diminishing circle, all the while doing mental arithmetic to estimate how much longer he could risk staying down.

He saw it suddenly, almost hidden in a vast clump of weeds that reminded him of overgrown jungle plants. Dipping down, he fumbled for the handle to which the rope had been attached. He grabbed it and pulled up hard, tearing it from the weeds, and kicking for the surface. As he did so, the night-sight showed him Farrar's body, waving like a dark trophy captured by the water plants and the fish in the dark, open-eyed and circling. He shuddered and kicked again.

His lungs close to bursting, he pushed desperately for the surface. Moonlight and false hope, he thought, as his head broke through the water. He thought of Nabila fighting death in the hospital and wondered if her lone struggle had been eaten up along with everybody else's.

He came up closest to the rowboat, which had drifted a little from the dinghy. Maddie was leaning over the edge, nervously awaiting his reappearance. When he finally did so, she sank back on the front thwart and breathed deeply to calm the thick patter of her heart.

He managed to get the box on board the rowboat, then climbed over the gunnel himself. He had never felt wetter or colder in his life. The bottom of the little boat was awash in water, and he began to worry that it might start taking on more with his extra weight.

The computer turned on without a blink. It was a Macintosh PowerBook G3, and David felt a surge of relief when he realized it was a machine he knew how to operate.

He found and opened the application that ran the entire arming, countdown and triggering procedure. Someone – probably not Farrar – had given it a nickname: 'Last Laugh'. It sounded like a regular computer game, and when he opened it – Farrar had not bothered locking it or using a password – it looked like a game. He was tempted to breathe a sigh of relief and discard it then, but for one thing: the programme contained two files, one in Chinese, one in Arabic, setting out the technical specifications for the weapon. A quick glance at the Chinese file showed David that, if this was a game, it could have massively fatal consequences.

Pulling down menus, he quickly located the programme's main control panels, and within those a clock showing the countdown. He had eleven minutes left.

The control panels also gave him access to the command sequence that would allow him to abort the entire procedure. Carefully, as water washed round his ankles and his teeth banged together from cold, he tracked his way through it, each step taking him nearer to the last. Then, just when he thought he'd done it, the screen flickered and there was an image of a hand. On the palm sat a flashing message that requested him to place his own palm on the screen. He stared at it for a moment, then corrected himself. Not his palm. Anthony Farrar's palm.

He thought it through in seconds, then started rowing back to the dinghy, positioning the rowboat roughly where it had been before.

'Maddie, are you OK?'

'Yes, I'm fine. What's taking you so long?'

'I'm nearly through. Look, I think I'd better come across to the dinghy.'

He rowed across the gap separating them and handed the lap-top to Maddie before stepping into the rowboat. The bag was in the rear of the dinghy, where he'd left it. Rummaging inside, he located the Ek knife, the same one he'd had in the Taklamakan, the same sharp blade. He clutched it tightly in one hand and removed the sheath.

'Dad, take care.'

Maddie kissed him on the cheek.

'I'll do my best,' he said, dropping over the side into the lake.

He went down like a stone, the night-sight in his left hand, the knife in the right, its cord tight round his wrist. For a few moments, it seemed easier to him just to let go, to flood his lungs with water and join Farrar at the bottom of the lake. The vegetation might hold them both down there for years, perhaps they'd just decay until their bones fell to the lake floor, never to be found. It was only the thought of Maddie in the dinghy, drifting without purpose as the sun came up and the day ahead lengthened into unimaginable grief that kept him to his purpose. That and the faintest flicker of belief that Nabila was alive and might go on living if he was fast enough.

He thought he'd been down eleven minutes and more, but that was impossible, so he went on searching, even though his lungs were screaming for air. He knew Farrar had to be there, but whichever way he turned, however hard he strained, he saw only fish and weeds. His lungs were burning as though on fire, and at the last possible moment he gave in, kicking away from the bottom. He shot towards the surface, but even as he rose he started to lose consciousness.

Then the water broke all around him, and he was in the air, gasping and spitting, gulping the air in greedily, the way he remembered drinking down water in the desert. Again and again he sucked down lungfuls of the stuff, until his head was spinning and his chest ached. When he glanced at his watch, there were barely seven minutes left.

He swam to the dinghy and saw Maddie looking down at him.

'I've got to go down again,' he said. 'What's it say on the computer screen?'

'There's a message in the middle of the hand. It says "Abort before final countdown. Six minutes remaining."'

He closed his eyes, sucked in all the air his lungs would take, and headed back under. This time, something curious happened. It was as if he could hear Nabila's voice inside his head, urging him on, telling him not to kick so much, but to let the panic subside and the water take him into itself. He heard her whispering, as though her lips were brushing his ear, words of caution and rebuke.

Next moment he was there again, swimming above that rotten prehistoric heart while the fish stared at him in open horror or fascination. He put the night-sight to his eye and started to scan in a slow circle. His eye felt tired, and at times the picture blurred, but he went on. 'Slowly,' whispered Nabila. 'Don't force it. Let it come to you.'

He saw him suddenly, as a priest might see a crucifix

702

in the near distance, after a long road, in a place where nothing might have been expected. In a matter of seconds, he was staring into the cold blank eyes.

As he reached out for the nearest hand, the chill thought came – What if I take the wrong hand to the surface? But he thought back to the lap-top and decided that Farrar had used his right hand.

Cutting without a hard surface underneath proved harder than he'd expected. The blade cut as well as ever, but it lacked purchase. He ended up with Farrar's arm between his legs, while one foot pushed down on his neck, clutching his hand while sawing hard through the wrist. He cut and sawed and splintered and snapped his way through a forest of thick and fine bones and tendons. Then there was a last sensation of tearing, and he realized he was losing consciousness from lack of oxygen.

He kicked and kicked again, pushing up in a last-ditch venture against death, Farrar's hand gripped tightly in his like a rabbit in an eagle's talon. He came crashing to the surface, and would have gone down again, drinking half the lake, had not Maddie caught sight of him at once and pushed for him, reaching him in time to grab his arms and haul him on board.

He retched and retched and retched, then pointed to the computer.

'Maddie, take it . . . take the . . . hand and . . . put it on . . . the screen.'

She backed away from him, all her terrors reviving, her barely dormant nightmares coming back to life.

'No,' she said. 'No, I won't touch it. It's horrible.'

'You have . . . seconds, that's all. Millions of people . . . will die. I can't live . . . with that, can . . . you?'

He struggled to get to a kneeling position, but he was still too disoriented to remain upright.

'You have to . . . do it, Maddie. Please.'

'Is she there?'

'She?'

'I don't know. The woman you wrote about. The one in your letter. That you love.'

He hesitated, then nodded just once.

'All right, then, I'll do it for her.' And she stretched out for Farrar's hand and lifted it to the screen.

'How long?' asked David. 'How long to abort?'

'Twenty seconds. It's accepted the palm print.' She threw the hand away in disgust. 'Now it wants a password.'

David looked up in pure horror. There was no way he could ever outguess Farrar, not with seconds to spare, but suddenly, it was as if every conversation he'd ever had with Farrar flashed through his brain, and the answer was in the last.

'Maddie,' he said. 'It's a name. A Chinese woman's name. Type it in carefully, you won't get a second chance. M-E-I-H-U-A.'

She did as he told her. The moment the 'A' was keyed in, a large message appeared: 'OPERATION ABORTED'.

Above their heads, the stars and the moon went on shining, unimaginable pleasures eternally denied. David wondered how beautiful Meihua had been, and how she had died. And he thought of Nabila, and how beautiful she was, and wondered if she was still alive. And Lizzie dead. And Maddie on the edge of insanity, the only part of his world he knew for certain. He drew up the anchor and started the slow pull back to the lights that waited on the shore.

CHAPTER NINETY-THREE

He went to the hospital alone. Maddie was still too ill to go with him, even if he'd wanted her to. She was having enough trouble coming to terms with her mother's death. Rose insisted she stay with him for the foreseeable future.

He looked for Blennerhassett as soon as he set foot in the unit, but the doctor was nowhere to be seen. The room where Nabila had been was just off the corridor. Already knowing what he would find, he headed there on his own.

The door opened on to an empty room. His heart skipped a beat, knowing now for certain what it meant. He stared at the bed, at the stands and trolleys and monitors and drips that still surrounded it.

He went back to the corridor. There was no one in authority to whom he could speak.

He'd go home now, and enquire later about what had been done with her, about the arrangements for her burial. He'd have to see to that. And a headstone with her name carved on it. He remembered that he didn't know her date of birth. And anyone who might have known was buried in the ruins of Kashgar.

He'd almost left the hospital when he heard a voice behind him.

'Mr Rodgers?'

He turned to see the Irish doctor. For a moment he could not remember his name.

'Dr Blennerhassett . . . I've just been to . . .'

'I've been trying to get hold of you.'

'I was away. My daughter . . .'

'Oh, yes, so you said. Have you seen her?'

'Maddie? Yes, she . . .'

'No, I didn't mean your daughter. Your wife. Aren't we all over the moon about it? You must be a happy man.'

'Happy? I'm sorry, but I don't understand. We're talking at cross purposes. I thought she'd died. Her room was empty.'

Blennerhassett's face changed colour.

'When did this happen? Jesus, Mary, and Joseph, I saw your wife no more than twenty minutes ago, and she was fit as a horse.'

David didn't know what to do or think. Had Nabila been alive and died within the past few minutes? Or had there been a ghastly mistake?

Blennerhassett dashed for a phone, while David sank on to a chair and tried to think of nothing. There was a quick burst of conversation, then the doctor slammed the phone back down.

'Jesus!' he said, 'I'll crucify you if you give me another turn like that. Your wife is perfectly well and sitting up in bed asking where you've gone. I think you owe her an apology. Ah, come on now, you'll be making me blub as well. They tell me if I ever show emotion on the job I'll get the sack. Isn't it a grand profession? Come on with me and I'll take you to her. By the way, there's a flower shop just over there, just in case you had it in mind.'

'Dr Rose? This is David Laing. How's Maddie?'

'Why ask me? She's very ill, you know that. Your wife and her idiot boyfriend have a lot to answer for.'

'It's my impression that's exactly what they're busy doing at this very minute. If you believe in an afterlife, that is.'

'I'm sorry, I didn't mean . . .'

'Of course you didn't. Look, there's someone I'd like Maddie to meet. It may do her some good.'

'Well, you can come over, but I can't promise anything. That cocaine did some terrible damage.'

'I'll be over soon.'

They scarcely spoke on the way across. Just being together and out of danger was enough for them these days.

'I like your parents,' she said. 'Your mother reminds me of an old aunt of mine. In fact, I think they're related.'

They stayed with Maddie for about an hour. Nabila found some sort of bond with her at once. As the visit came to an end, Maddie turned to her father.

'Are you two getting married?' she asked.

'Well, I . . .' David flushed. 'It's a bit . . .'

Nabila shook her head in disgust.

'The answer is, "Yes" – but only if you're happy. Take your time and think about it. If it's a "Yes", we'll get married the minute you leave this dump.'

Maddie smiled.

'I'll think about it,' she said.

'Well, don't be too long about it,' said David. 'I'm getting on in years.'

Nabila leaned across and kissed Maddie gently on both cheeks.

'Maddie, if you're willing, I'd like to try to help you. Would you like that, or would the herbs frighten you?'

'No. I'd give anything a try. Do you think you can do something?'

Nabila nodded gravely.

'Yes, I think I can do something. With that and . . .'

She turned to David.

'Oh, yes,' he said. 'Maddie, I've got a small present for you. All the way from China.'

He reached into his pocket and brought out a crumpled sheet of paper. Without a word, he passed it to Maddie. She held it for a moment without speaking, sensing, perhaps, what it was.

'Open it,' urged Nabila.

With shaking fingers she unfolded it. For a minute or more she stared at it, overcome with fear and longing.

'Is it . . . genuine?'

'Oh, yes. Very genuine,' David said.

'I can't read all the characters,' she said.

'That doesn't matter.'

Nabila smiled at him.

'Tell her,' she said.

'Well, I . . . I got some of our people on to this several days ago.'

'And?'

He broke into the biggest smile he'd ever known.

'You have another visitor waiting downstairs. Shall I show him up?'